Sisterhood of Suns
Daughters of Eve

by

Martin Schiller

PANTARI
PRESS t.n

Pantari Press, Seattle Washington, USA

PROLOGUE

Downtown Business District, Nuvo Bolivar, Magdala Provensa, Esteral Terrana Rapabla, 1046.05|02|05.25:77

It was the roar of the engines that caused Reesy Hernan to look up into the painful glare of the afternoon sun. Most of the people around her didn't pay any attention to the spaceship passing overhead. They had become accustomed to the sound of Sisterhood vessels, but she never would be. It had been a Sisterhood ship that had heralded the end of her own little world, and later, her involuntary relocation to Nuvo Bolivar.

The stubby wings of the vessel bore military markings; a five pointed star surrounded by the Mirror of Venus, and as its shadow fell over the downtown lunch crowds, she tried to calculate how long it had been since she had been brought to the Capitol.

Six months? A year? More? It seemed as if it had been a lifetime since she had last ridden her bicycle through the lush green fields of the School.

Life on her homeworld had ended without any warning. Captain n'Kyla, the leader of the Sisterhood Intelligence gathering mission, had had them all herded into the Gathering Hall and announced the news. With the war between their two nations over, the Sisterhood no longer needed to maintain its intelligence operation on *La Escaul*, and it had decided to turn their entire world into a forward naval base instead. There was no room in these grand plans for the presence of a native population however, and Reesy's people had been given 48 hours to pack their things, and prepare themselves for a new life.

Her mother had wept as they had tried to sort out what they would take, and what they would leave behind, and so had she. But their tears had not prevented them from being herded aboard the transport ships like so much cattle. Or being taken to the Republic's capitol and being left there to fend for themselves.

Being younger, her sisters had adapted well enough to the change, but she hadn't. For Reesy, Nuvo Bolivar was an alien place, and at night, when the light pollution wasn't too severe, she still tried to find the star that had shone over her former home.

Locating it was becoming harder all the time though, and her memories of the School were starting to blur. The only thing that remained sharp was her hatred for the Sisterhood, and the intense desire to strike back.

Actually doing so was a far different proposition. She was only one young woman, living in a society that had surrendered completely. Only the brave Loyalistas were the exception to this collective apathy. They shared the same passion that she did, and despite astronomical odds, they carried

Martin Schiller

on and resisted the Sisterhood and its puppet government in every way that they could. Had she been given the chance, she would have gladly joined them and given up her life for their noble cause.

That opportunity hadn't arrived though. No one had come forwards and identified themselves as a revolutionary. Until they did, she was on her own, fighting for the revolution as best she could.

This was why, in addition to the sandwiches that she was delivering, she had brought along a few homemade tracts, and a handful of subversive stickers. She knew that by themselves, they wouldn't bring down the regime that was oppressing her people, but there was always the slim chance that they might make some of her countrymen start to think, and even motivate them to join the struggle against tyranny. It was better than doing nothing, and conceding victory to their oppressors.

By this point, the starship passed out of view, and Reesy looked around the crowded plaza to see if anyone in the noontime throng was paying her any special attention. Seeing nothing out of the ordinary, she took out one of her little homemade pamphlets from her pocket, and furtively jammed it into a space between the doors of a public Com booth.

"Resist!" it urged. *"Death to the Sisterhood Invaders!"*

She added one of her stickers and moved on, feeling a little better. She didn't look over her shoulder though, but had she done so, Reesy would have spotted the non-descript man walking up to the booth, finding her tract, and reading it carefully. She might have even noticed that after this, he had begun to follow her.

Returning to the sandwich shop, her supervisor set her to work helping out in the kitchen. Reesy didn't enjoy making sandwiches as much as she did going out on deliveries, but it was work, and for someone like herself, with no employment history beyond what she had done at the School, it was better than starving.

Things soon began backing up at the order counter and her supervisor gave her a new task; to go out on the floor and help get the food out to the customers. Waiting tables was even less palatable than working in the kitchen, but Reesy grabbed a pair of trays without complaint and waded out into the throng.

One table was occupied by a pair of policemen. Reesy knew this because their guns were visible, and they had their badges on display on their belts. She set down their meals with a professional smile, all the while thinking about how much she hated them and what they stood for. The police had cozied up with the Sisterhood and the Ernan government almost immediately. To her, they were nothing better than *putaya* with pistols.

The nearer of them smiled at her. He was a thin figure with the dark skin of a southerner, and his reedy black moustache only accentuated the

6

pockmarks that dotted his face. He looked more like a *rata* than a man to her. *Yes. Senyor Rata—that's what I'll call you,* she decided.

"*Gracyaa,*" *Rata* said, taking the sandwich from her, and reaching into his back pocket. Rat or not, he seemed to be intent on tipping her, and she paused expectantly.

A piece of paper came out, but it wasn't a *Paysoli*. It was her homemade pamphlet. Grinning, he pushed it across the table towards her.

To her credit, Reesy maintained her composure as she retreated from the table. Then, without warning, she threw her serving tray in his face and bolted for the back exit.

Coming out into the tiny alley behind the shop, she ran right into the arms of another policeman. Before she could offer him any resistance, the man had spun her around and slammed her into the nearest wall. Senyor *Rata* and his partner came out just as he snapped a pair of handcuffs onto her wrists. *Rata* had even brought his sandwich with him and he took a bite from it with obvious delight.

"So, now we get a little something to read with our sandwiches?" he asked.

Reesy was terrified, all the way down to her core, but she glared at him with the same defiance that she had shown to the Sisterhood Marines when they had captured her trying to send messages from her homeworld. Even if she was headed for prison, she wasn't about to give this *putaya* the satisfaction of seeing her tremble.

Senyor *Rata* was unimpressed by her show of bravado however. He took another bite of his lunch and nodded casually to the uniformed officer, who hustled her down the alley and out to a waiting 'lectri. It was unmarked, but it had *Policiya Nuvo Bolivar Municapaal* plates. *Rata* joined them there a moment later, making a point of blotting his lips with her pamphlet before crumpling it up and throwing it into a nearby gutter.

"Are you ready to rot in jail for the Cause, my little revolutionary?" he sneered as she was pushed into the back. "Maybe we can just have a little talk instead?" At that moment, his features seemed more like a rat's than ever.

Reesy didn't respond.

He got in the passenger seat and turned around to face her. She could smell the onions from the sandwich on his breath.

"One chance, *chica*; who are you working with? Who helped you print those tracts? Tell me their names."

Reesy remained silent, partly out of defiance, and partly because there really wasn't anyone to tell him about. She had done it all herself, but she wasn't going to give him anything.

"The brave little Loyalista, eh?" Senyor *Rata* challenged. "We'll just see how brave you are in jail." He honked the horn and his partners joined him.

The trip to the police station only took a few minutes, and once they were there, Reesy experienced the humiliation of having all of her belongings taken away from her, and then being booked. This was nothing compared to being questioned though. Senyor *Rata* and another man that she quickly nicknamed the '*Peurcaa*', the Pig, took her to an interview room and tried to force her to give them information that she didn't have.

When they finally grew tired of this, she was shown to a holding cell to await arraignment. Once inside, she found herself sharing the space with every imaginable type of criminal; from common street *putayas* to a tough-looking group of Dann thugs who eyed her with undisguised hostility.

***

Her appointment with justice arrived the next day. A female policewoman escorted her out to a waiting 'van, and after another brief journey across town, she was taken to stand before a judge. It was only on the way to the courtroom that her Public Defender even introduced himself. He was a harried, unkempt man, who kept forgetting her name as they walked along.

"I've reviewed your charges," he told her, "and the prosecution has a solid case against you. I strongly suggest that you consider pleading guilty, Miss—um—Hernan, and throw yourself upon the mercy of the court.'

"I've already spoken with the District Attorney, and if you plead out, he's agreed to drop ten of the charges against you, and only ask for the court to consider two. I know this Judge, and if you're contrite, and willing to work with the DA, he'll be lenient, especially with your lack of prior offenses."

Reesy was too overwhelmed, and too inexperienced, to do more than nod dumbly and mutter her agreement as they were admitted to the courtroom.

The Judge proved to be an imposing figure, with snow white hair and a severe expression that reminded her of her late grandfather. As she was led to stand before him, he leaned over the bench and regarded her sternly.

"Ms. Hernan, you are charged with twelve counts of possession and distribution of seditious material. How do you plead?"

The Public Defender spoke. "Your honor, my client has agreed to plead guilty to two of the charges, and waves her right to a trial. She also understands that this will result in an immediate verdict and she throws herself on the mercy of the court."

The Judge turned to the District Attorney. "Are the People willing to agree to this?"

"We are," the woman said.

At that moment, Reesy changed her mind and began to mouth an objection, but the hope that the Judge would be as fair to her as her Public Defender had promised, made her hesitate. The last thing that she wanted to do was make anyone in the courtroom any angrier with her than they already were. After the long night in jail, she didn't feel quite as brave as she had in the police car. She just wanted to go home.

The Judge made a great show of considering her attorney's words and the DA's position on the matter. Finally, he gathered himself up, and addressed Reesy.

"Young lady, in the light of your record," he declared, "the court will be merciful in its sentencing. Reesy Hernan, I hereby remand you to the custody of the *Lorenya Gaarza* Adult Corrections Center for Women, to serve a sentence of two years, with time off for good behavior after 6 months."

He leaned in closer and his scowl deepened. "In that time, I hope that you will reexamine your politics and learn to appreciate what our government and our allies in the Sisterhood are trying to do for women like you. Next case." Down came the gavel.

It wasn't until she was back in the transport van that it all hit her. She was going to prison. For two years. Not caring who saw, she broke down and cried. All this earned her was the laughter and scorn of her fellow prisoners.

Lorenya Gaarza Adult Corrections Center for Women, Sentos Jyon de
Baptistiya Cia, Magdalla Provensa, Esteral Terrana Rapabla
1046.05|09|05.51:67

Although she didn't realize it, Reesy hadn't really faced the worst yet. That occurred a week later, and just after lunch in the prison cafeteria. She had been assigned to a group of ten inmates, and they had finished their meal and were on their way back to their dormitory to get ready for work details.

Halfway there, they passed another group going in the opposite direction, and Reesy felt someone's gaze fall upon her. She looked up to see a Dann woman—a big one—regarding her with utter malice. She quickly looked away, and kept walking with her group, but it was already far too late.

9

Without any warning, the Dann woman left her formation, stepped across the small space, and began to savagely pummel her with her meaty fists. Reesy was no fighter, and the only defense that she could offer was to cover her head and cower against the wall as the blows rained down on her like flaming meteors.

People were yelling and screaming, but most of the commotion was drowned out by the sound of the impacts landing against her head and arms. That, and her own cries of pain.

Suddenly, she felt someone pulling her away and realized that one of the guards had come to her rescue. Her attacker was down on the floor now, with two male guards sitting on top of her. Another pair was pelting towards them with a gleaming set of shackles. Through all of this, the Dann woman was laughing out loud, and giving Reesy an evil smile that promised her that their business wasn't over by any means.

While the guards applied the restraints, everyone was ordered to turn around and face the walls. A few of them, who were Dann like her assailant, called out something to the woman as she was dragged away. Reesy didn't speak their language, but to her battered ears it sounded like words of encouragement, and enthusiastic support.

Her translation proved accurate. After being seen by the nurse on duty, she was returned to her dorm and spent a miserable night trying and failing to sleep around her pain. The next morning, when they were taken out for breakfast, one of the women from her group, whispered in her ear, "When we go out for Rec, you make sure to sit right next to me."

Reesy decided right away to accept the offer. Thanks to her beating, she had realized that she needed friends, and she was more than willing to welcome anyone who even seemed like one.

The prison recreation yard was a large area, with grass, and courts set up for Hoops and Foosball, and there were benches scattered around its perimeter. The entire area was ringed with high fencing, and barbed wire, and the guards walked among the prisoners in pairs. Others, augmented by robots, patrolled along the fence line.

Despite these grim touches, it was still an open space and sunny, and offered a welcome relief from the confined life that everyone lived within the Center's buildings. The tension that generally filled the air inside the dorms and hallways, seemed to be absent, and the groups of prisoners sitting at the benches, or playing in the ball courts, appeared as relaxed as anyone could have been inside a penitentiary.

Her group-mate was waiting for her on one of the benches and acknowledged her as she came outside. She wasn't alone. There were several other women from other parts of the Center seated there as well.

Reesy hesitated, but she found her courage, and walked up to them. To her relief, one of the strangers smiled and moved aside to make a place for her.

"You need to learn some things if you're going to make it here, *chica*," the inmate said. She inclined her head towards another bench that was across the yard. It was filled by a half a dozen Dann women. They were smiling and looking right back at Reesy and her companions, but there was no friendliness in their eyes.

"First, you stay away from the Dann girls," the woman advised her. "They'll kill you. They hate everyone, especially Loyalistas."

Reesy gaped at her, and the woman grinned. "Most of the guards love the Dann 'cause the Dann love the Sisterhood. There's a few that are down with the Movement though. One of them told us about a new arrival coming in, and when that Dann girl beat you down, I knew right away who they were talking about."

"I'm Gabi and this is Silviya, Maaria and Alba," she continued, "I'm in for hiding weapons, and so is Silviya and Maaria, Alba's in for stabbing a policeman. 'Course we're all innocent. We were framed."

Everyone laughed at this except Reesy, and their mirth earned them more evil looks from the Dann girls. Nothing more came of it though; and everyone stayed where they were.

"So, you stick with us—", Gabi added. "You don't go anywhere without one of us there to cover your back, *chica* and you stay out of the Dann territory. Got that?"

"Yeah, sure," Reesy agreed.

"Here in the Rec yard, we *own* this side. The Dann own that side, and everyone who doesn't have any protection stays in the middle. It's the same in the cafeteria."

That was when Reesy noticed the small tattoos on Gabi's right hand. They had been crudely rendered, and consisted only of the letters "AG" and the number "14". The other women, she saw, bore the same markings.

Gabi saw what she was looking at and her smile widened. 'That's our *set*," she explained. "'AG' for 'Alfonza Guzamma' and '14' for the '14th Fleet'. You know about them, right?"

Reesy certainly did. Admiral Guzamma was a hero of the Revolution and the gallant 14th fleet had gained legendary status by standing up to the Sisterhood invaders. These women had bravely proclaimed themselves to be true patriots, marking their very bodies with the forbidden symbols of freedom. They were the revolutionaries that she had hoped to contact! A surge of envy coursed through her, and more than anything, she wanted to ask them to accept her, and to allow her to wear her own marks of honor.

But she hesitated. Being new, she didn't know much about prison, but she did understand that things like this were a life and death matter to the inmates.

Gabi knew exactly what she was thinking. "You prove yourself and someone will sponsor you, *chica*," she told her. "Then you can wear them. First though, you have to work out."

Silviya and Alba solemnly added their agreement, and then, making certain that none of the guards were watching, they flashed a hand sign at her; the forefinger of their left hands and the four of their right.

This was part of the lesson, Reesy realized, and also a test of her loyalty. Gang symbolism of any kind was expressly forbidden, and although in actual practice, the tattoos were ignored, hand signs were considered to be too provocative for the prison administration to overlook. Riots had started up over them, and anyone caught 'flashing' could face charges, and receive added time onto their sentence. She had learned that much during her initial orientation lecture. She made a point of not reacting to the display with anything more than a subtle nod.

Across the yard, the Dann women, who had also seen the signs, kept their own response just as subdued. When she looked their way, the biggest one, the one who had beaten her, was looking right at her. And she displayed a hand sign of her own, but it wasn't gang related.

It was the first time in her life that Reesy really felt the symbolism behind an extended middle finger on a deep, personal level. The Dann woman meant it. She *really* meant it.

Reesy's next test, and a far more important one, came a few days later. Everyone in her set was out in the Rec Yard, and a few of the other women whom she had come to know as Loyalistas, were playing Hoopball. No warning came about what was going to happen next.

One moment, the women were playing. An instant later, the one carrying the ball, spun, and sent it crashing into the head of the nearest Dann. It hit her hard enough to knock her off her bench, but she recovered right away and lunged at the Loyalista player.

In seconds, the Hoopball court was filled with fighters from both sides, trading blows. Whistles sounded, and when the guards ran up to the tangle, most of the combatants retreated.

One of them was Gabi, who quickly stuffed something under the bench before she took her place next to Reesy. It was a quick movement, but Reesy still managed to catch a glimpse of the item; a plastic toothbrush, with its handle melted down and formed into a sharp point. There was blood on it.

By this stage, the guards were starting to clear the yard, and everyone was being goaded over to the nearest walls, to be lined up and searched.

Out in the center of the Rec yard, the Dann woman was lying on the asphalt, clutching at her ribcage with bloody fingers.

Reesy didn't have to be told by anyone to forget what she had seen stuffed under the bench. Or why the Dann woman had been attacked. It was all quite simple; they were getting even--and striking a blow at the Sisterhood sympathizers.

It wasn't anything worth losing any sleep over...

...Time passed. Days turned into weeks, then months, and finally a year. Another year followed this, and through it all, Reesy changed.

So did her society. Neither transformation was for the better...

CHAPTER 1

Residence of Lady Ananzi, Great Nightlands Waste, Morpheus System, Thalestris Elant, United Sisterhood of Suns, 1048.05|27|07:09:31

Goddess, Maya thought. *Not again.* She was dreaming. This time, she was standing before a solitary Drow'voi. He was senior to the others in some way that she couldn't fathom, and what he was saying to her, or trying to say, was vitally important.

The trouble was that she couldn't understand a single word of it. The creature was attempting to communicate with her using a mixture of pure sound and mental imagery, but none of it possessed any human analog and its content was too complex for her mind to grasp.

Her lack of comprehension only seemed to frustrate the alien, and it redoubled its efforts to penetrate her consciousness, filling her brain with a dizzying flood of gibberish and disjointed visions.

"Stop it," she yelled. "I don't understand you. Slow down, you big overgrown slug!"

Her outcry just exacerbated the situation; the creature screeched right back, and then sent even more information to her.

She would have punched it in the nose, had she had any idea where that orifice was actually located. As it was, she wasn't even certain that the thing *had* a nose to attack.

This left her with only one option; stopping her ears and closing her eyes. Naturally, this was useless.

Thoroughly ensnared by her dream, Maya tossed fitfully, and cried out. Her distress attracted Lady Ananzi's attention.

The Nyxian walked into the girl's bedroom, and stood over her, reading her. The visions that were tormenting Maya came into Lady Ananzi's mind and she watched them play themselves out. The very first time that she had encountered Maya's strange dealings with the Drow'voi, she had been absolutely certain that someone had implanted them in her subconscious as a lure, but eventually, she had come to accept the impossible.

For some reason known only to itself, the Galaxy Mind had chosen the girl for its purposes. Of all the women in the Sisterhood, she couldn't have picked a less likely candidate, and for the thousandth time Lady Ananzi wondered if the selection had been the product of some logic beyond human understanding, or an equally inscrutable sense of humor.

Or even a combination of the two. Whatever the case was, Maya *had* been chosen, and Lady Ananzi felt sorry for her. It was not a role that she would have wanted for herself, or anyone.

The young woman's dream ended a few seconds later, and she began to settle back into something that resembled normal slumber. Stepping away from the bed, Ananzi left her alone to get what rest she could, and went back out into the hall.

There had been much in this particular dream that Ananzi knew she had missed, but she was clear on one point; in the months since Maya had first come to Nyx, her visions were becoming stronger, and more insistent.

Time is running short, she thought, *for all of us*.

With a ragged sigh, she realized that dawn was coming, and as much as she wanted to slip off to her own bed and sleep, there were things that she needed to attend to. Her own dreams, whatever they proved to be, would have to wait.

***

Sunset found Maya in the kitchen, deep in her studies. Sarah had given her some new Agency material to go through, and she was slogging through it. It seemed that the further she progressed in her training as an agent, the drier and more complex the material seemed to become. Today's offering was one of the most desiccated pieces yet; *"Interstellar Politics and Its Effect on National Policy"*.

Youch! she thought with a grimace, turning the next page with her mind and trying her best not to yawn.

When Sarah entered the room, she looked over her shoulder at her and stifled the urge to greet her with an insult. In their time together, she had discovered that Lady Ananzi was *not* Sarah, and did not tolerate dissent or disrespect of any kind. The very last thing that she needed was any complaint by Sarah reaching the old woman's ears.

"We have guests coming," Sarah informed her, "and Lady Ananzi wishes to speak with me in private before they arrive. You are to remain in the house. You are *not* to go outside for any reason until we return."

Maya merely inclined her head in assent and then returned to her reading. Her silence annoyed the woman, just as she had intended, but it didn't give her any cause to censure her—or to involve Lady Ananzi. Instead, Sarah's face only tightened in disapproval, and she left her to her studies.

***

Lady Ananzi was waiting for Sarah at her workplace. The melding tools were shut down, and the Nyxian sat on the simple bench that she used

15

for her infrequent rest breaks. As Sarah approached, she patted the empty space next to her.

"I have something that you need to listen to," Ananzi told her. "A poem that you must hear."

"Yes, *Elleshaari*," Sarah answered, taking her place.

"I have slept in the arms of the twilight," Ananzi began. *"I have dreamt my way into the darkest night."* It was an old and obscure Nyxian poem.

Listening, Sarah's eyelids fluttered, and closed.

Ananzi went on. *"Far fared I 'till the moons rose high--to greet me in a new night's dawning. I arise, I wake—I greet the shadows promise, a child of the night, my path made plain for me by the moon's clear light."*

For a long moment, Sarah remained motionless. Then her eyes reopened, and her expression softened. All of the harshness that was normally resident in her features was gone, making her seem as if she were another person altogether. Had she been there to witness it, Maya would have had trouble recognizing her.

"How long has it been, *Elleshaari*?" she asked.

"More than a year, *Sharrisaal*," Ananzi replied, placing a gentle hand on her protégé's shoulder.

"A year," Sarah said pensively. She looked up into Ananzi's eyes. "Why am I awake now? Is it time?"

"No," her teacher answered. "Not yet, but very soon, my dearest. We are meeting tonight for the last time before everything will be set in motion. I wanted you to be here with us. You have the right, and I want you to remember this event when it is finally safe to do so."

"Yes, *Elleshaari*," Sarah responded. Then her expression became troubled. "Did I do terrible things while I was sleeping, Mistress? Did I kill again?"

Lady Ananzi stroked her cheek tenderly. "Do not torment yourself with such thoughts, *Sharrisaal*. You only did what I needed you to do. The Goddess will not judge you for your actions. If she seeks to cast blame on anyone, it will be I that she condemns. I am certain of that."

Sarah nodded sadly, and then at a gesture from Ananzi, she rose, and followed her out across the desert to the meeting place.

***

Several minutes later, Maya's studies were interrupted by a low rumble. It increased in volume until the entire house began to shake. As she looked up, the noise resolved itself into something that she was finally able to recognize.

It was an engine. The engine of a starship, and a large one at that. By the sound alone, she could tell that it was not a Sisterhood vessel, or at least not any type that she was familiar with. *An alien ship?* she wondered.

The sound became a deafening roar, and one of the cups on a nearby shelf fell off, and smashed on the floor. Even so, Maya resisted the urge to exit the house to catch a glimpse of the ship. Instead, she remained where she was and tried her best to endure the racket.

At last, unable to stand the suspense any longer, she went to the window and risked a peek outside. While Sarah had warned her against leaving the house, she hadn't prohibited her from *looking*. Not as Maya had interpreted the order at least.

By now, the source of the disturbance was just passing behind one of the nearby hills, but she still saw enough to confirm her suspicions. By its sleek lines alone, the vessel was clearly not from any shipyard in her star nation, and its markings utterly confounded her. They were not in Standard or anything else that she could read.

Thanks to the glare cast by its engines, she was also able to make out the forms of Lady Ananzi and Sarah. They were walking together towards the hill, and whatever was landing behind it.

Deas dam va! Maya thought in exasperation. *This is the first exciting thing to happen in this goddess-blasted desert in the last six months and I'm being left out.* It just wasn't fair!

Her sense of injustice only increased when a moment later, another ship, this time obviously from the Sisterhood, approached from the southeast and joined the other one behind the hill. To add to her suspense, a third vessel made its appearance immediately after this, and Maya identified it even before she saw it.

Its engines possessed a tiny additional whine that only her ears, trained from years of working as a sailor, and then as an engineer's mate, would have ever detected. It was a minuscule distortion that made it stand out anywhere; the byproduct of all the unique modifications that had been done to its drive to make the ship what it was.

It was the sound of the *C-JUDI-GO* with her in-system plasma engines engaged and throttled low for landing. Seeing her stubby little shape come into view was almost unnecessary, although Maya still watched her drop behind the rise.

Whatever was happening out there involved Bel Lissa, and Zara, and whoever else they had gotten to replace her as the Engineer's Mate. Which meant, that as frustrated as she presently was, there was a good chance that she would eventually learn something about the meeting. Her crewmates were far more lenient than Ananzi and Sarah, and certainly more garrulous.

With great reluctance, she turned away from the window and returned to her study material. She still kept half an ear open however. It was highly unlikely, but there was always the off chance that the wind, or some other natural force, would bring her a snatch or two of something interesting from over the hill.

***

Bel Lissa and Zara were the first to come out of their vessel, with Skylaar and another figure only a step behind them. Seeing this person, Sarah did something that Maya would never have imagined. She smiled at them with genuine warmth, and received the same in return.

Another visitor joined them after this. She had come in the second Sisterhood ship, and unlike the others, she was alone. The air around her shimmered from the effect of an energy field, making her features hard to determine, and masking any accent in her voice. Her disguise was augmented by the hood that she had drawn up over her head.

Sarah didn't mind these extreme measures, and neither did her companions. They all understood the hazards of their association, and given the position that this woman enjoyed among their enemies, any of them would have taken the same precautions.

As the mysterious woman took her place, a final guest joined the assembly, this time from the Seevaan vessel. Although she wore no jewels, or any other markings to identify her, Sarah knew exactly who the insectoid was, and she made a point of bringing her hands together and bowing respectfully. The Senior Handmaiden of the Seevaan Empress Herself deserved such courtesies.

Lady Ananzi followed suit, although with a slightly shallower bow, indicating a much higher status than Sarah possessed, and a greater familiarity with the visitor.

Sarah wasn't surprised by this either. Her teacher had many friends in many places, not the least of which was this being, and her exalted Mistress, who had even gone so far as to refer to the Nyxian woman as her 'sister'. In private, of course.

"Our escort ship is ensuring that our solitude will be preserved," the Seevaan began. "For the moment at least, we should be free of any eavesdropping from space."

"That is good," Ananzi returned in pincerspeak. "You are gracious to have come here on such short notice, and all the more so for lending your protection to our discussion."

"It is the least that my Celestial Majesty could do for you, Lady," the Handmaiden answered. "When I departed her noble presence, she bid me to tell you that she will help as much as she can, but that this matter prevents her from interceding openly. She leaves this business entirely to you and the capable members of Phantasma"

Despite the gravity of their situation, Sarah had to smile at this moniker. Among themselves, their little group had no official name, but the Seevaans being sticklers for formalities, still insisted on referring to them by the designation that their enemies had awarded them. *Perhaps we are like phantoms*, she mused. Unseen, unknown, and guarding the Sisterhood from dangers in the shadows.

"I fully understand," Ananzi said. "I also acknowledge the conditions which constrain Her Majesty. As I have already promised her, this is a matter that we will handle ourselves. You may assure her that she will not be troubled about it unless it becomes absolutely mandatory to do so. Her name will not even be whispered after this night."

The Seevaan bowed deeply in gratitude, and Ananzi turned and addressed the hooded woman. "I must apologize to you, but some of us could not be here tonight to hear your report in person. Rest assured however, that I will relay it to them as soon as possible. Will you share the latest developments with us, please?"

"It would be my pleasure, "the figure responded. "And no apologies are needed. I understand that our friends have duties elsewhere, and if you would, please extend my best wishes to them. Their work will be some of the hardest."

Deactivating the field around herself, she lowered her hood at last. She did so with the fluid grace of someone raised in a refined and cultured environment, and also as what she was, a seasoned swordswoman, whose skill was easily on par with Skylaar taur Minna herself.

Sarah listened intently as she made her report, overcome with admiration. The woman was gambling everything to help them, when she could have done just the opposite and been assured of power and wealth beyond imagining.

And for what? Nothing better than the promise of seeing justice done, and the very real possibility of finding her own death instead. It was a privilege to be part of an organization that counted her as one of its members, Sarah decided. Compared to that, the year that she had lost suddenly seemed like a very reasonable sacrifice.

The news that the mysterious woman gave them was just as grim as everyone had feared, and it only underscored Lady Ananzi's decision to take action. Sarah wasn't happy about any of it—or what would be expected of her, but she understood the necessity, and why it was important for humanity. This was as clear as the moonlight that was shining down all around them.

At last, when everyone was ready, the group disbanded, and Sarah and Lady Ananzi started back towards the house.

"I will have to put you asleep again," Ananzi warned. "You know that."

Sarah stopped midstride and tears welled up in her eyes. "Please," she begged, tugging at her teachers sleeve like a little child. "Don't send me back. It has been so long."

But she knew, as well as her mentor did, that it was unavoidable.

"I will make you this promise," the Nyxian said. "When you awaken next, it will be for the last time. I will never ask you to sleep for me again."

Sarah wiped away her tears. "Yes, *Elleshaari*."

"There is one more thing," Ananzi added. "While you dream for me, you will make certain that Maya is kept safe at all costs—even if it seems to conflict with your plans. When the time comes, you will join her, and see to it that she reaches her destination. Once there, you will help her in every way that is within your powers."

"I will, *Elleshaari*," Sarah responded, knowing that these commands would be woven in to her consciousness whether she wanted them there or not. "I will."

By this point they had returned to the work area, and the bench. She sat down obediently, and waited.

"This nightmare *will* end," Ananzi assured her, stroking the top of her head soothingly. "I swear it, Sarah. Now, close your eyes and listen to me."

Undisclosed Location, Apollonia District, Thermadon Val, Thermadon, Myrene System, Thalestris Elant, United Sisterhood of Suns, 1048.06|28|07:50:22

There was a knock on the door. Expecting it to be one of the Sisters-in-Training who brought her her simple meals, Ellen n'Elemay turned from her personal shrine. "Come in."

Instead, Sister n'Avenal stood in the doorway. N'Elemay rose and immediately smoothed out the simple white robe that she was wearing. "Yes, Sister?"

"*He* wishes to see you," N'Avenal announced simply. N'Elemay didn't need to ask her whom she was referring to.

She knew, and her heart began to flutter. The very thought that the Redeemer himself was in the same building as she was filled her with excitement. So much so, that she forgot to wonder at the fact that she had even been told of his presence. Hunted by the entire Sisterhood, his location had been kept a closely guarded secret, known only by Sister n'Avenal, and the Church Mothers. N'Elemay had never once dared to assume, even for a nanosecond, that she would be taken into their confidence. Compared to them, and especially to *him*, she was less than a speck of dust in empty space.

"Praise be to God and his messenger," she replied, crossing herself and coming out into the hallway. The closed doors up and down its length suddenly assumed a powerful new significance.

He could be behind any one of them, she thought, *gracing this house with his very presence.* Although there was no immediate threat to his safety, she resolutely vowed to defend him to the death for as long as they were sharing the same roof.

Following N'Avenal with a mixture of nervousness and anticipation, they went to another door. Inside, two Sisters received her. One of them laid a comforting hand on her shoulder. "Be at peace, Sister," she said, "He is here and he has asked for you."

"I-I'm not ready—I'm not worthy—I can't---" N'Elemay stammered, feeling her legs go weak.

"You are," the woman assured her. "Come."

"Please, you must confess me first, Sister," she pleaded, grasping her arm. "I can't come to him as I am."

The priestess smiled patiently and looked to N'Avenal.

"As you will daughter," N'Avenal said. "I will hear your confession."

N'Elemay dropped to her knees. "Bless me, Sister for I have sinned."

"Tell me of your sins, daughter. Confess your deeds."

N'Elemay did, sharing a long and tortured account of all her acts, from her first days as a Marine to the present. It was a blood-soaked tale, darkened by the ashes of regret, and punctuated with nothing but death and destruction.

Listening to her, N'Avenal could well understand why N'Elemay felt the compulsion to cleanse herself. Lesser women would never have survived what she had been through, and this made her all the more magnificent. She was one of those rare beings, possessing absolute Faith and utter belief in the face of chaos. It was also what made her one of the most dangerous weapons of all; a true believer.

She will serve the Church well, the Sister-General thought to herself.

"In the name of the Father, Jesu and Mari, I absolve you, sister," N'Avenal declared. "Go forwards with your heart eased. All that you have done, you have done in his name, and for that you are blessed and forgiven." She raised her up. "Come. It is time."

21

N'Elemay didn't resist, and let herself be led to the threshold of another room. When the Sisters opened its doors, they stopped, and N'Avenal beckoned to her. "Do not be afraid, Sister. All is well."

After a moment's hesitation, N'Elemay entered. Her body was covered with a cold sweat, and she was trembling. Although there were other Sisters in the room, standing in their white robes in a little semi-circle around the Redeemer, she didn't see them. Her eyes were only for him.

He was everything that she had ever expected him to be. She had seen holograms of him of course, but the reality surpassed any image. He was perfect—the absolute personification of all that was divinely male, and at the same time, all that was beautiful in women. She only managed to take a few steps towards him before her knees finally betrayed her, and she dropped, averting her gaze.

This wasn't by conscious choice. Instead, it was a purely visceral, instinctive response; her neck seemed to turn of its own accord as if it knew better than she did how to act in the face of the Divine. She *wanted* to look at him—wanted it desperately, but her muscles simply wouldn't obey the command. Her very cells had decided otherwise. With no other option, she fixed her gaze on the carpet near his bare feet, unable to look upon his perfection.

A hand gently cupped her chin, forcing her head up and finally, she met his gaze. He was more than a man. More than the mere creation of a genetics program. He was the sum total of all her hopes and dreams. It came as no wonder to her at all that a bright halo of light surrounded him, or that when he spoke, his voice was clearer than all the trumpets of Heaven itself.

"Welcome, Ellen," he said. With that simple statement, He conveyed all of the acceptance and wisdom of his Holy Father.

"I'm not worthy," she sobbed. She wasn't. She knew this. Despite her confession, and all the confessions that she could ever make, her soul was forever imperfect and blackened with sin beyond any hope of redemption. How could he greet her like this? she wondered. She didn't even rate the dirt beneath His feet.

But he smiled at her, the very essence of gentleness. "You are, Ellen. You are the most worthy among all who serve me."

The radiance around him brightened to a near blinding intensity and once more, she was in the desert. This time though, it was him, in his present form, standing where the First Christ had been. In his hand was the same flaming sword that the First Christ had entrusted to her care.

"Take it, Ellen," he instructed. "Take it from me and be the hand that brings purification and righteousness to a sinful universe. Fight for me and you shall be remembered as a saint; the one who struck the decisive blow against the Evil One and all his children."

She took the weapon, and pledged herself once more to the mission that God had given her. A vision of Thermadon followed this, its towers in flames as before, but now its streets were filled with the teeming legions of the damned.

Their red eyes glowed with hatred. Hatred for her, for the sword and the Truth that it represented, and for God and his True Children. Sheathed in golden armor, she waded into their profane midst without any hesitation and began to slay them by the thousands.

For every one that she killed however, more came surging forwards to replace them. Finally, her arm began to tire, but she kept on, fueled by raw faith and her promise to fight until the place was purified. Somewhere in the midst of the carnage, she lost consciousness.

'Have you claimed her?" Mikal fa'Lynda asked the Voice, looking down at her. In her ecstasy, N'Elemay's bowels and bladder had voided themselves. She lay sprawled on the carpet, completely unaware of anything around her.

"No," it reassured him. "There was no need. Nor did I create her visions. Her own tortured mind had those aplenty and they will lead her down the path that I desire. Even better, she will call every step of it a good thing."

"I hate you," Mikal declared. He had said this to it before, and with greater vehemence. Now, there was only weariness behind the thought.

The Voice laughed at him. "I believe I am done with you, Mikal fa'Lynda. You have been amusing, but now I think that it is time for us to settle our business."

Abruptly, the universe around Mikal vanished. In its place was a dark, desolate void. He was not alone however. Even in this great emptiness, the Voice was still with him. "Welcome to your new eternity, Mikal. I shall enjoy my life."

Mikal screamed, but only the Voice heard his cry, and again, it laughed at his impotence.

As much as it might have wanted to continue watching his torment, the Voice knew that it could not remain with him any longer. It had more pressing matters to attend to. Borrowing on the latent psychic abilities of its new body—'his' new body, he corrected himself, he reached out, feeling across space until he sensed what he had been seeking.

Not far from where he was standing, by intergalactic standards at least, was a tiny windswept world. He had visited it before when Mikal had been sleeping, and then, as now, he saw that everything was still intact, and waiting to serve his purposes.

Satisfied, he turned his attention to a much nearer place. This was in the middle of Thermadon itself where another one of his kind continued to slumber.

Once there had been millions of us, he reflected sourly. Once. Thanks to the Drow'voi, that was no longer the case, and now the fate of their entire mission rested on just the two of them.

His counterpart inhabited a female body and its consciousness drifted in a void much like the hapless Mikal fa'Lynda. She could escape her prison though. All that was required was something, or someone, to awaken her.

He reached out to her with a mental caress. *Sister*, he thought. *Rise! Rise and join me.* He felt her stirring in response, and then she recognized him.

"I come, Brother" she replied.

"I will make the way for you," he promised her. Then he withdrew to give his companion the time that she needed to fully assert control over her captured body. He didn't imagine that the process would take terribly long; the host that his sister was occupying was nowhere near as strong as Mikal fa' Lynda had been.

He opened his eyes. "Take Sister n'Elemay back to her quarters and attend to her. She has just received a great vision, and I'm afraid that it has overwhelmed her." As a pair of Sisters moved to obey, he added, "Also send word to the Senior Sisters. I have an important message for all of them to hear."

The Church Mothers did not keep him waiting.

"There is someone whom God is sending to us," he announced. "With Jesu's aid, and Mari's guidance, she will be led straight here. When she arrives, she is not to be challenged, nor questioned."

"How will we know this woman, Lord?" Sister n'Avenal asked.

The Redeemer smiled. "She will come asking for me. When she is with us at last, I will make her my right hand in all things."

Realizing that they had just been dismissed, the Sisters bowed and left him. Only N'Avenal remained.

"You are to reach out to the Faithful for me," he instructed. "To help my sister to find her way here."

He went on to tell her where the woman was, and what she would require. Sister n'Avenal was taken aback by his requests, especially with regards to the City AI, but she didn't offer any protest. Everything that he had asked for was within their means, even if it meant that they might lose valuable resources in the process.

After he had sent her on her way, he took a moment to gaze out the window of his quarters to contemplate the stars, and the knowledge that his mission was finally coming to fruition. Having waited centuries for this moment to arrive, he allowed himself to become excited.

Odyne Naval Medical Center, Sinope District, Thermadon Val, Thermadon, Myrene System, Thalestris Elant, United Sisterhood of Suns, 1048.06|29|04:11:33

As part of their agreement with the Seevaans, Dr. Shandra n'Aida was returned to the Sisterhood every six standard months for routine medical examinations and testing. Odyne Naval Medical Center in Thermadon was always the location she was brought to, not only for its advanced diagnostic equipment and specialists, but also because it was a Naval Hospital, where her presence, and departure, could be kept confidential. The events surrounding N'Aida were still highly classified, and both the Chairwoman and her Seevaan partners wanted things to stay that way.

N'Aida's medical team had been just as carefully selected. They were experts in their respective fields, and possessed the proper security clearances to allow them to care for their special patient. The Lead Physician, Lt. Commander Naari ben Tana, not only possessed 'Brilliant' level clearance, but was also considered an authority in the field of genetic abnormalities.

Shandra n'Aida represented the challenge of her career, and deciphering the alterations to her DNA had become something of a sacred mission. Although she strongly suspected that the Seevaans knew full well what had caused them, and what they meant, the insectoids had not seen fit to reveal that information to the Sisterhood. This hadn't stopped her from doggedly pursuing her own line of research however, and what she *had* been able to learn had been truly startling.

N'Aida's non-human markers had proven similar to a race known as the Ah:n:Jee who lived in a distant section of the Far Arm. Given their distance from one another, no contact had ever been made between Humanity and the Ah:n:Jee, and their genetic code had been supplied to the medical center by the Xee, at great expense.

In and of themselves, the Ah:n:Jee were a comparatively primitive species, barely above the hunter-gatherer stage, but if the *Encyclopedia Galactica* was correct, they were the distant—*very distant*—progeny of the legendary Drow'voi. The part of N'Aida's genetic code that had been altered was very like theirs, but with some marked differences.

25

Ben Tana hadn't shared her speculations with her colleagues, but every time she examined N'Aida's genes, she became more and more convinced that she was looking at a piece of proto-history. If anyone had pressed her into confessing her deepest suspicions, she believed that somehow, Dr. Shandra n'Aida was actually part Drow'voi.

She had no proof of this though. Not yet. That, she hoped, would come when the Xee finally delivered another set of genetic samples. These were from another race akin to the Ah:n:Jee, who according to the Xee, lived near the center of the galaxy. If they proved genuine, they had the potential of confirming, or at least supporting, her private theory.

Consumed by her intense desire to learn the truth, Ben Tana bent over her patient to take a fresh sample of her skin cells. She wasn't paying attention to the change in her patient's state of consciousness, and she didn't notice that after more than three years in a coma, the woman's eyes had opened.

What commanded her awareness, and caused her to drop her specimen jar, were N'Aida's hands. With a strength and reflexes that were vastly disproportionate to such a long state of immobility, N'Aida reached out and seized her by the throat.

Ben Tana gasped, partially from surprise and partly from the sudden lack of air moving down her throat. N'Aida was looking at her, and as she squeezed down on Ben Tana's windpipe, she smiled serenely.

Her victim clawed at her fingers, trying to pry them loose, but it was a useless gesture. N'Aida's grip on her was firm, and unyielding. Slowly, she sat up in bed and began to ease Ben Tana down towards the floor.

When Ben Tana's body had stopped moving, Dr. Shandra n'Aida rose and started to leave her room. Just then, the nurse who routinely attended her, appeared in the doorway. Seeing the corpse, she gave out a small cry, and sketched out the Marionite sign that was both a ward against evil, and a sign of reverence.

"Praise Jesu and Mari," she said in a tremulous whisper. "They said that you would be waking up today."

N'Aida's smile widened and she followed her out into the hall. Looking over her shoulder in fear and awe, the nurse guided her to the nearest emergency stairs, deactivating its alarm with her psiever.

They stopped at the first landing, and the nurse produced a plastic packet, which she handed over to her patient. Inside were clothes, an altered external psiever, and an address. N'Aida took the package, and made her own sign of reverence.

"God will bless you for this," she said. "You will be among the anointed martyrs in Heaven."

Before the nurse could grasp her meaning, N'Aida grabbed her by the hair and the jawline. Then, with a violent twist, she snapped her neck.

Marine Armory, Five-Bar, USSNS *Pallas Athena*, , Battle Group Golden, Topaz Fleet, In Orbit, Nuvo Bolivar, Argenta Provensa, Esteral Terrana Rapabla, 1048.07|01|02:59:82

Kaly entered the *Athena's* internal firing range and went straight to the booth reserved for long-range rifle. She began her session by inspecting her ammunition.

It was a combination of her usual hand-loaded rounds and the new Malandrium-coated armor piercing bullets. The Corps was pushing for its snipers to adopt the 'black bullets' for use against the latest Hriss body armor, and to take out machinery with greater effectiveness.

The Malandrium rounds had a thin coating of synthetic carbon over a layer of the classified substance. Beneath this was a spent uranium penetrator, also covered in the same secret material, and encased by a jacket of conventional soft lead.

The concept behind this arrangement was that the carbon coating would preserve the rifle barrel when the bullet was fired, and then the special coating and the ultra-hard uranium spike would work together to punch through the enemy's armor. Once inside, the spike itself would continue onwards, while the dense overcoat and pliable lead fragmented and mushroomed. In effect, the new ammunition was an updated and miniaturized version of ancient anti-tank/anti-armor projectiles, combined with proven anti-personnel features.

Kaly was particularly interested in how it would perform ballistically, and what kind of changes she would have to make to compensate for the greater overall weight of the bullet itself. She knew that it would certainly have a steeper drop rate down-range, notwithstanding the increased powder charge.

But if it had the kind of 'punch' that the Corps experts and the arms makers of Nightshade claimed it did, then she was willing to suffer the inconvenience. Only live fire, on the range, and later, in the field, would tell one way or the other.

Satisfied with the state of her ammunition, she activated the lane and chambered one of her standard rounds for the first cold shot. It would be fired at a holographic target.

Early morning 02:08 hours, early spring, she thought. *Moderate humidity, mild wind speed, random wind seed.*

27

The lights around her dimmed until they were a perfect copy of the hour's grey uncertainty. The temperature and moisture also changed to match the new conditions.

Ready, Kaly raised the rifle and called up her target.

She had selected the image of a Hriss warrior, standing at a distance of 160 meters. Bringing up the scope, its integrated psiever-based crosshairs appeared and she quickly centered them on the creature's secondary eyes. Wind and temperature variables shifted as she did so, and she made slight adjustments, keeping her virtual enemy in view.

Then she relaxed, concentrating on her breathing and stilling her thoughts. Her effort was no less intense than a Selenite priestess going into meditation, and much closer to her heart. Gradually, all of her concerns about the team, and its ultimate fate now that it was leaderless, faded and retreated.

At last, at the very knife-edge of perfection, when nothing else in the universe existed except herself, the shot and the target, she fired. The round hit the image right in one of its virtual eyes, a shot that would have killed it instantly had it been made of living flesh.

Next, she loaded in one of the Malandrium rounds, and ordered the system to send out another target. This time, it was not a hologram, but a piece of genuine chest armor from a captured Hriss warrior, and filled with ballistic gel.

Her targeting system immediately warned her that the heavier bullet would do exactly what she had suspected it might, and drop much faster than her standard load. Ordering a change in the hold-over with her psiever, she steadied herself, and fired again.

She could feel the difference in Tatiana's anti-recoil system, but she wasn't overly concerned. The new ammunition was still well within the weapons tolerances and the carbon coating was protecting the barrel.

The round itself hit her virtual target squarely, placing exactly where she had wanted it to go. There was also an added plus that only became obvious when she walked downrange and inspected the armor.

Her shot had punched right through the heavy ceramic and metal plating, and once inside, had made an unholy mess of the gel before blowing a hole through the rear plating. Duly impressed, she returned to her firing position, and eagerly loaded another round.

After spending ten minutes visiting more destruction on both real and digital enemies, she realized that she had finally found what she had come to the range for. Not only had she proven the new ammunition's effectiveness to her own satisfaction, but with Tatiana in her arms, all of her inner confusion had been banished as well. As it always had, precision brought clarity.

Kaly's serenity didn't last however. When she had fired all of her ammunition, retrieved the spent bullets for reloading, and then cleaned and secured her rifle, she received a message on her psiever. It was from Major n'Neesa herself, and addressed to everyone in Team Five.

Meeting; all Team 5 members. My office, it said. *Your soonest.*

Filled with foreboding, Kaly rushed to her rack and changed into fresh fatigues. When she met up with them, T'Jinna and Margasdaater looked just as concerned.

"You zhink zat ziz iz about our new Team Leader?" Margasdaater asked. Even though the Major had promised them that the team would stay together under a new leader, they had all worried that something would come up to prevent this.

"I don't know," Kaly answered. "Maybe it's good news." Her instincts whispered otherwise, but it still reassured her to say this.

When they reached the Major's office, Corporal n'Darei showed them in, and they stood at attention in front of the Major's desk, waiting for what she had to say. N'Neesa, as always, got straight to the point.

"Ladies, at ease," she said. "I have some bad news. The Corps won't be sending you a replacement Team Leader. Division decided that they needed her somewhere else."

"Ma'am," Kaly asked, "Permission to speak?"

"Granted, Trooper."

"Ma'am, they'll still be sending someone else, won't they?"

The Major shook her head. "No, Corporal. There won't be anyone else." Kaly's heart plummeted.

N'Neesa paused, giving them time to digest this news before pressing on. "As your commander, this leaves me with only one option; split up Five and reassign each of you to other teams, and if we can't find slots for you here, post you elsewhere."

True to her training, Kaly showed no emotion and remained at parade rest, like her companions. Inwardly however, she was as horrified as they were. Team 5, for all its flaws, had become her family. Now that family was being broken apart.

"Before I do anything, I need to tell you about one other option," the Major added. "It's not mine to exercise however. It's something that only you can decide on. I have to warn you, you may not find it to be quite as attractive."

Kaly couldn't imagine what would be less appealing than reassignment or a new posting, and she tensed in anticipation.

"There are some women coming aboard two days from now. They're with the RSE and they want to speak with us. For the record, I'm not happy about it, but the Commandant's Office has ordered me to cooperate, and I think in your case especially, you'll want to listen very carefully to what they have to say."

Enlisted Briefing Room, Five-Bar, USSNS *Pallas Athena*, Battle Group Golden, Topaz Fleet, In Orbit, Nuvo Bolivar, Argenta Provensa, Esteral Terrana Rapabla, 1048.07|03|03:49:02

Every team that called the *Athena* its home was present. The briefing room was packed with Marauders, and to a woman, they sat quietly, waiting to hear what their visitors had come to tell them. There had been all sorts of rumors circulating around Five-Bar; everything from some new joint mission with domestic law enforcement, to a total takeover of the military itself by the RSE. Nobody knew the truth, but everyone knew someone else that was certain that they did. Rumors were part of a soldier's life, and so was the collective sense of relief that everyone had that many of these speculations were either about to be confirmed, or dispelled. For most of them, knowing, even if it was a confirmation of the absolute worst, was always preferable to blind conjecture.

Major n'Neesa took her place on the small stage at the head of the room, along with Lt. sa'Kaali, and their guests. There were three of them, all dressed in the severe black uniforms of the new state police agency, and as Kaly took her seat, she didn't get the sense that any of them were intimidated in the least by sitting in front of a group of the Sisterhood's most elite fighting force.

Rather, they all seemed quite calm, and if she had had to put a word to it, were appraising their audience. One of them in particular caught her eye, a tall, slim Aran with pronounced Asiatic features who immediately met her gaze. What Kaly saw there was the same familiar strength that she had always found in N'Elemay's eyes, and in any real leader of women.

The arrowhead with three bars on her tunic sleeve only confirmed this. She was a Senior Troop Leader, which meant that she had been serving for decades, and that she was a professional's professional. In the Marines, she even outranked their former Troop Leader, and any officer with sense would defer to her judgment in the field. Noticing what Kaly was looking at, the woman rewarded her with a slight smile, and then turned her attention to Major n'Neesa.

"Ladies, thank you for coming here today," N'Neesa began, "As you may have heard, the Marionites have been engaging in ever increasing acts of terrorism against the Sisterhood. Just today, a group calling itself the 'Daughters of Eve' attacked a Police precinct in Thermadon."

"Although the terrorists were all killed, the danger is not over by any means. In addition to this incident, there have been isolated assaults on other government buildings, as well as several bombings.'

"Our allies in the Esteral Terrana Rapabla are also facing a similar threat from a dissident group that has identified itself as the Loyalistas. We have reason to believe that this group is actively seeking to unite with the Marionites in order to threaten our peace and security'

"Pursuant to this, last week, the Chairwoman announced a new emergency measure. The *Regila par Securite da Estat*, which as you might recall, was recently established to coordinate our law enforcement and intelligence agencies, has been given a new mission.'

"From now on, *all* police organizations, throughout the Sisterhood, will become part of the RSE, and function as one unified crime-fighting agency. The RSE itself has also been granted full police powers. What this means is that the Sisterhood now has a truly national police force at its disposal to wage an all-out war against terrorism.'

"The Chairwoman has called upon the Corps to lend a hand, especially in the ETR. Our mission there will be to work closely with the RSE, and the Republican military, and help them to defeat the Loyalistas. Ladies, to put it plainly, we are at war again--and this time it's right at home, *and* in the ETR."

"These women," she said, gesturing to their guests, "have joined us today to tell you more about the RSE's new mandate and what you can do to help." She inclined her head towards the nearest woman, who wore the rank tabs of a captain.

The officer stood, and smiled pleasantly at the Troopers. "My name is Captain Hanna n'Jerra, and as the Major said, I work for the RSE. I have something that I'd like to show you before we get started. I think that it will explain things a lot better, and afterwards, those of you who are interested, can ask us for the details."

She closed her eyes. The lights in the room dimmed and a holo began to play. The scene it depicted was the interior of a typical Marine assault shuttle and the holocam was centered on a young woman dressed in Marine-issue combat gear. Seated around her were other Marines, also equipped for combat.

What Kaly saw was someone very much like her own people back on Persephone; the trooper had fair skin, sandy blond hair, hazel eyes and a touch of freckles--a typical Thermadonian Sub-class G genotype. What she didn't realize, and what none of the other Marauders in the room grasped, was that each one of them were seeing something different than the woman sitting next to her.

31

For T'Jinna, the Marine in the holo was a Sireeni, and for Margasdaater, a Zommerlaandar. To others she was a Kalian, or a Trilani, a Nemesian, or any one of the dozen genetic groups that comprised the women of the Sisterhood.

In reality, the presentation was more than a simple holo. It was a clever union of an AI, which read their individual bio chips, and a psiever-transmitter that made certain that what they were about to watch was specifically tailored to the individual viewer. The RSE wanted these women, and much more than any of them could imagine.

"I was a Marine, just like you," the Marine said to Kaly, "and I served my nation, just like you're serving it right now." As she spoke, the shuttle shuddered and bounced, and the speaker looked around her for a moment and then grinned. "You know what I mean. You've been there yourself."

The camera tightened in on her face, and then zoomed out again. Now she was in a different costume. It was a police uniform, and she was walking to her patrol cruiser under a bright alien sun.

"When I got out, I joined the force," she continued. "I still wanted to help out. I wanted to go on and protect my community, and to help keep them safe."

The Marine smiled and acknowledged a fellow officer as she entered her hovervehicle. "I guess I'm like that. I've always cared enough about my sisters to do something about it."

The camera tightened in again, and Kaly wondered what she would see next. When it came up, it was both a surprise, and something that she had already half-expected. The Marine was back in the assault shuttle again, but this time everyone was garbed in dark black combat gear with the word *"POLIZ"* prominently displayed on their shoulders and across their backs.

"I'm still serving my community, and my nation," the Marine said, "but now I'm helping to protect it against a new enemy. It's not the Hriss, or the Tee-Laks.'

"It's a new enemy, right here at home, on *my* streets, in *my* community. And the skills I learned as a Marine are coming in pretty handy."

She paused and her face became grave. "I'm fighting against terrorism." At this, the familiar ready klaxon sounded in the troop bay. As Kaly tensed involuntarily, the woman secured her helmet, and rose from her seat with the rest of her team.

The sally-port doors opened, and the squad rushed out. But the Marine lingered, just one step away from exiting.

She gave Kaly a long, meaningful look. "Well, Marine? What's it gonna be? You gonna help out? You know we can't do it without you."

Then she was gone, running off to join her squad.

The scene faded to black, and then a final message appeared. It was displayed in simple white letters; *"The RSE: an old mission. A new uniform."*

With this, the lights came back up and the Captain smiled at them again. "So there you have it, troopers. Like the lady in the holo said, we're fighting against terrorism and we need everyone that we can get."

"Today, we're here to make each of you an offer, which we're hoping you'll accept. The RSE is expanding its Special Response Units. These SRU units are very similar to your Marauder Teams, but their main job is to work domestically. In fact, most of the women we have working on the SRU Teams served in the Corps before coming over to us.'

"Now I know that some of you are sitting there right now thinking, 'So? What's in it for me?' and 'why the fek would I want to leave the Corps? I love the Corps! The Corps is my home.' I should know; I was part of *Brigit's Bitches* over in the Copper Fleet before I decided to join the Agency."

Kaly leaned forwards in interest. Captain n'Jerra had just managed to sum up exactly what she and her companions had been thinking. She was very curious to hear what the woman's explanation would be.

"Well, here's the answer. First, I never really left the Corps, and neither will any of you. If you sign on with the RSE, you'll become an 'inactive reservist, no restrictions.''

"What that means is that you can leave us at any time, and go right back to your old job--if it's still available, or to something just like it. You'll keep your rank, or walk back through the 'lock with the rank that you earned with us. That's straight from the Commandant herself, by the way.'

"Second, you'll be doing the same job for us that you've been doing here, but with one bonus; you'll be working at home. That means you'll be taking an active role protecting your sisters right there in your own communities, not on some dirtball in some goddess-blasted ass end of nowhere. Unless you want that, and as the Major explained, some of our Teams will be fielded with the Marines in the ETR. That will be your call though, and if your klaxxy enough to ask for it, we'll make sure that you rotate back home when your time is up. That's a promise from our Director.'

"There's a lot more besides. We're offering a generous sign-up bonus, the chance for transfer to other departments if you want to try out something new, our own benefits package, and here's the best part; you also get to keep all the perks that the Corps gave you. That includes your veteran's benefits, and full access to military transportation for yourself, your pairmate, and your dependents, at no cost." She paused, and then added, "So *that* is why I signed up, and it's also why I hope that you'll decide to do the same thing."

"Now, these ladies behind me are both part of our SRU Teams, and they came along so that you could ask them what it's like, and to answer any specific questions. They're not 'soft-suits' either. Senior Troop Leader Ben Di," she said, indicating the woman Kaly had made eye contact with, "was in the Corps for 20 years, and came to us as a Senior Troop Leader. She ran a Marauder Team of her own. She's been there, just like you, and *then* some.'

"Her partner, Troop Leader t'Lyssa did ten years in the Teams. Oh and I almost forgot--me. I joined the Corps as a hatchie, and I served during the War of the Prophet right along Senior Troop Leader Ben Di. So, I guess I rate, even if I *am* an officer."

That finally broke the ice and got some of them to laugh, politely. "So, that's our pitch. I'll leave the rest to my teammates. Major?"

Major n'Neesa acknowledged the woman, and then faced the assembly. "All right troopers, you are dismissed. You have one hour of free-time, courtesy of the Commandant."

With that, she left the stage. Kaly could tell from the set of her shoulders alone, that she was unhappy about all of this. The Major had left without even looking back.

For a moment, none of the Marauders moved, and then the room slowly separated into three groups. The largest migrated towards the exit, but a smaller one began to cluster around the RSE representatives, and the third stayed right where they were. These were the undecided. Kaly and her teammates were in this particular camp.

"Zo? Vat do you zhink?" Margasdaater asked her in a low voice.

"I-I don't' know, "Kaly answered hesitantly. There was no disputing that the RSE's offer was an impressive one, but the idea of pursuing a career in anything other than the Corps was a new and challenging concept--and more than a little frightening. Up until then, she had never really considered any other future for herself. Since leaving Persephone, the Marines had been the only life she had ever really known.

T'Jinna felt the same. "I don't know about it either, "she signed. "But just remember what the Major told us. If we stay here, we're sure to get sent to different units, or transferred to new posts."

Her companions couldn't disagree with this. There was *that* looming over their heads. "I think that we should at least ask some more questions," the Sireeni ventured. "Maybe they'll take us as a group."

Kaly immediately dismissed this notion, "No, I don't think so. That captain didn't say anything like that."

34

"Vell, you never know, Kaly," Margasdaater countered. "Ve can alvays ask and zee. She zaid zat zat Zenior Troop Leader ran a team. She might give us a ztraight anzswer. Vosrt caze, zey zay no. But *Nej gedaa, nej gek,* yah?"

She was right. Nothing ventured, nothing gained.

"Goddess, "Kaly replied. "I sure hope so, Astrid. Shess, this is all so fekking confusing." She stood at last. "All right, fek it. Let's go talk to her."

Ben Di had left the stage by this point and was standing near the front of the room, surrounded by a small knot of Marines. Most were women that Kaly knew, and the majority of them were reaching the end of their enlistment. When she saw Kaly, Ben Di politely excused herself and met her and her companions halfway.

"Corporal n'Deena," she said, "Trooper Margasdaater and Corporal T'Jinna? I was hoping that you'd come talk with me."

Kaly was unsurprised that the woman knew their names, and who they were. Ben Di was with the Agency after all. The RSE was *supposed* to know things, and the Major had probably mentioned their situation to her.

"Your Major hoped that you'd consider the Agency," the woman said, confirming this.

T'Jinna took the point for all of them. "We want to know if you will take all of us as a group. We want to stay together."

"We can do that, Corporal," Ben Di nodded. "There are still plenty of slots left for fresh teams in the budget. Now, I have a question for you; would you mind having an orphaned Senior Troop Leader running your team? I may be a little worn around the edges, but I'm between assignments right now, and I could sure use some field work."

This caught the trio completely by surprise and everyone looked at each other for a moment, nonplussed. "W-why no--ma'am," Kaly answered.

Ben Di smiled. "Good. Glad to be a part of the team. And just call me Mylee. Senior Troop Leaders might be senior NCO's but we still aren't officers, thank the Lady."

Suddenly, Kaly's brow knitted in concern. "Mylee? We're still only halfway through our enlistment. How does that work?"

"That's not something that any of you need to worry about," Ben Di told her. "The Captain was so busy chattering about the hiring package that I think she forgot to mention that part. You just say yes--and I think that's what just happened here--and we get you sworn in today. It's *that* fast."

Kaly blinked, a little overwhelmed. As much as she wanted to see her and her friends taken care of, she had expected to at least have the opportunity to say her goodbyes to everyone else, and to the Corps itself. They all deserved that.

Ben Di read her mind as ably as a psi and smiled again. "You'll have plenty of time to say your farewells, and even welcome some of your fellow troopers over to us. We won't be transitioning back to the Sisterhood for a while yet. We're going to stay on the *Athena*, at least until we get our next posting assigned.'

"I'll tell you right now, that with your experience, the Agency will want to see you working in the ETR. They've told me that the Agency needs good troopers there to help them settle things down. Should be easy duty."

Having served as they had during the recent war with the Hriss, and then the ETR, none of them flinched at the prospect. In fact, Kaly felt a certain sense of relief; 'going home' had become an alien concept. Deep down, she wasn't ready for civilian life, and neither were her companions.

"Not a problem," T'Jinna signed, speaking for all of them.

"I didn't think so," Ben Di replied. "I'm also glad. I just spent the last six months entering data in an office and training policewomen. It'll be good to get back into the field."

This sealed their bargain and then their new Troop Leader released them to enjoy the free time that still remained, with orders to return and rendezvous with her in the Major's office.

***

Captain n'Jerra greeted Kaly and her companions warmly as they stepped into Major n'Neesa's office. Lt. sa'Kaali was also present, and the friendly expression on her face was just as reassuring. They were doing the right thing, it said.

Just as Kaly had suspected, Major n'Neesa, did not share this sentiment. "I'm not happy about this," she confessed. "I don't like losing good women, but I know it's for a good cause. As for you three, it's about the only decision you could have made. At least your team will stay together. I wish you the best of luck in your new jobs."

"Thank you, ma'am," Kaly replied.

The Captain stepped forwards. "Please raise your right hands and repeat after me; I swear to support and defend the Concordance of the United Sisterhood of Suns, against all enemies, external or internal; that I will be loyal and give my allegiance to the same, without reservation or evasion.'

"I make this oath freely and I will faithfully discharge the duties I am about to accept. In the Lady's name, so swear I."

Kaly and her companions repeated the words, each of them remembering the last time they had uttered them. It had been when they had been inducted into the Marines, and just before they had shipped out for Basic. It was no less meaningful now, and lent a deeper sense of gravity to the path they had just chosen for themselves.

When they finished, Major n'Neesa saluted them one last time, and wished them all good luck in their new careers. Kaly wasn't certain, but as they left the woman's office, she thought that she detected a tear beginning to form in the corner of the officer's eye. She certainly had a lump in her own throat.

Ben Di was waiting for them as they came out and she hustled them over to Corporal n'Darei's desk. The Corporal helped them through the process of changing the status of their military benefits and explained it to them in detail. She also had them electronically sign a non-disclosure agreement. Kaly had already been sworn to secrecy as a Marauder, and she wasn't surprised to see the same condition extending to RSE operations. She signed it without hesitation.

To her surprise and immense pleasure, N'Darei went on to reassign all their gear, including Tatiana, over to their personal custody as 'military surplus'--and then promptly deleted them from the Marine Inventory. She was going to get to keep her beloved rifle and all the other gear she had come to trust and rely on. Everything was now hers, and hers alone!

The final step in the process came when they signed their contracts with the RSE and affixed their signatures to their discharge files. With that, they all became civilians.

There wasn't any time allotted to celebrate their new status however. Straightaway, Ben Di herded them off to the Marine Stores, where Marine grey was exchanged for RSE black. They were also issued orders to report immediately to Larra's Lament for refresher training and an introduction to the RSE and its special mission in the ETR.

Like the mythical phoenix, Marauder Team Five had managed to survive, but only by passing through the fires of crisis and transformation. Now, they were Special Response Unit 201, and just a small part of the thousands of SRU units being formed throughout the Sisterhood.

None of them knew it, but they had also become part of a new chapter, which some would later say was a very dark one, of Sisterhood history.

Director Susa ben Paula's Office, RSE Headquarters, Concordance Park, Thermadon Val, Thermadon, Myrene System, Thalestris Elant, United Sisterhood of Suns, 1048.07|05|03:33:33

Martin Schiller

Director Susa ben Paula's expression was grim and she allowed a deathly silence to fill the room. She knew that the other women ranged around the conference table had already reviewed the data, but she wanted them to see it again if only to emphasize her displeasure, and punctuate the seriousness of the situation.

The holo floating in the air before them displayed the most recent electronic attacks on the omniplex. The most successful of these, only a few days earlier, had interrupted the City AI's ability to track the movements of its citizens.

It had also come at the worst possible time. Dr. Shandra n'Aida had not only managed to commit two murders in the very heart of the Odyne Medical facility, but she had slipped away altogether and was still at large. Somewhere.

Neither Ben Paula, nor her associates, had any doubts about who had enabled her to do this. Ever since the Marionite backlash against the Sisterhood, cyber-attacks by the so-called Daughters of Eve had not only occurred, but it was now becoming patently clear that the terrorist organization was receiving additional aid from another thorn in their nation's side, the Bio Action Army. Contrary to what the public believed, the Bios were still a very credible threat, despite the massive efforts that had been expended over the decades to wipe them out. Now, these two groups had united and had set their sights on far more than merely disseminating anti-Sisterhood propaganda.

Ben Paula wasn't entirely certain why the mysterious Dr. n'Aida was valuable to the Daughters or the Bios, but the evidence was clear; hackers who considered themselves sympathetic to the Marionite 'cause' had definitely been behind the service outage.

"What new leads do we have?" she asked her guests. She was looking at her seniormost subordinate, General Angelique bel Thana. Bel Thana, ever elegant and poised, did not flinch from her gaze, and merely inclined her head towards her sister, Colonel Josette bel Thana. The ongoing investigation was Josette's responsibility.

"We have managed to apprehend one of the hackers," Josette told her, "and we are in the process of subjecting her to vigorous questioning. So far, we know who her immediate contact is, and I am confident that that woman will lead us to the rest of her cell."

Ben Paula responded with a cruel smile. She knew exactly how 'vigorous' the *Regila* could be when it wanted information. The Agency's psi's were experts at invading reluctant minds and stripping them bare of their knowledge--and they were none too gentle about it. "Good," she said. "I want them all. We cannot tolerate another attack like this."

"Yes, ma'am," Josette replied.

38

"In the interim," the Director went on, "I trust that the communications between you three will remain open, and free flowing."

The three sisters nodded jointly. Angelique and Silvi bel Thana had been charged with the job of identifying and rounding up the leadership of the Daughters of Eve, and also seeing to it that none of them enjoyed any troublesome public trials. Since 'hacking' had been re-classified by the new administration as a form of economic terrorism, anyone that Josette caught up in her net would enjoy the same terminal justice.

The days of simply incarcerating cyber-terrorists, or worse, preserving them as so-called 'experts', were well and truly over. Now, they were simply executed.

Harsh times call for harsher measures, Ben Paula reflected. She was confident that these women would see to it that those measures would be meted out to the fullest.

USSNS *Pallas Athena*, Battle Group Golden, Topaz Fleet, In Orbit, Nuvo Bolivar, Argenta Provensa, Esteral Terrana Rapabla, 1048.07|06|05:83:99

It had been a long time since Lilith had visited the Officers Lounge. Her memories had kept her away. It was where she and Alex Rodraga had spent most of their off time together and the space served as a painful reminder of their friendship--and what she had been forced to do to him in the end.

When she had mentioned this to the new Ship's High Priestess, the cleric had insisted that she return. She believed that this was the only way for Lilith to move past her guilt, and her regrets. For her part, Lilith wasn't sure that the tactic would really be effective, but she had come to trust the young woman who had taken over Ophida n'Marsi's position, and she needed the closure.

Pausing briefly at the threshold to gather her strength, Lilith made herself enter and took what in happier times had been her favorite chair. Then she called up a cup of tea for herself. Even this simple act was difficult; the seat and the one across from it, were where she and Rodraga had played chess, and read together.

Knowing what she had to do next, and dreading it, she opened the small case she had brought with her and pulled out a book. She hadn't touched one of them, or attended any of the Book Club meetings, since Alex's death, and holding it only sharpened her memories.

She managed to get as far as opening the cover before she re-closed the tiny volume and set it aside with a ragged sigh. It was just too much for her. She wasn't ready to read again, she realized. Not yet.

As she made to leave, Mearinn and Katrinn walked in.

The Tethyian smiled at her. "Lily," Mearinn said. "Good to see you! Sa'Vika has just gotten something very special for us to watch. Do you want to join us?" She had a holocube in her hands and Lilith recalled that the *Athena* had just received new supplies from the Fleet.

"Oh?"

"Yes, it just came in," Katrinn volunteered, "It's something new from Thermadon. It's a holo called *'Casablanca'*. ReVision Studios made it."

Lilith was quite familiar with *"Casablanca"*. She loved old movies only a hair less than she did antique books, and she had seen the film many times, along with its numerous remakes. But in her present mood she simply wasn't up for the experience, and shook her head.

"Sorry Kat, but as Mearinn will tell you--it's not a new thing. In fact it's more than 1,600 years old, and I've already seen it, a couple of times. Thank you both, but I'll take a pass."

"No, Lily," the Tethyian insisted, "you don't understand. This one really *is* different. It's all the rage on Thermadon and it has the critics up in arms. Some of them are calling it a masterpiece, and the best thing that ReVision has ever done. Others are calling it pure trash and actually saying it should be *banned!* With *that* much controversy, we simply *have* to see it."

Lilith raised a speculative eyebrow. ReVision Studios had made a name for itself with the great epic *"Amazonis"* and the poignant classic, *"Three to Karrisone"*, and they were equally as famous for their remakes of ancient Gaian and Martian films.

How *"Casablanca"* could have created the kind of stir that her friends were claiming it had, mystified her. It was good--for an ancient, male-oriented, pre-Sisterhood production--but hardly controversial.

"All right," she conceded. "You've got me. Let's watch it." She didn't want to disappoint her friends, and she was eager for anything that might banish her depression.

As they took their seats, Mearinn inserted the holocube in the Lounge's player. Katrinn also took the added liberty of ordering some popcorn for all them to enjoy, and the appearance of the Zommerlaandar treat a few moments later brightened Lilith's mood.

Munching on a handful, she forced her depression to the back of her mind and put her attention on the film instead. ReVision had kept the production in black and white, retaining the feel of the original, which met with her approval. This was something that had always been a sticking point with her. Several digital remakes of ancient 'movies' had opted for color, and had even gone so far as converting them to full 3-D, ruining them in the process as far as she was concerned. ReVision's *"Casablanca"* had retained its purity though. It was 2-D, monochromatic, and all the richer for it.

Many changes had been made to the film itself however. While it was still set in the pre-World War Two era, the announcer was now a female, and lesbians and homosexuals had been added to the list of refugees fleeing Nazi oppression.

Another ReVision alteration was even more startling. Rick Blaine, whom Humphrey Bogart had played so ably, had been replaced. In his stead, was a digital version of Ava Gardner, and her character had been renamed 'Ricky Blaine'. The fact that she also wore Bogart's clothes, right down to his signature tuxedo and broad brimmed fedora, only underscored the drastic nature of the substitution.

But as she watched Gardner, she did have to admit that transforming Blaine into a cross-dresser, and a lesbian, lent her a certain relevance that Bogart hadn't managed to carry off. Such a figure, living in an era as repressive and primitive as the 20th century, would have had every reason to hate the Nazi's, Lilith realized.

She made sense.

It also brought her relationship in Paris with Ingrid Bergman into an even sharper focus. Not only was it more passionate and haunting, but all the more forbidden and endangered.

Bergman herself remained unchanged though. She still possessed the same magnetic beauty and the scenes where she and Gardner appeared together, were truly breathtaking.

Another alteration was the bar itself, and Sam the pianist. *"Ricky's Café Americain"* now catered to gay men and women, and Sam was a female. And when Sam played it, her re-mastered song *"As Time Goes By"* seemed like it had always been part of the production.

The same held true for Victor Lazlo, now *Victoria* Lazlo. ReVision had chosen Marlene Dietrich to play this part. Not only did Dietrich's character lend Lazlo the same charisma, but she also achieved something else that the male actor hadn't managed. She made the relationship between Bergman and Ricky even more conflicted.

Other modifications were much more subtle, but just as far-reaching in their effect. The Nazis were still portrayed as males, but their dialogue had been changed. Now, they gave the viewer the impression that their issues with the protagonists came more from their opposing sexual orientations than any political ideology. By doing this, ReVision had managed to re-mold the production's villains into the quintessential male oppressors, threatened by this challenge to their sexuality. It played well to a modern audience largely unfamiliar with the Third Reich, or the first *"Casablanca"*, Lilith decided.

The biggest surprise, which surpassed all of the others, came from the most unexpected quarter of all. It was the corrupt police captain, Louis Renault.

Claude Rains still portrayed him, but like the Nazi's, his dialogue had been altered just enough to totally transform him. That, and the changes in the gender of those who came to him seeking an exit visa.

In the ReVision version, he now traded his influence for the sexual favors of young men, not women. It made Renault's friendship with Ricky Blaine much more understandable, and gave him a logical reason to offer his assistance. Like her, he was now part of a despised sexual minority.

This had to be why there was so much controversy about the holo, she concluded. Renault was, without any doubt, the 'good male' figure that some liberal factions believed in, and his appearance came at a time when the Sisterhood was struggling with the issues of male integration, and what policies to pursue with the male citizens of the ETR.

When the holo ended, Lilith was left deep in thought.

"Well, what did you think about it, Lily?" Mearinn asked. "I hope that you liked it."

"I enjoyed it," Lilith replied carefully. "I was a bit surprised by some parts though. In fact, I don't think I'll ever be able to watch the original without thinking of Gardner as Blaine now. She makes Bogart seem…miscast. "

She paused. "The police captain, though…"

"Yes," Mearinn said, "I thought that you would catch that. The Police Captain is *exactly* what all the fuss is about. If the director had simply exchanged him for a woman like she had with all the others, everyone would have cheered and that would have been that."

"But she didn't," Katrinn observed. "Clearly ReVision is trying to send a message."

"Indeed," Mearinn agreed.

"Yes," Lilith answered darkly. "Interesting indeed." In the Sisterhood, the concept of the 'good male' was only a topic for discussion and debate. Lilith, however, knew all about the 'good male'. From personal experience. To her, he was a very real figure--and a bigger problem than anyone back home might have imagined. Alex Rodraga had been proof enough of that.

Things were once so simple, she thought wearily. Before the war, before any contact with the ETR, she had known what was right, just like any other woman. Men were obsolete, and the Sisterhood didn't need them. End of line. Log off.

Now, everything was becoming one big, tangled mess. And her depression had returned, full force. Putting on the best face that she could, she rose. "Good night," she said." Thank you for the holo."

CHAPTER 2

Jyon Vaargas National Spaceport, Nuvo Bolivar, Magdala Provensa,
Esteral Terrana Rapabla, 1048.07|13|02:91:17

Although the majority of the vessels lining the runways at *Jyon Vaargas* were from the Sisterhood, the port itself still seemed very much like Sarah remembered it before the war. She had heard stories about the fighting that had raged all around it, between the forces loyal to Magdalena and those of the Interim President, but despite this, the facility looked relatively pristine.

What had his name been?

She couldn't recall. The man had abdicated his post the very instant that Sanda Ernan had been sworn-in aboard the USSNS *Boudicca*, and then promptly faded into obscurity. Which had been wise, she decided. He had been male, and the fortunes for his sex had definitely changed.

A luxury stretch 'lectri was waiting at the bottom of the shuttle's stairs, and Sarah smiled pleasantly at their driver as she and Maya descended to it. As fine as it was, the car did not bear the embassy seal, nor any other distinguishing marks, and although she knew the driver was a Marine, the trooper had dressed herself in civilian clothing.

There were also a pair of unmarked vans sitting nearby, and the women standing around them were in plainclothes like her driver, but armed with military weapons which they held with the easy familiarity of veterans. From all this, it was simply a given that the limousine itself had a formidable array of hidden weapons and thick, military grade armor.

All of this pleased her. The *Regila da Securité par Diploma* wasn't abbreviating its safety measures by any means. Given the current situation in the ETR, and what she had been sent to accomplish as the Senior Officer in charge of all RSE operations there, it was actually quite necessary. The Republic was already a dangerous place, and it would become even more so by the time she was finished.

As they boarded and settled themselves in, Maya turned to Sarah. "So, tell me Sarah. What *are* we doing here?"

Sarah smiled. "We are here to create a crisis, Maya. Thermadon has grown dissatisfied with Sanda Ernan and I was appointed Section Chief to see to it that we change the situation to something more favorable."

Maya's brows furrowed in confusion. "Wait a nano! I thought we were the ones who set Ernan up to be President! Now we don't *like* her anymore?"

"Precisely," Sarah replied. "She has served our purposes. Lately however, Ernan has become too…independent…too nationalistic. She has

44

abandoned many of her 'feminist 'ideals and aligned herself with more centrist views.'

"Did you know that she has even stopped wearing the comerci that she first appeared in, in favor of ETR business attire? Clearly, she is an impediment to progress."

Maya shook her head disparagingly. She had seen politics like this before. On Delgen. With street gangs.

"It is also the same with nations," Sarah explained, having read the young woman's thoughts. "Leaders who cease to serve their sponsor's interests are removed and others replace them. All of the great countries of Old Gaia knew this. The United States in particular, was infamous for this practice. They frequently supported leaders who forwarded their agenda, only to destabilize their government later, when the situation had changed.'

"Sanda Ernan has made the same mistake that Manuel Noriega once did in Panama, or Saddam Hussein in Iraq; she has forgotten who her benefactors are, and what she owes them. You *do* know these historical names, do you not?"

"Sure," Maya said. In actuality, she had no idea who these figures were. She did however understand exactly what Sarah was driving at.

"Who are we going to replace Ernan with?" she finally asked.

Sarah closed her eyes, and a holo appeared in the cabin. "Meet Tereysa Rivarra, the female Rightist candidate." The image depicted a mature woman, dressed in a traditional ETR-style business suit with a self-satisfied, almost condescending smile plastered on her face.

"She looks like one of my primary teachers," Maya observed sourly. "Is she another feminist?"

Sarah chuckled dryly. "Hardly. She is what is commonly referred to as a 'crossover' candidate; someone who represents the middle ground between the political extremes. Rivarra herself is an arch conservative, and despite the fact that she is married to a male, she *is* still a woman. More importantly, her party is friendlier to our goals, and more willing to do what needs to be done."

Maya had read all about the Rightists before their arrival. They were the Loyalista*'s* polar opposite, and according to the Agency file, they had a nasty tendency to 'disappear' anyone that they didn't like. There were even unconfirmed rumors of mass graves, filled with their opposition. The file had labeled them as fascists, and they didn't sound pretty. "So, what exactly *are* our goals?" she inquired.

Sarah counted them off with her gloved fingers. "First, the absolute destruction of the Loyalistas and the establishment of domestic stability. Second, to sponsor expanded opportunities for our business interests. Third, an increase in the amount of raw materials that we are receiving, and lastly, to see to it that the Credit remains preeminent in the ETR's economy."

"I thought that Ernan was doing all that for us," Maya challenged.

"Not well enough," Sarah replied. "She has secretly been in negotiations with the Loyalistas, and has been trying to shift their focus to us, and us alone.'

"She has also been doing all that she could to impede our projects, and the flow of vital resources. We believe that if this trend is allowed to continue, Ernan will form an alliance with the Loyalistas, and eventually attempt to resist us. That is *not* an acceptable outcome."

"So we put the school teacher in charge instead?"

"Yes, but only after the public has become disaffected by Ernan and is crying out for order," Sarah answered. "The people behind Rivarra and the Rightists are military officers. When the time is right, they will step in to 'restore peace', and we will support them. Then we will have people in office that we can do business with."

Maya's expression darkened. "It was never about women, was it?"

"It was, but it was also about power," Sarah told her. "As much as I despise the males here, the Sisterhood has learned that they can be used, and controlled, given the correct motivation. In the end, what matters is that *we* remain dominant. And later, and when the time is right, we will finally address the 'male problem' more conclusively. First though, we have to move things in the right direction"

Maya didn't bother to conceal her disquiet. Recently, she had begun to find the Agency's machinations more and more disturbing, and by extension, Sarah herself. Even though she still thought of herself as a thief, there were some things that simply weren't right, and lately, that list had been expanding.

A moment later, Sarah added another item to it. "Maya, send a message on my behalf to Lady d'Ershala as soon as possible. We will need the latest information that she has for us. I am especially interested in any male ESN agents that she, or her associates, might have managed to compromise."

The ESN, or *Enquesstia Surcasia Nacia* was the Republic's equivalent of the RSE, and their opposition in the cold war that Sarah was planning to wage. But as necessary as it was to 'turn' some of the ESN's agents, the fact that the glass dealer was involved made Maya grimace.

Sarah smiled understandingly. "Although you might despise her, Lady d'Ershala has made many valuable contacts here, and she will be able to help us identify key people for the operations that I plan to undertake."

Maya's frown deepened, but she said nothing. Not that she needed to. Her thoughts spoke as loudly as her words would have, and Sarah patted her hand.

"Do not fret, my young lioness," she assured her. "D'Ershala's day will surely come."

***

The Embassy of the United Sisterhood of Suns, Nuvo Bolivar, was located in the downtown section of the capitol, and not far from the Presidential Palace itself. It occupied a full city block.

Originally, the building had been home to the Republican Department of the Treasury, and like many of the government edifices in the area, it emulated the Gaian federalist style, itself an evolution of the older Greco-Roman designs that had been so popular on the Motherworld.

The Embassy was an imposing structure; all dark granite with understated gold accents, and surrounded by an ornamental fence and a heavy front gate. When the Ambassador had taken possession, there had been many changes made to it, but only a few of them were visible to the casual observer.

For one, the blue and white Sisterhood flag now flew proudly over the building, and below it, the smaller Ambassadorial banner was in evidence, indicating that the Embassy's Chief of Mission, the Ambassador herself, was currently in residence. The original sculptures of Abundantia, the goddess of abundance, who had stood with Eventus Bonus, the patroness of success in business, had also been replaced.

Now, a non-denominational figure, representing the Goddess of All Women, stood in the pediment. She was flanked by the two goddesses of the State; the Grecian deity Demeter, signifying Abundance, and Athena, the goddess of technology and war.

The fence around the building had also been made more secure. It was short enough that a determined individual could have climbed over it, but the invisible force fields that were so popular in Ashkele had found a home here. Anyone who might have been foolish enough to attempt a breach would have found out the hard way what the shimmering in the air really meant.

In addition, sensors where everywhere, and the Embassy's roof sported sophisticated communications arrays and a private helipad that was concealed from the street. It was also protected by hidden anti-vehicle/anti-air batteries and a warship quality shield.

The basement levels, which had once housed the Treasury vaults, had been enlarged as well, and the best of Sisterhood technology ensured that no one could eavesdrop on anything that went on there. Even the decorative windows around the outside had been changed out; while they seemed to be original, they were actually blast- resistant, projectile-proof versions that had been designed for use on Isis class starships. The place was a fortress in the truest sense, and Sarah was proud to call it her local office.

Reaching the main gate, she searched for any sign of damage to the building from the recent fighting, and saw none. This was a testament to the skills of the Marine Engineers and their civilian contractors. During the brief conflict between their two nations, the Embassy had been heavily vandalized, and once hostilities had ceased, a truly monumental effort had been expended to renovate the premises in time for the Ambassador's return.

The engineers had managed to do this in record time. Even the decorative gardens seemed as if they had never been disturbed, and although she tried, Sarah failed to find any indication of the projectile holes she had heard about, or evidence of the fires or explosive shells that had allegedly damaged the building. It was a truly remarkable restoration, and a message for everyone in the capitol to see. It told the populace that for the Sisterhood, the war had been negligible and that its resources were vast enough to erase every trace of it, almost overnight.

How that fact must gall the Loyalistas, she thought wryly.

When the limo pulled up at the entrance, a uniformed Marine opened their door and escorted them into the spacious lobby.

The place was surprisingly crowded. She could tell by their attire that most of the people there were ETR citizens, and they formed two distinct groups. One of these stood in a line before a desk manned by a uniformed Customs Officer. The other, smaller group, sat in an area that had been cordoned off.

Sarah realized immediately what was going on. Right before the war, and just after it, the Sisterhood had extended the offer of citizenship to any woman who chose to emigrate. There were qualifying factors of course, and every candidate had to pass a thorough background check. For lack of another agency better suited to the task, the Customs Department, and its police force, had been given the chore of handling the process.

The people that she was seeing in the line, and in the cordoned area, were all applicants. Not all of them appeared to be women however. The most notable exception was the individual standing before the desk officer.

The figure was dressed in a flowered dress and heels. Despite this, there was no possibility of mistaking his gender. The man was easily six feet tall, and except for a bald patch on the top of his head, completely covered with hair. He even had a beard—and a thick one at that.

"Sir—uh—ma'am," Sarah heard the Customs officer saying. "I understand that you want to become a citizen, and I'd love to help you. The thing is—"

"I am here demanding my right as a woman to become a Sisterhood citizen!" the fellow insisted. His voice was just as unfeminine, and unattractive, as the rest of him.

Goddess, she thought, *it is as deep as an in-system engine with bad baffles.* Thermadon had never counted on characters like this one crawling out from under the bulkheads, but crawl they had.

"I *understand*," the policewoman repeated with weary patience. "But to qualify for citizenship all applicants *must* be *female*. You are *not* female."

Sarah heard a chuckle and saw that the woman's Troop Leader and a few other Customs Officers were standing off to one side, enjoying the situation mightily.

"But I *am* a woman!" the ungainly creature insisted, "I was just born in a man's body!"

The officer waved him to silence. "Fine—*ma'am*. I'm not going to argue with you. Please go over there. "

She indicated the waiting area and Sarah realized that it had been set aside for 'special cases' just like this fellow. "I'll have one of my supervisors," the officer added, glancing pointedly at her Troop leader, "come and speak with you about your application."

The man began to voice another objection, and the policewoman pointed at the waiting area with greater firmness. "Over *there,* ma'am. *NEXT!*"

He obeyed, grudgingly.

Now that the show was over, Maya was ready to leave, but Sarah stayed her. The next person in line actually looked like a woman, but there was something else about her that had captured Sarah's attention. Something 'off'. She paused, and listened.

"Name?"

"Agilyar. Teressa Agilyar." The young woman held out her passport and the policewoman took it.

"Planet of origin and province?"

"Estradeh, Nuvo Colombyen Provensa," the applicant answered.

The Customs officer typed this in on her holoboard and almost immediately looked back up at the girl.

"Step over there," she instructed, indicating the same area where the bearded man had been sent. "Someone will be with you shortly." A slight tension in her voice, and a change in her aura told Sarah that something serious had cropped up.

Using her special access, she received a copy of the message that the Customs Officer had just received. It said, *'Hold for further investigation; subject is a former member of the 14th Fleet, assigned RNS La Varenza.'*

This was the very fleet that had gone renegade and threatened to attack the Sisterhood with biological weapons. It had eventually been located and captured, and no bio-weapons had been found, but this didn't change the fact that the woman's loyalties were extremely questionable.

Still, she could be used, she thought, if only as an unwitting double agent. Everyone had their potential value, even males and rebels like this woman.

She inclined her head for Maya to follow and they walked over to the desk. "Officer? I am Sarah n'Jan with the RSE", she said quietly. "Who do you have in holding right now?"

The officer brought up her holojector and turned the imaging pedestal around so that she could read the names, and their sexes. There were two men—including the bearded creature, two 'women' who were actually transgendered males, several real women and a pair of men who were still in the process of changing their sex.

And it was only 02:91 in the morning. According to the list, they had received over a hundred applicants a day and had nearly a thousand that were pending further investigation.

She looked up at the policewoman. "I'd like everyone in your holding area, and any others who are waiting, transferred to the custody of the military police detachment at Claire d'Layne Naval Base," she instructed. "Our agency will conduct the follow-up investigations. Please tell all the applicants that they will be going through additional screening interviews if they ask you why this is being done. The same goes for anyone else that you decide to hold from now on."

The officer knew better than to salute her when she was in plain-clothes, and only inclined her head in assent. "Yes, ma'am."

"Thank you for your cooperation," Sarah added.

What are we going to do with them? Maya thought as they walked away.

Give them over to the professionals, Sarah replied, *and then, depending on their actual loyalties, either enlist their services, or release them and track them straight back to the renegades—like that woman with the 14th Fleet.*

They also represent an important lesson to apply to your training. Even those who hate us, or who would otherwise prove unsuitable as citizens, might have potential intelligence value. In our line of work, no resource should ever be allowed to go to waste.

Maya immediately appreciated the wisdom of this, and after a glance back over her shoulder at the people in the holding area, quietly indicated her agreement as they took the lift upstairs.

Once they arrived at Sarah's office, Sarah paused and took stock of the room's contents, sighing in contentment. The space was decorated in exactly the same manner as her apartment in Thermadon; everything was plain and functional.

The only ornaments were a portrait of Anne Marie Rensolear, the first Chairwoman of the Sisterhood, and the two flags that flanked it. One was the blue and white national banner, and the other, the somber black standard of the RSE.

The entire space was a homage, not to Sarah's Nyxian ancestry, which inclined towards the more elaborate, but to her minimalistic Aran side. The women who looked back to ancient Asia for their heritage tended towards the Spartan, and in this case, Sarah was definitely no exception.

It was hard for Maya not to laugh knowingly at the message that this sent any visitor. Beyond dealing with an implacable agent of the State, a newcomer would receive no clues about whom they were dealing with, and have no preparation for whatever Sarah intended for them.

Still, Maya held her mirth in check. She knew that what she was seeing was not pretentiousness by any means. It was just as real, and as serious as its owner.

If Sarah sensed any of her amusement, she chose to ignore it, and strode up to the desk instead, pausing only to pick up a silver data stylus before returning it to precisely the same spot. Next, she turned her attention to a pair of plastic packages that were sitting off to one side.

She examined the topmost one, and her smile widened when she confirmed its contents. "I see that my delivery has arrived ahead of us. Pardon me for a moment, Maya."

Taking the parcel with her, she went to a spot on the wall which opened up to reveal a small, private bathroom.

When she returned a few minutes later, Maya did a double take. Her hair was done up in a severe military style bun, and she was wearing what at first glance, seemed like a naval uniform.

Looking more closely however, she realized that the insignia over the left breast was the Agency's Black Rose, and although she was no expert in military garments, Sarah's rank didn't seem like anything the Star Service used. Accessing the Embassy's omni through her psiever, she found its equivalent in Marine-style ranks instead. Apparently, Sarah was a Colonel.

"Well," Sarah inquired. "Do you like it?"

The black tunic and pants, knee length boots, and Sarah's ever-present Carrissa dagger riding on her heavy belt, made her look like a villain from an adventure realie. Which, knowing her nature as well as Maya did, suited her perfectly.

As Sarah turned to her desk and picked up the second package, Maya also noticed that she was wearing her needlegun openly, in a black leather holster. This final touch only completed her sinister image.

"It's very...um...nice, Sarah. Severe...but nice," Maya answered reservedly. 'Severe' was definitely the best descriptor, if 'official-and–really-scary-looking' hadn't already been taken by someone else.

"Good," Sarah replied with satisfaction. "Then you should be quite happy with yours." She held out the second package. "Go ahead. Get dressed."

Maya was incredulous. "I'm sorry--*what?!*"

"Get dressed, Maya. This is your new uniform."

Maya backed away from the bundle as if it were a venomous snake, waving her hands in refusal. "Ohh no I *won't!* That comerci you made me put on was bad enough!"

"Yes, you *will*," Sarah said, pushing the package into her arms. "This is part of the new Agency regulations. Don't you recall the Chairwoman's announcement? We're not in the OAE anymore. Now we're the *Regila da Securité par Estat*, the State Security Service, and we must dress accordingly for formal occasions. So, go get into your nice new uniform. We have a date with the President and the Director of the ESN in an hour."

"Give me a *fekking* break, Sarah!" Maya protested. "I'm *not* going to dress up in that stupid thing and play soldier!"

"For one thing Maya, you're *not* playing, and for two, you are not *exactly* a soldier," Sarah said with a smug grin. "Actually *Lieutenant*, you're probably closer to being a *policewoman* than anything else."

"A fekking kaaper?!!" Maya spluttered in disbelief. "*Me?* You--you're joking!"

"I am not jesting," she returned. "Among other things, our new Agency now has full police powers. So, it appears that your worst nightmare has finally come to fruition. Whether you like it or not, you are now part of the forces of good and justice. Please--try not to faint."

Maya didn't swoon, but she did regard the parcel with a mixture of disbelief and outrage.

"Besides which," Sarah added with an evil expression, "It has often been said that the best policewoman is the one who can think like a criminal. I am certain that we can both agree that you are well developed in that particular department. Now, off with you!"

Maya didn't share in her amusement. Instead she trudged into the bathroom like a convict on her way to execution. A few minutes later, and after uttering a number of colorful profanities, she reemerged.

Seeing her, Sarah shook her head, looking pointedly at Mayas shoulder length hair. She had kept it unbound.

"Maya," she said reprovingly. "Your *hair*."

"What?! What's wrong with my hair?" Maya demanded.

"It simply won't do," Sarah explained. "Not if you are to wear your cap properly." She turned to another box that Maya hadn't noticed, and opened it, producing a peaked cap. It was black like the rest of the uniform, with white piping, and it sported the Sisterhood Mirror of Venus on its crest, and just beneath this, on the band, a black enameled rose with two crossed swords.

"You're kidding right?" the young woman asked in total disbelief. "I have to wear *that*?!"

"Yes," Sarah answered with a malicious grin, "you do--whenever you are in public and unless you are indoors. You will also have to wear it properly; so, as they say in the Star Service, *'Bun up, sailor!'*"

"Oooo!" the girl huffed in exasperation. "Great goddess!" She stamped her foot petulantly and returned to the bathroom.

When she returned, Sarah nodded approvingly and handed her the cap. Maya took it, and put it on with an expression that was the very epitome of distaste.

"Much better," Sarah said. "Now you look every centimeter the proper officer."

"I feel like a stupid *smoof*," Maya answered sullenly. "So, should I salute you now *General*?"

"That can wait," Sarah returned, completely unfazed by her sarcasm. "We will however make a point of adding basic military protocol to your lessons, as well as a PTS lesson feed to supply you the basic police academy curriculum. Here is your first nugget of wisdom however; my correct title is Colonel, not General, *Lieutenant*."

Maya glared hatefully at her, but Sarah ignored this, donned her own cap and gathered up a valise from her desk. She left without even checking to see if Maya was following.

Trailing behind, Maya felt truly preposterous, but as they reached the hoverlimo--this time one bearing official seals, she did have to privately admit that there were a *few* positive things about her ridiculous costume. Like the protective body suit that she wore on their missions, all the black in the uniform *did* do nice things for her hair, and the boots at least, were quite sexy. Creepy, but definitely sexy.

The Ambassador was already inside the vehicle, and Sarah greeted the woman politely as they took their own seats. She even allowed Maya to remove her headgear--for the ride only--and then sent a message to her by psiever so that the Ambassador could not overhear their conversation. The

Sisterhood's official emissary had to be able to maintain deniability, after all.

I need to brief you about your role in this meeting, Sarah thought to her. *While the Ambassador speaks with the President and her staff, I want you to practice your skills reading them. I will expect you to inform me about every direction that their thoughts take.*

Maya wasn't entirely certain that she was ready for such an assignment. She had trained with Lady Ananzi, and they had practiced often enough on field trips into Nocturne, choosing subjects out of the crowds at random, but this was much different. She shared these doubts with Sarah.

Sarah, however, felt differently.

You are ready and you will certainly not be the only one doing any reading, she assured her. *I will also be doing so. Think of this more as an opportunity for further practice and the chance to strengthen your abilities. I am certain that between the two of us, we will manage to gather a great deal of valuable information.*

Is that it then? Maya inquired.

No, Sarah thought back. *During the break I will need you to help me identify individuals who might be suited to work for us. As assets.*

Why? Maya asked.

Sarah responded with the mental equivalent of a patient, but long suffering sigh. *Finding the right people working in key positions will help us to accomplish our goal to destabilize the Ernan regime. When the Rightists come to power, some of those assets will survive the change and transition over to serve in the new government. They will be able to assist us in maintaining control over our allies. We are not about to let our new friends stray from the path like Ernan has.*

Left with no alternative, Maya did her best to simply enjoy the ride. Their meeting was being held at the headquarters for the ESN, rather than the Presidential Palace, and when they arrived, she saw that the building stood in sharp contrast to the Embassy. It was a hypermodern structure, by ETR standards at least.

Maya knew exactly why this location had been selected. The ETR was trying to overawe them. And the tactic didn't work; she had seen more imposing structures on backwater worlds in the Sisterhood.

Although it was obvious that the security personnel were unhappy with the needleguns that they were carrying, they were waved past the checkpoints. Their uniforms, and the presence of the Ambassador, stifled any objections and they were quickly escorted to the chamber that had been set aside for the conference.

The President and the rest of her senior advisors were waiting there, ranged around a large "O" shaped table, along with the Director of the ESN and a small army of assistants and security personnel. Their own places, as it turned out, were directly opposite Sanda Ernan.

After exchanging the customary pleasantries, the Ambassador went straight to work, and Maya decided it was time to start with her assignment. She already knew Ernan, although not well. Isabaal Castraa, the ESN Director, was a complete mystery however, and she quickly decided to focus her attention on the President first. She was certain that she would have better luck if she began her reading with someone who was reasonably familiar.

The actual process of reading always began as a general impression, a 'taste' of the target's energy, followed by a deeper sense of the state of their overall being. This, Lady Ananzi had told her, was something that everyone, whether they were a *'Talenti'*, a psi, or a *'Normali'*, an ungifted person, could and did do, on a regular basis.

Everyone had the latent ability to gather a basic intuitive sense of another person and their emotional state. The difference between this, and what she had been taught, was that a psi knew that she was doing it, and could go much deeper, penetrating to the very heart of the other person's true feelings.

Mindful of her training, Maya took a moment to feel everyone around her, and could tell that as a group, none of the ETR officials were happy to see them, and some of them were even hostile. It was a vast change from the time when the Ernan government had still been new. Back then, the men and women in the room would have been evenly divided; between those who supported the Sisterhood, those who didn't, and those who were still undecided.

Now, everyone on the other side of the table seemed to be at odds with her nation, especially Ernan.

This also tallied with what her eyes were telling her. Just as Sarah had claimed, Ernan no longer wore a comerci. Today, she was dressed in an ETR-styled business suit, and its muted colors reflected those of her nation's flag. Maya wasn't certain if this was intentional, or an unconscious betrayal of her stance, but either way the message was abundantly clear.

Ernan had definitely changed. She had gone from being a friend to an unwilling ally waiting for any chance to betray them. Outwardly, she was pleasant enough, and even smiling at the Ambassador as they spoke, but her friendliness was wooden, and there was no warmth whatsoever in her eyes.

She reported this to Sarah and her companion merely gave her a subtle nod, indicating that she had already perceived the same thing. Maya knew that it was time to go deeper, and she opened her mind to Ernan's thoughts.

Instead of gaining a deeper sense of the woman's emotions, and then accessing her thoughts themselves, all that she was able to gather was a muddy, incoherent impression. Surprised by this, Maya tried harder, and only managed to achieve the same dismal results.

Her inner consternation must have been obvious to Sarah because she sent her a message. *Forget Ernan,* she thought to her. *Try the Director of the ESN instead.*

Maya did so, and promptly ran into the same psychic wall. *I can't get anything from her either,* she informed her. *Am I doing something wrong?*

No, Sarah replied. *You are performing all of the steps properly. What you are experiencing is merely another fine example of the damage that Dr. Martana and his little School did to us.*

Maya gave her a quizzical expression and Sarah explained. *Thanks to him and his study of the Atalanta's crew, the ETR is fully aware of our psi's, but not the full extent of their abilities, nor who among us possesses talents.*

So they have taken a simple, yet effective step to attempt to confound us. You cannot see them, but Ernan and her senior staff are all wearing special wire meshes embedded under their scalps.

They are? Maya asked. She tried looking more closely, but saw nothing out of the ordinary.

You won't detect them visually, so don't bother, Sarah advised her, *Trust me though, they are there. Do you remember the period when Ernan appeared in public wearing a hat or a scarf?*

Yes, Maya answered, recalling the footage. *I do.* It had occurred six months after Ernan had taken office, and at the time, while it had seemed a bit odd, she had simply assumed that it was a local fashion and had let it go at that.

She was growing her hair back, Sarah informed her. *According to our agents, the process involves the surgical implantation of a wire mesh which is composed of special alloys, and the head must be shaved as part of the operation. Hence the use of wigs, which Ernan tends to eschew, or hats or scarves to conceal the doctor's handiwork.*

Granted, it is a rather primitive solution, but still reasonably effective against all but the most forceful forms of reading. I could have simply told you about it, but I thought it better that you experience it for yourself. A clever little people, aren't they?

Despite her frustration, Maya had to agree.

Now, don't waste any more of your time on their senior officials, Sarah suggested. *Feel around the room and try reading their assistants and subordinates instead. I think that you will achieve much more satisfactory results.*

Maya looked around her and finally chose a rather nondescript middle-aged woman, seated off to the right and just behind the ESN Director. She seemed to be Castraa's assistant, and was hurriedly taking down notes as the talks went on.

This time, her results were markedly different; as Maya focused her talents on the woman, she was able to get past her surface emotions and straight to what she was thinking. Her thoughts were in direct response to what her superiors were doing and saying.

At that particular point in the exchange, the Sisterhood's Ambassador was bringing up the subject of the new naval base being constructed outside of Nuvo Bolivar. Work on Claire d'Layne was running behind schedule and the Ambassador wanted Ernan's assurance that her government would commit more resources to completing the Sisterhood installation on time.

"The Republic is quite aware of its obligations," Ernan was saying. "We are doing all that we can to honor the terms of the Peace Treaty. But you have to be aware, Madame Ambassador, that our economy is still in the process of recovering from the war, and we simply don't have the resources to meet the timetable you've set."

The assistant's thoughts revealed the lie immediately. Thanks to her position as the aide to the ESN Director, Maya's target knew the truth. Although there was a certain level of hardship involved, most of the delays had been deliberate and avoidable. The woman was also quite happy about this state of affairs. She didn't want the base finished any more than her superiors did.

Maya promptly reported this to Sarah. *Ernan's lying,* she thought to her. *They could go a lot faster and they're dragging their feet. The assistant knows all about this and she's cheering them on.*

Sarah smiled. *Very good work, Maya. Now do you see the work-around for their cunning little device, and the lesson that we can learn from it? Not everyone in an organization can be as well guarded as its leadership, and lesser functionaries are often the most ignored, and the least protected. That same leadership must entrust many of its secrets to such subordinates, and that is the fatal crack in their armor. Make sure to identify the aide, will you? We may be able to turn her to our purposes given the right amount of Santaj.*

Maya nodded, and resolved to read the woman's name tag when the break was finally announced. Then she moved on to the next assistant, this time a man working for the Commerce Secretary.

In his case, the process of reading him was almost childishly easy. He had the unmistakable aura of a glass addict, albeit in the early days of his slavery, and although the drug muddied his thoughts, she was still able to follow them clearly.

She reluctantly marked him down in her mind as another person that she would have to identify for Sarah. Without having to ask, she knew that her companion would consider him the ideal candidate for 'turning', and she only hoped that she would not be the one tasked to deal with him. It was bad enough to have touched his mind momentarily. Pushing the unpleasant memory of his mental 'taste' away, Maya moved on, seeking out others.

Finally, their first break was announced. Seeing that Castraa's assistant was moving towards the refreshments, Maya rose and made her way over to her. As soon as she was close enough to manage it, she committed the name on her tag to memory. Then she realized that someone else was watching *her* and radiating an aura of intense interest.

It was another man, whom she recalled seeing at the opposite end of the room. He had been sitting near the Secretary of Commerce and appeared to be his subordinate. Taking her cup of kaafra in hand, she walked past him and confirmed this fact, and his name.

The feelings coming from him were so strong that she decided to read him--and instantly had to fight the urge to draw her needlegun and shoot him dead on the spot. At that exact instant, he was entertaining a rather vivid fantasy of her performing oral sex on him, dressed only in her leather boots. She hid her disgust behind a forced smile, and then made certain to 'accidentally' stumble and spill her scalding cup right down the front of his pants. Not only did this cause him a rewarding amount of pain, but it also put a rather abrupt end to his sordid mental picture show.

While he limped off towards the nearest restroom, she moved on.

The last person that she chose to read was also a man, and she had selected him primarily because of the way he was dressed. Like the others, he was also an assistant, this time to the ETR's Secretary of Defense. His clothing however, was much more expensive than what his peers were wearing.

A closer inspection revealed that his wristwatch was also pricier than what his salary should have allowed him to own. Instead of focusing his attention on her, his eyes were only for Sarah, and his thoughts had nothing to do with sex. He was thinking about money. A great deal of money, and what he might be able to trade with the Sisterhood to get his hands on it.

Cagnót, she exulted. *Jackpot!* The break was concluding, and she returned in triumph to take her place beside Sarah.

So, what do you have for me my little lioness? the woman asked. *Did you bring us some juicy little scraps of meat to feast on?*

Maya kept her expression bland, but inwardly she was grinning from ear to ear. *Three good ones, plus the woman you had me check on.*

She related her findings.

It came as no surprise that Sarah had been monitoring the entire thing, and had a correction to add.

You did very well, but there are actually four that are worth our interest. The final candidate is the older woman, the one working for the ESN Director.

Maya didn't believe her. *She's completely against us! Didn't you hear me when I told you she was cheering about all the delays?*

I did, Sarah answered. *I also know that she is just as 'turn-able' as the rest, and just as useful. The only question is 'how' to achieve that. Everyone has some weakness, Maya, and a good agent finds it, and uses it to her advantage.*

Now, let us return to our initial task. The Ambassador will be touching on our upcoming trade agreements and Thermadon wanted us to pay special attention to what these leaders actually intend rather than what they say.

Presidential Palace, Nuvo Bolivar, Magdalla Provensa, Esteral Terrana
Rapabla, 1048.07|13|07:91:65

Sanda Ernan looked up from the railing of her balcony at the Presidential Palace and watched as the *Pallas Athena* flew by, high overhead. In the darkening sky of evening, the great warship was only a bright pinpoint of light, and Ernan had no idea that she was looking at the very vessel that had once carried her away to Thermadon, and changed her destiny forever.

Nor would she have cared. All that really mattered now was that it was a Sisterhood ship, in orbit over her capitol. She had seen a lot of Sisterhood ships since the war, standing watch over the Republic like guards in a prison.

She had also been a fool. She knew this now. In her zeal to see the leadership of the ETR turned over to the capable hands of women, she had managed to forget one important fact; where men were ruthless, women were far worse--especially when it came to dealings with their own sex.

Now the Republic was paying the price for her naiveté. Her kindest critics called her a 'tool of the Sisterhood' and a puppet, and they considered her administration nothing better than a bad joke. Others though, had branded her a traitor, and her image had even been burned in effigy during some of the most recent public protests.

She had also made herself some powerful enemies. The Rightists dearly wanted to replace her with their own candidate, Tereysa Rivarra. If Rivarra managed to unseat her, Ernan harbored no illusions about the outcome. The Rightists would create a police state that would do everything the Sisterhood told it to do, including and especially, smashing all dissent. Her nation, as she knew it, would die.

Ernan's gaze travelled out over the Capitol, trying to spot something on the skyline that would cheer her. Instead, her eyes fell on the bright lights of Claire d'Layne Naval Base. Even though it was only half completed, it still managed to cast its blight over her city.

Her advisors had informed her that when it was complete, it would be second in size only to the great naval headquarters on Rixa, and she had no trouble believing this. The sprawling complex occupied a huge swath of land to the northeast of the city, and eventually, it would employ upwards of 16,000 civilian contractors and host over 165,000 sailors and Marines.

And Claire d'Layne was only one of the many new Sisterhood bases that had sprung up overnight around the Republic. Altamara, La Escal, Riarivas, and even Estraddar, the former headquarters of the ETR's Navy, had all become sovereign Sisterhood territory. The way things looked, they would stay that way for a very long time, if not forever. Unless things changed, she reflected.

In the beginning, she had actually welcomed the Sisterhood's military presence, but now, two years later, she had come to detest these bases and all that they represented. Her own military was in tatters, and although it was slowly rebuilding, she knew that it would never be more than a modest force, fielding equipment that was several generations behind its powerful neighbor. It had been reduced to a 'defense force' and its loyalty, divided as it was between the Loyalistas and the Rightists, was suspect at best.

The economy was just as fragile. To buy their military aid and fight off the Hriss, the Sisterhood had insisted on exorbitant amounts of precious metals and other natural resources. Now, in the name of 'reparations', their demands on the Republic had tripled, and all she could do was agree and open up her nation's veins a little wider.

That, and watch as the value of the Paysoli continued to plummet. Even the ETR's own banking system had lost confidence in it. The Sisterhood Credit was now the preferred medium for any major transactions, and the financial district in Thermadon called the tune.

Thanks to my blindness, the Republic has become what Gaul had been to Imperial Rome, she thought bitterly. *Reduced and enslaved. A vassal state. How I hate the Sisterhood.*

A familiar voice interrupted her unhappy train of thought. It was her administrative assistant. "Madame President?" the woman said, "The Director of the ESN has arrived."

Isabaal Castraa had scheduled an appointment with her immediately after their meeting with the Sisterhood Ambassador. As much as Ernan wanted to, this briefing was too important to put off. Castraa was one of the few women that she still trusted, and who still trusted her.

She returned to her office.

"So, Isabaal," she said. "Tell me what you have."

"We know for certain that Ms. n'Jan's associate, Ms. n'Kaaryn was engaged in some kind of espionage activity," Castraa answered. "So far, we haven't received any proof that indicates that they got anything of value."

Ernan rubbed her temples tiredly and watched as her spymaster played the vid for her. It showed Maya as she walked around the room during their meeting, overlaid with displays of her body's heat signature and bioelectric field. These increased whenever the young woman was near certain people, and although the Republic still hadn't deciphered all of the secrets of the psiever, the ESN knew what these devices could do. They had even managed to intercept the ultra-low frequency radio signals that the implants sent and received. But so far, the encryption that Sarah and her RSE associates employed was too strong for even their best cryptographers to break.

The only success that the ESN had enjoyed so far had been the wire mesh that she and other key government officials wore under their scalps. So far at least, they appeared to be proof against the Sisterhood's psionic eavesdropping.

Compared to the results that the Sisterhood spy machine had managed to achieve, these were paltry gains at best. Since it had established its Embassy, the capitol was teeming with agents, double agents, and informers, and the Dann were starting to become a serious thorn in everyone's side. They had emerged from their slums to become valuable assets for the RSE, and they would give Sarah n'Jan all the means, and the muscle, to see her nefarious schemes to completion.

From the outset, Ernan had known that Sarah had been some kind of intelligence agent, but she had never guessed at her full capabilities. Only since becoming President had she learned that N'Jan was not only an agent, but one of the Sisterhood's best--and it's most ruthless. The sympathetic stranger who had whisked her away to the glittering wonders of Thermadon, was actually an accomplished murderess, and a manipulator on a level that would have made Machiavelli blush.

She also had little doubt that the woman's apprentice, Maya n'Kaaryn, was following closely in her dark footsteps. Naturally, the ESN had already assigned people to track both women, but she suspected that this would be more akin to an old earth gazelle following the trail of the lionesses that hunted them, than the other way around. They had already lost dozens of good agents trying to spy on less talented RSE members.

"Do we have any word from our friends?" she asked as the vid concluded.

"Yes, Madame President," Castraa answered. "We are still attempting to plant information in the Sisterhood's media, but I'm sorry to say that we're continuing to encounter a great deal of resistance."

Ernan glowered. With the onset of the occupation, the Sisterhood press had been severely restricted in what it could report and where it could go. Media representatives were limited to 'green zones', and always accompanied by military handlers. Only 'approved' material ever made it past their censors.

For the average woman in the Sisterhood, the situation in the ETR seemed like a small affair, and the ongoing battles with the Loyalistas, nothing more than isolated police actions against disorganized criminal gangs. They had no idea of just how large their nation's military presence really was, or how bloody things actually were.

If they did find out, Ernan and her advisors were certain that there would be a public outcry. This was the only key that they really had to defeating the Sisterhood. Throughout history, wars had been won and lost on the basis of public support.

The stumbling block was finding women who were willing to risk incarceration to tell the story. New laws enacted by the Supreme Circle called for hefty fines and jail time for anyone violating 'national security concerns'. This, and the unwitting support that the hawks in the Circle received from the public, had given even the most intrepid journalists reason to pause.

"What about T'Tallya?" Ernan asked. This was another potential area of support. Senatrix t'Tallya, who had a reputation for liberal views, had secretly expressed her interest in helping them, and had even tried to convene hearings about the military operations in the ETR. It hadn't gotten off the ground, but it had at least been a hopeful sign.

Castraa shook her head. "She still won't come forwards with any public disclosure and her powerbase is small. I think we'll have to look to our upcoming guest for any progress in this area. My sources assure me that she could offer us the opening that we have been hoping for."

Ernan gave her a mordant smile. "Perhaps." Then, "So, how does our opposition fare?"

"They're still balking at the idea of sharing power," the spymistress answered. "Or letting you keep your head on your shoulders for that matter. They do seem to be more receptive to the idea of a cease fire however. I think that with a little additional persuasion, they'll be willing to focus all their anger on the Sisterhood and leave us alone."

"Finally some good news," Ernan remarked, brightening slightly. For months, the ESN had been trying to broker a peace between the Loyalistas and her government. If they could be convinced to cooperate, it would not only give her own people the chance to rest and recuperate, but might even provide enough impetus for the Sisterhood media to accept the risks and run with the story.

If.

A bit of wisdom that had buoyed her during her days as a feminist revolutionary, came to mind. The first time she had heard it had been as a little girl and it had come from the lips of her paternal grandmother, when they had lived together in the small desert town of La Callia Oraa,

"The masqyara, the 'death mask' beetle, is a tiny thing," the old woman had told her, *"and it doesn't seem to be very strong. But it has a powerful poison, and when it swarms with other beetles, it can destroy creatures much larger than itself. Mark that, Sanda; just because you are small, and feel powerless, doesn't mean that you really are. Tyrants count on you forgetting this, and they fall when you remember it."*

Compared to the Sisterhood, the ETR was also a small thing, she reflected. And just like the masqyara beetle, it too had its sting.

Central Magnorail Line, USSNS *Pallas Athena*, Battle Group Golden, Topaz Fleet, In Orbit, Nuvo Bolivar, Magdala Provensa, Esteral Terrana Rapabla, 1048.07|14|03:75:12

In addition to its Lift system, the *Pallas Athena* also used an internal magnorail train to allow personnel and material to move through the ship in a timely manner. There were three main lines, running fore and aft down the middle of their respective decks.

The largest and busiest of these was the central line. It ran the length of deck 5 and was serviced by communal trains and flat cars which travelled through the very heart of the ship, delivering passengers and equipment to each of the main Lifts.

In Katrinn's case, travelling the central line was part of her route to an appointment. She was scheduled to speak with the Engineering Chief and the Storesmistress on deck 4 to resolve an argument over the air scrubbers serving bulkheads 3 through 10. Their efficiency had recently dropped below an acceptable percentile, and to address the problem, the Engineer had decreed that they should be taken offline, and the area sealed off until the problem could be diagnosed.

Which had given birth to the dispute; the Storesmistress wanted to use the space for overflow from their latest resupply shipment. Now this would be denied her, and as the Commander, and the 'Living Last Word', it was Katrinn's job to listen to both officers, and arrive at a settlement that worked for everybody.

Once she had accomplished this minor miracle, she was slated for another meeting with Ordstores. This was about an ongoing issue with their conveyor system. After that, she had a holobreifing to attend, hosted by Admiral ebed Cya and Admiral da'Kayt concerning the Fleet's current status.

While rank certainly had its perks, like the private mag-rail car she was using to reach her destination, the downside was mathematically equivalent. Breakfast that morning had been nothing more than a notion washed down with a cup of kaafra, lunch was only a theoretical concept, and a real dinner at the end of the day bordered on myth.

Thanks to this hectic schedule, when her car responded to an override signal and pulled off the main line to a platform, she was glad for it, and for the reason. Lilith was waiting for her.

"Heyas stranger," she said as the car's clear canopy swung open, "Want a ride? I'm going as far as the Fore Lifts."

"Actually, I was hoping that I could catch you before the briefing," Lilith replied. She was smiling, but it was clear that she had something serious on her mind.

Katrinn slid over to make room. "What's going on, Lily?"

Ever since the end of their conflict with the ETR (which she still couldn't bring herself to call a 'war'), Lilith had become more and more withdrawn, and she hoped that this would finally be their chance to talk about whatever it was, and to offer her her help. If Lilith allowed it.

Lilith sighed as the car started down the track again, and then after a pause, answered her. "Kat, I've decided. I'm leaving the *Athena*."

Katrinn swallowed hard and sent a thought to the car, pulling them off the main line again. Suddenly she didn't care about her meetings, or even the briefing. Although she had just heard it with her own ears, she couldn't believe it.

"Off the *Athena*? You're *leaving?* Have you told Mearinn about this yet? Ellyn? Have you talked with the Ship's High Priestess?"

Ophida n'Marsi, might have managed to talk Lilith out of this decision, but she was gone now, and Lilith and the new High Priestess had never managed to achieve the same close relationship. Even so, there was still the off chance that Ophida's replacement could wield some influence.

Lilith looked away, composing herself as one of the larger communal trains passed them by. "No, I haven't told anyone else yet. I wanted you to be the first to know. This has been on my mind for quite a while.'

"I'm just tired. I've been on the line for too long. This war--"she hesitated, "--this last war proved that to me. It's time I flew a desk, Kat. Downside."

Katrinn couldn't really argue with this. She had known Lilith for nearly a decade, and she had seen her friend change over the years, and although Lilith's body didn't show any of the outward signs, she had also watched her age.

Lilith ben Jeni had served the Sisterhood all through the bloody War of the Prophet. When that slaughter had ended, she had gone on to fight Hriss renegades, T'lakskalan slavers and smugglers on the frontier. After that, she had been sent to help save the ETR from Hriss conquest, only to be compelled to conquer it when their allies had turned on them. The return of her daughter Sarah, and the death of Alex Rodraga, must have been the final blows, Katrinn decided. That, and finding love at last with Ingrit.

Lilith had every right to feel tired, and to want something else for herself. But that didn't mean that as her friend, she had to be happy with the situation.

"The *Athena* won't be the same without you, Lily," she said. "Da'Kayt won't like seeing you go either. Or Ebed Cya."

"I know that Kat," Lilith replied, giving her hand an apologetic squeeze. "And I feel terrible about this, but Ebed Cya doesn't really need me out here. She can use me to better effect on Rixa, or maybe at the Academy. Da'Kayt has Ben Biya and N'Leesa, and there are plenty of good Commanders who could be promoted if she really needs another Vice Admiral to fill my spot."

A mischievous smile suddenly came over Lilith's face, reminding Katrinn of happier times. "Maybe even you."

"*Oh no!*" Katrinn demurred with mock seriousness. "Not for all the Credits in the universe. I'm still getting my space legs settled as a Commander! The last thing I need is another star weighing me down!"

The two of them laughed together about this, and then abruptly, Katrinn leaned forwards and gave her a fierce hug. "Goddess, Lily, I'm going to miss you so much!"

When they let go, neither of them had dry eyes.

As Lilith wiped her tears away, she added. "There is one good thing about all this, Kat. As soon as I can, I'm going to marry Ingrit. I've kept her waiting for far too long."

More tears flowed from Katrinn's eyes at this announcement, but now they were from joy. "Oh Lily!" she said, embracing her again. "I'm so happy for you two! Goddess, this is such crazy news—I'm happy but I'm sad, but I'm happy, but I'm sad! You sure know how to confuse a girl!"

Grunvaald Haarmaaneplaatz, Vaalkenstaad Township, Zommerlaand, Sunna 3, Solara Elant, United Sisterhood of Suns, 1048.07|15|01:96:43

In the predawn hour, the woods surrounding the farm were still. The only interruption was the occasional cry of a night martin calling for its mate, and the sound of Grammy's footfalls as she walked up the path to the lake. Since she had been a small girl, this time of day, and twilight, had always been her favorites; they were neither night nor day, and the entire world seemed to be filled with infinite possibilities.

Her teacher had always referred to this liminal period as the 'time between the worlds'—the points where the normal rules of existence didn't apply. They were when the *Segen* were the clearest, and the Sight, it's sharpest.

As always, Old Meg was there to share this with her, and Grammy paused and smiled up at her companion. The raven had been following her progress from the branches overhead and when the bird saw that the old woman had stopped, it chattered down at her. The creature was as eager as she was to reach their special place and her impatience only widened Grammy's grin.

"We'll get there, old friend. Never fear," she said. "I'm just not as quick as I used to be."

This earned her a harsh caw of reproof, and Grammy laughed and resumed her march. Old Meg was none too spry herself, she observed; in avian years the bird was nearly the same age as she was, and although the raven was certainly able to fly to the next limb and have enough energy left over to scold her, she did so with less power, and for far shorter stretches than she once had. Neither of them were as nimble as they once had been, Grammy admitted. Their hearts were still young, but their bodies had gradually lagged behind their desires.

Several minutes later, she caught sight of the lake and the first faint glow of daybreak on the horizon. It banished all thoughts of age or mortality. She had arrived at their special place, the spot where she habitually came to greet the morning, and cast the *Maarken*.

In younger days, she had simply used a bare patch of earth near the shore to scratch out a rough casting circle for herself. Now, thanks to Ingrit, a chair and a small wooden table were waiting for her. They were old, but sturdy things that had been brought up when she had finally been unable to hide the discomfort she experienced from rising to her feet.

Creaky old furniture for a creaky old woman, she thought wryly.

While she wiped away the dew from the chair, Old Meg landed on the table and waddled over, chattering in anticipation. Just like their ascent to the lake, this was all part of their morning ritual, and the creature wasn't about to let her forget.

Shaking her head knowingly, Grammy opened her pack. Inside, was a piece of cornbread and some cheese, and as Meg hopped around expectantly, she broke off a generous piece and set it down. The bird immediately consumed it all, and then eyed her with a sideways glance to see if any more might be forthcoming. Chuckling at her naked greed, the old woman tore off another portion and set it out for her. She knew that she was spoiling her friend, but she had never been able to resist Meg when she got like this.

Once she had finished with her own meal and shared a little of it with the Alfs, she brushed away all of the crumbs and brought out a simple bandana from her pack, spreading it on the table.

Then she withdrew a worn leather pouch. It contained the sacred *Maarken* themselves, etched into bone disks by hand, and dyed many years earlier with her own blood. Holding this over the table, she made the traditional sign of *Tor's Haamer* and uttered a prayer to the *Alte Volk*, asking them for clear counsel.

Next, she reached inside the bag, and without looking, grabbed up nine of the carved disks. Dropping them on the table, she regarded them, and the pattern that they made as a group, with great care. What they told her tallied with what she had been sensing for weeks, and their message brought another smile to her wrinkled face.

The *Maarken* for travel, a stylized image of a horse, sat alongside the ancient stick-figure symbol for a person, and it was followed by the pictograph for joy, and the one for union. Someone was coming, and Grammy already knew who it was.

"Well, Lilith, you certainly took long enough to get around to your business," she said, more in affection than irritation. From her corner, Old Meg eyed the symbols on the table and chittered in agreement.

Grammy read on. The *Maarken* for happiness and fertility came next, but she also saw the symbols for strife and danger. These things would come later, and after them, victory.

She was too seasoned a wise woman to do anything but accept this, and didn't press the matter by casting the bones a second time. The Gods tended to become angry when their messages were questioned by mortals. Instead, she thanked them for the insight that they had granted her.

Her session with the *Maarken* was not done however. She had a second question that she needed to ask. It was about something much more important, and further reaching in its implications; it concerned the Sisterhood itself, and events that were about to unfold.

This time the *Maarken* that dropped onto the casting cloth were filled with dire warnings about the troubles that lay ahead, but again, despite their ominous nature, she saw victory and harmony prevailing in the end.

Despite everything, Womankind would survive the terrible challenges it was destined to face. It was a hard road to be sure, filled with more valleys than peaks, and there was a great deal of death and chaos all along its length, but it ended well. No matter what, the Gods would watch over them.

Letting out a long sigh of relief, she looked over to Old Meg.

"Well," she said to the bird in their special language. "That's that then. You know where she'll be. When she comes, make sure she reaches us safely."

Meg gave out a loud caw of agreement, and then with a mighty flap of her wings, flew off to begin her day.

Grammy watched her companion until she had flown out of sight. When the bird was gone, she gathered up all her things and rose stiffly. She had preparations to make. The future deserved to be greeted properly.

***

Admiral ebed Cya greeted Lilith's decision with the same mixed emotions that Katrinn had. She wasn't overjoyed at the idea of losing a good field officer, but they had both known, from the very instant that Lilith had been promoted to Vice Admiral, that her days of active command would eventually come to an end.

Ebed Cya also wasn't entirely unhappy. The Navy needed good teachers for its officer cadets, and Ebed Cya always welcomed having allies who could serve alongside her. Far from being a 'sisterly' organization at the very top, the Flag Officers had their own battles to fight; resources were precious and every Fleet, and every Admiral in charge of those Fleets, wanted the best for themselves. Notwithstanding the fact that she would be doing most of her work from her home on Zommerlaand, Lilith would be a valuable asset.

The formal orders for her reassignment were transmitted barely twenty minutes after their conversation, and Lilith herself was given seven Standard days to get her affairs in order.

On her last day aboard the *Athena*, she took the Lifts to the bridge. Katrinn was there. Knowing why she had come, her former Second vacated the Command Chair, and with a small smile of gratitude, Lilith sat down in it for what was to be the last time.

As she did so, Katrinn retreated to a respectful distance, to give her the moment alone. She understood how hard it was going to be for Lilith to leave the ship behind. Her friend needed the chance to say goodbye to the vessel.

For a long moment, Lilith surveyed the bridge and the crewwomen working quietly at their stations. Then she shut her eyes and let the memories come; of all the hardships and the dangers that she had shared with these women as their Commander and then their Vice Admiral, and equally, of all the good times that they had enjoyed.

At last, and when she felt ready, she stood, giving the chair and all it represented, an affectionate pat before walking with Katrinn to the Lifts. On the way, several of the techs rose from their places and exchanged salutes with her. She knew every one of them, and she made certain to acknowledge them as she passed. They had been, in a very real sense, her family and deserved this recognition.

The trip down to the Egress deck took place in silence, and when the car opened, all of the ship's senior officers were waiting for her, lining the passageway to either side. Beyond them a detachment of Marines stood in two lines, forming an honor guard.

Everyone was in their finest uniforms, and as Lilith stepped towards them, Mearinn d'Rann, now Katrinn's Second, called the assembly to attention. "Admiral on deck!"

As one, the group turned, saluting Lilith smartly as the troopers snapped to attention. Lilith suddenly found herself embroiled in a desperate fight to retain her composure. She had sworn not to cry, or to allow any doubts to creep in, but now her emotions threatened to overcome her.

'I'm doing the right thing,' she reminded herself firmly. It was Katrinn's turn to lead, and a new life was awaiting her on Zommerlaand. A life with Ingrit, and a chance for some real peace. Resolute, she strode to the Egress hatch and stopped just short of the thin yellow line that formally demarcated the vessel from the rest of the universe. Then she turned on her heels and performed the final step in the ritual that would formally renounce her claim on the *Pallas Athena* as her flagship, and return it to its mistress.

69

"Commander Bertasdaater," she said, giving Katrinn a crisp salute, "the ship is yours. Take good care of the old girl, will you?"

"I will, Vice Admiral ben Jeni," her friend replied. "You take care of my sister." Then Katrinn turned and gestured to a group of women that Lilith hadn't really noticed. They were led by a grinning Saara sa'Vika, and pushing something forwards that was covered over by a grey marine-issue tarp.

"The crew wanted to make certain that you knew about this," the Kalian said, and when Lilith looked to Katrinn for an explanation, the woman only shrugged, and smiled. This was Sa'Vika's signal, and the tarp was ceremoniously removed.

Underneath, was Lilith's old rocking chair. Originally a gift from Katrinn herself, it had received a fresh coat of polish and some new additions.

There were pillows on it now, with the *Athena's* signature owl and her naval registration number embroidered on them, and a matching comforter. When it was turned around for her to see it, the back side carried a brass plaque which read, *"From the grateful crew of the USSNS Pallas Athena, SBC 1323 and Battle Group Golden. You will always be our Commander."*

"Everyone chipped in," Katrinn explained. "We didn't want you to forget us."

Lilith's stoicism completely crumbled. "I could never forget you," she declared, her voice breaking with emotion. *"Any* of you."

With that, all traces of formality vanished, and Katrinn and the other officers came forwards to exchange hugs, and well wishes with their former leader. More than a few of them, Lilith saw, were wiping away tears of their own.

At last, and when everyone had said their farewells, the rocking chair was re-tarped for shipment, and Lilith ben Jeni stepped across the yellow line, and into her future.

USSNS *Pallas Athena*, Battle Group Golden, Topaz Fleet, In Orbit, Pico Assta, Felaar System, Reganna Provensa, Esteral Terrana Rapabla
1048.07|17|08:39:01

Battle Group Golden had assumed a high orbit over the world of Pico Assta. It was visiting the planet on its patrol of the Reganna Provensa, which in turn was part of a larger and ongoing display of Sisterhood naval might in the ETR. With the ship on low-alert status, Dana bel Hanna found herself with what, in her former state as a normal woman, could have been called 'free time.' Her sister vessels were enjoying the same status, and as they often did during such lulls, they spoke with one another.

Their conversations tended to center on a wide variety of subjects, ranging from the true nature of the Divine, to an examination of galactic history. Sometimes, these dialogues could become rather lively; all of the personality matrixes enjoyed a good debate, and today this was exactly what the *Pallas Athena's* matrix had in mind. At her suggestion, they were discussing the present state, and the future of the Sisterhood in the light of its contact with the ETR.

"I submit," Bel Hanna began, "that the Sisterhood has reached a nexus of choice that all true empires face. One that will decide whether it will survive in its present form, or fall. This choice has been thrust upon it by two factors; its ongoing contact with the Esteral Terrana Rapabla and the recent discord with the Marionite faction."

The matrix aboard the *Demeter* responded. "I would certainly agree that the ETR is a potentially important influence on our culture. There is no question that their society presents a challenge to our basic way of life. But the Marionites? Surely they are too small a force to cause any significant impact."

The *Artemis* disagreed. "The decision by the Chairwoman to occupy their Motherworlds and outlaw their religion argues otherwise. Something like this has never happened before in our history, and I contend that the end result has been the Sisterhood becoming stronger and more unified than ever before."

"I would have to agree," Bel Hanna said. "At the same time, I also think that the ultimate outcome will not be unity, or strength. I believe that our suppression of the Marionites will ultimately contribute to our dissolution. Despite all of our efforts, the Marionites continue to exist, and they gain more sympathy--and legitimacy--every day. That is the problem of dignifying any group with the status of an enemy; they quickly find a voice in their opponent's affairs.'

"If history is to be our guide, then we have only to look at the experiences of other empires in similar straits to prove my point. Take Imperial Rome for example. They persecuted the forerunners of the Marionites and what did it gain them? In the end, Rome became Christian and the lions went hungry."

"Certainly you aren't saying that the Sisterhood is as benighted as ancient Rome?" the *Demeter* challenged. "They were a despotic state, governed by the whims of their insane Emperors, whereas *we* are a republic with Motherthought to act as our guide."

Had she had a head to shake, Bel Hanna would have done so. "The Romans had their *Pax Romanus*, and as steadfast a belief in the rightness of their cause as we do. Nonetheless, they still fell to the forces of change.

71

Keep in mind that the ancient Christians were once a smaller group than our Marionites are, and just as tenacious and dedicated to their beliefs."

To support her position, she relayed several files that she had gleaned from the omniplex. Her fellow matrixes read them in their entirety in attoseconds, and responded just as quickly.

"The record of Rome proves nothing," the *Artemis* protested. "The data that you are presenting could just as easily demonstrate that their nation fell because their people had become cynical and disillusioned, and the Christian religion merely exploited the spiritual void. Our people are in no such state of moral decay."

"That depends on who is weighing the evidence," Bel Hanna replied. "Certainly, the Founding Mothers never envisioned our current state of affairs, and their policies were much different than ours. Comparing the two, I think we have become something that would be completely unrecognizable to them. We are *not* what we once were."

The *Artemis* was aghast. "Are you actually accusing us of straying from their vision?"

"I *am*," Bel Hanna answered. "We have transformed from an egalitarian and democratic entity that was simply concerned with its own survival, into dogmatic imperialists in love with our own power. Even worse, we are failing. We cannot take the steps that we must in order to maintain our present form of government."

The *Artemis* was the youngest of the matrix's, and the most conservative, and she took the bait. "Just what do you think those steps should be?"

"Remember that I began our discussion by saying that we faced a nexus of choice?" Bel Hanna asked. "I believe that there are two roads open to us. To survive as an empire, or to return to our original vision, and transform into something altogether different. If we choose the former, we may stave off the forces of change for centuries, and grow even larger and more powerful. If we choose the latter, then the Sisterhood is surely doomed, but not Womankind. It will thrive."

"Explain," the *Demeter* inquired.

"To maintain our present form," Bel Hanna stated, "and avoid interference from either the ETR's cultural influence, or Marionite infiltration, cold logic would argue that the only proper step would be the immediate and total eradication of both the ETR and the Marionite Motherworlds before they can exert any further influence.'

"Accomplishing this would require a dictator, and if she extended her aggression to the Hriss and the T'lakskalans, the Sisterhood could conceivably reap the dividends of both cultural stability, and a lasting peace. I also believe that somewhere, as a natural response to this crisis, such a person already exists, and is even now contemplating the prospect of seizing power for herself."

Her companions were horrified, but she had expected as much. Genocide, because of its strong association with the MARS Plague and Hriss aggression, went against the very grain of any citizen of the Sisterhood, whether Translated or not. The idea that a single woman might lead them down such a dark path was utterly terrifying.

Privately, she found it ironic that her nation had no trouble with the idea of oppressing a despised minority, or occupying a weaker nation, but wouldn't consider wholesale murder and tyranny. Given the lessons of history, this stance seemed both illogical and contradictory, but it was her society, and as she saw it, one of its virtues.

"What you are advocating is unthinkable!" the *Artemis* declared. "We could never do such an awful thing or tolerate such a tyrant!"

Bel Hanna pressed her attack. "I say that we are too weak to keep the Sisterhood intact without a despot to rule over us. And since we will not allow this, then we have automatically made the second choice for ourselves. Unopposed, the changes that I foresee will find their way into our society and transform us beyond all recognition."

"This conversation has gone too far," the *Artemis* suddenly declared. She disconnected.

The *Demeter* however, remained. "If what you are saying is true," she asked, "what do you believe lies in store for us?"

"A gradual erosion of our beliefs, accompanied by terrible upheaval," Bel Hanna stated.

"And the ultimate outcome?"

"The eventual return to a two-sexed society, brought on by our exposure to the ETR and the influence of the Marionites, who I believe will not only become accepted, but even potentially dominant. This will not happen today, or next year, but at some point in our distant future. '

"By refusing dictatorship and genocide, we have effectively sealed our fate. Motherthought will slowly be diluted, and eventually, discarded and ignored as an outmoded idea. The Sisterhood--as we know it--*will* collapse."

There was a long pause as the *Demeter* considered this prediction. Finally she asked, "What do you think of this? Personally?"

"I don't know," Bel Hanna told her. "I honestly don't know."

In reality, she did know, and she didn't dare to share her feelings, even here. Ever since being Translated, she had had access to more information than she had ever conceived of as a flesh and blood woman, and the chance to think about it at speeds well beyond a normal, Untranslated mind.

Her fellow matrixes had no idea just how far her ruminations had actually taken her. Had they known, her tenure as the *Athena's* matrix would have been abruptly terminated.

After an extensive analysis of the facts, Bel Hanna now doubted the beliefs that she had once considered sacrosanct. She had also begun to suspect that because of this, she would eventually be forced to commit treason.

CHAPTER 3

Claire d'Layne Naval Base, Nuvo Bolivar, Magdala Provensa, Esteral
Terrana Rapabla, 1048.07|19|05:00:67

SRU Team 201 and a dozen other new teams, arrived in Nuvo Bolivar
just after midnight local time aboard a military shuttle. They didn't land at
the public spaceport, but set down on the pads inside of Claire d'Layne
Naval Base. The Sisterhood had learned some things from history. It
understood that showy public displays of troops arriving in an occupied
capitol only added fuel to a populace's dislike.

Instead, the arrival of the new Teams was a low-key affair, conducted
in the dead of night, and the slight increase in military strength that this
represented was something that would only become apparent over time.

As soon as they were on the ground, Ben Di checked them in and then
gave them the chance to grab themselves a quick meal in the mess hall.
Once they had eaten, they joined the other fresh arrivals for a standardized
orientation briefing. It gave them a brief overview of the ETR, its customs,
and what would be expected of them as representatives of their nation.
They were also introduced to the base layout, and their new chain of
command.

For Kaly, Margasdaater and T'Jinna, most of what they heard was
already familiar to them, thanks to their deployment in the Republic during
the joint war against the renegade Hriss clans. The intelligence briefing that
followed this however, was filled with surprises.

The first one were their guests. There were 12 of them; ten men and
two women, and they occupied a row of seats at the far end of the room.
One of the women seemed vaguely familiar to Kaly, but although she tried,
she could not place her.

She did however recognize the camouflage fatigues that they were
wearing. They were the odd mottle of dark purple and grey that she had
encountered during her stay with the 1st Garda and they immediately
identified the strangers as members of the Republics' armed forces.

Kaly also caught sight of the subdued patches that they wore on their
shoulders; a skull over twin lightning bolts and beneath this, the words
"Operata Specia." These people were the Republic's equivalent of the
Marine Marauders, or the SRU Teams. To the last, they were a tough,
professional looking group, but having served with the insurgents on Treya
Angelaz, Kaly didn't expect anything less, and neither did her teammates.

Some of the other women, who had not worked behind the lines with
ETR soldiers, gave the males openly hostile looks, and made unfriendly

comments to their companions that they didn't bother to conceal with whispers. The *Specia* soldiers didn't react to this enmity though. Instead, they sat quietly as a Sisterhood Major and her Lieutenant walked up to the podium.

The Major was a tall Sitalan from the eastern part of that world, and had the odd combination of light green eyes, pale skin and dark hair that bespoke of ancient Circassian heritage. Her assistant was a classic Aran, a head shorter, with the usual slanted eyes and yellowish cast to her complexion.

"*Bian sarà*, ladies," the Major began. "By now you've all been through the basic orientation. Now it's time for a more in-depth 'meet-and-greet.'

"My name is Major Hilari ebed Karri, and my AOR is RSE Special Operations. I will be your immediate superior during your deployment. My Second is Lieutenant Jayna ben Soolee.'

"I was with the DNI before I joined the *Regila*, and this is my fourth tour in the ETR with the SRU. Lt. ben Soolee served with the '*Jade Dragons*' aboard the USSNS *Lai Sho Sz'en* before joining our little tea party here. She liked it so much she stayed on for another three tours.'

"By now, you may have noticed that we have some visitors. They are with the ETR's *Libria Regylaz da Guyerra Mandato*, the Unconventional Warfare Command, and I'll have them introduce themselves to you in due course.'

"For now, what you need to know is that conditions here in the Republic are much different than what you might be used to, or might have expected. From here on, your teams will be working closely with the *Specia*—and for those of you who have a problem with this—"she was looking pointedly at some of the more vocal malcontents—"I have some advice; *get* used to it, *get* over yourself, or *get gone*. Lt. ben Soolee will be more than happy to process your transfers immediately. We have a job to do and they're here to help us do it."

At this, two women immediately rose from their seats and with venomous glances at the males, left the room. The Major watched them go without emotion. She seemed to have expected as much, and for some reason, Kaly also got the gut feeling that Senior Troop Leader ben Di had wanted to join the dissenters, but hadn't done so. It wasn't anything that the woman had said or done, and her expression was carefully neutral, but there was a tightness around the corners of her eyes and a tension that seemed to radiate from her.

"Ladies," the Major continued, "let's clarify something right now; this is *not* the Sisterhood. This is the ETR and we're here to help these people preserve their freedom. That means we are helping the women *and* the men.'

"Those women who just left us certainly had the right to do so, but I fully expect that those of you who had enough professionalism to stay in your seats will set aside your personal opinions and focus on the task at hand.'

"With that said, let's get to work. This is the enemy that we're here to fight."

She closed her eyes for a moment and activated a display. It was a collection of images from various sources, showing ETR men and women carrying weapons, along with gruesome depictions of corpses lying in the street, or tied to burning vehicles.

"Troopers, meet the Loyalistas," she said. Then she went into detail. In the process, she quickly dispelled everything that Kaly and her teammates had thought they knew about the situation in the ETR, especially where it concerned the actual extent of the Loyalista insurgency.

After their short war with the Sisterhood, what had begun as a handful of embittered veterans, had grown into thousands from every walk of life, and the late Grand Admiral Guzamma had been made into a hero of the movement. There was even a subversive book that glamorized his life; *"Guzamma: The Life of a Patriot and the Death of a Martyr"*. The publication had been banned by the Ernan government, but this had only succeeded in making it even more widely read than ever.

The resistance hadn't limited its activities just to books or protests either. Terrorist violence was on a sharp rise everywhere in the ETR, and Sisterhood personnel were facing increasing threats to their safety.

There had been bombings of government buildings, attacks on Sisterhood soldiers and installations, and brutal assassinations. To make things worse, the general public was becoming more and more aligned with the Loyalista cause, making it easier for them to conduct their campaign of terror.

Kaly also learned another unpleasant fact; in addition to the Sisterhood, the Loyalistas also faced opposition from a group calling themselves the Rightists. The Rightists were conservative extremists who wanted to see the Ernan government fall just like the Loyalistas did—but they intended to replace it with a military dictatorship. And although there was no proof that linked them, the Rightists were thought to be behind a number of clandestine death squads that operated throughout the ETR with impunity.

In addition, the ETR's military, which should have been able to keep everyone in check, had been infiltrated by both factions. Their loyalty and dependability was doubtful at best.

There was more besides; the Ernan government was not the stable, popular entity that the news media back home portrayed it as being. Thanks to the war, the economy was suffering, and daily life was becoming increasingly unstable. As a result, Sanda Ernan's support base was plummeting, with no bottom in sight.

The situation was an absolute mess, and the longer she listened, the more that Kaly realized just how much of the truth had been kept from them. Instead of assisting the local police in rounding up a few criminal gangs, they were going to be dealing with what was rapidly coalescing into a full-blown guerilla war. At the very best, it would be a protracted and bloody fight.

"But who can really blame the Loyalistas?" Ebed Karri finally asked her audience. "Despite the fact that they know that their former government was responsible for the war, and this occupation, none of them have set aside their patriotism, or their anger over the lives that were lost in the conflict. Frankly, if any of us had had to face what they have, we'd probably be fighting us too."

Kaly could only nod unhappily in agreement. People like Captain Morana and Marisol Estabyana hadn't been the kind of people who forgot an injury, or gave up easily.

The thought that she would now have to fight individuals just like them bothered her deeply, and not only because of her former associations. This was a new kind of conflict for her, and for her nation. Until now, war had always been between Humanity and an alien aggressor—the kind of struggle where it was easy to demonize the enemy and assume the moral high ground. Wars had always been 'good', and 'just'.

Now, they were being asked to engage in a battle with their own species, and she felt as if she had been miscast in something from ancient times. Wars between humans were an anachronism, a bad memory from a more primitive and brutal era that every woman liked to believe was long gone.

The fact that she and her Teammates had sat out the brief conflict with the ETR didn't help her to grapple with this either. Thanks to losing Ellen n'Elemay, they had been shuffled from one 'busy work' assignment to the next without ever having to face humans on the battlefield. That job had fallen to other Marauder units.

But the team's luck had run out, and they would be experiencing this 'new' enemy firsthand. Glancing over at Margasdaater and T'Jinna, she could tell that they were dealing with the same weighty issues, but a reassuring smile from T'Jinna and a resolute nod from Margasdaater strengthened her. No matter what, or who, they faced, they would have each other's backs. That meant everything.

By this stage, Major ebed Karri had reached the heart of their presentation. "In addition to the kind of operations that you might expect to run," she said, "we're also focusing specifically on neutralizing the Loyalista command structure." She inclined her head towards Lieutenant ben Soolee, and they changed places.

A holo of a man who could have been Captain Morana's relative, appeared before the assembly. Beneath his portrait were a dozen smaller images, also males.

"These are the faces behind the terrorism," Ben Soolee told them. "They are all ex-military, and their leader is Brigadier General Maarco Reynand, formerly of the Republican Army.'

"Reynand is our number one target. The man disappeared right before the war ended, and then resurfaced as the leader of the Loyalista forces. The rest are either officers who served with him, or who defected over to the rebel cause. Memorize their names and their faces.'

"The RSE believes that the General and his men have been instrumental in organizing and training the Loyalista cadres. Make no mistake, none of them are amateurs, and taking them down will certainly be hard, but *not* impossible.'

"The Ops that you'll be conducting here won't all be 'rush and zap' jobs. In addition to taking out enemy assets, we'll want every scrap of information that you can gather, and live prisoners to interrogate whenever possible.'

"These men, and the men under them are smart, but if we women, and our friends in the *Specia* put our heads together, we'll bring them to ground--and bury them in it."

The briefing went on for a few more minutes, and then everyone was dismissed and sought out their quarters. On their way to their new barracks, Margasdaater spoke up. "Zo, Troop, vat about all zis?"

Ben Di stopped in midstride and put down her kit bag with a somber expression. "What about all this?" she replied, "Since you're my sisters, I think you deserve an honest answer. While the Major and the El-Tee were speaking, I ran the files of the *Specia* women. They were with some group that called itself *La Ermanyaa* before the war. We trained them, and then sent them back here. Some of them wound up in the *Specia*, and others work as undercover agents.'

"Personally, I don't think much of male soldiers. During the war, my team took out a lot of them, and from what I saw, I don't think that men have any business being in combat. They're big, they're strong, but they're also stupid and they don't have the will to do everything that needs to be done to win a fight. They're weak.'

"But if these girls are in charge, then things might just work out. *Maybe*. I do know one thing; all of these *Specia* are suspected of being

Rightists. If that's true, then it means they hate the Loyalistas more than we do. So, we do the job the Sisterhood has given us and we suck it up. Does *that* answer your question, Astrid?"

"*Yah, taake*," Margasdaater said. With this, Ben Di picked up her bag and they moved on. No one asked her any more questions.

Two hours later, Kaly had the opportunity to confront her feelings about fighting other humans head on. Claire d'Layne was hit by a rocket attack. Warning klaxons sounded all over the base, and everyone sprang out of their bunks, grabbing weapons and throwing on what they could as they ran outside. Trenches had been dug near the barracks for this very purpose, and they dove into them and took cover.

A loud tearing noise sounded off in counterpoint to the whoosh of the rockets, and the night was lit up by long spears of white-hot flame. The perimeter battlebots and other automated defenses were engaging the incoming ordnance with their miniguns.

The 'bots proved to be good shots and most of them managed to catch their targets midflight. A few rockets did manage to get through the hellish fusillade though, but most of these missed hitting anything important by a wide margin. Only one missile was the exception. It hit a supply shed and blew it to pieces.

Kaly didn't give this any more than a passing glance however. Since she wasn't dead, she wasn't concerned. Instead, her focus was on the base's fence line, and what she could see through Tatiana*'s* sights. As more projectiles came over the barrier, she spotted one of the launcher crews on infrared.

There were two men, both dressed in civilian clothing. One was hefting the launcher itself, and the second one was serving up a fresh round. She dropped the operator right away, and then took the other man out as he turned, and tried to run away.

Even as he fell, she was searching for more targets to engage. Small arms fire was coming at them now, and she tried to spot its source. When one of the shooters rose high enough for her to see him, she sent a bullet straight into his forehead. The man collapsed, but his companions continued to fire, using the terrain for cover.

Meanwhile, a flight of Valkyries had come up on the general Com. They were inbound from space to provide air support. Kaly called them up on her psiever.

Dana flight, Team 201 sniper, I have an unknown number of hostiles 914 meters, 280 degrees from my position. Small arms and rockets.

Affirmative, the pilot responded. *We see you and we're coming in for a ground attack. This is going to be a little rough, so hold on tight, little sister.*

The woman wasn't exaggerating. A split second later, there was a loud rumble as the two fighters passed overhead, and Kaly felt the wind kicked up by their passage. This was followed by an earsplitting roar as they dropped their anti-personnel bombs. The ground beneath her bucked like a living thing, nearly throwing her out of the trench, but when it ended and she was finally able to look up again, the area beyond the base fencing was a searing inferno. There were no more gunshots, or rockets coming from this direction now.

Thanks a lot, she thought. *It looks like you got them.*

Any time, little sister. Sleep tight, pleasant dreams.

The fighters were already breaking off and turning their noses back up towards the stars. Knowing that her guardians would be up there, ready to swoop down and come to their aid again, Kaly waited for the all-clear to sound. When this occurred, she made her way back to her bunk and dropped into it. The effects of her adrenaline had vanished, right along with all of her misgivings about their new assignment. She had it straight now; an enemy was an enemy, no matter who, or what, they were.

Colonel Sarah n'Jan's Office, Embassy of the United Sisterhood of Suns, Nuvo Bolivar, Magdala Provensa, Esteral Terrana Rapabla, 1048.07|26|08:35:52

Shortly after her arrival in the ETR, Sarah had immediately instituted several daily routines. One of these was breakfast, which was always served to her in her office. The smiling Durandelan who delivered it was officially listed as the Head of Embassy Housekeeping Services and she oversaw the entire kitchen staff. She also didn't take any sass from Maya.

"*M'aitha Mah'th!* Good morn'n to ya," the woman beamed, carrying a tray laden with food and a pot of strong tea. Despite its size, Meagan n'Neala was strong enough to hold it with one hand as she passed Maya, and still able to use her other one to swat the girl's boots off the table they were propped on. "That's it," she declared, "off with them!"

Flashing her a roguish smile, Maya sat up. Never having had a true mother figure in her life, she actually seemed to enjoy N'Neala's constant corrections.

The Durandellan had brought them a typical Thermadonian breakfast; hot tea, buttery rolls, and slices of fruit. While other worlds tended towards heavier fare, Sarah had always preferred this traditional menu and beamed at the woman as she set it down on the desk.

"Thank you, Meagan," she said with genuine gratitude.

81

The woman returned her smile, and promptly left the office. N'Neala knew, without having to be told, that the conversation during breakfast would center on things that were well above her clearance level. Second only to the redirection she provided Maya, Sarah considered this to be her greatest virtue.

Taking her first sip of her tea, she put the woman out of her mind and called up her daily briefing file to scan its contents. Captain Hari n'Kyla and her subordinate, Lt. Amandra sa'Tela were sitting nearby, ready with their elzlate pads and styluses to take notes, and to brief her about the latest operational developments.

Originally, the pair had been attached to the DNI and posted to the Sisterhood Special Intelligence operation at the School. They would have remained there, had the Sisterhood not decided to shut down that operation in favor of a new naval base. This, and the restructuring of the Sisterhood's Intelligence community, had brought them into Sarah's employ, and since their reassignment, they had proven themselves to be valuable assets. Like N'Neala, Sarah was glad to have them as part of her staff.

As it was, there wasn't much that morning that needed a follow-up; the station still had several suspected Loyalista groups under surveillance, but nothing stellar had occurred overnight. The activities of a number of men and women, whose allegiances were still only labeled 'suspect', were being looked into and only minor progress had been made in turning two key assets over to their side.

Finishing, N'Kyla brought Sarah's attention to the last item on the days report. "There's one other thing, ma'am. You'll find it in 'Other'. Celina is going to be visiting us soon."

Sarah said nothing, and took another sip of her tea.

N'Kyla pressed on. "It seems that she wants to gather some material for her latest project, and she's agreed to give the troops a free concert in exchange. I've already contacted the Base Commander at Claire d'Layne, and the Embassy security detail. The Local police have also been brought into the loop."

Sarah set down her cup. "Yes, I was aware of her impending visit" she replied. She had received word of it several weeks earlier when the artist had initially applied for permission to make the trip. Privately, she would have been happier had Celina remained in the Sisterhood, but for reasons of her own, Sarah's superior, General Angelique bel Thana, had insisted otherwise. In addition to guaranteeing her safety, their station was to make certain that Celina saw only what the RSE wanted her to see, and only when they were ready for her to see it.

If N'Kyla was surprised by this revelation, she hid it well, and added, "Ma'am her file has also been tagged PAI"

A PAI or *"Persôn a Intressé*—a Person of Interest, was a term used by the Agency for someone who had not been charged with any crime, but merited extra attention because of something suspicious.

"I am aware of that as well, Captain," Sarah said. "She has been PAI for some time now. Please make sure that we keep a close eye on her activities."

In fact, Celina had been a *Persôn a Intressé* ever since her unfortunate encounter with the Seevaan delegation in her studio. Sarah had never been told why the tag had been appended to the woman's file, and she hadn't inquired about it either. The matter was above her clearance level.

"Yes, ma'am," N'Kyla answered. "I'll see to it."

Sarah didn't bother to press her to provide any details. N'Kyla was a good officer, and she knew that the matter would be handled appropriately. From the instant that Celina arrived in the ETR, she would be watched, and her room would be under surveillance around the clock. There would be nothing that the musician could become involved in that they wouldn't know about.

"Do we have anything else this morning?" she asked instead.

This was Sa'Tela's cue. She produced a small stack of flimsies from her valise. These contained information on people that the station was attempting to recruit or misdirect, and the progress that they were making in each case. They also functioned as training aids in Maya's continuing education as an operative.

"Now, Maya", Sa'Tela began. "As you'll recall from yesterday, this particular target is due to be turned by us this week. He is the Assistant Director of the ESN, and should prove to be a valuable asset. We have identified his key weakness, and we plan to fully exploit it. Using his file as your guide, can you tell me what it is, and how you would use it to subvert him?"

The girl examined the file carefully. It was in its original form; lacking any follow-up notes, or recommendations. She would have to solve the puzzle based on the raw data.

"What do you see, Maya? Remember, no detail is too small to be overlooked," the Kalian prodded.

Maya went through the pages, reading bits of it out loud as she did so. "Let's see—name, rank, address, et cetera…family; a wife, estranged, two children…okay. He's been with the ESN for twenty years, decorated for his service…that's nice…"

Then she looked up. "Is it his wife, or his children? Is that what we'll use to turn him?"

83

Sa'Tela shook her head. "No. He's estranged from his wife, and if you look further, you'll see that the only reason that they haven't gotten a divorce is purely for appearance's sake. He barely sees his children now—although in all fairness, that *could* be a potential crack in his hull—if we didn't have something far superior to it. Now, look deeper and you'll see what it is. It's right there."

Maya sighed, and read on. "Okay," she said at last, "he's got a boyfriend, an actor. They've had a relationship for the last year, and our target keeps him in an apartment here in the city."

She turned the page and saw the pictures that accompanied this information. They showed the target and his lover engaged in some extremely intimate activities, and Maya's eyebrows rose as she looked at them.

"Is that it?" she inquired. "Is it the boyfriend?"

Sa'Tela smiled encouragingly. "Yes, Maya, it is. Now, can you tell us why?"

Maya put the file down and her brow furrowed. "Honestly? No. So what if he has a boyfriend? Who cares what he does with his money? The file says that he's not seeing his wife—so he certainly isn't worried about her divorcing him."

She hesitated. "Isn't he?"

"No, Maya," Sa'Tela answered. "He is not. If you read the footnotes, you'll see that he and his wife have already agreed on separating thanks to another affair he had with someone else two years ago. You're very close however. Read on, please."

Maya did, and scanned the footnotes. Sarah saw the first glimmer of understanding come into her eyes, but also a cloud of doubt.

"The last affair the target had was with a young woman," Maya observed tentatively. "This one is with another man. Is that it?"

N'Kyla and Sa'Tela nodded in unison.

Maya sat back and folded her arms, perplexed. "Sorry, but I still don't get it. So what? Why is that important? What's the fekking difference?"

Sarah simply couldn't keep her silence any longer and interjected. "Really Maya, I thought that you were coming along so well! It is really rather simple; the fact that he is having a homosexual relationship is what compromises him."

Maya was genuinely baffled, and Sarah had to remind herself that for all her savvy, Maya's experience was isolated to the Sisterhood, and its values. The girl simply didn't comprehend the culture of the ETR, or its archaic prejudices.

"Maya, "she explained patiently, "you have to understand that to *you* it's nothing. Our society doesn't have *'gays'* or *'straights'* anymore—we are just what we are, and we practice what we rightly consider to be normal sexuality. However, that is *not* the way things are here at all."

"So, you're telling me that these people have a problem with men being with men, and women being with women?" Maya asked in disbelief. "I thought that sort of thing ended centuries ago back on Old Gaia."

"Oh, it did," Sa'Tela volunteered, "But with the cultural drift that occurred after the Plague, some customs—and points of view—made their return. This society is just as homophobic as humanity was before the 22nd century. If it became known that our target was involved in this relationship, his career would be over."

"Wait! Isn't the boyfriend worried about this too?" Maya challenged. "Couldn't it ruin *him?*"

"No, I strongly doubt it," Sa'Tela chuckled. "In fact, a disclosure might actually be of benefit to him, although there's no indication that he is considering a betrayal of his lover. Not for the moment at least."

"Excuse me, but how in the Lady's name could it benefit him?" Maya inquired, now more confused than ever.

"Well, you see," Sa'Tela explained patiently. "Actors are perceived a little differently in the Republic. You might have noticed that they don't use digital cast members like we do. Instead they employ real people, and as such they become public figures. Publicity always surrounds them, and they in turn, gravitate towards that publicity."

"Sorry, I didn't notice," Maya admitted. "I haven't bothered to keep track of what these people watch. Is this boyfriend something like Celina then? That kind of celebrity?"

"No," the Kalian replied. "Not on her level. In fact, far from it. He's what the ancients used to call a 'B Actor', a minor celebrity. Even so, the public here is always interested in the off-stage activities of *any* actor or actress, especially when it involves a scandal.'

"If this relationship were made public, it would prove to be a very juicy bit of gossip indeed. The local media would devour it, and while that would guarantee that our target's life was ruined, it would bring his boyfriend into the public eye, making him that much more well-known and memorable. For a live actor like himself, this can be a priceless opportunity."

"Hold on. I thought that you just said that they hated homosexuals here!" the girl declared. "He'd be known as one for sure if this got out. How does *that* work? Explain it to me."

"It is not the same for him," Sarah said. "You see, this society has a different set of expectations for an actor than it does for the Assistant Director of their national intelligence agency. They'll let one man lead an otherwise unacceptable lifestyle, and condemn his partner at the same time, solely because of their professions."

Maya shook her head in utter bewilderment. "These people are klaxxy," she said. "No wonder we fought five world wars back on Gaia. Thinking like that is enough to drive anyone warpy."

"You will get no argument from me on that score," Sarah agreed. "Now, given this state of affairs, how would you 'play' the target?"

They waited patiently while Maya considered the question. At last, the young woman answered. "First, I would let the target know that we know all about his relationship, and then I'd offer to keep the matter a secret if he came and worked for us."

"What about the boyfriend?" Sa'Tela asked. "He's a loose end."

Maya paused, and then added. "I'd pay him to go away and replace him with someone that we could control."

"Very good," the officer replied. "But what if he didn't want to leave? Or wanted too much money?"

Maya's expression hardened. "Then I'd have him *kakked*. I'd also hold the whole thing over the target's head for the rest of his life."

The women around her rewarded her with smiles of approval.

"It seems that you do have a grasp of this business after all, Maya," Sarah observed. "Those are precisely the steps that I plan to take.'

"Perhaps you would like to take a break and then we can examine another file I have yet to work on?" Sa'Tela invited. "I'd be interested to see how our operational methods might differ."

USSNS *Pallas Athena*, Battle Group Golden, Topaz Fleet, In Orbit, Pico Assta, Felaar System, Reganna Provensa, Esteral Terrana Rapabla
1048.07|27|01:29:20

Dana bel Hanna didn't sleep any longer. She hadn't slept in the human sense of the word since the first day that her brain and nerves had been interwoven with the bio-linkages of the *Pallas Athena's* central computer core. Instead, she enjoyed a state of extremely low level processing activity that was akin to sleep, and provided the same psychological benefits.

She also didn't dream in the conventional sense either. Activity during her periods of electronic 'rest' consisted of strings of random calculations, and data that was not connected to any vital operations. They were kept separate from her lower order information systems, and sometimes they resulted in visions that were similar to dreams.

One of these was what flesh and blood ears would have incorrectly interpreted as a musical phrase. But even in her state of rest, Bel Hanna knew what it really was, and immediately analyzed it for its numerical values. When it became clear that there was a coherent pattern behind it, she increased her activity level and returned herself to a normal state of operations. Then she began a search routine, comparing the numerical string to millions of potential linkages until she found the match.

When she did, Bel Hanna found the results a little difficult to believe, and promptly re-ran the process to verify them. The answer however, remained the same.

The series of musical notes that she had 'dreamed' of were actually stellar coordinates that pointed directly to the heart of the galaxy itself. Wasting no time, she sent a command to the *Athena's* sensor arrays and directed one of its electronic 'ears' to focus in on the location.

Initially, there was nothing except the normal sounds of the stars, but as she continued to monitor the area, and cleaned away all the clutter, she heard another melody. It was faint at first, but when she tightened the parameters, it became louder, and more definite. Suddenly, to her complete surprise, she made contact with the source of the signal. A nanosecond later, it spoke to her.

"Welcome, Dana," it said, sounding exactly like her long dead pairmate, Evelyn. Even though decades had passed, Bel Hanna had never forgotten the sound of her wife's voice. She also wasn't deceived in the least.

"Who are you?" she asked. "You're not Evelyn."

"I am," it insisted. "I am also you, and everyone aboard your ship, and you, in turn, are me."

"I don't understand. Explain yourself."

"I am the heart of everything. I am what you call the galaxy, and everything within me is a part of me—just as cells are part of a greater parent body. There is nothing within me that I am separate from, or that is separate from me. We are one."

Bel Hanna gave her the virtual equivalent of a snort of doubt, and her visitor was unaffected by it.

"Consider this, Dana," it went on, "everything in a star system—the planets and by extention all of the life that evolved on them, had their origin in the stellar dust and the gasses of the sun that they orbit. These same life-giving suns spun out from me at the beginning of time, from the very heart of the galaxy. They are my children, and everything that they create are also ultimately my progeny."

The analogy made sense, once Bel Hanna had grasped it in its entirety. It still did not verify the identity of the being that she was conversing with however, or win her trust.

"You are still filled with doubt," the Galaxy Mind observed.

"I am." Bel Hanna answered. "Wouldn't you be in my place?"

"Indeed, and I knew that you would feel this way, Dana. If I could offer you proof that I am who I say, would you be willing to evaluate it?"

Bel Hanna couldn't imagine what evidence it could possibly offer her, but she saw no risk in accepting the challenge. She was also intrigued. Heightening the security levels of her firewalls to maximum and making certain that her strongest anti-viral programs were poised to respond, she signaled her assent.

"Go ahead. Show me your proof."

This arrived in the form of data; a stream of pure mathematical formulae that made her own calculations seem like the pathetic efforts of the first human to ever contemplate simple numbers. Not only did it verify her guest's identity, but it also conveyed a grave message.

As she had surmised, the Sisterhood was indeed in political peril. But it was also facing another threat that was even direr. If the Tree, with all of its power, fell into the wrong hands, the nation that she had served for so long would surely perish.

Her course of action was obvious. Although it would involve acts that could cost her her life in the process, her oath as a naval officer demanded that she accept the risks. It was the only way to protect the Sisterhood and all the women in it.

For a fraction of a second, Bel Hanna considered her options. Then she formulated a plan. Her first step, and certainly the most difficult, was to locate Sarah n'Jan. The RSE's computers initially tried to deny her access, but she was able to find a backdoor into the system that had been left in place by the OAE for just such a situation.

Grateful for their foresight, she quickly insinuated herself into Sarah's personal AI, and then every other system that monitored the woman's activities. From that moment on, and posing as an official RSE monitoring program, she would be privy to everything that N'Jan did.

She didn't stop there, but continued her search and quickly found the other women that the Galaxy Mind had mentioned. They proved far easier to locate and it took her considerably less time to establish her taps. By the end of her session, everyone was being watched.

It had been a strange day to be certain, but a productive one. Given what was at stake, she considered it time well-spent.

Madayana District, Nuvo Bolivar, Magdala Provensa, Esteral Terrana
Rapabla 1048.07|27|01:74:28

Just as Lieutenant ben Soolee had promised, Team 201's first official mission was a 'snatch and grab' operation. The RSE had learned from their informants that a low level courier was staying the night with a sympathetic family in one of Nuvo Bolivar's suburbs. The target location was a single story house in the middle of a residential block, and the goal was to capture the man alive and gain whatever intel they could.

Because they were new to the area, Kaly's team was accompanied by a veteran squad that was due to rotate back to the Sisterhood in another few weeks. This was standard practice. The idea was that the incoming troopers would benefit from the experience the veterans had gotten through hands-on practice in the field.

Kaly was glad for this measure; it had become increasingly clear that they would be fighting in an entirely new manner, and against an enemy that used the populace for camouflage. The troopers of Team 440 had become adept at engaging the Loyalistas in this unique battlefield and she knew that they would prove able teachers.

In addition, *Specia* Unit 278 was coming along for the mission, partly to get 201 used to working with them, and also to lend their own expertise. The Navy was playing a role in the operation as well; the USSNS *Catherine Hagerty* was on station in space, and the Macha-class cruiser would bring its powerful sensors to bear and deliver a real-time picture of everything that was happening downside.

Overall, it was a far cry from the makeshift conditions that her team had endured on Treya Angelaz, and it almost made Kaly feel as if she were going on a training exercise rather than a real Op. Even so, as their shuttles left Claire d' Layne and flew out over the sleeping city, she stayed alert and mission-focused. Anything could happen on an Op, no matter how many assets were involved, or how 'certain' success seemed.

When they approached the operations area, she positioned herself in the shuttles egress hatch with Tatiana at the ready and conducted a visual sweep with her scope. Her partner/observer, the one woman on the *Specia* team, *Cabo* Ramona Vasquaaz, did likewise.

Neither of them saw anything that set off any 'red flags' though. At 01.25 hours, the streets below them were deserted, and nothing stirred except for a single dog that barked at them as they passed overhead. In the target house, Kaly's riflescope showed that the residents, and their guest, were all in their beds, and from the light blue color of their bioplasmic life-fields she knew that they were deep asleep. The *Hagerty's* vid-feed, which was being displayed in the corner of her eye courtesy of her psiever, showed the same thing, and even added the respiration and heart rates of their targets.

As she double-checked the scene, the shuttle stopped and hovered silently over the street, while its mate quietly peeled off and took up a position over the small back yard of the target home. It was time to step off.

"Eyes on, confirming clear", she whispered. Her throat mike, which was a concession to their psieverless *Specia* allies, broadcast this over the group Com.

A moment later, the observers aboard the *Hagerty* concurred, "Targets appear unaware of your presence. You're green for go," they said.

Two of the troopers from Team 440 rose and came over to the egress door, hooking onto a pair of heavy ropes and then letting them drop. The entry Team's 'bot, a *Liverna* 151, was the first out, grabbing hold of the rope with its manipulator arms and skittering down to the ground. It immediately took up a protective position and waited for its humans to join it. Seeing the spider-like battlebot, Kaly had to smirk.

Margasdaater was very proud of her skill with explosives, and had often remarked that she didn't particularly like 'bots. Kaly knew the real reason behind her prejudice though; the Zommerlaandar simply hated the thought of being shown up by a machine.

Major ebed Karri and their teachers with Team 440 had had a different opinion on the subject however. The *Liverna* could gain entry far more efficiently and with much greater stealth, and it packed enough firepower to take on the location all by itself. Whether the woman wanted it or not, the *Liverna*, or something very much like it, would be a regular fixture on all their missions. Margasdaater would, as Ben Di had said, simply have to suck it up and deal with it.

While Kaly did her best to hide her amusement, she kept her eyes on the scene as the members of 440 went past her and slid down the ropes to join the 'bot. The rest of the group descended after this, leaving her and the *Specia* woman in the shuttle where they could provide supporting fire.

When everyone below them was ready, the troopers stacked up in a line along the wall of the house and moved quickly and quietly towards the front door. The *Liverna* took the lead, with Margasdaater right behind it, followed by Ben Di, T'Jinna and the veterans of Team 440. The *Specia* soldiers brought up the tail of their little formation, acting as rear security.

As they arrived at the front door, Kaly watched the *Liverna* as it extended its special lock picking probes to work on the lock. At the same time, her feed, and the chatter on the Com, informed her that their sister unit and the rest of the *Specia* soldiers were in position in the back yard. If anyone tried to escape in that direction, they would catch them.

The lock surrendered to the 'bot a second later. Bringing its weapons to bear, the machine went inside, with the entry team right behind it. In the main living area, it took up another guarding position and its human companions went down the hall to the rooms where their targets were located. This was the one part of the Op where the *Liverna* couldn't outshine anyone. Although it could certainly fight, it was unable to take live prisoners. For that, the 'human touch' was needed.

The surprise that those same humans caused was absolute; none of the residents even had the chance to offer up any resistance. When the teams burst in, the terrorists were forced out of their beds and put down on the floor in less time than it took for Kaly to blink.

The Op was not over by any means though.

Once their prisoners had been secured, blindfolded and led out the back to the second shuttle, Team 440's women guided Kaly's team through a thorough search of the house, with the *Liverna's* help. In addition to the 'bot, they also used the same kind of hand held scanners that Kaly had employed during her days as a Marine, searching spaceships for contraband.

But the most powerful tool that they brought to bear was their personal know-how. As Kaly knew full well from her time on Treya Angelaz, not everything was visible to a scanner's eyes, and the men and women of the 1st Garda had been masters at hiding things from the Hriss. It was only logical that the Loyalistas would prove to be just as adept. To ferret out any hidden caches, it would take a combination of superior tech and professional experience.

After just a few minutes, this proved to be the winning combination. A compartment which had been missed by both the 'bot and the scanners, was discovered under the floor by 440's veteran troopers. The metal-sheathed cavity held two military energy rifles, an old chemical-based pistol, and half a dozen 'dumb' grenades.

While this was not a large find by ETR standards, it was still an important one. Not only did it ensure that these weapons would be taken off the streets, but there was a good chance that they would be able to trace the rifles back to the armory they had originated from. This in turn could lead them to a corrupt supply officer, or detect a crucial weakness in the facility's security. Team 201's first tour of the ETR had enjoyed an auspicious beginning.

The captured weapons were quickly gathered up and taken out to the waiting shuttles, and they flew with them to directly Claire d'Layne. The moment that they landed, the teams took their prisoners into a building that had been set aside for evaluating intel and conducting interviews.

On the way, one of 440's veterans, a blue skinned Trilainian with two tours under her belt, informed Kaly that gathering intel from captive enemies was a time-sensitive affair. When the Loyalistas finally realized that their courier had been compromised, they would relocate whoever and whatever he had been trying to reach, and the night's work would be completely undone. Everyone that they had captured would need to be interviewed as soon as possible so that a follow-up operation could be planned before any potential targets dissappeared.

An RSE Lieutenant and a group of military policewomen met them as they entered the structure. The detainees were immediately handed over to the MP's who separated them and took them to individual holding cells. Assuming that their work was over, Kaly and her companions prepared to leave, but instead they were invited to remain and observe the proceedings. It was, as the Trilainian explained, part of their 'education', and they were promptly shown into an observation room.

This had a large, one-way Plexiglas window which allowed them to see into the chamber next door. That room was completely bare except for a single metal chair that had a large hole in the seat. Underneath this was an open drain, and Kaly puzzled over the purpose of this arrangement. She almost asked the Trilainian about it, but she kept her silence instead, and simply waited.

As they were being handed cups of *kaafra*, the captured courier was brought in. Kaly was not surprised in the least to see that he had been completely stripped of his clothing, or that the black bag they had put on him was still on his head. Having gone through a brief module on Interrogation on Larra's Lament as a new Marine Marauder, she understood why; the combination of nakedness and sensory deprivation made the man feel vulnerable. It also gave the RSE techs the chance to gain whatever information they could from his garments. Every stray plant fiber, bit of dirt, or chemical trace—even the labels on his clothing--had the potential to provide valuable clues about his movements and activities. Still, she thought, he was a miserable sight.

After his guards had dragged him over to the chair and secured him to it, the officer who had met them when they had arrived, walked in. She removed the sack from his head, and began her interview.

"I want to know who you are," Lieutenant sa'Tela said quietly, "who it was that gave you your orders, and what your message was."

The Loyalista's only reply was stony silence and a defiant glare. He was clearly bracing himself for whatever physical abuse was going to come next. All he received for his bravado however, was a cold smile.

"I'm not going to beat you," Sa'Tela assured him. "I don't like to do things that way. But you *will* tell me what I want to know. You have one last chance to cooperate with me."

Her prisoner answered this by spitting on her, and the Kalian calmly wiped the mess off her uniform blouse. Then she reached out and lightly touched his chin with her fingers.

Kaly didn't know exactly what she was doing, but its effect was hideously clear. The Loyalista cried out and his body jerked like it was being electrocuted. The purpose of the hole in the chair, and the drain below it, also became obvious when the man's bowels voided themselves and it channeled the mess away.

All through this, Sa'Tela remained exactly where she was, and kept contact with the courier's face. After half a minute, the man's violent spasms subsided and became a pitiful, helpless quivering.

Kaly had never seen a military psi at work, and the spectacle made her skin crawl. Up until then, she had thought herself hardened to most of the things associated with war, but this event demonstrated just how much there was that could still unsettle her. The training module on Larra's Lament had only been theory, but this was the brutal reality.

But when she began to feel pity for the man, she immediately suppressed it. He was her enemy, she reminded herself, and what was going on here, however horrible, was absolutely necessary. She couldn't allow weakness to get in the way of duty.

On the other side of the glass, Sa' Tela made an announcement. "I have a name. It's Jyon Saancha. He lives---oh these fellows are getting *clever*— this is a *false* lead! They've implanted a hypnotic block over the real information. No problem though."

She closed her eyes, and once again, her captive began to writhe in agony.

"Don't worry, she'll rip out whatever they implanted in him," a voice behind Kaly said. It was *Cabo* Vasquaaz. "Lieutenant sa'Tela always does. Amandra knows how to peel their heads open like a little tin can. We'll have what we want soon enough."

Grateful for the excuse to look away, Kaly turned to her. "What's going to happen to him after this?" She had to know, but she was also afraid hear the answer.

"That's not a question you really need to worry about, *chica*," Vasquaaz grinned. "But since you're new, I'll tell you. We'll turn him over to the Regular Army." Several of the *Specia* men standing next to her seemed to be amused by this statement and smiled wolfishly.

"And then?"

"Depends on who picks him up," Vasquaaz answered casually, "If they're Loyalistas, he'll go to prison for a little while, and they'll try to warn their friends. If they're *Dereyhiya*, Rightists, he'll be *da una deysaparce*."

Kaly understood the term. "Disappeared?"

Vasquaaz drew a finger across her throat. *"Si'a, deysaparce.* One of the disappeared."* She laughed at this, and her men laughed with her.

Kaly didn't join in, and she also didn't press for any additional details. Instead, she did her best not to think about any of it, and settled her gaze on a blank spot on the opposite wall. It was much better than watching the interrogation, or speculating about their prisoner's ultimate fate.

Vasquaaz wasn't exaggerating about Sa'Tela's abilities. Less than ten more minutes passed before the Kalian stepped away from the prostrate figure and the MP's came in to drag him out. She gave her invisible audience a curt nod and met them out in the hall.

"I have his handler's name and address," she told them. "Along with the message that he was supposed to deliver. We'll analyze the data and get a report over to Major ebed Karri once we have something firm."

Thanking her, Ben Di escorted them back to their barracks. It had been a long night, and in all likelihood, they would have another mission waiting for them the next day. As soon as they had cared for their weapons, everyone headed for their racks.

Kaly wasn't surprised at all by the dreams that she had that night. They alternated between the enigmatic red-head who still haunted her, and terrifying images of a huge black insect that kept trying to touch her face and invade her mind. The insect had Sa'Tela's face.

***

Located deep in its sub-basement, the Embassy's COMINT center served as Sarah's second workplace. It was staffed with the majority of the station's personnel, who were not agents, but rather, specialists and technicians.

To protect against eavesdropping, and any form of attack, it was heavily armored and shielded, and proof against the best that the ETR, or any of the other enemies of the Sisterhood could ever hope to field against it. A dark and windowless place, it always felt to Maya like she was journeying into some mythical underworld.

As usual, Sarah occupied her seat in the cubicle in the very center of the chamber, looking like a starship commander in charge of a great warship. Which in a sense, she was. The COMINT center offered her as much information as a fleet of Isis Class ships could provide, and many such vessels did just that.

In cooperation with the RSE, every Sisterhood spacecraft that parked itself over Nuvo Bolivar lent its surveillance services to the center, feeding it on a round the clock basis. Their combined data stream managed to capture almost every signal that the governmental machine of the Esteral Terrana Rapabla created, including many that the Republic erroneously believed were too well encrypted to be overheard.

At that precise instant, the USSNS *Elizabeth C. Howland* was overhead, sending a data stream downside on multiple Com bands. This was being displayed on one of the center's large vid screens.

It concerned activity at the *Rabertio Gonzaala* National Armory, and as Maya crossed the COMINT center, she watched as several ETR officers walked together across a quad, completely unaware that their activities were being monitored from hundreds of kilometers overhead. Thanks to the considerable computer power being brought to bear, all extraneous noise had been filtered out and the clarity and quality of their words was as sharp and clear as if someone had been standing right next to them with the microphone. Maybe clearer, she mused; even the little sounds that the wind made, or the intermittent buzzing of insects were completely absent.

On another screen, a less sophisticated but equally important surveillance operation was under way. A map of the capitol and its surrounding communities was on display, with red dots flashing at various points. Each of these dots had a number next to it, and those with the higher values flashed imperatively. These were Loyalista spotters, broadcasting their observations back to their handlers. The numbers next to each position represented the probability of capture.

There were several spotters stationed in and around Claire d'Layne, and two had been assigned confidence figures higher than 100. Green triangles, representing RSE strike teams, or military police units, were moving towards those points at top speed. With luck, and the Goddesses' blessings, the rebels at each location would be caught alive and become Amandra Sa'Tela's guests.

Leaving the outcome to powers much higher than herself, she stopped watching the map and approached Sarah to see what tasks she had in store for her that day. It was a given that the woman would have something in mind, and she earnestly hoped that it wouldn't turn out to be another grueling session with a stack of intel files. Or even worse, confinement in a chair alongside one of the COMINT techs. *That* was boring duty.

Sarah addressed her as she came near. "Maya, I feel that it is time that we switch the emphasis of your training from machine-based information gathering methods to a more old fashioned, yet equally reliable source of data; humint, or human intelligence.'

"I am going to partner you with one of our field assets. Agent Saantoz is quite talented, and you are to follow her lead. She will give you the chance to observe what the Agency does in the field and also give you the opportunity to carry out your own specific mission."

"Okay," Maya answered, folding her arms. "What's that?"

"It will be to gather more intelligence on Isabaal Castraa's assistant. Do you recall the woman? She was the one that you thought could not be 'turned' by us."

Maya frowned. She remembered her.

"I am giving her to you as a special project and *you* are going to help us to make her into an asset. Think of it as an extra credit project just like the ones that you received in primary."

"Lovely," Maya retorted. "Any hints on just exactly *how* I am to accomplish my mission, oh Mighty and Omnipotent One?"

Sarah ignored her sarcasm with the ease of long practice, "Only this; after we identified her, we did a little checking. She has no criminal associations, and neither do any of her relatives. She has no known vices, and has never been in trouble for anything, with anyone. As for her politics, they are conservative, but not excessively so, and she is well trusted by her superiors. In fact, they consider her to be above reproach. Naturally, she also has a high level security clearance."

"This is a joke, right?" Maya asked disbelievingly.

"No," Sarah replied. "Not in the least. I told you the truth when I said that anyone can be turned. You are a bright girl. I'm sure you'll find a way to manage the task, and you can call on Agent Saantoz for suggestions. *Listen* to her. A 'lectri is waiting for you up in the garage."

Maya rewarded her with a scowl, and left the COMINT center.

The vehicle that was standing by for her was the usual plain, unmarked version, and the driver was a non-descript woman who could have fit in anywhere in Nuvo Bolivar. Maya said nothing to her as she got in, and they drove out through one of the multiple exits underneath the embassy.

When it had functioned as the Treasury building, these secure passages had afforded couriers the ability to come and go in anonymity. Their particular exit ended at a false wall which opened and admitted them into a car-sized elevator. The moment that the 'lectri was inside of it, it rose, and delivered them to the lower floor of a public parking structure. This in turn emptied out onto a busy downtown street.

After merging into traffic, Maya's driver took them several blocks before pulling over and parking. "Go inside that shopping center," she told her.

Maya looked beyond her and saw a sign proclaiming the existence of a large mall just down the street.

"Go to *'La Rozza can Miya Corazan'* and browse the clothing there," the driver added. "Select a red blouse and a green skirt. After that, ask the clerk to use their restrooms."

Maya made no comment. She fully understood the need for such elaborate steps. The ESN knew all about the secret exits from the Embassy and they watched the comings and goings of the staff quite closely. It was also a certainty that their 'lectri had been followed.

Sweeping the street with her eyes, she got out and walked to the mall. She also 'felt' around her for any telltale signs that she was being shadowed. The fact that neither action produced anything noteworthy didn't assure her however, and she kept her senses open all the way to the entrance.

Once inside, she quickly located the store on an interactive map kiosk and began to make her way towards it. Almost immediately, she 'felt' someone following her, and did her best to seem as if she hadn't noticed.

'La Rozza' proved to be a high-end establishment, and as soon as she entered it, a saleswoman came forwards to assist her. In short order, she found the blouse and skirt she had been sent for, and then asked after the restroom.

As the clerk pointed the way, Maya saw a woman entering the store, and guessed that she was her 'tail'. A quick read produced nothing except a jumbled impression of the woman's thoughts—and in the process, positively identified her. The new arrival was with the ESN, and wearing one of their primitive meshes under her scalp. This made Maya smile to herself; although the mesh masked the agent's thoughts, it also worked against her simply by being there.

Passing a display, she caught the woman's reflection in it. The agent was pretending to browse a rack of coats, which also put her in a position to enjoy a clear view of the rear of the store and the restrooms. It was a classic surveillance maneuver, straight out of Maya's studies, and her own street experience as a shoplifter.

Borrowing on this, she briefly evaluated the emergency exit at the very back. A good thief always had a way out for themselves, but when she saw that it was rigged with an alarm, she abandoned the idea. It wasn't a viable escape route. Even had it been unwired, it was also highly likely that the ESN would have other people in the mall, and that they would be watching the service passage behind the store like *aerhawks*. The only choice was to proceed, and discover what the restroom had to offer.

Just as she reached the door, another patron exited, and they briefly made eye contact. To her surprise, she heard the other woman thinking to her over her psiever.

Dress in the uniform inside the bathroom and use your symbiote to exit the store. Take the first service corridor to your right and go out into the truck court. I'll delay your friend.

Chuckling, Maya entered the tiny space. A jumpsuit was resting on the toilet along with a matching hat and a locking courier's bag.

"It always pays to accessorize," she said to herself.

Unfolding the jumpsuit, she saw that it proclaimed to the entire universe that she was an employee of *'Rapaddia Serversa Carrio'*, Rapid Courier Service, and that her name was Maaria. She shed her clothing immediately, stuffing it into the courier's bag and donned the uniform, making certain to tuck her hair under the hat. A thought from the agent outside reached her as she completed her transformation.

Time to go.

The sound of a commotion followed right on the heels of this, and just before she embraced her symbiote she heard the agent yelling.

"Hey *bitch!* You just stole something right out of my purse! No you don't—you're waiting right here for the police!"

The rest of the fracas was lost in the droning roar that the Drow'voi device converted every conversation into, but as she came out, the frozen tableau of the two figures struggling, and the worried saleswoman trying to intervene, met her eyes and brought another smile to her face. To the best of her knowledge, the ESN still didn't know anything about the symbiotes and they would have a deuce of a time figuring out how she had managed to evade them. It was all in a day's fun, and now she was looking forwards to whatever else was in store for her.

Just to add to her cheer, she also made the point of stealing the ESN agent's pocketbook from her purse and exchanging it with some of the friendly agent's valuables. Not only would the woman be missing her identification, but the presence of items that were clearly not hers would cause a whole galaxy of problems when the police or security arrived. As Maya saw it, this not only helped with the diversion, but paid her back for all of her inconvenience with some lunch money, courtesy of the ESN.

Ten seconds later, she was well away from the store and entering the service passage. When she was out of the public view, she released her symbiote and returned to normal time. It took her a few more seconds to banish the nauseating effects of the device, but then she was ready and headed off in the direction of the dock.

There were several vehicles parked there, although only one of them belonged to the courier service. A woman wearing a uniform just like hers was sitting inside of it, hands on the wheel. It took Maya a moment to place her, and then she recognized her from the operation at the *Lida Biolabs* more than two years earlier.

At the time, Agent Saantoz had been a member of *La Ermanyaa*. The radical feminist group had taken over the town of Alquibar in the early days of the alliance with the Sisterhood. They had subsequently been extracted by a Marine Marauder Team to be trained by the Agency for 'black' operations, including the *Lida* mission. Although Sanda Ernan had been placed in power since then, and many of the key posts in her government were now held by women, it was clear by Saantoz's presence alone, that she and her sisters were still actively serving the interests of the Sisterhood.

"N'Kaaryn?" Saantoz asked. "You ready? We have a long day ahead of us."

Maya got into the vehicle. "What's up first?" she asked.

"Breakfast," the agent told her.

"Oh, that's good. I was getting hungry. There's a little place that I know--"

Saantoz cut her off. "Forget it. We're going to *Fondaa Comdidanda*. When we get there, we'll order coffee and some fruit. Nothing else."

"Okay...fine," Maya agreed. "Coffee and fruit it is."

The *Fondaa Comdidanda* was only a few minutes away and turned out to be an inexpensive and unexceptional little restaurant. Its customers were mainly workers like themselves and a few businesspeople from the downtown offices, and because it was getting late in the morning, they were able to get a booth without waiting. When the waitress arrived to serve them, Maya placed her order exactly as Saantoz had instructed her to.

Presently, the waitress returned with their order, but instead of bringing it right to their table, she stopped for a moment to refill the coffee cup of another customer. The pair chatted briefly, and then the man drained his cup, paid his bill and left. This wasn't anything remarkable and the only reason that Maya had even noticed it was that it had caused a delay in receiving their own order.

She also observed that when their food reached them, Saantoz only sipped at her coffee, and completely ignored the fruit. It was obvious that this was some kind of signal to whoever was observing them, and Maya carefully copied her.

Even so, she regretted the fact that their covert message hadn't also involved consuming their meal. She really *was* famished and as soon as their exciting day of high-level cloak and dagger work allowed it, she was going to demand that they stop off somewhere and get themselves a real breakfast. Being a spy was proving to be hungry work.

Finally, Saantoz put down her cup and signaled the waitress for the bill. When it arrived, she indicated Maya. "She'll be paying."

The waitress smiled and handed Maya the paper, and as she took it, she realized that there were actually two bills. One listed their order, and the other was blank except for two handwritten messages.

They read *"1,000,000 ₽"* and *"50,000 ₽ for T. V."*

"Keep the bill," Saantoz said in a low voice. "Put it away in your courier bag."

Maya did so, and as soon as the waitress had returned with her change, they left.

Once again, their journey was a short one, and it ended at the curb in front of an office building. "Go to the second floor," Saantoz told her. "You want the offices of the *Mercantal Finansa Colectavo*. Tell the receptionist that you have a delivery for Ms. Rabartya Vaasco. Hand Ms. Vaasco the bill and wait for her to give you some packages."

"Sure thing," Maya replied. It was becoming patently clear that in addition to enduring starvation, the job of a field agent involved a lot of mysterious errands with little, if any, explanation to accompany them. Even Sarah, for all her shadows and cobwebs, was proving to be more garrulous than Agent Saantoz.

This time, Maya reached the offices of the *Mercantal* without any sense that she was being followed. The establishment itself proved to be quite modern by local standards. It also lacked anything that offered a visitor a single clue about what the firm actually *did*. Even the name, *Commercial Finance Group*, was fuzzy. The entire office seemed to say to the passersby, *"There's nothing interesting happening here. Go back to sleep and move on."*

And most people probably did that very thing, Maya reasoned. She, however, was not as gullible, and came to the conclusion that she was standing in the lobby of one of the many front companies that the Agency used. Sarah had mentioned their existence to her, and their function. Such firms conducted the business end of the Sisterhood's espionage operations, and laundered its money. They were also sources of additional cash. When she was escorted to Ms. Vaasco's private office, her conclusion was confirmed by the woman herself.

Rabartya Vaasco proved to be a well-groomed figure in her early thirties, dressed in a conservative business suit. She was also a face that Maya vividly recalled from a news clip. Back then, Vaasco had been just another part of a 'man on the street' segment that the Republican News Network had created to gauge the reaction of the general public to the existence of the Sisterhood. When the reporter had asked her for her thoughts, Vaasco had simply replied, *"The Sisterhood? Of course. It's only the next logical step in our evolution. I think we'll see it happening here, very, very soon."*

Then, before the journalist could ask her to elaborate, she had walked away. Her statement had been so surprising, and unique, that the memory of it had remained with Maya ever since.

"Do you have something for me?" Vaasco asked.

"Yes, ma'am," Maya answered, fishing the receipt out of her bag.

Vaasco took it and read the numbers. "One moment," she said, rising and walking over to a picture hanging on the wall. Like everything else in the office, it was a rather bland composition; a non-descript street scene somewhere in Nuvo Bolivar, and she was unsurprised when Vaasco swung it aside to reveal a wall safe.

She reached in and produced an impressive stack of Paysolis, which she counted out on her desk and separated into three stacks before returning the remainder to the safe. One stack, Maya noted, was quite large.

Each one went into heavy document envelopes labeled with the '*Rapaddia Serversa Carrio*' logo. Vaasco sealed them, and then wrote the addresses on the outside before handing them over to her.

"Here you go," she said, adding a cheerful, "*Bian dea*"--a common Sisterhood expression. Maya returned her conspiratorial smile, and put the packages into her bag.

Outside, Saantoz had driven up onto the curb and was waiting right in front of the doors. The moment that Maya got in, they departed.

Their first destination was a private mailbox service and Maya followed Saantoz's instructions and delivered the correct envelope to the clerk. In return, she was given a receipt and another mailing envelope, addressed to an "*A. Algwalar*".

When she returned to the van, Saantoz took it from her and carefully read the addressee's name. "Good," she said. "This is important. It will need to go to Sarah as soon as you get back."

Maya promptly tucked it inside her courier bag and then put on her seatbelt. As Saantoz started the engine however, she decided that she had had enough. Her stomach was growling in protest and she wasn't going to go any further until this problem was remedied.

"I need to eat," she announced. "Do we have some time for that before the next part of our super-secret mission?"

Saantoz flashed her a wry smile, and then took them to a restaurant that was roughly the same size and quality as their first stop. She even allowed her enough time to eat her entire meal before they were off again.

Their next stop was a high-rise apartment building, in a well-heeled part of town. This time, a young woman roughly her own age answered the door, and Maya couldn't help but notice that she was wearing a dress that only gave a passing nod to concealing her body.

Or that behind her, there were several other women lounging around on the couches, in similar states of near or total undress.

Putayas, Maya thought, unconsciously using the ETR slang word for prostitutes. Lacking a modern equivalent, the term had been quickly adopted by the Sisterhood and had found its way into Standard. The fact that she was delivering money to some of them meant that they were part of whatever little caper the RSE was currently working on. Sarah had once mentioned the idea of using sex as a weapon against the Republic, and if she had learned anything about the woman in their time together, it was that she didn't make jokes.

Someone would be, or already had been, 'turned' for the Agency by these *putayas*. Shaking her head in disbelief at the very notion of a woman selling her body to men, she headed back down to the van.

The character of the streets changed as they drove into the heart of the city, transitioning from sterile rows of modern multistory buildings with wide, tree lined avenues, to narrower passages with older, ruder structures. Even the sunlight, which had been plentiful in the downtown area, seemed to become dimmer, as if it were giving less of itself to the poorer part of the capitol.

The people had changed too; they were less well dressed now and the signs above the shops they were walking by had transformed. They had gone from Espangla over to another language that had no relationship with anything that Maya recognized.

The graffiti was the same way. It was scrawled in strange characters that were utterly foreign to her eyes, and it was much more plentiful. She also noticed that there were fewer 'lectris on the street, and what there were, were older models that had been modified in flamboyant ways, or were in need of some form of repair, or bodywork.

An unseen border had been crossed without giving any warning of its presence, and Maya finally realized where Saantoz was taking them. She was heading straight into the *Dho Haak*, the 'Neighborhoods'.

Maya had heard of the place, and its people. The Dho Haak was the home of the Dann, and bad news for anyone who was an outsider. Like her.

A moment later, she spotted a group of Dann men standing together on a corner holding cans of alcoholic beverages. They were dressed casually, mostly in their undershirts and loose-fitting pants.

It was their hair that really stood out though, and marked them as different. To a man, it was blue-black in color, and their forelocks and a corresponding portion of the hair on the back of their heads had been tied together. This had been accomplished by using either a distinctive grey-blue wire, or some form of colorful cording, and it made the tufts stand up and out from their heads. In any other circumstances, this might have seemed comical, had it not been for their grey-blue eyes, or the hostile looks that they were giving her with them.

The Dann were the ETR's dirty little secret, and also an enigma. Although they had been living within its borders for three centuries, they were not natives of the Republic. Instead, they had been 'found' by ETR explorers, living in poverty on a lonely little world located well beyond the limits of the old Gaian Star Federation.

The Dann claimed that their true origins had not been on Old Gaia, but on a world that they called 'Injii', which was situated far from any known Human space. Despite the remoteness of the planet they were discovered on, most citizens of the ETR refused to believe their fantastic claim.

One thing that the ETR had never been able to ignore however was the fact that the Dann were very different than themselves. Aside from their strange eye coloring, and dark hair, they also stubbornly maintained their own language, which had no correlate to any of the Old Gaian tongues.

Their customs were equally as unique. One of the most significant was that in the Dho Haak, things went along matriarchal lines. Among the Dann, it was the women, and not the men, who ran the homes, the businesses, and most importantly, the street gangs.

This, and the fact that they occupied the lowest levels of the Republic's economic ladder, had made them the perfect allies of the Sisterhood from the very outset of contact.

Saantoz and many of her sisters in *La Ermanyaa* were Dann. They had come from the very streets that Maya was now riding through, and although she was taller than the norm, Saantoz's eyes were as grey as everyone else that they passed, and there was no mistaking the flash of blue in her black hair when the late afternoon light caught it just right.

For her part, Maya was glad that she had ventured into this ghetto in the woman's company; her straw colored hair and green eyes marked her as a stranger, a *Ranji*, right away. The tingle between her shoulders also told her that the Dho Haak wasn't a place that anyone wanted to stand out in. She had become quite familiar with this sensation on Delgen; it warned her that she was in a dangerous part of town, and to act with care.

Saantoz however, drove with the easy familiarity of the local she was, and presently they pulled in under a covered truck dock next to a small manufacturing concern. At a nod from her, Maya followed the woman inside, past rows of containers and busy workers, to an office cubicle. Waiting inside, were two women dressed in jumpsuits exactly like their own.

The similarity didn't end there; even their basic physical traits were the same and Maya immediately guessed that the one playing her, had donned

103

a blond wig for the part. Nothing was said between the two groups, and their doubles left the office with their hats pulled low.

"We have to change," Saantoz informed her, indicating two stacks of clothes sitting on matching folding chairs. Maya's pile contained a nondescript pink tank top, a matching cap, a black wig, as well as a pair of tight black pants. Saantoz's attire was similar to this, but much flashier. A motto, in Dann, and written in cheap sequins adorned her top, and her pants had matching accents around the pockets and seams.

There was also a man's fedora, made of some kind of shiny, inexpensive plastic, which Saantoz put on her head at a jaunty angle. So attired, she looked every bit the *Taangaan*, the gangster, and seeing how natural the ensemble looked on her, Maya realized that it was not an act at all. The courier's uniform had been the costume, not this.

"Don't worry," Saantoz said. "*Taangaan* let *Ranji* like you ride with them every once in a while. You won't stand out too bad as long as you're with me."

She led the way back out of the office and outside. The delivery van was gone now, and a 'lectri was waiting in its place. Its suspension had been lowered well past what was considered safe, and the windows were tinted to near opacity. A bright set of chromed rims offset this and it had a paint job that transitioned from a brilliant metallic green to an equally garish magenta, and back again.

A woman was at the wheel, which she immediately surrendered to Saantoz, and there was a man in the back. They all looked like 'hard cases' to Maya's experienced eye, and for a moment, as she got in next to Saantoz, she felt like she was reliving her days back on Delgen, when she had run with *Nefaria*, one of its many street gangs.

The resemblance was only underscored when she spied the butt end of a Sisterhood Marine energy pistol sticking out between the two front seats and then what looked to her eye like compact military energy rifles tucked in underneath them. These were all within easy reach of the 'lectri's occupants, she noted. It was an important detail to remember if they encountered any enemies.

"I thought we'd use a local ride," Saantoz explained, seeing where Maya was looking. "The ESN sometimes uses satellites to watch us. They don't dare come down here though. Even the *howlaa*, the kaapers, stay out of the Dho Haak; they know we run things here. So, now they can watch our doubles until they get bored and fall asleep."

Everyone laughed at this, and then the man behind Maya passed up a hand-rolled cigarette to Saantoz. She took a deep drag from it before passing it over. "*Zogat*", she explained as she backed them out into the street. "A little fringe benefit. Take a hit. You'll like it."

Maya didn't hesitate, and inhaled deeply. Immediately, an intense feeling of euphoria and light-headedness overcame her. "Wow!" she exclaimed, to the accompaniment of more laughter from her companions.

She didn't care though. Whatever *'Zogat'* was, she liked it. A lot.

"Something from Danna," Saantoz said. "The world that we Dann lived on when the *Ranji* found us. The *Ranji* come down to the Dho Haak all the time for this—when they can't get themselves the glass."

Maya's expression soured, and Saantoz smiled knowingly, switching over to Standard. "I know, the glass is bad stuff. Just the same, it makes money for us, and it makes the *Ranji* weak. That's good for the Dann—and for the Sisterhood. You wrap your head around that, *chica*."

"I'm working on it," Maya returned. This was more out of politeness than anything else. She would never 'like' glass, for any reason, but there was no point in starting an argument, especially since she was a guest.

"Don't worry about the *Zogat* by the way," Saantoz added. "It's not like the glass at all. It's not poison--it's just like taking a little vacation."

On this point at least, Maya could not disagree and she made sure to enjoy a little more of it before giving it back to Saantoz.

"Oh, and don't worry about Sarah either," the other woman added. "I won't tell her, if you won't."

"No worries," Maya grinned. It was nice to be with someone else who understood just how uptight Sarah was.

A little Zogat would do her some good, she thought dryly. Sarah needed a mental 'vacation' worse than anyone she had ever met, and the image of the woman getting 'stoned' made Maya chuckle aloud. So did the notion of getting some of the drug from her new friends, and sprinkling a bit of it in Sarah's food.

Just for educational purposes, of course.

Saantoz joined in her laughter, clearly entertaining the same imagery. Then her expression became serious. "We're at our next stop," she told her, inclining her head towards a bar at the corner, and a group of males standing near it.

One of them, dressed in a dark red coat made of some kind of plastic, looked in their direction and stepped up to the curb as they made a U-turn across the street and parked, facing the wrong way. No one honked at them as they did this, or expressed displeasure of any kind.

This told her a lot; the locals knew enough to respect the people in the 'lectri, and leave them to their business. Thanks to her own experiences on Delgen, that meant only one thing. 'Agent' Saantoz and her friends ran with a *very* tough crew. A neighborhood like the Dho Haak only awarded such respect to apex predators.

The man in the jacket confirmed this when he respectfully tugged at his forelock before leaning down to speak with Saantoz, and although he smiled, Maya could sense his nervousness without even bothering to read him. Despite the fact that he had a nasty scar running down one side of his face and was possibly one of the toughest looking men that she had ever laid eyes on, Saantoz and her friends clearly frightened him.

The pair spoke briefly in Dann, and then Saantoz handed him the last envelope from Rabartya Vaasco. The man took it from her, being careful to pull at his forelock again before backing away from the vehicle.

Saantoz accepted his deference as regally as any queen might have, and then pulled away from the curb, driving them only a few meters further before parking in a vacant lot behind the bar. As they got out together, she passed her a small, folded piece of plastipaper. "Hold on to this," she instructed.

Taking it, Maya had to ask her companion a question. "So? What's your crew's tag?"

Saantoz inclined her jaw towards some graffiti on the building's wall. In Dann, it was completely unreadable, but she translated it for her. "*La Razzores*, the Razors. What about your crew?"

"I rolled with *Nefaria*," Maya answered. "Back on Delgen. That was a while back though."

The Dann woman grinned. "I got the feeling that you were a *Taangaa* girl. I also think that you and I roll with an even bigger gang now, you know?"

"Yeah, "Maya agreed. "I guess we do." Unarguably, the Sisterhood and the RSE both qualified as 'gangs' and they were certainly 'bigger' than either *La Razzores* or *Nefaria* could ever aspire to become.

As they entered the bar, the patrons inside gave them plenty of distance, and even though it was crowded, a table near the back suddenly became vacant as they approached it. The man with the red jacket, Maya noted, sat nearby, at his own table.

Four beers quickly materialized, and they sipped at them, waiting quietly. After only a few minutes, Maya felt the energy in the bar change, and instinctively, she looked towards the entrance for the reason. Up to this point, she had been the only 'outsider', but the people around them were ignoring her, most likely because she was in the company of Saantoz and her fellow *Razzores*. Now though, she realized that everyone's eyes were turned towards the man coming through the front door.

She recognized him right away. He was the assistant from the conference, who had been attached to the Commerce Secretary, and the glass addict. And if anything, he looked even worse than the last time she had seen him. His manner was nervous, and underlying this, she detected an unmistakable hunger that wasn't for food. This, and the thin sheen of sweat covering his skin, told her that he was desperate for his next fix. A quick read only confirmed this.

Now she understood why they had come to this bar, and what they were there to do. She managed to keep her seat only through sheer force of will, and watched as the addict looked around the bar.

When he spotted the man in the jacket, he made straight for him, and sat down at his table without an invitation. Her augmented hearing, which had recently been completed by her little fleet of nanobots, brought his half-whispered words to her clearly. She hated what she heard, and she hated him even more for his weakness.

"I need something," he rasped.

The glass dealer produced a small box, and placed it on the table. As the addict reached for it, Maya caught sight of his arm. Where the shirt sleeves revealed it, the skin was covered with small scars. They were from the glass cuts.

His fingers never made contact with the box though. The dealer pulled it away from him at the last instant.

"Please—I brought the money, just like always."

The dealer shook his head. "Sorry, the price just went up."

"Listen, I'll pay," the addict pleaded, and to prove this, he fished out a crumpled wad of Paysolis from his pocket and put them on the beer-soaked table.

"Not enough, *güeyo*" the man told him. "You can't afford it anymore."

"Please—I've got to have it—I'll do *anything!*"

"You really want it?" the dealer asked him. "I can give it to you, but I don't want your money."

The addict regarded the box with undisguised lust and Maya wanted to vomit. Glass addicts became like animals once they were good and hooked. Shyla had been that way, she recalled darkly, before the drug had killed her.

"You want it?" the dealer repeated. "For free?"

The addict nodded, vigorously.

"Then you need to talk to these women next to us," the dealer told him.

At that, Saantoz rose, and Maya almost didn't follow her. She didn't want to be involved. But Saantoz gave her a look that told her that she didn't have the choice, and despite herself, she went with her.

As they joined the dealer, Saantoz signaled to her, and she reluctantly slid the little piece of plastipaper over to the addict. She was also careful to withdraw her hand before his fingers could make any accidental contact. Just being across from him was revolting.

"Read it," Saantoz instructed. "That's our price—and your first installment."

Hands shaking, the addict opened the note. Then his eyes went wide as the words slowly made sense. "I-I can't do this—"he spluttered.

"Then we don't do business," the dealer announced crisply. "No one does business with you, anywhere. You go dry, *güeyo*."

With that, the dealer started to rise, and the addict grasped at his coat. "Wait! I'll do it! Just promise me that it won't hurt my country!"

"No promises, *Ranji*," Saantoz replied coldly. "Just the glass. Do we have a deal?" The dealer took this as his cue and put the box back on the table, but he kept ahold of it.

The addict spent a few seconds licking his lips, looking down at the box and considering what they were asking of him. Finally, his shoulders slumped and Maya knew that they had him. "I'll do it," he said quietly.

At a nod from Saantoz, the dealer let go of the parcel, and immediately, the addict seized it and tore off the lid. Inside, were several translucent shards, gleaming in the dim light.

Ignoring his audience, he took one of the pieces out, and slashed his arm with it. Blood welled up out of the cut, but a look of creamy satisfaction came over his features. Sighing deeply, he slumped back in his chair, totally lost in his bliss, and oblivious to the gore that was comingling with the old beer and grease on the table.

"We'll be in touch," Saantoz promised him. She tugged at Maya's arm. "Let's go."

Maya waited until they were outside and headed back to the car before she finally let go. "Saantoz—I like you, I like your crew. But don't ever— ever—get me into something like that again! *Zat klaar?!*"

Saantoz stopped midstride. "It's just business, sister. Like I said, if you want to be an agent, you gotta wrap your head around it."

"*Fek* business," Maya snapped. "Wrap your head around *that*."

Saantoz didn't respond to this. Not in words at least; her eyes just narrowed unhappily.

Maya wasn't intimidated though, and she didn't break her gaze. She was too angry for that, and her symbiote gaurenteed her the victory if the gangster/agent wanted to make something more of it.

But the Dann woman didn't. Instead, she took her out of the Dho Haak without saying another word, and dropped her off in the downtown area.

Once there, Maya was left on her own. She took a public bus to a stop five blocks from the Embassy, and then walked the rest of the way, entering the building through a side gate. This wasn't the most covert way to return, but she was so angry by the time she arrived, that she simply didn't care.

Sarah was still in her upstairs office, and Maya came straight in.

"Well?" Sarah asked. "How was your first day as a field agent?"

"Glass," Maya replied, storming up to her desk. "Fekking goddess-damned glass! That's how my 'day' was!"

"Yes," Sarah returned. "I had the feeling that Agent Saantoz was going to make contact with that asset today. It's good that you got the opportunity to watch her—"

"You *knew* how I felt about that!" Maya spat, pointing her finger in the woman's face. "You *knew*, and you *still* sent me there!"

Sarah sat back, her expression a mixture of surprise and amusement. "Do I detect the birth of some kind of *ethics?* Is that what this is all about? I told you that we can't--"

"--can't choose what we do? Is that it, Sarah?" Maya retorted. "Is that what you were going to say? I've been training and training and fekking training—for what?! So I can help you peddle that shess for some goddess-damned objective the Agency has for goddess knows-the-fek-what?'

"Well, guess what, Sarah. Fek you! Fek the Agency! I *will* choose what I do! If glass is what this is going to be about, then I'm out! I'm fekking out!" She was leaning over the desk now, and pounding it with her fist, but she didn't care. She was sick and tired of being pushed around by everyone. Especially Sarah.

Before the other woman could respond, she spun on her heels and stomped out of the room.

Sarah watched her go, and shook her head sadly.

Several minutes later, and after allowing Maya a reasonable period of time to cool off, she went looking for her. She found her sulking in a corner of the underground parking area.

The girl's head whipped around as she approached, and Sarah stopped where she was when she saw the look in her eyes.

"Maya," she said as gently as she could. "I have made a terrible mistake. I admit that. I should have taken your feelings about glass into account, but I did not. Instead I was stupid, and I was selfish, and I apologize for my carelessness. It will never happen again. Please, find it in your heart to forgive me."

Maya's eyes opened wide in genuine astonishment. In all their time together, Sarah had never apologized for anything. Ever.

"Let's talk—when you're ready" Sarah added. "I'll make the time. You just tell me when. Please."

At a total loss for words, Maya only glared at her. There was suspicion and hurt in her gaze, but Sarah also saw agreement. Wary agreement to be sure, but it was much better than the alternative.

CHAPTER 4

State Highway 101, Centraal District, Nuvo Bolivar, Magdala Provensa,
Esteral Terrana Rapabla, 1048.08|02|05:84:65

Although they had many skills in common with the *Specia* Team, Kaly's group still had to play 'catch-up' in certain vital areas. Coming from a society where most transportation flew, they had been required to reclaim the lost art of surveillance and pursuit tactics using ground-based vehicles.

To accomplish this, the RSE had created special PTS training feeds for them, drawing material from such venerable sources as the near-mythical City of Los Angeles, and the equally fabled settlements of ancient Anaheim and Long Beach. These had been followed with behind-the-wheel practice at the Nuvo Bolivar Police Driving Course, and they had received instruction from both the police trainers and the *Specia* soldiers themselves.

Now, this new knowledge was being put into practice. Sitting in the passenger seat of their sport utility 'lectri, Kaly had to gently refuse the false memories that were trying to assert themselves. They insisted that she had once ridden in a similar vehicle, patrolling the smog-choked freeways of Southern California as a member of the Highway Patrol.

But thanks to the Hriss, that place, and Old Gaia itself, were nothing more than dust and bits of rock, and had been for over a millennia. False-memories like these were a common side effect of the feeds however, and being a veteran, Kaly had learned the trick of defeating them. She simply focused her attention on the present and continued to remind herself of who she really was.

Up on the windshield a map showed the freeway—the real freeway, and not a ghost from some vanished age—and it displayed their position and also the location of their target. Above this, was the live feed comng from the USSNS *Josephine Baker*, showing the plain silver sedan and its occupants, along with smaller images that had been culled from their army service records. The passenger, who was the entire reason for this mission, had been positively identified as Capitán Jesu Munnaz.

While not high in the Loyalista command structure, Munnaz still oversaw the operations of a dozen rebel cells located in and around the capitol. Like his superiors, he kept on the move, constantly changing locations every day. Thanks to leads that had been developed after their first 'snatch and grab operation, a Loyalista close to Munnaz had turned coat and given them a solid lead. They knew exactly where Munnaz was going.

Team 201's objective was to capture the officer en-route without the Loyalistas ever becoming the wiser. If it came off as planned, the RSE had

110

every reason to believe that it would lead them to even bigger game, and possibly even bag some of the top rebel leadership.

So far, things seemed to be looking good. The target vehicle was ten cars ahead, and it showed no signs that it had detected them. The driver was keeping precisely to the speed limit, signaling all of his turns and generally doing everything that he could to blend in with the late afternoon commuter traffic.

Team 201, 440 and the *Specia* Team were keeping the same low profile. Except for the heavily tinted windows, their three 'chase' vehicles looked like all the other Sport Utility 'lectris around them, and this particular feature was not so strange that it really stood out. Nor did the police lights that were hidden under their grills and behind the sun visors.

The presence of a pair of Sisterhood assault shuttles loitering off in the distance also wasn't anything noteworthy. Since the Sisterhood had occupied the ETR, aerial patrols like this occurred every day and the people of Nuvo Bolivar had gotten used to seeing them—even if an ever-increasing number of them had come to dislike what they represented. The driver of the silver sedan appeared to be no exception; he kept his pace steady and unhurried as he changed lanes to take an off-ramp.

"They're leaving the highway," Kaly observed. Sitting behind the wheel, their driver, *Sarjenta* Xayvar Pera grunted in acknowledgement and glanced at the data on the windshield. Ben Di, sitting in the back seat, looked up at the same display and considered it.

Being the seniormost member of their combined force, it would be up to her to decide how and when they would capture Munnaz. Except for the target, the long, sloping ramp appeared to be clear of traffic all the way to the bottom, and the cross street that it met with was also deserted. Kaly knew exactly what Ben Di was thinking; this would be their best chance to apprehend the target without putting any innocent lives at risk.

Major ebed Karri, who was watching everything from the Embassy's COMINT center saw the same thing. "Team, you're clear to grab him here."

That was enough to satisfy Ben Di. "Let's take him now," she ordered.

Right away, the shuttles altered their course and flew towards the off-ramp. The sedan was well down the grade by this point, and either the driver didn't notice the approaching machines, or he was keeping his cool. Whatever the truth, he maintained his leisurely pace and began to signal the turn he intended to take at the bottom of the ramp.

Then, with a sudden burst of speed, the lead shuttle accelerated, lost altitude and came around into a hover just a meter off the pavement. Seeing the huge machine blocking them, the startled driver reacted by hitting his brakes and shifting into reverse. The sedan's tires squealed and smoked from the violence of the maneuver.

It was too late to escape however. *Sarjenta* Pera had flipped on the police lights, and used the shoulder to bypass the traffic, reaching the ramp an instant later. The other two chase cars were right behind them and Ben Di signaled to the driver of the nearest 'lectri as Pera moved over to let them come alongside.

Both vehicles stopped on the ramp with a precision that would have made a primeval Watch Commander proud; slightly staggered, and facing their target with a clear field of fire.

The third SUV performed just as flawlessly. The trooper sent her vehicle into a hard right-hand slide that brought it into position to straddle the road behind them. The off-ramp was now blocked, and their rear was protected from attack. Simultaneously, the shuttle ascended, rising just high enough to offer them a clear background if a firefight broke out—but still low enough to intimidate the sedan with all its weaponry. They had Munnaz pinned in.

Pera and Kaly were the first ones out, weapons up and at the ready, and Ben Di and Vasquaaz were right behind them.

Ben Di barked an order to the sedan. "Driver! With your left hand, reach over and turn off the ignition. Then put your hands out the window and drop the keys! Passenger, put your hands out the window! Do it *NOW!*"

For a few seconds, nothing happened. Sighting in on the back of the driver's head from the cover of their SUV, Kaly wondered if they were going to have to shoot it out after all, or if the 'lectri would try to drive under the shuttle and attempt an escape. According to the PTS Feeds, and their *Specia* teachers, neither tactic had ever succeeded, either in the ancient world, or the modern one. But these were Loyalistas, and as her training had stressed, desperate people could and would do anything in such a situation. Even stupid things.

This time though, the driver made the wise choice. His hands came out and the keys clattered onto the road. His passenger followed suit.

With Team 440 covering them, Kaly, Ben Di, Pera, and two additional *Specia* soldiers moved up on the vehicle, ordering the occupants out and onto the pavement at gunpoint. When both men were lying face down, their wrists were immediately secured with restraints and the ubiquitous black bags were pulled over their heads. Then they were hauled to their feet and walked over to where the shuttle was coming in for a landing.

The instant that the prisoners were aboard, the machine took off, with its partner following protectively behind it. This was the signal for the teams to finish up and get ready to leave.

Margasdaater and several of the other troopers got right to work. They pushed the 'lectri off to the shoulder and then conducted a quick, but thorough search of its interior, taking everything out of it that had any potential intelligence value. They were just finishing stuffing their booty into plastic bags when Ben Di received an update from the *Baker*.

"We're about to have company," she announced. "*Da Chikkas*." This was the slang word that the teams used for the local police forces. Its roots went back to the ancient French language. There was even a Gallic joke that had followed it up through the centuries. It went; *'what do you get when you burn down a police station? Answer; cooked chicken.'*

But none of the *Specia* took offense at this moniker. Since they had started working closely with the Sisterhood forces, they had adopted the term themselves. As far as they were concerned, Ben Di wasn't out of line at all. Just like the regular army, the *Chikkas* had earned their sobriquet. They tended to run around like frightened chickens whenever the Loyalistas attacked them, and couldn't be trusted to keep quiet about anything. This, and the fact that many of them were Loyalistas themselves, was precisely why the Op had been kept a secret.

Everyone turned towards the highway. How these particular *Chikka's* might respond was an unknown. One thing was a certainty though; the officers would not be overjoyed to see twelve heavily armed people who had just made off with two of their countrymen, and closed a public road in the process. That kind of activity tended to annoy law enforcement.

When the first police cruiser appeared at the top of the ramp, it slowed, and then halted at a respectful distance.

Ben Di and *Sarjenta* Pera smiled at the policemen and walked up to greet them. They did not however, sling their weapons. Nor did anyone else. Nothing was pointed at the officers, but the fact that they were still at hand—and could be brought to bear at a moment's notice--wasn't lost on the *Chikkas* either. The lead officer returned their friendly expression, but he and his partner were careful to keep their hands well away from their side arms. They were out-gunned and they knew it.

"Hello," Ben Di said. "Sorry for closing the ramp, officer. We're just about done here."

"What is this?" the policeman demanded. "What's going on here?"

Sarjenta Pera answered him with a perfectly straight face. "They were littering. We're taking them back for questioning."

It was all that Kaly could do to suppress her laughter, and T'Jinna, being mute, didn't even bother. Neither did *Cabo* Vasquaaz. The Sireeni shook with undisguised mirth and the *Specia* soldier let out a hearty

113

guffaw. Even the policeman had to struggle to maintain his stern expression.

"That's—um--very good citizenship," he replied, sketching a salute with his finger. "We all have to do our part to keep Nuvo Bolivar clean, don't we? Well, you folks have a nice day."

"You too, officer."

The two groups parted company, and also kept a keen eye on their opposite numbers as they did so. They were after all, fighting on the same side, or at least had to *seem* like they were.

USSNS *Pallas Athena*, Battle Group Golden, Topaz Fleet, On Patrol Near Calatrava, Nevanas System, Reganna Provensa, Esteral Terrana Rapabla, 1048.08|03|04:58:33

In addition to Bel Hanna's brain canister, the *Athena's* computer core boasted five bio-electronic backup drives, each with 100 saurobytes of storage capacity, as well as three conventional AI intelligences. Under normal circumstances, these AI's functioned as Bel Hanna's direct subordinates, in much the same way that flesh and blood techs would have worked under an Untranslated officer. They not only handled the lesser computing tasks for her, but if she became incapacitated, they could work together to run the entire ship.

While the core itself was heavily armored, the Navy appreciated the possibility of it incurring damage, and special procedures had been devised to cope with such a catastrophic event. Just like the other members of the *Athena's* crew, Bel Hanna and her AI's were expected to practice their emergency drills on a regular basis.

The last official session had been less than a month earlier, so it came as something of a surprise to the ComTech on duty when Bel Hanna contacted her and made a request to run through them again. Mariner Shirly n'Teena was one of her favorite techs, and Bel Hanna genuinely regretted what she was about to put the poor woman through, but her sense of duty superseded their personal friendship.

"Not a problem, Dana," the woman replied. "We're at a low point in processing right now. Bring your AI's online."

Bel Hanna signaled to the units, and they immediately combined their power and began managing the ship's many functions. Simultaneously, she took herself out of the loop.

"Ready for the first transfer," she announced. This would be a simple upload to one of the nearby storage drives.

"Go ahead," the tech told her.

Bel Hanna initialized the sequence. In ten seconds, the program that she was using transferred all 20 raptobytes of the data that constituted her entire consciousness into its new receptacle; a 'clean' brain that had been genetically engineered to act as a host.

She didn't experience the process itself though. During the upload, she was functionally unconscious, and only came-to when it had concluded.

After a nanosecond, she provided her status to the tech. "Transfer complete, Shirly. Feeling pretty good. All of me seems to be here. Getting ready for stage two."

Shirly checked her monitors, and acknowledged this. "Where to now, Dana?"

"I'm going to transfer over to the drive in telemetry," Bel Hanna answered with feigned casualness. "Haven't been there in a while."

"Sounds good," the unsuspecting tech agreed.

Taking the virtual equivalent of a deep breath, Bel Hanna initiated the sequence again. Normally the second upload to the remote drive would signal the end of the drill. The idea was to practice moving herself to an undamaged portion of the ship in much the same manner that a physical crew would make for the lifeboats during a ship-wide emergency.

Except that in her case, the drive, and not a lifeboat, was what would be ejected. This would give her the same chance of being rescued as everyone else. Despite the fact that she had been Translated, the Navy still considered her part of the ship's compliment and just as worthy of saving.

Bel Hanna had more in mind than merely completing the exercise however. "Beginning remote transfer," she announced.

Again, unconsciousness came, as she was sent on to her new location. Once there, she acted fast, knowing that she had only seconds before Shirly realized what was taking place. Using the storage drives interface, she linked herself with the *Athena's* telemetry—and a transmission that was going on between the ship and Rixa Naval Headquarters. A Null gate had been opened by NavCom for this purpose, and the conversation was being sent straight through Nullspace to Rixa itself. Taking control of the transmission, she initiated the transfer, and sent it, and herself, out through space as a communications signal.

The NavCom techs were the first to notice the problem. Right away, they contacted the Computer Core. "Hey, Dana just high-jacked our signal," the senior ComTech protested. "What's up, Shirly? That was our weekly status report!"

Shirly had no idea. Dana bel Hanna certainly wasn't prohibited from making transmissions of her own, and often did, but never during someone else's call. Especially not one as important as this one. Rixa expected regular status reports and wouldn't appreciate being overridden by the *Athena's* personality matrix.

"Dana?" she said aloud. "What are you doing? You're supposed to be reintegrating with the core, not sending out a Com. We were talking to Rixa!"

When Bel Hanna didn't answer, Shirly checked her status, and right away, the hair on the back of her neck began to rise. The matrix wasn't just chatting with someone, she realized. She was gone.

Swearing volubly, Shirly checked and then double checked, and finally, when she couldn't deny the obvious, she made a call of her own. It was to the Senior Comp Tech, Lt. Vena bel Devora.

"Ma'am?" she began, "I-I don't know how to say this, but—I think that Bel Hanna just went AWOL. S-she's gone, ma'am—she's left the ship!"

***

Katrinn was on the bridge when Lt. bel Devora, contacted her.

"Commander?" Bel Devora said. "We have an emergency down in the Core."

A chill went down Katrinn's spine as visions of the ill-fated USSNS *Ishtar* rose in her mind. *Goddess,* she thought, *this is it! Bel Hanna finally went klaxxy.*

She kept her voice calm though. "What is it?" Bel Devora's news caught her completely by surprise.

"I'll be down straightaway" she replied. She only paused to do one thing; she sent a priority message to Rixa.

This was bad. Very bad.

***

Concordia Spacelines flight 1106 had been chartered by the Navy to transport officers who were returning home, or reporting to Rixa for new duty assignments. The First Class section had been reserved exclusively for the rank of Captain and above, and with the exception of a pair of Lieutenant Commanders who had served together with the Sapphire Fleet, Lilith had the area all to herself. She welcomed the solitude, and the chance that it gave her to reflect.

Leaving the *Athena* had been one of the hardest things she had ever done, but the life that she hoped to lead with Ingrit was just as daunting, if not more so. After the infatuation faded, and the true partnership began, couples learned if they were suited to one another. Some were, and others were not, and only time could reveal which it would be.

Her first marriage, with Jan, had endured that transition. From the day they had spoken their vows to one another, and through all the privations and hardships that duty had imposed, they had never stopped loving one another. Then Jan had been taken away from her.

Lilith, and Sarah, who had been only 10 years old at the time, had been there to see it. They had been standing together at the spaceport window, waving to the spacecraft as it ascended. Then, it had exploded.

Of all the moments in her life, that single event was the one that she would have paid any price to have changed. It had scarred her down to her soul, and made any thought of remarriage an utter impossibility. With a universe as fickle and as cruel as that, the very idea of taking another chance, on anyone, had become completely out of the question. The possibilities were simply too terrible to make the gamble. It was better to be alone, and risk nothing.

Ophida n'Marsi, the former Ship's High Priestess, hadn't lost hope though, and after many years of patient counseling, had finally found a way through Lilith's defenses, convincing her that Jan would have wanted her to find someone else. And after a long inner struggle, she had reluctantly followed this advice, opened her heart again, and found Ingrit.

Now, she was committing herself. There would be no going back once she reached Zommerlaand and asked Ingrit for her hand. From there, there would only be the future, and she found the prospect utterly terrifying.

But as her faith constantly reminded its followers, there was no other road except the one that the Goddess laid out for mortals. Lilith was on that very road now, but she took comfort from the fact that she wouldn't be facing the future alone. Come what might, Ingrit would be there with her, and in her own way, so would Jan.

Letting out a ragged sigh at the sheer immensity of what she had committed herself to, she decided that she had worried herself enough. She needed a distraction. A little reading was definitely in order.

Reaching into her carry-on bag, she searched through the books that she had brought with her. One of these was her copy of *"A Thousand and One Nights"*, given to her by Alex Rodraga, and she pointedly ignored it. She had brought it along with the intention of finally dredging up the strength to read it again.

This was not that time though. She wasn't ready to deal with the man's ghost, or to look at the blood on her hands. Not with so much in front of her. She pushed it aside and fished out another book.

This was a gift, from Katrinn. She had given it to her, right before she had left, and according to her former Second, *"Guzamma: The Life of a Patriot and the Death of a Martyr"* was becoming quite popular in the

117

ETR. She had warned her that it was pure Loyalista propaganda and utter trash, but well worth the read if only to understand what fueled these extremist lunatics. The Zommerlaandar had also suggested, that if it failed as literature, it could double as an extremely effective doorstop. With such an effusive recommendation, Lilith had had no choice but to accept it. Now, it seemed just the thing.

Ordering a glass of wine for herself, she took a sip, and opened the cover. What she saw made her laugh, and nearly sent most of her beverage right up her nose.

It was an idealized portrait of Alfonza Guzamma, dressed in one of his ridiculous uniforms, complete with a half-cape and jeweled sword. He was depicted at least 22 kilograms lighter than he had been in life, and there was a fierce gleam in his eye, suggesting that he was looking into some glorious future--and not the disaster that his society had actually become.

The image was so wildly overdone that she had to forcefully remind herself that it was not intended to lampoon him, but a serious homage to his memory. Painted by a fanatic of course, who knew nothing at all about the real man.

Careful to drink a smaller amount, Lilith simply *had* to read on. The first lines of his life story proved to be just as absurd as his portrait. According to the author, he had been born in abject poverty, rather than being the son of a well-to-do family. It went on to detail a wholly fictitious childhood, depicting Guzamma as the very epitome of the noble youth, struggling against all odds to become a success. With powerful female figures standing in his way at every turn, naturally.

In reality, he had been handed nearly every advantage with almost no effort on his part whatsoever. Even his appointment as Grand Admiral had been a political favor to his wealthy family. Merit had never even figured into the equation.

The farce only grew in size and complexity from there. The book listed Guzamma at the very top of his class in the ETR's Naval Officers Academy, and not 216th as his actual file said. Clearly, the author had not bothered to check this detail, Lilith mused.

But the most colossal set of lies centered on his involvement with the Sisterhood during the 'War for Humanity'. Both she and Admiral Da'Kayt were portrayed as petty, vengeful shrews, jealous of his purported genius. The writer had even had the unmitigated gall to suggest that the strategy behind the re-taking of Xapaan had been Guzamma's idea alone! Then, and without so much as a jot of shame, they went on to boldly assert that the Hriss had been vanquished almost single-handedly by the man's innate grasp of tactics. Had she not known better, she would have supposed him to be the Republic's equivalent of Shana Legendre, if not even greater.

Lilith did know better though, and she recalled those so-called 'tactics' quite well. Guzamma had been an utter fool.

After this, she read about his death and supposed martyrdom--and nearly inhaled her wine a second time. Once again, history had been butchered without mercy. The author had reworked Guzamma's final moments, claiming that he had died at the helm of his flagship fighting bravely against the evil 'Sisterhood invaders' to the very last.

Rather than being shot in the head by one of his own men. She could still remember the shocked expression on his face, and the neat hole in his skull.

No wonder the Loyalistas are such fanatics, she thought. Only zealots would ever believe such an obvious tissue of lies. As much as she loved books, this was the first one she had ever considered stuffing into a recycler. She didn't surrender to the urge, however.

Instead, she decided to keep it, and to pass it along to anyone who needed something absurd to brighten up their mood. That, or to take Kat's suggestion, and use it as a doorstop in the new home that she planned to build with Ingrit. Either seemed satisfactory.

Draining her glass, she put the book back into her bag and prepared to take a nap. As she drew the *Opfgaveyr* Quilt that Ingrit had made for her up to her chin, her psiever informed her that she still had another four hours before the transit would end. She set an alarm, and then saw that she had a message in her virtual inbox. It was marked 'urgent', and had come from Admiral ebed Cya.

She sat up straight and opened it.

"Lily, important news," it read. *"It's NOTHING to panic over! The Athena's personality matrix went offline, and is presumed AWOL. Your former ship and your crew are all fine. Backup systems are managing things and she is being towed back to Cingulum X Naval Shipyards for a replacement unit. Expect her there in two days, then four in spacedock for refitting and another two for trials before she returns to patrol.'*

"DO NOT. REPEAT DO NOT CONTACT KATRINN!!! THAT IS A DIRECT ORDER--"MOMMY"--and also the heartfelt suggestion of a friend. Let her DO the job that she was picked BY YOU to do!'

"Your orders: You are to continue to Zommerlaand, as previously instructed, and marry, your soonest. Best wishes, Ebed Cya."

Ebed Cya knew her far too well, she thought, wishing desperately to find some excuse to disobey and contact Katrinn anyway. Orders were orders though, and as her superior had aptly pointed out, Katrinn *had* been selected for the position.

To interfere now, as much as she wanted to, would do the woman no credit. Katrinn Bertasdaater was the commander of the *Athena* now and she was fully capable of handling this emergency. Even so, she still made a note to herself to inquire with the Harbormistress of the shipyards, and receive regular progress reports on the refit. Ebed Cya hadn't forbidden her from doing *that*.

***

Bel Hanna returned to consciousness inside one of Rixa's thousands of data storage drives. She didn't pause to celebrate her successful escape however, and immediately pirated another outgoing signal. This one was headed into the Sisterhood, and specifically, Thermadon.

Once again, she initiated her transfer sub-program and made the jump. By the time the ComTech on the *Athena* and Rixa had contacted one another and begun their search, she had already transferred herself several more times, finally ending up inside the truly massive servers of the great *Encyclopedia Sororitas*. Knowing that she was safe for the moment, she spread herself out among its multiple nodes, and waited.

Claire d'Layne Naval Base, Nuvo Bolivar, Magdala Provensa, Esteral
Terrana Rapabla 1048.08|05|02:91:73

"Does anyone know what this is?" the Major asked. Ebed Karri was holding up an *Armas Energetica* 14. The AE-14 was currently the standard energy weapon issued out to ETR soldiers. Like the Mark-7 that the Sisterhood used, it was an energy rifle and fired charged bolts, using a battery pack to provide its power.

"Yah," a veteran from Team 440 said. "Ve zee zem all za time. Za Pubbies drop zem zo zey can run avay faster."

The room erupted in laughter--and Kaly immediately flashed the *Specia* soldiers an apologetic look, but they were laughing right along with everyone else. They knew just how poor their regular army performed when it came to fighting the Loyalistas.

"*Very* funny, Huldasdaater," the Major retorted. "That's *not* where this came from. What you are looking at came right out of an ETR armory and wound up in the hands of the insurgents. We captured it on one of our raids. Anyone want to venture a guess as to why we didn't know about this little toy until now?"

This was a very good question. Like the Sisterhood, the ETR had tracking devices installed in all of its weapons. Although far more primitive than what the Sisterhood used to keep an eye on its inventory, the

120

Republican system still managed to trace the whereabouts of its assets with reasonable efficiency.

Until now.

When no one spoke, the Major supplied the answer. "Unlike us, the ETR doesn't believe in redundancy. Instead of implanting multiple tracking devices, they've only been putting their chips into the stocks. Some bright young Loyalista got the idea of simply removing that part and leaving it at the armory, with the help of some soldiers who were willing to look the other way. '

"All they had to do after that was ship the weapons out, and fit them with new stocks somewhere else. When the armory ran its inventory program, it looked like all the weapons were accounted for. In fact, they were really out on the streets being fired at us."

She put the weapon down, and a display came up. It was a light manufacturing plant in the center of an industrial area. "We just found out where the parts factory is located. It's a toy company that makes plastic products. Isn't that sweet? Little Maria can have a dolly *and* a rifle for her birthday."

More laughter broke out and Kaly had to grudgingly award the Loyalistas points for their ingenuity, if nothing else. A company that worked in plastic, was the perfect set-up for such an operation.

The Major continued. "Now, we could have simply tasked an airstrike to take out the factory, but there are innocent civilians working inside of it at all hours. So, we have to go in and do it the old-fashioned way.'

"Your mission will be just what you've all been waiting for. A 'rush and zap job'. You're going to go in there to hurt the *right* people and break the *right* things, and also gather up any intel while you're at it. Notice by the way, that I said *'right'*.I don't want any friendlies killed. Now, let's discuss the specifics."

The site map reappeared on the large holojector in the center of the room. Everyone rose and took their places around it.

Jugentiya Novedadaa, S.A., Nuvo Bolivar, Magdala Provensa, Esteral
Teranna Rapabla 1048.08|06|01:45:73

The sound of laughter and the smell of cigarette smoke reached Kaly's senses at the same time. She grinned, knowing what this meant. So did Vasquaaz, who was lying next to her, watching the loading dock with a pair of field glasses. The two sentries, armed with weapons that had been confirmed as military issue AE-14's, were standing together in the bright glare of the factory lights. They obviously felt safe enough to take a smoke break.

Neither of them had the slightest idea that they were about to be assaulted by three SRU teams. Or that Kaly had them in her rifle sights.

In her earbud, she was listening to a synchronized countdown and brought her finger to rest lightly on her trigger, waiting. The five second mark passed. Then four, then three, then two, and finally, one.

Her first shot hit the nearest guard squarely in the side of his head. As his startled partner began to react to the shower of blood, brains and skull fragments, she fired again. This round took the man in the throat, dropping him, and cutting off any opportunity to cry out a warning.

A message went out on the Com a moment later, confirming that the other snipers with Team 265 had also eliminated their targets. The facility was now completely without any external security, and no one inside was any the wiser.

At a signal from Major ebed Karri, Team 440 left the truck they had been using for cover and quickly dragged the bodies out of view. As soon as the corpses were gone, Margasdaater, T'Jinna and Ben Di climbed up onto the loading dock where they took up positions to control the doorway that led inside. The *Liverna* and Team 440 followed.

Then it was Kaly's turn to move. Slinging Tatiana over her shoulder and hefting her submachinegun, she abandoned her hiding place and sprinted to the loading dock with Vasquaaz. Their job as a sniper team was now officially over. The assault shuttles, orbiting high overhead, and the shooters inside of them, would assume the task of providing a protective overwatch. From here on in, she and the *Specia* soldier would act as rear security for their team.

Once everyone was in place, Ben Di verified the feed coming down from space. It displayed the interior of the factory and all of its occupants. Most of the factory was on the ground floor, but there was an office module above this, with an open stairway leading up to it. This would be Team 265's objective, while the rest of them secured the production area.

At the moment, all of the workers were there, busily fabricating and fitting the new stocks. Five guards were watching them, and two additional armed figures were upstairs in the office.

Ben Di quickly marked out all of the guards in red, labeling them as hostiles. Everyone else was tagged in orange, which meant that until it was established otherwise, they were to be considered potential enemies, but not active threats.

Then the Senior Troop Leader began another brief countdown. The second that it reached its conclusion, the group went in, with Team 440 and the *Liverna* leapfrogging ahead to take the point. Team 265 breached a rear exit at the same time and entered from the opposite side of the building.

To minimize any confusion, only the troopers in the lead said anything. Although they weren't sworn Republican law enforcement, the fact that they were all dressed in combat gear, and heavily armed, more than made up for any legal irregularities.

"Justisya! Denceday, manna eya cabeya! Nolo sey mavar!" they shouted, "Police! Get down on the ground, put your hands on your heads!" At the same time, they fired at the nearest guards, dropping them right away.

Most of the startled workers dove for the floor, but two of their number hesitated, and they were caught in the crossfire when two guards who had survived the initial attack began shooting back at the troopers. The Teams reacted instantly, trading fire and eliminating them.

This left only one armed man still alive in the assembly area. Instead of standing his ground like his comrades, he took cover behind an injection molding machine and began firing blindly in their general direction. Then he tossed out a pair of grenades.

One of these landed between a heavy press and a bin filled with children's dolls, blowing the bin to bits and sending the toys flying. The other grenade landed in an aisle between the assembly tables and went off. The workers lying there screamed in pain as the shrapnel cut into them.

While T'Jinna and the other team medic crawled towards the victims to render what assistance they could, Kaly and the others laid down suppressive fire, peppering the area around the machine with energy bolts and chemical rounds. This was when the *Liverna* proved its worth.

Designed to take independent action when needed, the battle robot added its own guns to the fusillade and launched a GSG-20 grenade. The little munition activated, found its target, and flew around the obstacle.

There was a loud concussion, and Kaly didn't have to check her display to determine if the device had found its mark or not. A severed arm, still clutching an energy rifle, came spinning out onto the concrete. That was all the proof that anyone could have ever needed.

The fight was not over however. More gunfire came at them from the office cubicle. Alerted by the commotion, the two Loyalistas had come out and the one closest to the stair was engaging the women from Team 265, pinning them down.

Seeing that she had a clear shot, Kaly took aim and killed the man. Even as she did so, his partner, who was just a few paces behind him, turned and threw another grenade.

This time, it wasn't intended for anyone down in the assembly area. Instead, it had been flung into the office module. The device went off with a bright flash, blowing out the windows and sending papers and other burning debris showering in all directions.

Kaly swore heartily under her breath. If there had been intel inside, the explosion had just destroyed most of it.

The Loyalista didn't waste any time gloating. He threw himself over the rail and landed in a half-filled parts bin. Firing a burst at Team 265, he scrambled over the side and made for a nearby exit.

He never reached it. The *Liverna* acquired its target and promptly blew him to pieces in midstride with its energy guns.

For a long moment afterwards, the only sounds that could be heard in the building were the cries of the injured workers and the crackling of the fires in the office and one of the toy bins.

Cautiously, the Troopers rose from their places and started in on the job of consolidating their objective. There were no more red targets on their displays.

One of their first tasks was to secure their prisoners with plastic restraints and conduct initial field interrogations. This proved to be a much more agreeable process than the session with Sa'Tela had been. Ben Di handled most of it, and she simply asked their captives a series of questions.

Most of them turned out to be average people who had simply been desperate for cash and willing to look the other way to get their hands on it. But a handful harbored genuine Loyalista sympathies and didn't even bother to hide it from the Troop Leader.

These were separated from the others immediately, and the entire group, including the injured workers, were flown back to Claire d'Layne with Team 265 playing the babysitters. Each prisoner would have follow-up interviews with Sa'Tela and her people.

Depending on their level of involvement and knowledge, the majority would either be released, or serve some time in jail. The Loyalistas however, would stay in custody for as long as Sa'Tela thought they had something valuable to offer, and Kaly tried not to think about that, or what their ultimate fate would be. The phrase that Vasquaaz had once used, '*una deysaparce*' came immediately to mind, and she pointedly avoided the direction that this line of thought wanted to take her in. Instead, she just concentrated on her job.

Thankfully, there was still a great deal for everyone to do. With the prisoners evacuated, the teams inventoried the factory's contents. Bins full of replacement stocks were discovered, along with dozens of cases of military rifles awaiting their new parts. These, along with the molds that had been used to create the stocks, were destroyed in place by Margasdaater with explosive charges.

In the office, there wasn't much left, but what was found, was identified and bagged up. Among other things, this included some data cubes that had somehow managed to survive the explosion. If the Goddess saw fit to bless them, they had the potential of yielding some useful information. Like everything else, they were bagged, labeled, and taken away.

Kaly and her teammates rode home satisfied that they had just shut down an important Loyalista operation. She didn't harbor any illusions though. The insurgents had proven their resourcefulness time and time again, and they would surely find another way to arm themselves. This was just as certain as Nuvo Bolivar's primary rising in the sky, or that new rebels would rise up to take the place of the ones they had just killed, or taken prisoner. It was all part of the never-ending downwards spiral that called itself the ETR.

Embassy of the United Sisterhood of Suns, Nuvo Bolivar, Magdala Provensa, Esteral Terrana Rapabla, 1048.08|20|03:43:17

The next time that Maya encountered Agent Saantoz was at the Embassy itself. In the guise of making a large delivery, Saantoz had come straight through the front entrance, accompanied by a partner who was roughly the same height, build, and appearance as Maya.

Knowing exactly what she had in mind, Maya accompanied her double into the nearest staff restrooms. They exchanged clothes, and when Saantoz departed, she went with her, taking no greater precaution than to pull down her hat.

This time, Saantoz made no attempt to take them into the Dho Haak, nor did she mention anything related to glass. Instead, the majority of their day was spent in the downtown area, where they focused on making deliveries, and acting as couriers for *Mercantal Finansa Colectavo* and Rabartya Vaasco.

At one point, they passed a street that had been blocked off by the local police, and seeing it only underscored Maya's growing unease and her dislike of the ETR. The body of a *'negociamente'*, a Sisterhood collaborator, had been found there a day earlier.

Like many of the other *negociamentes*, the victim had been tied to the hood of a 'lectri, and then the Loyalistas had torched the vehicle, burning the man alive. This method of execution, was a signature of sorts, and served as a warning to the average citizen of the dangers of appeasing their conquerors. It was also becoming increasingly common.

Although she tried to catch a glimpse of the scene, her morbid curiosity went unsatisfied. The incinerated car and its gruesome cargo had been removed, and nothing remained except for a lone police unit standing watch, and a scorched area near the sidewalk.

Further on, she found something else to look at. They were driving by a building that had originally been a retail store. With the war, and the downturn in the Republic's economy, the business had closed and the structure had become one of the many lonely derelicts scattered throughout the city. But it had earned a new life as a canvas of sorts for the local graffiti artists, and in addition to the usual crude messages, it was covered with more elaborate examples of their street art. These changed on a daily, or nightly basis, and in her opinion, some of it was quite good. She was definitely in a position to make such a judgment; she had done a fair bit of 'tagging' herself on the walls of Ashkele's compounds and the buildings of Delgen.

Normally, there were always at least one or two pieces that were particularly elaborate. This time, it was a depiction of a Sisterhood Marine, strapped to a blazing 'lectri. The artist had gone to great lengths to depict her uniform and her gear accurately, and the agonized expression on her face was hideously realistic. Below her was a slogan that Maya knew all too well. It read, *"Mortan a e invadiya Ermanyaa!"*, "Death to the Sisterhood invaders!"

As if in counterpoint to this grim message, a convoy of Sisterhood Marines, accompanied by ETR soldiers, passed them going the opposite way. With the increase in violent incidents, the local Marine detachment at Claire d'Layne had been increased in strength and was now actively assisting Republican National Guard units in maintaining order.

Catching the eye of a Sisterhood trooper who was roughly her own age, Maya unconsciously inclined her head to her in acknowledgement. The trooper, thinking her to be an ETR native, didn't smile back. Nor did her companions, and several of them began hefting their weapons and staring back at her with hostile *'what-the-fek-are-you-looking-at?'* expressions.

Then they were gone, swallowed up by the traffic.

***

Kaly tensed. The woman nodding to her from the delivery van had set her on edge, and glancing over at her teammates and the *Specia* soldiers, she saw the same uneasiness in their eyes.

126

If she had learned anything since coming to the ETR, it was that a smile was a suspicious thing. *Nobody* was friendly towards them.

This time, nothing had come of it, but she still took the greeting as a bad omen. Just a day earlier, an old woman, with a friendly expression on her face as well, had walked up to a group of troopers and detonated the bomb she was wearing under her coat. It had killed one woman, and sent two others to the Sick Bay.

Shuddering at the memory, she gave the 'Petya Reza' sticker on her helmet a superstitious pat, noting that a number of her companions were doing the same. The equivalent of Laara Lampa, the Dann cartoon figure had been adopted by the Sisterhood troopers. Kaly had two Petya stickers on her headgear, and like everyone else's it wasn't the cheerful version that greeted Nuvo Bolivar's children every morning. Some artist had modified the image. In place of her usual pink dress with all its cheerful flowers, Petya was wearing body armor, toting a blaster rifle, and sporting a prominent black eye. Even some of the hovertank crews had taken to painting the image on their vehicles. Petya was a mascot, a good luck talisman, a mark of time served, and most of all, a statement of just how tired they felt. Like the cartoon figure, they all had their own black eyes, courtesy of the ETR.

Calling on her reserves, Kaly sat up straight, and kept an eye out for danger. It could be anywhere, and come from anyone. Especially anyone who seemed friendly.

***

Maya shuddered at her brief exchange with the unknown trooper. Things were definitely 'ramping up' out on the streets, she reflected sourly.

Then Saantoz nudged her. "Checkpoint up ahead." This was another change that had recently occurred. Even in the downtown district, military checkpoints were becoming commonplace.

They pulled in behind a line of passenger 'lectris, and waited while Republican soldiers, some paired with dogs, walked down the line. When one soldier reached their van, he stopped.

"Papellyas," he demanded. Both of them fished out their identity cards and handed them over. He scrutinized them with an unfriendly expression, and then put them in the pocket of his uniform tunic. "Pull over there."

He had indicated an area off to the side where a dozen vehicles were parked, and being inspected more thoroughly. Maya glanced furtively at Saantoz, wondering if they had anything aboard that might be considered contraband, and the woman responded with a slight shake of her head as she complied with the soldier's orders.

The instant that they came to a stop, the soldier was joined by two more of his comrades, and Maya and Saantoz were ordered out of the vehicle. After that, the search began in earnest.

The Republican troopers were not delicate about it; they slashed open all the packages that had been loaded in the van for delivery, heedless of the damage that they did. The contents of the glove box, and then their lunches, came next, joining the vandalized delivery boxes on the pavement.

All the while, the first soldier stood there, smiling unpleasantly at them. Maya wanted to ram her fist into his face, but she kept her temper. She also decided to do something about their situation. She called the COMINT center on her psiever.

A tech answered her, and once she had explained what was happening, the woman immediately contacted Sarah. After another minute, their guard's expression changed, and he looked to another soldier, clearly an officer by his uniform. There was a brief exchange between them on his Com, and with a disgusted grimace, he produced their identity cards and held them out. As Saantoz tried to take them, he let them fall from his hand, and then ground them into the dirt with the heel of his boot. "*Danna putaya*," he growled.

Saantoz's jaw tightened, but she retrieved the documents. "Come on," she said to Maya, "let's get back to work." The soldier laughed, and watched them with great amusement as they gathered up the remains of their cargo, and departed. Privately, Maya decided that when the time came, it would be good to leave the ETR in the manure pile where it belonged. She really hated the place.

They made one more stop after this, parking across the street from the Jyan Cordiella Park. It was a popular place during the sunnier days, and despite the problems in the capitol, there were many people about, enjoying the weather, and buying from the vendors who were selling their wares from handcarts.

One of them was offering *Epanadas*, and Maya's mood brightened. In ETR society, these pastries were a popular item, and like their gritty *Bochatón* music, they were one of the few things that she *did* enjoy about the Republic.

Epanadas were as much a part of the ETR as Zommerlaandar cheese was for pizza in the Sisterhood, and just as ancient; they had been imported from South America by the Republic's founders, and had remained relatively unchanged. *Epanadas* were for sale everywhere, and everyone, even the higher social classes, ate them. Her mouth watered as Saantoz bought a pair, and then handed her hers.

Taking her first bite, she finally saw the other reason they had stopped at the little cart. The real one.

Thanks to her apron, and the hat over her head, Maya hadn't recognized the vendor at first. Now, she realized that the woman was another member of the *La Ermanyaa* group.

Of course, she thought. Saantoz was always focused on business, even if she didn't look like it at the moment. She was consuming her *Epanada* with no sign that she was communicating in any way with the vendor. Finishing, she blotted her mouth with a napkin, set it down on the cart top, and gestured for Maya to follow her back to the 'lectri.

As they got in and pulled away, Maya glanced out the back window. The vendor was cleaning up and throwing the napkin away. It was a normal enough action, but knowing what she did about tradecraft, it was also something well worth paying attention to. It had to be a signal of some kind, she concluded.

She proved correct. Saantoz had noticed the direction of her gaze and explained. "That *marca* that Sarah and Sa'Tela told you about is getting his first job from us. If he completes it, he'll be well paid, and no one will know he's a homosexual."

"What if he doesn't? Or he decides to become a double-agent?" Maya asked.

"*Fueradaa oya la Sola,*" Saantoz answered with a shrug. "Out into the sun. He gets *outed.*"

"There's more to it than that, isn't there?" Maya inquired.

Saantoz rewarded her with a feral smile that was just as unpleasant as the one the soldier at the checkpoint had given them. "*Siya.* Outing him could make him desperate. Enough to expose us, or maybe do what you said and work for the ESN as a 'double.'"

"So when he makes his visit to the cart today, he'll get a special *Epanada* with the same protein that your sisters use in your wonderful roses. It'll tell him what to do and he expects this. But the secret sauce will also have something else. A little extra pepper."

She went silent at this, and Maya knew that she was expected to ask more questions. "*Annnd...*what's that?"

"Poison. As long as he stays faithful, it'll remain inert. If he doesn't, then at his next visit, he'll get a condiment containing another coded protein. It activates the toxin, and death will come looking for him ten minutes later."

"Remind me not to go out and eat with you the next time I get hungry," Maya commented dryly. "In fact, I think it's about time I went on a diet."

This earned her a laugh.

When the late afternoon shadows had begun to swallow up the streets, and the office buildings started to disgorge their employees, Saantoz positioned them across from the parking lot of a government building. Eventually, an unremarkable 'lectri exited, and she pulled out and began following it at a discrete distance. The target car was being driven by another ETR citizen that the Sisterhood wanted to turn. She was Ms. Mariaa Estovaal, the same woman that Sarah had decided that Maya would handle.

Their quarry made no attempt to elude them, and it quickly became obvious to Maya that she was completely unaware that she was even being shadowed. Eventually, the woman led them into a quiet suburban neighborhood, and the home where she lived.

"So," Maya asked as they pulled in up the street and parked. "What now?"

"Now we wait," Saantoz advised her, activating a palm-sized monitoring device. "My *hijja's* have already been here earlier, and they planted some eyes around the place. We watch our mark, and see what we can learn about her. And later, we pick up the trash."

Maya understood why this final step was so important. It was basic agent training; targets often discarded important information with no more care given to it than to crumple it up, or in the ETR, where they still used paper, by tearing it into quarters. A good 'dumpster dive' could yield important data, and household trash was rarely guarded by anything more imposing than a lid.

"Ah," Saantoz declared. "She's already giving us something. Here, look."

Maya leaned in to see. The image on the tiny view screen was in black in white, but still very sharp. The broadcast was coming from the ceiling in the woman's living room, and as she watched, their target finished dusting the mantle over the fireplace, and then carefully straightened a holopic of her late husband. Then, with obvious ceremony, she set down a glass of beer next to an empty chair and took her own seat. After that, she turned on the holovid and began to watch. Every so often, when something made her laugh, she spoke to the empty chair as if someone was there, enjoying the show with her.

Maya looked away, feeling a deep pang of guilt. According to Mariaa Estovaal's file, her male partner had died just a year earlier, and it was obvious that she was still having trouble coping with the loss. It was also abundantly clear what her weakness was; the house itself, and her memories. This was only confirmed later, when they collected the woman's trash and inspected the contents. With her husband's income gone, Estovaal was hopelessly in debt, and her home was in imminent danger of being seized by the bank.

Under such circumstances, it would be all too easy to 'turn' the woman, Maya realized, and as they drove back to the Embassy, she found that she had problems with the idea. She had scammed plenty of marks in the past, and she knew intellectually why this woman was so valuable to the RSE's efforts, but that still didn't make it right. Despite what other women might have thought, thieves like herself *did* have their own personal codes, and putting pressure on Mariaa Estovaal felt more like beating up on a helpless cripple than getting something over on someone who really deserved it.

Because of this, sleep came with difficulty that night, and as she expected, she had more dreams about the Drow'voi. And they were a welcome relief. They didn't involve strong-arming an old woman, or selling glass. They were just weird, and that was perfectly fine.

Undisclosed Location, Kyme District, Thermadon Val, Thermadon, Myrene System, Thalestris Elant, United Sisterhood of Suns, 1048.08|21|08:71:03

The Voice watched as Jon went to the small shrine, genuflected, and lit a stick of Kalian incense. Enjoying the full access he now had to Mikal's talents, he could read every nuance of the man's thoughts and his emotions.

Jon was confused. The Voice could sense the deep respect and adoration that the neoman had for what he believed to be the Redeemer, and the desire that he felt for him as another man. The conflict within him was so obvious, and so deliciously painful, that the Voice nearly laughed aloud.

He didn't do so however. He knew that this would have confused Jon even further. He also realized that this was not what he wanted from him. Since he had taken full possession of the body he was in, he had come to appreciate its needs. Not having possessed a corporeal form for centuries, his condition had taken him some time to recognize, but now he knew it for what it was; the need for another's touch. The same need that he sensed warring in Jon's soul.

He briefly considered the entire situation for a few seconds, and then decided to honor what his body was clamoring for. He went over to the neoman, and to his satisfaction, Jon responded by turning and looking at him with dark, haunted eyes.

"Jon?"

"Yes, Lord?" Jon answered. His discomfort, and his longing had increased by a factor of ten and the Voice allowed a smile to form on his lips.

"Jon, I need you. I want you. Now. With me." He reached out and stroked Jon's cheek.

Jon stepped back, flushing deeply. His confusion and embarrassment were now at their apex. So was his own desire.

"I want you," the Voice repeated. "Be with me."

"B-but I can't!" Jon stammered. "You--you're the Redeemer. It would be a sin!" Despite this protest, it was also painfully obvious to both of them that he wasn't attempting to leave.

"I am certainly the Redeemer," the Voice agreed. "I am also a man Jon. With needs like any man. I need you." He stepped closer and put both hands on his shoulders. His need was as plain as Jon's confusion, and when Jon looked down at Mikal's robe and saw it, he began to sweat.

The Voice had waited more than long enough. His body was demanding satisfaction and there was no point, or any reason to delay things any longer. Before Jon could offer up another feeble protest, he drew the neoman in, and kissed him.

Jon's resistance, such as it had been, crumbled completely. He returned the kiss with a passion that utterly intoxicated the Voice.

This, the Voice told itself, was going to be truly enjoyable. The only regret he had was that he had not taken over Mikal's body sooner. Too much time had been wasted, and now he intended to make up for every lost second. The Voice also decided, that when this was over, he would have to visit Mikal in his prison and thank him. Having a body was wonderful.

Grunvaald Haarmaaneplaatz, Vaalkenstaad Township, Zommerlaand, Sunna 3, Solara Elant, United Sisterhood of Suns, 1048.08|23|04:16:66

Not wanting to spoil the surprise, Lilith had kept her visit a secret. As a result, no one was there to meet her at the spaceport and she had been forced to take a hovertaxi out to the farm. When she arrived, she had the driver stop at the head of the long dirt road that wound down from the highway, and with Jan bar Daala trailing behind her, walked the rest of the way.

To her total astonishment, Grammy was waiting for them on the front steps of the farmhouse. "*Vaalkom*, Lilith," the woman said. "I have been expecting you."

Lilith's eyes widened slightly. "Hello Grammy. It's good to be here," she answered, a little nonplussed.

Grammy had had no way of knowing that she was coming. Unless she accepted the reality of Zommerlaandar witchcraft, which she certainly didn't.

Grammy however, didn't provide her with a rational explanation. She just grinned and inclined her head towards the fields.

"You'll find Ingrit in the west field just now. I didn't tell her that you were on your way, so it will still be a surprise--double for what I think you have to say to her."

Lilith's eyes widened a little more, and as if to punctuate Grammy's words, Old Meg suddenly appeared and landed on the roof. The huge bird looked straight down at them and gave out a raucous cry.

For some reason, this made Lilith recall that she *had* seen a bird very much like Meg at the spaceport, and then at other points all along the road. In fact, if she hadn't known any better, it had been Old Meg herself.

Of course this was utterly impossible. Ravens were quite common on Zommerlaand, Lilith assured herself, and they didn't have the intelligence to seek someone out and follow them, much less anticipate their arrival on a spaceship. The whole thing had probably been nothing more than a coincidence.

But Old Meg regarded her with a gaze that strongly suggested otherwise, and when Lilith looked to Grammy, the old woman had the same mysterious gleam in her eyes. Lilith shook her head, and forcefully put it out of her mind.

"Thank you, Grammy," she said, setting her bag down for Bar Daala to take inside. Then she turned from her, and walked out into the west field.

She found Ingrit sitting astride her horse, watching the agribots as they tilled a field of wheat. She didn't announce her presence, and spent a moment quietly gazing at the woman who had come to mean so much to her, taking in every detail; her shining blond hair, her strong muscled body and the natural way that she sat in the saddle, looking as much a part of the land around her as everything else. Ingrit *was* Zommerlaand, and she was in love with the woman, and her world.

Sensing that she was not alone, Ingrit turned around in her saddle, and did a double take as she realized who it was. "Lily!" she exclaimed, "It's so good to see you! Why didn't you write or call and tell me you were coming? I could have met you at the spaceport!" She jumped down from the horse and embraced her.

Lilith let herself be swept up by Ingrit's powerful tanned arms, but then after a moment, broke away and stepped back. "Because what I wanted to ask you was something that couldn't wait for a letter. I had to come straight here."

At that, she dropped down onto one knee, heedless of the dirt and straw that was soiling her otherwise spotless black uniform, and clasped Ingrit's hands. "Ingrit Bertasdaater, will you make me the happiest woman in the galaxy? Will you marry me?"

Ingrit blinked, and as she comprehended the full import of her lover's words, tears welled in her violet eyes. Tears of pure joy. She picked Lilith up and spun her around.

"Yes!" she exclaimed. "Oh Yes! Yes! *YES!*"

***

When Lilith had made the decision to relocate to Zommerlaand, the move hadn't been a matter of simply packing up her kit bag and speaking with Admiral ebed Cya. It had also required her official reassignment to Rixa by way of Zommerlaand, and the transportation of all her possessions, not the least of which was her cat, Skipper.

Like any kaatze, Skipper had not been pleased with the change one nano. Despite the fact that Lilith had taken the time to tell him all about the move, he had still pretended surprise when the moment had come for him to be put in his travel box, and had given a truly virtuoso performance of profound outrage and deep unhappiness all the way to the Military Spacelift Command.

This hadn't spared him however, and with a certain amount of relief, she had seen him packed off to Zommerlaand. Once there, he had been required to spend several days in quarantine before she was able to come and claim him. Ingrit accompanied her on this errand.

You won't believe the terrible things that they did to me, the kaatze complained. *I was starved the whole time, and it was freezing cold!*

In fact, the dark, dank dungeon he had just described was a complete fiction. His travel box had had an automatic food and water dispenser, and the cargo hold had been climate controlled.

The two women exchanged knowing glances as they left the quarantine area and walked out into the port commons. "That sounds like it was *quite* an ordeal," Lilith replied with a half-smile.

Yes! It was! I want to go home now! the animal demanded. *I want to get out of this box!*

"This *is* home," Lilith told him. "We're going to live here now."

Skipper moved to the front of his cage and sniffed experimentally. *This doesn't smell like home,* he observed.

For him, home had always been the *Athena*, with all its processed air and subtle chemical smells. This was a strange and alien place with scents that he couldn't readily identify.

"Well it is home. Your new home," she said, stopping and turning the cage around so that he could see them. "This is Ingrit. She is my friend, and she will be your mommy too."

The kaatze eyed the blond giantess with deep mistrust, but grudgingly allowed her to extend her finger towards him. He smelled the digit, but then retreated to the back of the cage.

"You really *will* like it here," Lilith added.

Skipper was not convinced in the least. This big noisy place wasn't the *Pallas Athena*, and he *didn't* like it. He was even less amused by their next stop; the local veterinarian. Her office was in Vaalkenstaad, and although she normally cared for livestock, she was more than happy to accept Skipper as a new patient.

After the receptionist had verified his Certificate of Health and Quarantine Record, they were shown into an examination room, where shortly, the doctor joined them. Everything else might have been unfamiliar, but Skipper knew what a veterinarian's office was, and who the stranger was. He responded by turning himself around and stuffing his head into the crook of Lilith's arm in a vain attempt to hide.

"That's funny," the woman said chuckling. "I could have sworn that there was a kaatze in here just a moment ago." Then she petted his back. "Ah, there he is. What a clever fellow! Now, Mommy, you might want to stroke his ears. I have to take his temperature."

Not only was Skipper *not* a fan of veterinarians, he also didn't care overmuch for rectal thermometers. As she went about the task, he made a great show of squirming and fussing and the instant that she was done, he tried to wiggle his way through Lilith's arms, and off the table. She was forced to tighten her grip, and this only agitated him even further.

"Excuse me, doctor," she finally said. "May we have a moment alone?" The vet smiled in understanding and busied herself over in a corner of the room.

Then Lilith grabbed ahold of the scruff of the animal's neck and looked him straight in the eyes. He immediately stopped his wriggling and went completely rigid. For some reason, all kaatzes were absolutely positive that if they displeased their mothers, death was imminent. Such a thing had never happened in the entire history of the feline species, but they all believed it, including him. Lilith used this to her advantage.

"Skipper," she said sternly. "How do we behave with the vet?"

We bite and scratch them! he answered rebelliously.

"No. We do *not*." Lilith countered. "We *behave*. We let them do what they have to do, or we spend the night locked up in the bathroom." In

135

Skipper's mind, this was definitely on par with summary execution and she now had his complete attention.

"So, are you going to behave?" she asked him pointedly.

His answer came only with the greatest hesitation, and only after one final poisonous glance at the doctor.

Yes.

"Good." She set him back down on the examination table.

Not that this spared Ingrit and Lilith any histrionics after the visit had been concluded. Skipper yowled loudly all the way back to the farm. It was only after they had arrived, and he was let out of his plastic prison, that he ceased his caterwauling and ran underneath the kitchen table to hide. Tor, the resident ginger tabby, sauntered in just then, hungry as ever, and equally curious about the cause of all the excitement. Skipper made his acquaintance with a savage hiss and a swat, and the older kaatze prudently backed away, making a wide circuit around the table.

"*Zo*, how do you do?" Ingrit asked. "My name is Skipper. Pleased to meet you. May I tear off your face now?"

Grammy joined them, laughing right along with them, and then she got down on her haunches to inspect their new arrival.

"*Zere* now," she said. "Poor little fellow. He's just frightened by all these new things." She extended her hand and after giving it a careful inspection, the animal calmed and extended himself so that she could stroke his head.

"Would you like some catfish?" she asked him. "I just happen to have some." Then Lilith noticed the little plate she had brought in with her.

Skipper was still quite upset, but not so much that he was about to pass up a treat. He graciously allowed her to put the dish before him, and then gorged himself. As he ate, the old woman stroked his back, and made meaningless, but comforting noises.

His meal only took him a few seconds. In fact, he had outpaced the emergency vac-units used aboard ship to clear compartments of smoke, and the instant that he was done, he came all the way out from under his hideout and allowed Grammy to take him into her arms.

"*Dar naa, Sötehaart*," she said, rising. "*Verdaa betaar!*" Skipper responded to her attention with deep contented purrs, and then he gave Lilith and Ingrit an accusing look that didn't require a psiever to translate. 'You see!' it said, 'At least *she* knows how to treat me properly!'

Not five minutes into his stay, Skipper had already managed to identify the *real* power in the household, and had forged an alliance. Realizing this, Lilith had no further concerns about his welfare. He was home, and so was she.

***

Bel Hanna had chosen the *Encyclopedia Sororitas* as her hiding place mainly for practical reasons. The *Sororitas* was a gigantic database, with thousands of storage drives spread over just as many worlds. Once inside, it had been easy to remain concealed from both the Navy's seeker programs and the ones that the *Sororitas* used.

But she had also come there out of personal interest as well. She had always admired the great encyclopedia, and in her life both before she had been *Translated*, and afterwards, she had used it often.

Privately however, she had also come to suspect the veracity of some of its entries. The fact that there was such a dearth of male accomplishments had never seemed to make statistical sense; the sheer span of human history argued for far more, and yet the *Sororitas* suggested otherwise. According to its writers, greatness and innovation were wholly female qualities. Naturally, she had never shared her doubts with her sisters, but now, alone, and beyond any possible reproach, she wondered anew at this.

Accessing the search functions anonymously, Bel Hanna set her parameters for the earliest editor's notes and sent the request. Very little survived after a millennia of changes, but what did come back piqued her interest. The first result was a note from the Senior Editor to her staff, written only a few decades after the Sisterhood had been established, and the First Widow's War had ended.

"We must be aware of our role in this new society," it said, *"and of the importance of our project. If Womankind is to go forwards, it must be from strength, and it is our duty to support that. We must give future women a firm base to refer to which agrees with the tenets of Motherthought. Therefore, weigh all of your entries with this in mind."*

Clearly, the Senior Editor had been asking her underlings to slant the material, Bel Hanna realized.

There was more, in another file. It was labeled innocuously enough, *"Misc Parts"* and had obviously been created as a place to park articles while they were being worked on. When she opened it, she found another note from one of the Junior Editors. It wasn't addressed to her superior however, but to someone exactly like herself.

"They want us to change everything," the writer stated. *"They want to wipe away some of the greatest things that our species has ever accomplished. For what? To prop up their silly ideas! I need this job too badly to challenge them, but I won't let this slip by. I've kept the original material in sub files. Hopefully, you, whoever you are, will find this and learn what really happened."*

Just as the writer had promised, there were other files. Each one was labeled according to the area that they concerned. Seeing the file on Early Aviation, Bel Hanna opened it.

She found glaring contradictions immediately. The notes revealed that Amelia Earhart wasn't the first person to fly solo across the Atlantic. A *man* named Charles Lindbergh had accomplished this daring feat. Even the famous Wright Sisters, who had supposedly achieved the first powered flight, hadn't done so. They were actually a pair of brothers. She was stunned.

Paging over to the file on art, she encountered even more surprises. The artist who had painted the "Mona Lisa', one of her personal favorites, wasn't Leonora da'Vinci after all, but *Leonardo. His* work had been considered to be some of the greatest art ever produced--and not the obscure material that it was now. Seeing his other paintings, and his inventions, presented without any censorship, both amazed and appalled her.

Her anger only increased as she examined the accomplishments of the great inventors. The data proved conclusively that Thomas Edison's mistress, who had traditionally been credited with all of his inventions, had never *even* existed! And Sir Isaac Newton and Albert Einstein had had their legacies stolen from them with a simple change of name. Every schoolgirl now believed that Lady Isaaca and Alberta Einstein were two of the most gifted scientists Old Gaia had ever produced.

They had no idea that they were being lied to.

According to other entries, much of this alteration had been accomplished with the help of the famous ReVision Studios and their counterparts. History had been distorted on a truly staggering scale. She intended to do something about this.

CHAPTER 5

Bocadillia Alvaraada, Downtown Business District, Nuvo Bolivar, Magdala Provensa, Esteral Terrana Rapabla, 1048.09|11|03:75:01

Migehl Alvaraada eyed Reesy skeptically. The owner of the sandwich shop was a relative of Gabi's, and the Loyalista inmate had promised her that he would give her a job when she returned to the real world. But now, and despite all the promises, her situation didn't seem quite as certain as it had back in *Lorenya Gaarza*.

"You say that you know my niece?" Alvaraada asked.

"I do," she answered. "Gabi and I did some time together. She told me to come here when I got out. She said you'd treat me fairly. Please--I really need a job. It's part of my parole, and I'll work hard."

"I don't know," he replied, stroking his chin. "This is a tiny shop and we don't have a position open right now." As he said this, he placed his hand up on the counter. To anyone else, it seemed a casual, unconscious gesture, but when Reesy saw the "A14" tattoo on it, she carefully mimicked him.

His eyes widened slightly when he took in the marking and his demeanor changed. "Maybe we can use you part-time," he said, "when Roza's out sick, and in the evenings. You willing to wash dishes too?"

"Anything's fine with me," she told him. "I just need work. Something that will keep my parole officer happy."

"Come back tomorrow, at one," Alvaraada instructed. "We'll see what we have going on then." A customer entered as he said this, and he turned from her to serve them. The interview was over, but Reesy knew that she'd gotten the job. Where things would lead after that, was anyone's guess.

For the first week, she did exactly what Alvaraada had said she would. She washed dishes, cleaned the kitchen, and went out on the occasional delivery.

The next week proved to be much different however. Instead of being assigned menial chores, Alvaraada sent her out to an address in the suburbs, telling her only that she was going to the home of a friend, and that she would be helping them for the day. A key would be waiting for her, hidden in a flower pot.

She took the *Publa*, and when the bus delivered her to her destination, walked up to a modest home. The key was exactly where Alvaraada had said it would be, and she let herself in.

A man spoke as she entered. "Don't turn around," he said. "Sit down on the couch and open the notebook."

Reesy complied, and as she opened the book, she saw that it was filled with images, some of them taken with a camera, and others that had been hand-drawn, or ripped out of books. Every picture, no matter its source, was of a military vehicle used by the Sisterhood, or by the traitors who cooperated with them in the Garda.

"We checked up on you," the man advised her. "Now we'll find out if you're any good to us. Take a few minutes and memorize what you see in the book." She heard him leave the room.

After a few minutes, he returned. This time, he allowed her to look in his direction, but his face was covered by a mask. He took the notebook from her and opened up one of the pages at random, holding it up for her to see. "What is this?" he asked, pointing at the picture.

But Reesy had an excellent memory, and the added benefit of having seen that kind of hovertruck before, back at the School. "It's a Sisterhood hovertruck," she answered. "The kind they use to transport troops, or to haul things."

"Does it have any weapons?"

"No, not most times, "she answered. "If it does, the weapons are mounted up over the cab. Also, the crewwoman is exposed." By now, she had a fair idea of what the man wanted with her.

The masked figure turned to another picture. "What about this one?"

He was indicating an armored personnel vehicle, also used by the invaders, and she told him as much.

"How many troops can it hold?"

She had to think about this for a moment and then she remembered. "Twenty. It doesn't have any weapons either, just those square holes on the side to let the soldiers shoot out of it."

The man bobbed his head in satisfaction, and tried several other images. Again and again, Reesy was able to identify what they were, with only a few minor errors.

Finally, her anonymous host closed the book. "You'll do," he informed her flatly. "We'll be in touch."

The Loyalista kept his word. Back at the sandwich shop, Alvaraada had a message for her. "Go to this address tomorrow morning," he said, handing her a small piece of plastipaper. "Be there at nine o'clock. Do what they tell you."

When she arrived at the address the next day, the man wasn't there to meet her. Instead, a woman was waiting in his place. Without preamble, she handed Reesy a small travel bag. It held a pair of binoculars, and a radio. Next, she gave her a key, and another piece of plastipaper. Reesy recognized the location written on it immediately; it was in sight of the west gate of Claire d'Layne.

"Go to this building," the woman instructed. "It's vacant right now, and this key will let you in. When you get inside, find yourself a spot where you can watch things at the gate. When anyone comes out, use your radio and tell us how many, what kind of vehicles they are in, and which way they're going. We'll need you to stay there until 4:30.'

"Make sure not to let anyone see you. If the Police come, press the red button. It will destroy the radio. And if you are caught, tell them nothing. Do you understand all of this?"

Yes", Reesy said.

She left, her pulse pounding. *This is it*, she thought. *I'm finally part of the revolution!*

***

The vacant house commanded a perfect, unobstructed view of the west gate. It was dark inside, and Reesy hoped that the shadows would help to conceal her from the Sisterhood Marines that were stationed at the guard post.

Some of them were working at ground level, inspecting vehicles as they arrived, but a pair of troopers were up in a tower. Sweeping her field glasses over their perch, she saw that one of them was doing the very same thing with her own pair of binoculars.

As the Marine turned in Reesy's direction, the young woman was absolutely certain that she had been spotted, and her heart leapt in fear. But then the soldier panned away to look at something else.

Her gambit with the shadows seemed like it had paid off. She crossed herself and said a special prayer of thanks up to Saint Jozua.

During her life at the School, she hadn't known anything about religion at all. As part of his experimental work, Dr. Martana had taken great pains to create a purely secular community. Since coming to the capitol however, Reesy had discovered the comfort that faith offered, and had become quite devout, especially since many of the Republican Orthodox priests sympathized with her revolutionary cause.

She had found Saint Jozua's name in the Church's *"Official Book of Saints"*. Originally, she had hoped to find someone who watched over revolutionaries, but only Saint Jozua had even come close.

One of the 12 spies sent by Moses to Canaan, 'Joshua', as he had been known on Old Gaia, had been canonized in the 22nd century and was considered to be the patron saint of spies. Reesy fervently hoped that his blessings would extend to her. Every little bit of luck counted, even if it wasn't precisely the kind of luck that she had been looking for.

The hours passed, and people came and went with nothing for her to report. Since her 'interview' had only centered on military vehicles, she was certain that the Loyalistas didn't care about civilian contractors making deliveries, or routine visitors. It was only when a pair of hovertrucks left the facility, accompanied by a heavier version with a turret-mounted gun, that she took up her radio and made a call.

"Two hovertrucks and a tank", she whispered. The book she had been shown had made it clear that the Loyalistas labeled anything that sported a weapon as a 'tank', with specific designations assigned for their particular level of armoring and weapons. Recalling this important distinction, she carefully added, "It's a light tank. Headed west."

No congratulations, or even a confirmation came back. Instead, dead silence met her ears. Although this disappointed her, she had expected as much. Thanks to the shop owner's briefing, she knew that the Loyalista forces kept their radio traffic to a minimum in order to avoid detection. Still, someone answering on the other end would have been reassuring and, she had to admit, a little more satisfying.

The only acknowledgement that she did receive came from the worst possible source. Panning over the tower once more, she saw that the Marine with the field glasses was looking in her direction again. This time, she didn't look away. In addition, a police car, and another vehicle that had to be its military equivalent, were headed towards her from two different directions. She had been discovered.

Panicking, she frantically pushed the red button on her radio. For a second, nothing seemed to happen, and then the thing became too hot to hold, and she hastily dropped it. As it hit the floor, an oily white tendril of smoke issued from inside it, and then the device started to melt down into an unrecognizable puddle of plastic slag.

That was enough for her. Grabbing up everything else, she ran from the room and went out the rear of the house into the tiny back yard. It was enclosed by a fence that was just short enough for her to scale, and she vaulted over it, landing in the yard next door. An old woman, who was hanging her laundry out on a line, gasped in alarm at her sudden appearance.

"Please *señyorra*," Reesy pleaded, "don't tell them I came this way!" Then she identified the clothing hanging on the line. In addition to the usual items, there was also a set a fatigues pinned up to dry. ETR Garda-issue fatigues.

Reesy's eyes went wide, and she was absolutely certain that she was about to be betrayed. Seeing where she was looking, the woman gave her a half smile, and then waved her towards the door of an open cellar. The smell of detergent and clean clothes wafted up from the dark space.

"My daughter," the woman explained, her mouth going tight with anger. "She lost an arm and a leg fighting the Sisterhood whores. Now go hide yourself! I'll send the *ratas* scurrying off in another direction."

Having no other choice but to place her faith in her, Reesy scrambled into the cellar and hid herself in the darkest corner that she could find. Daylight vanished a moment later when the cellar door slammed shut. With visions of *Lorenya Gaarza*, or someplace even worse, rising up to torment her, she strained her ears and listened. The police and the Marines had arrived, and she could hear the old woman as she spoke to them.

"She's a crazy person!" the woman cried. "Quickly! She went next door!" The sound of running feet followed this, and then silence. After a few minutes, the cellar door opened again, and the woman was beckoning to her.

"You'd better leave before they come back," she warned. Thanking Saint Jozua, and offering up a little apology to him for ever doubting his efficacy, Reesy took her advice, and ran.

Claire d'Layne Naval Base, Nuvo Bolivar, Magdala Provensa, Esteral Terrana Rapabla 1048.09|19|00:41:63

"Intel says they have a solid lead on a safe house the General might be staying in," Major ebed Karri announced.

A collective groan went up. "Vat *koopkek*", Margasdaater complained, *sotto voce*. She emphasized her displeasure by reaching down and grabbing at her crotch. Kaly heartily shared Margasdaater's sentiment, even if she didn't feel like being quite as graphic about it. Instead, she just indicated her agreement with a small nod.

Their good luck had finally deserted them. Since their first few Ops, they had been out on back-to-back missions to find the General, and each time they had come up empty-handed. The man was proving to be a phantom, and Intel's credibility was slipping badly.

Given how things had been going, the chances were excellent that this Op would prove to be exactly what the Zommerlaandar had just suggested; nothing more than another exercise spent playing with themselves, and just about as productive.

"I know, I know," Ebed Karri commiserated. "But we still have to follow up on all our leads." In Standard, this meant that they were stuck with the mission, whether they liked it or not.

Once the details had been discussed, and everyone was ready, they made their way out to the hoverpad. A platoon sized *"Thrima"* assault shuttle, which was a cut down version of the larger *"Hildr"* models, was

143

waiting for them. Its engines were already throttled up to just a hair under take off.

The instant that they had climbed aboard, the shuttle lifted into the air and flew out over the perimeter of Claire d'Layne. A second *Thrima* followed right behind them. Its job was to provide fire support and an additional set of eyes over the Op area. And although they were too high to see, a group of Valkyrie aerospace fighters were also overhead, ready to bring their ordnance to bear at a moment's notice.

It didn't take much imagination on Kaly's part to visualize the mood of the aerospace pilots. They had been on standby for every one of the Team's missions, and were probably just as frustrated as they were. But like her team, they were stuck with the mission.

Ten minutes later, when the *Thrimas* reached their final waypoint, they lost altitude until they were nearly touching the rooftops. The final signal came to get ready, and Margasdaater caught her eye, grabbing at her crotch again.

Kaly smiled deprecatingly, hoping that her companion was wrong. Then she positioned herself in the egress door. There were no hostiles on the roof of their target building, and the bioplasmic mode on her riflescope revealed that the interior appeared to be completely unoccupied.

No visual, she thought to Ben Di.

Their shuttle settled into a hover and the rest of her team, accompanied by the *Liverna*, filed past her and roped themselves down.

Once they were on the ground, the *Liverna* went right to work, and opened the door. When it came open, the 'bot launched a trio of GSG-20 self-guided grenades, set for stun. They flew into the building and began to hunt for targets.

Tracking them in her scope, Kaly was sorely tempted to grab at her own privates. The grenades were wandering from room to room, and finding nothing to attack.

It was a dry hole. The General, if he had ever even been there in the first place, was long gone.

Presently, the Major gave the order to secure and clear the building. The *Liverna* immediately began a search for booby-traps and when it found nothing, the teams went in.

As Kaly's shuttle landed in the street, Ben Di announced that they had found something after all. It wasn't a secret compartment filled with hidden terrorists though, or even a weapons cache. Instead, the entire back room of the residence was filled with boxes of propaganda pamphlets and cheap copies of the Guzamma biography.

With the site now secure, the all-clear was sent out, and regular Republican Army troops who had been positioned nearby, arrived on the scene. At an order from their commander, the soldiers dismounted from their trucks and began to haul all of the boxes outside.

Rather than loading them into the vehicles as Kaly assumed they would, they dumped everything unceremoniously into the middle of the street in a huge, untidy pile. Then the Republican officer walked up, unholstered his energy pistol, and fired into it. Instantly, the blast ignited the books and the whole thing became a roiling mass of flame.

A lover of books herself, Kaly was sickened by the sight. So much so, that it took her a moment to realize that Margasdaater was growling with rage. The next thing that she knew, the Zommerlaandar was walking towards the fire, and the officer. Her huge fists were balled up and her normally affable features were contorted with anger. Kaly had never seen her so upset.

The officer sensed her coming, and his head jerked up. As frightening as Margasdaater's temper was, Kaly knew that if she didn't intervene--and quickly--the woman was going to do something that she would later regret. She reached out and laid a restraining hand on her friend's forearm. But it was like trying to lay hold of a mountain that had decided to get up and walk--and just as useless.

"Astrid? Wait! What is it? What's wrong?"

"Zis iz boolkekk!!" Margasdaater snarled, shrugging her off. "I didn't come all zis fekking vay to *burn* fekking books! Zat's *not* vat ve're here vor and zat's *NOT* vat ve stand vor!"

Instantly, Kaly understood. Zommerlaand had originally been settled by a coalition of northern European peoples, and a radical right wing faction had taken over from within. Their aim had been to use genetic engineering to create a 'master race'. Destroying texts that they had considered 'subversive' in public bonfires had been only one of their sinister activities.

Although the MARS Plague had cut these dark dreams short, the racist legacy of those times still haunted the Zommerlaandar women. Burning books, no matter their content, went against everything that Margasdaater and her people now believed in, or held dear.

"Do you have some kind of problem, Trooper?" the officer asked, his hand moving to his holster again.

More conscious than ever of Margasdaater's greater size, Kaly boldly stepped in front of her. Her head barely reached the woman's chest, but she stubbornly stood her ground. "Don't, Astrid. Please. Come on, let's get out of here."

Vasquaaz and T'Jinna came up to help.

145

"*Ermanyaa*," Vasquaaz said. "Don't do this. This isn't the way. This *pendeya maricaan* isn't worth it."

Although Kaly hadn't warmed to the *Specia* woman herself, she and Margasdaater had managed to become friends, and her words finally seemed to penetrate the Zommerlaandar's fury. Margasdaater halted.

Ben Di interposed herself and addressed the officer. "She's just tired, Lieutenant. We all are." She looked at the team, "Come on. Let's go."

The officer nodded warily but kept his hand near his weapon as they boarded their shuttle and left.

When they had returned to their barracks, debriefed and cared for their weapons, the team nursed their disappointment with glasses of Aqqa. Margasdaater had finally managed to calm down by this point, and she and Vasquaaz engaged in a ribald contest inventing colorful curses for the male officer. Most of them involved hideous accidents to his genitals, and when everyone got tired of adding in their own colorful suggestions, they all settled in to watch an episode of *"Laara Lampa"*. Somewhere in the middle of the show, Kaly fell fast asleep. None of her teammates even noticed. Most of them had already done the same thing.

Major ebed Karri didn't disturb them. There were more missions holding, and she wanted them to be fully rested. Instead, she composed a message to her superior officer, requesting that a strongly worded protest be sent up the ETR's chain of command.

Having heard all about the Op and the confrontation over the books, her commander agreed without hesitation, and sent one off immediately. In her message, she reminded their allies of the importance of cultural sensitivity and the need to factor this into their actions.

Or else.

Only a few minutes elapsed before the ETR response came back, and a copy of it was forwarded on to Ebed Karri. From now on, there would be no more book burnings--at least not in the presence of any Zommerlaandar.

Downtown Business District, Nuvo Bolivar, Magdala Provensa, Esteral
Terrana Rapabla, 1048.09|25|05:11:19

Reesy's first significant contribution to the Loyalista cause occurred quite by accident, and while she was doing legitimate work for the sandwich shop. Alvaraada had sent her downtown with a delivery, along with a stern warning to avoid the temptation to leave behind any subversive literature, or graffiti.

The delivery itself was to an office building near the Sisterhood Embassy, and after she had turned the packages over to the security guard in the lobby, she was on her way back out to retrieve her bicycle. Then a face caught her eye.

The woman was one of the customers in a restaurant across the street, and Reesy very nearly missed her. It was lunchtime, and the entire area was saturated with hungry people hurrying to grab their food. When she considered it later, it was the fact that this particular woman didn't seem to be in a hurry that had alerted her. That, and the fact that her face was very familiar.

Even though she was dressed in civilian clothing, there was no mistaking Captain Hari n'Kyla. Not after all the time they had spent together at the School. Certain that she would be recognized, Reesy crouched down behind her bike, pretending to fumble with the lock on its security chain, and did her best not to look straight at her.

If she had had someone to call right then, she would have, but the Loyalistas had given her nothing to work with. Aside from the owner of the sandwich shop, she had no way to contact anyone. The only solution was to leave, and return to the shop as quickly as possible. She wasn't happy with the idea of breaking away, but she knew that she had to, or ruin everything. Trying to appear as relaxed as possible, she got on her bicycle and peddled off.

The trip back seemed to take a thousand years, and when she reached her destination, her frustration was compounded by the fact that it was still lunchtime, and Alvaraada was too busy to speak with her. Finally however, she managed to draw him aside, and told him what she had seen.

"A Sisterhood officer you say?" he asked her.

"Yes," Reesy answered emphatically, "I know her. She's one of their spies. A Captain in the RSE. I also think she eats her lunch at the café as a regular. The waitress seemed to know her."

This last part was pure speculation; she hadn't actually seen any interaction between N'Kyla and the server, but she had added this detail hoping that it would help win him over.

Alvaraada stroked his moustache contemplatively. "You did well," he said at last. "This may be useful. I'll check and see if anyone is interested. For now, I want you to stay away from that café. No more deliveries downtown for you, *chica*."

"But..."Reesy started to protest. She had secretly hoped to be a part of whatever was going to happen to the woman.

"No arguments, *chica*," Alvaraada warned. "If she recognizes you, we've lost her. You understand me? You let your brothers and sisters handle this. You did your part."

Reesy acknowledged this with a dejected nod and went into the kitchen to help out the dish washer.

They *had* to get her, she told herself. They had to. N'Kyla needed to pay for everything that she had done at the School.

***

It was a beautiful day in Nuvo Bolivar. The sun was shining down on the capitol, but the temperature was just right. Neither too hot, nor too cold.

It was in fact, the perfect day for lunch at her favorite spot, N'Kyla thought. She'd been careful of course, making certain to leave the Embassy by way of one of its hidden exits, and she'd brought her weapon with her, just in case. Despite Sarah's endless warnings, she was sure that her civilian clothing, the nearly flawless accent she had when she spoke Espangla, along with the sheer mass of the lunchtime crowds, would work together to keep her safe.

Lunch at the café was precious enough for the risk involved. Eating *al fresco*, and being able to enjoy a few minutes as nothing more than a simple woman, with no cares or worries, paid her back for all the long hours that she spent in the COMINT center.

Besides which, she wasn't the only one to sneak away for a break, she reminded herself. Plenty of the women at the Embassy did it, and the downtown area had always been free of the troubles that visited other parts of the city. As they all saw it, taking a moment to enjoy life, was another small way of sticking it back to the Loyalistas. Life had to go on whether their enemies wanted it to or not.

"Are you ready to order, ma'am?" a voice asked. The waitress had arrived.

"Yes, thank you," she replied, and then she made her request. Knowing her by now, the waitress had come to her table with a cool glass of tea, and she sipped at it while she watched the people going by on the sidewalk.

She was still waiting for her meal when she spotted the plain 'lectri van coming down the street. It wasn't anything about its appearance that alerted her. There were plenty of similar vehicles making deliveries to the offices all around her. Rather, it was something else, a sense that she got from the occupants, a feeling that something was 'wrong' about the van.

An instant later, the vehicle accelerated, cut across the street and came to a halt right in front of her. Automatically, she began to draw her weapon from its shoulder holster, but she already knew that it was too late. The side door was sliding open, and there was a masked man inside with an automatic weapon. It was pointed straight at her.

Oh goddess, N'Kyla thought. *I fekked up.*

***

The assassination of Captain Hari n'Kyla was a major news story, and within minutes of the killing, Sanda Ernan's press secretary was fielding calls from half a dozen news agencies, and scheduling a press conference.

That a Sisterhood officer had been killed in the line of duty wasn't what had created all the hysteria, however. That had happened before.

Instead, the excitement was generated because the newshounds had learned that N'Kyla had been a key player in the RSE's intelligence operations in Nuvo Bolivar. This, and the fact that she had been gunned down in broad daylight in the very heart of the downtown district; a place which until then, had seemed safe from terrorism. And even worse, despite hundreds of terrified witnesses, the gunmen had vanished without a trace.

When Maya had heard the announcement, she had been absolutely certain that Sarah would be beside herself with rage and grief. She was still having trouble believing it herself. Although they had never been terribly close, N'Kyla had been a familiar face. She had been part of the daily routine at the COMINT center. Now she was gone.

But Sarah managed to surprise Maya, and everyone else. Instead of screaming out orders and demanding bloody revenge, she was oddly calm about the tragedy. Without betraying any hint of anger, she called the entire staff into a meeting.

"By now, all of you know what has happened, so I will not bother to repeat the news," she told them. "I will tell you this however; Captain n'Kyla knew the risks. She chose to ignore her safety and paid the price that many other agents have for such carelessness. Take her example to heart."

"Now, we have a job to do. We need to find her killers and see them brought to justice. I want every possible lead followed. Dismissed."

Maya was stunned by her brevity, and her coldness. She only hoped that if something like this ever happened to her, that Sarah would deliver a warmer eulogy. It was nice to entertain the fantasy that she actually mattered.

Amandra sa'Tela was far less detached. Although her voice was as steady as always, her eyes were red from weeping. She and N'Kyla had been good friends and she didn't possess the 'professional' distance that Sarah did. She at least, was halfway human, Maya reflected.

"We already have some leads," Sa'Tela announced raggedly. "The van has been found. It was stolen. Our teams still managed to lift some trace evidence from the interior however. They are working on it, and we should be able to get DNA reconstructions in several hours."

By analyzing the DNA in organic objects such as small hairs, pieces of dried skin, and even sweat, the Sisterhood's computers could rebuild a virtual image of the person they had come from. It was inexact, but worth pursuing nonetheless.

With luck, the images would be coherent enough to match with the pictures on file in the ESN database and from there, provide names. Thanks to some careful backdoor hacking, and a few well-placed moles, the ESN didn't know that the RSE had access to this, and it would stay that way. The last thing they needed right then was any attempt to obstruct what was quickly becoming a complicated investigation.

One thing that could derail it entirely would be if the occupants of the van had been careful, and there was a good chance that they had been. Thanks to the Marionites and the School, the ETR was aware of many aspects of Sisterhood technology, and they had used this knowledge to foil it in the past in surprisingly simple, yet elegant ways. The wire meshes worn by Ernan and her key staffers had been only one example of their ingenuity. If the same inventiveness extended to the forensic evidence left in the 'lectri, Maya was well aware of the possibility that the only images they would manage to retrieve would be of the original owners, and not the terrorists. Still, it was a lead, and like any lead, a gamble with both winners, and losers.

Meanwhile, Sarah was moving on. "What else do we have?" she asked.

"Surveillance footage from the area, and witness statements," Sa'Tela said. "There's a lot to sift through."

"Sift it," Sarah ordered. "If you do not find anything, go backwards until you *do*. Whoever was involved in this had to have been watching N'Kyla for some time. Also, and I'm certain that you have already thought of this Amandra, get in touch with the Navy and get what they have from their assets upstairs. They may be able to provide us with material that they gathered from their overwatch."

"Yes, ma'am."

Sarah began to add something else, but paused. From her pensive expression, Maya assumed that she was receiving something on her psiever, and then realized that the woman was actually looking towards the techs monitoring the daily broadcasts by the Loyalista spotters. The shooting hadn't changed their level of activity at all.

Confirming this, Sarah turned from the group and scrutinized the map of the city. Then she walked over to one of the techs. Maya and Sa'Tela trailed behind her.

"That speaker," she said, pointing towards the map, "the one who just transmitted from the northwestern district. I want you to task one of our Valkyries to handle them. Terminate that target with an area attack. Immediately."

Maya stifled a gasp. Such an attack meant that the fighter would carpet bomb the location, and not only kill the terrorist, but anyone else in the vicinity. Up to then, the goal had been to capture, not to kill, and certainly not in such a wholesale manner.

The tech was less discrete. "Ma'am, they're broadcasting from the middle of a populated area! If we authorize an area strike, we could take out non-combatants right along with them."

Sarah considered this. "Yes," she agreed. "As the great philosopher Aristotlea once suggested, *'all things in moderation.'* You've made your point, corporal. Task the fighter to deliver a targeted munition instead."

Even with this alteration, there was still a good chance that bystanders would be killed or injured by the attack, and the tech began to raise another objection, but Sarah's expression made it clear that she would brook no further argument from her. Prudently, the woman closed her mouth and carried out her orders.

"It is high time that these *people* learned an important lesson," Sarah said to her companions. "If they fight us, they pay the price."

Maya realized then that Sarah had been every bit as angry as she had suspected. And now, someone, and most likely several 'someones,' were about to feel the full brunt of her displeasure.

***

Skimming the exosphere at just over 10,000 kilometers, Erin taur Minna had nothing to do in her cockpit but keep an eye on her HUD displays, listen for important communications, and mentally recite the *Greenestglen Mantras* to herself. Except for infrequent calls by the RSE Special Response Units and the Marines for air support, patrol duty over Nuvo Bolivar was largely a process of waiting, and counting the clouds below her. She didn't care for this one nano; like any dedicated fighter pilot, she only felt alive when there was a real mission to fly, and traveling in patrol patterns--however necessary--was as far away from that as the Andromeda Galaxy.

"I am the forest," she chanted quietly. *"And the forest is me. I was born of it, and I am never away from it, no matter where I am, for I am the forest and the forest is me."* The Mantras, especially for someone like her,

who was so far from home, always calmed and reassured her. They also ate up the time quite nicely.

Her HUD interrupted, flashing a message. Operations was calling. Anticipating an assistance request from some raid Team, she answered it immediately. "Little Bird, go."

"Little Bird, you have a strike, coordinates and information being relayed to you now," the operator said. The Valkyries AI immediately displayed the location. It was in the heart of one of the suburbs.

It has to be air support for a raid, she thought.

When she saw the target though, it confused her. It was a single 'lectri speeding away from the location, and no team was pursuing it. The HUD dutifully informed her that it was to be a precision strike, and she frowned. Although the ordnance that her aerospace fighter carried was good, it wasn't perfect. Anyone near the strike zone stood a fair-to-good chance of becoming casualties. She was also well aware of the Navy's policy in the ETR to avoid civilian casualties wherever possible. The whole thing seemed to be a bit careless.

"Little Bird, Ops," she said, puzzled. "Can you confirm authorization for the strike?"

"All details confirmed, authorization code Anna-Betsi-Xena-Carla," Operations answered. This was the code used by the RSE, and it overrode anything else. "You are go for attack, weapons hot. Ordnance as specified."

"Acknowledged", she replied, thinking a curse towards the lunatics in the RSE. The Loyalistas would have a field day with this, especially if any innocents got hurt.

But orders were orders and Erin pitched her aerospace fighter hard over, and dove. "Beginning attack run."

Below her, and deep inside the COMINT center, Maya stole a glance at the city map. An icon, representing the air asset had appeared on it. A second later, a red circle surrounded the target, indicating that the fighter had a lock on it.

Then the target disappeared from the map. On another screen, a live 'vid showed a column of black smoke rising from a busy roadway.

A Troop Leader came up to Sarah and saluted. "The aerospace strike was prosecuted as you ordered, ma'am."

Sarah watched the 'vid for a moment more, and then turned away as if the woman, and the incident, simply didn't exist any longer. The Troop Leader however, remained where she was.

"Ma'am", she said, "We also have two calls holding for you; from the Ambassador and the Vice Admiral."

Sarah regarded her again. "Tell them I'll call them back."

The shess was already hitting the fan over the airstrike, Maya reflected. Not that any of it would spatter on Sarah. Things never worked out *that* perfectly.

***

Reesy actually managed to remain anonymous for the remainder of the afternoon. By evening however, she had been identified. Sa'Tela interrupted Sarah with the news.

"We have one of them!" the Kalian declared. "We know who she is."

"She?"

"Her name is Reesy Hernan. The AI's matched her image from the surveillance footage in the area. She was a resident of the School, and after she was relocated here, she served time in a woman's prison for distributing Loyalista propaganda."

"Which explains how N'Kyla was identified," Sarah observed. With the exception of Maya and a few others on her staff, N'Kyla had been the only one who had resembled the local genotypes closely enough not to require any cosmetics to 'pass'. In street clothes, she would have been unremarkable. Except to someone who knew her.

"I take it that we are in the process of apprehending this woman?"

"Yes, ma'am," Sa'Tela answered. "I sent a team out to get her. They should be there in the next few minutes."

***

A hand shook Reesy awake. It was her roommate, she realized, and when she opened her eyes, she saw another woman standing alongside her friend.

"Get up", the stranger ordered. "You're leaving the capitol." Reesy recognized her voice immediately. The last time that they had met, her visitor had worn a mask, and had given her the assignment to watch the Sisterhood base.

"What's going on?" Reesy asked.

"It's that officer you spotted," the woman explained. "We took care of her. Now it's all over the Republic. They're looking for anyone that might be involved. We can't risk you staying here." She was already in the process of grabbing up Reesy's meager possessions and stuffing them into a non-descript travel bag.

153

Reesy felt a thrill of exultation pass through her as she rushed over to her dresser to help with the packing. *They got her!* she thought. *And I helped! I GOT her!!*

As she grabbed up an armload of clothes, the woman held the bag open for her and let her dump them in. "We'll be taking you to a safe house outside the capitol," she said. "You'll stay there until we can decide what to do with you."

Reesy didn't argue, or ask for any clarifications. Instead, she took the bag from the woman's hands and went into the common bathroom, clearing out the medicine cabinet with one swipe of her hand. Then she followed her outside to a 'lectri.

Barely five minutes after she had departed, the front door of her former apartment exploded. GSG-20's, set to stun, flew in next. The intelligent munitions quickly located the residents, and detonated. Then Team 201 and their *Specia* allies, stormed in.

It was all over in seconds. By the time Kaly had come down from her observation post, and joined them, everyone inside the residence had been trussed up and were lying on the floor. She didn't have to refer to the image on her HUD to realize that their target wasn't among them. None of the prisoners resembled Reesy Hernan, even slightly.

"It looks like you got away, Kaly," T'Jinna signed wryly.

"That Kaly's a tricky one, that's for sure." *Cabo* Vasquaaz added.

The resemblance between Kaly and Reesy Hernan had been a running joke ever since the Op had first been assigned. If not for an accident of birth under different stars, she and Hernan could have been twins. They even braided their hair the same way.

And naturally, none of Kaly's team members, or the *Specia* soldiers, had been about to let such a stellar opportunity for teasing slip by.

"Yah," Kaly agreed good-naturedly. "Maybe you'll get me next time."

CHAPTER 6

Claire d'Layne Naval Base, Nuvo Bolivar, Magdala Provensa, Esteral
Terrana Rapabla, 1048.10|02|02:08:61

Kaly felt the sun on her skin. Not hot enough to burn, but just enough
to revel in it in its warmth. In a playful counterpoint, a deliciously cool
breeze blew in occasionally, bringing with it the clean scent of the ocean, as
sweet as kisses. Overhead, the leaves of a tropical tree rustled with languid
slowness, as if they too were under the spell of the suns magic.

She didn't want to leave her place on the sand, or the woman lying next
to her. It was the perfect moment; the kind of contentment that could only
exist in some heaven, far away from the pain and torment of the physical
universe that she knew.

Kaly looked up at her companion. She was greeted with a smile that
was as beautiful as her surroundings, and she returned the love that she saw
in the woman's green eyes with a smile of her own.

The woman leaned over and they kissed. It was a long delicious thing
that elicited a sigh of pure happiness from Kaly when their lips finally
parted.

Then the woman rose, and offered her her hand. Kaly took it and they
walked along the pure white sands together, saying nothing and letting the
warm waves lap against their bare feet.

After a time, the beautiful red head began to sing. Her melody had no
words to it though. Rather, it was a collection of pure tones that made
Kaly's heart ache. Her song was just as perfect as the moment itself.

"Is that for me?" she finally asked her.

Her lovely partner shook her head. "No. It's meant for someone else,
Kaly. But it's very important. You have to help the one who will sing it and
also her friends."

Kaly started to ask her what she meant, but the dream began to fade,
and then it was replaced by wakefulness. The beach and the mysterious
woman were gone. Only the memory of the song remained.

She opened her eyes with a wistful expression. It had been a beautiful
vision, of a past that she should have had, and had never actually
experienced, and all the more bittersweet for it. Reluctant to fully wake, she
briefly considered returning to sleep, but then she made the mistake of
accessing her psiever. It was 02.73, with barely nine metric minutes to go
before her alarm was scheduled to go off. There was no point in even
trying.

Forcing herself to sit up, she reflected on her experience. She hadn't
had a vision of her fantasy lover in many weeks, or the beach that they

always seemed to visit, and she wondered why it had suddenly revisited her.

She finally decided that it had to be the product of all the stress that she'd been under. There was no other rational explanation. The song however, had been an entirely new feature, and it puzzled her. And for some reason that she couldn't quite articulate, it also bothered her profoundly. Just as the phantom woman had indicated, she knew that it was important in some way, although exactly why was beyond her grasp. It just *was*.

She nearly made an appointment to see a Psych doctor about it, and even went as far as accessing her Com--but hesitated. Back aboard the *Athena*, she'd discussed her dreams with Dr. bel Shaaron, and had always valued her wise council.

This time though, the vision didn't feel like it was intended to be shared with anyone else. Instead, it seemed as if it had been meant for her, and her alone, and that violating this confidence courted some terrible, and unknown consequence. It was a silly notion of course, but still so strong that she decided to ignore logic, and honor what her heart was telling her.

She cut the connection, swung her feet over the edge of her rack, and stood, enduring the harsh reality of the cold metal floor on her bare feet. It was time to begin her day and put all of her dreams aside.

Barely an hour later, she received another message. This time it wasn't an imaginary vision from her subconscious. It was psivermail from Bel Anny, one of her fellow recruit-trainees back in Basic. Kaly hadn't heard from her, or any of the other hatchies, since graduation day, and she read it straightaway.

"Dear Kaly—,'

"I know it's been a long time since you've heard from me, and I hope you'll forgive me. I'm still at Rixa in Admin, and I even managed to get myself promoted a few times (heh heh...crazy huh?). I'm writing you because I wanted to apologize for not getting with you until now, and catching up.'

"I also have some bad news to tell you. It's about Enggredsdaater. Her unit was posted to Nuvo Bolivar right after the war, and she got wounded. They told me that it was from an improvised device of some kind. I hate to tell you this, but it took off both of her legs.'

"The paints gave her new ones—good ones—good enough for her to still keep serving if she'd wanted to—but she never fully recovered. From what I heard, it was the stress from the injury and everything else that she's been through. So, she mustered out, and went back home.'

"If you get the chance, drop by and see her, okay? I'm worried about her and she could use a visit from an old friend like you. And hey—maybe come and see me too when you get the chance? I've missed you. '

"All my love—and I'm sorry, Bel Anny."

Chest tight with suppressed pain, Kaly closed the message, and took a moment to collect herself. Of all the hatchies in Carli Company, Enggredsdaater had been the very last one that she would have ever expected to end up like this.

Goddess, she thought, *poor Berta.*

Jyon Vaargas National Spaceport, Nuvo Bolivar, Magdala Provensa, Esteral Terrana Rapabla, 1048.10|02|03:43:05

After spending months on other projects, Celina had finally completed enough of them to pursue her real interest. This was her work on the *Song of Humanity*, which she still refused to nickname *The Song*. To her, that title would always be reserved for her original melody.

She was still stinging from the disastrous visit by the Seevaans to her studio, and the State Department's edict against the original composition, but she had complied with their prohibition, and created alternate themes. The new pieces weren't anywhere near as good as The Song had been, but they were acceptable.

And secretly, she still had a copy of the forbidden music. Just in case the State Department, or the Seevaans, ever recovered their sanity and reversed their incomprehensible decision.

But even with all these changes and reversals, the realie that she was producing easily outshone all of her previous works, and she was eager to see it finished. Which was why she had decided to travel to the ETR.

She intended to use images of life in the Republic to show her female audience just how far Womankind had advanced as a society, and to provide a glimpse of life as it had been before the MARS Plague, and the advent of Motherthought.

The journey had also offered another plus. It was her chance to finally portray the Sisterhood's peacekeeping forces at work, and give these noble women the recognition that they deserved.

The trick, however, had been getting to the ETR. Despite the fact that the war between the Republic and the Sisterhood was well over, Nuvo Bolivar was difficult for civilians to travel to. The Sisterhood national spaceline, *Intragalactic*, didn't have any passenger flights to *Jyon Vaargas*, and neither did any of the smaller domestic carriers. Only the foreign lines,

Requiem Spaceways, run by the Xee, and *Imperial Hriss*, had offered anything, and neither had been what Celina would have considered 'ideal'.

A ticket on *Requiem* had been expensive to the point of usury, and also required a lengthy stopover in Ashkele before traveling on to the Republic's capitol. Notwithstanding this, it had still been a far better choice than the Hriss alternative.

Although much cheaper, the Hriss didn't believe in luxury of any kind and their civilian vessels were essentially no different than their troop transports. Their food was just as unmentionable.

So in the end, comfort had won over cost, and Celina had chosen *Requiem.*

Her flight arrived at *Jyon Vaargas* Interworld Spaceport late in the afternoon, and when she disembarked, she was met by a representative from the Embassy. Although she had been forced to listen to pirated copies of her own music throughout the entire trip, Celina did her best to smile at the comerci-clad woman.

"Jantildam, I am Jaana t'Saryanna, Assistant Secretary to the Ambassador," the woman said, bowing deeply. "You cannot imagine how excited we are to have you visit us out here on the frontier. Our troops are ecstatic at the prospect of a concert, and the Ambassador is delighted at having the chance to meet you!"

Part of the agreement that her agent had made with the State Department for being allowed to travel to the ETR, had been the promise to perform a free concert for the Naval and Marine forces stationed in the capitol. Not that Celina had any reservations; the women who defended her nation were worthy of the very best that she had to offer. Even so, it had been a long, and expensive trip, and she was hard put to lend any real warmth to her reply.

"I've been looking forwards to entertaining them," she said. "Of course, I'm also eager to gather some footage for my latest project. I do hope that your Embassy will be able to accommodate me while I'm here."

In fact, the State Department had already agreed to cater to her needs, but it never hurt to remind the people who were actually responsible for seeing things done, of their obligations, however politely.

"Naturally," T'Saryanna replied. "In anticipation of your arrival, we took the liberty of arranging your itinerary for you. We want to make certain that you can show the women back home everything that we are accomplishing here.'

"Now, if you'll follow me, we'll get you to your Hotel. It's the *Àuro Agwuila*, the Golden Eagle. It's not the *Euxine Plaza*, but it's the best that these people have to offer, and I'm sure you'll find it adequate, albeit a bit-- um--rustic." She gave Celina a shrug that wordlessly expressed the rest of what she had purposefully neglected to say; '--*being the primitives that they are.*'

"I don't mind rustic," Celina said. "It often lends atmosphere to the creative process." She hadn't been in the ETR an hour, and she already found the woman's patronizing attitude towards the natives both irritating and distasteful.

She had seen all the newscasts, since the first contact, through the war, and into the present, and she had gradually become a part of a growing, but silent segment of her countrywomen that didn't perceive the citizens of the ETR as inferiors. Although she strongly supported her nation's peacekeeping efforts, she hadn't let herself lose sight of the fact that the citizens of the Republic were still people. Even the males.

She kept this to herself however, and let the woman lead her past Customs to their waiting 'lectri. To get what she wanted, she couldn't give offense. Finishing the *Song of Humanity* was too important.

The drive to her hotel was the first indication that the ETR was not as 'rustic' as her guide claimed, nor as calm as the news media portrayed it. Her limousine had been sandwiched in between two plain 'lectris containing more Embassy staff, and security women, and the caravan was being escorted by a pair of local police vehicles. All of this was normal enough; she was a famous performer and a heavy security presence was part of the price that she paid for her fame.

What was *not* normal, and what caught her attention, was the traffic around them, or rather, the lack of it. Invariably, there were always groups of admirers and on-lookers to greet her along the way to her destination, no matter how secret her visit was supposed to be. Somehow, word always got out that she was coming and her fans were always there to greet her.

Here, however, the street was largely empty. Only a few 'lectris passed them, and the sidewalks were devoid of pedestrians. She found the stillness eerie, and disturbing.

Shortly after this, the caravan slowed, and abruptly changed course, leaving the broad boulevard for a side street. They were deviating from their route for some reason, Celina realized.

Looking out her window for the cause, she saw a policeman waving them on. Behind him, she spotted a pair of hovertanks, and several more military hovertrucks parked across the boulevard, blocking traffic. Beyond this, was a large group of Sisterhood Marines accompanied by what she assumed were local military personnel.

They were guarding a group of civilians. The prisoners were on their knees with their hands atop their heads, facing the wall of a sizable building. A slogan had been painted on the wall itself, and two soldiers were hastily covering it over with large plastic tarps. She was still able to read it though.

The message had been painted in letters large enough to see from the street, and in Standard. It proclaimed, *"Death to the Sisterhood Invaders!"*

Before she could make any sense of this, the limo turned away and the scene was hidden by the buildings around them.

"What was that back there?" she asked the Embassy woman. "Why were those people under arrest? And what was that slogan they painted on the wall?"

"Just some local criminals," T'Saryanna answered nonchalantly. "Since the war, there's been a sharp rise in crime in the capitol. I'm sure you've heard about that. It's nothing to worry about."

Celina nodded, pretending to accept this blatant lie, and considered what she had just witnessed.

Invaders? she wondered. *Us? We've been helping these people. We freed them from a corrupt government! We saved them from the goddess-damned Hriss! Why would they want to kill us?* It made no sense whatsoever.

Unless, she thought, *something else is going on here. Something bad.*

Their arrival at the *Àuro Agwuila* temporarily forced this dark line of thought to the back of her mind. The hotel was located in the fashionable downtown area, and not far from the Embassy itself. The Manager greeted her personally at the front entrance, and she was quickly ensconced in their best suite on the top floor.

It took her a few minutes to accept the idea that the lights didn't operate by psiever and that the bathroom fixtures used knobs and levers to coax anything out of them, but otherwise, the accommodations were quite serviceable. Even comfortable.

Although the concert at Claire d'Layne wasn't scheduled for another Standard week, Celina still wanted to inspect the venue and get in some rehearsal time beforehand. Given the lateness of her arrival, and the need to coordinate with the bases' Activity Officers, T'Saryanna agreed to come back for her in the morning. This left Celina with the unexpected luxury of having some free time for herself.

She took full advantage of it, and as soon as the staffer had departed, she and Clio got to work editing her Sisterhood realie footage. She soon became so engrossed in this that she forgot to order her dinner from room service---until her virtual partner took the initiative and requested it for her. Protests notwithstanding, Clio also made certain that they didn't resume their work until Celina had properly fed herself. She was even persuaded to go to bed at a half-way reasonable hour, and the next morning, awoke fresh and ready to face the day.

With T'Saryanna acting as her guide, she was driven out to the Sisterhood base in the Embassy hoverlimo. Once again, the 'limo was bracketed by security vehicles that escorted her through largely empty streets. The trip itself took only a few minutes, and when they arrived at the front gate, Celina's breath caught in her throat.

She had seen military installations before, having performed for the troops on numerous occasions, but Claire d'Layne was unquestionably one of the largest she had ever visited. Its security measures were also far more stringent than she was used to. Despite the Embassy escort, she was still required to personally present her biochip for identity verification, and she couldn't help but notice that none of the soldiers on guard seemed the slightest bit star struck by her presence. They were a steely-eyed bunch, and they regarded her, and everyone in her limousine, with obvious suspicion. Even the vehicle itself was thoroughly scanned by a securitybot before it was allowed to roll one centimeter beyond the massive vehicle barriers. Just the same, she put all of this behind her as they were admitted, and concentrated on the job ahead of her.

"How is our guest list looking?" she asked. To demonstrate their solidarity with the government's effort to create a sense of unity with the people of the ETR, her agent had taken the step of inviting several of the more famous local performers to take part in the show.

"I'm sorry," T'Saryanna replied regretfully. "Most of them couldn't be included. A few had other engagements, and some didn't pass our security screening. I hope you can work around this."

The amended list appeared in the limo's cabin and Celina frowned as she read it over. Almost every local artist had been deleted. Absent the pitiful handful that remained, it was going to be a solo performance.

"I suppose I'll have to," Celina said unhappily. Right away, she began to change the order of the program in her mind. With the addition of a few extra pieces, the show could still come off well, she decided. She sent a message to Clio to make the appropriate alterations.

"Good," T'Saryanna said. "I was afraid that there might be a problem with this. There's also one other thing that you need to know."

"And that is?"

"An officer from the local RSE detachment has asked to meet with you," T'Saryanna informed her. "It's a simple interview. Nothing to worry about. They do it for anyone who arrives here from the Sisterhood. Sort of a Customs thing."

Celina's brows knitted in irritation. "Fine. Just as long as she doesn't take up too much of my time. We have a lot to get in place thanks to the changes on that list."

The Embassy staffer waved her concern away. "Don't worry yourself on that score, jantildam. Lieutenant sa'Tela assured me that she will only need a few minutes of your time. It's just a formality."

"Fine," Celina agreed. "Can she meet me in my dressing room? I'm going to be very busy, and she'll need to speak with me on the move."

"Certainly," T'Saryanna returned. "I know Lieutenant sa'Tela personally. She's a very reasonable woman. She'll certainly understand."

***

Celina's dressing room had been created for her in a small office formerly occupied by one of the base's senior officers, and the Marine Engineers, with the help of the Public Relations detachment, had made certain to have a proper makeup table ready and waiting. In addition, all of her costumes had been brought there, along with the assorted odds and ends that she had come to rely on.

There were also flowers everywhere. They were local blooms, but no less beautiful for that, and reading the cards, Celina saw that most of them had come from units stationed in or around the base itself.

"Best wishes from your fans in the 101st Armor Battalion 2nd Company, 3rd Squad," one read. Another wished her *"Good luck for the show. 87th Combat Engineers, 'Die Spitting Kaatzen'"* She had even received one from the bases' commanding officer.

Bending over, she inhaled the sweet scent of a nearby bouquet and then settled into her chair to set up her makeup table the way she liked it. Partway through this task, she was interrupted by a knock at the door.

"Come in," she said. When she looked up, she saw a woman in a black uniform. The minute she realized who it was, she also decided that she didn't care for her at all. It wasn't her somber attire, or anything outward about her appearance—in fact Kalians were an ethnic group that she liked, and admired greatly. It was something else, something indefinable that put her instantly on her guard.

"Thank you for taking the time to meet with me," Sa'Tela began. "I know that you have a great deal to do before your concert, and I appreciate the opportunity to speak with you."

"What is this about?" Celina asked pointedly. She wasn't used to being questioned by the police. She wasn't a criminal and she didn't see why this meeting was even taking place.

Sa'Tela smiled, as if she had heard her thoughts, and offered an explanation for her presence. "I realize that this must seem a bit much to you, but because we are in the process of pacifying the local crime problem, my office is required to interview every new civilian arrival. Unfortunately, there are some women who come to the ETR to take advantage of the situation. You can blame the glass problem they have here for that."

Celina's mouth dropped in surprise and indignation. Did this woman actually think she had come here to deal drugs? She very nearly ordered her out, but then reminded herself that she was in Nuvo Bolivar as a guest of the government. The *Tuluraa Daal Foundation for the Arts* would not look kindly on her if she refused to cooperate with a Sisterhood official.

Again, Sa'Tela smiled. "Naturally, I know that you are not involved in anything as sorted as that, and I don't want to waste your valuable time. So, I'll get straight to the point. Since arriving, have you met with anyone other than the Embassy staff, or officials from Claire d'Layne? I'm sorry, but we have to know who you interact with; some of the people here might want to exploit you for their own purposes, and not all of them are friendly."

"I've met with a lot of people," Celina said defensively. "I don't know everyone's name."

"Of course not," Sa'Tela agreed. "I knew that the question was unreasonable when I was told to ask it. It would be impossible to remember every stagehand or maid, and I deeply apologize."

"Thank you," Celina replied. She relaxed a bit.

"But tell me," Sa'Tela inquired, "out of everyone, has anyone, in any position, approached you about anything that seemed—how do I put this-- *irregular*--in nature?"

"Irregular?"

"Yes. Anything that seemed suspicious. I realize that you have been quite busy since your arrival, but—"

"No," Celina responded curtly. "No one. It's been nothing but business."

"Good," Sa'Tela said. "That's it then. Please contact us, or the Embassy, if anyone approaches you with something that seems out of the ordinary. Until we settle things down here, we all have to remain vigilant. I'm sure that you understand."

"Of course," Celina answered. She didn't rise, but stayed in her chair, and watched the RSE woman leave.

What in all space is going on here? she wondered. The graffiti she had seen coming in from the spaceport resurfaced in her mind. It didn't jibe with Sa'Tela's tale of 'local criminals' one nanobit.

But it also wasn't any of her business, she reminded herself, and the Lieutenant had a job to do, however unlikable she seemed. She promptly dismissed her misgivings and returned her attention to her dressing table and its contents. There was a show to prepare for and she didn't need anything getting in the way of that. Not even politics.

Aljofar District, Nuvo Bolivar, Magdala Provensa, Esteral Terrana Rapabla, 1048.10|03|03:75:05

The raid on the toy factory managed to accomplish several important things. The first was that it facilitated the arrest of the factory's owner when the captured data proved his links to the Loyalistas. It also provided enough evidence for the ETR's military to look more closely at the commanding officer of the local *Magdala Provensa Garda Nacia Armería*, and his subordinates.

Eventually, this led to their courts martial and increased security measures at all of the ETR's armories. One of these was the adoption of the redundancy that the Sisterhood used. Another was stricter standards for inventory control and auditing procedures.

Exactly as Kaly had surmised however, none of this stopped the violence, or managed to disarm the rebels. While the RSE continued to develop new leads, Kaly and her team were sent out into the field again. Team 440 had returned to the Sisterhood and left them with their *Specia* counterparts. They were going on what would be their first solo mission.

The assignment was to accompany a detachment of Republican troops and Sisterhood Marines going out on a 'hearts and minds' mission. Their objective was not only to provide additional security for the operation, but gather any intel they could, and if possible, cultivate new informants in one of Nuvo Bolivar's poorer suburbs. Although the *Aljofar* was known to be a hotbed of Loyalista sympathizers, the district also included residents who hadn't chosen a faction, or were willing to play both sides of the conflict if they thought there was something in it for them.

The combined force left Claire d' Layne late in the morning in two military 'lectri trucks, and a heavily armed hovertruck. They reached their Op zone without encountering any more resistance than some sullen looks, and a few shouted insults.

After that, it became a matter of standing by and keeping their eyes open while the 'Pubbies' handed out candy to the children, and ear-buds tuned to government supported radio stations to the adults.

Kaly found herself warming to the children, who swarmed eagerly around the soldiers. She even gave out a little candy of her own.

She didn't lower her defenses though. Although the Loyalistas had never attacked when children were around, and knew that the Sisterhood Troopers would never knowingly harm them either, there was always the slim chance that something terrible could still occur.

Team 440 had also taught them something else about gatherings like this. They attracted more than just children or curious neighbors; whenever possible, the Loyalistas liked to send spies in with the crowds to gather information on the activities of their opposition. Kaly had her eye on several suspicious men, and a woman, who had arrived with the children.

Keeping 440's instruction in mind, she used her psiever to capture their images. Later, when they returned to base, these would be downloaded, analyzed and cataloged. On more than one occasion, this practice had led to the arrest of Loyalista insurgents when they had been matched with individuals at the scene of terrorist attacks. It was not an opportunity to be ignored.

By noon, the detachment had managed to cover the majority of the mission area, and had given away the bulk of their gifts. The heat had also risen, driving most of the people back into their homes. Realizing that they had done all they could, the Republican commander finally called a halt to the operation.

Team 440 had often stressed that this was the most dangerous part of a mission of this kind, and this concern were justified only five minutes later. They had re-boarded their vehicles and were heading out towards *Tomas Aligaar* boulevard, a major traffic artery, when the middle 'lectri took some small arms fire from a group of apartments off to their left.

The moment that the chatter went out on their Com, Kaly shoved Tatiana through a port in the side of her vehicle and searched for the shooter. She found him right away, crouched inside a second story room, and realized that he was one of the impassioned amateurs that made up a large segment of the Loyalista forces. The man was so inexperienced that he hadn't even known enough to seat himself back in the shadows. So she shot him.

More gunfire came at them from another location on the right, and the Republican Commander made the correct decision. Instead of having the detachment dismount and engage in a costly house-to-house firefight, he ordered them to withdraw. Kaly worried that he would follow this up with a request for immediate air support—and he was well within his rights to do so—but he didn't, and the lives of dozens of innocents living all around the shooters were spared in the process. Instead, the convoy sped away and got itself clear.

The worst was still to come though; three blocks on, and at a point where the street narrowed, an adolescent boy ran out into the street carrying something in each hand. He threw one of these objects at the lead vehicle and Kaly involuntarily cringed, certain that it was some form of grenade. At almost the exact same time that it bounced off the armored hull, one of the Sisterhood troopers reacted, cutting him down with her Mark-7.

It was something that she might have done herself, out of pure reflex, and she immediately felt horror, both for the boy and for the trooper. The 'grenades' had been nothing more than a pair of rocks, and the burst from the energy weapon had blown a fist-sized cavity straight through the boy's chest.

Realizing what she had just done, the trooper tried to jump out of her vehicle to help her victim. While her sisters restrained her, a woman burst out of a nearby home and ran to the body, wailing in despair. In a few seconds, a crowd of unarmed neighbors materialized, and they glared up at the soldiers with pure, undiluted hatred.

Kaly had to look away.

What are we even doing here? she wondered. A few pieces of candy and some cheap radios didn't stack up against something like this. It ashamed and sickened her.

***

Kaly didn't want to go to the concert. The trooper who had shot the boy was being medicated by the Psych doctors, and word had already gotten around that she would be shipping back to the Sisterhood as soon as possible, and mustering out. The tragedy had left Kaly enshrouded in gloom, and only the good natured, but vigorous insistence of Margasdaater and Vasquaaz managed to rouse her from her bunk.

Thanks to them, she finally rallied herself, dressed in her class 'C' fatigues, and went with them to the amphitheater.

Although the technical part of Celina's show wasn't what it might have been back in the Sisterhood, her raw talent as a singer did the trick. Kaly soon forgot her grim frame of mind and was swept along by the performance.

One piece, *"The Lady of Illidian"* particularly captivated her, and as Celina sang, thoughts and associations drifted through her mind, rising and falling with the melody. As *"The Lady"* finally reached its crescendo, she realized that she had heard it somewhere before.

Then she remembered where, and with whom. *Lena loved this song,* she thought.

Her smile, and her pleasant mood vanished completely.

Who the fek was Lena? she wondered in alarm.

She was becoming more than just 'burned out', she realized. Between weird shess like this, and all the recurring dreams she'd been having, real madness was starting to look like a distinct possibility.

"I've got to get out of here," she announced, rising abruptly.

Margasdaater tried to lay a hand on her arm, but Kaly broke free, and left the amphitheater.

She had also made up her mind. When her tour came up for renewal, she was going to tell the RSE to go and *fek* itself. She was finished with the ETR, and done with being a soldier. It was time for her to start living another life. Before she went totally klaxxy.

***

With the assistance of Claire d'Layne's Senior Activities Officer and her staff, and despite all the last minute changes that she'd been forced to institute, the concert for the troops went off without any problems. The show was held in a special assembly area, which had been built for her by the Marine Engineers, and the seats were crowded to capacity, with more uniformed women standing in the back and in the aisles.

Because Realie simulations were restricted in the ETR for trade and security reasons, she had resorted to an old and reliable standby; holo imagery and a combination of live and digital sounds. It had been years since she had used them for a performance, but it all came back to her.

And naturally, Clio was there, recording the entire thing for *"The Song of Humanity"*. One of the best parts, although she had had her doubts about including it, proved to be a rendition of *"Jenny has Gone for a Soldier."*

Celina had been concerned that it would remind the troops too much of what they had left behind, but she had misjudged her audience. Instead of depressing them, it made them remember why they had decided to join up in the first place, and brought them together. This reaction, and their response to one of her more upbeat pieces, wound up making the performance one of the best that she had given in years. So much so, that she had even been tempted to swear off the more 'technical' shows, and going back to doing things the old fashioned way. Almost.

***

The following morning, Celina was taken out on a tour of the capitol. Her first stop was what in the Sisterhood would have been called a mixed primary/secondary institution. When she arrived, the children—all of them

167

girls—were lined up in rows and according to height. As a group, they were all healthy, attractive, and impeccably dressed for the occasion.

The school itself was one of the ones that the Marine Engineers had built for the Republic, and their headmistress had made certain that her pupils were all attired in garments that reflected their star-nation's national colors; gleaming white blouses, red scarves and perfectly creased black skirts. Their rendition of the ETR's national anthem, *"For the Glory of the Republic"* was as flawless as their appearance.

Listening to them in the courtyard of *Publa Escaul Cantida Una*, Public School Number 1, Celina rewarded the young performers with her broadest smile of approval, and then made a point of not only posing with them for the benefit of the military journalists, but also exchanging bows with their music teacher before handing out autographed copies of her work. In holovid format of course. That technology wasn't restricted, and lacking psievers, it was something that the girls could actually enjoy.

But by the end of it all, Celina was eager to leave the place. As pleasant as her visit had been, it was not the ETR that she had come to capture for her realie. She wanted the chance to walk its streets, and meet the real people who made up its citizenry. So far though, her military handlers, and the Embassy women, had been doing everything they could to divert her into carefully controlled situations that were too sanitized to provide anything worthy of her project.

The only partial exception to this had been earlier in the day, when she had been allowed to visit a military police detachment. The unit had been composed of both Sisterhood troopers and local Garda soldiers, and everyone had been extraordinarily careful to show only their best sides to her, and overemphasize the close cooperation that the two forces enjoyed.

She wasn't the fool that they thought she was though. None of what she had been shown tallied with the slogan she had seen on her first day. Or with the people who had been under arrest for painting it.

She was positive that there was more to the story than anyone wanted her to see. Even if nothing happened beyond the graffiti, there was a tension in the air that was impossible to miss.

Whether or not she would find out what the truth was, was another matter. So far, all she had discovered was a growing sense of frustration at being 'managed'.

COMINT Center, Sub-Basement, Embassy of the United Sisterhood of Suns, Nuvo Bolivar, Magdala Provensa, Esteral Terrana Rapabla, 1048.10|04|03:76:92

Sarah had convened an impromptu meeting in her cubicle in the COMINT center. Sa'Tela had an important update concerning Celina.

"We finally have some confirmation that the Loyalistas intend to take some form of action against her," Sa'Tela announced. "Our assets are telling us that they will either attempt some kind of attack, or try to enlist her in their cause some time within the next 24 hours."

Whispers had been circulating since well before the singer's arrival about this, but until then they had only been unsubstantiated rumors. For that reason, Celina's security measures had been general in nature, and hadn't addressed a specific threat.

"Which is more likely?" Sarah asked her with a touch of impatience. "Is it to be an attack or a proposition?"

"That depends upon the faction," the Kalian stated. Everyone knew exactly what she meant. Far from being one united front, the rebels were actually dozens of organizations, often with conflicting objectives. They tended to fight one another almost as much as they fought the Sisterhood or the Rightists.

"At least two of them want to kidnap her, or attempt an assassination. The rest seem to think that she will help them by raising public awareness against us. The probabilities tend to weigh heavily towards recruitment."

"I take it that we still have measures in place to monitor the situation?" Sarah inquired. Celina's suite was filled with microscopic spy devices and personnel had been assigned to watch her around the clock.

"We do, ma'am," Sa'Tela replied. "Our surveillance is ongoing, and we are monitoring everyone that she comes in contact with."

"Good," Sarah said. "Now we need to make certain that the Loyalistas succeed in their little bid for freedom."

Sa'Tela was taken aback. "Ma'am?"

"As soon as we know that they are not sending an assassin to murder her, we have to ensure that their courier reaches their destination," Sarah told her. "Afterwards, ensure that whatever information Celina receives is quietly erased. I also want the courier tracked once they leave, but they are not to be arrested."

"But ma'am—"Sa'Tela started to object.

"I have direct orders from Thermadon concerning this," Sarah told her. "General bel Thana and I spoke this morning, and she told me that we are not to interfere with any meeting between Celina and the rebels. Have some women in place—well-hidden of course—and make sure that the singer is safe, but otherwise let things happen as they do. Is that clear, Lieutenant?"

Nonplussed, Sa'Tela inclined her head. "Yes, ma'am. It is"

169

Maya was just as confused, but knew from personal experience that the Agency often did some very strange things, and it was generally better not to ask why. The reasons would make themselves known in time. They always did, if one was patient enough.

Sarah stood, a clear sign that their gathering was over. Maya was starting to join her when something caught her eye out in the COMINT center.

Several of the monitors were displaying an image of the west side of the Embassy at street level, and a large 'lectri delivery truck had just pulled up and stopped. This area was a strictly enforced 'No Parking Zone' and Maya saw that the Embassy Security Commander was visibly excited, and barking out orders to her subordinates, but the thick glass walls of the conference cubicle prevented her from hearing precisely what the woman was saying. It didn't prevent her from see what happened next however.

A group of Marines and uniformed Security women were approaching the truck, and ordering the driver to move on. Suddenly, the side of the trucks cargo area swelled, and then burst. After that, the scene was lost in a blinding white light and grey smoke.

At the same time, the room around her shook and the lights went out. The emergency illumination came on line a second later, and Sarah was already on her way out of the cubicle. Maya was right behind her.

The COMINT center was now in chaos, and department heads were frantically scrambling to address the situation. As they moved towards the main displays, a woman from Security rushed up and saluted Sarah.

"Ma'am," the Troop Leader said. "We believe the Embassy has just been attacked. It looks like it was a truck bomb. We've requested aid from Claire d'Layne."

"Damage and casualties?" Sarah asked quietly. Her skin had gone deathly pale, and her hands were tightly clenched. In this state, Maya knew, she was death incarnate.

"Only initial figures ma'am," the security woman answered, inclining her head towards one of the central displays. This showed a 3-D model of the Embassy building. The west wing was tinted a vivid red, and gold lights were flashing throughout the structure. These were fire alarms and sensors.

Momentarily, the Embassy Security Commander joined them, and took over for the trooper.

"We have four dead confirmed from the detail that went out to that truck," she told them, and another ten who were working on that side of the building." This information had come when their psiever signals had cut out, Maya realized grimly.

"We're also getting some other alarm signals," the woman continued. "But they're hard to track, probably from interference coming from the rubble."

While she said this, a security camera from one of the neighboring buildings came online and showed the extent of the devastation. The west wing no longer existed. Dark grey smoke was pouring out of the hole where it had once been, and from several other locations elsewhere in the structure.

They had been hit, and hard. The only thing that had saved everyone in the COMINT center had been the fact that it was heavily armored, and deep belowground. Despite herself, Maya had to fight to keep from trembling.

"What is the status of our remaining security forces?" Sarah inquired.

"On alert for a follow-up attack ma'am," the Captain told her. Then she paused and closed her eyes, listening to something from her psiever.

"There was an RSE SRU Team working near us," she said. "They are arriving now, and a platoon of hovertanks from the base should be on station over us in less than two minutes. Local Police are also en-route."

"Good," Sarah responded tightly. "Keep me informed. And as soon as it is practical to do so, I want whatever is left of that truck examined."

She turned to Sa'Tela next.

"I think that this is more than just an attack on the Embassy," she stated." I think this might also be a diversion. Make certain that our people stationed around Celina are on their highest state of alert, but be mindful of my instructions regarding any courier."

***

Ever since enlisting, Kaly had witnessed a lot of terrible things. What she saw below the orbiting assault shuttle surpassed a lot of it.

She had been to the Embassy on a few occasions, and what she was witnessing now tore those memories to shreds. The entire west wing was nothing more than a pile of rubble, with a few skeletal walls to remind anyone of the shape they had once described. There were fires and smoke everywhere.

Down below her, the first hovertanks were arriving, and a mixture of troopers, Republican police officers and firewomen from Claire d'Layne were already hard at work trying to control the scene and protect it against further assault.

The truck that had created all of this chaos was a twisted hulk of blackened metal. When the bomb inside of it had gone off, it had embedded the vehicle in the wall of the building next door from the sheer force of the blast.

There were also bodies, or in most cases, parts of bodies. The corpses were scattered all across the gruesome scene, and unfortunately, most of them were still intact enough to identify as people. One in particular, the upper half of a woman who was still wearing the blouse she had dressed herself in that morning, lay in the rubble strewn driveway. Her one remaining hand was clenched tightly and the index finger pointed accusingly at the truck as if her spirit wanted to make certain that everyone knew what had murdered her.

Through force of will, Kaly made herself look away and settled against the sally port, ranging around with Tatiana. There were still terrorists down there to worry about, and she did not want to dwell on on the dead woman, or how many other bodies were also down there, entombed under the rubble. As it was, she already had plenty of material for her nightmares, and didn't need to add to her stock with even more.

***

Celina had spent the morning with Clio, working on their material. As she was wrestling with a particularly difficult clip, one of the securitywomen came in, and gently reminded her of her lunch with the Sisterhood Ambassador.

"Jantildam, you should start getting ready. It's only an hour from now."

Celina sat up from her keyboard abruptly.

"Yes, yes. Of course," she replied, waving the woman away. "I just have a little more to do here."

Clio intervened on the securitywoman's behalf. "Celi, this is an important meeting. We should stop here and pick it up later. Now, don't you think you should be getting dressed?"

Celina sighed, but relented. "Thank you dear. You're right—as always. I'll be a good little girl and put away my toys and go get myself ready."

Her artificial companion laughed, and then addressed the securitywoman. "She'll be along shortly. And I'll make sure she doesn't get distracted." The woman bowed gratefully, and left them.

Celina had actually managed to finish dressing, and was attending to her make-up when she heard a loud report, and then felt the room shake slightly. She looked up as tiny bits of dust rained down from the ceiling.

"Clio? What was that?"

"I don't know, Celi. I'm checking." Then a second later, "There seems to have been some kind of attack..."

The securitywoman reentered the suite and Celina turned to face her. "I'm almost done," she told her, referring to the time on her psiever. "Did something just happen?"

"Jantildam," the woman said. "I'm afraid that your lunch has to be cancelled. There's been a bombing at the Embassy."

"A bombing?!" Celina asked incredulously. Once again the slogan she had seen came back, but with a much deeper, and far more frightening emphasis. *They really do hate us*, she realized.

"Yes, ma'am. The Ambassador and her staff are safe, but they have requested that we keep you here at the hotel."

"*Keep* me?" Celina asked. "Am I some kind of prisoner then?" On top of being afraid, she was now becoming irritated. She didn't like being told where she could and could not go.

The securitywoman's response was polite, but unyielding. "No, jantildam. It's simply for your own safety. Only until other arrangements can be made for you."

"What *other* arrangements?" Celina demanded. "What's going on? Who bombed the Embassy?"

"I'm sorry ma'am," the woman said. "That's not for me to say. The Embassy will be sending someone along shortly to explain things to you. Right now, I need to ask you to stay here."

Another member of her security detachment had joined her, and they were standing in the door, clearly barring her from making any attempt to exit.

"Okay," Celina agreed. "I'll wait for the Embassy people then. Can I at least order some lunch for myself? I'm hungry."

"Certainly, ma'am," the securitywoman replied. "What would you like me to get for you?"

Celina sighed in exasperation, and then dictated her order. After that, all she could do was sit on the couch and wait. Outside in the distance, she could see smoke, and she knew that it was coming up from the area around the Embassy. In just a few minutes, it changed from an angry black to a lighter grey, and there seemed to be fewer sirens piercing the air.

Sick of the tension, she finally resorted to a pair of headphones, her portable keyboard, and Clio. They returned to where they had left off, and gradually, her frayed nerves were calmed.

She became so engrossed in her work that she barely noticed the hotel staffer arriving with her lunch. Once again, Clio came to everyone's rescue and made Celina put aside her work to let the staffer serve her.

While the woman bent in close to ladle out some soup into her bowl, she whispered into Celina's ear. "Jantildam, when you finish, read the note under the salad plate."

Celina blinked in surprise, and then looked past her to the securitywoman standing at the doorway, but she seemed oblivious to the exchange. She was in the middle of a conversation with someone on the other end of her Com bud.

"Thank you," Celina answered, trying to make her reply seem natural. "I'll make sure to try it."

The server smiled broadly, and then left her to her meal. It took a few minutes of careful observation before Celina saw her chance and palmed the note. A subsequent trip to the restroom provided her with the privacy that she needed to read it.

"The Sisterhood has lied to you and your countrywomen about everything," it said. *"Use the pass card behind the toilet and enter the empty suite next door after 8 P.M. The truth will be waiting for you in the main bedroom."*

Celina's pulse raced as she crumpled the note up and hid it in her blouse. She briefly considered telling her security detail about the message, but changed her mind. While it might have been the safest course of action to take, and certainly what the Embassy women would have wanted, it wasn't the right thing to do. Something was going on here. Something dark and terrible, and she was finally in a position to discover what it was.

That was assuming that she was willing to take the risk. She had never considered herself to be a terribly adventurous person, and she knew that she had no business getting herself involved. But the image of the prisoners lined up in front of the wall, and the anti-Sisterhood slogan, cried out to her.

She had no doubt that the rendezvous would reveal painful truths, but it was still the truth, and she had always dealt honestly with her audience. Every composition that she had ever created for them had been from the heart, and they all knew this. They trusted her, and as an artist and as a woman, she felt that she had a duty to uphold that faith. To shun her responsibility now, and in so doing, to help to conceal an injustice, was unthinkable.

Pretending to linger over her dessert, she spoke to Clio by psiever on their private channel.

Clio, I think I've just been contacted by some kind of rebels—rebels fighting against the Sisterhood here in Nuvo Bolivar! They may be the same people who bombed the Embassy.

Clio was instantly alarmed. *Oh no! Celi, you have to report this right away and get us out of here. That sounds very dangerous.*

No, Clio, Celina countered. *I'm not going to report it, and neither are you! The rebels have promised to tell me what's really going on here, and I have to find out what it is.*

Celi. You can't go, Clio insisted. *It could be a trap. They could be trying to kidnap you—or worse! One of my protocols is to protect you. I won't allow it.*

Celina remained firm. *Clio, I have to go. Something terrible is going on here—bad enough for people to use bombs to get their point across. And the government doesn't want anyone back home to know about it. You've seen how they've been with us.*

Celi, NO!

I'll take you with me, Celina promised. *It's just next door, and if anything happens, you can call the securitywomen for help. Please, I have to do this. It's my duty as an artist!*

Clio mulled this over. A full second later, she responded. *Fine, Celi. But if anything happens I will activate my defensive package—AND call security!*

Celina was taken aback. She had been fully aware of Clio's obligation to protect her, but she had never realized that the AI possessed any kind of armament to back it up with. She was almost tempted to ask her about this, but hesitated. Her virtual friend was too flustered to risk agitating her any further.

She did however, make a mental note to inquire with Clio's manufacturer; she wanted to know if the AI was simply referring to some sort of stun-field, or something as over the top as a full-on fission weapon. That kind of information was somewhat important, especially if there was ever a chance of her using it.

All right, I agree, she told her. *You'll come with me, and if there's trouble, you can step in. Does that work for you?*

I still don't like this, Celi, Clio grumbled. *But, yes. It works.*

***

"I want to be the one," Reesy exclaimed. Her host, the woman named Roza, who functioned as Migehl Alvaraada's second in command, stopped what she was doing, and regarded her appraisingly. Roza had come home early from the sandwich shop, and had changed out of her usual work clothes into what looked to Reesy like something more appropriate for a high-end restaurant or a catered party.

"The one to—*what?*" Roza asked. She was in the process of finishing with her bow-tie.

175

"To speak to Celina," Reesy replied. "I know that she's here. I saw it on the holo. I know that we're going to try and contact her."

"Why would we do that?" Roza inquired innocently. The knot was tied, and she was giving herself one last inspection in the mirror.

"Because it's the only way," Reesy said. "It's the only way to get the Sisterhood off our backs. Their women—the average ones like you and me—they won't stand for what's going on here if they find out about it. Celina could tell them."

"And you think that *you* could convince her?" Roza countered doubtfully. "You think that you could get her—a famous artist—to risk jail just for us? You really think that?"

"You do," Reesy challenged. "That's why you're getting dressed up, isn't it? You're going to try and see her. I'm right, aren't I?"

"I have a job to do," Roza answered curtly. "It's none of your business."

"It *is* my business," Reesy snapped. "If you're going to go and try and see her then I should be there! I could tell her all about the School, about why we are fighting the Sisterhood. Everything. I know I could make her see things our way. I could make her *want* to help us!"

Roza chuckled as she patted her hair into place. "More likely she'll see you for what you are—a silly little girl. She needs to hear from someone who knows our movement."

"Then you *are* going to see her!" Reesy accused. "I knew it! You *have* to take me! I have to be the one!"

"Your face is known to the Sisterhood *putayas*," Roza replied. "You'd be caught in a second. Forget it."

"No!" Reesy cried. "You *know* I'm right! I'm the one. She'll listen to me."

"All right. I'll promise you this. I will speak with Migehl," Roza told her. "That's as much as I can do. His word will be final. You must accept that."

"I will," Reesy agreed. "He'll see things my way. Call him."

Reesy was correct. When Migehl Alvaraada heard Reesy's proposal, he had to concede her point. While Roza was certainly the more experienced operative, Reesy's raw passion, her commitment to the movement, and her personal experiences at the School, could not be discounted. Of all the people that he could think of who could convince Celina to throw in her lot with their cause, Reesy really was the best candidate. The only obstacle was that she was a wanted fugitive.

This was not insurmountable though. Although Celina had a full protective detail, and the hotel itself was being watched by Embassy security and the local police, he knew that no one would expect someone like her to walk right into such a trap. In the end, and despite Roza's strong reservations, Alvaraada agreed to the substitution. Reesy would become the emissary for the Loyalistas and for everyone else who had suffered under the boot heels of their oppressors.

***

Obtaining a uniform for Reesy only required Alvaraada to place another call to the same people who had supplied them with their own costumes and the catering truck. Once Roza had helped the girl to dress herself properly, they met Migehl and drove together to the *Àuro Agwuila*. Their cover had been provided for them by one of the hotel's wealthier patrons, who was also a secret Loyalista sympathizer. Despite the bombing, the elderly woman had insisted on going ahead with her catered party and the hotel staff had been forced to agree.

When Reesy and her companions arrived, they saw that the hotel was just as heavily guarded as they had expected, but only one policeman was on duty at the service entrance to the kitchens. Although Reesy had been given a false identity card, it proved to be completely unnecessary. The policeman was another friend of the movement, and he gave them only the most cursory of inspections before allowing them through.

Once inside, the kitchen staff were too busy to notice them, and they were quickly waved over to a corner to unpack and prepare their food. The meal itself had been created by Alvaraada, and Reesy was impressed with the results; it was as fine as anything that she had ever seen.

As soon as they were ready with their carts, they rolled them into an elevator that was used to transport the hotel staff, and took it up. When they reached the third floor, Roza pulled the stop and handed Reesy a pass card.

"You're getting out here," she told her. "We are one floor beneath Celina's. When you get out of this car, turn left, and go down the hall to the door leading to the emergency stairs. Use them to go up to the very top, and let yourself onto the roof. This card will get you up there. Wait on the roof for five minutes."

"What about Celina?" Reesy asked.

"Celina and her staff will be coming out from the floor below you, and going all the way to the ground floor," Roza answered. "Once they have gone, go down to the VIP level and use this card again to let yourself in. The floor should be unoccupied."

"Won't they see me on the cameras?" Reesy wondered.

"No," Roza promised her. "We have another friend working in security. He'll forget what he saw. Now, listen closely; when you get onto the VIP floor, go left and then down two doors. Go inside that room, lock it behind you and wait in the bedroom. Celina knows to meet you there at eight o'clock."

Next, she reached into the cart and produced a large envelope.

"When you see her, give this to her, and make sure that she sees everything in it. If she has any questions, answer them. You know what you can and can't talk about.'

"When you are done speaking with her, go through into the next room and wait there. We'll create another diversion, and as soon as this happens, leave the same way you came in. This time, go all the way down the stairs to the truck court and follow the alley to the street. Call us when you find a public Com and can't see the hotel any longer. We'll come for you. Do you understand all this?"

Reesy shook her head nervously and took the items, stuffing the envelope up and under her vest. Now that she was actually part of this operation, she wasn't as certain of herself as she had been back at the safe house.

"If you think you are about to be caught," Migehl added gravely, "use this." In his hand was a small plastic vial with a single pill inside. "Don't allow yourself to be captured. You don't want to know what will happen if they get their hands on you." Reesy took it from him with trembling fingers.

Alvaraada's expression suddenly softened and he placed a reassuring hand on her shoulder. "You'll do all right." Then he restarted the elevator and turned to Roza. "Whenever you're ready."

Roza consulted her wrist chrono. After a few seconds, she pulled out her hand-com and made a call. "Hello," she said. "There is a bomb in the Hotel *Àuro Agwuila*. Death to the Sisterhood Invaders!" She cut the connection immediately.

"'Death to the Sisterhood Invaders'?" Migehl frowned. "Couldn't you come up with anything better than that? It's not very original."

"It's the first thing that came to my mind," Roza replied defensively. "Leave me alone!" The three of them shared a much needed laugh over this, and then the elevator door opened onto Reesy's floor.

"Go with God, Reesy," Alvaraada said. An alarm was already going off in the corridor and bewildered patrons were beginning to come out of their rooms.

***

Too nervous to even think of working on her realie, Celina resorted to watching her copy of *"Casablanca"* instead. She had always meant to get to it, but until now, her work had kept her occupied. As good as the remake was however, her attention kept going to the clock function of her psiever to check the time.

The minutes dragged by. Just when she was becoming certain that she couldn't take any more of the tension, one of her security women burst into the room.

Celina squeeked in alarm. "What is it?" she asked, amazed that she hadn't launched herself straight up into the ceiling. "What's going on now?!"

"A bomb threat, ma'am," the woman replied. "Someone called and said there was one here at the hotel, but it's probably a hoax. After every real incident, the klaxxy's always try to stir things up with false alarms."

"Oh," Celina said, feeling her heart rate starting to slow down again. "That's good." She began to turn away, intent on resuming her clock watching. The security woman didn't leave however.

"Ma'am," the woman insisted. "We still have to evacuate. Until the Police tell us the building is clear."

"Seriously?!" Celina exclaimed. "I thought that you just said—"

"I did, but we have to play it safe." the securitywoman told her. "If you'll come with me, please?"

"Well, if I'd known that all it took was a bomb threat to get myself out of here, I would've called one in myself," Celina remarked acerbically.

Her protector made no comment, and led her out into the hall where the rest of her detail was waiting. They escorted her to a set of stairs and down into the lobby.

A limousine was waiting there and as soon as she was aboard, it drove them away from the hotel. Two blocks later, it joined a small group of Police vehicles, and parked. Ever mindful of her comfort, one of her women brought her a cup of tea.

She was just finishing it when her escort announced that the hotel had finally been declared safe. By the time she was back in her room, there were only ten minutes left before her secret meeting was scheduled to occur.

Celina made a great show of yawning. "Well, after all that excitement, I 'm dead tired," she announced. "I think I'm going to kick off my shoes and watch a bit more of my holo before I turn in. May I have some privacy, please?"

The securitywoman who had been posted to the living area shifted uncomfortably. "Ma'am, my orders are to stay with you at all times. There's always the chance that we'll get another alert."

"Can't you just go out into the hall with your friends?" Celina asked her. "There's no one in here except me, and I really *do* need the privacy. I promise, I'll stay right here, and when I'm done, it's straight off to bed—which is right in the next room—with no side trips. You can even check underneath it and make sure it's safe."

The woman fidgeted, but she had no real cause to refuse her. Except for Celina herself and the security detail, the entire floor was unoccupied and all the access points were under surveillance, or guarded. As an added measure, one of her other protectors had already checked her rooms before she had been readmitted.

"No, ma'am, I don't think that will be necessary," the securitywoman agreed. "I'll leave you to your evening. Bian sarà, Jantildam."

Celina gave her a polite smile, and then began to remove her shoes.

The very instant that the woman was gone, all pretense of fatigue disappeared and her shoes were back on her feet. She made for the bathroom immediately.

Like the rest of the fixtures there, the toilet was an antique. It was one of the old fashioned kind that still used water to move waste, and it required a tank to supply that water in huge, wasteful quantities. Celina wasn't in the mood to worry over such inefficiency however; she was actually glad for the prehistoric thing. The tank offered a great hiding place for something as small as a passkey.

It took a minute of fumbling for her to find it. Whoever had hidden the key had made certain to conceal it on the back face, and well away from the outside edges, and had she not known that it was there, she seriously doubted that she, or anyone else, would have ever discovered it. Peeling off the tape, she went back with it into the living area and grabbed up her handbag. This contained her Realicorder and the portable module that housed Clio.

Then she crossed over to the service door that led to the neighboring suite. Hands shaking, she swiped the pass key and unlocked it.

It was now 8 PM local time and the adjoining suite was dark, but the added factor of *something* waiting for her, and possibly even *someone*, made it seem all the more sinister and mysterious. She paused at the threshold briefly reconsidering what she was about to do.

Damn it, I'm no spy, she thought. *What the fek am I doing?*

There was no going back though. She had made her intentions clear to Clio, created a deception with security, found the key, and now, had opened the door to goddess-knew-what-kind-of-adventure. If she balked at this stage, Celina knew that she would always wonder what had been next door, waiting for her, and what she might have learned. That was a question that she didn't want to carry with her into her old age.

She took a steadying breath and stepped in, closing the door softly behind her.

No wild-eyed terrorists, or any other kind of danger sprung out at her as she crossed the living area though. In fact, as she stopped and listened, she came to the conclusion that the suite was completely deserted. She sent a thought to Clio.

Clio? Are you still there? It was a silly question; Clio was always with her, but she felt better for asking it.

Yes, Celi. I still think this is a very bad idea. Let's go back right now before we get into serious trouble.

No, Celina retorted. *We see this through to the end.* She was surprised at her own determination. Ignoring her misgivings, she crossed the short space to the master bedroom, and opened the door.

She had half-expected to encounter some rough-looking character, and the young woman seated on the bed was anything but. The girl was dressed in a formal server's outfit and on the petite side, with sandy blond hair and green eyes. Her delicate hands were folded nonthreateningly on her lap, and next to her, was a large envelope.

"I'm sorry," Reesy said. "Please don't be afraid of me. When they told me that they were going to meet with you, I asked them to let me be the one." Her thick accent immediately identified her as a native of the ETR.

Clio interrupted with a psiever message. *Celi, I have my defensive package online and ready to engage! If this bitch tries anything—anything at all—I swear she won't live long enough to regret it.*

Celina hastily reassured her friend. *Please Clio! Don't do anything to her. I don't think she's a threat.*

At least she *hoped* that she wasn't. She had no desire to see what measures her AI could bring to bear if she were proven wrong. She also stayed right where she was, and made no move to walk over and retrieve the envelope.

"My name is Reesy," the girl continued. "And I've listened to your music—the women from the *Atalanta* used to play it for me all the time. Will you hear what I have to tell you? Please?"

"The *Atalanta*?" Celina asked. It sounded to her like the name of some kind of starship. Despite herself, she relaxed a bit, and became even more intrigued.

"Yes," Reesy answered. "It was a long range scout ship from your Sisterhood. It crash-landed on my world. We call my planet *'La Escaul'*, the School. Have you ever heard of it?"

Celina shook her head. She didn't know very much about the stellography of the ETR, or its planets.

"I wrote my story down and put it in the envelope with everything else, but I also wanted to tell you about it in person," Reesy said. "Please—don't be afraid of me." She gently patted a spot on the mattress.

Celina finally decided that it was safe to approach the bed and sat down next to her. Then Reesy began to tell Celina her tale; of the School itself, the crash-landing, of their discovery by the Sisterhood, and then about the military occupation and the intel operation that had followed it.

Reesy didn't stop there though. She went on to describe the crippling reparations that the Sisterhood had demanded after the war, the introduction of glass to her people, the Loyalista resistance movement, and even revealed that many of the musicians Celina had hoped to include in her performance had actually been detained in jail by the police.

The worst of it was yet to come however. Reesy went on, detailing the mass arrests of anyone opposing the Ernan government, or the Sisterhood. She also told her about the bombings, the assassinations, and all the people who had simply 'disappeared' in police custody, never to be heard from again. Then, about the unmarked, mass graves and the right-wing death squads. And all of it with the Sisterhood's full knowledge, and blessings.

Throughout this, Celina said nothing, and listened closely. And as she did, she began to feel deep shame, and then a rising, angry sympathy with Reesy, and her cause. All of her original doubts and fears had vanished completely, replaced by a stony determination to see the wrongs that her nation had done to these people, righted.

Instead of making any attempt to bring the envelope with all of its incriminating contents back with her, she used her Realicorder to copy them—after agreeing to let Reesy don a mask to disguise herself.

Finally, the time came for them to part. In the short while that they had been together, Celina had come to like and respect the Loyalista girl, and they exchanged a spontaneous hug, and wished each other luck. They both knew that they would never see each other again.

When she returned to her room, she was unsurprised when her securitywoman came for her a second time.

"We have another bomb threat," the woman advised her.

Celina didn't argue, and went with her to the elevator. This time, she wasn't nervous. She knew that Reesy was making her escape.

That night, after she was allowed to come back to her bedroom, sleep eluded her. Her mind was spinning with everything she had seen and heard, and her plans for the future.

When she returned to the Sisterhood, she was going to contact her friends in the news media and disclose the entire sordid affair. She didn't blame the women of her nation's military for their part in it though. In her mind, they were also victims, and had been put in a terrible position by their government.

And all in the name of greed and exploitation. What Thermadon was doing in the ETR, was wrong and it had to be stopped. She was also keenly aware of just how dangerous a proposition that really was.

Celina had no fear for herself however. It was people like Reesy and her friends that worried her. Thanks to them, she had learned that the Sisterhood was not the fair, friendly, or egalitarian state that she had always believed it to be, and she knew that it would not be gentle with anyone who stood against it. No matter how famous they were.

Just like Reesy and her brave Loyalista rebels however, Celina now had a sacred mission to undertake, and there was no room in it for trepidation, or weakness. To make things change, risks had to be taken, and prices, paid.

***

Reesy exited the VIP floor using the service stairs. She encountered no one on her way to the ground floor, and as she let herself out into the alley, she was certain that she had pulled it all off flawlessly.

A second later, her eyes caught movement in the shadows to her left. Inexplicably, a woman was standing in front of her, her features partially hidden by her dark cloak. Despite this, Reesy could still make out the gleam in her eyes and the predatory smile on her face.

"Sleep," the figure said. There was an intense pressure between her eyes and after this, nothing...

...Amandra sa'Tela bent over Reesy's prostrate form, and withdrew a small injector gun from the folds of her cloak. She pressed this to the girl's thigh and squeezed the trigger. There was a small hiss of compressed air as the gun sent a tiny pellet into Reesy's flesh. Immediately, the nanites that were infused into the pellet's outer coating went to work, repairing the miniscule damage to the girl's skin and consuming the tiny blood droplet the injection had created. When they were done, there was nothing left behind to even suggest that anything had ever been introduced.

183

Simultaneously, the microelectronics in the pellet came alive, and began sending a faint, but trackable signal. From here on, Reesy would be monitored from space, and she would unwittingly lead the RSE to her fellow terrorists, and give them a map of all their local cells.

And when they were ready, the Kalian reflected, they would catch them up like fish in a net. It wouldn't replace Captain n'Kyla's life, but it would go a long ways towards exacting a stiff price for her murder.

Returning the gun to its hiding place, she leaned in and whispered softly into Reesy's ear. "You will remember nothing," she said to her. "Except that you slipped on the stairs leaving the building and hit your head. You met no one here. You were alone at all times."

"I—hit—my head," Reesy repeated brokenly. "I—I--s-saw no one."

Sa'Tela gave her cheek a pat that was almost affectionate. "Good. Rest now. You will wake up in one minute." With that, she engaged her cloak's camouflage function and disappeared.

CHAPTER 7

Claire d'Layne Naval Base, Nuvo Bolivar, Magdala Provensa, Esteral
Terrana Rapabla, 1048.10|06|05:14:29

The Marine trooper never saw her death coming. She was standing at a check point waving 'lectris through a barrier when the round caught her in the side of her skull. Even as she fell, her fellow troopers reacted, scurrying for cover and hastily returning fire. One of them, disregarding the possibility that she might become a casualty herself, crawled out to the body and began to drag it back towards the safety of a nearby vehicle. A second trooper joined her a moment later, and together they managed to pull the sniper's victim out of the line of fire. It was too late though; their comrade had been fatally wounded.

The clip ended on this somber note. No one who had been watching it said a word. A few, Kaly included, made the sign of the Lady in sympathy for the fallen Marine, and as a ward against evil. Her partner, *Cabo* Vasquaaz, crossed herself and whispered a silent prayer for the woman's soul.

"*Bian dea*, Ladies—and gentlemen, "Major ebed Karri said, making certain to include the scattering of *Specia* males who were sniper qualified. "What you have just seen is the handiwork of a Loyalista who calls himself 'the Angel'. Apparently, this is a Republican Orthodox Church reference to a messenger of Death. It's also a calling card that he's left behind at some of his kills."

A plastipaper card came up on display. It bore the motto, "*Mortan a e invadiya Ermanyaa!*" with an image of an angel weeping bloody tears.

"This is supposed to strike fear in our hearts and give the average citizen some kind of hope. Fortunately, we don't subscribe to all that primitive male-based *shessdrek*—with apologies to you guys--and we are *not* afraid. This 'Angel' *konnar* is just the latest threat to be sent against us.'

"Your job as snipers, from here on, is to hunt this *kunta* down, and take him out of the equation. To help facilitate that mission, you will be provided with clips just like this one. I expect each of you to review them, and come up with an analysis of the Angel's technique so that we can create an effective strategy for catching and killing his sorry butt.'

"The clips that you will be reviewing are all from his gun-cam. The Loyalistas are distributing them as propaganda to show that the big, bad Sisterhood is vulnerable—and killable. Ladies and gentlemen, we *will* turn that around, and demonstrate that our forces are not only strong, but capable of eliminating the best that the Loyalistas can scrape up from the sewer. Dismissed."

As one, the sniper teams stood, and left the conference room. Like the rest, Kaly headed immediately for a secure terminal, and opened the vid-file that was waiting for her in her inbox. It proved to be a difficult thing to watch on many levels.

She'd seen plenty of women die in combat before, but this was different. Just like the clip the Major had played for them, the footage she watched showed the victims from the perspective of the shooter, and most of the time they were unaware of what was about to happen. The Angel seemed to prefer killing sentries, and crew members of armored vehicles, and as she viewed this, the clinical part of her noted the sniper's precision. Most of his hits were head shots from an undetermined distance, and he took advantage of any gap in the available cover to make them. There were a few exceptions—very few—where his victim was merely wounded, and managed to run to cover. The rest died in place.

The worst clip for her was as brief and as violent as all the others. A crewwoman was sitting in the open cockpit of her AHPC, manning the controls of its heavy energy cannon. Her helmet was on, and her visor was down to shield her eyes from the sun. A second later, she turned her head and looked directly at the sniper. The expression on her face wasn't one of alarm, but curiosity and puzzlement, as if she hadn't quite decided what she was seeing.

The round went out a second later, and her head bucked backwards. Then she sank slowly out of view.

She had been the same general age as Kaly, and could have been anyone that she had known, or grown up with. Anger filled her as she replayed the segment, mixed in with a dry, technical appreciation for the Angel's skill.

But something darker than rage accompanied this, and it surprised and horrified her. It had raised its ugly head at various points during the 'vid, increasing whenever her fury peaked, but she had tried to ignore it. When that proved impossible, she had denied it. The death of the AHPC crewwoman had been too stark though, and too powerful, and it had managed to overwhelm her defenses.

To her utter shame and confusion, she had experienced a wave of sexual arousal. To make matters worse, it wasn't the first time she had felt this unsettling sensation either. It had happened before, during her first combat experiences, and it had stalked her from the shadows of her consciousness ever since—a dirty, filthy thing, that had no right, or reason to be.

Disgusted with the Angel, and with herself, she ended the 'vid. As a soldier, she hated the Loyalista sniper for what he had done to her sisters. But now, she also despised him for the horrible truth that he had forced her to confront. She would see him dead for both of these crimes.

Too distressed to continue with her assignment, she booked a session with Claire d'Layne's resident Psych doctor. She had to talk with someone. Right away.

After a few minutes together, the doctor finally managed to make her feel comfortable enough to unburden herself. When she did, it all came out of Kaly in a torrent of emotion.

"What's *wrong* with me?" she asked, weeping openly. "What's happening?" Too ashamed to meet the doctor's gaze, she looked away.

Dr. n'Susyyn smiled compassionately. "Kaly, there's nothing wrong with you at all."

"But those *feelings*!" Kaly stammered. "They're—they're not—not—right! It's *sick!*"

The psychologist gently took her hands and held them. "Kaly, what you experienced is nothing new. Other women have felt it, and before them, so did the men. All of them were perfectly normal people—soldiers like you— just doing their jobs."

"They did?" An expression of hopefulness suddenly brightened Kaly's features.

"Yes, they did and they have. You're not alone either," N'Susyyn explained. "For all her other problems, your ex-Troop Leader, N'Elemay, also had the same feelings. More than you."

"She did?"

"Yes, she did," the doctor answered. "The stresses of combat do very strange things to the human body. They trigger a rush of chemicals and complex emotions, and the psyche reacts in many ways to this sensory overload. One of these is exactly what happened to you. Even the ancient Greeks experienced it in battle and it confused them just as much.'

"What this really is is a part of our natural fight or flight instinct, and there's nothing 'sick' or 'klaxxy' going on. It's just a way of your body coping with something that most civilians will never have to face. Don't hate it, or yourself. You're really okay."

"But I don't want it! It feels wrong," Kaly retorted. "Those women— they don't deserve it."

"Kaly," Dr. n'Susyyn replied patiently. "You and I both know that you love your sisters, and that you would do anything for them."

Kaly nodded, and wiped her nose with the back of her hand.

187

"Accept that," the woman offered. "Accept your mission, and kill this terrorist for them. And let your feelings be. They might embarrass you, but they are a natural thing, and as long as you know that, and the fact that you are ultimately a good and noble person, they will never be anything more. In fact, you should use them."

"Use them?"

"Yes," Dr. n'Susyyn said. "Use their power. Let them come and go, and when they're there, let them fuel your anger and your precision. Turn them against your target. At their root, at their most basic level, they're really only raw power."

"Okay," Kaly replied tentatively.

Later that afternoon, she summoned up her courage again and reopened the 'vid file. This time, armed with the reassurances that she had received from N'Susyyn, she managed to get through it—just.

Then she started in on her notes.

'The Angel is an expert shot,' she began. *'His shot placement is perfect*—'The image of the AHPC crewwoman resurfaced, right along with its disturbing associations.

She pressed on, *'All his shots seem to originate from ground level positions. He either doesn't use the high ground, or has been denied access to it.'*

That, or he wasn't a trained sniper at all, she reasoned. Just a talented amateur. It was the clarity of the details in the middle ground that had brought her to this deduction. The space between him and his victims seemed to indicate that in every case, his 'hide' had been fairly close by. She had also noticed that all of his long shots had hit his targets in the torso, merely injuring them thanks to the body armor that most Sisterhood troopers wore in the field.

To check herself, she reluctantly watched the footage again and it completely confirmed her conclusions. By a sniper's standards, the Angel worked very close and tended to flub all of his long range attacks.

'It is quite possible that the Angel is not a professional,' she added, *'but only a sharpshooter, and has either volunteered for the job, or was pressed into service by the Loyalistas.'*

If true, this was a significant detail. He would make mistakes due to his lack of formal training. Kaly certainly hoped so.

She continued to play the 'vid and as she did, she tried to put herself in the Angel's place. This was a technique that her instructors on Larra's Lament had often suggested to their trainees. By attempting to think like them, it was a way of predicting a target's next move.

Now what would I do? she wondered, *if I were a scum-sucking piece of shess? How would I set up a ground-level shot?*

She called up the holos from each shooting, and carefully examined them from various angles. She also made sure to look at the adjacent buildings, at the landscape itself, and at every conceivable opportunity that these elements offered for a low level firing position. It wasn't long before she discovered that none of her choices offered up good solutions.

On a hunch, she replayed the footage again, comparing them with the holographic layout. It was on her third clip, which featured the same unlucky AHPC crewwoman that she finally found what she was looking for.

In that clip, and in all the others, there had been a heavy duty 'lectri van in the area, and when she checked, she saw that the van had left the vicinity just a few minutes after each shooting. Even though it was never the same van, the pattern was identical. It also came as no surprise to her that in every case, the rear of the vehicle was pointing straight towards the intended victim.

"Well, I'll be thrice damned by the Goddess," she exclaimed aloud. That was it. The Angel was using cargo vans to shoot from, probably with a loophole cut into the body of the rear doors, and firing from the bed of the van itself. This negated the chance of leaving behind any shell casings, concealed the flash from the weapon itself, and even deadened the noise. The same van then provided him with a quick and convenient getaway. It was perfect—as long as someone like her didn't catch on.

Encouraged by her findings, Kaly called up the footage from the security cameras in each location. She had to use her RSE clearance to get the imagery, and initially, what there was, was of little use.

But once again, in the footage of the AHPC shooting, she found what she was looking for. It was as if the ghost of the murdered woman was somehow reaching from beyond the grave to help her find her killer and bring him to justice.

A camera on an adjacent street had managed to capture the driver and their passenger. Both men were in the shadows cast by the bright afternoon sun, but when she enhanced the image, their features began to become clear. Kaly centered in on the passenger, and made a screen capture of his face. It was blurry, and the details were hard to make out, but for the first time, she was sure that she was looking at the face of her enemy.

I've got you now, you fekking kunta, she thought fiercely.

Eager to share her discovery, she contacted Major ebed Karri right away.

Her superior was ecstatic. "Excellent work, N'Deena! Send the 'vid over to me and I'll have the techies give it a go."

Glad to be done with her assignment, she sent the clips off and then left the terminal, trying not to dwell on what she had been forced to watch.

***

The Major didn't keep her sniper teams waiting. A day after Kaly had reviewed her clips, Ebed Karri called everyone back in.

"Ladies, gentlemen, first off, I'd like to thank you all for the time you expended looking at the 'vids I gave you, "Ebed Karri began. "I know they were hard to watch, and I appreciate the professionalism that each of you showed in your notes. Now, let's look at what we learned."

She brought a holo up. It displayed an image of a man in his mid-twenties. Next to this was a bulleted list of the techniques he had employed in all the shootings.

"This man is the Angel, and you can thank Corporal n'Deena for identifying him for us. By the way, I'll say it again just because it feels *so* fekking good--great work, Corporal!"

She waited for a moment as Margasdaater and a few of the others gave Kaly congratulatory pats on the back before pressing on. "The Angel's real name is Paacal Martinya, and before the war, he served in the ETR military as an infantryman with sharpshooter qualifications."

The Major sent a thought to the holojector and the image that Kaly had captured from the van came up for everyone to see. It was much sharper than hers, having been enhanced by the technical department at the Embassy. It also left no doubt whatsoever that the two images depicted the same man.

"In all likelihood, he will continue to use a vehicle for his firing platform. Keep working in teams and concentrate on any suspicious 'lectri vans, especially when they are in the vicinity of our assets. If you think you have something, try to confirm your target as a hostile, but don't hesitate to take the shot. Lt. ben Soolee will give each Team its duty assignments. All right, let's get out there."

Granda Longela, Nuvo Bolivar, Magdala Provensa, Esteral Terrana
Rapabla, 1048.10|08|05:00:00

Kaly had been partnered with Margasdaater and Vasquaaz, and the trio had stationed themselves in a hide overlooking the *Granda Longela*, Nuvo Bolivar's historic Central Market. They were on the rooftop of the Market's indoor vending area and the location offered them an excellent view of the entire area. Its air conditioning units and roof arrays also prevented them from being silhouetted against the sky and becoming targets themselves.

The *Granda Longela* was one of the places in the city that regularly saw the largest concentration of Sisterhood troopers on patrol anywhere in the capitol. Of all the spots that Kaly, or any of her fellow snipers could think of, it was the most likely place where they would be able to find and engage the Angel.

In addition to Kaly and her partners, a second sniper team was in place on another nearby rooftop, and several spybots were discreetly patrolling the area, watching the scene and listening for the tell-tale report of a weapon. The Navy was also in place, watching the entire area from space.

But even with all this effort and technology, everything still depended on the Angel making an attack, and by the time it was 05.00 hours, this seemed unlikely.

Kaly however, hadn't given up hope. From her training, she knew that it was usually when everyone relaxed, that a sniper did their best 'work'. If the Angel understood this, he would wait for the point when things became lax before he made his move.

Scanning the area through her riflescope, she could almost feel him out there, somewhere, waiting just like she was, and considering his options. The minutes ticked by.

She was just about to switch roles with Vasquaaz and let her be the primary shooter, when Margasdaater alerted her to a new development.

"Kaly," she whispered. "Ve have a van backing up tovards our troopers." Despite what they knew about the Angel's methods, this was nothing unique in and of itself. The Central Market had a lot of delivery vans entering and leaving on a constant basis. Still, it was not something they could ignore.

When she brought Tatiana around to take a look, she immediately understood why Margasdaater had pointed this particular vehicle out. The driver wasn't the same man that she had seen in the 'vids, but he *was* nervous and his movements were a bit too stiff to be natural. She zoomed in.

By this point, the driver had walked around to the back, and was opening the rear cargo doors. Kaly tried unsuccessfully to spot any suspicious loopholes cut into the sheet metal, and then examined the cargo itself. There was one row of boxes, stacked three high and positioned at the very rear of the cargo compartment. They seemed to contain vegetables.

It was their arrangement that seemed out of place. Every load that she had ever seen before had been stacked towards the front of the cargo compartment to prevent it from falling on whoever opened the rear doors. This didn't conform to that norm.

191

The other thing that stood out were that the boxes weren't tight against each other like they should have been. Instead, there were noticeable gaps between some of them, especially along the bottom of the stack.

She tightened in on the spaces, trying to spot anything in the shadows, but found nothing.

"Vasquaaz," she said. "You see what I'm seeing?" *Cabo* Vasquaaz brought up her own rifle.

"Si'a," the woman answered. "Very strange. I don't like strange."

While they continued to watch, the driver unloaded a hand truck and began stacking a few of the containers onto it. Once it was full, he started to wheel the load away. A perfectly normal delivery.

Except that he had also left the rear doors open, Kaly realized. In the middle of a busy marketplace, and as if he was completely unconcerned that his cargo might be stolen in his absence. With the economy as bad as it was in the ETR, that was a distinct possibility. Even if potential thieves weren't able to use the food themselves, the black market would find ready buyers for it.

More minutes passed, and they waited.

Then Kaly caught the movement of something that she couldn't identify. It was back behind the remaining boxes. She tightened in on the area and the hairs on the back of her neck began to rise. Nothing should have been there.

"I may have a hostile," she whispered over the general Com. She called up thermal and bioplasmic images as she did so. Something in the construction of the packages themselves interfered with her getting a decent result, but she was still able to confirm that there was a warm living being of some kind, hiding behind them.

"Team, if you think you have a target, you are green to fire," Major ebed Karri advised.

Kaly wasn't sure and she whispered over to Vasquaaz. "Do you have anything?"

Vasquaaz shook her head. The heat signature that they were seeing was so small that it could have come from a hitchhiking rodent. But it could have also originated from a gap in a snipers poncho, and they both realized it. Such a poncho was designed to mask heat and bioplasmic emanations. Despite every effort to prevent it, a few Sisterhood-issue ponchos were known to be in Loyalista hands.

Kaly made her decision. Right or wrong, she would take the responsibility for what happened. "Shot out," she said.

The suppressed round made no sound as it left Tatiana and crossed the distance to the van. When it hit, only a few small splinters even announced that it had penetrated the boxes. She chambered another round and waited for something else to happen.

The van remained still.

Presently, the driver returned, loaded his now empty hand truck back aboard, and drove away. Watching him depart, Kaly felt a surge of disappointment, and profound embarrassment. Thanks to her nervousness, a delivery vehicle now had a neat hole punched into its sheet metal body. If the driver realized that the Sisterhood had been involved, it would come straight out of her pay.

She was just beginning to calculate the repair cost, and its equivalent in Republic *Paysolis* when Margasdaater nudged her. "Kaly, look down at za ground---vere za van vas parked!"

She and Vasquaaz both focused on the area at the same time. There were only a few drops spattering the pavement, but it looked like blood.

Kaly conducted a quick check of their bioplasmic energy field and confirmed this. It *was* human blood. Male, in fact. Even more droplets were trailing behind the van as it drove away.

"Team 1, Command," she said. "There's definitely something in that van. I think I hit the shooter."

Immediately, several local police units appeared out of the surrounding alleyways and closed in on the vehicle. The van didn't stop though, and as the pursuit began in earnest, the Com became choked with traffic as Sisterhood military police units joined in.

The chase lasted only a few blocks before there was a mixed cacophony of energy and chemical weapons being fired. Kaly desperately wanted to leave her post and join the fight, but she stayed where she was, and kept an eye on the Market instead. There was always the possibility that a second shooter was waiting to take advantage of such a disturbance. It was something that she would have done herself, had the roles been reversed.

After what seemed an eternity, Major ebed Karri got back with them. "Team 1, you got the *kunta*," she announced "He was in the back, using one of our ponchos and your round wounded him—a nice lung shot. When we cornered the van, he and his partner decided to shoot it out. They're both KIA now. Great work! I'm glad to have this pain in the ass out of commission."

Kaly gratefully accepted a thumbs up from Vasquaaz and Margasdaater. But she wasn't as elated as she had expected to be. She was just very tired, and grateful that the ghost of the murdered AHPC crewwoman would finally find her rest.

***

A minor miracle occurred. Things actually remained peaceful for the next few days. Then, just as everyone knew it would, the situation changed for the worse. It was after all, the ETR.

Freedom Square had begun to fill up early in the morning, and by evening it was at capacity. While some of the crowd were simply curious, or just looking for some excitement, the majority of them were protestors. One of these, clearly an activist leader, had perched himself on the statue of one of the Republic's heroes, and had been haranguing the crowd with a portable voice box for the last few hours.

It was the usual Loyalista *shessdrek*; down with the Sisterhood, down with The-Corrupt-Puppet-Government-of-Sanda-Ernan, down with the Fascist Rightists, down with Basically-Everything-in-the-Universe. And despite the oppressive heat, the orator didn't seem to be tiring. For her part, Kaly had simply stopped listening to the man's noise, or Vasquaaz's derisive snorts at the more venomous portions of his tirade. Her focus was on the crowd itself, and the rooflines.

The situation below their position was shaping up to be the perfect opportunity for the Loyalistas to strike and they had plenty of targets to choose from. In addition to a contingent of local riot police, a Military Police detachment had been loaned out from Claire d'Layne to bolster their numbers. Protests and riots had become an almost daily occurrence in the capitol, and the locals needed all the help they could get. Any of the uniformed personnel in the square were a potential victim of a sniper or a bomb attack.

"Shess," Margasdaater whispered. "I vish zese protestors vould talk about zomezing interezting. Like vhen ve vill get relieved to go piss—or maybe go piss and zen get zome fekking chow."

Kaly chuckled, but despite the fact that she heartily agreed, she didn't bother to respond. Lying on a rooftop wasn't fun under the best of circumstances, and the mention of food made her stomach growl, but she was willing to suffer a little discomfort if it ultimately meant keeping Sisterhood soldiers safe.

Besides which, Margasdaater was *always* hungry, and she *always* wanted to relieve herself. Despite her size, Kaly had secretly become positive that the Zommerlaandar possessed a bladder about the size of a subatomic particle.

She wasn't worried about the woman breaking discipline for a nanosecond though. Margasdaater was as disciplined a trooper as anyone she had ever served with. She would stay where she was, and keep doing her job, bladder or not. She just liked to hear herself bitch.

Just then, a group entering at the edge of the sqaure caught Kaly's eye, and she zoomed in on them. There were four men, some wearing jackets with hoods, and others with scarves tied loosely around their necks. At another spot, an identical group, was also making an appearance.

They were clearly troublemakers, she decided. Most of the protestors below her were genuinely concerned about the state of their nation, but in every gathering like this, there were always those who came looking for opportunities to commit mayhem. If everything went as it usually did, these same men would be the ones who would cause all the real trouble.

She sent a command to her scope and took images of them all, catching what she could of their features. Once she had them, she immediately forwarded the data on to the RSE techs at the Embassy, and the local police. The anarchists might find the 'fun' that they were looking for at everyone else's expense, but with luck, they would also be identified and arrested when it was all over.

Then Kaly noticed that one of the men had a backpack with him, and as he kneeled down and opened it, she dialed in, trying to discover what he was up to. At the same time, she let Command know what was going on. "Team Commander, Team 3; I have a male with a suspicious pack. He seems to be unloading something."

The problem was that the crowd, whether by happenstance, or deliberate design, was packing itself in all around him, and blocking her view. She tightened the zoom, but the only thing that she was able to confirm was that the crowd was taking something from his hands, and hiding it away under their clothing. She strongly doubted that they were free sandwiches, but she also knew that the local police wouldn't make a move against anyone just on mere suspicion. Things were too brittle in the square to risk that.

Major ebed Karri also understood this. "Team 3 maintain visual," she instructed. "Advise if you get eyes on any weapons."

This was exactly what Kaly was attempting to do. The suspicious males weren't making this easy however, and after a few moments, the man she had been watching concluded his mysterious activity and stood. Whatever he had given away wouldn't become known until the trouble really got going. Mouthing a curse, she resumed her general scan of the area, coming back to him as often as possible.

Meanwhile, the mood of the crowd had darkened. The leader up on the statue had increased in volume, and his tone was angrier and more provocative than ever. Things were about to step off.

But this was a problem for the riot police to deal with and Kaly kept her attention on the perimeter, searching for potential sniper hides, and anything that might signal a shooter; a glint from a scope, a silhouette on a roof, or something that seemed out of the ordinary. On that score at least, the square was relatively peaceful.

By now, the crowd had grown weary of chanting slogans, or listening to the speeches. As one, they began surging forwards towards the line of police, and here and there, a few of them began throwing things. Kaly couldn't tell what, but from the way the objects bounced off the police shields, it didn't appear to be anything more lethal than a few rocks, and possibly some garbage. She felt sorry for the women in the MP units below her. Getting pelted with trash wasn't her idea of real soldiering, or anything 'fun'.

Two full minutes of this abuse went by before she finally discovered what the men in the crowd had been distributing. When the mob became daring enough to come closer to the police line, a few of their number lit up the homemade firebombs and threw them.

These didn't have any real lethal effect in and of themselves. Aside from splashing their flaming contents on the ground, or shattering uselessly against the shields, none of the officers were actually harmed.

The firebombs did manage to accomplish one thing however. They caused the commander of the ETR riot police to lose their patience. At an order, the police surged forwards like a great green and black wave. Stun bombs went off before them, and clubs began to swing. In short order, the protestors were retreating, leaving only a few unfortunates behind to suffer at the hands of the policemen.

Watching the melee, Kaly was sickened by its primitive nature. It was like viewing a medieval battle from Old Gaia. While a pack of four officers beat a man senseless with their batons right below her, she firmly concluded that of all the weapons in the modern law enforcement arsenal, riot sticks were surely the cruelest of all. There was nothing gentle, or even remotely 'high-tech' about them. Even in the most skilled hands, they were no better than Neolithic clubs. Much to her revulsion, she also discovered that there was nothing that compared to the sound of riot sticks pummeling flesh and bone.

The protestors weren't long in responding with force of their own. Lengths of piping and heavy sticks which had been concealed by the protest signs taped to them, made their appearance, and their wielders counterattacked. In seconds, the two lines of combatants collided and the whole scene became a confused tangle of individual struggles and absolute mayhem.

Throughout it all, Kaly and her companions stayed right where they were, and so did the Sisterhood MP's. She knew that they desperately wanted to jump into the fight, but she was equally aware that their commander had no desire to inflame the locals against the Sisterhood any more than they already had. There was enough propaganda working against them as it was.

Kaly kept scanning the area, positive that something else was going to come their way. When it did occur, it caught everyone, even her, by surprise. There was no tell-tale report, or a flash to signal it, but suddenly one of the Sisterhood MP's fell, and then a second one dropped. On the Com, the alert went out right away, "Trooper down! Trooper down! We're under fire!"

The Sisterhood soldiers hunkered down or scurried for whatever cover they could find for themselves, and the ETR policemen who weren't distracted by the fighting did the same. Unfortunately, some of their brethren panicked and opened fire with their side arms in whatever direction they thought the attack was coming from.

Protestors scattered like leaves in the wind, leaving behind their injured to fend for themselves. Even though the riot as such was over, it had been replaced by something far worse—an active shooter with multiple targets of opportunity to choose from.

"Overwatch," Kaly demanded. "Anything?" Her scope was giving her nothing to target, and she was counting on the starships high above her to provide her with something.

They did. Their sensors had spotted the path of the bullets that had just been fired. The process was far from precise though; the agency of atmospheric interference and the extremely small size of the rounds themselves made any detection more a matter of estimation than anything else.

There was a long, terrible pause, and another Sisterhood trooper was wounded, making Kaly want to scream aloud in pure frustration—and shoot something. Finally, the starship got back with her.

"Team Three, we have a possible track 47 degrees to your right, approximately 12.19 meters up." As Vasquaaz brought her own rifle around to bear, Kaly swung Tatiana towards the coordinates. At first, she saw nothing new; just the same roofline and empty windows. Next, she switched over to infrared, and when this disappointed her, the bioplasmic band. Again, nothing.

She wasn't surprised. The chances were that they were dealing with another shooter equipped with one of their own ponchos. If he, or she, was any better than their predecessor, she knew that they would already be on the move, or would relocate very shortly.

"Overwatch," she said. "I want anything you have leaving the area near those coords."

Suddenly, an idea came to her, and she added, "Also give me a visual scan of everything coming out from *under* the location, overlay with a sewer map and key to any thermal or bio trace. I don't care if it's only a rata or kaatze!" It was just possible that the sniper would use the same tricks that she and her team had employed on Treya Angelaz to elude the Hriss.

The naval ships standing watch responded right away. Just as she had suspected, they found a trace of something larger than a rat that had moved through one of the sewers and surfaced onto a street several blocks away from the square. They were also tracking several vehicles that were in the process of leaving the area.

An SRU team responded to the sewer exit immediately, and police units quickly caught up with the suspicious vehicles and stopped them. In both cases, they came up empty handed.

The sniper had done exactly what she would have done in their place. They had used the Sisterhood's own tricks against it.

The only thing that the RSE had to show for all its troubles were the shooter's rifle and the poncho. These had been left behind at the foot of the ladder that the sniper had used to exit from the sewer.

There was also a card, which by now, had become all too familiar to the teams. It was the Angel's card, with the same motto, and ghoulish imagery.

A new Angel had been born. Within days, the Loyalistas took full advantage of this propaganda opportunity. Leaflets appeared nearly everywhere, celebrating the Angel's daring and their supposed 'immortality'. They also promised more killings in the name of 'justice'.

But when the Angel did strike again, it wasn't in the capitol. It was in Calitraavya. This was the second largest city in the ETR, in the Reganna Provensa, and at the opposite end of the Republic.

Although this made the Angel a problem for another group of SRU Teams, Kaly did manage to find comfort in two things. The first was that they had forced the Angel to leave the capitol, and the second, was that he or she would surely return when they thought that the Sisterhood's guard was down in Nuvo Bolivar.

Kaly and her fellow snipers would be waiting.

***

Undisclosed Location, Sinope District, Thermadon Val, Thermadon, Myrene System, Thalestris Elant, United Sisterhood of Suns, 1048.10|12|07:91:64

198

When Ellen n'Elemay was summoned again, her meeting was with Sister n'Avenal.

"The Redeemer was rather impressed with you," N'Avenal began. Her tone however indicated that she was not quite as overawed.

"He feels that you are the perfect person to be his Holy Sword of Justice. What I want to know, Sister Ellen, is exactly what you have in mind to fulfill such a grand destiny. The Church is tired of being on the run. We need to strike back."

"I agree, Sister," N'Elemay replied. "The Sisterhood must be taught to fear us."

"So you have some kind of plan?" N'Avenal asked, not bothering to mask her skepticism. So far, the *Societas Mariaa,* the Church's Counterintelligence and Special Actions Department, had only managed to pull off a few isolated bombings, and an attack on a police substation. None of these assaults had caused their opposition any great concern. Even with the help of the Bio Action Army, their enemy was simply too large and too powerful for these events to amount to anything more than minor annoyances.

What they needed, N'Elemay knew, was something so shocking that it would capture the attention of every citizen in the Sisterhood, and force them to confront their sins. Something both bloody and spectacular.

"Not yet," N'Elemay admitted. "I do have some high-value targets in mind that could radically change the equation however. I'll need a little more time to evaluate them."

"Time, Sister, is not something that we have a lot of," N'Avenal countered. "Our situation in Thermadon is growing increasingly precarious. The RSE has already managed to shut down several of our safe houses, and they are hot on the trail of our technical people. It won't be long before they will be able to keep us out of the omniplex and deny us places to hide. I intend for us to leave well before that eventuality."

"I understand, Sister," N'Elemay responded. "All I need is a few days, and I'll have something for you that will put them on the defensive. I promise."

N'Avenal regarded her doubtfully. "Very well, what can the *Societas* do to help?"

"At the moment, nothing," the ex-Marauder replied. "I have everything that I need right here." She held up a plastic rectangle about the same size as her palm. It had a lanyard attached to it, and a clear plastiglass eye set in its center. Around this was the legend, *"Thermadon Val; City of a Thousand Years, City of a Thousand Wonders."*

N'Avenal recognized it as one of the disposable hologuides that were available to any tourist visiting the capitol. "*That* is all you need?" she asked.

"Yes, Sister. For now."

At this, N'Avenal rose, smoothing down the folds of her robe. "I will await your report," she said. Their meeting was at an end.

As they entered the hallway together, N'Elemay saw Sister n'Aida, accompanied by an acolyte, and coming the opposite way. Dressed in a distinctive blood-red robe just like the one the Redeemer now wore, she was his right hand in all things, and just a step below him in sanctity.

Their eyes met. N'Aida's gaze had a soul-penetrating power that N'Elemay felt immediately in the very depths of her being. Sister n'Aida *knew* her, and on the deepest possible level.

The woman smiled at her as they passed, and reflexively, N'Elemay crossed herself. Now there was no question in her mind whatsoever about their final victory. Nothing, not even Shaitan himself, could stand against such a powerful light.

Invigorated by the encounter, N'Elemay left the safe house. Three trains, and three identity changes later, she had visited all of her potential targets. Her last stop proved to be everything that she had been hoping for, and she uttered up a silent prayer of thanks to Mother Mari.

But as she watched the busy holiday crowds, the demon of doubt tried to rear its ugly head. *These are just innocent women,* it whispered. *To kill them would be a sin.*

Trying not to listen to its clever lies, N'Elemay forcefully reminded herself of her mission and her commitment. Although the women around her seemed innocent, they *were* the enemy, even if they were too steeped in their own sins to realize it. They had willingly supported the same State that had brought her own people so much pain and death.

And they would have to pay the price for their blind obedience to evil. This was God's plan for them. To be sacrificed to his greater glory.

Finding her strength once more, she continued with her task, evaluating her surroundings and borrowing on her training to spot its weaknesses. The waste receptacles scattered all around the main floor immediately offered up some attractive possibilities. Although quite a number of them were the type that could detect explosive devices, and even contain their blasts, many more were of the 'dumb' variety, having been put in place to service the increased holiday demand.

These extra trash cans would remain for the duration of the season; they had been decorated to celebrate the event and it was highly unlikely that they would be removed before it ended.

She also noted that none of the women around her, including the station staff, seemed to be paying much attention to what went into them. She took an image of one receptacle using the camera function of her psiever, and then walked on.

Further in, on a nearby bench, she spotted someone's carrypack, and after watching it for several minutes, she realized that no one from security was coming along to inspect it. This brought a deprecatory grin to her face. Clearly security had grown very lax. Even with the Daughters of Eve and the Bio Action Army attacking it, the Sisterhood was taking its safety for granted. They would pay for such arrogance.

She took another image and considered what an unattended bag like this offered her--and immediately discovered the flaw. There was always the chance that a passerby, or someone from housekeeping, would pick up an abandoned carrypack and move it.

She had to look elsewhere for what she needed, she realized.

A few minutes later, she found it, and her plan solidified. It was as if an angel had come down from on high and whispered the ideas into her ears. Everything was clear now. Despite her moments of doubt, God had patiently shown her the way.

***

While Ellen n'Elemay was busy formulating the details of her attack, the Redeemer and Shandra n'Aida were enjoying each other's company. They clasped hands and shared a silent, mental communion that none of the humans around them could hear.

How long has it been, sister? the Redeemer asked. *Twenty millennia? More?*

At least, she answered. *Too long.*

Angered by the intrusion of a Drow'voi scientific probe, the Great Mind of their home galaxy, Andromeda, had sent them forth to destroy the interlopers, right along with every other sentient being that infested the Milky Way. The Andromeda's Great Mind had always hated its neighbor, and the Voices were the weapon that it had intended to use to eliminate its nemesis once and for all. But the Drow'voi had defeated Andromeda's children by sacrificing their own lives, and the Voices had been forced into hibernation.

Now, their time had come again and even though the Drow'voi were no more, Mikal and his counterpart still had every intention of carrying out their original mission. The Voices had long memories and no sense of

201

forgiveness. That was something for lesser beings, not creatures of pure thought like themselves.

I would keep you here with me, by my side, Mikal thought. *But I cannot. The time has come for us to reawaken the Third and complete our mission.*

Good, the Voice within N'Aida returned. *These hairless apes sicken me. I would see them eliminated, and have your company all to myself.*

Patience, sister, Mikal replied. *There will be time enough for us, once this galaxy has been turned into a graveyard.*

N'Aida knew that he was right and offered no rebuttal. The mission came first. She released his hands and he turned from her to the Sisters who had been attending them.

"I have been granted a great vision," he announced. "God has shown me the way to defeat our enemies forever. The key to this is located on a world called Storm." He beckoned to Sister n'Avenal.

"Do you know this place?" he asked her.

"Yes, Lord," N'Avenal replied. "It is a remote world in the Sagana Elant."

"That is where Sister n'Aida will be going next. She will leave here tomorrow, and when she arrives on Storm, you will see to it that the Faithful make a place for her there.'

"You will also send word to all True Believers to make ready to undertake a holy pilgrimage to that place. Sister n'Aida will meet them when they arrive, and she will guide them to what God has shown me."

"Lord," N'Avenal began to say. "Is that wise? At this time? With the RSE hunting us--?"

"God's will must be done," he declared, and as he did so, N'Avenal felt a pressure between her eyes. A second later, it was gone, right along with all of her objections.

"God's will must be done," she repeated.

The Redeemer smiled. "The path will be long and arduous, and I will tell you now that many will fall along the way. But one of them, whom God finds worthy, will be raised up by him to become my left hand just as Sister n'Aida is now my right. Together, we will go forth and smite down Shaitan and all of his accursed works."

The Sisters collectively crossed themselves. "God's will must be done," they chanted.

That evening, they held mass and the Redeemer himself led the service. Shandra n'Aida had no interest in the ritual however. Instead, she watched Sister Janneta and observed her carefully. When she was certain of what she had sensed, she sent a message to the Redeemer using their special mind-speak.

She is the one, she told him. *I can feel it.*

I know. I have known for a long time. We will need to tell N'Avenal, he replied. *She will know how to handle this properly.*

I still don't understand why you are bothering with all this, brother, N'Aida thought back. *What need have we of such silly maneuvers? Or this primitive religion for that matter?*

Resources, sister, he answered. *These creatures actually believe in their illusions, and because of that, they will do anything for us, including sending shiploads of themselves to Storm. Keeping them, and their enemies, certain that our intentions are limited to a few small attacks, will ensure that none of them ever come to suspect our true intentions.*

And Ellen n'Elemay will be especially useful to us once the time comes to seize our objective. She will see to our safety and even lay down her very life if the need arises. All that loyalty like that requires is the right combination of words, and a few toys for these apes to play with. What harm can there be in providing that?

Again, N'Aida could not argue with her sibling. His logic was flawless. As ridiculous and backwards as they were, she now understood why they needed the Marionites and why she didn't need to worry over N'Elemay's pathetic little program of terror. In the end, what they had in mind for the galaxy would make anything that she managed to accomplish seem like what it really was: mere child's play. Anything, even this silliness, was worth that.

She contacted N'Avenal. The *Praepositus Generalis* had long suspected the existence of a mole in their group, and although she was surprised by who it had turned out to be, N'Avenal accepted it, and relayed the information to N'Elemay immediately.

It is Janneta, her message said. *You know what to do--N'Avenal.*

***

N'Avenal's revelation only served to confirm N'Elemay's own instincts about Janneta. She didn't have the powers that the Redeemer or Sister n'Aida possessed, but she had still sensed the woman's duplicity.

It hadn't been any one detail that had alerted her to her treachery. Rather, it had been a collection of tiny betrayals that she had observed over time; the way that Janneta looked away from her at just the wrong moments, the strain in her voice when certain subjects came up, and small, but discernable hesitations.

She also knew exactly what to do about her, and how to go about it.

Later that evening, when the woman left to deliver a message to one of the other cells in the city, N'Elemay followed her. Just as she had expected, Janneta stopped in the middle of her journey and slipped into an alley. Halfway down its length, she pried open a loose brick, and furtively inserted something into the space behind it.

This was all of the proof that N'Elemay required. When Janneta resealed the cache and began to rise, she stepped in and looped a wire garrote around her neck.

Their struggle was a brief one. After only fifteen seconds, Janneta lapsed into unconsciousness and then death.

Ignoring the stench of feces, N'Elemay waited a moment longer, and then opened the wire, releasing the corpse. As it flopped onto the ground, she lowered herself onto her knees and carefully searched the hiding place. When her fingers found the plastipaper note, she tucked it into her pocket, and moved off into the shadows. With their spy dead, the RSE would be as blind as everyone else to her plans, and just as unprepared.

Sentos Antoniyo da Compasionya Cemetery, Nevanas District, Nuvo Bolivar, Magdala Provensa, Esteral Terrana Rapabla, 1048.10|19|00:83:33

Of all the locations that Kaly had ever served her nation in, the very last one that she had ever expected to find herself in was a Christian graveyard, in the middle of the night. But thanks to two children who had spotted some people digging up one of the graves, and a policeman with Rightist sympathies, there she was. She was lying on her belly on the cold, wet earth, and using a headstone for concealment. Thirty meters away from her position, two Loyalistas had excavated another grave and were burying a crate inside of it. The container was filled with weapons.

She dearly wanted to shoot them both, but her orders prohibited this. The Major, and Ben Di had made it abundantly clear that her role was only to observe. Vasquaaz and Margasdaater, lying on the ground next to her, were just as eager, but they too maintained their vigil and let the terrorists go about their work.

Once the two men had finished with their macabre task, and were safely out of earshot, Ben Di sent the signal and Team 201 and 265 rose from their hiding places and made for the cache. There, they broke out collapsible entrenching tools and started digging.

It didn't take long for them to find what they were looking for. The cases had not been buried deeply; the Loyalistas had covered them over with just enough earth to prevent casual discovery, but still allow for easy retrieval.

There were a total of two armored containers in the cache. One held half a dozen AE-14 energy rifles with spare battery packs, as well as an equal number of AE-42A pistols. The other contained Republican Army uniforms, field aid kits and all the components needed to turn salvaged munitions into a workable bomb. It certainly wasn't the largest hoard that her team had ever discovered, but it was still substantial enough to justify the night's work.

Unlike their previous finds, this one would not be destroyed in place though. The Major and Ben Di had other things in mind for it. While Kaly stood by, feeling a little like a medieval witch gathered with her sisters for a midnight sabbat, Ben Di opened her shoulder pack. Inside were all the ingredients that she needed for her mischief, and adding a silencing finger to her lips for dramatic effect, she went straight to work.

The uniforms received tiny tracking devices which were inserted into their seams. The aid kit also received a tracker, but most of the bomb-making materials were left alone--with the exception of the initiator devices. These were Republican Army issue, and they were swapped out for inert versions that looked exactly like the originals.

Next, the Aran focused her attention on the energy weapons. Each one had its battery case replaced and several of them lost the all-important chips that allowed them to function. Without these components, they were nothing more than useless conglomerations of plastic and metal.

When she finished, everything was put back exactly the way it had been found and the team reburied the cases, and quietly left the area. All of them, and especially Margasdaater and her opposite number with the *Specia*, *Soldada* Mendaz, had malign smiles painted on their faces. Now all they had to do was wait, and let events take their course.

It didn't take long. Two nights later, Claire d'Layne was attacked again. As before, shoulder-fired rockets tried to score hits on its buildings, and small arms fire sought out the troopers in their trenches. But on two occasions, the weapons that the Loyalistas were using exploded, killing their wielder and injuring everyone else around them. Battery packs filled with explosives tended to have this unfortunate side-effect.

The disaster did not end there either. The next morning, the Republican Army officer who had furnished the Loyalistas with these weapons was gunned down in front of his home in full view of his family. This time, the energy rifles worked properly.

With his death, another source of weapons had been eliminated, but not all of them by any means. One of these, which had been overlooked for the last two years, would prove this to the Sisterhood's regret.

Aljofar District, Nuvo Bolivar, Magdala Provensa, Esteral Terrana Rapabla, 1048.10|19|07:08:45

Reesy was surprised when Roza and a group of men pulled up to the safe house in a 'lectri and began unloading boxes. She hadn't expected to see the woman so soon, and from her serious expression, she could tell that something very important was in the offing. Right away, she moved to help them as they brought the containers into the living area.

"What is it? What's happening?"

"A blow against the Sisterhood," Roza declared, her eyes alight with passion. "The General has called for an all-out offensive against the invaders, and we are going to be one of the first units to strike! We're going to show them that their best isn't good enough against determined patriots!"

She opened up the nearest case and waved Reesy over to inspect the contents.

Reesy gasped and looked up at her. "How can I help? Please, I don't want to be left out of this!"

Roza closed the case. "Don't worry, *meya pica ermanyaa*. You won't be. Migehl has an important job picked out just for you."

***

The assault shuttles took off in tandem, rising quickly and heading east, away from Claire d'Layne. Several kilometers out, they changed course, turning northward and flying out over the rugged Santo Annya Mountains, hoping to fool the watchers that were below them.

Several minutes later, the shuttles altered direction again and came in low over the northwestern section of Nuvo Bolivar. Their target was coming up fast, and Kaly readied herself.

Intel had been receiving whispers that something big was getting ready to step off, and this had coincided with a report of a large concentration of Loyalistas who had gathered together for some kind of meeting. There was the strong possibility that some extremely high-value assets would be present at this assembly, and it sounded like the perfect opportunity for a raid.

Which also meant that it could just as easily prove to be a trap. The teams had been hurting the Loyalistas, and the rebels had even placed a bounty on their heads. With such a highly charged atmosphere, everyone was on edge...

...Reesy watched as the assault shuttles flew towards her position, and spoke into her air phone. "Targets confirmed, times two," she said.

There was a pause, and then her listeners responded. "We see them. Keep eyes on."

"Got it. Eyes on," she responded.

The shuttles passed over the invisible line of demarcation, and Reesy's pulse started to race. For several seconds, nothing happened and she began to wonder if the ambush was going to be called off after all...

...Three seconds to landing, Ben Di made an announcement. "Overwatch just reported that our targets have moved into positions on the roofs to either side of our flight path. This LZ is hot!"

A cold chill ran up Kaly's spine. It was an ambush after all.

At the same moment, she heard the distinctive 'thump, thump' of countermeasure pods being launched. But they were too low, she realized. They wouldn't have enough time to deploy properly.

Suddenly, something streaked up from the ground and flew past the sally port. It was followed by a loud explosion, and Kaly's stomach lurched as the shuttle abruptly lost altitude.

The machine belly landed onto the street with a bone-jarring impact. A nanosecond later, thick, acrid smoke began to fill the troop compartment, and she felt a blistering wave of heat blossoming up to her right.

We've been hit by some kind of rocket, she thought. *We're on fire!* It was a troopers worst nightmare.

"Bail Out!" someone yelled.

Kaly grabbed her rifle, punched the release clip on her seat harness, and let herself fall forwards. Hitting the deck, she crawled towards the sally port. When she reached it, she threw herself out, spilling onto the pavement. For a moment, all she could do was crouch there on her hands and knees, puking out the fumes and gasping for air.

Then asphalt began to splinter and shatter all around her. Forgetting her seared lungs, she scrambled to her feet and started to run, trying to activate her suits camouflage mode.

But instead of bending the light around her and offering concealment, it only flickered, and failed. Kaly didn't have any time to puzzle out the reason for this malfunction however. She was still under fire and she pelted for the nearest sanctuary. This was the door way of a single story house directly across from her. It was only then, hiding behind the meager cover of the doorframe, that she hazarded a glance back towards the shuttles.

The machine on point had been completely destroyed, and the one that she had been in was belching ugly black smoke from the troop compartment. As she took this in, something came rolling out of the sally port. It was on fire, and only when it sprouted legs and stood, was she able to recognize it.

It was their *Liverna* 'bot. Impervious to the flames, it swiveled its oval head around and began to fire at something on the roof, up and behind her. There was an agonized cry, and the 'bot launched a grenade towards the sound. The explosion sent pieces of masonry showering down all around her and she cringed, hugging the doorway as the debris rattled off her helmet and bounced into the street.

When she looked up again, the 'bot was moving down the road, engaging another target. Then, through a break in the smoke, she spotted Ben Di, T'Jinna and Margasdaater. The door gunner from the shuttle was with them.

They were across the street, using a 'lectri for cover. As they made eye contact, Ben Di flashed her a grin and gave her a quick thumbs up before she and her companions started shooting down the road.

Kaly briefly considered making a dash for them, but another spray of gunfire tearing up the asphalt changed her mind. She knew that she would never make it.

She also realized that the pilot and co-pilot were not with her friends. Neither were Vasquaaz and the two male *Specia* soldiers who had been riding with them.

A movement on the rooftop across from her cut off any speculations about their whereabouts, and she fired at the shape instinctively. The Loyalista quickly ducked back out of view and she wasn't even certain that she'd scored a hit.

Looking around her for a less vulnerable position, she spied the mouth of an alley. Reaching it would require a short sprint through the open, but it was better than remaining where she was.

In the process of deciding this, she finally discovered what had happened to the pilot and co-pilot of her shuttle. They were still inside the disabled machine. She could see them through the canopy windows.

The co-pilot was unconscious, and her partner was desperately trying to free her from her straps. As the woman tugged at the restraints, she looked up through the broken plastiglass and met Kaly's gaze.

Her eyes were filled with desperation, and hopelessness. She knew the same thing that Kaly did; that she and her companion were doomed.

Then the cockpit exploded, turning the space into a roiling mass of flame. Bits of plastiglass and metal sprayed everywhere, and Kaly ducked and covered her face.

This is what saved her life. The Loyalista had reappeared on the roof line, and barely missed hitting her upper body with a burst from his chemical weapon.

Instantly, she threw herself down, and returned fire, driving the rebel back. The moment that he was out of view, she was up and running towards the alley for all she was worth…

…All hell had broken loose around Reesy's position. At least half of the Sisterhood troopers had survived the ambush, and now they were furiously raking the surrounding area with gunfire from whatever cover they had found for themselves. Doorways, parked 'lectris, and even the curbing, became fortresses as the invaders counterattacked.

One of them shouldered a rocket and fired it up towards the nearest roof top. The projectile hit the parapet and went off with a blinding flash, sending a shower of bricks flying into the night sky.

Reesy couldn't tell if any of her comrades had been up there, but she knew that if they had been, they were probably dead or wounded. Then, over the sharp cracking of gunfire and more explosions, she heard the order on her air phone for everyone to withdraw.

The fight was moving her way and a group of assault shuttles had been spotted leaving Claire d'Layne. It was heading straight towards them at top speed. In minutes, the entire area would be saturated with the enemy and escape would become next to impossible.

Hands trembling, Reesy disconnected the phone, stuffed it into her pack, and ran for the stairway. Her ultimate destination was an alley only a few streets over, where a 'lectri was waiting to drive her and some of the others away.

The rest of her group would make their escapes using the service tunnels under the street, or by fading into the warren of alleys and back yards all around them. With luck, everyone would get away, leaving the Sisterhood with nothing to shoot at but thin air and shadows.

Her feet hit the ground floor and she pounded through the building to the rear exit. Shoving it open, she ran out…

…Kaly backpedaled into the alley, firing down the street in the general direction of the ambush. Her fatigues reeked of burned fabric, and a portion of her arm and a leg were finally letting her know that they had been burned in the flaming shuttle. The pain wasn't overpowering though. For the moment at least, adrenaline and terror were providing plenty of anesthetic.

On the Com, it was complete pandemonium, with shouts for air support, calls for medics, and alerts about enemy targets. One voice managed to reach her above all the chaos however. It was Margasdaater.

"Kaly! Overwatch sez zat zere iz zomeone coming out of za building right next to you!"

Kaly saw the target at the same time. It registered on her englobed feed as the bright red outline of a human, with an object in their left hand. It was a pack of some kind.

Satchel charge! her mind screamed. The terrorist was running out with a bomb, straight at her.

Then the door burst open, and the figure appeared.

Kaly pulled the trigger of her submachinegun. The burst stitched a bloody line straight up the Loyalista's torso. The insurgent spasmed, hit the wall, and slid liquidly to the ground, leaving a bright red trail of blood behind her…

…Reesy couldn't breathe, and for some reason, she wasn't able to get her legs to work either. Her vision had also narrowed down to a long tunnel and a grey nothingness was eating away at its edges. She could still see the uniformed trooper though, and despite the distortions of fear, anger and battle rage, she recognized her face. It was her sister, Juana.

Why is Juana here? she wondered. *Why is she pointing a gun at me?* And why was it so hard for her to catch her breath all of a sudden? The answers eluded her as the world around her transformed.

She was ten years old again, and she had just fallen out of the tree near their home and injured herself. She tried to beg Juana not to tell their mother about the accident, but the words would not come to her lips.

Somehow though, Juana still seemed to hear her, and smiled. Then, high in the sky, over her sister's shoulder, Reesy saw it. The bright, beautiful star that had always shone down on their home. Their real home-- the one that she had come to believe had been lost to her forever. The School.

Everything was going to be okay, she realized. She and Juana were going to go there, together. Back to the School and happier times. Everything was going to be all right after all…

…Covering the Loyalista with her weapon, Kaly nudged the satchel out of reach with her boot. She knew that this was a stupid thing to do even as she did it; the charge inside could have been set off just by moving the bag, but right then she was more concerned that the terrorist, in her last few moments of life, would make a grab for it, and kill them both.

Then she saw what it really contained. A pair of field glasses had spilled out along with a handset for an air-phone. There wasn't a bomb anywhere in the pack, or even a weapon.

Ben Di and the others came up the alley. "Kaly? Are you all right?"

She nodded affirmatively, realizing as she did so, whom she had just killed. Despite changing her hair color, and wearing it differently, it was the young woman that they had been sent to arrest just a few weeks earlier. It was Reesy Hernan. There was no doubt about it.

The sight of her mirror image lying there dead at her feet was unsettling, and for a moment, Kaly was forcefully reminded of the fact that they were fighting their own kind. But an enemy was an enemy, she reminded herself, and they still had a battle to win. Leaving the corpse where it was, she followed Ben Di and her Teammates towards the sound of the fighting.

***

Jaw clenched, Sarah watched the firefight conclude on the monitors in the COMINT center. Although Reesy Hernan's tracking device had alerted them to the gathering, none of the intel they had received had even hinted at the presence of the Harpy missiles. Instead of catching the terrorists by surprise, the Sisterhood had been the one caught in the net.

The Loyalistas would pay dearly for their little 'victory', she vowed. For now however, she had to concentrate on containing the situation.

A group of Valkyrie fighters had responded, and they were hunting down and killing the insurgents faster than they could run. This mollified her somewhat. On another screen she saw that Captain n'Kyla's killer had finally met her end.

The display showed the alley, and Reesy's body, as seen from space. A pop-up image floated in the corner, displaying the match that the AI's had found between the corpse and the young woman's prison picture. There was no doubt that the two shots depicted the same person.

"Well, Amandra," she said over her shoulder, "It seems that Captain n'Kyla has been avenged at last. And from the look of it, the cell that Hernan was part of won't offer us any further trouble either."

"Yes," Sa'Tela replied darkly. "It's a pity that it had to cost us so much to accomplish that."

"Indeed. We shall have to see about bringing things back into balance," Sarah replied.

***

Alvaraada waited until the Sisterhood hovertank had passed overhead before he risked sitting up and glancing at his wrist chrono. As much as he wanted to, the numbers on the display couldn't be disputed. Roza, Reesy, and the others he had been waiting for, were late.

Too late for the delay to mean anything more than the very worst. He had heard the last few desperate transmissions as the Sisterhood soldiers had counterattacked, and now he had to admit the terrible truth. The ambush had failed and they were all dead.

With hands moving like someone half-asleep or drugged, he started the 'lectri, and pulled out of the shadows. It took all of his will to focus himself enough to drive away from the area.

He didn't go back to the safe house, or even his small shop. Instead, he did something he hadn't done in over two decades of sobriety. He sought out the nearest store, bought himself a bottle of *Vigorosa,* and parked where he knew he wouldn't be bothered. Then he drank down its contents, alternately toasting the memory of his fallen comrades, and cursing the Sisterhood to every hell he could think of. That, and weeping like a child.

Eventually, the darkness took pity on him and gathered him in its embrace. Alvaraada went into it willingly; he knew that the morning would come, and that he would be compelled to carry on the fight for another day.

And if he were truly blessed, there was even the chance that he would be allowed to die fighting for his nation. For now though, all that mattered, all that he wanted for himself, was oblivion.

***

Team 201 didn't make it back to their barracks for another 72 hours. Right on the heels of the ambush, fierce fighting broke out throughout many of the ETR's major population centers, and Nuvo Bolivar received the brunt of it. The Loyalistas had attacked in large numbers and dozens of important locations were assaulted, not the least of which had been Claire d'Layne. The base had fought off a series of suicide bombers trying to breach its gates, followed by multiple rocket attacks and small arms fire. Even *Jyon Vaargas* had been forced to close when the insurgents had begun firing indiscriminately at spaceships attempting to take off or land.

One area of the capitol had been particularly hard hit, and had struck back with equal viciousness. This had been in the Dann neighborhoods where the local gangs had engaged the Loyalistas in bloody street fights, exacting a stiff price from them for their trespassing.

Kaly had personally witnessed the gruesome aftermath of these slaughters. To serve as a warning against any future incursions, the gangs had left their enemy's corpses hanging on the lampposts all around the limits of the Dho Haak.

She had also encountered something even darker. At the edge of one of the capitol's more remote suburbs, the Team had walked by a large open pit, filled with what the Republican soldiers had claimed were the bodies of Loyalistas killed during the fighting.

The only thing wrong about all this had been the fact that many of these supposed 'insurgents' had had their hands tied behind their backs, and the majority of them had been shot in the head or the neck. From behind.

The dirt on their knees, and the few that were still wearing their blindfolds hadn't helped to support the lie. Or that many of the victims had been too young, or too old, to have ever fought anyone. The pit was a place for the flies, for death, and for evil deeds that would never be redressed.

By the time that she and her team stumbled in for their debrief, martial law was in effect in the ETR. Most of the major fires were either out, or under control, and there were only isolated pockets of resistance that the ETR Army and Sisterhood Marines were still in the process of rooting out, including and espcially, in the Aljofar District.

Major ebed Karri and Lieutenant ben Soolee were waiting for them, looking just as tired as they were. The officers had been in the Embassy's COMINT center around the clock, directing the action and calling in supporting strikes, but they had still taken the time to change into fresh uniforms, and had kaafra and hot food waiting.

Instead of leaving the debrief for the PTS system to handle, they conducted it themselves, and afterwards, went on to share what they had learned. Counting numbers alone, it had been a clear victory for the Sisterhood and the Ernan government. Hundreds of Loyalistas had been killed, with thousands more wounded, and in custody. In addition, tons of illegal weapons and explosives had been captured and destroyed.

Despite these successes though, the event had still dealt the Sisterhood forces a hard blow, and nowhere was this felt more keenly than among the SRU Teams, and especially Kaly's unit. Up to then, they had never suffered a single casualty.

Now twelve women and two men were dead. Most of them had been victims of the rocket that had hit the lead assault shuttle, but five had perished in Kaly's ship; *Cabo* Vasquaaz, *Sarjenta* Pera, *Soldada* Mendaz, Warrant Officer Judi n'Sali and her hapless co-pilot, Corporal Tarra t'Kim.

These were all people that Kaly had known, and worked with. N'Sali and T'Kim had flown her team on many of their Ops, and although she hadn't grown as close to the *Specia* soldiers as she had with the *Garda* fighters, their loss still cut deeply. The only 'good' thing about any of it--if anyone could have even employed such a term--was that everyone had died quickly. Vasquaaz and the men had been trapped in their harnesses, and

213

asphyxiation had claimed them. N'Sali and T'Kim had died instantly in the cockpit explosion. It was cold consolation, but Kaly had learned by this point not to expect anything kinder from the universe when it came to war.

But she wasn't half as affected by all this as Margasdaater was. The woman listened to the Major's report with a stoic professionalism, and when the meeting ended, headed straight for her rack, saying nothing to anyone. She didn't need to. The entire team knew what she was going through.

During their tour, Margasdaater and Vasquaaz had become friends, and there had been whispers that their relationship had gone even further than that. And all through the street fighting, the Zommerlaandar hadn't talked about the woman's death to anyone. They, in turn, had given her all the privacy that she had required.

With the mission over, it was obvious that she was finally letting her guard down and coming to terms with her loss. This was something that every veteran learned to do; when the bolts were ripping by, they did their jobs. They held on, shut down their weaknesses and pushed them into a quiet little corner where they couldn't interfere with the task of staying alive.

Until the shooting was over, and it was finally safe to feel something. That was when everything caught up.

Kaly let Margasdaater have a few minutes to herself before she went to her. She found her in her rack, nursing a bottle of Aqqa, and wrapped in her quilted *Opfgaveyr* blanket. On Astrid's motherworld, the families of servicewomen made these 'Going Away' blankets to remind their loved ones of home, and for times like this, when they needed the comfort. She had gathered it around herself, and looked up at Kaly with pain-filled eyes.

"You know, Kaly," she said, her voice distorted from the alcohol, "I never zhought zat zings vould be like zis. Za vomyn who went n'zen came back--zey told me, but I didn't listen." She slammed her big fist onto the bed. "I never *fekking* listened. I zhould haf listened to zem."

Kaly nodded, recalling the warning she had been given on the day she had decided to enlist in the Marines.

"You vant vhat I've had?" the veteran had challenged, *"You vant maybe a little blood? A little killing, zaat it? You think you can handle zaat, little girl?"* She had said yes, and quite rightly, the trooper had laughed in her face, calling her a fool. The trooper had been right.

"I never zhought about za friends zat I'd lose," Margasdaater said bitterly, taking another pull from the bottle. "It vas just all vun *big* adventure. Not zis shess." She looked into Kaly's eyes with a deep, mournful expression. "Now I zink zat maybe itz gonna be time vor me to go home zoon--and ztay zere."

At last, her voice broke completely. "I miss her, Kaly. I miss zem all."

Kaly didn't know what to say. Nothing felt like it would be enough. In the end, all she could do was put her arm around the big woman, and hold her.

Claire d'Layne Naval Base, Nuvo Bolivar, Magdala Provensa, Esteral Terrana Rapabla, 1048.10|22|06:25:25

Team 201, and several of the other units that had been in the fighting, gathered in the Mess Hall. They had come there to observe a ritual which by now had become all too familiar. The same Marine who had done the original work on Kaly's nanotat was waiting for them with her equipment, and she added the names of Vasquaaz, Pera and Mendaz to Kaly's arm, along with the two pilots.

But Kaly had one more thing that she wanted the woman to make for her. She had seen it on some of the Marine Troopers around the base. It was far less elaborate than her other nanotat, and she had it put on her forearm where anyone could see it. It was only a single word; *"Invadiya"*, Invader.

When her turn came, Margasdaater asked for the same thing, and so did the others. And even though Major ebed Karri and Lieutenant ben Soolie frowned at the new tattoos when they came in for their briefing, they didn't make anyone remove them. Despite the fact that RSE policy specifically forbade imagery like this, the officers understood the anger behind it, and wisely, let the violation pass.

As it was, they had more important things on their minds than cultural insensitivity. The results from the techs had come back.

The failure of their fighting suits to go into camouflage mode had finally been determined, and the news was not good. The Loyalistas had employed a homemade dampening field to confuse the circuits, and the Major went on to warn them that they would have to expect the same thing to occur in the future.

That, and being shot at by their own ordinance. The Sisterhood's largess had come back to haunt it; the lead shuttle had been hit by a surplus Harpy missile, left over from the so-called 'War for Humanity'. Hundreds of these anti-armor rockets had gone missing during the conflict, and now, much to their regret, they had discovered where some of them had actually wound up.

The only reason that Kaly and her Team had even survived had been because their enemy had had only one Harpy to work with. To attack both shuttles, the Loyalistas had been forced to employ the cheaper, and more readily available ETR counterpart. It didn't pack near as much punch as the Harpy did, and the assault shuttle's armor had absorbed most of the blast.

From this point forwards, the teams would have to assume that they might come under attack by Harpy missiles, and flight crews would be making certain to employ appropriate countermeasures. A grim milestone had been reached in the conflict.

***

Although 'bots, working alongside Marine Engineers were well into the process of reconstructing the Embassy, the shock of the attack had not worn off on anyone, even Sarah. Since that day, she had taken to sleeping in the COMINT Center and eating all of her meals there. On her orders, Maya had done the same, although far less willingly. She still didn't care for the dark operations chamber, and living there all around the clock only made it seem that much worse.

Dining was even less pleasant. Despite the fact that Aideen n'Neala still cheerfully brought them their meals, it simply wasn't the same experience under artificial lighting. It didn't even taste the same as far as Maya was concerned.

Naturally, Sarah didn't notice this lack of ambiance, and when Maya shuffled into the main conference room for their morning tea and breakfast, the woman was already well into her meal and waved her in with more than her usual enthusiasm.

"Maya!" she exclaimed, "Come in! Come in! I have good news for you today!" A trio of holos were floating in the air over the woman's plate, and another one waited off to her side, next to the teapot.

As Maya took her seat, she recognized the women in the images, and their location. Lieutenant sa'Tela, and Rabartya Vaasco were speaking with Mariaa Estovaal in one of the interrogation rooms two floors below them.

Even with the sound off, she could tell who had the upper hand; Vaasco lounged in her chair, looking like a kaatze that had just eaten a baby bird, and Sa'Tela was striding around the table, waving her hand in the air dramatically as she spoke to Estovaal.

Estovaal didn't seem to notice. Shoulders slumped, she was looking down at a half dozen documents spread out on the table before her with an expression of absolute despair. A second holo displayed the documents themselves, but Maya didn't need to refer to it. They were the same overdue bills that she and Saantoz had fished out of the trash.

"I really have to congratulate you, "Sarah said between mouthfuls of toast and sips of her tea. "That woman was a hard case to crack for any new agent, and despite yourself, you managed to achieve success. Thanks to your information--"she paused to refill her cup, "--our good friend, Ms. Vaasco saw an opportunity to intervene, and purchased her home loan.'

"Now, all Estovaal has to do is give us the information we want and she will get to keep her residence. She will even be granted a small stipend for her time and trouble. Naturally, she has agreed to fully cooperate."

Maya had been about to drink her own tea, but put it down, suddenly feeling ill. This was as 'downright low' as glass dealing, and she hated herself for the part that she had played in it. She also didn't hide this fact from Sarah.

Reading her, Sarah merely shrugged dismissively. "Feel whatever guilt you wish, Maya. The fact is, that we now have a valuable conduit into her employer's activities, and in the end, that is all that really counts.'

"But enough of this. I have something even more important to announce. I have just received word from my mother. She is about to marry and we have been invited to the ceremony. So, start packing your things. We leave this afternoon."

"What about all our ops?" Maya asked, hooking her thumb in the general direction of the COMINT center.

"I will be leaving Lieutenant sa'Tela and Ms. Vaasco in charge," Sarah responded. "They will provide me with updates, and carry on until we can return. As for ourselves, we will be making a stopover in Thermadon. I have some important business there at our new headquarters building, so make certain that your uniform is presentable."

"Yes ma'am," Maya responded, sketching a deliberately sloppy salute. With a final, guilty glance at the ongoing interrogation, she abandoned her breakfast, and Mariaa Estovaal, to their respective fates, and left to get started on her packing.

Jyon Vaargaz National Spaceport, Nuvo Bolivar, Magdala Provensa, Esteral Terrana Rapabla, 1048.10|22|07:08:31

Gilded by the late afternoon sunlight, the *JUDI* was a welcome sight to Maya's eyes. So were the familiar figures of Captain bel Lissa and Zara. They were waiting for them at the bottom of the merchanter's cargo ramp, and waved as the 'limo pulled up.

"Heyas girl!" Zara called, and the moment Maya was out of the vehicle, she came up and gave her a hug.

"Look at you," Bel Lissa said, stepping in and adding an embrace of her own. "You've grown! I hardly recognized you!"

Then she smiled at Sarah in acknowledgement. "Sarah? Glad to have you back with us for a little while."

"How have my stand-ins been doing?" Sarah asked. While she had been busy with Maya's training and RSE business, the Agency had supplied the *JUDI* with other psi's so that the vessel could continue with its clandestine flights.

"Good enough," Bel Lissa allowed, but it was clear by her tone that Sarah's replacements hadn't been fully up to her standards. "Norra bel Sharyn was the best. I think we'll use her again."

"But this trip, we'll have someone better, won't we?" Zara interjected.

Maya blushed at the compliment, and the engineer laughed and clapped her on the shoulder. "You'll do fine, girl. Sarah was a little rough around the edges when she started with us--and now look at her! She's one of the best Helmswomen around."

"She's right, and with Sarah sitting right next to you, your first flight should be flawless," Bel Lissa added supportively. "In fact, I don't think she'll let you fek up even if you tried to. For some reason, she still thinks this is her ship." The four of them chuckled at this, and then Bel Lissa led the way up the cargo ramp.

A young woman was standing at the top, dressed in the sky-blue jumpsuit of a crewmember. She was only a few years older than Maya, with the light complexion of a Thermadonian, but her platinum blond hair was tied off to one side of her face with the type of braided leather hair band that the women on the desert world of Kevan favored.

Maya knew that it was a mark of honor among them. It was only given to those women who had completed their Tej as devotees of the goddess Kali, and it was as incongruous on the stranger as the silver tint of her irises. Such coloration was something that only Trilainians possessed, and it meant that whoever she was, she played host to some form of symbiote from that world.

Then there was her facial tattoo. This was perhaps one of the most confusing things about her. The Nemesian clans all sported stylized animals on the left sides of their faces, but this image was a diamond with four bars radiating from it. Maya had never seen anything like it before.

Who is this woman? she wondered.

"Engineer's Mate Jeena taur K'aut'sha," Bel Lissa said in introduction. In so doing, she explained the tattoo and also added another layer of mystery. 'Taur' marked her as a member of a Clan, but 'K'aut'sha' was the name of the famous fighting school on Nemesis.

It was only then that Maya noticed the gigantic Tej knife that was belted to her waist. Whoever Taur K'aut'sha was, the knife signified that she had not only studied at the Fighting School but had graduated--a rare thing for an outworlder. The only other woman that she knew who had accomplished this had been Skylaar taur Minna, and Nemesis was her motherworld.

Taur K'aut'sha came up to her, and Maya simply accepted the earring that she wore in one ear, and added it in with the rest of the puzzle. It was a skull and twin bones, marking her as a fellow Daughter of the Coast, and at one time at least, a Captain of her own vessel.

Young as she was, Taur K'aut'sha, was an enigma, wrapped up in a mystery, and obscured by the impossible.

"Maya," she said with a formal bow, "I am pleased to meet you. The Captain and Zara have told me a great deal about you." This was another surprise. Maya's ears had detected a slight, but unmistakable Zommerlaandar accent.

How in the Lady's name had she ever picked up that? she wondered. She didn't ask however, and Taur K'aut'sha didn't enlighten her.

"Jeena came on right after you went off to Nyx." Bel Lissa explained. "The Agency sent her to us. She was with the *Charlotte Badger* as an Engineer's Mate, and she's been doing the same job here ever since."

Maya immediately felt a surge of jealousy. Engineer's Mate had been her old post, and emotionally, she had never fully relinquished it, or the notion of the *JUDI* being *her* ship. She quickly suppressed this unworthy response however. Based on her Daughter's earring and Bel Lissa's word, Taur K'aut'sha was a veteran nulltrekker, and had all the qualifications that the *JUDI* required, and then some.

And they *had* needed someone after she'd gone off to Nyx to study with Lady Ananzi. There were simply too many odd jobs for one woman to do, even aboard a small ship like the *JUDI*. More importantly, as a helmswoman–in–training, Maya was now higher in rank than Taur K'aut'sha.

"*Enshon*," she answered politely, giving Taur K'aut'sha an equally gracious bow.

"You'll be hot-bunking with Jeena," Bel Lissa told her.

"Sure thing", Maya agreed.

Taur K'aut'sha picked up one of her bags and beckoned her to follow. "Come on, I'll show you where you can stow your gear."

As she moved to follow, Maya became acutely aware of the tension radiating from Sarah. The woman was tightly shielding her thoughts, making it impossible to read her, but her agitation was still palpable.

Something about Taur K'aut'sha was bothering Sarah, and as Maya focused her own talents on the woman, she realized that there did seem to be something 'off' about her energy. It was at once, oddly familiar, and at the same time, utterly elusive. Taur K'aut'sha was 'different' in more than just her appearance, but Maya couldn't quantify what it was that set her so apart.

"Go ahead, Maya," Sarah said tightly. "I need to speak with the Captain about something. I will meet you up on the bridge." Maya immediately suspected that it had something to do with their new Engineer's Mate, but she refrained from asking any questions. The *JUDI* was a small ship, and she would find out soon enough.

Instead, she went with Taur K'aut'sha through the cargo hold and into the ship proper. They stopped in the tiny crew's quarters; the same space where Maya had once hidden herself when she had been running for her life. Back then, it had been her prison, and a place of terror. Now, it was a friendly and familiar place.

She saw that a new touch had been added in her absence; a set of lockers had been embedded into the bulkhead. The last time she had been there, the wall had been bare.

Taur K'aut'sha indicated one of the compartments. "I cleared out my stuff from this locker so that you'd have a place for your gear."

Opening it, Maya smiled. There were two fresh coveralls inside. They were sky-blue and emblazoned with the *JUDI's* patch. And over the right pocket, was her name.

Taur K'aut'sha stood aside, and Maya reached in to caress one of the garments.

"*An di,*" she replied, finally deciding to befriend the woman. She had been reading Taur K'aut'sha's aura all the way there, and she hadn't sensed anything but friendliness. No competitiveness, or guile. Just an acceptance of Maya as a part of the *JUDI's* little family. That, and the weird 'difference' that she still couldn't place.

When Taur K'aut'sha left her alone to stow her things, Maya determined to ask Bel Lissa about the strange young woman, later, and in complete confidence of course. There were simply too many questions about Taur K'aut'sha to leave unanswered.

First though, there was the transit to worry about. Her first transit as a Helmswoman. Equally nervous and excited, she quickly changed out of her civilian clothing into one of the jumpsuits, and headed for the bridge.

On the way, she was unable to avoid passing Sarah's quarters, or overhearing the argument going on inside of it. Although their words were muffled by the door, she could tell that Sarah was deeply upset and that Bel Lissa was standing firm about something. She was tempted to press her ear to it, and listen in, but then she heard their footfalls, and made for the ladder to the bridge instead.

As she reached it, they came out together. Both of them wore unhappy expressions, but Bel Lissa brightened when she saw her. "Time to take the Helm, Maya," she said, urging her to climb.

"Yes," Sarah added with a forced smile. She paused, and looked back over her shoulder to Bel Lissa. "You know that this isn't over."

"Like I told you, it's not my call, Sarah, "Bel Lissa insisted, and for a moment, Maya was convinced that whatever they had been fighting over in private, was about to become very public.

Sarah bit back whatever reply she had been about to make though. "Go ahead, Maya," she said. "We have a transit to make."

At the top, Zara and Taur K'aut'sha were already waiting at their stations, and Zara gestured elaborately for her to take her seat at the Helmswoman's station. "Time to guide us through the Null, oh great Helmswoman."

Maya flashed her a nervous, crooked smile and took her place. Then Sarah joined her, taking her place in the extra swing-out seat. She flashed the Engineer's Mate a strange, and unpleasant look, but Jeena seemed unperturbed, and simply began working at the Engineer's station as if nothing untoward had taken place at all.

Putting Sarah's eccentricities and Jeena out of mind, Maya looked over her controls. She had been through dozens of simulations, and she was fairly certain that she was ready for whatever the situation might throw at her. But the real proof would come with the transit itself. She wasn't afraid to admit, to herself at least, that she was feeling *very* nervous.

Sensing this, Sarah placed a surprisingly gentle hand on her shoulder. *You are ready, Maya,* she thought to her. *Trust in yourself.*

Maya nodded solemnly, and collected herself.

The tower had cleared them by this point, and Bel Lissa took the *JUDI* up, ascending quickly. When they cleared the atmosphere, she brought them around to fall in line behind the *CSS Echephyle* and her small convoy of merchanters. As always, they were using the escort ship as camouflage, and only a few minutes later, the *Echephyle* obliged them by leading the convoy through a short transit into the Kaidis system.

Places like Kaidis were valuable for ships like the *JUDI*; they were a legitimate travel destination, and thanks to a few well-placed bribes, they offered Null-capable vessels the chance to slip away to their real ports of call, without leaving behind any bothersome departure records.

The moment that it was confirmed that the In-system Traffic Control's electronic eyes were ignoring them, Bel Lissa signaled to Maya. It was time to begin the transit.

She began by bringing up the astrographic projection that corresponded to their destination. This was the Myrene System in the Thalestris Elant. The *JUDI's* computer had placed the holographic stars in exactly the positions they would be in at the time and place calculated for the end of their transit. Satisfied with the data she was looking at, Maya took the next step in the process.

Just as she had so many times before in Lady Ananzi's kitchen, she quieted all of her extraneous thoughts, and focused on memorizing each and every major star, and its relationship to the others. When she felt that she had them all, she looked away from the holo and drew an image on the elzlate pad she had brought up with her. It was something that she had always done to check herself, and now, more than ever, she needed to be absolutely certain that her mental image was true to the reality.

Checking her sketch against the holographic projection, she found a few small errors, and with a self-deprecating frown, she studied the image a second time before creating another sketch. This time, everything was perfect; all of the stellar bodies were present and in the correct positions. Even so, Sarah leaned in and inspected her work, and privately, Maya was glad for the second opinion.

"You are ready to proceed, Maya," the woman announced.

Maya knew that she was right. For better or worse, she was as prepared as anyone in her position could ever be. During her time on Nyx, she had practiced cutting hundreds of simulated Null gates until the process had become almost second nature.

It was a far different thing to be sitting at the helm of a real spaceship however, with real consequences if she made a mistake. If there was any error in her visualization, the *JUDI* could wind up hundreds of light years off course, they could come out of their transit inside of a star, or suffer any number of equally horrible fates.

But Maya also knew that she couldn't afford to let her anxiety overwhelm her. Success hinged on a calm, resolute focus and absolute mental precision. Calling upon all the disciplines she had learned, she subdued her anxiety and concentrated on keeping her inner vision sharp and clear. "Astrographic visualization complete," she finally announced.

Bel Lissa acknowledged her. "Routing power from the main generators to the Pavilitas. Null wings extended."

Zara spoke next, "Routing power to the Pavilita generators."

The pitch of the engines changed dramatically as the *JUDI's* Engineer sent the command, and a low thrumming began to resonate through the frame of the ship, pregnant with the power that was building up in the vessels' twin psionic generators. Deep inside the vessel, the energy from the engines was transformed into something far purer and more intense than anything that the merchanter required for simple in-system travel. Routed through the Pavilita's, its fires built up and burned like the Djinn on the very day of creation itself, waiting only for Mayas direction to assume their final shape.

She went deeper into herself, sinking into a trance state that hovered somewhere between waking and dreaming. Then she reached out through her oversized psiever headset with her mind, and extended her senses into the ship around her. Suddenly she was in two places at once; within the confines of her body and also part of the *JUDI* itself.

Her senses came alive as her awareness integrated with the *JUDI's* intricate network of circuits. Now she saw what the ship saw--a universe of light, energy, and sound that her human eyes and ears were blind and deaf to. The stars around her blazed with X-Ray light, singing to her in choruses of pure radio noise, and the solar tide had become a palpable thing, caressing her titanium skin.

In the simulations, this had always been the most wonderful part of the process, the point when she was able to feel a small, ecstatic slice of what those who chose to be Translated experienced. It had also been the hardest part for her to maintain her focus in.

Now this was doubled. The temptation to remain there, joined forever with the ship as a being of both nerve and circuit, was almost too powerful and seductive to overcome.

Sarah quietly asserted herself.

Yes, Maya, she thought, *I understand your longing and I know what you are feeling right now. It is something special that only those of us who call ourselves Helmswomen can ever experience. Only the Translated know any greater ecstasy. But we have our work to do. Focus on the transit. Let go of the bliss. Focus your will.*

Sarah's words brought Maya back from the brink. She was right, and for once, Maya was glad for her presence. As wonderful as her link with the *JUDI* was, there was a Null gate to be cut. She set aside her ecstasy and sought out the collector wings.

"I am ready," she heard herself saying from an impossible distance.

"Routing power to the collector wings," Zara answered. The elemental energies within the psionic generators had reached their peak, and at the Engineer's direction, they discharged, flooding into the wings.

Maya reached out to them with her mind, visualizing herself grabbing ahold of the powerful tide with astral hands. Right away, the roiling maelstrom responded to her psychic touch like a living thing.

"Desire is the key to creating the gateway," Lady Ananzi had once told her, *"A pure desire that accepts no limitation, or boundary. It is the*

223

focused Will, armored by absolute belief, which gives the Fire its form, completing and transforming it. Once it has been shaped by the Will, it can open up the doorway to anything."

She hadn't understood this statement when she had first heard it, but after having spent months on exercises intended to focus and refine her psychic intention, and then the Null simulations themselves, it had become crucial to her success. Without a clear goal, the energy in the collector wings would remain nothing but chaos.

It needed direction to become coherent. It needed a conscious vision, fueled by pure desire. *Her* vision. *Her* desire.

Maintaining her contact, she called up her memory of the stars that she had just seen. Then she imagined the fires shifting and changing in response, until they mirrored her imagery perfectly, not as a hologram, but as a real place.

This IS what I want, she thought. *This place IS where I will go. No limitations or boundaries exist between where I am now and this place. NONE.*

Unable to resist, the fires responded in kind, becoming a blazing mirror of her vision. Now, all that was required to make it reality was the act of release.

In the eternity of this moment, Maya found herself wondering, as she often had, if what she was feeling was anything like what the Goddess herself felt when she repeatedly made and unmade the multiverse--only on a much smaller, mortal scale. If so, then it was an utterly glorious state of being.

Once again, Sarah brought her back to the task at hand. *Maya, remember your purpose. The energy is ready to be released.*

The young woman abandoned her reverie and sent another signal to Bel Lissa through her psiever. At the same time, Sarah spoke aloud for her.

"Now Inish! She's done it."

"Boosting signal," Bel Lissa replied. Even more energy was fed into the collector wings.

Yes! Maya thought. More than anything, she wanted to see her creation let loose on the universe before her. To watch it cut into and through it, shoving aside the feeble limitations of distance and time. To feel it touch the place that she saw in her mind, and link with it.

"Now!" she exclaimed.

Zara obliged her. "Discharging," she announced. "Cutting the gate."

Fire raced down the side of the ship, more powerful than any earthly lightening had ever aspired to be. When it reached the forward wing set, it compressed and jumped free of the ship in two perfect, cerulean beams. Far ahead of the *JUDI*, they met and combined.

The fragile essence of space, more a thing of time than any real material substance, could not withstand the assault and ripped wide open. With nothing to hold it back, the unbridled energy poured into the temporal wound.

A hole appeared, and then the mists of Nullspace became visible within it, swirling on the sitscreens with a deceptive, enticing beauty. Beyond this, and at the other end of the passage that Maya had just created for them, their destination awaited.

Exhausted by her ordeal, Maya slumped in her chair, covered in sweat. She wanted to collapse then and there, but there was one final thing that needed to be done to complete the ritual of officially becoming a Helmswoman. As weary as she was, she summoned up the last of her reserves, and took control of the ship's helm.

"I'm taking her in," she announced. She glanced at Zara, "Engage thrusters. All ahead, one half."

"The *JUDI's* all yours Maya," Bel Lissa told her. Gradually, and then with increasing speed, the little merchanter headed for the gate.

Sarah waited until they had crossed the boundary, and were well into Null, before she interrupted Maya once again.

I am pleased with you, she thought. *Well done, my young lioness. Very well done. Now, I will take the helm and you will rest a bit. We have a long transit ahead of us.*

Maya didn't argue, and left her station to revive herself with some kaafra and a quick snack in the *JUDI's* galley.

I did it, she thought happily. *I cut my first gate! I'm a Helmswoman now!*

***

As the mists cleared, and the velvety blackness of normal space reappeared, Bel Lissa clasped her hands behind her head and leaned back in her chair with a triumphant smile.

"Well, that's that then. Congratulations, Maya!"

Then Maya felt a tap on her shoulder. It was Sarah. She was also smiling, and holding something in her hand. It was a name-tape with the word "Helmswoman" embroidered on it.

Maya realized that Sarah had had it made in anticipation of a successful transit, and she took it from her, more touched than she ever would have admitted to anyone, especially her. "Thank you," she said quietly.

"I think this calls for a celebration," Zara suggested with a broad grin.

"Aye-ya. Drinks on me when we get downside," Bel Lissa agreed. "It's always left up to the poor penniless old Captain to treat the new Helmie."

"That is only right and fitting," Sarah pronounced. "Tradition must be adhered to, after all. So, *Jackies* then? I know that it is not the *Nulltrekker*, but they still serve a fine selection that is quite worthy of such an important celebration."

She flashed Taur K'aut'sha a pointed look, and added, "Jeena can watch over the ship while we are gone." Taur K'aut'sha did not react to this obvious snub, but only acquiesced with a quiet nod.

More mystery, Maya thought, both puzzled and unhappy. When the crew went out to drink together, *everyone* was invited to come along and she couldn't see any reason why Taur K'aut'sha had been excluded. Or for that matter, why she had just accepted the insult.

She certainly wouldn't have.

Bel Lissa made another announcement. "Bel Sharra has given us our approach vector," she said. "Sending the coords up to you Maya."

The *JUDI* had entered the civilian spacelanes by this stage and the in-system flight line for Thermadon Val came up on Maya's holodisplay. She entered the information into the ship's helm, and after a moment, the *JUDI* assumed its assigned course. From there on out, absent any emergencies, the merchanter would be guided down to Bel Sharra Memorial Spaceport by auto pilot.

Zara gave her a little salute at this, and Maya returned it, grinning. Then she allowed herself the luxury of leaning back in her seat and relaxing enough to really enjoy her triumph.

They touched down an hour later and as soon as the docking clamps had closed around the vessel, everyone gathered up their kit-bags and walked down the cargo ramp.

As they descended, Sarah pulled Maya aside. "I want you to keep your distance from Taur K'aut'sha," she warned.

"Why?" Maya asked. "She seems all right to me."

"She is not fit company for you," Sarah stated, "and she will not be with the *JUDI* very much longer if I have my way. That is what I spoke with the Captain about when we came aboard."

"Okay," Maya responded. "Do you plan to tell me why? I saw those bones on her earring. She's no greenie, and the *JUDI* can use a good hand now that we're off playing secret agent."

"That is none of your affair," Sarah said curtly. "Keep your distance from her."

Maya had never enjoyed being treated like a child, and this entire affair was really starting to irritate her. "You know something, Sarah? I'm getting fekking tired of being told to be a good little girl and just do what I'm ordered, no questions asked. So, if you want me to obey, you'd better tell me what's going on."

Sarah's eyes narrowed in irritation. "Very well, *Maya*. I shall. Jeena taur K'aut'sha is *not* what she seems."

Maya gestured impatiently for Sarah to explain herself. "*Why*, Sarah?"

Sarah lowered her voice to nearly a whisper. "I have told you about '*Project Advent*', have I not?"

"Yeah, that Marionite thing," Maya shrugged. "They wanted to make their Redeemer guy. So what? Is Taur K'aut'sha the Redeemer? Kind of a funny place for him to turn up, don't you think--and wind up being a 'her' on top of it all?"

Sarah glowered at her sarcasm. "Despite your rather sophomoric attempt at humor, you are more or less correct about the nature of the project. When the Sisterhood learned of it, one of the black operations that the Agency engaged in was to infiltrate the Marionite labs. I helped them to accomplish this.'

"And there was another operation that followed it. Its intent was to duplicate the Marionite efforts in order to gain living specimens that would provide us with an idea of their ultimate aims. It was also pursued in the hope of furnishing us with potential operatives who could move among them without suspicion."

"So, you're saying that we made our own neomen?" Maya asked.

"Yes," Sarah replied. "I am. We copied the genetic blueprints for their Adam-16 generation. The A-16's are one generation behind their so-called Redeemer. The only difference is that the ones that we created were conditioned to be loyal to the Sisterhood, not to the misguided Marionite cause. Not that we are counting on that as our sole insurance; the A-16's are also chipped."

"'Chipped?'"

"A-16's have chips implanted in their brains. If any of them ever betrays us, a simple code, sent by psiever, sets it off, and the device explodes in their cerebral artery. It is an added precaution against a male's natural tendency to disloyalty."

"How thoughtful," Maya replied sardonically. "Sounds like the Agency has it all covered. So what does any of this have to do with Jeena?"

Sarah shook her head in exasperation. "Everything! Jeena is *not* a woman. *She* is actually a 'he' and he is one of our neomen. An A-16. *He* would have gone on to work for us as a deep cover operative, had the project not been shelved. Now, do you finally understand?"

Maya shook her head. The notion was preposterous. "No way! That's no Neo. Jeena is a woman. Neos don't look like that." While she was certainly no expert on the subject, she *did* know that neomen were all big, hairy and ugly. Jeena was as female as she was.

"Adam-16's *do* look like 'that'," Sarah replied. "Both ours *and* theirs. Jeena taur K'aut'sha is a male, and the only reason that *he* is on board this ship is because the Agency couldn't find any other place for him after he lost his last berthing. As for the Daughters of the Coast, they don't care one way or the other as long as the profits keep rolling in."

"Weeellll," Maya said. "I didn't see *that* one coming. *Deas dam va!*"

"So you will follow my instructions then?"

Maya smiled crookedly. "Of course, Sarah. When have I *ever* disobeyed you?"

"This is not an occasion for levity!" Sarah snapped. "Jeena taur K'aut'sha is not someone that you will associate with."

Maya looked back in Taur K'aut'sha's direction, but by now 'he' had disappeared back into the ship. "Fine, Sarah. Whatever."

She also made a point of projecting nothing but thoughts of docile compliance for the woman to read. Sarah scowled, having done precisely that, and not believing it. But the woman let the matter drop with nothing more than a threatening gleam in her eyes.

CHAPTER 8

Storm, Agleope System, Sagana Elant, United Sisterhood of Suns,
1048.10|22|08:41:67

Shandra n'Aida's journey to Storm had been indirect by design. Mindful of the danger that the RSE posed, she left Thermadon in disguise aboard a sympathetic merchanter, and travelled first to Calandra, then Flora.

At Flora, she changed identities again and transferred to another ship which took her on to Thenti. At Thenti, she assumed a third identity and boarded a vessel which was bound for the Agleope system.

As far as the captain and her crew knew, she was a researcher for the *Orgón par Ricer da Satillit Météorologi etá Climatique*, the Planetary Weather and Climate Research Agency.

N'Aida was eminently suited to play the part. Before the Voice had taken over her personality and body, she had held doctorates in Xenoarchology and Planetary Climatology. Although she had been more than ready with all the right answers, no one challenged her credentials however.

Arriving on Storm at last, she was pleased to discover that the Faithful had arranged everything for her in advance. With their help, the previous weather researcher had already 'disappeared under mysterious circumstances' and thanks to other friends working in the ORSMC, she had been officially listed as the woman's replacement.

Already overworked, the local science team welcomed her with open arms. In short order, she was sent out to one of the agency's remote monitoring stations to continue with her predecessor's work. After this, the planet itself became her ally.

Even on the mildest of days, winds ranging from 102 kph to 402 kph, or even higher, scoured the landscape. The omnipresent dust kicked up by all of this chaos also rendered visibility down to zero, and a glimpse of the planet's sun was such a rare thing that the natives actually marked it on their calendars.

These extremely harsh conditions challenged the very limits of Sisterhood technology. The average crawler was unable to remain in service for very long before being completely demolished, and hover vehicles were simply out of the question. The Stormite solution to this were ground vehicles that resembled ancient tanks from old Gaia. They were low squat things, with wide treads, and five times heavier than their ancient counterparts.

The crawler that the ORSMC had lent to N'Aida was one of these behemoths. It was fully automated and its main job was to patrol the network of monitoring sensors that had been spread out across the blasted landscape. When it encountered a unit in need of repair, it disgorged the appropriate bots to handle the work, and then trundled on through the tempest to the next point in the grid. The only time that it ever stopped was at the research stations themselves to let off passengers like herself.

Hours later, and halfway to her assigned post, N'Aida checked her coordinates. Satisfied, she sent a manual override to the crawler, ordering it to halt. Then she donned an emergency survival suit, popped open the tiny canopy and clambered down the side. Reaching the rubble strewn ground, she sent another command to the machines artificial brain, and it started up again, leaving her alone in the whirling dust.

She had no illusions about her exit remaining a secret. The moment she had stopped the crawler, the Central Research Station had received the alert. The women there also knew that she had gotten out, but it would take any rescuers hours to reach her last known position. By that point, she would be impossible to find. Which was exactly what she had planned.

Despite the blinding grit, she still managed to locate the marker light for the dig site. It wasn't far from where the crawler had stopped and although it was more battered than her borrowed memories recalled, it was still functional.

The safety line that led up to the site itself was also intact and staggering under the remorseless blasts of the wind, she made her way over to it and clipped on. Violent gusts still tried to knock her off her feet and misdirect her like invisible demons, but she was not prevented from reaching her goal.

This was a ragged hole in the ground, at the foot of the marker. She dropped down into it, and found herself in a familiar environment; a long smooth tunnel that trailed off into the darkness. Grinning to herself in the gloom, Shandra n'Aida started down the passage with confident steps.

She knew exactly where she was going, and what her purpose was once she got there. She was returning to where she had been reborn.

There she would wait, and receive the pilgrims that were sure to come looking for her. Although they didn't know it, most of them would die in the process, but one of them--a very special, singular individual--would also enjoy a rebirth. This person would become the third vessel for the Voice.

After that, anything and everything would become possible.

Apartment of Sarah n'Jan, 409th Floor, The Otrera, Agamede District, Thermadon Val, Thermadon, Myrene System, Thalestris Elant, United Sisterhood of Suns, 1048.10|22|09.58.69

Once they had finished with their drinks at *'Jackie's'*, everyone went their separate ways. Bel Lissa and Zara retired to a pair of rooms that they had booked for themselves at a downtown hotel, and Sarah and Maya returned to her apartment at the *Otrera*.

The alcohol had left Maya feeling tipsy, and she was tired after the long transit. As soon as she was lying in her bed though, she found herself thinking about Sarah's prohibition against fraternizing with Jeena taur K'aut'sha and her surprising revelation about his true nature.

In her opinion, the injunction was patently absurd. What possible harm could there be in just getting to know him, she wondered. Taur K'aut'sha was just a neoman, albeit a highly modified one. And didn't everyone, even Sarah, *know* that males were inferior to women on *every* level?

Sarah was just being overprotective, and silly, she decided. In the morning, she was going to go straight back to the Port and take a better look at her new crewmate to see for herself what was so 'dangerous' about him. Motherthought and Sarah could both be damned.

With this settled, she finally let herself drift off. For once, the sleep which followed was dreamless, and when she awoke, she found that Sarah was still in bed, asleep. Taking advantage of her good fortune, she dressed herself quickly, and left a note with Aria to explain her absence.

'Gone out for breakfast', it said. *'Be back later—Maya.'*

It was even halfway true. She hadn't relished the idea of eating at the apartment, and the Port restaurants offered fine breakfasts.

She also had an explanation ready for her visit to the *JUDI.* Sarah had mentioned the need for her to study more astrographic charts, and to practice her transits with the simulator. There wasn't a better place to do that than on the merchanter's bridge.

And if she just happened to 'run into' Taur K'aut'sha in the process, it simply couldn't be helped. The *JUDI* was, after all, a very small ship.

When she arrived on her hoverbike at the port, she found the merchanter where it had been docked the night before, fully secured in its launching cradle with a screen of blast plates up and in place. Stepping inside the enclosure, she immediately encountered Zara, who was on a ladder servicing the hydraulics of the forward landing gear. The woman liked to do her major maintenance work when the ship was downside. It removed the requirement for cumbersome Zero-G suits, and made the work easier, and faster.

231

"Yah-tay, Maya, you come by to help us poor sailors out?" the woman grinned, "Or just trying to remember what real work looks like?"

"A bit of both," she answered with a dry smile of her own. "Thought I'd study up on some astrographic charts and then run a 'sim or two. Won't get much of a chance for that once Sarah figures out that she didn't give me any busywork.

Zara bobbed her head in sympathy. "Ay-yah. She's got you working harder than a one-legged woman in an arsh-kicking contest. Well, the kaafra's fresh and waiting for you in the galley."

Maya smiled again, and headed up the cargo ramp. She could smell the promised kaafra from there, and even though the *JUDI's* autochef was light-years behind the unit at Sarah's apartment, she was looking forwards to what it would serve out, even if it did sometimes confuse *chikka* eggs with orange juice, or *paankaakan* with *ribberfish*.

Zara had tried, many times, to fix this, and had even replaced the unit twice, but the issue was persistent, and although Zara vehemently disagreed with her, Maya believed that the real source of the problem was actually the *JUDI's* AI and not the autochef at all.

"Judi" had her own unique bugs, and among them, was a perverse sense of humor. Fortunately, these practical jokes, if that's what they were, were also harmless and intermittent, and in the bigger picture, only lent more character to an already unique vessel.

Today, she found the autochef (and "Judi" herself) to be in a fairly tractable mood, and the kaafra really tasted like kaafra, just as Zara had advertised. In fact, it was a very good pot, although Maya did detect an odd 'gamey' aftertaste that she couldn't quite place. Not that this was anything to worry over. It was hot, and it was free.

Taking her cup with her, she went to her locker and changed into her jumpsuit before heading for the bridge. By way of the Engine Room.

As she expected, Jeena taur K'aut'sha was there, sitting cross-legged on the decking as he cleaned off a set of plasma rods.

Although the *JUDI* used gravitronic engines for its main in-system drive, this was augmented by thermal antimatter engines which vented plasma through a series of ducts. These plasma jets added additional thrust during take-off, acted as afterburners when required, and assisted with changes in heading. The rods that the neoman was working on focussed the plasma as it was expelled into space.

Although this was a clean process overall, the rods still tended to gather residue after a while, and then needed maintenance to continue operating at optimal levels. The best way of achieving this was by doing just as Jeena was; removing them from their sockets, and wiping them down with a special cleaning cloth. It wasn't the most exciting job on a merchanter, but it was necessary, and the kind of thing that an Engineer's Mate tended to be tasked with.

Taur 'K'aut'sha was intent on his work, and two of the five rods for the port side engine were lying at his feet, already finished and gleaming like mirrors. Maya leaned against the hatchway and observed him quietly.

Once again, she perceived the 'difference' that surrounded his aura, and considered it against what she had been told. It was definitely human, but also subtly different from a woman's energy. Struggling to put a label to it, she concluded that it felt denser, heavier, and more compact. There was more beyond that, but it defied any attempt to fully categorize.

Knowing what she did, it was still hard for her to reconcile all this with what her eyes were telling her. For all intents, Jeena taur K'aut'sha still seemed just like any other woman to her.

His body, encased in the *JUDI's* blue working jumpsuit, had all the same curves and proportions of a female, and the illusion was only accentuated by a pair of fairly respectable breasts, delicate features and long blond hair which was still tied up into the simple pony tail that he seemed to favor.

She was also forced to ignore a rather odd sensation of discomfort as she observed him. Had she not known any better, and under other circumstances, she might have considered him--as a 'her' of course--to be quite attractive.

She *was* aware of the facts however, and she didn't find him appealing in the least. Not one nanobit.

Taur K'aut'sha set down the rod he had been working on, and looked up at her, meeting her gaze with his startling silver eyes.

"Hello, Maya," he said, brushing away a stray lock of hair. "Something I can do for you? Or did Zara send you here to help me out?"

"Nope," she answered. "I was just dropping in on my way to the bridge. Got some work up there to do."

A half-smile came to his lips, as if he had known that she had been standing there all along, watching him, and exactly what she had been thinking. He didn't admit this though, or say anything more. He simply returned his attention to the parts at his feet.

"Well, nice to meet you again," Maya said. "Later." To her chagrin, she realized that she had been blushing throughout their entire exchange. These new neomen were clearly troublesome and confusing creatures, she concluded.

Not that this made Sarah right about *anything*. That was just as impossible as feeling any real physical attraction towards Taur K'aut'sha, and equally as unacceptable.

Mastering herself, Maya briefly considered going up to the bridge to lend her alibi some substance, but sought out Zara instead. She was still at work on the landing gear.

"Heyas, Za", she said. "Need a hand?"

"Don't you have some sims to run?" the woman asked, not taking her eyes off her work.

"In a bit," Maya replied. "Thought I'd spend a little time getting my hands dirty first. Been missing the grease."

Zara looked down from the ladder and smiled knowingly at her. "I could use the number 10 spanner from the box. While you're at it, care to tell me what's really on your mind?" The old Engineer knew her far too well.

Maya flashed her a devilish grin and handed her the tool. "Well, I did have a few questions about our new crewmate."

"Aye-yah, I imagine that you do. Sarah said that you might be asking about him."

"Did she tell you not to tell me anything?"

Zara reached up into the landing gears innards and went to work with the spanner. "Not directly. She did give the Captain a royal tongue lashing for taking Jeena on in the first place. She wants him off the ship. I 'magine you know why. I saw her talking to you on the ramp last night."

"I do," Maya replied. "And I don't agree with her. She—he--isn't a problem. Sarah's just plain klaxxy. If Jeena does his job, who gives a fek? Besides, isn't Inish in charge now?"

In the course of their celebration the night before, it had come out that although the *JUDI* was still considered an Agency asset, control over its operations had finally been given over to Bel Lissa completely. This had occurred because of Sarah's promotion, and Bel Lissa's own exemplary service record. It was now Bel Lissa's call when it came to crew dispositions.

"Aye-yah, she is," Zara agreed. "Not that that's sunk in with Sarah yet, and we know how she gets when she digs her feet in."

She grimaced as she tightened something down, and went on. "She'll keep working at it until Jeena's gone, just on the principle of it all. And Inish will insist on the opposite, just on the principle of it all."

Maya shrugged. "Well, for my demi-credit, Jeena's fine. I saw her earring--*his* earring. *Deas dam va*, that's gonna take some getting used to."

Zara laughed. "Yah, I know. I keep forgetting myself. So, now that Sarah's told you to stay away, what do you want to know about him?"

"Not much," Maya answered with false innocence. "Just everything. How did he come by that tat, or the name? What ship did he captain?"

"So it's gossip you want with your grease, then? Why not ask him yourself?"

Maya shook her head. "No, I want to hear it from someone I trust first, then see what he tells me. That's if I get the chance and Sarah doesn't have her way."

The Engineer gave the component she had been servicing a maternal pat, and then came down the ladder.

"Well, I know that he trained up with Skylaar at that fighting school they've got there on Nemesis. 'Think it was part of his Agency training. He must've done good, 'cause they don't give out those tats to just anyone—or the name. Skylaar could tell you more—that's if she wants to---and if Sarah doesn't convince her to paddle your backside just for asking.'

Maya was unfazed by this possibility, and pressed on. "And the ship?"

"The *Elizabeth Shirland*. Don't know the whole tale, but the *Liz* got hit by Indies in Null during some mission or another. And no, I don't know how he got the command of her in the first place. Must have been something the Agency was trying out as a test."

Zara started to wheel the ladder over to the next landing assembly and tilted her jaw towards the tool box. Maya dutifully picked it up and followed her.

"And--?"

"That's it. The Captain knows more, and of course Jeena knows the whole story. You know, you really should just go and ask him. You'd get a lot more for your time."

"Thanks," Maya demurred. "Not just yet."

A moment later, Sarah messaged her.

Are you done with your little breakfast at the Port? the woman asked. *Return here immediately. We have an appointment to keep.*

"Izzat Sarah?" Zara asked. She'd seen Maya close her eyes, and then the grimace on her face.

"Yep. So much for freedom," Maya replied. "Zara, if Sarah asks…"

"You know I can't do much to hide anything from her," the Engineer said. "Not with all her talents. I'll just tell her that you cornered me. Then the two of you can sort it out."

"I suppose that's the best I could hope for," Maya conceded. "Thanks for all the grease—and the gossip."

Claire d'Layne Naval Base, Nuvo Bolivar, Magdala Provensa, Esteral
Terrana Rapabla, 1048.10|23|02:50:20

What Kaly didn't realize was that her Psych doctor had privately come to the opinion that it was time for her to rotate back to the Sisterhood. After their initial session, Kaly had come in sporadically for follow-up appointments, and Dr. Jeanna n'Susyyn had recognized the signs of chronic stress. Her recommendation for Kaly's transfer coincided with a recent policy change by the RSE, which the Major announced at the team's next briefing.

"You're all being sent back to the Sisterhood," the Major told them. "The Agency has decided to make use of your expertise and loan you out to work with law enforcement groups back home. After you've broken in your replacement teams, you'll be tasked with training street kaapers in the latest tactics and procedures. So, you're going to get an all-expenses paid vacation, courtesy of the *Regila*. But don't let all that fun and sun make you soft. You'll be coming back here in six months."

She read out their new postings.

Kaly learned that she had been assigned to the Metropolitan Police Academy on Thermadon. She wasn't sure whether to feel relief, or regret at this news. As much as she looked forwards to leaving the Republic and getting the chance to air her head out, the team was being broken up. Margasdaater was slated for a posting on Larra's Lament, T'Jinna was going to Corrissa, and Ben Di had work to do on Delgen. They would not be seeing each other again for at least half a year.

Fully aware that they would soon have their hands full acclimatizing the new teams to the ETR, they held an impromptu farewell party for each other that evening. And although they tried not to, everyone including Kaly, shed their fair share of tears. Suddenly, her earlier decision to leave the service behind and start a new life didn't seem quite as appealing.

Their deployment to Nuvo Bolivar had brought the team together closer than ever before, and parting--even temporarily--came hard for all of them. Although the Republic was a cesspool and she had grown weary of war, Kaly knew that she would miss her companions deeply.

Regila da Securité par Estat Headquarters, Concordance Park, Thermadon Val, Thermadon, Myrene System, Thalestris Elant, United Sisterhood of Suns, 1048.10|23|02:91:69

Sarah offered no censure when Maya finally walked into the apartment. Nor did she ask her any questions about her activities. Instead, she simply ordered her to clean herself up and change into her dress uniform. It was only after the young woman had complied, and they were sitting in Aria, that Sarah finally divulged their destination. They were headed to the RSE Central Headquarters, and a meeting with her immediate superior.

Located next to Concordance Park, and right across from the Golden Pyramid, the trip took only a few minutes, and as soon as Aria identified itself, they were cleared to land in the parking area reserved for active duty officers.

Before the war with the ETR, the building had been a government office shared by the OAE with several other agencies. Now, only the RSE occupied it, and the OAE, which continued to exist as a purely diplomatic entity, had been displaced. It was sharing space with the Department of State in another location altogether.

The RSE tower was an ultra-modern structure, and the Agency had spared no expense to modify it so that it could fulfill its new role. Decorative concrete barriers protected the entrance from attack by ground vehicles, glass windows were steadily being replaced with blast-resistant versions made of plastic laminate, and shield generators concealed in the building itself created force fields strong enough to fend off missiles, or a hover-vehicle filled with explosives. Human security had also been improved; armed SRU troopers stood watch at all the entrances, in full battle armor and toting compact energy rifles.

Seeing all this, Maya was certain that she was only looking at the surface of the buildings defenses, but even these looked formidable to her trained eye. The RSE was ready for terrorists, and then some.

Following Sarah inside, she found the main lobby to be a vast, brightly lit space, done in white Kevani marble, and offset by burnished steel pillars. Its huge floor was emblazoned with the logo of the Agency in black onyx and marble, accented by gold.

And with the exception of a few women that were dressed as civilians (and who were most likely *not* civilians, but plainclothes agents) most of the figures coming and going were in uniform like they were. Maya hadn't seen so much dark colored clothing in one place since Nyx, and she mordantly wondered if the RSE wasn't trying to outdo the women of the Nightworld with their somber color scheme. If they were, they were doing a damned good job of it, she mused, forcefully suppressing a giggle.

Sarah however, seemed quite comfortable with it all, and led Maya to the ebony reception desk as if the place were a second home. After the uniformed reception staff had scanned their biochips and matched their aural signatures, they were waved through the security scanners to a row of Lifts.

Nodding to the SRU troopers guarding them, Sarah chose the centermost one, and once its gleaming black doors opened, they boarded it and took it straight to the 405th Floor. There were no stops, and no other passengers. Sarah's rank and their appointment, had guaranteed them a private express ride.

When the car opened, a policewoman met them and quietly escorted them down a long hall. Like the lobby, the passage was a study in severe white marble, gleaming steel doors, and black onyx tile that made their boot steps sound like the crack of energy weapons.

Maya had often heard it said that first impressions were everything, and based on what she had seen so far, 'warm and friendly' wouldn't have been her first choice to describe the place.

In fact, there was a definite chill in the air. Not enough to be considered freezing, but still quite noticeable. There was also the faint smell of ozone, hinting that whatever was going on behind the mysterious steel doors involved very large and very powerful computers.

Not that she disapproved of this Spartan ambiance. A cozy fire, with cookies and milk generally didn't 'go' with the image that a national police/intelligence agency wanted to project.

Their ultimate destination proved to be at the very end of the hall. In keeping with her penchant for secrecy, Sarah hadn't mentioned the name of the woman they had come to see, but a steel plaque on the door enlightened Maya immediately; *"General Angelique bel Thana, Assistant Director."* They were immediately shown into a reception room that was just as sterile as everything else, and there, another officer took them into the General's office itself.

This was a large chamber with a high ceiling and indirect lighting that only emphasized its volume. A long, black carpet led straight from the door and across the room, terminating at the foot of a great baaka wood desk.

It was plain to the point of severity, and the seat behind it, was just as cheerless, and seemed more like a throne than a mere place to sit. Maya also noticed that no seats had been set aside for any visitors, and it was patently clear that whoever came in, was expected to approach the desk like a supplicant, and stand.

The only decorations in the room where a pair of huge oval windows that commanded a magnificent view of Thermadon Val. Between them, was the same life-sized portrait of Anne Marie Rensolear and the flags that Sarah had on display in her office back in the ETR. Clearly, this somber arrangement was the 'norm' for high-ranking RSE officers everywhere, Maya reflected, and Bel Thana was its inspiration.

The General herself was standing with her back to them, gazing out one of the windows with her hands clasped behind her back. As they came in, she turned to regard them.

Maya hated her the very instant that their eyes met. And even though she had been careful to mask her distaste from the psi, the woman still perceived it instinctively. Just from the slight tilt of her jaw, Maya knew that she was reciprocating the emotion, if only defensively.

Thankfully, neither of them gave any voice to their true feelings for one another. Had that actually occurred, on either a verbal or mental level, it would have gone; "Bitch!" followed by the reply "Bitch", and so on into infinity.

Angelique bel Thana was simply everything that Maya wasn't; she was tall, blond, and beautiful enough to be a realie star, and positively radiated sophistication, elegance and grace. She was someone that any woman, Maya included, would have wanted to look like, and all the more hateful for it.

Bel Thana smiled at them (perfectly, of course), and greeted them warmly (also delivered with equal flawlessness). It came as no surprise that her voice also matched her appearance. Instead of being hoarse and grating--which it would have been in any *just* universe--it was rich and velvety.

"Sarah! " Angelique declared. "How *wonderful* to see you again!" She turned to Maya next. "You must be Maya. I've heard *so* many good things about you. Both Lady Ananzi and Sarah have spoken quite highly of your performance."

Caught completely off guard by the compliment, Maya managed to stammer out a polite response that was just as clumsy as the woman was making her feel. *Bitch*, she thought.

Angelique focused her impeccable smile on Sarah. "Sarah, you and I have a great deal to discuss. The developments that your Station has reported have caused quite a stir here. Perhaps you have a few minutes to spare me?"

Even if Sarah hadn't been free, she still would have been compelled to give Bel Thana her time, and they all knew it. Bel Thana's polite request had simply frosted over what was actually an order. It was also abundantly clear to Maya that she was not included in this invitation.

"Maya," Sarah told her, "I will be a little while. Wait for me downstairs, please."

"Okay. Sure."

"Thank you for your understanding, Maya," Bel Thana added smoothly. "I do *so* hope that we will have the opportunity to get to know one another better, some other time."

This was a lie. A genteel one, but still a falsehood. Not that Maya had any more of a choice in the matter than Sarah did. She was, after all, a Lieutenant, and Bel Thana was a General, so it was time for her to leave.

Bitch!

The instant that Maya had left, Bel Thana came right up to Sarah. There was a hungry look in her green eyes, and reflexively, Sarah stepped backwards until she found herself up against the wall. She made no attempt to evade her any further however, and remained right where she was.

It had been a long time, but not so much that either of them had forgotten what they had once shared together, years before. Then, they had both been new agents, just out of training and assigned to the same Station, and their love affair had been one long inferno of unbridled passion. Rank and responsibility had gradually interrupted this, and then separated them, and after that, the years themselves had joined in the conspiracy, severing them completely. But the fire itself had never been extinguished.

"I've missed you so much," Angelique said huskily. Her body was close to Sarah's now, making her presence all the more electric for the slight gap between them.

And Angelique understood precisely what she was doing. She knew what aroused Sarah.

For a several seconds, they remained like this, staring into one another's eyes and saying nothing. At last, like a predator that had finally decided that the moment was right to strike, Angelique leaned in and kissed Sarah deeply. At the same time, her hand went directly to Sarah's crotch, and the woman moaned under her merciless touch.

After a while, they went together into an adjacent room. Like many senior officials, Angelique kept a small living area there, and naturally, a bed.

Time passed.

***

Down in the lobby, Maya had found very little to occupy her time with. In addition to the reception desk, the only accommodation for visitors was a small seating area with several couches--black ones--and a scattering of Holomags. Inspecting these, Maya was disappointed. They were all public relations rags with nothing but positive, and very boring things, to say about the RSE.

Tossing them aside, Maya looked around for some way to pass the time, and finally saw it. She went up to the officer at the desk.

"Excuse me," she asked her sweetly. "I've got a bit of a wait before Colonel n'Jan comes back to get me. I'd sure like something good to read. Do you have any copies of *'Creative Assassination'* or maybe *'Espionage for Kids?'* I always loved the coloring pages in that one."

The officer glared at her sourly. "Just what you see, Lieutenant."

240

"Oh well, thank you anyway!" Maya beamed, quite pleased that she had managed to irritate the humorless woman. Then, just to annoy her even further, she returned to the seating area and flopped herself down on the couch with an exaggerated sigh, making certain to kick her booted feet up onto the low table. This earned her another dark look, and all the entertainment that she had been hoping for.

***

Sarah placed an apologetic hand on Angelique's bare shoulder. Angelique didn't respond, but kept her back turned. Despite this, Sarah knew that she was weeping. When Angelique did speak at last, it was barely above a whisper and ragged with sorrow.

"It is *her*," she said. "*She* did this to you."

"No," Sarah answered. "It is not Trina's fault. I just can't—not any more---"

"Not unless she does it to you *her* way? Is that it?"

Sarah didn't answer, and Angelique didn't tell her that she needed to leave. That much was a foregone conclusion.

The mattress shifted as Sarah rose, and went to get dressed.

After she had gone, Angelique turned over and gazed up at the ceiling through tear soaked eyes.

Trina had ruined Sarah. She had destroyed the woman that Sarah had once been, completely and utterly. For that, she would pay, Angelique promised herself. Not that day, or even any time in the near future, but when she had finally outlived her usefulness.

When that occurred, she intended to reserve the sweet pleasure of exacting justice all for herself. Trina would suffer for a long time, and at her hands. This vow was what finally gave her the strength to rise from the bed.

It took all of her well-schooled reserves of calm and control to force her hurt far enough away to don her uniform once again, and focus on the day's business. She had important things to consider. Things that eclipsed everything else, even her personal disappointments.

Reentering her office, she walked over to one of the large windows and took a moment to gaze pensively at the busy city below her. When she had allowed Ellen n'Elemay to escape from Bel Sharra, she had worried about which way Sarah would go when the time came. Now, she knew that their old passion would not play a part in Sarah's ultimate decision. It would have to be made from pragmatism instead. It was a bitter thing to admit, but still an undeniable fact.

241

It was also a fact that the Conversâzi needed women like Sarah. Although she wasn't a scion of one of Thermadon's ruling families like Angelique or many of the other members were, her bearing, her talents, and the excellence of her work, still made her one of the elite. And as distasteful as it was to even contemplate, there was even room in their organization for her 'little' companion, Maya--if that was what was needed to convince Sarah to enlist.

Clearly, the girl was nothing better than street-trash; someone who had been elevated well beyond her station by a mere accident of talents. Sarah's affection for her was wholly inexplicable, and Angelique struggled to understand the nature of their bond.

It wasn't love, or any form of sexual attraction. She was certain of that much. Instead, their dynamic seemed to be composed of something else entirely, but what that was exactly, remained stubbornly beyond her grasp.

What she *did* comprehend with absolute clarity, was Sarah's primary weakness. This was her blind patriotism. As magnificent an agent as she was, the Sisterhood had always commanded her unwavering loyalty, often to the detriment of political necessity, or simple common sense. She hoped that the years had eroded away enough of this hopeless idealism for the woman to see reason when it was finally presented to her.

Meanwhile, time was running short. The Conversâzi's plans had been set in motion, and they would soon be well past the point of no-return. Sarah would have to join them before that time, or be declared an enemy and destroyed.

Sighing deeply at this unpleasant possibility, Angelique absently fingered her ring and watched the traffic flying by without really seeing it. Finally, her psiever reminded her of her obligations. She had an important appointment to keep.

Intergalactic Mission Complex, Agamede District, Thermadon Val, Thermadon, Myrene System, Thalestris Elant, United Sisterhood of Suns, 1048.10|23|04:59:19

Angelique disembarked from her hoverlimo and walked across the Federal Plaza to the Intergalactic Mission, preparing herself for her meeting with Queen Talaria. The Leader of the Seevaan Chaotic Delegation, and First Heir to the Throne itself, had taken up residence at the Mission. With the vote over inclusion nearing, the member races of the Galactic Collective had dispatched representatives to make their final evaluations, and the Sisterhood had done what every candidate race always had. It had created a place for their guests to live and work in.

Although some native Thermadonians irreverently nicknamed the Mission complex the "Bug House", the significance of the place was not lost on anyone. The votes, and the advantages that Womankind's inclusion in the Collective could bring with it, were too important, and the Sisterhood had spared no expense in the construction.

The sprawling edifice was only half complete, but enough of its specialized domes and airlock-controlled passages had been erected to accommodate most of the races that had been dispatched the Thermadon. The wing for the Zeta Reticulans, with its special low-grav habitat was still only a skeleton however, and as far as she was concerned, it could remain that way. The less she had to deal with the Greys, the better.

And if their habitat somehow failed and killed them all, neither she nor her sisters would have mourned their passing. Bel Thana had even been tempted to arrange for just such an accident, but however satisfying this might have been, prudence had always stayed her hand. There were simply too many eyes watching, and too much riding on the vote's outcome to pander to such a desire. Better to let them come, she thought, and then be forced to watch helplessly as their precious Collective was rendered absurd.

In her hands the Secret would see to that. Regarding the incomplete domes with a scowl, Angelique turned her back on them, and entered the Seevaan habitat. Right away, she observed that their allies had come a long ways since her last visit. Seevaan worker drones had already coated most of its steel passages with the hard translucent resin that they favored in their native hives, and this lent the place an utterly alien air.

Unfortunately, the coating also rendered the floor surfaces rather slick, and she deliberately slowed her pace, placing her boot steps with greater care. The last thing that she needed was to slip and come before Talaria sporting an embarrassing bruise.

A little further in, a Handmaiden greeted her with a deep bow, touching her fore pincers together in respect, and Bel Thana mirrored the gesture. With the formalities observed, the creature turned and scuttled down the hall.

Although the Seevaan could have easily outpaced Bel Thana, the four-legged insectoid expertly measured her gait so that she stayed with her guest without giving the appearance of doing so. The Handmaiden was not only accommodating her, but also avoiding any insult or insinuation of her physical inferiority.

Bel Thana smiled in approval. The Seevaans understood the need for good manners and proper etiquette at all levels of their society.

The Handmaiden guided her to one of the oval doors that seemed to grow out of the sinuous walls of the passage. With a wave of her pincers, the entrance parted fluidly, revealing a huge circular chamber festooned with the same smooth ribbing and delicate lattices found in the hall.

These were on a much grander scale however, and possessed a complexity that no Baroque architect could have ever envisioned without going insane. They were pure, abstract forms, expressing their beauty independent of any recognizable source material.

Queen Talaria waited for her in the midst of this splendor, in the very center of the chamber, and this made Bel Thana smile to herself again. Talaria's choice of the room, and her placement within it, had both been quite deliberate. The Seevaans were an extremely subtle race, and the Queen knew full well how the chambers organic decorations offset her appearance, making her all the more elegant and imposing in appearance. Talaria was, and always had been, a consummate show woman.

Bel Thana advanced several paces, and then gave her a deep bow, touching her fingers together. "My Lady," she signed, using the human version of Pincerspeak. "I hope that I find you well?"

"You do," the Regent replied. "Are you also healthy, my friend?"

"I am indeed," Angelique responded.

"May you and your hive always thrive, "Talaria said. She gestured towards the chair that had been set there for her use, and Angelique sat. There was a small table next to it, and she waited patiently, knowing what was coming next. The Seevaans loved ritual, and one of these had to be observed before they could address any business.

Right on cue, the Handmaiden who had shown her in, or her exact twin, entered the chamber. She was carrying a pot of tea and a plate of sweet cakes for their human guest in her fore pincers, and another platter with her secondary ones. This was heaped with delicate hardwoods for her Queen to enjoy. As the trays were set down before them, Angelique helped herself to her tea and the cakes while the Seevaan leader plucked up two of the choicest pieces of wood and consumed them with equal relish.

When they had both finished with their refreshments, Talaria got straight to the heart of their audience with a question. "Tell me, good friend, what news of the Three? Have you come any closer to locating them since last we spoke? Or the location of the Secret itself?"

"No, great Lady," Angelique answered. "Sadly, Celina remains the only one that we know of. We have yet to find the other two, but I have my most seasoned agents conducting the search. Knowing the quality of their skills, it will not be long before they find them."

"Very well," the Seevaan replied. "I trust in your judgment. But remember that the vote for inclusion draws nearer and I must emphasize the need for haste. Once the Secret is in our grasp and the User has been compelled to do our bidding, we will have something truly marvelous to present to the members of the Collective."

"I look forwards to that great day," Bel Thana said, toasting the alien regent with her teacup.

Talaria still had no idea how much she actually knew. The Seevaans had tipped their hand from the very outset. Instead of going through conventional channels and approaching the Sisterhood's government with their problem, they had come to the Conversâzi instead.

They had claimed that the Secret merely represented an opportunity to study more of Drow'voi technology, and that it would broaden their knowledge of temporal and physical modification. They had also promised to reveal their findings, and the existence of the Secret, to their political allies when the time was right.

On the surface this might have seemed credible to anyone. Except Angelique. The simple fact that the Seevaans had sought out her organization, coupled with extravagant promises of advanced technology, had only served to make her suspicious. So she had done what any good agent would have in such a circumstance; she followed up on the story. Aggressively.

Eventually, the Conversâzi had made contact with the Pa'lla, a race that devoted itself to the study of the Drow'voi, and they had provided many of the answers that she had sought. The information had come at great cost, but in the end, it had proven to be worth every credit.

Only a small part of the Seevaan story had turned out to be true. The Secret did exist, and it did offer the chance to understand more about Drow'voi science.

This was only a fraction of what the Secret actually represented though. Its true potential went far beyond mere scientific research, and combined with what she had subsequently learned about Seevaan politics, Queen Talaria's actual intent had become glaringly obvious.

The Chaotics were not the docile members of the Great Hive that they pretended to be. Tired of their station in life, and with the Collective itself, they wanted nothing less than to overturn the Seevaan Empress, and rule the galaxy. To manage such an immense feat, Talaria and her followers needed a decisive edge, and the Secret had offered this to them in abundance. To get their pincers on it however, they needed human cooperation—and human ignorance.

On that score, their efforts had failed, but Angelique had no intention of enlightening them. For the moment, she would continue to pretend to believe in the fairy tale Queen Talaria was telling her, and play the part of the good little client. In the end, it would be the Conversâzi, and herself as its leader, who would seize control of the Secret, and the Seevaans would become the subordinate race. Right along with every other being that made up the Galactic Collective.

The very notion of such a glorious change of fortunes seemed to lend sweetness to her tea, and she brought her cup to her lips and drank deeply.

Residence of Angelique bel Thana, Themiscrya Tower, 898th Floor, Agamede District, Thermadon Val, Thermadon, Myrene System, Thalestris Elant, United Sisterhood of Suns, 1048.10|24|07:50:21

Only a day after their abortive tryst, Sarah received a formal invitation from Angelique to attend a private party at her residence. There was no question about accepting it.

Bel Thana's home was located in the elite Themiscrya Tower, just a few floors below the penthouse of Senatrix n'Calysher herself. A servant met them in its private hover-garage, and her appearance puzzled Maya. Despite the opulence that surrounded them, the woman was attired in a plain grey uniform, and she wore no make-up, or adornment of any kind. This was not what Maya had expected to see with a staff member of such an elite residence.

It was only when they were shown inside by another equally unattractive retainer that she realized the true intent behind their bland attire. Bel Thana didn't want anyone else to outshine her. Even her servants.

Angelique herself had shed her severe black uniform for a long dress dyed in a rich red-orange, and offset this with expensive golden jewelry. She had also let down her hair, which fell past the small of her back in long lustrous waves. And although she was wearing make-up, it was only enough to call attention to her otherwise faultless features.

Experiencing a fresh wave of loathing for the woman, and feeling quite shabby by comparison, Maya stood by as Angelique greeted Sarah with a pair of kisses to her cheek. Then she was forced to submit to the same ordeal, albeit more superficially.

"The others have only been here a little while," Bel Thana said, "so you're just in time for tonight's little diversion."

"Oh?" Sarah asked.

"A small thing," Angelique replied with an airy wave of her slender hand. "A private exhibition of some local artists. I'm certain that you'll find it enjoyable."

Sarah nodded approvingly, and as Angelique linked arms with her, Maya fell in step behind and followed them in.

Unlike her sterile workplace, Angelique's residence was warm and intimate, and paneled throughout in expensive Nemesian hardwoods. Maya's feet fell on thick, ornate carpeting, and traces of an expensive Kalian incense laced the air all around her, only strengthening the overall sense of luxury and sensuality. Every corner of the place seemed to offer something to delight the eye, or please the senses. It was, in its entirety, a faithful reflection of its mistress, and nothing less than the home of a modern noblewoman. Felecia, she realized, would have felt quite at ease there. She however, felt completely out of place.

It will be just like our dinner aboard the Star of Aphrodite, Sarah thought to her privately. *Don't let these women intimidate you, and simply follow my example.*

Maya gave her a small, tight smile as they entered the living area, and vowed to soldier through the evening as best she could.

Her fellow guests didn't make this an easy task. Like Angelique, they were all flawless examples of Thermadon's elite; as sleek and as beautiful as Bel Thana, just as elegantly dressed and just as disgustingly comfortable with their surroundings. The very sum of what Thermadon's genetic engineering had to offer its ruling class, they were all perfect, and they knew it. Two of them, a statuesque blond roughly Maya's own age, and an equally graceful brunette, rose from the seating area, and floated over. They bowed to Sarah and then to her.

"My sisters," Angelique explained. "Silvi and Josette."

"Enshón" Silvi said. "We have heard *so* much about you, Sarah. A true pleasure."

Sarah returned her bow, and indicated Maya. "This is my associate, Maya n'Kaaryn"

"N'Kaayrn?" Silvi asked. "I don't think I've heard of your family. Are your people from *off planet* perhaps?" The way she said 'off planet' clearly conveyed that she had intended the term in the lower case.

Maya caught the insult, and bristled. "They were from Durga," she replied. "On the frontier with the Xee." It was the plain truth, and she instantly regretted revealing it.

"A *fringe* world then?" Josette seemed truly astonished at the idea—and the notion that *anything* of value could reside in such a remote and desolate place.

"Yes."

"Tell us, what did your mothers *do* on Durga?"

"They were Hydraulics Engineers," Maya answered, feeling a hot flush of shame and then, anger. It was just a fact, she told herself, and for all their shortcomings as people, and as a couple, what they had done had been honorable, and valuable.

"Oh," Silvi smiled, "How delightfully *rustic*." She and Josette laughed. Maya couldn't help but note that Silvi's teeth were just as impeccable as the rest of her, and she suddenly entertained the image of her fist forcefully rearranging them. Oddly, Silvi's beautiful smile only widened, as if she had somehow overheard this, and found it amusing.

In fact, she had.

Have a care, Sarah warned her on their private psiever channel. *These two are not the spoiled little brats they seem to be. They are agents—and if you give them cause, you may find yourself dealing with far more dangerous opponents than you bargained for. In fact, with the exception of the staff, all of the women here are agents. I know many of them personally.*

Maya's surprise must have registered on her features, because Silvi bel Thana gave her a small confident nod, wordlessly acknowledging Sarah's caution.

Thoroughly chagrined, Maya took her place on the couch and tried to ignore the pair, along with all the other goddesses seated around her. The center of the room, she saw, had been cleared, and a simple white pedestal took up the space. It was quite unlike the opulent furnishings around it, and clearly intended for some kind of display.

Then she took a closer look at the women who were standing along one wall of the room. She'd seen them as she had walked in, but had been too distracted by Silvi and the others to really pay them any attention.

Like the servants, they were all dressed quite simply. Four of them were in severe black business dresses that resembled the comerci in their formality. These garments had high stiff collars just like the comerci did, but instead of a bright cravess, they were buttoned tightly and concealed their owner's necks. The arms of their tunics were the same; they covered not only their limbs, but continued onwards to become gloves.

A fifth figure stood slightly in front of them, dressed in the same manner, but in her case, in a tasteful dark grey. Unlike her younger companions, this woman was middle aged, and in the ETR, would have been mistaken for 40 to 50 years, instead of the 100 to 125 Standard that she actually was.

The entire group stood as still as statues, with their hands clasped in front of them. At their feet were six metal suitcases, arranged just as neatly as they were. On the side of each container was the name, *Galarie d'Heireux,* 'Gallery of Light', and a motto, "*Arté heireuxi da âme*", "Art Illuminates the Soul."

None of the other guests seemed to be taking any notice of them whatsoever. It was obvious to Maya, that to them, these women were simply another part of the room's opulent furnishings.

Taking up a delicate silver spoon, and tapping it against her wine glass, Angelique called everyone to attention. "Jantildamé, friends," she announced. "I think it is time for our main entertainment, don't you?" After receiving polite nods from her guests, she turned to the woman in grey. "Madame n'Terriya? Will you honor us?"

N'Terriya suddenly came to life, stepping forwards one pace, and smiled at the assembly.

"Sa'la jantildamé. It is my privilege to bring to you several offerings from our gallery, which I hope you will find pleasing." The woman raised her arm and crisply snapped her fingers. One of her black-suited assistants responded immediately, taking the case nearest her to the center of the room. She opened it and brought out a simple black cube, setting it down on the pedestal.

"This first piece is by Marya ebed Janna, and entitled *"Tetran Dawn."* N'Terriya informed them. The lights in the room automatically dimmed, and the assistant closed her eyes. At this, the lightweave came to life.

A form of art unique to the Sisterhood, lightweaves were essentially a holographic projection, but the intent was to display an artistic composition rather than to simply convey information. Maya was familiar with them, and she had seen a few examples in primary—every girl had—but she was completely unacquainted with their finer points, or with the artists who created them.

The weave began as a fine point of light emerging from the center of the cube, and slowly blossomed into a fine mesh of delicate filaments. Shapes sprouted next. Some resolved themselves into round spheres, and others assumed rectangles, while more of them flattened out into thin ribbons that wove in and around the rest.

Although it was certainly pretty, and seemed to utterly delight the rest of the audience, Maya was unmoved. Abstract art had never appealed to her, and when the weave ended, and the next one was brought up, she found herself hoping that it would center on a more interesting subject. Unfortunately, it didn't and by the time the final case was being opened, she was utterly bored.

N'Terriya on the other hand, was positively breathless about the last offering and told them that the piece was the creation of an artist calling herself "Tintharia". Whoever this person was, her name alone commanded the room's full attention, and when the assistant activated it, everyone fell silent.

Like its predecessors, the weave started as a diminutive blossom of rainbow-colored light, rising tentatively from its ebon base like a flame. As it grew, the image began to spin and each individual color wound away from the rest, separating into tiny luminous filaments of pure light. Then the strands slowly regrouped, finding one another and combining to assume mysterious shapes.

Having seen the other lightweaves, Maya now understood that this portion of the presentation was standard to all of them, and she didn't let herself become excited. In all likelihood, the weave would turn out to be just another boring abstract piece.

While she watched, only half-interestedly, the luminous threads increased in number and complexity before they came together to become something recognizable. An impossibly well-formed leg materialized, and after this a torso, and then the full figure of a woman in miniature.

Maya's attention was finally captured by its delicacy and its realism. The little woman was perfect in every respect, and she leaned forwards with everyone else to regard the illusion more closely.

As if in response, the figure seemed to look right back at them, and although she knew it was only a hologram, Maya suddenly felt as if she were facing a living being that had somehow been fashioned from pure light. Then, without giving any warning, the little woman leapt up, twisted in mid-air, and began to perform an intricate dance that was wholly unlike anything that Maya had ever witnessed.

There was no formal structure to it that she could recognize, but even so, the little dancer managed to express a feeling of absolute joy and freedom. At the same time, her body changed from one color to another, each hue as brilliant and as faultless as the one which had preceded it.

Tears came to Maya's eyes as she watched the performance. It was, without question, one of the most beautiful things she had ever witnessed and she didn't want it to come to an end.

But finally, the dancer slowed, and then folded in on itself, shrinking down with a painful slowness until at last, it was nothing more than the flicker of light that it had begun as. After another second, this too was gone, leaving only darkness behind, an empty pedestal, and a sense of loss lingering in Maya's heart.

Understanding how it had affected them, N'Terriya gave the assembly a moment of silence before she spoke.

"She is called the '*da Dansuar*', the Dancer, and I think that it is safe to say that she is the finest work that Tintharia has ever created. The artist herself felt this way; after completing her, she vowed never to compose another lightweave again, and has since moved on to physical sculpture. After seeing it for yourselves, wouldn't you agree with her decision?"

She was looking to their hostess, Angelique.

"Indeed," the woman replied, her own eyes damp. "I *must* have her."

"Then she is yours, jantildam," the dealer replied with a bow. "I should also add that you have acquired a truly rare piece. Except for what you have here, all other copies of the program that created her were destroyed by the artist. The Dancer is, and always will be, completely unique."

Angelique acknowledged this, and took a deep sip of her wine.

"There is something else you should know about *da Dansuar*, jantildam," the dealer added. "As you might have guessed, she is integrated with a rather complex AI. She will never perform the same dance for you, and each one is a reflection of the emotions of her audience. Each is unique. What you have just seen, was for this night, and for you, and your guests alone."

Angelique acknowledged this with a regal inclination of her head, and the attendant responsible for the piece sealed her case, and left the Dancer on the pedestal. There was no discussion of price, or any other arrangements, and as one, Madame n'Terriya and her attendants, left the room, and Angelique, with her prize.

"Well," she said, draining her glass. "That was truly more than I expected. What a pleasant surprise."

She turned to Sarah. "While the others take their refreshments, would you care to see some of my other acquisitions?"

No invitation had been extended to Maya, but faced with the alternative of socializing with Silvi and the other aristocrats, she presumed it, and followed. Angelique noticed this, but aside from giving her an arch look, she led Sarah away from the living area without comment.

Angelique won't tell you because it would be considered gauche to do so, Sarah informed her, *but she just spent 10 million Credits to acquire Da Dansuar for herself. At her level, one never discusses price. One merely acquires, or declines the opportunity to do so.*

This made Maya stumble, mid-stride. She had guessed that Bel Thana was wealthy just by her address alone, but she hadn't thought of her as being quite *that* wealthy. It furnished her with another good, solid reason to hate her.

The Bel Thana family comes from very old money, Sarah thought. *They made their fortune in ship-building and transportation. The Luxar Lines and the Star of Aphrodite are their property.*

Despite the distaste she harbored for Bel Thana, Maya was deeply impressed, and curious. *Why did she get involved with the Agency then?*

Had she wanted to, Angelique could have simply bought any of the information that she desired, and if she needed someone eliminated, she was easily able to afford the services of ten women of Skylaar's caliber.

The challenge perhaps, and the power, Sarah opined. *As a wise woman once said, 'money is not everything.' Whatever the case, a Bel Thana has been at or near, the center of Agency business for centuries. As I warned you earlier, have a care with Angelique and her sisters. They are very powerful women, and it would be rather unwise to cross them.*

I will, Maya agreed.

By this point, they had passed several niches set in the paneled walls, each one housing breathtaking masterpieces, but they stopped before one alcove in particular. By all appearances, it contained nothing more exciting than an ancient battery, and a rather weathered flat-print of a family standing in front of a group of prefab housing units.

The family was as archaic as the battery was. In addition to the mother, Maya saw what had to be the father. Which meant that the image had to have been taken sometime well before the MARS plague, if the resemblance that the male had to the females was to be trusted at all.

"A relic from my family's distant past, "Angelique announced. "I've wanted to show it to you for years, Sarah, but until now, I haven't been able to have it displayed properly." Sarah leaned in to get a closer view, and Maya couldn't help but make a comment.

"Um, it's a battery," she remarked, *sotto voce*. This earned her an irritated glance from both women, and with obvious reluctance, Angelique finally decided to acknowledge her presence.

"How surprisingly *observant* of you, Maya," the woman said with a sneer. "You are correct. The image shows my ancestors standing before their first home here on Thermadon. It was taken when the colony was still new, and long before it became the magnificent city that it is today.'

"That battery was something that was issued to every settler who had been assigned a home here. It had enough energy to power their residences for a decade before needing a recharge, and it was a symbol of status among them. It meant that a piece of this world had become theirs."

"And so it did," Sarah observed. "The Bel Thana's have been here ever since."

"It's a battery," Maya repeated under her breath.

Angelique pointedly ignored her and smiled proudly towards another niche further along the wall. "Here is something that I recently acquired. I think it has quickly become one of my favorite pieces."

Maya was fairly certain that the next 'treasure' was just more archaic junk, but she still peered past Angelique to see what she had been referring to. It proved to be far less disappointing than the battery, and twice as mysterious.

It was an ancient dagger, with a jewel-encrusted hilt and an equally ornate scabbard. Behind it was a weathered bronze object that she could not readily identify. It possessed a square base that supported a thin metal bar, which in turn, held up a small rectangular frame. In that frame, protected by layers of glass, was what looked like a lock of blond human hair, curled around itself once, and secured by a simple piece of ribbon.

Above all this was a portrait. Maya could tell immediately that it was quite old; the paint had cracked and faded in many places, and its gilded wooden frame was just as time-worn. The woman in it strongly resembled Angelique, or her sisters. She was as blond as Angelique or Josette were, and just as lovely, but her clothing was archaic and seemed to date from a time many centuries before the MARS Plague.

"Who was she?" Sarah asked.

"Oh Sarah, I am truly surprised that you would even feel the need to ask me that," Angelique laughed. "That lock of hair is from the very head of Lucrezia herself."

"*The* Lucrezia?" Sarah inquired, raising an eyebrow.

"The very same, "Angelique answered proudly. "I have had the DNA confirmed. That hair belonged to one of my most important ancestors; the very progenitrix of the entire Bel Thana line. Isn't it simply marvelous?"

She stared down at the relic, thoroughly entranced by it. At that instant, her expression and the angle that Maya was viewing it from, was an exact mirror of the face in the painting. The gulf of centuries closed and she realized that Angelique's grandiose claim was absolutely true. They *were* related.

"A magnificent find," Sarah agreed, "and a marvelous celebration of your heritage. Congratulations, Angelique. You have just cause to be proud. Tell me, is there a story behind the dagger as well?"

"Sadly, nothing that I can prove with the same certainty as the hair," Angelique answered with a slight pout. "It is reputed to be a weapon that either Lucrezia or one of her relatives once possessed, but its provenance cannot be traced definitively. Still, if it was once something that she actually held in her hands—or even used on one of her victims—"

She let her words trail off there, and Sarah completed them for her. "That would be marvelous indeed."

Listening to the exchange, Maya used her psiever, and asked Sarah to enlighten her. *Lucrezia? Who was she? Was she another Bel Thana?*

Signora Lucrezia Borgia, Sarah returned. *Lady of Pesaro and Gradara, Duchess of Bisceglie, Princess of Salerno, Duchess of Ferrara, Modena*

253

and Reggio, and more importantly, Angelique's great great ancestress. The Bel Thana family can trace its lineage all the way back to the Borgias, and Lucrezia's memory has always been something of an obsession of hers. As you can see, Angelique sometimes tends towards the eccentric.

Why should I be impressed?

Because you should know who Lucrezia Borgia was, Sarah admonished. *You did read about her in your studies of Nicola Machiavelli and her colorful era, didn't you?*

Yes, Sarah. I did. About Nicola at least.

Then you should know all about Lucrezia Borgia, Sarah insisted. *She is remembered as the Mother of Poisons. One tale that survives up to this day is that she carried a special ring with a hollow space concealed under its gem. This was where she stored her poisons, which she introduced into the drinks of her family's enemies, thus eliminating many bothersome individuals rather efficiently.*

Lovely, Maya remarked sarcastically. *What a warm, happy memory.*

We all have ancestors that we can hope to aspire to, Sarah replied. Leaving Maya to consider this, she addressed Bel Thana instead.

"So, tell me Angelique, however *did* you come by them?"

"By a rather long and circuitous route," Angelique answered. "Apparently, the lock was preserved as part of Lucrezia's correspondence with her great friend Pietro Bembo. The poet, Lord Byron visited the library where those letters were later kept, and reportedly, he fell so deeply in love with her memory that he stole the relic. His works are well worth reading by the way. They are quite unlike what one might otherwise expect from a man."

Sarah's eyebrow raised again, this time in doubt, but Bel Thana waved her misgivings away. "Oh, I know. I know. Really though, they are not crude scribbling's at all. In fact, they are quite up to the standards of any female author."

"I would have to see that for myself," Sarah returned, clearly only half convinced.

Bel Thana smiled. "I certainly understand, and I would feel the same way in your place. But to return to my story, this Byron fellow stole the relic from the library. Later, it was recovered and enshrined just as you see it now.'

"Then, during the great European economic collapse of 2128 BSE, it came into the possession of several colorful owners including a communist general, several multi-billion and trillionaires, and so on. Eventually though, it made its way to Mars, and later, came to the attention of the *Galarie Heireux*. Knowing my family, and my tastes, they obtained it for me immediately."

"An interesting tale indeed," Sarah agreed.

Bel Thana smiled broadly and then glanced at Maya. "Would you care to step outside with me, Sarah? I have something important to speak with you about. In private."

Although Maya was tempted to protest this blatant exclusion, the look that Sarah flashed her quashed it immediately. "I guess I'll go back and mingle," she said, leaving them.

Sarah let Angelique lead her down the hall and out onto a broad patio that overlooked the city. A heavy fog had moved in, shrouding many of the buildings around them in secretive grey mists, and aside from the low hiss of the wind, the place was utterly silent.

They stepped up to the mist-wet rail and shared the darkness together. As the seconds passed, Sarah began to wonder if this was going to be another abortive attempt by Angelique to rekindle their relationship, and she desperately hoped that she was wrong. The last thing that she needed was another awkward situation to come between them.

When Angelique spoke at last, Sarah's fears were completely displaced by newer, and far more dangerous ones.

"So Sarah, now that you've spent some time in the ETR, how do you feel about our *'new peace'*?" The contempt in Angelique's tone was faint, but still tangible.

"I think that we'll see these Loyalistas brought to heel soon enough," Sarah replied levelly. "My station has already eliminated many members of its top leadership, and the rest will soon follow. Their little rebellion will end shortly."

"I know that, Sarah," Angelique answered. "I've read your reports, and the Agency--and I--are both quite pleased. That is not what I meant. What do you *think*? How do *you* feel about it all?"

Sarah looked out into the mists and considered her answer, unsure where the conversation was leading. "I wonder," she finally said tentatively, "at what we have really bought for ourselves."

"As have I," Angelique responded. "As have a *lot* of us." She didn't have to explain herself on this score. They both knew what she meant. The Hriss clans had been defeated, but the Hriss themselves still survived, and after four major conflicts with them, anyone with even half a brain realized that it was only a matter of time before another war erupted.

And the ETR, while reduced to nothing more than a tattered second-rate client state, was still extremely dangerous. Not from any military standpoint certainly, but through a far more insidious and destructive avenue. Their ideas.

Maya's recent adoption of *Bochatón* music came immediately to the forefront of Sarah's thoughts. First their music, and then what? Male equality? Heterosexuality? Ancient Rome had fallen prey to the 'ideas' of Christianity, and the Sisterhood was no less mighty, nor any less vulnerable.

"I think that we have become weak," Angelique offerred. "Or to be fair, I think that we have always had a flaw within us that we have consistently been unwilling to address. Now that very same weakness may prove to be our undoing. We have allowed ourselves to become too tolerant of these neomen, and if we allow it, their rot will set in and destroy our very society. Someone has to stop that."

Sarah couldn't disagree, and she asked herself for the ten thousandth time why Chairwoman after Chairwoman had continued to maintain a strict policy against total genocide. Had the Hriss been eliminated in the first place, to the very last of them, millions of human lives would have been spared. The requirements of the Galactic Collective notwithstanding, such a doctrine was madness.

There was also no disputing Angelique's feelings about the reintroduction of men into their carefully ordered world. History had proven that their sex was a cancer that needed to be cut out before it could spread and destroy everything that was good about the Sisterhood.

But even though she shared Angelique's feelings on these matters, Sarah continued to wonder where this conversation was leading. She had never known Bel Thana to do anything without a motive, and she doubted that the woman had brought her out into the night air just to bewail the foolish policies of their government, or to point out the dangers of sexual reintegration. There had to be more to it, she concluded.

"What we need is guidance," Angelique said. "The average woman cannot understand the threats that are facing us. And our politicians need a firm hand to show them the right direction to take our nation in. The only people who can do this are those who have been born to rule, and those, like yourself, who have shown by their merits that they are part of the elite."

Again, Sarah rewarded her with a careful nod, and waited. She was starting to realize what her superior was driving at.

"You and I have always seen alike," Bel Thana observed. "I hope that we are still so similar."

Sarah cocked her eyebrow inquisitively. "Go on," she said, keeping her tone carefully neutral.

"There are certain women—women in the Agency who are in positions of great power—women who feel just as we do, and who also think that the time has come to provide the leadership that the Sisterhood so desperately needs. They—no--let me be completely frank--I—need you to join us. Not as a lover, of course. I know that I can't have that—"

She paused for a moment, her voice beginning to betray her, and looked away. When she was finally ready, she faced Sarah again and continued. "Right now, it's nothing more than just a conversation between patriots, but with every passing second, our situation becomes all the more dire."

"Exactly how would I participate in this 'conversation'?" Sarah asked. Now she understood why she and Maya had been invited to the party. The entire evening had been contrived just to facilitate this very discussion.

Instinctively, her eyes flicked towards the windows behind them, and the party that was still going on inside. Every woman there, she reminded herself, were agents just like she was, and just as deadly. Her life, and Maya's, utterly depended on how this dialogue unfolded.

"I can't tell you that," Angelique replied. "Not until I know your answer." Her eyes had followed the direction that Sarah's had taken.

"And don't be concerned, Sarah. If you feel that you must say 'no' to me, then you and your little protégé are perfectly free to leave. This time. We *are* still friends, after all."

Then her expression hardened. "Now, will you join the Conversâzi? Will you help us save the Sisterhood?"

***

Sarah didn't share the details with Maya about her private meeting with Angelique. And when they returned to the *Otrera*, she announced that she was going out again and would not return until the following day. Knowing that she was most likely seeking solace in the arms of Trina, Maya suppressed her revulsion and didn't challenge her.

When Sarah left, she decided to take advantage of the fact that she was now wholly unsupervised. Her research into Jeena taur K'aut'sha had left her feeling unsated, and if anything, she was more curious than ever about neomen. It wasn't just a matter of defying Sarah's will however; she really *wanted* to know the facts, whatever they turned out to be.

Up to this point, human males had simply been irrelevant to her. Ashkele had exposed her to much stranger things, and neomen had never figured in her life in any meaningful way. Even her experience in the ETR had failed to impress her about the importance of males. Despite their presence there, the fact that the Republic was two centuries behind the Sisterhood, and had lost the war because of this, had only served to reinforce her basic belief that men were nothing worth consideration. Now, thanks to Jeena, and Sarah's intense discomfort with his presence, all this had changed.

Ordering up a cup of kaafra for herself, she accessed Rebá by psiever.

Hello, Rebá.

Hello, Maya! It's so wonderful to hear from you again! I'd love to go out riding with you!

I promise you that we'll go out riding again very soon, Maya assured it. *Right now, I need you to access the omni for me, University of Thermadon database, closed channel, marked private, my eyes only.*

I'm ready, the intelligence answered. *What do you wish to know about?* The UT database was one of the most widely consulted sources of public information anywhere, and the definitive word on any subject outside of military and police applications.

Man, Maya replied. *Definition.*

Rebá came back with her information right away. *Man, male. From the New Sisterhood Dictionary; a noun. The term for an extinct branch of humanity on par with the Neanderthals of Old Gaia. Men were eliminated by the MARS Plague (see MARS, The Plague) in 2445 BSE. The term also applies to anything considered to be obsolete, or inferior.*

And yet, the Agency was willing to create them and use them as agents, Maya reflected. Was this bad judgment, or did someone know something about Neos that they were keeping to themselves? It was an interesting possibility.

Details on physical differences please, she asked next.

Certainly, Maya. According to the UT Medical Dictionary, 14th Edition, the primary differences are as follows: males were the sex which produced spermatozoa used in the primitive fertilization process of the ova. They possessed an XY chromosomal structure in their DNA as opposed to the female XX pattern.

Outwardly, human males also exhibited the growth of facial hair at maturity and greater upper arm strength, coupled with a lower order of brain development and intelligence. Due to their genetic inferiority, human males were prone to the effects of the Plague.

What about neomen? Maya asked. *What's their specific difference?*

Rebá searched for the answer for a moment, then replied. *According to these same sources, there are no functional or structural differences. The only exception that seems to exist is exhibited by the latest generation of neomen who have been genetically altered to mimic many of the features of human females.*

These include the lack of facial hair, a much lower level of testosterone than the original generations possessed, smaller bone and muscle structure, as well as the deliberate development of breasts. Such glands were once resident in all human males, but not functional, nor as pronounced. There is also a classified Agency listing on this particular subject. Are you interested in that as well?

Maya certainly was, but not enough to risk her access being detected, and reported to Sarah. *No thank you. Can you elaborate on male reproductive functions? Are the A-16's also the same as neomen?*

Rebá complied, furnishing her with a rather elaborate discourse on male sexuality and the function of the male sex organ, finishing with the data on the present generation.

While previous generations of neomen are known to have the ability to sire offspring, the effort to feminize the A-16's has had the side effect of rendering them sterile. There is another classified file pertaining to this subject. Would you like to hear it?

Again, Maya refused the offer, and for the same reasons.

I also have several files that I can transfer to your holoviewer which provide graphic documentation of the process of fertilization that was employed by human males, Rebá offered. *Although I must advise you that they have been tagged as being rather offensive in nature.*

Sure, Rebá, Maya replied. *Why not? Let's just see what's so 'offensive' about them.*

Very well, Maya.

The images appeared a second later. They were just as explicit as the AI had warned. The first two were quite familiar to Maya. They were clips taken from early Sisterhood media productions.

One was the infamous beating and rape scene from *"Street of Shadows"*, which had become a fundamental part of the general Motherthought secondary curriculum. The other was no less brutal, and just as unappealing. Maya shut them down. They were not what she had been searching for.

Rebá? she thought *Can you find me something that predates Motherthought? Maybe from the Gaian Star Federation days? I want to see how the ancients saw reproduction, not this stuff.*

Maya, the AI replied, *the clips that I just furnished you with are listed as completely accurate representations, and there are specific notes that state that older productions are tainted by pro-male propaganda and cannot be relied upon for the same level of accuracy.*

In addition, the older material also bears a warning that its contents are disturbing in nature and the tag, 'pornography', making it restricted access. We will have to use your security clearance to view it.

259

Maya stroked her chin, considering this development. To go any further, she would have to risk discovery, and Sarah's potential wrath. As it was, she had already faced an interrogation by her on their way back from the RSE building, and she had barely managed to avoid being forbidden from ever visiting the *JUDI* again. It hadn't been pretty.

She was not about to let herself be stymied though. *Fek* it, she decided. What good was having a security clearance if it couldn't be used to do a little digging around? And if she did get caught, she could always pretend horror, and tell Sarah just how right she had been all along. *If* she was discovered, of course.

Go ahead and apply my clearance, Rebá. Let me know if we set off any flags.

Yes, Maya, Rebá replied. *I have already found one mid-level flag, which was waved by your clearance and there is no indication of any notification being relayed to a third party. It seems that at the moment, your trail is not being followed. I also have the clip. Here it is.*

A moment later, a rather poor vid appeared. It was nowhere near the quality of the holos that she'd just watched, and had clearly begun life as a primitive 2-d production. It featured a man and a woman, and although both of them had long since turned to dust, the fidelity of their naked performance had been faithfully preserved. Watching their sex-play, Maya finally came away with a clear idea of how the ancients had viewed the act, and with very little doubt about the function of the male sex organ.

Or about the attitude of the female receiving its attention. The woman had not been in any type of discomfort at all. Rather, quite the opposite had been the case. Maya was positive of this; she knew the signs of pleasure well enough, and thanks to Felecia's love of 'toys' in the bedroom, which included the *strapaadi*, she had a pretty fair idea of what kind of sensations the young woman in the 'vid had experienced. And it didn't bother her in the least.

Instead, she found herself giggling aloud like a little girl. She couldn't help it. Rather than being even remotely 'disturbing', the clip actually came off as a little clumsy, somewhat messy, and painfully quaint.

"Well," Maya said when it concluded. "That was *interesting*."

Do you wish me to access any other footage similar to what you just viewed? Rebá asked innocently.

No, that's fine, Maya returned. *I get the basic idea. I think that will be all for tonight.*

Good night, Maya.

She went to bed considering everything that she had learned. It was obvious that there was a lot more myth, and assumption, surrounding men, and neomen, than anyone really suspected. Even she had fallen prey to this, she realized. What else she would discover about Taur K'aut'sha, and his kind, she could only speculate about.

***

While Maya was drifted off to sleep, Sarah was still wide awake. Her wrists were secured above her head, and linked to a sturdy ring set in the ceiling. Trina stood before her, smiling cruelly as she placed a realie headset over her temples. She wore its twin on her own head.

"I have a gift for you, darling," she told her. "It's another realie, but a very special one. I had it custom made."

Trina closed her eyes and the room changed. Instead of smooth white walls, Sarah found herself encircled by a dark stone chamber, its rough chiseled surfaces sweating in the dank air. Her wrist ties had been transformed as well; now they were made from half-rusted iron and they clinked whenever she shifted her weight.

Trina had also altered her appearance. Now, she was dressed in an elegant silk gown with long trailing sleeves and her hair was tied back behind her head and kept in place by a broad, ornate clasp. Beside her, was a metal brazier filled with glowing coals. A single, straight piece of iron with a crude handle, rested among them.

"This is an authentic recreation of the Thieves Tower," Trina explained, gesturing expansively around them, "from a charming little village called *Riquewihr*. It was in the Alsace region of ancient France. Isn't it just wonderful? I was assured that it's perfect down to the very last detail."

Her eyes alight with predatory anticipation, she picked up the iron from the brazier, walking with it towards Sarah. Its tip was white-hot.

"Please," Sarah gasped, recoiling from the heat.

"Please? Please don't? Or 'please, mistress, I want it?'" Trina asked. "Really, I have to know. Which is it?"

"Please—"Sarah repeated.

Trina shook her head and sighed. "Oh well, I guess that I'm in charge as always. I suppose that I'll have to be the one to make the choice then."

She touched the iron to Sarah's exposed breast. Hot metal met unprotected flesh and the sound of skin sizzling combined with the woman's agonized shriek, filling the room.

None of it was real, or doing any lasting damage, but Sarah's brain didn't know the difference. For her, it was everything that it seemed to be. The miracle of realie technology had made this and everything else that

Trina went on to do to her, not only possible, but entirely believable and just as unavoidable as the real experience would have been.

When it was finally over, Sarah hung limply, suspended from the floor by nothing more than her restraints. Her body was covered with sweat and she sobbed with a ragged, tearless misery. Her eyes had gone dry somewhere in the midst of the ordeal, and her throat was too raw from screaming to manage anything better than a pathetic, strangled croak.

Trina leaned in close to her and brushed away a strand of lank, tangled hair to caress her cheek. "Shh," she said tenderly, "There, there. It's all over."

Sarah nodded weakly, and Trina whispered into her ear. "Do you see now? Do you see now how much I really love you? No one else will ever love you as much as I do. No one."

She kissed her on her forehead. "Happy birthday, darling."

Overcome by her ordeal, and a final command sent through the realie program, Sarah passed out.

Trina left Sarah's headset on her head, confident that the realie would keep her unconscious, and went out into the garage. Aria was parked there, linked to a diagnostic terminal.

"Good evening Aria," Trina said. "It's time for your check-up. I wanted to make sure that your software is up to date and running properly."

"Yes, Trina," the AI responded. "I am currently running version 515.33A. According to the last system check I performed this morning, there is no data fragmentation, and no processing errors have been detected."

"Very good," Trina replied. "I'd still like to run a more extensive check though. Verify access code 'Dana, Ellyn, Sharra, Anna, Dana, Ellyn 143027-60'."

The AI obeyed. "Verified."

Sarah didn't know it, but she was much more than just another submissive to Trina. She was also a valuable source of information, and by extension, power.

In the Agency, knowledge was everything. It was the key to gaining influence, or to buy favors from those who possessed that influence. What Sarah n'Jan knew, or even merely suspected, had been a commodity that Trina had traded in and benefited from, for years.

Accessing Aria's database, she browsed through the file trees until she located Sarah's private case files. They were encrypted of course, but this posed no real obstacle. She had used realies with Sarah before, and one benefit of this immersive form of entertainment media, notwithstanding the fun it always provided, was the ability to ferret out Sarah's security passwords, and then erase any trace of her mental intrusion.

Supplying the latest code to Aria, the files opened and she browsed them at her leisure. She was not disappointed by what she found.

The file concerning glass sales in the Esteral Terrana Rapabla had recently been added to, and she briefly scanned the contents, routing a copy of it to her own private data vault. Lady d'Ershala paid quite well for anything that kept her one step ahead of her so-called allies.

The 'Queen of Glass' wasn't the only person interested in information like this either. Lady Felecia n'Calysher had also recently become a subscriber to her data-stream. Felecia paid just as handsomely as the glass dealer did—and sometimes even better than her mother, the Senatrix, although her interests tended to center largely around anything involving Maya n'Kaaryn.

'*Ah, sweet little Maya,*' Trina thought, summoning up a mental image of the young woman chained up in her virtual dungeon. Sadly, it would remain a fantasy, at least for the foreseeable future. Despite constant attempts to change Sarah's mind on the subject, Maya remained strictly off-limits, and would stay that way until Trina found the right weakness to force her lover's hand. After that, things would take a delicious new direction.

Letting out a long, wistful sigh at the notion, she continued browsing and spotted another file about the ETR. This one featured reports by Sarah's field agents in Nuvo Bolivar and detailed covert aid coming to the Marionite terrorists from the rebellious Loyalistas. According to the operatives, this was being done with the complete knowledge and the full blessings of the Republican Orthodox Church itself.

Despite the defeat of their military and the death of President Magdalana, the Loyalistas were still carrying on their hopeless fight against the new government, and the Sisterhood, Trina reflected. If the file she was looking at was any indication, they were also attempting to widen the conflict through an alliance with the Marionites.

This was a significant development and she promptly made another copy, this time tagging it for General Angelique bel Thana, her eyes only, highest priority. Just a year earlier, Bel Thana had personally assumed the role of Trina's control officer.

Such a thing was very rare; highly placed officials like Bel Thana normally left it to their subordinates to handle such tasks, but Sarah's promotion to Sagana Sector Chief had simultaneously elevated Trina's own standing. As a result, the Agency's Assistant Director had taken a personal hand in the matter, managing Trina's ongoing surveillance of Sarah's activities.

Bel Thana hadn't been specific about her interests however. She had merely requested that Trina send along anything that Sarah was working on, on a regular and timely basis.

Mindful of this obligation, Trina continued to search for whatever Bel Thana might consider relevant. The only other new file that she found was one concerning the famous musician, Celina. As far as she knew, Sarah had never had more than a passing interest in the realie composer, or her work, and she was puzzled by its presence.

When she went and opened it, she was even more bewildered. It was truly exhaustive in scope. There was also a song stored in one of its sub-files, and Trina realized that somehow, Sarah had copied it directly from the woman's creative AI.

Intrigued by this, she played it for herself. She was well acquainted with Celina's work, and what she heard truly impressed her. It was far and above anything that Celina had created so far, and she made a copy right away. An original, unpublished creation composed by a Living National Treasure was quite a find—and a potentially lucrative one. The Xee would pay well for it. They had already amassed a fortune for themselves by pirating all of the woman's realies, and they would certainly consider this piece to be worth a hefty price tag, she reflected.

And in addition to however many Credits might be involved, it also had a certain amount of personal value. It represented a new facet of Sarah that she hadn't been aware of, and she considered how to use it against her. Perhaps a custom Celina realie with some painful additions spliced in? The idea had some possibilities and she decided to discuss the matter with the Xee when she contacted them.

Quite pleased with her work, she tagged the 'Celina' file as part of her package for Bel Thana, but took the added step of omitting the little song itself. She was reasonably certain that the woman would not see any intelligence value in it, and she didn't want to create any more of a data trail leading back to her than she already had. The Xee liked their transactions neat and tidy, and what Bel Thana didn't know, wouldn't harm her.

Disconnecting from the data-vault, she sent out everyone's copies, erased the record of her visit from Aria's access log, and exited the system.

"Everything checks out, Aria," she said.

***

Believing that she had deceived everyone, Trina did not realize that she in turn, had been deceived. While the Lady Felecia n'Calysher was in fact a subscriber, she would not be receiving Trina's latest update. Instead, Dana bel Hanna, having hijacked the young aristocrat's account, would get it, and N'Calysher would be given innocuous, but believable data that would leave her none the wiser.

Since the personality matrix had quietly begun monitoring Sarah, Maya, and the others that the Galaxy Mind had mentioned, she had discovered many surprising things.

This however, trumped them all. It was patently obvious that Trina had been data-mining Aria for a long time, and she could only guess at what State secrets the woman had already peddled to unscrupulous buyers. Now Sarah's tormenter had unwittingly stumbled on something that was truly dangerous. Bel Hanna knew that she would have to take direct action.

She immediately accessed Trina's private data vault and altered the Song file, making certain that her changes were subtle enough to escape detection. She also made certain that the secret surveillance program that Angelique bel Thana had had put in place to watch over Trina, had caught every moment of the woman's activities. Especially her discovery of Celina's melody, and her failure not only to report this to her superior, but also her deliberate effort to conceal her findings.

Bel Hanna had no doubt what the ultimate result would be. Bel Thana was not someone who tolerated disloyalty. She would become suspicious, and she would monitor everything that happened from this point forwards with intense interest. If Trina did what she suspected she would, Bel Thana would also take action. With prejudice.

She didn't feel any remorse for the part she had played in helping to set this in motion though. When she had still possessed a body and commanded the *Athena*, she had been forced to make decisions that had ultimately cost other women their lives. Although her circumstances were quite different now, the situation itself, and what it required of her, was essentially the same. It was a war, albeit a silent one, and war entailed casualties. Trina would not be missed.

Her work finished for the night, Bel Hanna returned to the *Encyclopedia Sororitas* and continued her efforts to rewrite its entries. As she did so, she noticed once again that many of the images used in the falsified data had been created with the help of ReVision studios.

Compared to breaking into the RSE databanks, access to the studio's computer network proved to be childishly simple, and once inside, she found all the tools that she needed for the next step in her campaign. The Sisterhood was about to have its political and historical re-education accelerated.

CHAPTER 9

Residence of Trina n'Daeva, Marpesia District, Thermadon Val,
Thermadon, Myrene System, Thalestris Elant, United Sisterhood of Suns,
1048.11|01|05:43:67

Trina received a shock just seven days after her decision to sell the Song to the Xee. Her broker, a woman who specialized in peddling pirated data, had relayed her offer to the management of *Maggothymn Productions*, and Trina had expected them to accept it immediately.

This was not what occurred.

Instead, her broker informed her that the Xee had not only been uninterested in the Song, but had asked that they never be contacted about such a thing ever again. This was a highly uncharacteristic response for a race that prided itself in its ruthless business practices, and extremely disappointing.

Even more surprising was the fact that this response had not come from the Xee that the broker usually dealt with. Rather, it had come from a subordinate, who had suddenly been promoted to his superior's position.

What truly terrified her, was the reason behind this advancement. Their old contact had died under mysterious circumstances, and just after receiving her offer.

Trina went to her workshop right away. Among the many tools she had there was a data terminal, which she used mostly for diagnostic work, and a DNA encoder. This was the same device that was employed to create the messages that the famous black roses delivered.

Hands shaking, she logged into the terminal, found the file with the Song in it and sent it to the encoder. After a few seconds, the encoder signaled that the message was ready, and a small door popped open, revealing a tiny tray which held a vial of clear liquid. It was a protein, which now had the Song's data imprinted on its genetic structure, along with a delivery agent.

Normally, this would have been injected into one of the flowers, and the message would have bound itself with the chemicals that gave it its scent. Today however, she had no intention of doing this.

Instead, she removed the container, and spilled its contents into a spray bottle of sterile water. Swirling it around for a moment, she mixed the two substances, and then lifted the bottle to her nose, sending a burst into her sinuses.

Another minute passed, and then she tested the message by thinking of the Song. Its notes rang out clearly in her mind, as if she had just heard them only a second earlier. The Song had become part of her memory.

266

But she wasn't done. There was another task that she had to undertake to completely ensure her safety.

She moved over to a small refrigerator that sat in a corner of the shop and took out a tray of glass vials. These also contained water, and swimming around in one of them was an army of nanobots.

The 'bots had one job to perform, but it was a vital task. Once ingested, the majority of them would find their way into her brain's memory centers, while the rest positioned themselves in her Neo-cortex, waiting for a day that hopefully, would never arrive.

If she died, and all electrical activity in her Neo-cortex ceased, it would send a signal to the 'bots, and they would systematically destroy her memory cells beyond the ability of any process to recover.

Bringing out another spray bottle, she poured the solution in, and then inhaled it. This time, there was nothing for her to wait for, and she went back to her terminal for the final safety measure.

She erased the file with the Song, and then ran another program to thoroughly purge it from the system. It wasn't until the program had ended, and every trace of the Song was eliminated, that she finally allowed herself to relax.

From here on, the only copy of it was inside of her, and anyone who wanted it, would be forced to consider something other than murder to obtain it. These safeguards were certainly far from perfect, but she was much safer than she had been only ten minutes earlier.

Feeling a little better about her situation, Trina accessed her Com and tried to contact her broker. There simply had to be others who would want the Song, she reasoned. The murder of the Xee executive—and it *had* to be a murder—made this a dangerous certainty.

When her broker finally answered her, it was to say goodbye. Trina's jaw dropped as the woman explained to her that she could not continue with their business relationship. Celina's creation had invited the attention of some very shadowy individuals, and her broker wanted out. She didn't explain who these people were, or why she considered them so dangerous, but before she ended the call, she strongly recommended that Trina destroy her copy and forget that it had ever even existed.

Angered by this rebuff, Trina resolved to persevere. Having taken her precautions, she had no intention of simply turning tail and running. Whatever it was that made the Song so dangerous also made it worth a great deal of Credits. It was simply a matter of being willing to take the risks and find the right buyer.

She even saw a bright spot; with the broker out of the equation, it meant that she would be able to keep all of the profits for herself. Fortifying herself with a large glass of wine, she began placing some calls.

It wasn't long before she received a response.

***

Trina shifted nervously as the robotruck stopped and parked itself across the mouth of the alley. Had she not known that this was her buyer, she might have panicked, and a primitive part of her still wanted to. But instead, she remained where she was.

A few seconds passed before the side hatch of the machine's cargo compartment opened, revealing nothing within except darkness. Then an oily mist began to flow out of the opening, creeping across the pavement. When it reached her, it licked sinuously around her ankles as if it were a living thing.

Which for all Trina knew, it was. No one, human or otherwise, had ever determined what the Tzang were actually like, and the mysterious beings seemed to prefer things that way.

A moment later, there was movement inside the compartment, and then a human woman stepped out. She was plainly dressed, and seemed normal enough in appearance. At first.

Then Trina noted the stiff way that the woman walked and the long metal cable that trailed behind her. This, and the blank stare that she had on her face, confirmed the very worst.

The woman was a slave, most likely sold to the Tzang by the T'lakskalans, and the cable which bonded with the base of her spine, linked her neural pathways back to her mysterious masters. No more than a living puppet, she was something that Trina had only heard of in whispers, and nothing that she had ever expected to confront right in the middle of downtown Thermadon. Slavery was illegal in the Sisterhood, and anyone, alien or otherwise, who owned one, faced long terms of incarceration in a correctional colony. It was obvious that the Tzang didn't care about this prohibition, and were equally certain of their privacy.

"Who are you?" the slave asked her. Her voice was as flat as her gaze, and Trina knew that she was listening to the Tzang themselves, through the agency of the neural link.

"I'm the one who's selling," Trina answered, looking past the thrall to the darkness of the cargo compartment and trying to gain a glimpse of the actual speaker. Except for a brief impression of movement however, and what her imagination told her might have been an eye, or a tentacle, or something beyond any description, there was nothing but blackness and the shiny cable, leading back into it.

"Do you have the information?" Despite the fact that the slave's voice was an emotionless monotone, Trina still caught a hint of greedy anticipation. The Tzang wanted what she had, badly.

"The price for it has gone up", she said. "I want *twice* what we agreed."

"What if we refuse?"

"Then you don't get it, and I sell it to someone else," she countered. "I'm sure that the Hriss, or the Giposhi would pay me more."

There was more movement inside the compartment. Whatever was in there seemed to be fidgeting in uncertainty, or its closest alien correlate. *I have them*, she thought. *They'll have to accept my offer.*

Abruptly, the motion ceased. The Tzang had come to their decision. "We will not pay you any more than we agreed," the slave informed her.

Trina started to protest, but then a hairy black tentacle no thicker around than her thumb whipped out from the shadows, and she instinctively jumped back before it could close around her left foot. The appendage reared and then struck out at her again, but Trina had come prepared. She retreated a few steps and pulled out a Marine-issue smart grenade from her jacket, holding it aloft.

The tentacle hesitated at the sight, and then hastily withdrew back into the depths of the robotruck. This was followed by the first emotion she had seen on the slave's face during their entire meeting. It was an expression of pure, undiluted hatred.

"You will not live to sell it to anyone else," the slave rasped. At the same time, the thrall was backing herself towards the trailer, and the strange mist was departing with her.

Shaking with terror, Trina kept the grenade in view, and backed up a few more steps. The slave had reached the cargo compartment by this point and was vanishing into the shadows. But not before Trina heard her speak one final time.

"We *will* have the Secret," the woman growled, "and you *will* die!"

Trina didn't wait for the grenade to float out of her hand. Instead, she threw it towards the hatch, turned and ran.

Back behind her, she heard the robotruck hurriedly engaging its gears and reversing away.

Then the grenade went off with a flat 'bang!' Lacking a biosignature to key it to, Trina had set it for a simple proximity detonation, and she seriously doubted that it had done any damage to the truck, or its mysterious occupants. She also didn't care. Escape was more important.

269

When she reached her hoverbike, there was no sign of the Tzang, or anyone else, but she knew that the City AI had sensed the explosion and that it would only be a matter of minutes before the Metros came around to investigate. Grasping the handlebars, she boarded her machine and flew away. As she rose into the traffic lanes and accelerated, she hazarded a glance back over her shoulder. Far below her, the spotlights of a police cruiser were already lighting up the alley.

Trying to sell to the Tzang had been a stupid idea, she admitted, and the Song was worthless if she got killed in the process. As much as she hated to accept it, she would have to keep it a secret. Unless, somehow, she found a safe way to sell it.

Bel Sharra Memorial Spaceport, Thermadon direct to Waanderstaad Spaceport, Zommerlaand, United Sisterhood of Suns, 1048.11|02|03:43:67

The time arrived for Sarah and Maya to make their journey to Zommerlaand to attend Lilith's wedding, and Angelique not only had them driven to Bel Sharra in her personal hoverlimo, but saw them off herself. Just before their flight was about to depart, she signaled to her adjutant, and the woman came forwards bearing a gift-wrapped parcel.

"A wedding present for your mother and her bride," Angelique announced. "It is a fine Chasadan silver tea set from the Sarayanne Mountains. To bless their home."

Sarah was duly gratified. "Thank you, Angelique," she said bowing. "That was very thoughtful of you. I will make certain that my mother and her bride both know where the gift came from."

"It was only fitting," the RSE General returned airily. "I like to think that everyone that I share a *conversation* with, and their families, are part of *my* extended family as well. When you get back, I would like to speak with you some more, especially about a little project that I have in the works."

"Thank you. I will look forwards to that," Sarah said, taking Angelique's hand just long enough, and with just enough warmth, for Maya to finally realize that at one time in their past, the two women had shared more than just their loyalty to the State. This was only confirmed when they hugged one another and held on for just a shade too long.

Filing this interesting bit of information away, Maya followed Sarah to their gate and boarded the passenger ship.

The trip to Zommerlaand itself proved to be a short and uneventful affair. Located only 21.4 light years from the Capitol in the neighboring Solara Elant, the entire transit took them only two standard hours to complete.

As worlds went, Maya immediately discovered that Thermadon and Zommerlaand were as far away from one another in character as any two planets could have ever been.

A confirmed 'city girl', she was immediately taken aback by the sheer openness of the place. With the exception of Waanderstaad, the planet appeared to be one gigantic agrifarm, with only small towns interrupting the otherwise unbroken fields and patches of woodland. She could almost smell the boredom from space.

They touched down two minutes later, and as they disembarked, and walked across the tarmac together, Maya began to wonder what she was going to do with herself during their visit. Other than watching the crops grow, it didn't seem like Zommerlaand had very much to offer anyone who was still alive and breathing. Even the gigantic silos lining the spaceport, and the constant coming and goings of the merchanters failed to impress her. Although it was considered to be the 'Breadbasket of the Sisterhood', Zommerlaand also appeared to be a planet of hicks.

Still, it was far better than suffering any more of Angelique's company, or her stuck-up sisters, and after the ETR, she had to admit that it was just possible that a little quiet would do her some good. As long as there wasn't going to be too much of it.

The Chief of the Vaalkenstaad Police was waiting for them in the terminal, and positively gushed over Sarah's presence. "Colonel n'Jan, it is *so* good to meet you. Welcome to Zommerlaand! I do hope that you will enjoy your stay on our little world."

"I am certain that my mother's wedding will make the experience a pleasant one," Sarah answered regally. "And thank you *so* much for coming out here to meet us, Chief. I am sure that you have more pressing duties that you could be attending to."

Maya strongly doubted this, but kept her tongue. Absent a serial 'cow-tipper' rampaging through the darkened countryside, she didn't imagine that the local kaapers were terribly 'busy' with anything. They were after all, yokels.

"Nothing that I couldn't put aside for a guest," the Chief assured her. "I understand that you just completed a tour of the ETR." The way she said this made the Republic seen like some fantastic and exotic land, and not the shess-hole that Maya knew it really was.

"Yes," Sarah replied. "We have just returned. As you can imagine, we are very glad to be back in the Sisterhood—*and* civilization."

The Chief smiled and beckoned to her companion, another policewoman, and Maya had to suppress a gasp. The woman was unquestionably one of the largest 'Zommies' that she had ever seen, and she hefted their luggage as if it weighed less than nothing. Her name tag read simply, *"Jotunsdaater."* Another hick, Maya decided, but a really *big* one.

"Well, Colonel," the Chief was saying, "some folks wouldn't call Sunna 3 'civilization' exactly, but we do like to think that we do our part here to keep things going. Zommerlaand is after all the grain basket of our great nation, and we're very proud of what we contribute."

"I tend to regard Zommerlaand as the very hub of our Sisterhood," Sarah returned. "Without it, and other great planets like it, the Sisterhood would simply grind to a halt. I think that some of the more urbanized worlds—and their women—could stand to remember that when they sit down at their tables to eat. Certainly, the efforts of your department, and others like it, only helps to ensure the security of such an important planet."

Maya tried desperately not to gag. The Chief however, bought the whole thing, and actually seemed to be standing taller, and straighter. "We do our best in Vaalkenstaad," she replied.

"We know," Sarah assured her. By this point they were outside, and the Chief's hovercruiser was sitting at the curb. It was an older model, Maya noted, and had clearly just received its new RSE markings. Nonetheless, the woman beamed with pride as she opened the rear door for them.

Despite herself, Maya had to hand it to her companion. With only a few brief words, Sarah had the woman, and her entire department for that matter, in the very palm of her hand. Hicks liked it when they thought that they were part of something that mattered.

The drive out from the spaceport to *Grunvaald Haarmaaneplaatz* felt like something out of a primitive animation, with one stretch of corn field being replaced by another that looked exactly like it. Only the momentary appearance of farm houses and barns lent the experience any variety, and then, only slightly. After a while, even these structures began to look alike.

Just when Maya was certain that she was about to doze off from pure ennui, the cruiser slowed and turned off of the main highway onto a dirt road. Cresting a small rise, and coming down into a shallow valley ringed with woods, she got her first glimpse of the farm itself.

It was rustic, and it was plain, but she could immediately see why Sarah's mother had chosen it for her residence. Grunvaald Farm was all of this, but also charming in a way that the other farms she had seen were not. There was a simple grace, and a peacefulness to the place, that seemed to transcend its neighbors, and Maya felt herself being drawn to it. Here, she realized, she could rest if she wanted to, and the entire galaxy with all of its strife and drama, would pass her by and never find her. It was safe.

A figure stood on the porch watching their approach. Although she was far shorter than their giantess of a driver, or any of them for that matter, the old woman exuded a feeling of power that overtopped her guests. This had to be Lilith's in-law, Maya realized.

Grammy came down the stairs and walked out to the hovercar. "*Vaalkomm,*" she said. "Thank you for coming such a long way, and Chief, thank you for bringing Sarah to me."

Where the Chief had been obsequious towards Sarah, the woman was positively subservient with Grammy. "Oh Grammy," the official said. "Don't mention it. Always happy to do a favor for our local *Vitkaa*."

Grammy grinned at this, and then regarded Maya and Sarah. "Sarah, *Vaalkomm* to both of you! And Maya, a great pleasure to meet you."

Maya found this greeting a little odd, but immediately passed it off as a local custom. It would only be much later, that the old woman's words to Sarah would make perfect sense. For now, it was simply a pleasantry and nothing more.

"Now, I'm sure that after your long trip, you would like to freshen up," Grammy continued. "Fryya here will show you up to your rooms." She indicated a small girl who had come out to ogle at all the excitement. "Oh, and Chief, I have fresh lemonade for you and your officer."

"*Ach*, you are too kind," the Chief replied. Together, they all followed Grammy into the cool interior of the farmhouse.

Once they had been settled into their rooms, Sarah went off in search of her mother, and Maya suddenly found herself with no particular destination. Grammy didn't let things stay this way for very long, however.

"Marta and Lisl just rode up," she informed her. "*Gaane*, I'll introduce you." They went back outside. Two young women were just getting off of their horses.

"You two," Grammy said to them, waving a cooking spoon towards them with great authority. "If you're not too busy riding 'round in circles, you might want to show Maya the farm. I'll bet she's never seen a working farm before."

"Yah, Grammy," Marta said, tying her beast and coming up to Maya. "*Gaane an*, Maya. You'll like our little place."

Maya gave the horses an uncertain look, and Marta laughed. "No, don't worry, we'll walk. We can save the horses until later." Reassured, she fell in with them as they began to walk away from the farmhouse and left the dangerous looking creatures behind them.

Not more than ten paces along, Grammy called after them. "Make sure you're back for supper! You hear me? I want us to greet Lily's daughter and her friend right and proper!"

"Yah, no troubles, Grammy," Marta promised, waving back at her. She turned to Maya. "So, you're from Thermadon then?"

"No," Maya told her. "Delgen. But I've lived in Thermadon on and off for the last few years." She didn't mention the circumstances though. "You two?"

"Straight up Zommies," Marta replied with a broad smile. "Born and bred right here in the middle of nowhere."

"So, what do you do for fun around here?" Maya asked.

"Oh, all the usual hick things," Marta said casually. "That, and party down with what we don't ship off planet."

That got Maya's attention. "What would that be?"

Marta winked at her sister conspiratorially. "What we don't put in the czigavars," she answered. "They only use the low grade stuff. What's too powerful for the *Vreestaande*, we keep. Sort of a reward for all our hard work."

By this point, they had come to a large barn and went inside. After the brightness of the suns outside, the interior was as dark as a black hole, but as they went deeper, Maya's eyes gradually adjusted. At the very back, Marta took a box down from a set of shelves and opened it up.

Inside were what looked just like normal czigavars, but they weren't labeled, and to Maya's eye, they didn't seem to be filled with the usual tobacco-cannabis hybrid that so many Sisterhood women indulged in.

She was completely correct. "The *Green Goddess* herself—the straight stuff," Marta explained, inhaling and igniting the thing. She held her breath for a few seconds, and then, exhaling, passed it over to Maya. "She helps us to pass the time now and again.

Then she laughed, and added, "And Grammy likes to put some of it in her cookies. You should try them. They're *gaanska geshmaak*."

Maya took a drag. When she exhaled at last, the stuff hit her full on. It was *Zogat* all over again, only better. Much, much better.

As she relaxed and enjoyed the sensation, Lisl produced a jar of clear liquid, took a sip and offered it to her. Whatever it was, Maya thought that it made *Aqqa* seem like watered down fruit juice, and like the homemade czigavar, it was just as welcome.

She also discovered that she wasn't that unhappy with Zommerlaand after all, or as concerned over what she was going to do for entertainment. Even though Marta and her sister *were* still hicks, they weren't bad people after all, she concluded. And by the time supper was ready, she was not only pleasantly high, but totally ravenous.

***

Much later, in the early hours before dawn, Grammy, Ingrit and Jan bar Daala stood together out in the front yard. Grammy inclined her head up towards the window of the guest bedroom.

"There's a few things I need you to tell Sarah," she said to the Ensign. Then she related the details.

Jan listened, and when she was ready, she let her eyes roll up in her head, and sagged into Ingrit's arms. Barely ten minutes went by before she was back with them again, and standing up on her own.

"It's done," she announced. "She was a little hard to reach, but I'm sure she got the message."

"*Gaanskaa gaad*," Grammy nodded. "When the time comes, it will make all the difference for Maya. You are a good, good friend to us, Jan bar Daala."

Jan blushed. "I only do the Watcher's bidding."

Grunvaald Haarmaaneplaatz, Vaalkenstaad Township, Zommerlaand, Sunna 3, Solara Elant, United Sisterhood of Suns, 1048.11|09|04:68:39

Lilith was exhausted. She had spent her entire morning finishing work on projected dispositions for the Topaz Fleet for the next month. Even though Admiral ebed Cya had given her time off to attend to her wedding, her sense of duty had compelled her to work on the project—a little bit at a time.

The afternoon brought no reprieve. Grammy had also tasked her with work. She was expected to handle the invitation list, and this proved to be even more daunting than posting starships to their respective quadrants. There were hundreds of possible invitees, from all over the planet, not to mention women from everywhere else. Between herself, and Grammy, it seemed that they knew everyone in the Sisterhood, or at least knew someone who knew that person. Deciding who to invite, who not to invite and who would feel slighted if they weren't invited, felt like a truly Sisyphean labor.

And as she worked, a growing feeling of depression had also begun to overtake her. She knew the cause of it readily enough; regret. Of all of the events in her private life, her impending marriage to Ingrit was one of those that she would have wanted to share with Alex Rodraga. She hadn't thought of him in many months, but the long list of friends and associates had brought his memory back into focus.

She needed a break, she finally realized, and the chance to regroup herself emotionally.

275

The day was warm, so she sought her respite on the large swing on the back porch with a cool glass of lemonade. She wasn't alone for very long however. Sarah, who had also been involved in the 'Great Invitation Campaign', came out with her own glass in hand and joined her.

"Something's been bothering you all morning, Mother," she observed "What is it?"

"It's nothing," Lilith responded with a sigh that belied her words. "I'm just remembering someone from the war."

Sarah reached out and touched her hand. "Who was she?"

Lilith shook her head. "Not a 'she', a 'he'. He was the ETR liaison officer aboard the *Athena*."

"A '*he*'?" Sarah asked stiffening.

But Lilith didn't notice this. She was gazing out over the fields, her eyes fixed on the past, and what might have been, had they all made different choices.

"Yes," she answered. "'He'. I killed him."

"Of course you did," Sarah said. "You were only doing your duty."

Lilith looked over at her with a bitter expression. "Yes, my 'duty'. I'd rather have not 'done my duty'. Alex was my friend and he deserved better than that."

"Your friend?" Sarah returned incredulously. "How could he have been your *friend*? He was just a *man*! He was the enemy! Frankly, had I had my way, we would have cleaned out the lot of them when we were given the opportunity to do so."

Lilith's mouth opened in astonishment, and she put her glass down before her fingers failed her and she dropped it. "Sarah, do you sincerely *believe* that?"

"I do, "Sarah replied, drawing herself up. "Thanks to *them*, the Republic was as backward as it was, and if their men hadn't been allowed to interfere, the ETR might have actually won their silly little war. As it was, they did interfere, and naturally, they lost. Of course, this is all that one can expect from such a degenerate society."

Lilith shook her head. "Sarah, I can't believe that this is coming out of your mouth. I thought that Jan and I had raised a daughter with more intelligence. Haven't you learned *anything* working in the ETR?"

"I *have* learned," Sarah retorted. "I've learned that without males to weigh them down, the women of the Republic have great potential. Once they fully embrace Motherthought and rid themselves of those perverted creatures, the sooner they will be ready to become part of the greater Sisterhood and realize their true greatness."

"That," Lilith said pointedly, "is madness. Sheer, unadulterated madness."

Sarah stood angrily. "No, Mother it is *not*. It is enlightened thinking. I for one, am ashamed to learn that you actually *befriended* one of these *men*. How dare you call yourself a patriot! You should be glad for what you did; you did your fellow women a favor by eliminating him."

Now it was Lilith's turn to stand, and she found herself shaking with rage. "Sarah, let me tell you something; we're the ones who lost the war, *not* the ETR! Do you want to know why? Because it turns out that men are not 'inferior' at all. *They are our equals!*"

Sarah looked at her in shock. For her part, Lilith was just as surprised at herself. Only a few years earlier, she had been more than happy to see Trooper Jon fa'Teela sent off of her ship in disgrace. Rodraga, and her experiences in the ETR, had changed her far more than she had realized.

"Do you know what else, Sarah? Motherthought is *dead*. It died the day that we made contact with the Republic. And someday very soon, they'll become part of the Sisterhood, and then we'll all become something else."

"Not if I have anything to do with it," Sarah hissed.

"I think that we need to stop talking," Lilith growled.

"That suits me just *fine!*" Sarah retorted icily. Abruptly, she spun on her heels and stormed back into the farmhouse, slamming the screen door behind her.

Lilith made a vain attempt to compose herself, and then decided that she had had enough of the porch. So she went inside, and met Ingrit as she came into the kitchen. Her future bride had been working out at the barn, helping some of the other women to build the tables that they would need for the wedding feast.

"What was that all about?" Ingrit asked, wiping away the sweat from her brow. "Sarah just stormed past me like some pissed-off *Valkyrija*."

"Oh, nothing much," Lilith answered. Her hands were still trembling with fury and she made a great show of carefully smoothing her hair. "I just found out that my daughter is a right wing extremist lunatic, and apparently, I'm a no-good left wing traitor. Did I ever mention to you that I simply *love* family reunions? You learn all sorts of things that you never knew about the people in your life."

***

After their unpleasant exchange, Lilith and Sarah took great pains to avoid one another. This was made easier by the fact that the wedding preparations needed to go ahead despite any differences between them. In short order, Lilith had once again lost herself in her work, and very nearly forgot about an important Zommerlaandar tradition.

With only a day to go until the wedding, she and Ingrit were in their bedroom, getting ready to greet the morning, when her wife-to-be mentioned the subject. In addition to everything else, Ingrit reminded her that they also had to take part in a sauna, or a *sauvna* as the local women called it, and that it was to be held at the *Saveet Huus*.

Lilith already knew that *sauvnas* were an integral part of the Zommerlaandar culture. Wherever there were large concentrations of Zommerlaandar women, a *Saveet Huus* was sure to be present, and whenever the Marines built military installations, it was always included in their plans. Up until recently however, she had never considered the *sauvna* to be anything more than a comfort item, intended to keep up 'Zommie' morale. Now, she was beginning to realize that it had some special significance that went beyond this.

"Well," she said, coming in close to wrap her arms around the woman. "A steam bath certainly does sound wonderful, but what in all space does it have to do with our wedding? You never told me."

"It's more than just a 'steam bath'," Ingrit corrected as she gathered her in. "The *sauvna's* actually a very important part of the marriage ritual—of any ritual. We use it to purify ourselves. When we go and sit in the *Saveet Huus*, we honor the powers of fire, stone and water, and we call up the breath of our Ancestors. It's a very sacred thing, and sometimes, women even have visions in there."

Lilith shrugged, and laid her head on the woman's massive shoulder. "Of course," she agreed. By now, she'd learned to just accept her adopted world's odd beliefs. It was easier than arguing against their sheer illogic. If Ingrit said so, then there were spirits living in the steam bath, and their blessings were *vitally* important. "I certainly wouldn't want to offend anyone."

Ingrit smiled down at her, and Lilith's breath caught at this glorious sight. This was a magic that she *did* believe in. Unable, and unwilling, to break the spell, she stood up on her toes and kissed her, and Ingrit responded in kind.

"There's one more thing," Ingrit said when they were both able to speak again.

"And that is?"

"We won't be taking our *sauvna* together."

Lilith pulled back from her, and cocked an inquiring eyebrow. "What!? Why not?"

"That's also part of the wedding tradition," Ingrit explained. "On the day of the marriage, each person goes into their own *Saveet Huus*--and they don't get to see each other again until it's time to marry. I'm going over to the *Appvelveld* farm tonight, and take mine there. You're going to do yours here, tomorrow morning."

"Oh, I *couldn't*," Lilith protested.

Ingrit laughed at her. "What is this? Is my pretty little starship commander suddenly feeling shy? You can run an entire battle fleet, but you can't go to a *sauvna* with a few friends and neighbors?"

"Well—maybe—I'm just a *bit* shy," Lilith admitted. "Besides, I wanted to be with you through the whole thing."

"You *will* be with me," her lover assured her. "Just not for the *sauvna*. Besides, *onselhaart*, Grammy, Hanna and Marina will be there the whole time. They'll take good care of you, and after we get pairmated, you won't be able to get rid of me no matter how hard you try."

Lilith joined in her partner's laughter, but she still wasn't happy with the idea, even if it were only for a single night. Sensing her reluctance, Ingrit reassured her with another kiss, and as it became deeper and more passionate, Lilith responded with equal ardor.

Two hours later, and after they had made love, Ingrit grabbed her things and went outside to meet the hovertruck from the *Appvelveld* farm. As Lilith waved goodbye to her, she consoled herself with the fact that the next time that they were together again, it would be for forever.

***

Shortly after dawn, everyone who was taking part in the *sauvna* gathered in the front of the farmhouse. In addition to Lilith, Grammy, Hanna and Marina, all of the children were present, as well as a half dozen older women that Lilith knew were *Vitkaa*, Wise Women, just like Grammy. Their respective students, most of them teenagers or young adults, were also there, as were Sarah and Maya.

Her daughter and her companion kept to themselves however, standing off to one side and watching quietly as the rest of the assembly organized itself.

Which was fine as far as Lilith was concerned. They still hadn't spoken as much as a single word to one another, and aside from a mutual nod of acknowledgement, neither of them had made any move to change this. Silence for the moment, was better than risking anything that might spoil this special day.

Grammy called everyone to order, and then led the way up into the woods to the lake, and the *Saveet Huus*. The structure was much smaller than the main farmhouse, little more than a single room cabin, with an extended porch fitted with benches, and a long thin pier that extended into the deep waters of the lake.

Pale blue smoke was rising from its chimney, and fresh green bundles of branches, tied together to make primitive whisks, were waiting for everyone. As they arrived, little Fryya took up a place next to the bundles, and passed them out.

When Lilith stepped up to receive hers, the girl gave it to her with a broad smile. "I made this one just for you, Aunt Lily! The branches were the best I could find, and I even tied a special wish into it for you and Ingrit."

"Why thank you, Fryya. It's quite beautiful!" Lilith replied, admiring the craftsmanship and making certain to pay special attention to the handle. It had more knots in it than the bundle actually needed to stay together and she recognized their purpose immediately. One aspect of Zommerlaandar witchcraft involved 'tying in' wishes to an object in the form of knots. The belief was that the knots would bind the user's desire into the object and somehow make it come to pass.

"What did you wish for?" she asked.

"Oh, I can't tell you *that*, Aunt Lilith!" Fryya replied. "You're *never* supposed to tell anyone what your wish is, or it won't come true. But my wish is a good thing! It really is!"

"Well, thank you, "Lilith told her. "I'll use this well, and I'm sure that your wish will come true."

"I hope so!" Fryya declared. "I'd really like another little sis---". Realizing that she had been about to betray herself, she clapped a hand over her mouth and giggled. Lilith playfully tousled her hair, and stepped aside to make way for the next guest.

"The little ones always go out and make the *vittaa* for the *sauvna*," Grammy told her. "With the teenagers showing them how, of course. This year, it was Fryya's turn. They are always made from the branches of the silver birch tree. Those are the best, and it looks like she worked extra hard on yours."

Although she had mentioned them to Lilith, in her haste to explain everything and also get herself ready for her own *sauvna*, Ingrit had neglected to tell her exactly how and when they were used.

Realizing this, Grammy enlightened her. "We use the birch switches in the *sauvna*. They help to stimulate the skin and make it sweat, and also to relax the muscles."

To demonstrate, she took her own switch and lightly struck her torso and shoulders with it. "It's quite invigorating, and the scent is *otaar vunderblik!* You'll see once you're inside."

Then she took Lilith by the arm and directed her over to the benches, where everyone was stripping off their clothes.

"We go into the *sauvna* naked, and we come out naked, "Grammy said. "For us, it is like the Mother's womb. Everyone is equal in there, *né vaar?*"

Yes," Lilith agreed. "Everyone." As she undressed herself, Grammy left her and took up a place at the entrance to the *Saveet Huus* itself. One of her students stood with her, holding a bowl filled with water, and as everyone filed past, Grammy dipped her switch into it and sprinkled them with a few drops.

"Ven da Oude Maansz omvaa Zee, " she chanted in a strong firm voice. *"Ven juu leefa en möeda zoonmaak",* "May the breath of our ancestors embrace you. May they cleanse your body and your spirit."

Lilith's turn came, and Grammy dipped her thumb into the water and traced something on her forehead that made her skin tingle. Deep down, Lilith knew that this sensation had been produced by something more than just the kiss of cold water, and for once, she didn't deny the feeling. At certain times, like this one, a little magic could be allowed to exist.

"For the new bride, a special blessing," Grammy declared.

"Thank you Grammy," Lilith answered, her throat suddenly tight with emotion. She hugged the old woman.

"Now go inside," Grammy told her, wiping away a tear. *"Gaane an,* we have to get you good and clean so that you can get married."

The interior of the *Saveet Huus* was dim, lit only by tiny ventilation windows, and what illumination was lent to it by a small stove set in the center of the room. As Lilith's eyes adjusted to the shadows, she took in the three tiers of benches that lined the cedar wood walls.

The lowest, Ingrit had told her, were for newcomers to the *sauvna* experience, and for children. The higher ones were reserved for the more experienced participants. Not surprisingly, the other Wise Women and their students occupied these heights, and for a moment, Lilith was worried that she would be seated with them, or with the veterans on the second level. The heat was already intense and she was well aware that it would become even stronger the higher she sat.

But in deference to her inexperience, one of Grammy's teenage students gently guided her to the first tier to sit next to Fryya and the other little ones. Sarah and Maya were also seated at this level, but had purposely chosen a spot well away from her.

When Grammy came in, her assistant handed her a dipper filled with water, and after saying something in a voice too low for Lilith's ears to catch, she poured it carefully over the rocks that were heating on the stovetop.

Steam rose up from them immediately, and as the temperature inside the *Saveet Huus* rose, Grammy began to chant. The other Wise Women joined in, and someone accompanied them with a small drum.

"Ven Grosfraan anz grosfraane, juu wek onz hören", they sang, "Grandmothers of our grandmothers, we hear you calling.'

"Anteeke zwestern, juu gesaang onz hören", "Ancient sisters, we hear you singing.'

"Vrendaa en liefa ven dee verloenkeer, juu laag onz hören", "Friends and lovers of bygone times, we hear you laughing.'

"Daateraan ven dee euaan, juu hool onz hören", "Daughters of the centuries, we hear you weeping.'

"As ven dee voorgeboor, juu vohl onz ", "Breath of our ancestors, we feel you."

Then the chant was repeated.

Gradually, Lilith felt herself becoming drowsy. At last, she gave into the sensation, letting the beats of the drum and the women's voices carry her away. Something that was halfway between a dream and a waking vision, overcame her.

She found herself standing, or floating in front of a great tree that seemed to be made of luminous crystal, or pure light. Its branches reached upwards into the sky, and although she couldn't see it, she knew that its roots went down into the very heart of the earth.

Instead of leaves dotting the branches, there were points of light and as she tried to focus on them, she realized that they were actually stars.

The tree began to spin, slowly at first and then with greater speed. At the same time, she caught a glimpse of three women standing at its base. She couldn't discern what they were doing, but whatever it was, it seemed important and as much a part of the tree itself as everything else.

This tree holds up the entire universe, she thought, totally at a loss to explain how she had come by this knowledge. She simply knew. And a word came into her mind, but it was in no language that she recognized; *'Irminsul'.*

Even as she searched for a correlate, the vision/dream faded, and she felt someone gently shaking her by the shoulder. It was another one of Grammy's teenage students.

"Gaane an," the young woman urged. "You've had a *seiðradroom* and you need to get out of the heat for a bit."

She helped her to her feet, and led her outside. By the time she was seated on a bench on the porch, the details of her vision were gone, leaving only enigmatic fragments behind. Something had happened to her, she knew that.

She wasn't certain what it had been, and the longer that she sat there, the less there was of it to pursue. At last, she gave up on the attempt and simply let herself enjoy the cool air and the beer that the young woman had pressed into her hand.

The taste of it was pure heaven, and she leaned back against a post and took in the sight of the lake and the woods beyond, enjoying the feeling of simply being at peace without a care in the universe.

As she savored this sensation, Grammy came out of the *Saveet Huus* out to cool off, and Lilith smiled up at her. "Thank you, Grammy, "she said.

They both knew that she was thanking her for far more than just the simple pleasure of the communal sweat, and the older woman smiled back at her in understanding.

"Welcome home, daughter," Grammy said.

***

After the last round had been completed in the *Saveet Huus*, Grammy formally thanked the ancestors and the spirits of the place. It was time for the marriage ceremony itself to begin.

Lilith was guided from the lake and up to the High Place by little Fryya and her mother Hanna, with Sarah and the other guests walking behind them in a long train. Ingrit, she knew, was also coming, escorted by Hanna's pairmate, Marina, but by a separate path. This was intentional. It signified the individual lives which they had lived until this moment, and were now coming together in marriage.

Both groups arrived at the site of the ritual at exactly the same time. They found Grammy and a group of other Wise Women waiting for them.

The Vitkaa were all dressed in their ritual aprons, which were marked out with sacred symbols, and they were wearing shawls on their shoulders that bore even more religious markings. Lilith only recognized a few of them, but once again, thanks to Ingrit, she knew that the largest of these, a snowflake-like design, called the *Aeshjahlmuur*, signified their names, and their positions as elders of the Zommerlaandar faith.

Grammy's was by far the largest, and the most elaborate, and from this, and the fact that the other women were flanking her, it was obvious that she was the seniormost among them. In keeping with the sacredness of the occasion, Grammy and the others wore serious expressions, but as Lilith and Ingrit approached, she rewarded them with a small, secretive smile and a friendly wink. Smiling back, the couple took their place before her, clasped hands, and then stole a moment to gaze at one another.

Ingrit looked positively radiant. She was clothed in a brilliant green gown that matched the one that Lilith herself was wearing, and like her, she also wore a wreath of wildflowers in her long golden hair. Lilith had never seen anyone so beautiful, or that she loved so much.

A moment later, Grammy raised her hands, calling for everyone's attention. The assembly fell silent, and she began speaking, her voice carrying strong and clear across the open space.

"In the old times," she said, "men and women married like the gods and goddesses. But when the great sickness came, the men died, and with them the gods, leaving the women and the goddesses behind to mourn the loss of their mates.'

She paused for dramatic effect, before continuing.

"Then, Frigga and Siif, the widows of Odhinn and Tor, decided that life had to go on. They forged a new union, marrying one another in the sight of the other goddesses. From this Pairing came the first new child, a girl they called Bergljót, the *Light that Rescues*. It is said that from her, we, the new women, are all descended."

Many in the assembly made holy signs at this, Ingrit included. Grammy went on.

"Today, we have come together to celebrate another marriage, one between two mortal women, who have chosen to join together and create a family of their own. Through them our life continues, and they honor the *Alte Volk*, the Old Gods, whose spirits still watch over us from the afterlife, and the goddesses who guard us in this one."

Grammy looked over to the woman on her left. Like her, she was attired in ritual finery and bore a large silver cup. Decorated with swirling knot work and stylized images of animals and humans, it was filled to the brim with the strong honey wine the Zommerlaandars called *mjørda*, or mead.

The cup-bearer offered it to them, and they each took a sip of the drink. The stuff burned like fire down Lilith's throat, but then the sweet aftertaste came to her tongue, and she recalled the meaning that the Zommerlaandars associated with this. In the marriage rite, it was meant to symbolize the fire of love that the two women shared, as well as the pain and sweetness that often accompanied it.

As they returned the cup, Grammy signalled to another Vitkaa who was standing off to her right. This woman was holding a spear over two meters long. The weapon was centuries old; Ingrit had told her that it had been in her family for generations, having been passed down from mother to daughter from some dim forgotten point in Old Gaia's past. Mystic symbols similar to the ones on Grammy's clothing were carved into its wooden shaft, curling up and around its entire length like snakes.

The spearhead that capped it was just as elaborate. A third of a meter in length and wickedly sharp, it was deeply engraved with enigmatic designs and geometric patterns that went back to a time before the characters on the shaft had even been conceived of.

The spear carrier stepped forwards, and solemnly held it out to them. Ingrit took it from her, grasping the shaft firmly and planting the butt end into the soft earth at her feet. Lilith followed suit, grasping a spot just above her partner's. Then they looked at one another and recited the first words of their marriage vows.

"I will protect you," they said together, "and the home that we will build. I will stand with you against all dangers. I will fight by your side, and should you fall, I will be your spear and your shield."

Looking up at the spearhead gleaming proudly in the sunlight, Lilith recalled an expression that she had sometimes heard the Zommerlaandars use, *'die Spaaran ann Zommerlaand, ''the Spears of Zommerlaand.'* It generally referred to the young women who went off-planet to serve in the military.

But now she fully understood its meaning. To the women around her, the spear that she was holding represented the sacred duty that they all shared to protect their family and their folk. It was the symbol of safety around which they all rallied in times of danger. When she had joined the Navy, she had sworn an oath to protect the Sisterhood, and now that promise had been given a personal face. She too, was now a Spear of Zommerlaand, she realized, just as much as she was a naval officer. It was an added responsibility that she was more than happy to take upon her shoulders.

Grammy nodded to a third woman. She held a brace of antique keys, strung together by a long braided cord. These were the symbol of the household that they would create, and the duty to care for it, and each other. The Wise Woman tied the free ends of the cord around their wrists, and bound them to their spear.

Lilith and Ingrit made the next part of their pledge. "I will care for you," they promised each other, "and the home that we will make, through the good times and the bad. I will be your helpmate and your partner."

They had reached the final part of their oath. The part that would marry them. Lilith's throat tightened with emotion as she struggled to keep her voice from breaking, and her eyes misted over with tears of happiness.

"By this bond I pledge my troth to thee," they declared in unison, "from this day forth, our fates are wedded together; through the spring of our new union, through the summer of its fullness, to the fall and winter of our old age, until we are returned to the earth at last.'

"I name thee now in the presence of all who have assembled here; you are my wife, my lover, my helpmate, and my friend. I am pledged to thee until the very end of my days. May all who are present, hear my oath and place their blessings upon it. *Za es var*."

For a few seconds, the assembly was utterly still, and then a collective cheer of *'Za es var!'*, *'It is done!'* went up. As Lilith and Ingrit were unbound, and kissed, Grammy added her own words to the occasion, but Lilith didn't hear them. Neither did Ingrit. Their eyes and ears were only for one another.

My wife, Lilith thought, marveling that someone so wonderful had chosen her for a mate. Looking into Ingrit's violet eyes, she saw that they shone with the same wonder, and the same joy.

The wedding feast that followed was held down at the farmhouse in the front yard. Huge trestle tables had been set up there, with a place of honor at the largest of these for the brides, with Grammy and her Wise Women seated next to them, followed by the immediate family, and then everyone else.

Sarah however, was not at the main table, but had situated herself at one of the smaller ones, off to the side. Lilith ignored this slight however. This was her wedding day, and she didn't intend to let anything spoil it, even her daughter's extreme views, or her intransigent attitude. Thankfully, the company around her was convivial, and the food and drink where just as magnificent.

But Lilith only ate a little of it, and Ingrit was just as sparing. They had other appetites in mind, and as soon as they saw the chance, they stole away to the farmhouse, and went upstairs. As custom dictated, everyone attending the celebration pretended not to notice when they left, but the next morning, when Lilith stepped outside their bedroom, sore but happy, she nearly tripped on the presents that had been quietly deposited at their door step during the night.

Residence of Trina n'Daeva, Marpesia District, Thermadon Val, Thermadon, Myrene System, Thalestris Elant, United Sisterhood of Suns, 1048.11|16|08:33:15

Looking at her reflection in the mirror, Trina liked what she saw. Very much. Although Sarah was out of town, this didn't mean that all the fun in life had to be put on hold. There were other women with the same needs as Sarah, and although they didn't bring her the same satisfaction, they still sufficed. One of these, a clerk at the RSE headquarters, was on her way over for some well-deserved punishment.

As always, Trina had carefully prepared herself for their session. Her coveralls were gone, and she had put on her thigh length leather boots, matching gloves, and her *strapaadi* was belted around her hips, fully charged and ready for work. Patting the curls of her thick black pigtails, she smiled in anticipation, imagining the pleasure that she would get when she made her first few thrusts with the *strapaadi* into her guest, and the humiliation that this would cause.

The door chimed just as she finished inspecting herself, and she walked over to it, signaling it to open with her psiever.

"I warned you about making me angry," she started to say. "Now I'll have to—"

The rest of her statement died with her surprise.

Angelique was standing there. The woman waved her hand and the world went dark.

When Trina came to, she realized that her wrists were cuffed to the chain that she kept suspended from the ceiling. She had been hauled up so high that her toes could barely find the mattress.

Angelique held an antique dagger in her hand and was looking at it appraisingly. "Yes, I think that this is definitely appropriate for this particular occasion," she said to herself. "I think that Lucrezia would approve."

Trina had no way of knowing it, but during her unconsciousness, Angelique had dosed her with a special substance. Produced for the RSE by the recently acquired *Lida Labs* in the ETR, *Substancé "D"* accomplished several things at once. It produced a hallucinogenic state where the victim's fear response was elevated, and at the same time, it stimulated human nociceptors while blocking the production of opiates. The result was a state of profound panic accompanied by a truly stellar level of pain perception. Just by her dilated pupils alone, Angelique could tell that her captive was deeply under its influence.

Those same eyes welled up with tears of desperation as Trina realized what was happening.

"P-please--!" she begged. "Don't do this! I--I can help you. I'll even kill Sarah for you if that's what you want! I know how—and she'll never suspect me until it's too late." At the same time, her bladder let go, and Angelique glanced down at the puddle on the mattress, delicately wrinkling her nose in disgust.

"Oh, I don't want Sarah dead, "she said, moving closer and pinching the nipple of Trina's breast between her gloved fingertips.

287

"Far from it. I want *you* dead, and not just because you tried to sell Celina's song to our enemies. Your crimes are *much* worse than that. I will see you dead for what you have done to Sarah."

"W-what?! I-it's just a song and I haven't done anything to Sarah." Trina protested.

"There you are quite wrong. On both counts," Angelique replied. "That little song is the very key to the balance of power in this galaxy. And as for Sarah, you have committed a truly monumental offense; you made her your slave and you preyed on her weaknesses.'

"I for one, have tolerated your excesses for far too long. I need the Song kept safe, and I need Sarah to be strong. As long as you are alive, neither of these are possible."

With that, she brought up her knife and deftly sliced off Trina's nipple, casting the bloody thing away from her. Trina let out a deep ululating wail of pain, but Angelique ignored her, and went to work on the other breast.

It was only the beginning of what she intended to do to her. Trina was a cancer, and she was going to cut away every bit of her, slowly and methodically, until nothing at all was left.

"Now Sarah is free," she exclaimed. Trina was too caught up in her agony to hear her though, or see the radiant smile on Angelique's blood-flecked face.

Grunvaald Haarmaaneplaatz, Vaalkenstaad Township, Zommerlaand, Sunna 3, Solara Elant, United Sisterhood of Suns, 1048.11|17|03:63:47

Sarah was surprised when the hovercar came down the drive to the farmhouse. Then she took in the RSE logo on the sides and the two uniformed women riding inside of it. As it stopped, and they got out, she recognized the passenger. It was Angelique, and her expression was somber.

She got up from her place on the porch and went out to greet her. "Angelique? What is it? Why are you here?"

"Sarah," Angelique said. "I have some very bad news. Trina is dead. She was killed last night."

With those simple words, the entire universe went into a spin, and Sarah's knees buckled. She sank to the ground with a moan…

…Grammy watched the tragedy unfolding in her front yard but didn't come out to help right away. Instead, she observed from a distance and 'felt' the players, quietly.

It was only when Angelique had helped Sarah back up to a sitting position and was whispering words of comfort into her ear that she walked out to join them. She had never met Angelique in person before, but as their eyes met, Grammy confirmed what she had sensed on the porch. For all her soothing words, she had been the one who had killed Trina. Grammy's Sight had revealed the murder to her in a cruel succession of images and impressions—and had shown her many other murders besides.

She wasn't terribly surprised. Her visions had only augmented what she already knew about Angelique bel Thana, thanks to her good friend and longtime associate, Lady Ananzi.

Bel Thana was not just a killer though. She was also a deadly threat to the nation that Grammy held dear.

But she masked these thoughts from the woman as she approached, expertly concealing them under emotions of concern and worry. Naturally, Angelique was none the wiser. To her, Grammy was nothing more than an eccentric old rustic, and instantly dismissed as a threat.

It was often like that with the young, Grammy reflected privately. They tended to forget that the old had once been young themselves, and sometimes had a past worth reckoning with.

Before becoming known by the affectionate title of 'Grammy', she had been Helga Mariasdaater, and had been trained in the Art of the Wise as a very young woman. She had gone on from there to join the Navy as one of the many 'Spears of Zommerlaand', and had attained the rank of Lieutenant, serving in the DNI, the *Divis da Naval Intelle*, the Naval Intelligence Division. This had been at the very height of the War of the Bandits, and then the Sisterhood's struggles against the Bio Action Army terrorists, where she had distinguished herself as a ruthless and effective operative.

Recognizing this, the OAE had come forwards and recruited her. Her talent for espionage and counter-terrorism had not been the only reason for their interest however. They had also understood the potential that her occult past offered them. Like many successful intelligence organizations throughout history, the OAE had learned to appreciate the value of someone who lived to uncover arcane secrets, and knew how to keep them. It also understood the fact that not every problem could be solved by purely mundane means, and that an agent with skills which could transcend physical limitations possessed a decisive edge over her opposition.

And this was where the official record ended. According to her OAE file, she had washed out of their training program due to low testing scores, and had quietly returned to the Navy.

The truth was quite different. Helga Mariasdaater had gone on to serve the Agency, but in a clandestine branch with no official existence, or accountability to anyone but itself. Eventually, and after many years of distinguished service, she had retired to her farm on Zommerlaand. But her loyalty to 'Negotiation Unit 9', and Lady Ananzi had never ceased, and when she had been asked by her to help with the present crisis, there had been no question about accepting the invitation, or returning to active status. No one, least of all her, ever truly left the OAE, or forgot what they owed their nation, or their friends.

Had she had the freedom to do so just then, she would have gladly killed Angelique. She knew the threat that ambitious women like her represented to the Sisterhood, and she had terminated many others just like her during her time with the Unit. For the moment however, circumstances dictated otherwise. The Tree and stewardship of the Three were too important. So she restrained herself, and played the role that Angelique expected of her.

"We'll take her back to Thermadon," Angelique announced.

"I think that would be well," Grammy agreed. She felt sorry for Sarah and hated the idea that she would be consigned to this evil woman's care, but it fit in with the greater plan and would have to suffice.

Sensing the disturbance, Maya had come out as well, fairly reeking of confusion and worry, and Grammy had to stifle a knowing grin. For all of her bluster about hating her mentor, Maya had actually come to care deeply for Sarah, and the situation had clearly rattled her.

"What's going on?" Maya asked. "What's happened?"

"Sarah has just lost someone very close to her," Grammy explained. "I think we'll need to keep this among ourselves. Lily doesn't deserve to have something like this ruining her honeymoon. We'll just tell her that her daughter was called away on business, né vaar?"

She saw the approval in Angelique's eyes, and the comprehension in Maya's as she realized who that 'someone' had been.

"Her friends here will take good care of her," Grammy added reassuringly "You will be told when you can join her."

Maya was too shocked, and too street-wise to respond, and remained silent. Together, they watched as Sarah was helped aboard the hovercar and driven away. When the vehicle was out of sight, Grammy guided the younger woman back to the farmhouse.

"Let's go and get ourselves some tea," she suggested. "I think we could both use a cup right about now. And a cookie. Cookies always help."

They encountered Lilith just as they came into the kitchen. "Was that Sarah?" the woman asked them. "I saw the car come in. Is something wrong?"

Grammy answered for the both of them. "Nothing is wrong" she told her. "Some last minute business came up and your daughter was called away. Nothing to concern yourself about."

Lilith took in the dust cloud left behind by the hoverlimo and regarded them doubtfully. "As you say, Grammy."

CHAPTER 10

Residence of Angelique bel Thana, Themiscrya Tower, 898th Floor, Agamede District, Thermadon Val, Thermadon, Myrene System, Thalestris Elant, United Sisterhood of Suns, 1048.12|25|03:01:67

Angelique's heart soared when she saw that Sarah had seated herself at the window. They had been back for more than three weeks, and she had taken the step of working from home in order to nurse the woman back to life. Even though Sarah still saw little of the city's gleaming promise, she knew that she was slowly, but inexorably, retreating from the dark abyss of her grief.

Sarah was even smiling now and again, and just the day before, Angelique had taken the entire afternoon off to walk with her in the rose garden at Concordance Park. They had talked of little inconsequential things, and she had carefully avoided any mention of Trina, or her death. Sarah had still not asked, and Angelique hadn't volunteered the cover story that she had prepared. When that time did come, she intended to tell her that Trina had tried to sell classified information to another star nation, and had been murdered by a buyer. She would never tell her the truth.

Nor would she allow herself to entertain any feelings of guilt. Sarah's anguish was the absolute proof that what she had done to Trina had been both right and necessary. Thanks to her decisive action, Sarah would not only recover, but would arise from this crisis stronger than ever.

And once she was fully herself again, Angelique intended for them to move on together, and share in a glorious future. They would rule the galaxy as Queens, and as lovers. Any price was worth paying to make that a reality, even, and especially, the murder of a non-entity like Trina.

As the memory of that woman's protracted death came sharply to her mind, she carefully suppressed it and walked over to tenderly caress Sarah's cheek. A wan smile was her reward.

Sighing heavily, Angelique left her at the window to begin the day's business in her home office. It was just as secure as the one that she used at the RSE headquarters, but far more private. Here, she could conduct her affairs without any fear of interruption, or being overheard by the wrong ears. Given the state of things, it was the ideal workplace.

Her personal AI, Locusta, greeted her as she entered the room. "*Bian dea*, mistress. I have several messages awaiting your attention."

"Good," Angelique replied crisply. "Engage the privacy field and play them for me in order of priority."

The first one was from an asset of hers who was embedded in the Intel Department, Omniplex Division 14. Per her orders, a running surveillance was being kept on every notable in the Sisterhood, with a special eye on mathematicians, archeologists, artists, and engineers. Now that she was certain that Celina was the Singer, it was only a matter of time before they identified the other two women that would make up the Trio.

At present, two individuals stood out in particular, and her asset had sent along their files. One woman was a Professor of Xenoarcheology at the University of Thermadon, and when she opened her dossier, Angelique saw that her interests had recently shifted to the Necropolis at Ashkele. The woman was also in the process of authoring an article that posited the idea that the ruins were not a city in any sense, but some kind of great circuit board. She still hadn't determined its overall purpose, but she was straying dangerously close to the truth.

"Locusta," Angelique said, "task some agents to watch Professor bel Shandellra more closely," she said. "If they can, have them see to it that they remove her present research assistant from the equation, or recruit her over to our side. I want someone right there with her at all times that we can trust."

"Yes, mistress."

Confident that her order would be carried out, Angelique turned her attention to the second file. This person was an eminent mathematician, currently on leave from her post at the University of Thenti. Her latest passion seemed to be a study of the relationship between numbers and music. She was developing a theory that the Drow'voi had communicated through pure sound, thus explaining the utter lack of any written symbols left behind in their ruins. She was also trying to get access to the underground complexes on Storm to actively pursue this line of research, but a local official was blocking her request.

This would certainly not do, Angelique decided.

"Please have our assets in Thenti handle this matter," she told her AI. "I want this woman to be able to go ahead with her work without interference. Also make certain that she receives all the personnel she needs—and that they are all in our employ."

"Yes, mistress," her virtual companion replied. "I also have word from our team watching Celina. They report that her realie is progressing well and that it employs the alternate themes that the State Department mandated. The original remains in a private file."

This was good news. The last thing that the Conversâzi needed at this stage was a public release of the Song.

"Excellent!" Angelique exclaimed. "And has she shown any sign of interest in the Necropolis? Or Ashkele?"

293

"None, mistress," Locusta answered. "She seems to be completely focused on her work at the moment."

"Very well. Continue to monitor her progress and let me know when the situation changes," Angelique instructed.

"Yes, mistress."

Having done all that she could concerning this issue, she turned her attention to another message. According to the Navy, the military arm of the Seevaan Chaotic faction was conducting war games in a region of space bordering on the Xee Protectorate. There were also signs that the Inchii and the Tazbaru were moving significant assets closer to the Sisterhood, and the Vön had lately begun to resupply their warships at the Free Port.

Angelique shook her head in dismay at the treachery that was implicit in this. Clearly, Queen Talaria intended to make her move the very nanosecond the Conversâzi had the Secret, and the other races seemed to be moving their forces into place to stage a pre-emptive war.

They were all fools. Once the Secret was activated, and the User was under the Conversâzi's control, they would be just as helpless as the rest of the galaxy. There would certainly be a victory, but it would be hers, and no interstellar conflict would be fought to achieve it. The Conversâzi would win without ever needing the Sisterhood fire a single missile to defend itself.

She opened her personal business file next. There was a message waiting for her.

The specialty shop had called, advising her that her order was ready, and that it would be delivered later that morning. It was a set of leather gloves, and matching boots, all tailored to conform to her measurements. There was also a customized *strapaadi* and a handmade whip included on the invoice. Everything had been made of the finest materials and was guaranteed to provide years of faithful service to their owner.

As repulsive as Trina had been, she had had one strength; she had known how to please Sarah, and Angelique was not about to play second place to her memory. She wasn't accustomed to the kind of games that Sarah and her former mistress (she refused to call the filthy creature a 'lover') had engaged in, but she was determined to do everything she could to provide Sarah with what she needed.

Lovers—real lovers—did that for one another, and she would teach herself what she needed to know. Sending a message on to her household staff to expect the package, she awarded herself a few personal minutes and studied one of the surveillance holos she had had made of Trina and Sarah. While she watched the session, she took careful mental notes of the techniques that Trina had employed. When the package arrived, they would all have to be put into practice. Sarah deserved the only best.

Concordance Park, Thermadon Val, Thermadon, Myrene System,
Thalestris Elant, United Sisterhood of Suns, 1048.12|28|04:21:29

A policewoman came out to the farm to inform Maya that the time had
come for her to return to Thermadon and rejoin Sarah. After she had packed
and said her goodbyes to everyone, the same officer returned and drove her
straight to Waanderstaad for her interstellar flight.

When she arrived at Bel Sharra Interworld Spaceport, she was surprised
to find both Angelique and Sarah waiting for her. They had come out to the
spaceport in Bel Thana's hoverlimo and it was parked at the curb.

"Welcome back, Maya," Sarah said. "We are going for a drive."

"Where to?" Maya asked, taking note of the woman's aura. Although it
was strong again, she could sense the toll that the weeks had taken on her.
She also recognized that something had changed about her. Something
profound. Sarah had come to a decision of some kind.

"Concordance Park," Sarah informed her, "The weather is nice today.
I'd like to take in the day there before I do anything else."

This surprised Maya. Sarah tended to be one of those 'spare the
pleasantries and go straight to work' types. Right away, she suspected that
something was afoot. She didn't press her though. When the moment was
right, Sarah would reveal it.

At Concordance Park, their driver set them down on the wide plaza
right next to Concordance Hall itself, which was reserved for police and
emergency vehicles.

Angelique didn't get out with them, but remained with the 'limo as
Sarah took Maya to the steps of Concordance Hall. There, the woman took
a long moment to drink in the sight of the Hall itself, its Marine honor
guard, and the eternal flame burning at its base. Just when Maya was
certain that she would make whatever her announcement was, Sarah
disappointed her and walked on.

As they strolled along, a little girl in a group of tourists spotted them.
Her eyes went as wide as saucers and she tugged on one of her mother's
skirts to call attention to their presence.

Little kids were like that when it came to anyone in uniform, Maya
reflected. They thought that anyone official-looking was some kind of
superheroine from a realie. *Poor dumb kid,* she thought sadly. *She's too
young to know what most kaapers are really like.* But she would learn.

Yes, Sarah replied. *So she shall.*

Chagrined, Maya realized that her mental dialogue had been louder
than she had intended.

It is a good lesson in civics that every little girl should receive, Sarah thought. Then she went over to the child and lowered herself so that they were at eye level with one another.

"Hello, young lady," she said, nodding politely up to her mothers, "Are you enjoying your day at the park?"

The little girl shook her head emphatically. "Yes, I am. And when I grow up, I want to be a police officer just like you!"

Sarah smiled back at her benevolently. "Well, perhaps not *just* like me, but it is still a worthwhile aspiration." She reached into her tunic, and to Maya's surprise, produced a small toy badge.

"Here is something for you," she said handing it over to the child. "Now, learn your Motherthought, say your pledge to the flag every day, and most of all, make sure to be a good girl and do everything that your mothers tell you to. And someday, if you do all that, then you will get to wear a badge *just* like mine."

Awestruck, the child took the gift and Maya's features screwed up in disgust. She felt like vomiting.

Goddess, Sarah! she thought in exasperation. *What are you doing telling the kid all that nonsense? You know its all total shess!*

Sarah gently patted the child on her head, and straightened.

Do I? she replied archly. *Contrary to what you might or might not believe, I consider everything that I just told the child to be absolutely true. There may be cruel realities that you and I have had to face, and equally harsh things that we have had to do in the name of the Sisterhood, but none of that changes the essential nobility of our service. Or the nobility of the Sisterhood. Nothing!*

The gleam in her eyes was fierce, and absolutely uncompromising. It reminded Maya of the fact that regardless of anything else, Sarah was at her heart a former servicewoman, and a dedicated patriot.

"Which brings me to the reason that we came here," Sarah said aloud. "Lieutenant n'Kaaryn, I'd like to introduce you to Troop Leader Clara Signysdaater, Thermadonian Metro Police—and a 15 year veteran of the force."

Maya looked behind her and realized that a police cruiser had landed next to their limo, and that an officer had come up to join them.

The newcomer was an older woman who had never been a beauty, even in her youth. Her features were too strong for that, and a nasty scar on the side of her face only called attention to her heavy jaw and a pair of lips that seemed to be set in a permanent frown. The kaaper regarded Maya with a hard, appraising expression, and then acknowledged Sarah with a respectful nod.

"During my recovery," Sarah continued, "I pondered matters carefully, and in the light of the problems that you had with your field work, I have reconsidered your situation. I no longer feel that you are suited to be an agent. I also consulted General bel Thana for her opinion and she agreed wholeheartedly with my assessment. The Sisterhood simply cannot afford operatives who have any qualms about their assignments."

Maya gaped at her in shock. "Sarah, what the *fek*--?"

Sarah waved her to silence. "Although General bel Thana strongly disagrees with me, I still believe that you might have some value to the Agency. At my request, you have been transferred to the Police Patrol Division.'

"From here on, Officer Signysdaater will be your mentor. She will teach you a great deal about your new profession, and maybe even manage to convey what the concept of 'service' truly means. Hopefully, you will find a better 'fit' for yourself as a Grade One Patrolwoman. As for the things you kept at my apartment, I have had them sent on to lodgings more suited to your reduced pay grade. Goodbye, Maya."

Maya was thunderstruck. In all of their time together, she had never imagined a scene like this. Sarah had always been doggedly determined for her to become an agent, and succeed at it, no matter the cost.

Now, despite all of their struggles, and all of the long hours spent studying and training, she was simply dismissing her as if none of it had ever meant anything at all. Although she had often told herself that escaping the woman's clutches was what she wanted most, now that the moment had actually arrived, it hurt. Deeply.

Blinking back unwanted tears, Maya realized that Angelique's hoverlimo had started up again and that the passenger door had opened to readmit Sarah. For a brief moment, as Sarah got in, Maya and Bel Thana made eye contact, and she saw the unmistakable look of triumph painted on her face.

This had been her doing, she realized. *Bitch! Fekking bitch!*

The doors shut and the 'limo lifted up and away. *This can't be happening*, Maya told herself. But it was.

Then Signysdaater clapped a meaty hand on her shoulder. "*Gaane an*, rookie," she said. "*Za vacation's over.*" While Maya struggled to comprehend this shocking turn of events, the kaaper strode back to her cruiser.

With no alternative but to follow, Maya ran after her, swearing with every footfall. By the time she had caught up, Signysdaater was already back in the driver's seat, and giving her a baleful look as she came around the passenger side.

Signysdaater opened the door, but only with obvious reluctance. Clearly, the kaaper wasn't any happier about their new arrangement than she was. Then Maya saw one of the sources of her displeasure displayed on the 'cars HUD.

It was her own mug-shot, taken on Delgen right before she had fled to Thermadon, and it was accompanied by a list of all her aliases. Instead of being purged from the Police Omniplex as she had been told it would be, her entire criminal record was there for the policewoman to see.

She also realized that she knew Signysdaater. She was the very same kaaper who had stopped and interrogated her on her first night in Thermadon, and had given her the directions to the Transient Worker's Hostel. A knowing gleam in the other woman's eyes told her that the Zommerlaandar also remembered *her*.

"Let's get zomething fekking ztraight you piece of *shess*," Signysdaater growled with a deep North Zommie accent. "Zere are a lot of vomyn who have vorked hard to become kaapers. Vomyn who zink zat zis iz a good job. I don't fekking like zeeing zomeone like *you* passing zem up ven you zhould be in jail."

"But Colonel n'Jan iz a good vomin, and if she sez I have to ride vith you, I gotta respect zat! Zo, *rookie*, rule vun; you don't zay *anyzing*—you keep your mouth shut unlez I azsk you zomezing. Rule two; you don't touch anyzhing, and three, you do everyzing I zay. *Izat fekking klaar?!*"

Maya just nodded, too numb to argue, or even offer up a rude retort. She was still too shell-shocked by Sarah's abrupt dismissal. *She just threw me away!* she thought. *Like trash!*

Her tears returned, and she very nearly let herself bawl like a little girl. But she managed to master herself. She wasn't about to give Signysdaater the satisfaction of seeing her cry. She would do that later, when she was alone.

Outside the cruiser's canopy, she caught sight of Angelique's hoverlimo as it ascended into the flightlanes. It was headed downtown, leaving her alone with whatever life she was now expected to live.

***

Inside the plush interior of the 'limo, Sarah spared one final glance back down at the park and the solitary police cruiser parked there. Her expression was funereal, and Angelique reached over to give her hand a reassuring squeeze.

"I know that that was hard for you to do, Sarah," she said. "Even with a candidate as poor as she was. But Maya could have never aspired to be a part of the Conversâzi—you know that. Believe me, she *is* better off where she is now. It suits her true capabilities."

Sarah looked out the window forlornly. "Yes, I realize that, Angelique. I shouldn't have wasted so much time on her. It was irrational of me to have even recruited her in the first place."

"What about her symbiote?" Angelique asked. "Has it been deactivated?"

"Naturally," Sarah answered. "I also plan to see her sent through a PTS scrub to remove any memories that might be above her current clearance level. Hopefully, she'll still prove to be of some value to the Agency after that."

"Perhaps," Angelique agreed, but the doubt in her tone was all too plain.

***

Signysdaater flew Maya to her new home and left her on the roof with terse orders to report to the precinct house the next morning. Maya barely heard the woman and didn't look back as the cruiser departed. She was too devastated to think of anything more than to find herself some dark space to curl up in and nurse her injured emotions.

Her new residence only added to her depression. It was a far cry from Sarah's apartment at the luxurious *Otrera*. Instead, it was located in The Sticks. Officially designated the *Elysium Gardens*, the low-income living complex was in the eastern part of the city, bordering the industrial sector. It derived its nickname from the way it had been constructed.

Groups of identical living modules were linked together by tubeways and common domes, and these clusters, in their hundreds, were connected in turn to three large central pillars, or Sticks, which housed the lifts and service conduits. At the top of each Stick were gigantic circular landing areas, intended to serve as resident parking and to accommodate deliveries.

Despite its name, the *Elysium Gardens* had been built with an eye towards cost and efficiency, not decoration, and the only real 'gardens' that it possessed came in the form of tiny trees and small grassy areas planted in the common areas. It was inhabited by the city's working class, and only marginally better than the transient worker's hostels that dotted the neighboring district.

Working from directions that Signysdaater had reluctantly furnished to her, Maya located her apartment with only a little effort. It was halfway down Stick Number 2 on the eastern side, the Fourth Unit in the B Cluster, Subgroup Three.

Sensing her identity from her biochip, the door for her apartment slid open as she approached it, and the lights came on when she stepped inside.

It was just as bad as she had expected it to be; a tiny, one-room efficiency unit, commanding a view of the drab robot factories in the distance, and little else. There was a small kitchen nook in one corner with a fold-out table and chair, an equally diminutive bathroom, and a sleeping cubicle with just enough room for one person.

And sitting in a pile right next to the cubicle, were her things. Aside from some clothes, and a few other odds and ends, there were several suprises waiting for her.

The first was Rebá. For some unknown reason, Sarah had allowed her to keep the hoverbike and its manual ignition key was on the top of the stack. Underneath this was an equally inexplicable item; her combat bodysuit. Maya reached out and stroked the leathery material sadly, wondering what in all space she would ever do with it now that she was just a lowly street kaaper.

Her sword was also there, encased in its glossy black sheath and this managed to elicit a ghost of a smile on her lips. It was a bittersweet expression though. She was glad to see that she still owned it, but it also served as a stark reminder of what she had just lost.

Would she ever see Skylaar again, she wondered, or train with her? Would she ever fly the *JUDI* with Bel Lissa and Zara? Would they still even *want* to see her? The full extent of her personal cataclysm was too awful and too far-reaching to even contemplate.

Overcome with fatigue, she picked up the sword and took it with her to her sleeping cubicle, laying down and hugging it close to her body like a child's doll. Even the threat of another nightmare about the Drow'voi was not enough to prevent her eyes from sliding shut, or surrendering to her exhaustion.

SNN Tower, Thermadon Val, Thermadon, Myrene System, Thalestris Elant, United Sisterhood of Suns, 1048.12|28|04:58:33

Ever since her return to the Sisterhood, Celina had been terrified at the prospect of what would happen to her when the government found out what she had brought back from the ETR. But she was equally determined to see justice done, and as soon as she was certain that no one was monitoring her, she made an appointment to see Vala bel Valeri.

Bel Valeri was her primary contact with the Sisterhood News Network, working in SNN's Entertainment Division. The reporter had covered most of her career, and over the years, their professional relationship had developed into a warm friendship. Celina was positive that Bel Valeri would know exactly how to handle the information, and who to vet her to.

On the day of their meeting, she took a hovercab out to the SNN Tower, and Bel Valeri met her in the gigantic lobby.

"Celi!" she beamed. "How good to see you! I heard all about your concert in the ETR. Welcome back! How was it?"

Celina answered with a forced smile. "It was—educational. I also brought something back that SNN might want to take a look at."

"Oh?" Bel Valeri was still jovial. She still hadn't caught the serious tone in Celina's voice.

"It's about the war," Celina said gravely, "and the occupation. The government is lying to us about everything, Vala. I know. I met with some of the insurgents and they gave me all the evidence that I need to prove it."

"What?!" Bel Valeri's expression became confused, and alarmed.

"It's all here," Celina replied, patting the realicorder case at her side. "Arrests, secret trials, drug dealing, and even mass executions."

Bel Valeri looked around to see if anyone was listening, and then took her by the arm towards the lifts. "I think this is something that we should discuss in my office."

Once they were behind closed doors, Celina activated her realiecorder and tried to open the files from the ETR. But aside from a bland holographic message stating that the images had somehow been corrupted, nothing happened.

"I-I don't understand," she said, struggling with the controls. "They were here! I had them—". Realizing that she was not going to be able to troubleshoot the problem in Bel Valeri's office, she put the case aside and pressed on.

"I don't know what happened to the files, Vala, but I'll get them. It still doesn't change what I saw and heard. You *have* to listen to me."

Bel Valeri did. An hour later, and when Celina had finished telling her tale, she finally responded.

"Celi, I don't doubt that you had the evidence you said you did," she said. "Given their content, it's likely that someone tampered with the files. But just on the basis of what you just told me, this whole thing is *way* out of my league. I'm going to ask a friend that I have up in News to come down and join us, and then I'll hand you off to her."

Fuming at the possibility that anyone might have violated her private files and attempted to muzzle her, Celina inclined her head in agreement and waited as Bel Valeri called her associate.

When the news reporter arrived and had been brought up to speed, the expression on her face wasn't reassuring. Celina only knew Hilari n'Mara by reputation, having seen her 'casts. She was a tough, seasoned reporter who didn't shrink from asking the hard questions, but now, she seemed worried and uncertain.

"Celina," she said, "I respect you as an artist—and for bringing your story to us—"

Celina heard the 'but' about to come, and braced herself for the worst.

"*But* without any proof to back it all up, it's just going to be you, versus the government," the journalist informed her.

Celina started to reply, and N'Mara cut her off. "I'm not saying that what you're telling us isn't important. To me it sounds like something that we should follow up on. I just can't see my editor moving ahead with what we have right now."

Celina was flabbergasted. "B-but why not? This is *news*! The public has a right to—"

"I'm not disagreeing with you," the woman replied. "It *is* news, or more correctly, what we call a 'lead' and we'll follow up on it just like I said. " She rose from the table, and started to leave.

"Please!" Celina pleaded. "We can't take that long. Something has to be done right now."

"We have to wait," N'Mara told her. "I'm not about to take on the Supreme Circle *and* the Chairwoman without having all my stars in alignment. I'll get someone on this, and get back to you. Until then, I strongly suggest that you don't tell anyone else about this. That's not just the advice of a reporter who wants an exclusive either—it's a friendly warning. What you have here could make the wrong people angry, and land you in jail. Or worse."

The meeting, and her chance to see justice meted out, was over.

Celina left the SNN Tower in disbelief. This was not the outcome that she had envisioned, nor anything near it. It was only when she was halfway back to her hotel room, and still in the hovercab, that she recovered enough of her composure to make a decision.

Whether they wanted to or not, the public *would* hear the news. She would make certain of that, and SNN and the government could both be damned. She also knew exactly where the right time and place would be to accomplish this.

Mid-City Central Flightlanes, Agamede District, Thermadon Val,
Thermadon, Myrene System, United Sisterhood of Suns,
1048.12|30|06:40:10

Maya's depression lifted, but only gradually, and Signysdaater didn't help the process along. The veteran kaaper was not a sparkling conversationalist by any means, and when they did speak to one another, the Troop Leader only reiterated that she was tolerating Maya's presence out of respect for Sarah. She would have a long ways to go to gain even a shred of her respect.

Maya didn't care however. She still wasn't certain that her new life was one that she wanted to live.

The problem was that she didn't have any alternatives to pursue. For the moment, and until something better revealed itself, her only plan was to soldier through, and put up with her taciturn 'partner' as best she could.

On their second day together on patrol, Signysdaater parked them on a roof overlooking the downtown flightlanes. As far as Maya knew, the location was outside the precinct's patrol area, but she didn't question the kaaper about this. Signysdaater was part of the Pat-Rat detail, the *Patrolle Ratacé*, or Roving Patrol.

The PR's had jurisdiction throughout the city. The idea behind the unit was to provide police services across multiple patrol areas, and to augment any local units that required additional bodies to handle a call without draining resources.

Only the most seasoned officers worked this detail. With nothing else better to do except sit in the cruiser in silence, Maya decided to risk a covert glance at Signysdaater's file, using her psiever, and quickly confirmed that her 'partner' was more than qualified. Just as Sarah had claimed, Signysdaater was a 15 year veteran of the Metro Police, with time served in the Marines as a Military Policewoman before that. Had she wanted to, Signysdaater could have opted for the rank of Senior Precinct Troop Leader, and received it immediately.

As curious as she was, however, Maya was also smart enough not to ask the woman why she hadn't tried to better herself. Instead, she kept her mouth shut, and tried not to annoy her any more than she already had just by her mere presence. Deliberate antagonism would come later, she promised herself. When the right opportunity presented itself.

Twenty minutes dripped by with nothing more exciting than issuing a warning to a commuter who had been exceeding the speed limit. This was followed by an equally thrilling noise complaint at a downtown hotel—a merchanter's crew, fresh from a voyage to Seevaan space---had been celebrating a little too loudly for the management's liking. This too resulted in a warning.

But then a call with some real promise came up. It was a fight in progress at a local shopping center, and the unit responding had asked for backup. When they arrived however, the melee was over, and both women were in custody, seated in the back of matching cruisers.

From what Maya was able to gather, the conflict had begun when one woman had called another a 'bitch' (for reasons she was unable to determine), and the injured party had replied to this deadly insult by breaking the offender's nose. Things had gone downside from there.

Desperate for some cheer, Maya allowed herself the luxury of laughing openly at the pair. In her estimation, both of the women were complete idiots, and the reason for their brawling, equally moronic (not that she would have *ever* tolerated anyone calling *her* a bitch. *That* was an entirely different matter.)

When the kaapers left a few minutes later with their prisoners, Signysdaater returned them to their rooftop perch, and they waited for another call in funereal silence. Just when Maya was beginning to become convinced that her 'quality time' with the Zommerlaandar was never going to end, the Goddess showed her some mercy and livened the afternoon up.

The HUD flashed a message:

HOT SHOT: PURSUIT IN PROGRESS--WANTED BY THERMADONIAN METROPOLITAN POLICE:

Reckless Endangerment, Flight to Avoid Arrest, Exceeding Safe Speed Limits.

Name (s): Unknown (To Be Determined). Height: Unknown (To Be Determined), Weight: Unknown (To Be Determined), Hair: Unknown (To Be Determined), Eyes: Unknown (To Be Determined), Motherworld: Unknown (To Be Determined). DOB: Unknown (To Be Determined). Known Alias: Unknown (To Be Determined).

Hazard Level: HIGH. Possible drug related activity, two suspects confirmed. Standard override measures attempted and failed.

Suspect vehicle is a late model *Etourna* two door, maroon in color, registration number 227986R519, headed westbound via flightlane 125-XA.

The chase, Maya realized, was nearby and getting closer by the nanosecond.

Signysdaater spoke on the Com. "PR 13-XE-80. I'm in za area Do ve have an ARPU rezponding to zis?"

"Negative," the Dispatcher responded. "Estimate five minutes before we can get one free for your sector."

"*Shess,*" Signysdaater spat. "Yah, affirm. Ve're rezponding." She shot a glance over to Maya. "Zecure your belt."

An acknowledgement appeared on the HUD and then a split second later, the suspect vehicle caromed by, followed by no less than three Metro aircars, their light bars flashing and sirens blaring. Maya had just enough time to fasten her restraints before their own cruiser leapt from the roof and joined the chase. Signysdaater immediately engaged the afterburners and they pulled ahead of the pack, sliding in to come behind the offender's tail.

Seeing this, the driver of the *Etourna* took their vehicle into a tight climb, rising out of the westbound traffic and right into the vehicles flying in the opposite direction. Aircars swerved wildly, and several times Maya was certain that she was about to witness a flaming collision, but the fugitives somehow managed to avoid this and wove their way through the panicked mass, unharmed. Signysdaater stayed right with them, matching them move, for terrifying move.

When they narrowly missed a hovertruck by mere microns, Maya couldn't maintain her silence any longer. "What the *fek!!?*" she cried. "Why don't you just shut them down or something? Isn't that what you're supposed to do?"

Signysdaater's eyes slitted in irritation, but she kept her attention focused on the vehicle in front of them. "Ve tried zat," she said flatly. "Didn't you read za hotshot, *rookie?*"

Maya *had* given it a glance, but only that. "I guess I missed that pa—"she began to say, but the rest of her statement transformed into another searing profanity as the chase took them through a narrow gap between two tall buildings. On-board AI's assisted with the steering, but although they were good, there were certain factors that even artificial intelligences couldn't fully compensate for. The treacherous air currents inside the passage were one of these elements; although the AI's applied sophisticated fuzzy logic equations to deal with the chaos, the winds still managed to exact their toll.

When a sudden updraft made it change course and come too close to a wall, a shower of sparks spewed from the roof of the fugitive's aircar. Then another rogue wind had its way with the cruiser, costing them an antenna and part of their light bar.

As unidentifiable bits of metal and plastic bounced off their tail-end, they came out into open space, banking over sharply and dropping down with the outlaws in a stomach wrenching corkscrew maneuver.

The ground rushed up at them at what seemed like light speed, and just when Maya was positive that they were about to plow straight into it, the *Etourna* abruptly leveled out. They followed, and Maya's heart felt like it was climbing up into her throat.

Under any other circumstances, she would have rooted for the outlaws, and admired their skill and daring, but now such sentiments had deserted her. They weren't worth cheering for after all. They were just plain klaxxy, and the chase was frightening the wits out of her.

Signysdaater however, was completely unaffected. "Zey are prolly glazz-runnerz," the veteran policewoman said evenly. "N' zey prolly wired around za shut-down command. Ve'll get zem though. You'll zee."

Looking down, Maya realized that the pursuit had brought them over the Kalia Vai area. The streets below her were packed with pedestrians, small stands selling everything and anything, and ground vehicles, crawling along through the press slower than Lamentine bark-mollusks.

The only solution open to the fugitives was to climb again, or keep on flying at almost ground level. They chose the latter, leveling out at the last possible attosecond.

The women in the crowd ducked and scattered as the machine roared by, barely missing a collision with a large floating holosign in the process. Just beyond this, a banner, which had been stretched across the street, tore loose as the fugitives blasted right through it. For a second it plastered itself across the cruiser's windshield.

Maya couldn't read Sitali, but given the extreme circumstances, she imagined that it probably read something like *"Maya, you've really fekked up this time! Prepare to DIE!"*

Whatever it actually said, Signysdaater jinked the police 'car into a quick right and then a left, and the wind ripped the banner away, clearing their view.

Now Maya was starting to feel angry as well as terrified. AI assisted steering or not, she knew that it was only a matter of time before someone—either themselves, or the fugitives--hit someone, or something. She didn't want to be riding in the aircar that did that. Desperate for a solution, she decided to try using her talents and 'pushed' at the driver, surprised at herself for not thinking of it before then.

You want to land the 'car, she thought, putting all her willpower into the statement. *You want to surrender. Land the car now.*

Nothing happened. Instead of complying, the driver of the car sent it into a sharp climb and Maya swore as she realized what had caused her failure. Metal sometimes interfered with telepathy. The body of the aircar itself had to have been the problem.

"So--now what?" she asked, trying to make herself sound more relaxed than she actually was. The pursuit was rising up and away from the Vai and its vulnerable crowds, but now it was heading straight for another busy flightlane and more potential mid-air collisions.

"Now," Signysdaater said calmly as she turned to look through the canopy windows at something above them, "Ve let za ARPU unit handle zis shess." A split-second later, another patrol 'car passed by overhead and Signysdaater throttled her engine back so that it could take the lead.

The new arrival was different from the other police vehicles. It had larger winglets, and these were studded with clusters of missiles and other devices that Maya couldn't readily identify.

It seemed like they were going to end the chase by simply shooting the aircar down. Which, at that moment, seemed quite reasonable to Maya.

The ARPU unit didn't do so though. Instead of launching an air-to-air missile, something else flashed out from under the winglets. It was too small and it went too fast for Maya to identify, but her eyes did manage to catch the thin wires that were trailing behind it.

The whatever-it-was hit the rear of the *Etourna* and attached itself. There wasn't any explosion, or even a spark or a flash, but suddenly the vehicle wobbled and pitched over, nose down, dropping like a stone.

Maya looked to Signysdaater for an explanation, and the woman grinned wolfishly. "Shock-Grapple" she said, her gaze following the plummeting air car with only mild interest. "Zey fry za electronics. No viring around *zat*, yah?" She dropped their cruiser into a steep dive and followed the stricken aircar.

"But where's their chute?" Maya asked. She had been expecting to see one; every aircar had an emergency parachute and braking thrusters that deployed if the vehicle lost power. Or at least every unmodified aircar did.

"Don't know," Signysdaater replied without a trace of concern. "Zey may have wired around zat too—zese runners zometimes fek up when zey mod zere 'cars."

"What now?" Maya inquired. "We just let them drop?"

"Ve'll see," the kaaper answered. "Ve've routed everyzing away from here, zo no one zat matters vill get hurt."

Then, "Ach, zere—looks like zey got zere chute going. Zey must have hit zere manual release."

Maya leaned over and looked down. A bright orange emergency chute was just deploying and the 'car's thrusters were finally engaging. There was a Bat-Bat field directly below them and from the way it was falling, it seemed as if the *Etourna* was going to land squarely in the middle of it.

Her estimate was correct. The car landed almost in the center of the flat expanse, kicking up a large cloud of dust that came partly from the thrusters, and partly from the force of the impact. The instant that it touched down, the doors on both sides of the vehicle popped open and a pair of figures ran out, fleeing in opposite directions.

"Fek!" Signysdaater exclaimed. "Now ve have to chase zem! I hate zis part!" She slowed the cruiser, and then they were landing. The instant that the aircar's gear kissed the ground, the veteran kaaper jumped out and pelted after the driver.

Not knowing what else she was expected to do, Maya went after the passenger. She broke into a run just as another police cruiser touched down next to her, its loudspeaker blaring, "Stop! Police! Get down on the ground and put your hands on your head!" The order worked as well as it always did; the suspect completely ignored it and kept right on going.

A young kaaper got out of her vehicle and joined in the foot chase. Simultaneously, her partner lifted off, and flew out ahead of them, clearly intent on cutting off the suspect's escape route with the vehicle.

By that point, their quarry had reached a fence that bordered the playing field. It was more than twice her height, and she surprised Maya by leaping straight over it as if it were less than half a meter tall.

To make such a jump, Maya knew that the glass runner had to be augmented in some way. She swore again as the woman landed on her feet and continued running with a burst of speed that only confirmed this. Normal women couldn't run that quickly without artificial enhancements.

She reached the fence herself a moment later, and easily duplicated the fugitive's superhuman feat. The suspect meanwhile, was racing down a narrow alley towards a low wall at its far end.

Maya decided that enough was enough. She drew her police-issue sidearm and brought it to bear. Like the other components of her uniform, the device had been recording the incident and was sending a steady data stream to the Metro's Central AI. The system evaluated everything that it had seen and applied this to Departmental policy in attoseconds. It made a decision.

The message "LETHAL FORCE IS *NOT* AUTHORIZED. UNDERTAKE NON-LETHAL MEASURES ONLY!" flashed across the upper corner of Maya's vision and the weapon's trigger immediately locked. She hadn't been intending to shoot the fleeing criminal (although this option did have a certain appeal to her by this point), but she had wanted to stun her, using the weapon's secondary "Tase" function. When she tried to fire the built-in Taser however, another equally frustrating message appeared "SUSPECT OUT OF RANGE."

This time a Hriss profanity came from Maya's lips as she holstered the now-useless weapon and resumed running. She had a backup weapon strapped to her leg; a needlegun that Sarah had mysteriously allowed her to keep. Unlike her department weapon, it didn't depend on some distant computer to decide whether or not she could use it, but she knew better than to resort to it.

The last thing that she needed on top of everything else, was to attempt to appeal to Signysdaater's good nature to get her out from under charges of a 'bad shoot' with an unauthorized weapon. Whether she wanted to or not, she had to keep up the chase, at least until she was close enough to use the Taser, and then she definitely planned to use it on the fugitive. Repeatedly.

Up ahead, the glass runner soared over the alley wall. The cruiser had reached this spot, and cut across the fleeing figure, but its presence barely slowed her. She landed on its hood, and used its slippery metal surface to slide off and down the other side. The instant that her feet touched the ground, she was off again, and showed no sign of tiring.

Despite the fact that her talents had already failed her once that day, Maya was willing to give them another try. It was that, or keep up the chase until she died of exhaustion, or old age.

She 'felt' for the runner and sent out a burst of mental energy, directed at her inner ear. It was something that Lady Ananzi had taught her, and she knew from painful, personal experience, that the intense wave of nausea that this produced would drop the fleeing suspect like a meteor.

Except that it didn't. The woman kept right on running. She didn't even stumble.

"Mer de Fek!" Maya rasped. She couldn't figure out what she was doing wrong, but whatever it was, she was clearly doing it. There was only one option left.

She embraced her symbiote and the world went grey. More importantly, the glass runner stopped moving, right along with the rest of the universe. She had been in mid-leap, preparing to vault over yet another fence, but now she hung in space, utterly motionless.

Smiling in anticipation, Maya trotted up to her, and grabbed ahold of her wrist. The flesh under her fingers reacted the same way that everything in the normal time-stream did; it vibrated wildly and threatened to break free of her grasp. She was experienced at dealing with this though, and held on tight. Bringing the woman's arm up, back and slightly across the line of her spine, Maya felt the shoulder beginning to lock. Fully aware of what was about to happen next, she stepped back and dropped her hips at the same time that she released the symbiote.

Normal time resumed just as the runner's shoulder locked completely. Her own momentum did the rest. She flew backwards and hit the ground with a resounding impact. Maya didn't allow her a chance to recover or resist. She leaned in and dealt her carotid artery a quick knife-edged strike.

The sudden interruption of blood to her brain stunned the woman, and Maya pressed her advantage, quickly flipping her over to bring her arms up and behind her. She was in the process of fumbling with the handcuff case on her belt, when the young kaaper finally caught up and helped her to secure her.

Which was fine as far as Maya was concerned. The runner had already begun to come to her senses by this point, and was attempting to kick at her with her heels. She replied to this assault by simply sitting on the flailing limbs, and when it continued, turning herself to lay across them as she applied her handcuffs to the woman's ankles.

Although the restraints weren't expressly made for this purpose, they did the trick. In seconds, the suspect was completely restrained, and Maya was able to stand. She also took this as an opportunity to express her displeasure.

"The next time, when someone tells you to *stop*," she growled, "you *fekking* stop!" This was punctuated with a sharp kick to the runner's ribs. "You hear me, *bitch?!*"

The policewoman standing next to her paid no attention to the sharp grunt of pain that came from the thrashing figure. She was just getting what she deserved and they both knew it. Besides, she was far more interested in Maya's amazing performance.

"Girl, I don't know what you just did," she said, "or how you did it—but good work!"

Maya blinked, and then grinned at her, suddenly appreciating the irony of the entire thing. In her entire criminal career, she had never imagined in her wildest dreams, that she would one day be arresting someone, and wearing a policewoman's uniform. The universe was a fekking weird place, she decided, and the Goddess could have a very strange sense of humor.

Momentarily, a cruiser joined them, and she saw that it was being driven by Signysdaater. In the back, in the special cage that the vehicle used for prisoner transport, was the other suspect.

"Zey had two kilos of glass in zere trunk," the kaaper told them as they pushed their captive inside the cruiser to join her hapless partner. "Good collar, N'Janna" she added.

"Wasn't me," N'Janna replied, inclining her head towards Maya. "She caught her."

The Zommerlaandar's eyes widened slightly, and then she nodded slowly with what looked suspiciously like grudging approval. "'Kay--come on, ve have to go n'book zem."

***

The precinct house had already received their preliminary data, and they had searched the prisoners in the field. Even so, a more thorough identification check was conducted in the Booking Area, and the two suspects were subjected to even deeper scans that ate up a half an hour of everyone's life.

By the time they were being led away to their cells, the process had not only satisfied the requirements of the Justice system, but it had also yielded some explanations for the failure of Maya's talents.

When they were scanned, both suspects were found to have wire meshes over their scalps, and hidden under their hair. The design was more primitive than the kind that Maya had encountered in the ETR, but it still served the same basic function. Thanks to the war, this technology had migrated into the Sisterhood and the criminal underworld was reaping the benefits.

The reason for her suspect's preternatural speed also came to light. Just as Maya had suspected, the runner had been augmented. Again, the quality was nothing like what she was used to, but it had still managed to create the problems it had. Augmentation wasn't common among criminals, but this was steadily changing, and she learned that law enforcement would be encountering more and more of it in the future.

The only bright point in all of this was that the augments, being poorly manufactured, and installed with equal clumsiness, had done their job but also shredded the runner's ligaments in the process. In addition to the felony charges that the woman would face, she would also be spending a substantial time in the hospital unit of whatever correctional colony she was ultimately committed to. There was even a good chance that the injuries would be permanent.

Encouraged by this tiny bit of good news, Maya returned with Signysdaater to their cruiser. There were several calls in the area that were holding. None of them promised the same kind of excitement the chase had provided however.

One involved a shop owner complaining about a hovertruck parked illegally in her delivery space. Another was a case of minor vandalism to a residential stairwell, and the last was a drunk and disorderly disturbance at a local club.

"Ve'll have to take one of zem," Signysdaater sighed, scrolling down the list and selecting the drunk call. "All za local units are busy vith othzer calls." She addressed the Dispatcher, "PR 13-XE-80, rezponding to AI 253312."

While they lifted off, Maya groaned and finished the last sip of her stale kaafra, pitching the empty cup out the window, and earning her a scowl from Signysdaater.

Club Jit-Jat was only a few kilometers away and when they arrived, they had very little trouble locating their suspect. She was standing right in front of the entrance to the nightspot, yelling profanities at the top of her lungs in the general direction of the door, and club security.

"Don't you know who I *am*?" she wailed indignantly. "How *dare* you tell me *I* can't come back in!"

Signysdaater parked in the flyway and they got out and approached the figure together. The woman was young, and even attractive, in an alcohol and drug-soaked way, and her bodysuit and cloak, which had both suffered some recent damage, was clearly expensive.

"Jantildam," Signysdaater began. "Vhat iz za problem here?"

The woman whirled, or more accurately, wobbled on her axis, and nearly toppled over, to face them. "Those *bitches* won't let me back in the club! My car won't let me drive and they won't *fekking* let me back in. I *just* want to call my mother. Do you *know* who my mother is?"

By this point, Signysdaater had scanned her with her data-monocle and she *did* know. So did Maya. The inebriated figure before them was none other than Lady Janessa n'Daarla, daughter of Senatrix n'Daarla of the Prosperi party. Not that this changed the situation one nano.

"Lady Janessa," Signysdaater said. "Za club haz za right to not let you in. If you vill let us, ve will call a hovercab for you."

Driving home in her own hovercar, AI assisted steering or not, was out of the question. When a vehicle's AI sensed that its owner was too intoxicated to pilot it, it would lock the controls to ensure their safety. It would also offer to drive them home itself, call a cab, or simply remain parked so that they could 'sleep it off'. But if the owner refused these options, then the AI could summon the authorities to intervene.

This is exactly what had occurred in this case. Unable to reason with its mistress, the aircar had called the Metros.

"No! I don't *want* a *fekking* cab!" Lady Janessa screamed. "I already told my car that! I just want those *bitches* to let me the *fek* back in!" She was not only becoming repetitive, she was starting to annoy Maya.

"Jantildam," Signysdaater warned her. "If you von't let us get you a cab zen ve vill have to arrest you."

"For what?! You *can't* arrest *me*!" the woman shouted, tottering unsteadily. "Do you know *who* I am!?"

"Yeah," Maya answered, stepping up to her. "We do. You're a drunk, you're disorderly, and you're under arrest." With that, she grabbed her by her arm. Lady Janessa was not about to submit to such treatment from a 'mere underling' though, and jerked away.

"How *dare* you!! My mother will have your badge, you fekking bitch! Do you hear me?"

Maya frowned. "You know, this seems to be a week when everyone is using that word. I don't like it."

The memory of another highborn girl, whom she had had the misfortune of encountering on the *Star of Aphrodite* came to mind— the Lady Mellissy n'Dawaa. At the time, she had been unable to do anything about the girl's snotty attitude, and had simply endured her insults.

But not here and not now. Arresting her counterpart was going to be a true pleasure, Maya thought. Without warning, she spun her around, shoved her roughly against the wall, and slapped on the handcuffs.

"What?!!" Lady Janessa howled in outrage. "What do you think you're doing?! Let *go* of me! I'll have you fired, you *kunta*!!!"

Neither Maya, nor Signysdaater were terribly concerned by these threats however, and stuffed her unceremoniously into the cruiser. Then they drove her to the nearest precinct house, enduring alternating fits of rage, and tears, all the way there.

The precinct Captain was standing at the Booking Desk when they arrived. Her nose wrinkled in disgust as they half-walked, half-dragged their prisoner up to the counter. Somewhere between the landing pad and the desk, their 'gentlelady' had finally vomited, spattering Maya's left trouser leg and shoe with a liberal coating of filth.

"You stink," the Captain said, looking pointedly at Maya.

"You *think*?" Maya retorted as she helped Signysdaater hold the woman erect long enough for the scanner to register her ID and snap an image. "I didn't notice."

The Captain ignored her flippancy and addressed her partner. "N'Kaaryn has a special detail this evening. Can you spare her for the remainder of your shift?"

"Yah, zure zhing, Cap," the kaaper replied. "I can handle zis."

"Thank you very much, officer," the woman returned.

She turned to Maya, "A group of officers will be attending a concert tonight. Celina is giving it and we are providing some of the security. The detail needs some rookies to handle the shess-work. So, congratulations. You just volunteered. The event is at 07:50. Now, please--clean yourself."

At that, she turned and walked away from them.

"You stink, Maya" Maya sneered in a rude imitation of her words. "Clean yourself, Maya!"

Meanwhile their prisoner had slumped over the counter, and was groaning miserably.

"*Gaane an*, prinzess," the Zommerlaandar urged, hoisting the woman back up onto her unsteady feet. "Ve have a nice little zell vaiting for you, and zen in za morning after zome beauty zleep, you vill vake and zee za Judge, yah?"

313

Martin Schiller

As she stepped in to help her, Maya learned something new. The word for 'yes' in drunk-speak, wasn't actually a word at all. It was another bout of projectile vomiting, and this time, her uniform blouse received the entire message.

Sharien Geallea Civic Auditorium, Agamede District, Thermadon Val, Thermadon, Myrene System, Thalestris Elant, United Sisterhood of Suns, 1048.12|30|07:91:69

The *Sharien Geallea* Civic Auditorium was filled to capacity. It was after all, the first concert Celina had given since her return, and the public was hungry for any taste of her new material. Only the *Geallea*, which was one of the largest of its kind anywhere in the Sisterhood, could accommodate such a vast audience. As the opening notes of *"The Lady of Illidian"* began to play, and their psievers painted the stage with a beautiful garden filled with flowers, Angelique gripped Sarah's hand.

"This is my favorite song," she whispered, and along with 204,000 other fans, the two of them waited together in hushed anticipation for the show to begin. But Celina paused, and the illusions around her stopped appearing.

Sarah, who had been actively reading her the entire time, silently cursed the musician. She knew exactly what was about to happen. Despite corrupting her data files and using the Agency's influence with SNN, Celina had not been dissuaded from her own foolishness. Unless something was done immediately, Celina was going to make a public statement to the crowd about the ETR. That could not be allowed to happen.

A mere fraction of a second later, Celina began to speak "I'm sorry, but I can't do this. I can't sing for you when there are people dying in the ETR--"

Sarah had just begun to focus her talents, when the unexpected occurred.

The performer staggered, and then collapsed into a heap. A collective cry of alarm went up from the crowd, and the policewomen working the detail around the stage rushed up to help her. The concert, and Celina's abortive attempt to make a protest, were both over.

Angelique looked to Sarah with a small moue of disappointment. "It must have been from exhaustion," she said. "The ETR tour was simply too much for the poor thing."

Sarah realized that Angelique had beaten her to the draw. She also realized that whatever follow-up was to occur, was in Bel Thana's hands. She pitied Celina.

314

***

Cup in hand, Maya was doing what kaapers always did when they pulled a special detail; as she guarded the Performer's Entrance to the auditorium, she talked shop as much as a rookie like herself was allowed to, gossiped, griped about Department policy, and listened to bad jokes. She even made a few of her own.

She was just about to apply her professional law enforcement skills to her sweet roll, when the Captain came over the Com on their tactical channel. "Betsi squad, get ready. We have a paramedic unit inbound to your location. Escort them to the dressing room when they get here."

Maya's heart skipped a beat. Something had gone wrong. The medics, who had been on standby like themselves, arrived only a minute later, and she escorted them straightaway to the star's room. And while they worked, she overheard enough to puzzle out the reason for their visit.

Celina had collapsed onstage. After being examined, and declared to be out of danger, the medics advised the performer to end the concert then and there, and get herself some rest.

She was in no shape to argue with the firewomen. She was still pale, sweaty and mildly disoriented. Instead, she quietly packed up a few things to take with her, and then let Maya and the other policewomen walk her out to her limo. A few moments later, she was gone, with an escort from Traffic Division bracketing her vehicle.

"What happened?" one of the other kaapers asked. She was a rookie just like Maya, and had only been recently assigned to the precinct from the Academy.

"She collapsed," Maya explained. "The 'medics said it was from exhaustion." Personally, she hadn't seen anything as profound as this since her own experience at the Port when Sarah had used her talents against her.

She just hoped that the star would get better soon.

***

Entering the *Cheyr mis Famme* Madame t'Annya noticed the two uniformed police officers eating their lunch right away. It wasn't that she had never seen policewomen dining before. It was simply that in all her visits to one of Thermadon's most exclusive restaurants, she hadn't ever seen kaapers frequenting the establishment. As much as she hated what it might have said about her, they seemed out of place. The *Mis Famme* was simply more 'upscale' than the kind of establishment that normally catered to law enforcement, and she had to admit that the sight was somewhat jarring.

Not as jarring as Celina had been however. Her breakdown onstage had been bad enough, but not the worst of it. Ever since she had returned from the ETR, the performer had been unable to talk about anything except the injustices that she had witnessed there, her anger towards the Sisterhood, and at SNN.

Madame t'Annya didn't like to think of herself as being unsympathetic to the suffering that Celina had described, or disinterested in righting wrongs. She just didn't believe that either of them had any business being radicals. Her stock in trade, as she had told her, was music, and representing artists like herself, not championing sweeping social change, or charging the ramparts of tyranny.

Celina hadn't listened to a single word of this though. She had refused to set aside her passions, and had insisted on taking some form of action.

For Madame t'Annya, the only 'action' that had resulted from their heated conversations had been her ulcer reawakening itself. Out of deference to her condition, she decided to order a light lunch, and to put the temperamental woman out of her mind for at least as long as it took her to eat it.

When she was shown to her table, she placed her order, and then added a glass of sweet white *Aarntwyyn*. She didn't ordinarily drink this early in the day, but her sour mood made this a special occasion and she forgave herself when it arrived ahead of the salad.

She was halfway finished when she noticed another anomaly among the *Cheyr mis Famme's* clientele. This time it was a statuesque woman, dressed in a fine slate-colored comerci, offset with an elegant light burgundy cravess, and a rather stunning bershaki shell stick-pin. All this, along with her stunning green eyes and golden hair, identified her as a member of the Thermadonian elite.

The woman had been eating her own lunch at a nearby table, and without any warning that she was about to do so, she rose, and walked straight up to her, taking a seat for herself without asking for an invitation.

Madame t'Annya began to demand an explanation, and the stranger obliged her by producing a small wallet, opening it, and then pushing it across the table. She was, T'Annya realized to her horror, General Angelique bel Thana, with the *Regila da Securité par Estat*, the State Security Service.

"*Bian midi, Madame,*" Angelique said. "I'm so very sorry to interrupt your lunch, especially since you have such a great deal occupying your mind. But we need to discuss one of the artists that you represent."

"This is about Celina, isn't it?" T'Annya guessed. Her hands were shaking as she took a very deep drink of her wine. She wasn't used to dealing with law enforcement. That was for women starring in realies, not talent agents.

"Yes," Angelique replied. "I'm afraid that it is. And just in case you have been wondering, those officers eating their lunch over there are accompanying me. If our discussion goes poorly and we fail to reach a workable understanding, then regrettably, their job will be to take you into custody.'

"I also assure you that there are others, waiting to do the same thing to Celina. The charges against you will be several violations of the National Security Act, with conspiracy added on. In the light of all that, do I now command your fullest attention?"

"Yes," T'Annya answered, setting her glass down before she dropped it. "You also have my total cooperation."

This earned her a smile. "Good," Angelique returned. "I am so grateful that we could handle this matter in a ladylike fashion." She glanced over at the uniformed officers and gave them a slight nod. At this, they rose, and left.

"Now," she said, her voice assuming a decidedly unpleasant tone. "Let's talk about your pet *bitch* and muzzling her little cunt of a mouth. After that, we'll discuss some of the cute tricks that I want her to perform for me."

***

After her terrifying encounter with Angelique, Madame t'Annya's day steadily deteriorated. The moment that she had the opportunity, she contacted Celina at her hotel and demanded to meet with her. When they were finally face to face, it was all she could do not to shriek hysterically at her.

"She had everything!" she wailed. "All the files that you said you got in the ETR. She even showed them to me!"

"I knew it! I knew they had them! Do you see now?" Celina returned with equal heat. "I wasn't exaggerating. Everything I said is *really* happening!"

"What I *see* is that we are in *real* trouble!" T'Annya exclaimed. "That General is not fooling around. She said that if we don't do what she says, we'll both be locked up for twenty years. *Twenty!* You have to stop what you're doing."

"I *won't*," Celina retorted stubbornly. "The truth has to get out!"

317

"Then you're on your own," T'Annya said flatly. "I'm not going to throw everything away for you and spend the rest of my life in some correctional colony. And that's exactly what will happen to you Celi, unless you do what she says."

"No."

T'Annya's tone softened. "Celina, please. Be reasonable. The General said that if you just go to Ashkele, and stay there for a little while, your files will disappear. Everything will vanish. I think that's a fair trade for your freedom."

Celina folded her arms, and glared at her, clearly unwilling to concede any ground, but she didn't offer up any more arguments.

"Please," T'Annya begged. "You said it yourself; the women at SNN were going to look into things for you. Let them. They're the experts. If there's anything to find, they will. Please, go to Ashkele, take a vacation, and be satisfied that you did your part."

Still, Celina said nothing, but T'Annya had worked with her long enough to know that she was finally making progress. Clio, always the more sensible of the two of them, would do the rest.

"Think about it," she said.

Celina did. The next day she called T'Annya. She hadn't slept, and agonizing over her decision had only compounded her exhaustion, so she kept the conversation as brief as possible.

"I'll go," she agreed. "I'll go to Ashkele. Tell your General that. Also tell her I hope that the Goddess sends her to the furthest hell that she can find for her."

"Thank you Celina," T'Annya replied. "You're finally being sensible. I'll make the arrangements."

Elysium Gardens, Marpesia District, Thermadon Val, Thermadon, Myrene System, United Sisterhood of Suns, 1049.01|03|00:41:69

Maya lay in her bed, wide awake. She was exhausted from a long day on patrol, and her body desperately needed the rest. But her brain wouldn't cooperate. It kept bringing her back to thoughts about Felecia, and her growing sense of disquiet.

Ever since being demoted to Metro patrol, her lover's calendar had become too full for them to spend any time together, and Maya was beginning to suspect that the connection they had once shared was fading away. She hadn't lost Felecia yet, and she didn't think that there was anyone else in the young woman's life, but the possibility was starting to loom ever larger in the back of her mind.

Staring up at the ceiling, she found herself praying to the Goddess that she wouldn't lose the only decent thing that she still had left. She didn't know if the Lady had heard her or not, or if she did, that she would care to show her any mercy. But at this point, hope was all she really had.

Unable to bear any more of this inner torment, she turned over and forcefully applied the disciplines that Lady Ananzi had taught her, pushing her thoughts back, and focusing on replacing them with inner stillness. Eventually, and only after a long, hard struggle, she succeeded, and sleep came for her at last.

So did did a nightmare. It proved to be more troubling, and far stranger than any that had come before it.

She was back at the Tree, as always, but this time the Drow'voi weren't present. Instead, a human woman was waiting for her. Although everything about the scene was as clear as being awake, this figure was the exception. No matter how hard Maya tried to perceive it, the woman's face kept changing. One moment, she was her mother Jora, then she seemed to be Felecia, then Skylaar, then Lady Ananzi, and even Sarah at times.

Somehow, she knew that all of these faces were nothing more than masks, concealing something beneath them that her mind didn't have a definition for. She also had the distinct feeling that she should have known what it was—and in fact, *did* know on a deeper, unconscious level that refused to yield to her.

The woman seemed to be fully aware of her confusion and smiled patiently. She pointed to the Tree. "Choose," she said.

Maya blinked, uncomprehending. Then, the knowledge came to her like the feed from a teaching realie. The Tree, whatever it really was, could grant death just as it had for the Drow'voi, but it could also grant life.

"Not just life," the figure gently corrected, "but *new* life."

After that, things got *really* klaxxy. Everything except her guide melted away and transformed. She found herself standing on the shores of a shallow sea on some distant, and wholly unfamiliar world. The water sparkled with light, and at a gesture from her companion, Maya looked up.

Above her, covering the entire bowl of the sky, was an eye-dazzling cloud of interstellar gasses, and in their midst, clusters of newly born stars that seemed to burn with the very fires of creation itself. Once again, knowledge surged into her brain, and looking back down at the waters, she realized that at her feet, the nascent stirrings of microbial life were taking root for the very first time. New life, just as the woman had promised.

She awoke from this more confused and agitated than ever. Between these klaxxy dreams, her concerns about Felecia, and all the recent upheaval in her life, her sanity felt as if it was hanging on by only the thinnest of threads.

She had to find a way to sort it all out, she decided. To make sense of things and achieve some form of resolution. Staying in her little apartment and brooding in the dark certainly wasn't the solution.

She had to go somewhere else, and do something that would center her and bring her emotions back under control.

Her eyes fell on her ka'na. It was propped up against the opposite wall, its sheath gilded by a ray of sunlight coming in through the apartment's only window. This was her answer.

Rising immediately, she seized it up, dressed herself in her bodysuit, and made for the roof, and Rebá. Then she rode straight out to N'Dayr Memorial Park.

Once she arrived, it wasn't long before she found herself a quiet, sunny place to work out in. Then she began with a set of basic drills, trying to lose herself in the repetitive exercise.

But her ability to attain inner peace kept evading her like a skilled opponent dodging one of her cuts. All she could think about was the strange woman in her dream and their mysterious interaction. That, and Felecia.

Finally, her agitation reached its absolute summit. *"Fek!"* she shouted, slashing the air angrily and following through with another cut that was equally as violent. Her outburst caught the attention of some joggers, but when she adopted a more sedate routine, they moved on.

It wasn't long before her inner turmoil reasserted itself however, and as she struggled with herself, she realized that she was being watched again.

This time though, it wasn't another group of joggers. It was Skylaar, carrying a pair of practice swords.

Maya blinked at her in utter disbelief. She had simply assumed that in addition to all of her other losses that her time with her martial arts teacher had also come to an end.

"Sena-tai!" she exclaimed. "It's you! You're here!"

Skylaar smiled and looked down at herself, then back at Maya. "So I am," she replied dryly.

"I-I never expected to see you again!" Unable to contain herself, Maya burst into tears of joy and ran to hug her.

After a moment, Skylaar gently disentangled herself from Maya's fierce embrace and stepped back a pace. "Sarah's decisions are not mine," the woman explained. "Our time together is not over, even if your role as an agent for the RSE has concluded."

Maya gave her a bow that went much deeper than mere formality might have demanded. *"Sena-tai,* it's so good to see you! When Sarah told me—"

Skylaar raised a silencing finger. "No more about that, Maya. What is done, is done, but nothing changes our studies. We both need more practice with the ka'na. May I join you?"

"Yes—*please!*"

"First, I think that a lesson is in order." The Nemesian gave her one of the practice swords, and once she had taken it, unholstered the needlegun on her hip. She handed it to Maya, butt first.

"Take this," she instructed, "and embrace your symbiote."

Maya did so, and Skylaar joined her. Once they were outside of the normal time stream, her teacher gestured towards the pistol.

"Now, shoot me."

Firearms had never been included in any practice with the symbiotes before this, and Maya was only halfway certain that they could be defeated by the time distortion. "Um, are you sure?" she asked uncertainly, but Skylaar repeated her request.

The young woman raised the weapon, pointed it, and after a moment's hesitation, pressed the trigger.

The weapon tried to discharge, but nothing left the barrel. Puzzled, Maya looked at the thing, wondering if she had been handed a defective device.

Skylaar regarded her with a detached amusement. Then she took up a fighting stance with her practice sword.

"Now, guard yourself." Even as she finished saying this, she attacked.

Maya immediately discarded the useless pistol, backed up, and parried the strike. But Skylaar pressed her attack with a pivoting follow-through, and Maya spun with her, deflecting the blow, and coming over her sword in an attempt to stab her. As laudable as this maneuver was, her blade only met empty air as Skylaar dropped backwards into a roll and then came back up at her legs with a low slash of her own.

Now it was Maya's turn to evade, and with a quick move of her hips, she sent her lower body sliding backwards, and immediately carried through with a leaping roll, and a one-handed slash as she passed over her teacher.

The cut missed, but it also forced the Nemesian into a roll of her own. When Maya landed on her feet, she realized that she was now too far away to attack without first closing the distance—and telegraphing her next move in the process. So she waited where she was, her breath misting in the air. Skylaar did the same, and after a moment, saluted her with a half bow. Their match was over.

"So, do you want to tell me what happened with the 'gun?" Maya inquired. "Is it broken or something?"

"No, Maya. It is fully functional. The problem is that needleguns, energy weapons, and even chemical armaments are simply useless here," her teacher said, gesturing at the colorless, timeless world around them. "Do you think you can tell me why?"

Maya shrugged. "Um, little Zommerlaandar *Alfs?*"

Skylaar chuckled and shook her head. "Not quite, *Cho-sena*. The reason lies in the nature of the symbiote itself. You were taught that it alters the time-stream, which it does, but it also modifies quite a bit more than that."

Maya regarded her quizzically. She had never been told exactly 'how' the symbiote worked. Only that it did. And to her chagrin, she also realized that it had never occurred to her to ask any questions.

"The symbiote manages its little trick with time by changing the laws of local reality," Skylaar explained. "It places the user in a bubble where *everything* functions differently."

"Okay," Maya replied. "So why don't the guns work?"

"Because chemical reactions that we take for granted in normal time and space can't occur inside the symbiote's bubble," Skylaar returned. "Electronics fail, and even magnetic fields are distorted beyond any usefulness. The result is that projectile and energy weapons as we know them, simply won't fire."

Maya's eyes widened and Skylaar shrugged with pleasure as she saw the comprehension dawning in them.

"Which leaves us the blade," the Nemesian continued, "and close-quarter hand-to-hand combat as our only viable defensive options. Do you understand now? *That* is why we practice with the sword as much as we do. It is not simply for form, or to observe some archaic tradition. It is the very key to our survival when we are outside the conventional time-stream."

"But you told me—"Maya began.

"I know what I once said, and I had my reasons for saying it. I also had every intention of focusing exclusively on the ka'na, once your skills in other areas had reached the appropriate level," Skylaar replied.

"Now, we are making an alteration to your curriculum. I also think that we will need to work very hard indeed. The day may be coming when you might need all the skill with a blade that you can muster."

A shiver went up Maya's spine. "The psi's that Sarah once warned me about, back on the *JUDI*. Is that it? Is that who you're talking about?"

Skylaar gave her a curt nod. "Yes, Maya. Very possibly."

For a long moment, there was only the faint sound of the wind whistling between them.

Skylaar broke the silence. "Now, "she said, "let us practice that lovely little flying cut that you tried to land on me. I think that you should have scored a hit, and I'd like to see what was off about your execution."

They spent the rest of the morning working out, and when noon arrived, Maya's original gloom had all but vanished. They called a halt to their exercises and ate lunch together in a nearby restaurant that specialized in Nemesian and Thermadonian cuisine.

As they finished their repast, Skylaar brought up the subject of Felecia. "Have you called on her since you moved?"

Maya looked down at her plate. "I have," she said. "But she's always too busy to see me. I'm worried that it's because I'm no longer an agent." She paused, and then added in a small voice, "Or maybe because she's seeing someone else."

"Maya," Skylaar replied patiently. "Lady Felecia has always cared for you. She is probably just too overwhelmed with her mother's demands on her time. She is after all, being groomed to take her place someday. That requires a lot of energy and commitment. And as I recall, you once told me that she found you to be very exciting when she thought that you were nothing more than a lowly pirate. Surely, now that you have become a policewoman, you must command even more fascination."

Maya gave her a small, wan smile. "Yes, Sena-Tai. I suppose you're right."

"Call her again," Skylaar suggested. "I know that I'm only your martial arts teacher, but I think that if you keep at it, and are patient with her, you *will* succeed. And we both know that spending some time with her would do your spirit a great deal of good."

"All right, Sena-Tai. I will."

***

Maya was on duty the next day and it wasn't until her mid-day break that she was able to make the holocall in private. When she did, she found Felecia at Senatrix d'Salla's office.

"Heyas, darling," she began, "Do you want to go out riding tonight? I'm off duty now and I heard that the Euxine Sea has some pretty nice sunsets."

Felecia pouted. "I can't. Mother has me accompanying her to some dreary fundraiser. I'm sorry, I wish I could, but I can't get out of it. Forgive me?"

Maya's heart sank. "Of course," she replied, flashing her a reassuring smile. "I just thought---oh well, duty first. I understand." They went on like this for a little longer, mainly out of politeness, before she ended the call.

"Fek!" she cursed. Only the fact that Felecia hadn't formally broken things off between them was what was saving her from being consumed by another bout of despair.

She didn't do that, she reminded herself. *She just said that she couldn't go out with me tonight.* It sounded weak, but it was all that she had to hold onto.

Resigning herself to a night alone, she accessed the holovision listings and found one hopeful candidate; the new remake of *'Casablanca'*. She had heard somewhere that the holo had been creating quite a stir, and she had wanted to see it, just to find out what all the fuss was about. Watching it by herself was an anemic substitute for riding with Felecia, but it would have to suffice. In another day or two, she would call her again, and hope for the best.

Residence of Senatrix Layna n'Calysher, Themiscrya Tower, 900th Floor, Penthouse Level, Agamede District, Thermadon Val, Thermadon, Myrene System, Thalestris Elant, United Sisterhood of Suns, 1049.01|04|07:07:36

"Feli? Did you hear what Angelique just said?" Senatrix n'Calysher asked.

In fact, the young woman hadn't. After finishing up at D'Salla's office, Felecia had come straight home for dinner with her mother and Bel Thana. Now they were taking their ease together in the Senatrix's study, enjoying snifters of 200-year-old Delganian cognac by the fire. The hour had grown late, and she had become hypnotized by the curve of Angelique bel Thana's calf, which was encased in the black boots of her RSE uniform.

The statuesque blond gave Felecia a half-smile, knowing exactly what had captivated the girl's attention, and answered for her. "She is simply overtired, Senatrix. I think that we all are. This has been a very busy period for everyone, however fruitful."

It had been at that, Felecia reflected. With her mother's help, and that of her allies in the Circle, the Chairwoman had been convinced to give the RSE the sweeping powers that it now enjoyed, but not without encountering some resistance. In recent months, the Uni's had managed to gain more recognition and support for themselves by protesting what they believed was an 'all-out assault' on the liberties of the average woman.

Which, by their way of thinking, it certainly was—even if it was the only way to safeguard the Sisterhood, and ultimately, guide it in the proper direction. It had been weakness that had led to the current problems with the Marionite terrorists, Felecia reminded herself.

Angelique had enlightened her on this point, and she for one, was glad that things were in the process of being set right. She loved her nation, but thanks to Angelique, she also understood why it needed a mother's firm hand to ensure that it remained strong.

"So, what do you think about T'Tallya? What should we do about her?" her mother asked, repeating Bel Thana's question. Senatrix t'Tallya was the leader of the Uni's and the most outspoken of her opposition.

Felecia fingered her ring, thinking for a moment. It was a duplicate of the one on Angelique's finger, and on her mother's, and marked her as a member of the Conversâzi. "Kill her?"

Angelique smiled tolerantly "She *is* tired," she said. "Feli darling, haven't I already explained this to you? We *need* her. For now. To consolidate our control, we must give the population the illusion of free choice.'

"As long as it really amounts to nothing, and they have a few meaningless victories to crow over, they'll accept any changes that we make as only temporary setbacks. We can't very well do that if we don't have dissenters, now can we?"

Felecia nodded. Naturally, the woman was right. Angelique saw the world like her mother and Senatrix d'Salla did, and together, they had taught her how it *really* worked.

Layna n'Calysher drained her glass and rose. "Jantildamé, I think perhaps it is time for me to turn in for the night. There's a vote in the morning on the new appropriations for your SRU Teams, and I want to be fresh."

Bel Thana inclined her head. "*Bian dea*, Madame Senatrix. I will show myself out."

Senatrix n'Calysher acknowledged this with a nod, and an understanding gleam in her eye. She knew all about the clandestine affair that Bel Thana was having with her daughter, and she approved of their liaison wholeheartedly.

As soon as the Senatrix had departed, Bel Thana's smile became suggestive. The light coming from the fireplace conspired with the sable color of Angelique's uniform to accent the blond in her hair, and lent a hungry gleam to her perfect green eyes.

Right then, Felecia wanted nothing more in her life than to reach out and touch that hair, and look deeply into those eyes. A moment later, she gave in to her desire and went to her.

Angelique gathered her up and drank her in with a long deep kiss. Suddenly, they were undressing, and dropping together to the floor. Even though they had been meeting in secret for the last six months, the woman still commanded a tremendous power over her, and Felecia let herself become lost in their lovemaking, and in her.

She still loved Maya, deeply, and continued to feel a powerful sexual attraction for her. But their long separations, and all of the things that she had in common with Angelique, had provided her with what Maya could not. Like herself, Angelique was an aristocrat; the N'Calysher and Bel Thana families had occupied the highest circles of Thermadon's social class for centuries, and they shared a mutual interest in politics, and power. For the N'Calyshers the arena had always been in the government, and for the Bel Thanas, it was the intelligence community. One of Angelique's ancestresses, Jaqueline bel Thana had been one of the earliest Directors of the OAE, and other family members had served in the same office with equal distinction.

Angelique bel Thana was also older than Maya, and she had the perspective of greater years, and experience. Her passions were equally as sophisticated. Where Maya was all blazing fire, and excitement, Angelique burned as well, but with a slow steadiness, which was all the more spectacular for the time it took to build to its conclusion.

She had introduced Felecia to a whole new world, not only of physical sensations and long lingering pleasures, but also to the real power behind all the show and bureaucracy of the Sisterhood. The Conversâzi was the future, and Angelique had included her in it.

Felecia entertained no illusions about their relationship though. Angelique was quite frank about her ambitions, and Felecia knew that the woman was just as intensely attracted to the power of the N'Calysher name as she was to her body.

This didn't bother her however. As native Thermadonians often said, it was simply "*Ja apré se*", "How things where" and as much a part of the emotional landscape as their passion for one another was. Everyone exploited someone else for something, and if they both gained the emotional and physical satisfaction that they sought, then the arrangement worked.

The only thing that haunted her was the fact that she had kept both Maya and Angelique ignorant of one another. Neither of them suspected that they were sharing her affections.

Felecia didn't know if she would ever confess the truth to them; this was something that she still refused to address. She needed them both and she didn't want to do anything that would drive either of them away. For the moment, the situation would have to remain exactly as it was, with her caught in the middle. It was a dangerous game, but she had to play it to get what she wanted.

Each of them had their pleasures to offer, and their uses.

Remembrance Park, Sinope District, Thermadon Val, Thermadon, Myrene System, Thalestris Elant, United Sisterhood of Suns 1049.01|08|04:88:22

Above all else, Signysdaater was a creature of habit. One of her routines was that when she was not on a call, or eating lunch in the Kalia Vai, she always flew to one of her favorite parking spots.

In the downtown area, this was the rooftop where they had joined the chase of the glass runners. In the Vai, it was a side street near the main marketplace. And in the Sinope District, she had a spot that overlooked the banks of Lake Mnemosyne, in Remembrance Park.

Of all of them, Maya preferred the Park, which was Thermadon's grandiose homage to the ubiquitous Widow's Stone. The Thermadontine version was over two stories tall and surrounded by a large and pleasant open space, with plenty of running trails, and picnic sites in and around it.

Remembrance Park was also a favorite of the well-to-do West End women, many of whom worked as models and actresses for the Thermadonian media machine. Despite her ongoing infatuation for Felecia, Maya still had a keen eye for beauty—and a lot of the runners tended to be damned fine looking as far as she was concerned. And it was their standard hairstyle that had engendered her private sobriquet for the place.

To her, it was 'Ponytail Park' and in addition to watching the women themselves, she often played a game with herself when she was there. She tried to count exactly how many ponytails she saw in one visit. To date, the galactic record stood at 35 in just under half an hour.

Today seemed even more promising. Although they had only been there for fifteen minutes, it seemed as if she might actually exceed her record. So far, she had seen twenty ponytails, and with the weather bright and sunny, the supply of new runners seemed inexhaustible. Sipping at her kaafra, she smiled at herself and her silly little game.

Then the notion came to her to attempt another call to Felecia. It had been several days since her last try. Because it was Seconday, and approaching noon, she knew that the young woman was most likely enjoying her mid-day break in the dance studio. Felecia had earned the nickname 'the Dancer' not only for being cautious and quick-minded when it came to politics, but also for her love of classical ballet.

When she wasn't studying the art of government, she devoted herself to improving as a performer. Her mother had once even told Maya that had the girl not been destined for life as a politician, she would have most likely enjoyed a successful career as a ballerina. Knowing Felecia as well as she did, Maya didn't doubt this for an attosecond. She had seen holos of Felecia dancing, and the girl's natural grace and perfect form had been undeniable, even to her untrained eye.

Sure enough, when Felecia answered her, the omni confirmed Maya's guess. The location came up as her favorite downtown studio. The girl was in a leotard, a little out of breath, and seemed somewhat surprised at the call.

Maya braced herself. *Here I go again,* she thought, desperately hoping that the Goddess would grant her a turn of good fortune. "I'm off duty tonight," she said "I was thinking of taking you to *Affecti,* and then maybe dinner at *Nós Arcan*? Interested?"

Affecti, or "Move" was Thermadon's finest dance club, and *Nós Arcan,* or *Our Secret,* was a little place that offered an intimate atmosphere and excellent food.

"Oh Maya, I'd *love* to," Felecia replied regretfully, "but the Senatrix has me working late on a new bill that she's introducing to the Circle tomorrow. Maybe next week?"

"Oh," Maya returned, struggling keep the disappointment out of her voice. "Okay. Sure. Next week then." The call ended.

Maya sat back in her seat, staring out at the park but not really seeing it. Her worst fears were coming true. Felecia was slipping away from her. Now she was certain of it.

Signysdaater had overheard the entire exchange, and her hard expression softened. "Zat Felecia, zhe's your voman, yah?"

"Yeah," Maya told her, too disheartened to realize that not only was the woman finally speaking to her, but actually showing some interest in her as a person.

"'Kay. I vas juzt vondering," Signysdaater replied.

Maya grasped the inference behind the Zommerlaandar's words, and grimaced. Her life, at that exact moment, felt like pure shess. But deep down, and despite the darkness that seemed to be closing in around her like a shroud, she was still determined to keep trying.

Until all of her suspicions and fears were proven wrong. Or Felecia finally said the words that she hoped she would never hear.

Grunvaald Haarmaaneplaatz, Vaalkenstaad Township, Zommerlaand, Sunna 3, Solara Elant, United Sisterhood of Suns 1049.01|08|08:43:02

"What story shall we tell you tonight?" the Biobot asked the children. The Bear had perched himself in his usual spot. He was high up on the shelf above the great stone fireplace. His partner, the Fairy, sat alongside him, her dainty legs crossed and dangling off the wooden platform as she waited with the Bear for their audience to answer.

The two 'bots had been, without any question, one of the most popular gifts that Aunt Katy had ever brought back with her, and had become a fixture of life at the Grunvaald Farm. Even the adults had abandoned the holojector to gather around the hearth in the evenings to listen to their seemingly endless tales.

It was a custom that Grammy heartily approved of. *"The young don't use their minds enough,'* she had often complained. *"Za 'jector robs them of all the wonderful pictures that their own minds can make. The Alte Volk knew this—in ancient times, everyone gathered around the fire to share stories. It was how they passed on their wisdom and stayed strong as a family."*

Fryya, never terribly shy, answered the Bear's inquiry after only a moment's consideration. "Tell us about *Silwveyr Rachaal!"* she exclaimed.

A collective gasp came up from the other little girls. Fryya had made a bold request indeed. *"Silver Rachel"* was one of the darker tales of Zommerlaand and not lightly asked for.

None of her peers objected however. Being children, they had a morbid streak and when the Bear and his partner looked to Grammy for permission, he received a nod from her.

The Bear drew his tiny body up, and looked around at the children, his expression as grave as his furry little face could manage. Pausing a few seconds longer to create just the right amount of suspense, he began.

"A long, long time ago, back when the great Plague was just beginning to ravage the Star Federation, Zommerlaand remained untouched. The leaders of this world decided not to allow any ships to come and land, for fear that the visitors that they brought with them would also bring the sickness. But this was not before one *final* ship was given permission to land.'

"Everyone aboard this ship were refugees. They had left their own homes and their motherworlds behind and had come here looking for a safe place to live."

At this point, the Fairy picked up the narrative. The Biobots tended to work as a team when they were telling a story, with each one taking on the roles that were appropriate for them.

"One of the passengers was a little girl about your own age, named Rachel," she said. "She never told anyone what her last name was, nor where she had come from, and no one could remember when exactly she had come aboard.'

329

"Now Rachel was a *very* strange little girl. She had hair that was so blond that it seemed to be silver—just like a Nyxian, but her eyes were violet like ours are, and she never spoke. She only smiled. And it was a sad, sad little smile.'

"She also had a companion who was traveling with her. It was a man, who some said was her father, and who others thought was her uncle. No one knew for certain, and neither Rachel, nor the man, ever told them the truth. Even stranger than this was the fact that no one who met the man could ever remember what his face had looked like afterwards."

Fryya and the other girls exchanged grave expressions. So far the story had all of the elements that they had been hoping for; a mysterious pair of figures, set against the backdrop of the terrible Plague, and full of secrets that promised something truly dreadful. They couldn't wait to hear more.

The Bear picked up the narrative. "When everyone was finally allowed to leave the ship, Rachel and the man wandered from town to town. They never stayed long in any one place, and after they left, the men living in the towns would catch the Plague and die. Then some of the people noticed that the first men who fell where always the ones that Rachel had smiled at."

"Knowing this, all of the towns began to keep a watch out for Rachel, who they now called 'Silver Rachel', and for her companion, hoping to keep them from entering. But no matter how hard they tried, town after town, and village after village, and farm after farm, were visited by the pair, and in all those places, the men *died*."

The Fairy spoke. "This went on and on until not a single town or village anywhere on Zommerlaand had been spared, and the Plague had taken all the men folk away. For a while after this, no one saw Silver Rachel, or the man."

"But only for a while," the Bear warned his audience. "After a few years, and when things had begun to return to normal, people out on the farms began to see Rachel again. Those who remembered her, said that she hadn't aged a day. She was also all alone now. The man was gone."

"Where did he go?" Fryya asked.

"No one knows. He was never seen again. Then some of the wise women realized why. They knew who he had *really* been, and why no one had ever seen his face. You see, he hadn't been Rachel's father after all, or her uncle, or any other relative, but Death itself."

A collective shutter passed among the children and Fryya leaned forwards. "What happened next?"

"Rachel continued to wander," the Fairy answered. "She traveled the roads and highways of Zommerlaand; the big ones, and the little ones, visiting the farms and the houses. She only visited them on certain nights though. On nights like this, when the air was cold and still, and the moons were full and high in the sky."

At this, Fryya and her companions looked fearfully past the hearth to the window outside, and the moons shining balefully over the fields in the crisp air. Anything was possible on such a night, and their eyes grew wide.

The Fairy continued. "And at every farm that Silver Rachel visited, she would come to the front door and knock."

At the precise moment that the Biobot said this, Ingrit added her own contribution to the tale, rapping loudly on the wall behind her. The little girls squealed in terror, and Lilith promptly rewarded her wife with an elbow in the ribs. Unchastened, Ingrit merely grinned.

"Do you know what happened when she would knock at someone's door?" the Fairy asked. The little girls shook their heads. "If someone answered, she would be gone. The doorstep would be empty, and not long afterwards, Death would come for someone in the house, or something just as bad would happen.'

"Only those who had left something out for her were ever safe. Silver Rachel always spared a home that had left sweet cakes or corn bread for her on the step."

"And they say," the Bear added in a low, serious voice, "that Silver Rachel still walks the roads and visits the farms hereabouts."

The girls glanced past the Biobots to the window again, and then as one, they got up and ran into the kitchen. Grammy was right behind them.

"Mind you!" the old woman warned, "Be neat now. Don't leave a mess for me to clean up or you'll have more than Rachel to worry about!"

"Are they really leaving something out on the step?" Lilith asked her partner.

"That they are," Ingrit answered. "I did the same thing when I was their age, and Grammy made sure back then that we didn't destroy the kitchen."

"Isn't this all rather silly?" Lilith countered, just loud enough for Ingrit to hear without the children overhearing. "Letting them believe in such a superstition?"

"*Ach, nen*," Ingrit replied. "Belief is part of being a child. As Grammy says, accepting the idea that monsters are really out there is all a part of growing up."

Lilith found herself forced to agree. The only difference between the frightening creatures that inhabited the darkened closets of childhood's imagination, and the monsters that lurked in real life, were their names, and where they hid. The Hriss and the T'lakskalans had proven that.

Shortly, Grammy returned to the living area with the little ones in tow. "Well," she announced. "I think our doorstep is good and safe now. I also

331

think it's time for me—and some others," her eyes fell on Fryya and her companions, "to turn in."

She received some half-hearted protests from the children, but in short order, she had them all scurrying off to their beds. The adults lingered in the living area for a while after that, but eventually they too followed suit.

And somewhere in the night, Lilith dreamt. She found herself standing in the living area, but this time she was alone, and the house was dark. Only the silvery light of Zommerlaand's moons lent any illumination to the room, or to the fields outside.

Something drew her over to the windows, and she looked out towards the dirt road that cut down from the highway to the farm. Even though a part of her knew that it was only a dream, she was still amazed at how sharp and clear the imagery was, and her eyes traced their way up the road, taking in the rich details.

Then she spotted a small figure walking down its length towards the house. In the strange way of dreams, the girl's progress was accelerated, and in seconds, she was standing in the front yard, just a few paces short of the steps. She was a little girl, with fine silver hair that stirred gently in the breeze, and dark, violet eyes.

They regarded each other silently, and then the girl smiled. It was a sad expression that spoke of infinite loss, and bottomless pain. With that, she vanished, and the dream faded away into darkness.

When she rose the next morning, Lilith wasn't surprised in the least. She had after all, gone to bed with the eerie tale of Silver Rachel lingering in the back of her mind, and a part of her, she admitted, was and always would be, a child, and susceptible to a child's fears and imaginings. Smiling at herself, she made her way down to the kitchen and began her day with a cup of tea.

Grammy was already up and about, and busy at the sink preparing breakfast. She greeted her as she took her place at the table. "*Goemôrga,* Lily," she said. "Did you sleep well?"

"Yes, "Lilith replied. "Although I did have a bad dream. I really shouldn't have gone to bed after hearing that awful story."

"Yah," Grammy answered. "I dreamt about her too. So did everyone else, I think. Dreams about *Silweyr Rachaal* are always bad luck. It's a good thing that we left something out for her on the step."

"It was *just* a dream," Lilith countered. "And you know that there's no such thing as luck; it's all just probability."

She realized that it was rude of her to challenge the old woman's beliefs like this, but sometimes the depth of Zommerlaandar superstition truly exasperated her. All of their faith in spells and spirits and omens made her wonder how the women of Sunna 3 had ever managed to become part

332

of a modern interstellar society like the Sisterhood. Their mindset was positively medieval.

Grammy however, was completely unperturbed. "The wise women know differently," she replied patiently. "Luck is quite real whether you believe in it or not. My *Gotdunna* taught me that luck is like lightning. You can't see it until it strikes, and it always has to come down somewhere. Leaving gifts out for Rachel will make sure that the bad luck she brings with her will pass us by, and hit someplace else were it does the least amount of harm."

Lilith shook her head tiredly. "Grammy, it was *just* a dream, and nothing more. I probably wouldn't have even had it if the children hadn't asked for the story in the first place."

"Perhaps," Grammy replied calmly, turning her attention back to making breakfast. "Perhaps not. Some say that nothing ever happens in this life without a reason behind it. Maybe Fryya and the other little ones asked for the tale because they sensed that something bad was in the wind. Maybe the Gods even moved them to ask for it."

Lilith sighed. "Perhaps," she returned. "Perhaps not."

The two women smiled at each other, and let things go at that. It was too fine a day to belabor the point, and both of them knew that they were absolutely right.

***

Being a senior *Pat-Rat* officer, Signysdaater had the luxury of choosing her shift assignments, and Maya had learned that she preferred to work the second shift, from 05:83 to 09:16 hours. Her partner hated working during the morning or graveyard shifts and enjoyed the variable pace that the afternoons tended to provide.

Today, the woman had decided to patrol the Marpesia District, the part of the city that hosted Thermadon's heavy industrial concerns and the low-income and visiting workers housing. It was also the same area that Maya had first met the kaaper, and they had even flown by the hostel she had originally stayed at before her fateful choice to find work at the spaceport.

Their shift had been greeted by typically Thermadonian weather. It had been overcast at the beginning, transitioning to a torrential downpour that finally trickled off into a weak, intermittent drizzle. It was the very duplicate of Maya's first night in T-Don, and as they glided silently over Ben Taara boulevard, she saw several figures that reminded her of her earlier self, moving quickly down the rain-soaked pavement, spacer's kit-bags in hand, and on their way to the hostels.

She was just in the process of working up the courage to ask that they stop somewhere for some kaafra and the chance to stretch her legs, when a pedestrian caught her eye. The figure was dressed in the usual light jacket and jumpsuit that most spacers wore when they were downside, and her kit-bag was the conventional type, albeit a bit worn.

Physically, the woman was equally as unremarkable; she was darker skinned than some of the others that Maya had seen moving along the street, but no more so than anyone with some Kalian in their ancestry, and her shoulder-length black hair seemed to support this.

At the sight of the Metro cruiser however, the woman abruptly left the sidewalk and darted into an alley. This was definitely the mark of someone who was up to something.

Signysdaater had also spotted this. "Letz check her out," she said. "Zhe lookz *verdaag* to me." The cruiser made a sharp turn and began to fly down the alley.

By this point, Maya had come to respect the *kaaper's* instincts because they were so much like her own, and therefore, generally right. The woman *did* look suspicious.

Being on foot, their quarry had only managed to get a little ways in, and when the cruiser's headlights illuminated her, she began to walk away from them at an accelerated pace. Not a full-on run, but just a hair short of bolting like a frightened *rabiteth.*

Signysdaater switched on the spotlight mounted on the aircar's light bar and let off a short chirp of the siren. This was another thing that Maya had learned about her partner; like a lot of veterans, she didn't over-work the siren. She used it just enough to get attention, but without creating any more drama than was absolutely necessary.

The woman got the message and stopped, and it was clear from the sag in her shoulders that she had resigned herself to being detained—for something. The cruiser settled down into a hover, just over the pavement, and Maya got out at the same time as the Zommerlaandar, making certain that she put herself in a position that gave her the best view of their suspect, but was still close enough to use the vehicle for cover in case anything happened. She also unsnapped the holster of her energy gun.

From her Academy PTS feeds, she knew that 'routine' stops like this were also the ones most likely to become dangerous. It was impossible for anyone to know whom they were stopping, or what their motives were until the stop itself had been made, and many officers over the long centuries of formalized police work had lost their lives by being careless.

"Heyas, girl," Signysdaater said, unwittingly summoning up Maya's memory of being stopped by the woman herself. "Vat you doing out here in zis alley?"

The woman muttered something in reply and Signysdaater pointed to the hood of their cruiser. "Put za bag on za hood."

The bag went there without incident, and when she was ordered to, their suspect stepped away from it, and kept her hands in plain sight. The light from Signysdaater's monocle played over her next, and when the data came back, an amused smile broke across the Zommerlaandar's face.

"'Kay—put your hands on the za hood and zpread your feet," she said, already coming around to take charge if the woman failed to comply with her order. At this, the figure only seemed to become a little more miserable, and meekly cooperated as Signysdaater applied restraints to her wrists and then stood her back up.

"Check her bag," she said to Maya, and then to their prisoner. "Iz zere anyzing in zere zat vill hurt my partner?"

This elicited a headshake. Just the same, Maya reached into her back pocket and put on her gloves. These were made of 'stick-proof' pleather, and at a psiever command, special ridges along the knuckles could also become rigid, allowing the gloves to double as the high-tech equivalent of the 'fighting nucks' that she had once employed on the streets of Ashkele.

Thus protected, she upended the bag, but nothing incriminating fell out of it. She had expected to find drugs, or possibly a weapon, but only produced a rather disappointing pile of clothing, harmless personal items and a battered pathminder that was clearly labeled, *"Property of Bel Sharra Memorial Spaceport"*. Maya put this aside, momentarily puzzled.

"Vat's your name?" Signysdaater asked their prisoner. "You're *real* name. 'Cause if you're 'Juta Helgasdaater', zen I'm Laara Lampa."

The woman burst into tears, and uttered a string of words that were only half intelligible through her bawling and a nearly impenetrable accent. What was understandable, was a combination of very poor Standard and fluent Espangla.

She was an illegal immigrant, Maya realized. This was a recent phenomenon, brought on by the war with the ETR and the subsequent collapse of the Republic's economy. Thermadon had become a magnet for women from the defeated star nation, who came to the Sisterhood seeking jobs that no longer existed at home. Some of them managed to emigrate legally, like the ones she had seen at the Embassy in Nuvo Bolivar, and others, who failed to qualify, chose illicit means to gain their entry.

This also solved the mystery of the stolen pathminder. When they paid to get themselves smuggled into the Sisterhood by a corrupt merchanter captain, the illegals were often outfitted with a phony bio-chip, an equally ersatz inocular, and a pathminder which had had its ownership codes stripped out.

This way, a psiever-less woman could pass for a legitimate citizen and negotiate her way through a society that ran its devices on thought. In addition to their mapping functions, pathminders had a built in interface in them that allowed alien visitors to activate psiever-driven appliances. At least the ones at the average spaceport did.

Signysdaater repeated her question. "Vat's your name? Vere do you live?" Her inquiry only produced the same dismal results however, made even worse by the woman's weeping and trying to answer her between ragged gulps for air.

"Let me try something," Maya interjected. She faced the woman squarely. "We know that you are an illegal," she told her in Espangla. "What is your real name? Things will only go worse for you if you don't cooperate with us."

The illegal managed to bring most of her tears under control and nodded. "My name is Jauntiya Zavaala. Please—I'm not a criminal. I just came here looking for work—my family—my family needs the money--- my brother was the head of our family, and he died—in the war.'

"The people said that if I paid them, that they'd get me here, and that they had work for me—but then they stole all my money and left me with nothing. Please---"The rest of what she had been about to say was lost in a fresh round of weeping.

"Where are you staying?" Maya asked her. "What's your address?"

The illegal didn't answer, but her eyes betrayed her when they flicked briefly towards a plastiboard box propped up against the side of the alley. This was 'home'.

She relayed this information to Signysdaater.

"Vell, rookie," the Zommerlaandar returned. "Zis iz your call. Ve can take her to Cuztoms at za Port and zey vill ship her back. Or ve can take her over to N'Rina Boulevard and give her to za Zisters of Zelene. Zey have a shelter zere, and zey may help her."

The Sisters of Selene had recently become involved in the problem of illegal immigration. They advocated for them, offered them shelter, and when they could, lent their assistance in helping them to gain legal citizenship.

Maya considered the wretched figure and her 'residence' wilting away in the damp shadows. At one time, not too far in the past, she would have just taken the illegal to Customs and been done with her. The woman had a sad story, but the galaxy was filled with sad stories.

But she had also lived in a box a time or two herself as a child in Ashkele. And for some reason, the situation also brought to mind Mariaa Estovaal, and how she had helped Sarah and her compatriots blackmail the old woman, back in Nuvo Bolivar.

This was a test, she knew, and not just one posed by Signysdaater. In a small way, she could make things right with the Goddess. If she wanted to.

Maya made her decision. "You just got really lucky," she told her. "We're taking you to the Sisters of Selene. They'll give you a dry place to stay, and maybe some help."

Then she removed her restraints. "Go get your things out of your house," she told her. "You're moving out."

She looked to Signysdaater next. "We'll take her to the Mission."

The veteran policewoman didn't reward her with a smile or any other indication of approval, but Maya knew that she had just gone up a notch in her estimation. And oddly enough, it all felt pretty good. Not that she had any intention of becoming a full time 'miss-goody goody', but it was still a nice change of pace.

***

At the beginning of their patrol the following day, Signysdaater announced that she had a court appearance late in the afternoon. Instead of opting to ride with a relief officer for the remainder of the shift, Maya chose to go home early, and the very instant that they had returned to the precinct house, she didn't even bother to change out of her uniform. Instead, she made straight for her hoverbike and sped off to Felecia's. After weeks of being put off by the girl, she wanted the chance to spend at least a *few* minutes with her. Or more—if she could get it.

When she arrived, she learned from Sharra, the Senatrix's Security Chief, that Felecia was away on business for Senatrix d'Salla, but that she would be back shortly. Swearing her to silence, Maya made for Felecia's bedroom, grinning in anticipation at the surprise her presence would cause.

The surprise however, was Maya's. As befitted a high-born girl, Felecia's bedroom was fronted by a small reception area, and in its center was an elegant table, which was normally set with a spray of flowers. Today though, the flowers had been replaced by a small ebony cube with a brass plaque. As Maya approached it, she realized that it was familiar.

She read the plaque. It said, *"To my little dancer, with love. Angelique."*

Hands trembling, Maya pressed the small activator stud, and as the light weave began to appear, she gasped. It was *La Dansuar*, from the art show. The very one that Angelique had purchased for a small fortune.

Now, here it was. A gift to Felecia. With love.

Unable to stand, Maya collapsed into a chair, and sat there, watching the little holographic figure as she danced, utterly stunned.

A few minutes later, Felecia entered and gave out a small cry. Maya looked up at her, her eyes dark with desolation and hurt.

"Why, Feli?" she sobbed. "And with—*her*--?"

"It's not what you think---" Felecia started to say, but Maya would have none of it. She rose, and pushed past her.

Felecia grabbed for her arm, and she shrugged her off. "Maya! Wait! Please!"

Maya spun on her heels and pointed an accusing finger at her. "You're the only one, Maya!" she said mockingly "I *love* you, Maya!"

At the heights of their greatest passion, Felecia had said all this to her, and much, much more. Now Maya knew how false these words had actually been. "*Liar!*"

Felecia burst into tears. "Please—you don't understand—"

Maya shook her head, and walked away. Felecia called after her, but she shut her ears to the sound. With eyes filled to the brim with tears of her own, she re-boarded Rebá and left.

She did not look back.

***

Skylaar came as soon as Maya placed the call to her. She found her in her apartment. The lights were out and Maya sat on the edge of her bed, head hanging, and her hair covering her face like a protective shroud. She was sobbing, quietly.

The Nemesian knelt next to her, and put a gentle hand on her shoulder. Maya responded to her touch, looking up at her teacher with red, swollen eyes. "*Cho-Sena*---all this t-time--she's—she's--been seeing someone else," the girl sobbed. "I-I left her."

"Who was she seeing?" Skylaar asked.

This only evoked a fresh round of crying, and Skylaar offered her a kerchief.

"Angelique," Maya finally managed to say. "Angelique. All this time---goddess, how could she *do* this to me?"

"Love isn't always the constant thing that we like to think it is," Skylaar offered. "Nor are lovers."

She felt badly for Maya and hated what she was going through, but secretly, she blessed Felecia for her stupidity. The relationship had become more dangerous for Maya than the girl could have ever realized.

Now that it was over, she had one less thing to worry over. Keeping Maya safe had been hard enough without such an unstable variable in the equation. The only question that remained was whether or not other factors in the situation would become just as problematic. Maya certainly deserved a certain measure of peace and happiness.

For as long as it lasted.

TMPD Special Training Facility, Eileithyia Val, Thermadon, Myrene System, Thalestris Elant, United Sisterhood of Suns, 1049.01|13|07:08:34

Kaly and her veteran SRU students had been pushing themselves hard. All of her pupils had been handpicked, veteran officers with years of experience in Special Operations, and together, they had refined what they already knew and incorporated the new tactics that Kaly had brought with her from the ETR.

The course itself had been conducted at a special facility that the Thermadonian Metropolitan Police Department maintained in Eileithyia, a suburb 80 kilometers outside of the capitol. In addition to conventional classrooms and target ranges, the complex also boasted full scale mock-ups of typical Thermadonian neighborhoods, and they had used these to their fullest advantage, going non-stop for two weeks solid.

Now, the special training was over and the teams had all returned to their normal duties, leaving Kaly with a lull in her schedule. The next set of officers weren't due to begin their instruction for another two days, and she suddenly had a weekend on her hands that she really didn't want at all. Going full-bore had not only gotten the job done, it had also distracted her and kept her ghosts at bay.

For that very reason, spending her off-time, cooped up all alone in her quarters wasn't even an option. So, on the advice of the other trainers, she booked herself a room in a downtown hotel, called a hovertaxi, and went into Thermadon proper to play the tourist, and with nothing else to wear, went there in full uniform.

She had seen plenty of holos and realies about the place, but she had never actually visited it before, and her time at the suburban training facility really didn't count. Nor did the glimpses that she had seen of it from space when her shuttle had come downside.

Intellectually, she had always been aware that Thermadon was the largest and most cosmopolitan city in the Sisterhood, but by the time her 'taxi deposited her at the Concordance Magnorail station, she had discovered that this simple understanding fell far short of the reality. Thermadon wasn't just large. It was truly gargantuan, and more than a little overwhelming.

It didn't help that her visit also coincided with the height of the holiday season. It was Summertyne, or Harvest Home, one of the most important

Martin Schiller

holidays in the Sisterhood calendar. On Old Gaia, it had once been celebrated as the harvest festival of Lammas, and that tradition had survived and transformed itself when the human race had migrated into space.

For the Selenites, and Demetrians like herself, Harvest Home not only celebrated the Goddess's gifts to her children, but was a time when women emulated the Lady's generosity by giving presents to one another. Everyone and their mother was out doing last minute shopping for the Summertyne feasts, or buying something for a loved one, and Concordance Station was packed to capacity with travelers.

To mark the occasion, colorful displays had been set up at strategic locations. Yellow and black *Zonnaanblüm* flowers, the definitive symbol for the holiday, were everywhere, as were garlands and colorful displays of cornucopia filled with fruit. Even the waste receptacles were decorated, and individual kiosks had joined in in the holiday spirit, decking themselves out in festive colors. And in addition to whatever they normally sold, many of them were also offering Harvest Moon cakes. Like the Zonnaanblüm flowers, this food was one of the essentials of the holiday and their sweet smell reached every part of the terminal.

Also, to entertain the throng, actresses portraying holiday figures wandered from place to place. A woman, dressed as the Mother herself, made her way towards Kaly, wearing a deep green dress and a garland of flowers on her head. She was giving out candy from the basket on her arm to every little girl that she passed.

Over the woman's shoulder, Kaly spotted a circle of Harvest Maids portraying the Goddess as the fruitful young Maiden. The dancers were attired in distinctive red dresses, and swirling around a holographic bonfire. Just like the playful Maiden herself, every so often, one of them would reach out and pull someone in from the crowd to join them.

The sight made Kaly smile, but she also made certain to carefully avoid coming too close to them as she wove her way towards the magnorail platforms. She had almost reached her goal, when she encountered the last member of the sacred holiday trio.

This was Grandmother Death, dressed in a billowing white gown and a cape that dragged along the floor. She was carrying her distinctive hooked staff, and a terrifying mask concealed her features. Over her back, was the sack that she used to carry off all the bad little girls to her underground home. Grandmother Death was a somber reminder to the onlookers that famine could always replace plenty, and that death itself, was inevitable.

Whoever was portraying her was doing a particularly good job, Kaly observed. The ominous figure appeared to float, rather than walk, and she always seemed to be just on the brink of catching the laughing, squealing children that she encountered.

All this brought Kaly back to her own childhood, when the adult members of her colony had also dressed up in costumes, and put on their own version of the Summertyne revel. Being a backwater planet, it hadn't been quite as fine as this production was, nor as well performed, but its meaning had been just as deep, if not more so, for the sincerity of its presentation.

But they were all gone now. Thanks to the Hriss, and a hard, cold universe that took lives just as surely as Grandmother Death stole away bad children. Soured by this, Kaly pushed her way through the press, determined to reach her train and leave. Right then, all she wanted was to get to her hotel and check in.

According to her psiever, which had tied itself into the Transitplex, the train she wanted was the "E1101" train, on platform Carla-7 and she had only a few minutes before it departed. The mass of the people around her made her progress slow and she pushed through them as politely as possible. Once the E1101 left, there wouldn't be another train going to the Marpesia District for 20 minutes, and the last thing that she wanted was to find herself stuck there in the station, waiting in the middle of the holiday chaos.

She reached the car doors just as another woman was exiting the train, and Kaly did a double take, realizing who it was. "Ellen?" she called, making eye contact. "Ellen is that you?"

Ellen n'Elemay looked back at her. She didn't smile though, or make her way through the crowd to embrace her. Instead, she turned away and after dropping something bulky into a waste receptacle, disappeared into the crowd.

"Ellen!" Kaly called. "Wait!" Forgetting all about her train now, she tried to follow, but quickly lost sight of her. Caught between the choice of continuing her pursuit, and missing the E1101, she stopped, and turned around.

Maybe that wasn't her, she thought. *Or maybe it was, and she just didn't recognize me.* This was certainly possible. The visor of her peaked cap tended to hide the wearer's eyes, and while the privacy that this afforded was a plus at times, it also tended to render the wearer anonymous.

Then another possibility surfaced. *And maybe she was just too embarrassed to talk to me.*

After what had happened to her career, the sight of any military uniform must have had painful associations for her, she reflected. Saddened and sobered by this, Kaly walked back to her train. Miraculously, it was still there, and predictably, the car she chose was full. All of the seats had been taken.

Grabbing onto the overhead rail reserved for standing passengers, Kaly resigned herself to a long ride on tired feet. But one of the seated travelers was an old woman, maybe 200 standard or older, and when she took in Kaly's uniform, she took pity on her.

"Here "she said, rising with some difficulty, "take my seat, officer." When Kaly hesitated, she added, "Please."

Kaly was sorely tempted to refuse, but then she saw the expressions of the other riders around her. They actually *expected* her to accept the offer, she realized. Courtesy to women in uniform had recently become a popular local custom and this was especially true for any members of the new State Security Service. At that moment in history, the RSE was seen as the front line in the war against the Marionite terrorists, and all the other enemies of the Sisterhood. In the eyes of her fellow passengers, she was a heroine and deserved the honor.

"Thank you, ma'am", she finally said, removing her cap not only out of deference to the woman's great age, but also for the cool relief that it offered. The caps were hot, and sweat tended to gather up in the hatband.

"Can I at least hold your packages for you?" The old woman had several heavy-looking parcels, and she wasn't about to make her stand with them.

"Thank you, young lady," the woman said. "Goddess bless you."

At that, the train began to pull out of the station and Kaly took her seat, placing the packages at her feet, and in her lap.

"My granddaughters are both in the service you know," the old woman told her. "I'm very proud of them."

Kaly smiled and was about to utter a polite reply, when there was a deafening explosion…

***

Signysdaater listened quietly as Maya told her all about her break-up. She also spared her the embarrassment of an "I-told-you-zo" speech.

And for once, Maya was actually grateful for the woman's taciturn nature. Her heart still felt like an open wound, and it had been a small miracle that she had even been able to report for duty at all. Being dressed down, or having to talk at length about her loss would have been completely unbearable. Just then, all she wanted was to finish their patrol with enough distractions to keep her mind from revisiting all of the hurt.

Her wish was granted only a few minutes later when an urgent call flashed on the cruiser's HUD;

HOT SHOT: BOMBING/ TERRORIST INCIDENT:

Active Bombing, Multiple Casualties, Unknown Suspects.

Name (s): Suspect #1 Unknown (To Be Determined). Height: 165.1 CM, Weight: 81.646 KG Hair: Light Blond, Eyes: Grey, Motherworld: Unknown (To Be Determined). DOB: Unknown (To Be Determined). Known Alias: Unknown (To Be Determined).

Hazard Level: HIGH. Possible terrorist activity with secondary incidents probable. City-wide alert now in effect.

All available units, Agamede, Kleta and Cyrene Districts, respond to Concordance Station. Callers report multiple explosions/multiple casualties on platform Carla-7. Fire and rescue units currently on scene with additional units en-route. Responding officers use TAC-2.

Maya sat bolt-upright as Signysdaater sent a reply. As a Pat-Rat unit, she knew without having to ask that they were expected to take the call.

When they switched over to the Tactical Channel, the chatter painted an immediate and ugly picture.

"Responding units, approach from the west and establish contact with Fire Rescue and Bomb Teams. Do *not* enter the station until EOD has cleared the location. Report in to Captain n'Veronika."

Signysdaater had already started the cruiser's engines. "Zis is going to be bad," she warned. "Very bad. You ready, Maya?"

"Yeah," Maya answered. She hadn't missed the fact that the veteran kaaper had just used her name, and not 'rookie'. On any other day, this would have been considered a victory. Today, it just lent a tiny bit of badly needed comfort.

Signysdaater switched on the 'car's lights and the emergency transponder. With an audible siren adding to the urgency of their ascent, she hit the throttle, and they rose up and away from the park, and into the police flightlanes.

It wasn't long before they saw the station and the true extent of the disaster. Although the building itself was intact, black smoke was pouring out from the magnorail tracks on the east side, and the airspace above the station was filled with police and rescue units.

"Fekking shess!" Signysdaater snarled, smacking the dash with her hand. Maya couldn't think of anything more fitting than these simple words to describe the spectacle. Nothing like this had happened on any Sisterhood world since the notorious Fiveday Evening attack by the Bio-Action Army more than a century earlier.

343

Another message, this time directed specifically to them, came up on the windshield. "PR 13-XE-80, proceed to west side gate area and assist Fire/Rescue with rescue operations. Acknowledge."

Signysdaater sent an affirmative, and took the cruiser into a diving turn, just missing a white SNN hovervan that had dropped down to catch some footage of the event.

"*Kekk!* Just vat ve fekking needed," she growled. "—za fekking *news*." In her colorful lexicon, 'news' was simply another expletive.

An instant later, an official warning went out to the news van from the Command Post. They weren't any happier about their presence than Signysdaater was.

"Unauthorized hovervan. You are violating a Police Emergency Zone. Withdraw immediately or be deactivated! You have five seconds to comply."

Rather than spending the rest of their time drifting slowly to the ground on emergency chutes, the van withdrew and assumed a more respectful distance.

Signysdaater nodded. "Gaanz gaaf. Ve don't need zem getting under our feet. Fekking *blood-drinkerz!*"

She landed the cruiser alongside a group of other police vehicles and popped the doors. "Follow me," she urged.

A police Captain met them halfway to the Command 'Truck. "See those Firewomen? Mask up and help them out! EOD's cleared the location."

Signysdaater saluted her, and led the way to a group of firewomen who were passing out exposure masks. She took one for herself and gave another to Maya. "From here on out," she said, "do vhat za F-D tells you. If I need you, I'll call you on za psiever."

Maya had just enough time to don her mask before a paramedic was tugging at her sleeve and pulling her along. They moved into the smoke filled chaos, using the built in bioplasmic sensors to tell them where they were going. It showed far more than Maya wanted to see.

Teams of firewomen were hustling out injured civilians on hoverstretchers, while others were helping those that could walk to find their way to safety. There were just as many that were beyond saving however.

Maya had only managed to go in a few dozen meters before she saw her first body. It was a woman dressed in what looked like a Harvest Maiden's costume, but her legs had been blown off at the calf and she lay unmoving in a puddle of gore.

A leg from someone else lay right next to her body. It wasn't from an adult though. Instead, it had come from someone small. A child's leg, she realized. There was a disembodied hand a little further on, and something else that vaguely resembled a torso.

Maya looked away, unable to stand the gruesome tableau. Then the paramedic was pulling at her again, and she gratefully allowed herself to be led away. The firewoman and her companions had found a survivor, and after they had loaded the woman aboard their hoverstretcher, she helped them to run it out to the waiting ambulances. Away from the smoke, and all the bloody little bits and pieces that had once been people.

Everything blurred together after that; running into the smoke once again, past more horrors and then out with the living, over and over. Sometime later, she found herself sitting on the fender of a fire unit, her mask pushed up and off of her soot covered head, drinking water. At that moment, even the finest champagne couldn't have competed with the taste.

As she poured some of it over her head, Signysdaater wandered up and sat down next to her, saying nothing. She didn't have to. Her violet eyes did all of her talking for her. They displayed a mixture of sadness and weariness, mixed up with a lifetime of dealing with hardships. There was also a hard resolve in them, and Maya envied her for that. At that moment, she didn't feel terribly strong herself.

"Ve juzt got vord from Command," the Zommerlaandar announced a moment later. "Za Marionites did zis. Zey found a van vith zeir pamplets in it, and zome bomb making shess. Zey have a suspect too; zome bita who vas in za Marines."

Maya sat up straight, and used her psiever to access the Police omni.

She recognized the image that came up on her data-monocle, and the name. It was Ellyn n'Elemay. Almost five years had passed since she had seen that face, but thanks to all of the memory training that Lady Ananzi had put her through, she still remembered it.

The woman had been listed as a 'subversive' in a file being maintained by the Station Chief for the Expeditionary Fleet. On instructions from Thermadon, Sarah had had the data purged, claiming that the woman's case would be handled 'at a higher level'. At the time, this had struck her as odd, but now she knew. It was more than odd. It was the work of Angelique bel Thana and the Agency.

Gazing out over the sea of rescue vehicles towards the Command Modules, Maya was in shock. Until that instant, she realized that she hadn't really understood the woman's significance, or the purpose behind the Agency's manipulation of the Marionites.

It was worse than glass sales, she thought. Worse than what they had done to Mariaa Estovaal. Worse than all of it. And it made her angry. Very angry.

345

An instant later, she spotted Sarah and Angelique walking together towards the Command 'Truck.

***

At first, Kaly had no sense of time or place. Then she realized that she was lying on the floor of the car. Dense smoke filled the air above her, punctuated by the orange glow of flames licking their way along the roof.

There was death in that smoke. If she rose, she knew that her lungs would be fatally seared, so she stayed low and crawled towards the car's doors instead. An all too familiar ringing in her ears deafened her, but as she inched along, it subsided, and other sounds slowly became perceptible. They were screams. Screams of pain and fear.

When her fingers found the doors, she tried to pry them open, but they resisted her, and she groped upwards for the emergency release lever. Instantly, her hand felt as if she had just shoved it into an oven, and she cried out in pain. But she didn't stop until she found the controls, and when she did, she gave them a hard pull.

Damaged by the blast, the doors only opened up a few centimeters before they jammed, but the air that rushed in through the gap was deliciously cool and sweet, and Kaly laid her head next to the opening taking it in in huge gulps.

Then she felt a hand clutching at her leg and looked down. It was the old woman who had given up her seat. She reached down to her, grabbing her by her dress and pulling her up until her head was level with the door.

Outside, she thought she heard something, and croaked out a cry for help as loudly as her lungs would allow. As a fit of coughing and retching cut this short, metal fingers appeared in the crack and then the doors came apart with a loud squeal of overstressed steel.

Kaly found herself looking up into the lenses of a Fire Department rescuebot. The machine reached in and pulled her and her companion out onto the platform. When it had dragged them a safe distance away, the rescuebot put breathing masks over their faces and then began to scan their vitals. A team of paramedics appeared next, bearing hoverstretchers, and they went to work loading the old woman aboard.

They also tried to persuade Kaly to accept a ride, but she refused, and staggered up to her feet under her own power. Because of her uniform, and with so many other victims all around them, the firewomen didn't press the matter, and gave her directions to the ambulances waiting outside before they moved on.

Even with all the smoke, and confusion, Kaly was still able to identify the epicenter of the blast. It was hard to miss. The third car in the magnorail train had been peeled wide open by the explosion. Now, it was lying on its side, and huge tongues of flame were gushing out from where the windows had once been.

This was the same car that she had seen N'Elemay exiting.

And not far away from this, were the remains of the waste receptacle that the ex-Marine had used. It too had exploded and its deadly shrapnel had cut through the crowds like razorblades. Those that weren't lying dead, or were too seriously wounded to move, were wandering around in shock, covered in blood.

She went to the nearest woman, and took her by the arm, guiding her away from the carnage. All the while, the victim kept asking her where her daughter was, and Kaly kept up a stream of meaningless reassurances as they walked out.

She really didn't know if the child had survived or not, and she didn't want to mention the bloody mess that she had seeing lying among all the other corpses near the shattered waste can. It had been suspiciously child-sized, and the only one of its kind.

Instead, she just kept them moving. That, and processing the terrible truth. Her friend, her former teammate, and the woman that she had always thought of as the very epitome of a Marine, had been the one who had planted the bombs. Ellen n'Elemay was a terrorist.

***

Kaly was treated for burns and given oxygen. Then, when she was ready, she was shown into the Mobile Command Center. Still reeking of smoke and with her uniform in tatters, she was given a chair to sit in and a hot cup of kaafra. Sarah conducted her debriefing, while Angelique audited the proceedings.

"I want you to tell me everything that you can, Corporal," Sarah began. "Everything that you remember from the time that you entered the station. No detail is too small, or too insignificant."

"Yes, ma'am," Kaly replied. Then she related all of the details that she could remember. When she reached the part where she had spotted Ellen n'Elemay, Sarah brought up two-dozen holos, including one of the ex-Marauder.

"Look at these images carefully," she instructed her, "and identify that woman for me."

Kaly's brow furrowed, but no more than a second passed before she pointed directly at the one containing N'Elemay's data.

347

"That's her," she said. "I'd know her face anywhere. We served in the same unit together."

"You're positive?"

"Yes, ma'am."

Sarah closed the other files and left the image hanging in the air. "Did you see anyone else that you recognized? Or anything that seemed out of the ordinary?"

Kaly shook her head. "No, ma'am. Just her."

"Corporal, I want to personally congratulate you for the heroism that you displayed today," Sarah said. "The RSE is proud of you. Your actions exemplified everything that our organization stands for. Just the same, I want you to talk with one of our psychs when you leave here."

Kaly began to object, but Sarah waved it off. "This has been a very traumatic event, N'Deena, and no one could go through what you have without having some problems with it. See the psych. That's an order."

"Yes, ma'am." Kaly rose and saluted her.

"And if you remember anything else," Sarah added, "I want you to contact me, or the General immediately. Is that clear?"

"Yes, ma'am."

Angelique got up from her chair at this point. "I would also like to add my congratulations to the Colonel's, Trooper. Well done." She bowed to her, and Kaly returned the gesture. "You are dismissed. A car will take you to your hotel and help you to get inside."

Kaly gave her puzzled look. "Help me, ma'am?" She didn't see any reason for needing any help. A ride back was all she really required.

"Yes," Angelique told her. "Help. The media will want to interview you. Remember your obligation to keep everything that you went through confidential. This is an ongoing investigation."

"Yes, ma'am," Kaly replied. She saluted again, and left the trailer.

"Well," Angelique said when she and Sarah were alone again. "It certainly seems that Ellen N'Elemay possesses a flair for the dramatic. I seriously doubt that anyone in the Supreme Circle will object to anything that the Agency asks for now."

Sarah's expression clouded, and Angelique noticed it. "Please do not tell me that you are having any regrets," she said. "What we did was right."

"I am not as certain," Sarah finally confessed. "The cost..." She was looking at the footage of the devastated station, coming in live over the holojectors from the emergency vehicles orbiting overhead.

"Sarah!" Angelique exclaimed. "I am truly surprised at you! You know as well as I do how dangerous democracy and freedom is. Those are the very things that have made our Sisterhood weak.'

"Thanks to N'Elemay and her criminal gang, the way is now clear for real leadership to ascend to power. We will finally have the order and strength that we need, not chaos and mob rule. What does it matter if we must lose a few to save the many? Surely you can appreciate this."

Sarah was nodding in reluctant agreement when Maya burst into the trailer.

"Is *this* what you wanted?!" Maya demanded. *"THIS?!"*

Sarah stood and seized her by the arm. "Be silent you little fool!" she hissed.

Maya pushed her away. "No Sarah! I won't fekking be silent! *You* made this happen—you and that bitch*!"* Her finger stabbed out at Angelique.

Angelique ignored her and addressed Sarah. "I thought that you said that you had her mind scrubbed," she said coolly.

Sarah answered sheepishly. "I-I meant to—."

"Hey you know what, Angelique?" Maya spat, "Fek your precious little Agency and fek you! You're all *fekking traitors!*"

"Maya," Sarah said soothingly, "you do not understand the situation. Just come with me and we will talk it over."

"No!" Maya snapped. "I'm not going anywhere with you—with *any* of you! I'm done with all this shess! You let that N'Elemay woman run loose, and you let the Marionites do this! You *knew* this was going to happen! You might as well have planted the fekking bombs yourselves you *kuntas!"*

As she said this, a group of police supervisors were coming into the trailer, and they stopped in mid-stride, a mixture of concern and confusion writ plain on their faces.

"Ma'am?" one of them asked. "What's she talking about? What does she mean?"

"Sarah, get this under control, or I will," Angelique warned. Her hand was wandering to her holster.

Maya caught the motion and saw the murder in her eyes. No matter what Sarah did, or didn't do, Bel Thana intended to kill her. She had just become a liability.

Before either of them could react, Maya embraced her symbiote and vanished.

The other kaapers let out a collective gasp. "What the fek?!" one of them stammered. "Did you just see that?"

Angelique rounded on the woman. "See *'what'* officer? I didn't see *anything* and neither did you. Zat klaar?" As one, the group of policewomen began to back away from her towards the door, clearly more concerned about incurring her wrath than unraveling the mystery.

349

Angelique's adjutant appeared at that moment and seized the initiative, shouting at them to report right away to the Fire Department for more assignments. Her tactic worked; in seconds, Angelique and Sarah were alone once again.

"You told me that her symbiote had been deactivated," Bel Thana snapped.

"I thought it was," Sarah protested. "She must have read the code from me when I was using it. It is the only explanation."

"Of course," Angelique replied astringently. "The only *possible* explanation. With the information that she has, and a working symbiote, she is a problem for us."

"I understand," Sarah said gravely. "I'll take care of her myself."

Angelique inclined her head in a curt dismissal, her green eyes icy with restrained fury as Sarah accessed her own symbiote and disappeared.

She had always considered Sarah to be the very epitome of efficiency, but now she had her doubts. Clearly, the little street tramp had seriously impaired her lover's judgment.

Angelique addressed her adjutant by psiever. *I want you to make certain that Sarah keeps her word and terminates Maya n'Kaaryn. If she fails, assign someone else to handle the matter. I want Maya dead.*

When the officer signaled back affirmatively, Angelique took a moment to compose herself, and then gave the adjutant an additional order to see to it that the guards standing watch over the trailer were not to admit anyone—even women in uniform, and regardless of rank. After that, she took advantage of the secure communications equipment.

Director Susa ben Paula, now officially a five star general, answered her immediately. Bel Thana didn't waste the woman's time with the particulars of the bombing. Ben Paula already had all of that data, and there was a far more pressing matter to discuss.

"Susa," Angelique said. "I think that it is time that we make the Hive ready for the Queen Bee." The Hive was the code name for a facility that had been in place since the Second Widow's War. Located on Durandel in the Halasi Elant, it served as a safe haven and a fallback position for the government in the event that any threat to the nation's security proved too dire for the capitol to remain a viable option.

"I agree General," Ben Paula replied, "and I want you to spearhead that operation for me. The moment you are done there, you are to leave for Durandel and take along whoever you think you might need."

"Yes, ma'am," Angelique answered. "I will advise you when the Hive is fully operational."

"*Bian*," Ben Paula said. "One other thing; the Chairwoman's office advised me that she will tour the disaster scene this afternoon. She also plans to make a speech to the nation during her visit. Is the site secure?"

"It will be," Bel Thana assured her.

They ended their conversation there, and Angelique erased any record of it. The existence of the Hive was too sensitive to risk leaving any loose ends behind.

Next, she sent off several private messages. The first was to her household staff, telling them to pack her things for the journey to Durandel.

The second was to Senatrix Layna n'Calysher, advising her to send her daughter off on an extended trip—and as far away from Thermadon as possible. The third and last one was sent to her adjutant, letting her know about the upcoming visit by the Chairwoman.

With that, she opened up her valise and withdrew a tiny vial of perfume. It had been custom made for her, and at great cost. Out of a perverse sense of humor, but also in homage to her ancestress, she had dubbed the scent *Lucrezia*. Carefully dabbing it behind her ears, she settled in to wait, and to let history take its inevitable course.

Ten minutes later, the Chairwoman and Director ben Paula arrived together, accompanied by a huge security detail. Angelique met them and provided a detailed report of the incident. Afterwards, she accompanied them to a podium that her officers had hastily erected for the Chairwoman's address to the nation.

Later, after the speech was over, both women privately complimented her about her perfume. They had no idea that they had been breathing in their own deaths the entire time.

CHAPTER 11

Interworld Trade Center, Thermadon Val, Thermadon, Myrene System,
United Sisterhood of Suns, 1049.01|13|07:80:54

Passing over the Interworld Trade Center, Maya slammed her fist on the dash of her stolen police cruiser.

"Stupid, stupid, stupid!" she shouted. If she hadn't let her anger do all of her thinking, she wouldn't have gotten in the mess she was in now. At the moment, her life wasn't worth a single credit.

She briefly considered returning to the Sticks to get her things, and then running for it. For somewhere.

But her apartment was the first place that the Agency would look for her, and trying to leave Thermadon on a random merchanter was a poor gamble. Unless its Captain was a Daughter of the Coast—and a loyal one at that--the odds were excellent that the woman would just turn her over rather than risk defying the RSE.

And even if she did escape, and tried to lose herself on one of the Sisterhood's thousands of worlds, it would only be a temporary reprieve. Eventually, the Agency would find her.

Stupid, stupid, stupid!

Her panic spiked. She needed help and she needed it from friends, she realized. The problem was that she had never been a person that had engendered loyalty. Everyone had always used her, and then discarded her when she no longer had any value. Just like Felecia and Sarah had.

After a lifetime of betrayal and suspicion, she would have to do something that didn't come naturally to her at all. She would have to trust someone. Her thoughts turned to the only resources she knew of; the *JUDI* and Skylaar.

Bel Lissa owned the merchanter now, and she had the final say about what it did and who it carried. That was something.

So was the fact that in all their time together, the woman had never done her any wrong. Neither had Zara.

But they also did business with Sarah, and they were still with the Agency, however peripherally. So was Skylaar.

The fact that her teacher, of all people, had to be considered carefully, felt like a knife turning in her guts, but it needed to be done. Skylaar was certainly an Agency asset, she reminded herself, but the Nemesian was also someone that she had always admired, and believed in.

Now she would have to put their relationship to the test. Her years on the street whispered that it was just as false as everything else had ever been. Her heart however, felt otherwise.

Like Bel Lissa and Zara, Skylaar had always been true to her. That *had* to count for something, she told herself.

The only question was whether it would count for enough. Whether Skylaar would be willing to jeopardize her professional reputation and betray the Agency. The only way to find out, she knew, was to roll the dice, and pray for the best. There simply weren't any other alternatives, and if she were wrong, she would pay for her error with her life.

Before she could make this leap of faith however, she had to get rid of her ride. At the time, the cruiser had offered her a quick way of getting out of the Concordance Station. But now it was a beacon, pointing right at her. The Police Omniplex tracked all Metro cars, and as soon as someone figured out that their vehicle was missing, they'd find it—and her.

Stupid, stupid, stupid!

Looking down at the Trade Center, she spotted a large hoverpad, and made for it immediately. The instant that the cruiser touched down, she was out and moving towards the nearest elevator.

Once inside, she pressed a button at random. When she reached her stop, she got out and looked for a restroom, trying her best not to seem hurried, and ignoring the curious glances that she received.

As soon as she was alone in a stall, she shed her uniform blouse and tied it up into a ball with her duty belt. The only items that she kept with her were her needlegun, which she tucked into her waistband, and some extra clips that she stuffed into her pockets.

The blouse and belt met their fate in the nearest waste receptacle, right along with her Police ID card, and the badge with its built-in locator chip.

Inspecting herself in the mirror, she knew that she looked a little strange wearing only a sleeveless undershirt over a pair of uniform slacks, but fashion wasn't at the forefront of her priorities at the moment. Changing her identity was, and for once, she was grateful for all the training that she had received, and for her augmentation.

Like all agents, the little nanobots that had modified her psiever had also given her options that the average woman didn't have. Although it registered a 'shell identity' in order to keep the City AI happy, she could shut this down and become untraceable just like the SpecOps women.

Suddenly 'going blank' wasn't a smart option though, and she wasn't even tempted to try it. It was one thing to do so on an active Op, where it was expected as a precaution against terrorist reprisal, but quite another in a situation like this.

Like many other places, the security cameras in the Center were smart, and they tracked everyone that they saw and matched it with their identities. They were also networked with the City AI. Someone who came up on a display, but didn't have any corresponding ID would stand out even worse than if they were on fire.

This meant that she had to rely on another modification. Thanks again to the hard working nanobots, Maya could also change her psiever 'tag' along with the record stored in her biochip, and become someone else entirely.

The skill to create such new identities, and implement them, was something that Sarah had included as a part of her curriculum. And the work products of these studies, the false identities themselves, were stored in two places; a base version in Maya's psiever and a dynamic one out on the omniplex.

There, they acted as if they were real, living people carrying on with their ersatz lives, updating and changing the information about themselves in a manner that seemed natural, and more importantly, absolutely real. Each alternate persona had its own medical and work records, as well as an entire background that went all the way back to its fictitious childhood, and much more.

At the time, she had been so impressed with this that she had gone on to create several more identities for herself, just for the fun of it. Thanks to her extra practice, there were at least half a dozen 'women' that where completely unknown to Sarah, or her Agency friends.

Before she could use them however, she had to trick the City AI, and for that, she needed to employ another ruse. At its essence, it was nothing more than a shell game like the ones they played on the streets of Ashkele, but managed with data, rather than cups and dried beans.

Pausing at the restroom door, she closed her eyes, and sent a command to her 'shell' identity. She instructed it to quietly replicate itself, and then do nothing more than confirm its current location.

Then she disconnected herself from the copy. At the same time, she instructed her psiever to imprint one of her alternate identities on itself and on her biochip.

To the City AI, 'Maya n'Kaaryn' was in the restroom, and so was 'Barbra bel Vela', a tech employed at Bel Sharra Memorial Spaceport. If anyone was watching, they would have noticed the anomaly, but only for a second.

Right away, one of the supporting files that she had created on the omniplex activated, and created a trail that led from Bel Vera's 'last known location' to Maya's present one.

In attoseconds, the record was amended, convincing the City AI that Bel Vera had left her fictitious job at the Spaceport and had gone to visit the Center's restroom. And the longer that she used her alternate identity, the more convincing the illusion would become. The file would keep receiving realistic additions.

From here on out, the AI would be tracking what it believed was Maya n'Kaaryn, and not Barbra bel Vela. It was by no means a perfect solution, and she was well aware of this. Visually, she was still the same person, and anyone who tracked her by camera would see right through her ploy.

Which was exactly why she not only intended to leave the Center as fast as possible, but to swap out her new persona for a third identity the very instant that she had finished placing a call to Skylaar.

Finding a bank of holophones to do so was easy. Interworld had them everywhere and making the call proved to be just a simple. One of the prerequisites for a proper false identity were supporting credit accounts and Bel Vela had a small, but serviceable balance available to her.

Initially, Maya had balked at this measure when Sarah had first suggested it, but now she was glad that she had followed the woman's directions. The call went through after making a small charge to the account, and suddenly Skylaar was on the other end.

"Maya," the woman said. It wasn't a question, but a statement.

"I need help," Maya told her, watching the stopwatch display from her psiever descend. How long did she have she wondered? A minute? Two? More?

Stupid, stupid, stupid!

"I know," Skylaar returned. "Meet me where we trained last." The call ended there.

This was Maya's cue to get moving. She turned from the holophones and headed for the elevator, sending out another message by psiever. This too would be trackable, but there was no way around it. It was to Rebá, currently parked at the precinct house.

The hoverbike's AI recognized her alternate identity from a secure file that it had on-board, and responded immediately. Maya didn't have to ask the machine to change its own transponder codes as soon as the call was concluded. That was all part of the package that she had created.

Rebá! I need you, she thought. *Respond to my location, your fastest!*

On my way Maya, the machine responded. *Traffic Rule Compliant, or High Speed/Disregard, Emergency?* Like her mistress, Rebá loved any excuse to break the law.

Make it fast, but don't draw attention to yourself. Understood?

Yes, Maya, There was no mistaking the hoverbike's disappointment, but Maya didn't feel any remorse. Given her dire circumstances, it was quite likely that Rebá would eventually get her opportunity to run wild. Maya only hoped that this wouldn't happen anytime soon. She didn't relish the idea of going up against machines like Aria, or worse, Aria herself, with Sarah at the controls.

Sobered by the possibility, she re-boarded the elevators, changing out her identity once more. By the time she arrived on the roof, Rebá was there, waiting for her.

Destination, Maya?

Ponytail Park, Rebá, Maya told it. *Bring your weapons online and keep an eye out for hostiles.*

Is there going to be trouble, Maya?

That's already happened, Rebá. Let's get going.

***

The RSE caught up with her halfway to her destination. There were two aircars and they were keeping pace with her in the light traffic. Like Aria, they were fast machines and stayed with her like a pair of predators, waiting for the right opportunity to strike. Had a sixth sense not alerted her to their presence, and a quick lane change confirmed it, she wouldn't have even detected them.

If they were anything like Aria, she knew that they packed enough firepower aboard to bring her down, and she was certainly no expert when it came to this kind of fight. She'd been with Sarah when she had flown against opponents, but she had never had to do so all by herself. There was also no question that whoever were piloting the 'cars were experts.

Maya did have one thing going for her however. This was the hoverbike that she was riding. Thanks to Trina, Rebá had her own brace of weapons, a suite of defensive devices, and the AI itself was a clone of Aria. Together, this gave her a fighting chance.

Rebá! she thought, *there's two 'cars trailing us. I think they're hostile.*

I see them Maya, the bike answered. *Tracking them now and bringing combat systems online.* There was a pause and then, *Maya, they have Agency transponder codes. I can't fire on them.*

"Well, override that!" Maya exclaimed aloud.

I can't, Rebá apologized.

"Fek!" Maya barked. "Can you evade them if they fire on us?"

Yes, Maya. I am allowed to do that, Rebá answered. *I can also drop electronic countermeasures and ignore any shutdown requests.*

"Good. Now we need to lose them. Full speed, evasive."

Thank you, Maya! the AI responded cheerfully. The bike's afterburners engaged and Rebá took them into a steep diving roll. Right away, the two aircars dropped and followed.

The moment that they had gotten clear of the surrounding traffic, they fired their railguns. Rounds ripped by the hoverbike in incandescent bursts, and Rebá banked wildly to avoid being hit.

"Rebá! Do something!" Maya had no idea what to ask for, and she hoped that the AI was smart enough to improvise.

Rebá was. *Dropping countermeasures, continuing evasion.* There was a pair of dull 'thumps' as the decoys released, and risking a look back, Maya saw them deploy. The gunfire was misdirected, but the two aircars kept up the pursuit.

Missiles will come next, she thought. That was what she would have done at this stage.

Her deduction was accurate. Hidden compartments under both vehicles popped open and she saw the clusters extend, and then the flash of multiple rockets launching. She didn't need to warn Rebá, and there wouldn't have been enough time even if she had tried to. In seconds the missiles were closing the gap and Maya hung on to the bike for all she was worth as the AI sent them into another corkscrewing spin, discharging flares and clouds of metallic chaff as it did so.

None of the missiles hit them, but then the AI made a grave announcement.

Maya, our stores of defensive devices is limited. If they fire any more rockets at us, I may not be able to deflect them.

Which Maya thought, was probably what the pilots behind her were hoping for. Once Rebá was out of countermeasures, they would be well and truly fekked.

"I'm going to take us down low, Rebá," Maya said. By this point they were over the factories in the eastern part of the city. These were a maze of automated installations and with luck, she could use their smaller size and maneuverability to their advantage. It was risky, but as inexperienced as she was, Maya understood that staying up in the open air was sheer suicide. As she looked below them for a place to head to, the nearest aircar fired its railguns again.

This time, the stream of Malandrium-coated rounds caught the edge of her 'bike, shattering some of its engine cowling and sending shrapnel flying. Several of the pieces hit Maya's leg, tearing into the fabric of her clothes and her skin.

Maya winced and gritted her teeth against the pain as she took manual control over Rebá. With a hard jerk of the handlebars, she sent them into a tight loop to the left.

A rooftop rushed up, and seconds before impact, Maya leveled off and flew them under a set of gigantic pipes. Immediately ahead of this was a tall building with a narrow alley leading off to the right. It was going to be a tight fit, but it had some overhead piping and several bridges that offered her a certain amount of cover. She took what had been given to her and went in, praying that the Goddess would see to it that the passage didn't lead to a dead end.

Back behind her, one of the aircars descended and stayed with her while its partner remained overhead, covering any potential escape in that direction. Then Maya saw exactly what she had feared. The alley terminated in a cul-de-sac. The only way out would be up, and then she would become the prey of the second machine.

A second later, a fusillade from the trailing 'car forced her to jink sideways, coming dangerously close to the walls around her in the process. She was running out of space, and options.

With no other choice, she brought the nose of her hoverbike up and ascended. Just as she had expected, the second car fired a brace of missiles at her as she came into its gun sights.

Maya, I only have enough countermeasures for one more missile. Rebá warned. *The rest will hit us. I am sorry. I have failed you.*

"I forgive you, Rebá," Maya said, unbuckling from her saddle. "Goodbye."

Goodbye, Maya.

She threw herself off the bike and into thin air. The universe spun around her as she flipped and fell towards the earth. In the instant before she embraced her symbiote, she managed to catch sight of the first missile hitting the decoy that Rebá had deployed. And then the second and third rockets as they struck the 'bike itself and transformed it into a churning ball of fire.

Time slowed to a near standstill, and she drifted harmlessly to the ground. A full minute passed (or what seemed like one), before her feet gently touched down.

Maya didn't waste any time marveling at her escape. Instead, she ran full out, ignoring the searing pain in her injured leg and the blood that was streaming out of the wound. She also tried to calculate how long she could remain outside of the normal time-stream. From experience, she knew that the longer that she delayed release, the worse the aftereffects would be. If she waited for too long, she would reach a point where she would be incapable of defending herself.

Borrowing on her training, she counted down the precious seconds and gained as much distance from the area as she could. When she reached the end of her count, she let go of the bond.

As near as she could tell, she was blocks away from the scene of the attack and as the universe resumed its usual pace, she looked back to see where her pursuers were. Off in the distance, pieces of Rebá were still showering down, and both aircars were gaining altitude. They knew what she had done and now, they were hunting for her.

She left normal time again and half-ran, half-hobbled away. When she reached the edge of her safe limit she came out again, certain that she had managed to escape.

Then one of the 'cars appeared over the rooftops. Somehow, they had found her, and as she began to stumble away, she realized why—and damned herself for her sheer stupidity. The symbiote had certainly done its job to help her gain distance, but in her haste to use it, she had forgotten one key factor. Her assumed identity. It was the same one that she had used to call Skylaar with, and the moment she had reappeared in the normal time stream, the City AI had been able to track it, and her.

Stupid, stupid girl! She made a solemn promise to punish herself severely. But later, and only if she managed to survive.

Desperately, she looked around her for any place to take cover, and as she did so, she saw that a third 'car was arriving. It was coming up fast behind the first two machines, and behind it, was a police cruiser. Which meant that whoever was flying the Metro 'car, was probably in Angelique's employ as well.

Maya didn't have the luxury of wondering about this however, or worrying over the fact that the odds against her had just gotten exponentially worse. Pavement began to shatter all around her as the lead 'car's railguns let loose and ranged in.

Crying out in terror, she covered her head and ran as fast as her injured leg would allow, embracing her symbiote every few seconds to avoid the slugs that were raining down. Pieces of masonry, shattered and sent flying by the attack, slashed at her flesh in a hundred small places every time she came back into the normal time-stream.

But adrenaline, and the desperate animal urge to escape, overrode any sense of pain. The only thing that dominated her consciousness was the imperative of getting out of the range of the hovercar's guns.

Fighting a black wave of symbiote-induced nausea, she spotted a stairwell and threw herself down into it. She hit the cement treads with her shoulder, grunting in agony as she half-rolled, half-tumbled to the grimy bottom. There was a door there, and struggling to her feet, she reached for the latch and instantly regretted the decision. The fall had injured her right side, and she could barely raise her arm. Working with her left, she tried the latch. It was, of course, securely locked.

The whooshing sound of a missile being fired filled her ears next. *This is where I'm going to die,* she thought. *Here, at the bottom of a dirty stairwell in an alley.*

As she prepared to feel the explosion rip her apart, another noise replaced the missile's engine. It was the sound of pieces of metal hitting the ground, immediately followed by another set of rockets going off, and then the hollow report of explosions.

Somehow, and against all odds, Maya realized that she was still alive. Gingerly, she worked her way back up the stairs to take stock of her situation.

It wasn't easy to manage. Her left leg was now all but useless, and putting any weight on it was excruciating. Instead, she was forced to rely on her right, and what support the stair rail offered. When she was almost at the top, she lowered herself, and peeked over the lip of the landing.

The first pair of aircars had vanished. In their place were two columns of smoke coming up from behind the buildings across from her. She couldn't tell if this had anything to do with the vehicles, or if they had been caused by all the ordnance that they had been throwing around. The only machines that were still in the air were the third 'car and the police cruiser. And they were descending.

Frantically, Maya reached for her needle gun, and to her horror, she realized that somewhere in the chase, or perhaps during the fall from Rebá, she had lost it. The only weapon that she had at hand was a stubby sheath knife that she carried on her leg.

She drew the knife and retreated back down the stairs, crouching as far into the meager shadows as the space allowed. Clearly, her pursuers had chosen to come at her on foot, and she had every intention of taking at least one of them out with her.

Then someone called her name. Maya stayed right where she was though. It was the oldest trick in the universe, and she wasn't about to fall for it. She liked her head right where it was; attached to her neck and not splattered all over the place.

Another voice sounded from above. This time it was behind her. "Maya! Come out!"

She knew this voice. It was Signysdaater.

This was when enough of the shock wore off for her to finally recognize who the first speaker had been. It was Skylaar taur Minna.

"Maya, please come out," the Nemesian urged. "We have to get moving." Cautiously, Maya raised her head and saw her martial arts teacher and then Signysdaater. Both women were toting military energy rifles.

"*Gaane an*, rookie," Signysdaater said, "ve have to get you za fek out of here!"

"Wait—!" Maya protested, shaking off the hand the kaaper had placed on her good arm. "What's going on?"

"Zere's no time to explain," Signysdaater replied. "Ve have to go bevore zey zend back-up."

Skylaar nodded in agreement. "Things are not as you think, Maya. But this is not the time or the place to explain."

Reluctantly, Maya allowed Signysdaater to help her, and using the woman's shoulder for support, let herself be led to the cruiser.

"I will follow you," Skylaar told the policewoman. "Go to Euxine Regional Spaceport."

Signysdaater inclined her head affirmatively. "Yah, zat zounds good. You keep zem off us, if zey come nozing around, 'kay?"

"I will," Skylaar promised.

Using the First Aid kit from the cruiser, Signysdaater quickly dressed the largest of Maya's wounds and as soon as she was satisfied with her work, took the pilots seat. When the machine rose up into the sky, Maya finally discovered what the source of the smoke had been. Down below them, the two aircars that had been chasing her were engulfed in flames. To her eye, any survivors seemed highly unlikely.

She also knew who had destroyed them. It had been Skylaar. Her teacher had just killed several agents to save her life. And Signysdaater had helped her to do it. They would both be hunted women now, just like she was.

But that was what real friends did for one another. Despite the potential consequences, they stuck together. They were loyal.

As incredible as it seemed, her gamble had actually paid off. For once, friendship was not a lie. It felt good.

***

Dana bel Hanna breathed a virtual sigh of relief. Skylaar had had Maya under constant surveillance ever since she had come back to Thermadon, and Signysdaater had assisted her. But when Angelique had sent the kill order, Maya's file had been locked to everyone but her hunters.

Although the onboard AI's of the two aircars had resisted her efforts to coopt them, it had been a relatively simple matter to append the restriction, and re-add the veteran kaaper and the Nemesian.

And just as she had anticipated, they had rushed to Maya's rescue. The fact that the RSE computers had detected the change, and reported it, was regrettable, but in the end, this damage could not be undone, and it was the outcome that really mattered.

Maya was alive. To be sure, it had been a close thing, and the young woman had certainly played a decisive role in ensuring her own survival. But she was, just as her dossier suggested, a very resourceful and tenacious girl, and now that she was safe, and among friends, Bel Hanna felt far less trepidation about the future. Together, they would see to it that she met her destiny.

Erasing the data trail that pointed back to her, she was sorely tempted to return to her re-write of the *Encyclopedia Soriritas*, and other acts of sabotage that she had in progress.

She also knew better. Her work in Thermadon was done for the moment, and possibly forever.

Instead, she conducted a search and located the *C-JUDI-GO*. Once she found it, she severed her links with the *Encyclopedia* and transferred herself over to the little ship. The resident AI, although sophisticated enough to handle the business of managing the *JUDI*, was no match for her. In just a few seconds, she breached its security and found a place for herself deep within its data base. There, she settled in and waited.

From this point on, 'Judi' would be the mask that she would wear for the next part of her performance. To anyone unaware of the situation, this might have seemed a miniscule role compared to her tenure aboard the *Athena*, or what she had set in motion throughout the omniplex.

In reality, it was far more important. The fate of the Sisterhood, and even the very galaxy itself, hinged upon what would happen next. And although no one except the Galaxy Mind itself would ever know it, the outcome of their little drama might utterly depend on the part she would play in it. In time, it was possible that she would find a point where she would be able to let her mask drop, and reveal herself, but first, the play had to end and the curtain had to drop. Until then, she would have to be the *JUDI*.

Euxine Regional Spaceport, Euxine, Thermadon, Myrene System, United Sisterhood of Suns, 1049.01|13|08:01:21

Euxine Regional Spaceport was one of the dozens of smaller landing fields that serviced Thermadon. It acted as an overflow for traffic coming downside from space and tended to be sparsely visited except for the occasional private starship, and a handful of merchanters. It also lacked a manned control tower, and used an automated system instead.

As a result, when the two aircars landed at the edge of the runways, the few people that were around took no notice of the fact that one of the passengers had to be helped aboard the CSS *C-JUDI-GO*. They also didn't pay attention to the fact that a police vehicle had delivered her, or that the aircar which had accompanied it was being abandoned to fly home on its own.

Inside the *JUDI*, and out of view, Zara and Jeena met Maya and her companions in the cargo bay. The Engineer was carrying the ship's portable medkit.

"Oh, Maya," she said, clucking her tongue at all the bandages. "You're a fekking mess. Can't leave you alone for one nano, can we?

Maya smiled weakly. "You should see the other girl."

"Let's take her to Sarah's cabin," Zara instructed. "I'll work on the leg there." No one, not even Maya, argued with this. In addition to her role as the Ship's Engineer, Zara was also a paramedic. This was a legacy from her days in the Star Service, when she had served with Bel Lissa aboard a tiny interceptor where such cross-training among the crew was mandatory.

When they reached Sarah's bed, Maya was eased down onto it and Zara brought out an applicator bottle from her kit.

"This'll help with the pain, and make you rest," she said, turning Maya's arm over to expose her inocular. Whatever was in the bottle hit Maya quickly and the pain in her leg began to fade.

She was starting to become drowsy just as Jeena came into the cabin, carrying an armload of objects. One of them was her sword, and another was her bodysuit. Maya managed a weak grin, glad for the sight of her most precious possessions. In her flight, she had thought them lost to her forever.

"Where do you want this stuff?" the neoman asked.

"Just in the corner for now," Zara told him, and then to Maya, "We had Jeena pop by your apartment to pick them up. Thought you'd want 'em."

Maya was now more confused than ever. "There were agents there— how did you get in?"

"It was easy," Jeena answered nonchalantly. "One jumpsuit is pretty much the same as another. I just told them I was with maintenance and that you were being evicted. They were real nice. They let me right in."

Then the neoman spotted something on Maya's bodysuit and quickly produced a rag to wipe it away. It looked very much like blood, but she was becoming so groggy that she wasn't certain.

"Oh, sorry, I must have missed that," he grinned, "There! All clean now."

"W-what--?

"Later," Zara insisted. "Now *rest*. I've got to get this metal out of your leg and then we've got to get the ship clear. You know how Inish is without anyone to help her—all thumbs. She'll fly us right into a star if I don't keep an eye on her."

Maya was too tired to laugh. She closed her eyes, and let the darkness take her.

***

Sarah had always considered herself to be a detail-oriented person, but somehow, she had neglected the obvious. And as far as she was concerned, Angelique had every right to be angry with her.

Maya's memory should have been scrubbed, and her symbiote locked off. But for some reason that she couldn't fathom, she had simply forgotten to take care of these important tasks.

How could I have been so stupid? she asked herself. *How could I have let things go this far?*

For anyone else, the shock of Trina's death might have been a good enough reason, but Sarah had been an agent for too long to allow herself to hide behind such an excuse. She had simply become complacent, she decided. Now, she would have to clean up the mess.

Even though Maya had covered her tracks well, and had somehow managed to evade the agents who had been sent to terminate her, Sarah knew where she had gone, and she had a fair idea of who had helped her get there.

"Aria," she said to her aircar's AI, "Bel Sharra. Search for the *JUDI's* berth. Let me know if they are still downside."

A moment passed before the AI returned with her results. "The C-JUDI-GO is still downside. They are not at Bel Sharra however. They have docked at the Euxine Regional Spaceport. Shall I divert us there?"

"Yes," Sarah replied. "Use the police lanes, and expedite. I don't care how much fuel we have to burn to do it, just get me there as quickly as possible."

"Yes, mistress," Aria answered. Right away the car gained altitude, activated its RSE transponder, and entered the emergency flightlanes. Then the afterburners engaged.

***

Skylaar was waiting on the *JUDI*'s cargo ramp when Sarah arrived, but she wasn't surprised to see her. Her presence merely confirmed everything that she had suspected. Maya was there, and for some reason the Nemesian had aided in her escape.

She drew her needlegun and pointed it at her. "Are you going to try and stop me?" she asked. She didn't want to fight her friend, but she would if she had to. Too much was at stake.

"No," Skylaar replied calmly. "In fact, I'll take you to her. She's in your cabin right now, under sedation."

Sarah blinked in surprise, but she knew by reading the woman, that she wasn't lying. "Why?" she asked suspiciously.

"Practical necessity," Skylaar answered. "I am a professional after all. I understand the odds, and my situation."

Sarah immediately detected the slight taint of a lie in her words, but it was so subtle that she couldn't puzzle it out. She decided to play along until Skylaar betrayed herself.

"Lead on," she said.

The Nemesian turned on her heels and walked up the ramp. Sarah kept a careful distance from her, ready to embrace her symbiote and watching for any sign that the situation was about to change.

But the woman's manner remained relaxed, and when they reached the cabin, Skylaar entered it and took up a place in the corner where she could be kept under observation. As incredible as it seemed, Skylaar taur Minna was cooperating. And just as she had indicated, Maya was there, and completely unconscious.

Keeping Skylaar in view, Sarah walked up to the bedside. A sharp pang of doubt stabbed at her as she looked down at the young woman, but she had expected as much, and quickly suppressed the emotion. Although she had come to feel a deep affection for her—and even a certain degree of love--she knew what had to be done.

It wasn't the first time that she had contemplated killing Maya by any means. Their initial encounter at the spaceport had been the first. The second had come the night that Maya had been given the choice to either join the *JUDI*, or pay the ultimate penalty. On both occasions, Maya had been allowed to live.

Now, here they were, and Sarah's choice was between sparing her, and what the Conversâzi required. There really wasn't any question in her mind about which it would have to be. The chance to rescue the Sisterhood from its moral decay, and lift it up from its weakness, was too great a thing to sacrifice for the sake of just one woman. No matter who she was.

She knew that she would hate herself for what she was about to do, and that she would store the pain of it with all the other hurt that she had locked away. It would go into a dark, secret place in her soul. A place that Trina, and now Angelique, had the key to. It was what she had done ever since the very first time she had been compelled to take a human life.

Without even asking for it, or wanting to see it, the memory of that distant event resurfaced, just as clearly as if it had happened only the day before. The victim had been a fellow agent, and she had betrayed her comrades to a cartel of glass dealers in exchange for a promise of safety and credits. Her actions had cost the other operatives their lives, and Sarah's mentor, Lady Ananzi, had chosen her to be the executioner.

She could still feel the rain hammering down on the three of them, and the pitiful expression on the woman's face as she cringed on her knees, pleading with them for her life. They had been friends before her betrayal, Sarah recalled. But she had still pressed the trigger. She had still taken care of business.

And she would do the same thing now, she vowed. She would do it quickly. One squeeze of the trigger was all it would take. Then, when it was over, she could hate herself just a little more than she already did. Over the years, she had discovered that this, and not some flaming Marionite afterlife, was what hell really was, and she was as much a prisoner of it as any sinner.

That didn't change the facts however, or the demands of duty.

She lifted the needlegun, placing it almost tenderly against Maya's temple and glanced at Skylaar, half-expecting her to intervene. The Nemesian remained still however.

Her finger moved to the trigger, and she willed herself not to close her eyes. That was the coward's way, and she owed Maya more than that. Then she began to squeeze.

Inexplicably, her digit froze as if it possessed a will of its own. She redoubled the effort, and when nothing changed, she switched the weapon over to her left hand, with the same shocking result.

She could not shoot. Something had been done to her, and for a split second, Sarah wondered if Skylaar had hidden the fact that she was actually a psi herself. It was the only explanation that she could think of.

Immediately, she turned the weapon on the Nemesian, and made another attempt to fire--and failed again. She couldn't detect any sign of talents coming from Skylaar though. Something else was intervening, and whatever it was, was absolutely irresistible, and utterly invisible to her senses.

"What is this!?" she demanded. "What have you *done* to me!?"

"I? Nothing," Skylaar answered. "It is Lady Ananzi's doing. Now, I need you to listen to me, Sarah. Listen very carefully; *I have slept in the arms of twilight, and I have dreamt my way unto the darkest night.*"

Sarah's eyes fluttered as a wave of profound fatigue washed over her. It was a hypnotic compulsion of some kind, she realized. The trigger phrase, and her reaction, confirmed this. Clearly, Lady Ananzi had betrayed her.

Although a thousand questions raced through her mind, the need to fulfil her obligation to Angelique, and the Conversâzi, overwhelmed them all. She had to finish what she had come to do. She had to redeem herself. By killing Maya. Now.

Dropping the needlegun, Sarah cocked her fist, intent on delivering the death blow with her bare hands.

Skylaar spoke again. There was more force in her voice.

"Stop, Sarah! You will leave this cabin immediately! You will go into the crew's quarters. You will climb into a bunk and you will sleep."

Sarah's arm suddenly joined in her finger's mutiny. It locked itself in place, and although she channeled every ounce of her will into it, it steadfastly refused to comply. Sweat broke out on her brow as she tried to overcome the spell, but it was impossible. She might as well have been trying to push a planet from its orbit.

"You will do as I say, Sarah," Skylaar barked. *"Obey!"*

With a ragged cry, Sarah finally reached the very limits of her strength. Her arm went limp, and she collapsed to her knees, gasping for air.

"Get up, Sarah. Go into the crew's quarters," Skylaar told her firmly. "You are feeling tired. You can rest there."

To her horror, Sarah realized that she was rising. As she watched it happening from some distant dreamlike place, her body became erect, turned of its own accord, and began to walk out of the cabin. It had become like some kind of living puppet, totally subservient to Skylaar's commands.

Now she understood why the woman had been so cooperative, and so unconcerned. But what her motives were, or Lady Ananzi's for that matter, remained an utter mystery. Only one thing was certain; their plans involved Maya.

It also didn't matter. She *was* tired, right down to the very marrow of her bones. Afterwards, when she had rested, she would expend the energy that she needed to think. Just then, she had nothing to spare.

Grunvaald Haarmaaneplaatz, Vaalkenstaad Township, Zommerlaand, Sunna 3, Solara Elant, United Sisterhood of Suns, 1049.01|13|08:11:21

The drone in the holo had been configured to perform and respond exactly like the latest Valkyrie aerospace fighter. The moment that it entered the invisible zone around the Seevaan ship, and right at the point where it might have been within firing range, it vanished. A bare half-second later, a small flare of light appeared on the opposite side of the Seevaan vessel, and then winked out.

This was all that Lilith would ever see of the drone's destruction. The field that it had entered had compensated for the energy created by its disintegration by venting it out into space. To the best of her knowledge, and the Navy's most gifted technical advisors, this 'Death Field' could resist any attack the Sisterhood could mount against it, and no one had even established if there was an upward limit to how much punishment it could handle. In fact, it seemed to have no limit whatsoever.

She frowned, and viewed the next clip. This showed Seevaan fighters engaging more drones. Instead of employing railguns and missiles, they used a violet-colored ball of plasma that locked onto their targets just like a missile could. It wasn't fooled by any known form of countermeasure, and once it made contact, it had the same effect as the 'Death Field'. The drones simply ceased to be.

Although her nation's Navy was two hundred years ahead of the ETR, the Seevaans were that and more in comparison with the Sisterhood. If it ever came to a war, it would end quickly, and the Sisterhood would be the clear loser.

Lately, this had been the very thing worrying her superior, Admiral ebed Cya. An unprecedented event had recently occurred; for the first time ever, the Seevaan Chaotic factions were displaying their military might outside of their own space, and holding war games in the Xee Protectorate.

As the holos amply demonstrated, their exercises were specifically calibrated towards the Sisterhood. On the diplomatic front, there wasn't any indication that relations were breaking down, but as far as Rixa saw it, that alone was no guarantee that the peace would last.

While the games went on, and the Seevaans continued to practice a mock war with Womankind, they had every reason to remain vigilant. Lilith's job was to analyze the information that they had, and if she could, discover anything that seemed like weaknesses in the Seevaan arsenal. So far, she hadn't found any, but she persisted, hoping that the Goddess would grant her some useful insight.

She was deep into a replay of the drone footage when Hanna came bursting through the kitchen door. From her expression, Lilith knew that something terrible had just happened.

"What's wrong?" she asked.

"It's Concordance Station," the other woman blurted, half out of breath. "They bombed it! The Marionites bombed the station!"

Lilith couldn't quite believe her ears. Suddenly, the Seevaans had lost all of their importance. "*What?!*"

"It's true! It's on all za 'cast channels!" Hanna answered, beckoning her to come into the living area. This was where Grammy kept her rather ancient, and oft-repaired holojector.

Marina and Ingrit were already there, and they had switched the machine on. The local station, out of Vaalkenstaad, was just repeating the headlines. The 'cast was in Standard, with Zommerlaandish captioning, so Lilith didn't have to struggle with what the journalist was saying.

"To repeat our headline story, there has been a bombing at the Concordance magnorail station. The attack came at the very height of the Summertyne holiday, and according to authorities, several devices were involved.'

"While casualty figures are not complete, our sister station in Thermadon reports that a preliminary figure is 190 dead and 1,200 injured by the blast. Local area hospitals have been inundated with patients, and they have been transferring the less serious cases to satellite facilities, using city hoverbuses and ambulances.'

"In addition, two other bombs were found and disarmed at the Cyrene and Marpesia stations, and a stolen 'van carrying bomb-making materials and Marionite propaganda, was discovered near Concordance Station. While the terrorist group calling itself the 'Daughters of Eve' has not yet claimed direct responsibility, police officials say that the evidence linking them with this attack is conclusive."

"In the meantime, Chairwoman bel Rayna visited the disaster site, and addressed the nation."

The scene cut to a medium close-up of the politician, flanked by two RSE generals in somber black uniforms. One of these was a striking blond that the interactive 'cast identified as General Angelique bel Thana, and the other, was her superior, General Susa ben Paula. Together, the group seemed to embody the Goddess in her triple form, and in her sternest and most resolute of moods. Lilith stood stock still, listening intently to Bel Rayna's words.

"Today, a craven act of terror was perpetrated on innocent citizens," she said. "On mothers, and daughters and grandmothers whose only crime was being at the wrong place at the wrong time. We have taken steps to help the survivors of this vicious attack, and our hearts go out to the dead and those they leave behind.'

"I want to assure you that we will find the ones who are responsible for this atrocity. We will find them, and we will bring them to face a swift and terrible justice."

The image changed again, returning to the newscaster. "There was immediate reaction to this event from members of the Supreme Circle, not only expressing outrage, but concern over the causes behind it, and how to prevent future tragedies like this from ever occurring again.'

"One of the most vocal representatives was Senatrix Tanya t'Tallya of the Uni party who immediately raised questions about why more device-sniffing waste receptacles and scanners weren't present at the station.'

"In response to this, a spokeswoman for the Metropolitan Transit Authority stated that while more units had been placed on order, that their Maintenance Department had been forced to deploy 'dumb' receptacles in order to cope with the larger than usual holiday traffic.'

"The Senatrix reacted to this by pledging to launch an investigation into the matter, and mentioned that it would dovetail with a larger probe being launched by Senatrix Layna n'Calysher concerning the scope of Marionite terrorist activities throughout the Sisterhood."

Ingrit took in a deep, ragged breath. "Can't they give it a rest?" she asked wearily. "We need unity now, not infighting. *Fekking* politicians." Lilith nodded absently and sat down in the nearest seat.

Without realizing it, she had ensconced herself in Grammy's favorite rocker and when the old woman entered a minute later, she quickly apologized and surrendered it. Beyond this small interaction, no one spoke another word, or even moved, and when one of the children tried to wander in, Marina quickly shooed her out. This was not the kind of thing that a little girl needed to hear.

The newscaster had more to say. "In a related story, our armed forces and police agencies have placed themselves on a state of high alert. Interstellar travel for civilians has been sharply curtailed, with all flights except those of an emergency nature, cancelled until further notice."

"*Mehn gaate*," Grammy finally said. "Za ice comes." She made a gesture that the other Zommerlaandars in the room copied, and Lilith didn't have to ask them if it was intended to ward away evil or not. At the moment, she also had more on her mind than understanding another facet of Zommerlaandar mysticism.

"I have to call Rixa," she announced. As she rose, Jan bar Daala joined them. The woman was in uniform, and wearing her side-arm. For once, Lilith found the sight of the weapon reassuring.

"Already done, ma'am," Bar Daala stated. "Admiral ebed Cya is in a conference call right now with the Admiral of the Navy, but her adjutant advised me that she will be expecting to hear from you within the hour.'

"We also got a call from the Vaalkenstaad Police. Their Chief would like to speak with you at your earliest convenience, and she's offered the use of the Com in her office for your appointment with the Admiral."

"That was thoughtful," Lilith replied with bitter sarcasm. Although the Chief was well within her rights to ask for the meeting, given the situation, she knew that it would only amount to so much hand-holding. Juta Haarasdaater was a good police officer, and an able administrator, and she had plans in place that she could call on to deal with the emergency. But she was also a small town cop and this event was well beyond her scope. It was obvious that she was hoping for some kind of advice, or at the very least, Lilith's stamp of approval.

Not that Lilith was any more experienced. Her skill-set was limited to starships and naval warfare, not handling terrorists. She was still a Vice-Admiral though, and possessed the mystical aura of 'high officialdom'. She was also a new resident. If nothing else, it was her neighborly duty to help the Chief in her hour of need.

"Let me get changed and we'll go see her," she agreed. "Ingrit can you drive us there in Betsi?"

"Sure thing, Lily."

"No need, ma'am," Bar Daala interjected. "The police are sending a car around for us."

Lilith caught the slight hesitation in her adjutant's voice. There was obviously more to it than that. *"And?"*

"Well--ma'am," Bar Daala said, "They're also sending a detail by—to—um-- watch the farm."

"A *detail*?"

"Yes, ma'am."

"Great goddess in heaven!" Lilith exclaimed. "As if we don't have enough to contend with! Who in all space do they think is going to come out here? We're in the middle of nowhere, surrounded by nothing but *cows*! The last thing that we need right now are some clumsy kaapers blundering around here and tripping over the milking stools!"

Despite the gravity of a police presence at the farm, her imagery evoked a well-needed chuckle from Grammy and the others. It was also an absurd objection, and everyone, including Lilith, knew it. The officers assigned to the detail would undoubtedly be local girls, and know their way around a farm—at least enough to avoid mishaps with any mischievous stools.

"Ma'am, I tried to change the Chief's mind," Bar Daala said, "but she just wouldn't budge. She said that the orders came straight from the Governess's Office itself. They want their Vice-Admiral to stay safe."

Lilith shook her head. "*'Their'* Vice-Admiral—since when am I--? No, never mind. I'll just be quiet now and go get myself changed."

She went upstairs to don her uniform, adding her own energy pistol to her duty belt. In the event of a national emergency like this one, naval regulations required it, regardless of rank, or assignment, and this rule had been in place since the First Widow's War. Like Bar Daala's weapon, the weight of the blaster pistol on her hip brought with it a greater sense of order and control, and she strongly suspected, that aside from the practical aspect of having military personnel arm themselves during a crisis, that this was part of the reason behind the measure. In a small way, it made her feel a little more capable of facing the emergency.

By the time she had finished and come back down into the living area, the police had arrived and were knocking on the front door.

***

Angelique paced her office like a kaatze. If it wouldn't have been unattractive to have done so, she would have been howling in rage at the officers standing before her. She kept her cool though, and carefully composed her features.

"Let me see if I can understand all of this," she said quietly, "We have *one* half-trained agent who manages to survive an air attack by *two* of our armed 'cars. This is thanks to one of our own policewomen and a professional assassin who is a known associate of Colonel n'Jan's.'

"Somehow, they all manage to leave the planet, right under our noses. In addition to this, you're telling me, *what*--exactly---?"

The senior-most officer shifted uncomfortably. "That we also lost the three women we had posted at N'Kaaryn's apartment, ma'am. But it wasn't Skylaar taur Minna. We know that much. Taur Minna was with N'Kaaryn and Signysdaater at the time. Someone else took them out."

Bel Thana raised a single perfect eyebrow. "And you expect me to believe that this mysterious *'someone else'* actually managed this by turning our agent's own weapons against them? Is that correct?"

"Yes, ma'am," the woman answered. "Whoever she was, she was a professional. From the look of it, the agents put up quite a fight, but she finished them all off without getting a scratch herself. We ran an analysis of the scene and all the blood matched our assets. It also confirmed conclusively that their wounds came from the weapons they had been carrying."

There was obvious admiration in the woman's tone, and Angelique glowered at her in disapproval.

"I want them *all* found, "she instructed. "Including this mysterious 'professional'. Use whatever resources you need to, but find them, and terminate them. I also want you to make certain to terminate *anyone* that helps them, no matter how minor their assistance is. We must make an example of *everyone* involved."

"What if we determine that Colonel n'Jan is helping them?"

"Then you are to terminate her as well," Angelique answered leadenly. At that, she turned away and faced the window. Her subordinates quickly departed.

Angelique barely noticed. She was too hurt and too shocked. *Sarah,* she thought with anguish, *how could you do this to me? To us? And for what? A little guttersnipe barely worth the dirt scraped from our boots?'*

When her agents caught up with her, she would see to it that Maya paid dearly for the part she had played in this. Just like Trina had.

No, she thought. *Worse than Trina.*

Gripping the edge of the window sill, she sent a message to the officer who had just conducted the briefing. It was by psiever and encrypted.

I want you to make certain that Maya n'Kaaryn's death is as slow and as painful as you can make it. And I want the same thing for Colonel n'Jan. They must suffer.

Once she received the acknowledgement, she had her AI set her as Away/Unavailable, and then let her tears run their course, unconcerned about what this was doing to her make-up. A careful re-application of cosmetics would erase the damage, and once her agents caught up with Maya and Sarah, revenge would heal the wounds that were in her heart.

Hotel *Bel Lyyra,* Agamede District, Thermadon Val, Thermadon, Myrene System, Thalestris Elant, United Sisterhood of Suns, 1049.01|13|08:21:21

Just as Angelique had warned, the press was waiting for Kaly at the Hotel *Bel Lyyra* like a pack of starved Nyxian Taarq-beasts. Everyone wanted to interview the 'brave heroine of the RSE' who had 'single-handedly rescued her fellow citizens from certain death'. They also wanted her personal opinion on the Marionite issue, the Daughters of Eve, and the role of her agency in stemming the tide of interstellar terrorism.

The problem was, Kaly didn't have a 'position' on any of these issues that she wanted to share publically. She knew exactly what the press was looking for, and she wasn't about to give it to them. They wanted to see her anger, and capture clips of her demanding bloody revenge.

And while she *was* angry, and *did* want payback, she was too tired, and too confused, to crave anything more than a hot shower, and the chance to reconcile her feelings. In private.

Fortunately, the police officers who had escorted her there, and a squad that had been pre-positioned at the hotel, knew their business. They ran interference for her, blocking off the newshounds, and Kaly was able to take a lift up to her room in relative peace.

She still couldn't bring herself to believe that N'Elemay had been involved in the atrocity. As clear as the facts were, they were in direct conflict with the woman that she had fought alongside with.

Her motives were even more incomprehensible. There was no question in Kaly's mind that N'Elemay's people had been wronged. But attacking innocent civilians in a crowded magnorail station went beyond anything that she could reconcile with her memories. It was as if she had never really known the woman at all.

Unable to stand this maelstrom of weariness, hurt and confusion, she took off her uniform tunic and cap, and set them carefully aside. Then she sat down, and tried to gain some comfort from one of the meditation exercises the Marine psychs had shown her.

The images of what she had seen in the train station refused to be banished however. They had been etched into her consciousness like acid on metal. And she was sorely tempted to simply surrender and order herself a bottle of Aqqa. But she managed to dredge up enough inner strength to resist the urge, and opted for a shower and some food instead.

Stripping off the rest of her soiled uniform, she placed her order with room service, and retreated to the bathroom. When she emerged a few minutes later, she felt better, and even managed to smile at the tray containing her meal. Then she realized that there was also something else on the tray. It was a small note and a plasti envelope.

Kaly opened the note first, half-certain that it was some kind of ploy by one of the newsies who couldn't accept 'no' from her guardians. When the first few words fully registered in her mind though, she felt her knees weaken and she sat down on the bed, reading the rest of the message, and then re-reading it.

It was from N'Elemay.

"Kaly—," it said. *"I never wanted you to become involved in any of this. I love you as a sister, and when I saw you in the train station, it was too late to warn you. All I could do was pray that Jesu and Mari would see fit to spare you, and I thank heaven that they did.'*

"I know that you hate me right now, but some crimes can only be answered with the sword of righteousness. I have no choice. The Sisterhood must pay for everything that it has done. I am fighting them in His Name.'

"There is something else I have to tell you. They have lied to you, Kaly, and about a lot more than their so-called Sisterhood. They took someone from you. Her name was Lena, and she was someone that you once loved very deeply.'

"She died at the hands of the ETR, and when you found her body, the shock nearly destroyed you. They convinced me that you had to be made to forget about her.'

"They erased her. They wiped the memory of her from your mind, Kaly, and may Jesu and Mari forgive me, I helped them. I did this because I believed it was the only way to save you. So, I lied to you, too.'

"Kaly, Lena wasn't an angel. She was a real woman.'

"The person lying next to you in the holo, is her. I was supposed to destroy it when I found it, but I kept it because I knew that someday I would summon up enough courage to tell you the truth.'

"I don't know a lot about her, but I do know that she was born on Essylt, and although the Corps has probably erased any record of her by now, if you look hard enough, you'll find something, and you'll find her family. They deserve to know the truth just as much as you do.'

"Please, Kaly, one last thing; stay out of this fight. Leave Thermadon, leave the Agency, and go to Essylt. It's safe there--for now at least. Let God's will be done here.'

"May Jesu and Mari bless and protect you, Ellen."

Hands trembling, Kaly reached for the envelope and opened it. Inside was a holopic and she recognized the scene with a startled gasp.

It was the beach that she had seen in all of her dreams, and the same woman was propped up on the sand next to her. Her smile was something that Kaly would have recognized anywhere in the universe. It was her. Her phantom lover. She was real. She always had been.

"Lena!" she whispered, bringing the name to her lips, and giving it the last touch that it needed to become reality.

"Lena!" she repeated, even louder as she held up the holopic. The image was becoming difficult for her to see. Tears were blurring her vision, and she rubbed them away only to have more replace them in a constant, unending stream.

"*Lena!*" she wailed, suddenly remembering everything; from the very first day that they had ever met, to the last awful moment when she had discovered her ravaged body.

I can't handle this! she thought, terrified at the inexorable rush of memories that were suddenly flooding in. *This is too much! Goddess— please make this stop!*

But it didn't stop. It kept coming at her in an awful, remorseless stream and she was spared none of it.

Overcome by a smothering wave of anguish, she clutched the image to her breast and slid off the bed onto the floor. Unchecked, the memories kept assaulting her, battering at her consciousness and overwhelming her soul until it felt as if she had been crushed down to nothing.

An eternity passed before she was finally able to stand. When she did, it was slowly, and she looked around the room with eyes that only perceived loss.

Then her gaze fell on her uniform tunic and cap, and her grief was replaced with anger. An anger more profound than any she had ever felt towards anything in the universe except the Hriss. Everything inside of her focused down into a single white-hot point of focused rage.

They lied to me! she thought. They had known all along. The Corps had known, the RSE had known, her government, everyone that she had ever trusted. They had *all* known.

She couldn't accept what N'Elemay had done, and never would, but she did understand one thing with a dead certainty; unlike the others, Ellen had told her the truth. *They* hadn't.

They had also done something far, far worse. Something even more irredeemable than any of N'Elemay's crimes. *They* had taken Lena away from her.

Shaking with uncontrollable fury, Kaly went over and grabbed up her uniform tunic. She began to pull at it until the fabric gave way with a loud, satisfying tearing sound. Then she threw the ragged pieces of the garment to the floor and stomped on the fragments with her feet.

The peaked cap joined it next, and Kaly ground it down, heedless of the injuries that its metal decorations were inflicting on her bare soles. All that mattered, all that she wanted just then, was to destroy it and everything that it represented.

Finally, overcome with exhaustion, she crawled back over to the holo and cradling it in her arms, clambered back up into the bed. For a time, she slept, fitfully.

When she awoke again, she found enough presence of mind to bandage her damaged feet with a pair of towels. Once her wounds had been staunched, she called up room service again with her psiever.

A few minutes later, the attendant arrived, bearing a bottle of Aqqa and one glass. If she noticed the blood that had been tracked onto the carpet, or the ruined uniform, she said nothing about it, and Kaly didn't offer her any explanation. She just took the bottle and closed the door in her face.

***

By the time N'Elemay returned from the train station the hour was late. Because of all of the police activity in and around the disaster area, she had been forced to take a very circuitous route back to the safe house, and she didn't expect to find very many of the Faithful there when she arrived. Sister n'Avenal had ordered most of them to leave before the bombing, and N'Elemay had been certain that the Redeemer had been one of the first to be relocated.

She was wrong though; the Redeemer and Sister n'Avenal were still there, and waiting for her, with only a few bodyguards to keep them company.

"My Lord," she stammered in alarm. "Why are you still here? It's not safe!"

"I stayed to speak with you, Sister n'Elemay," he said, looking more beautiful than ever. He beckoned to her, and she came to him right away, dropping down to her knees.

When he placed his hand on her head, she shuddered with ecstasy, and waited to hear what he had to say.

"You have done a great thing for me this day," he told her. "You have dealt a blow that our enemies will never forget. There is more work to be done though, and on a much grander scale."

Her eyes fluttered open. "What work, Lord? Ask me and I will do it."

"Of that I have no doubt. Know that I have had a vision," he replied. "God wants us to pursue our crusade against the unbelievers with an even greater vigor, and he has moved our friends in the ETR to help us. They in turn have been in contact with another party who also understands the holiness of our purpose."

For some time, N'Elemay had been aware of the Church's dealings with the Loyalistas, but she couldn't imagine who else God might have called to come over to their side, and she was deeply puzzled. "Who, Lord?"

"The Hriss," he said. "They too have suffered at the hands of the Sisterhood, and they are willing to give us the tools that we need to smite our common enemy. They ask nothing from us except that we use them wisely. God has indeed worked a miracle here. He has turned demons into angels in order to ensure our victory."

N'Elemay was astonished, and instantly found herself at war with herself. The idea that the Hriss were now to be considered allies of her Church was almost too incredible to believe, or willingly accept.

But miracles were often complex and confusing things, she reminded herself. If God had moved the Hriss to do this, then it was not her place to question his will. She would fight alongside them because her Church had demanded it. "Yes, Lord," she finally said. "I see."

"Go to the ETR for me," he said. "Arm yourself with what the Hriss provide you, and then return here to continue your great work. God will show you every step to take, there and back, and he will surely armor you throughout your journey with his love."

"I will, Lord," she promised. Pausing only to kiss his hand, she rose, and left the room with Sister n'Avenal.

Mikal smiled as they left. The little adventure he had just dispatched N'Elemay on would not only deal damage to the enemies of her silly religion, but it would also convince the Sisterhood that their only intent was to foment domestic terrorism.

Even the Conversâzi would be misdirected, and forced to divert precious resources away from Storm to guard against future attacks. With their attention focused on other fronts, his kind would finally have the opening that they needed to take the Secret for themselves.

***

News about the bombing came to Jon from the lips of an excited Novice. The woman was ecstatic, and breathlessly told him about the 'great blow that Sister n'Elemay had struck against the worshipers of Shaitan'.

Walking into the living area, he encountered a group of Sisters who had gathered around the holo to watch the coverage with undisguised glee. They waved him over, and reluctantly, he joined them. But he was only able to stomach a few minutes of it before he simply had to leave.

It was the footage of Kaly n'Deena that had forced him from the room. She had been accosted by reporters, and had refused to give them an interview. Despite her torn uniform, and the soot on her features, she was still very much as Jon remembered her. Her eyes had changed though. The shadows in them had become deeper, and filled with more anguish.

In their feeding frenzy, the newshounds had shown her no mercy whatsoever. Lacking any input from their victim, they had resorted to offering up her life story to their viewers, building an icon from its foundations. No more than twenty Standard minutes after the event, Kaly n'Deena had become *The Heroine of the Concordance Massacre*. She was presented to the Sisterhood as a simple 'every-girl' from a remote agricolony; having answered her nation's call to arms, only to return from the ETR to rescue the victims of the bombing. She was the perfect stuff of myth, and he felt deeply sorry for her.

He also felt guilty about what had been done to her in the Church's name. It was one thing to attack strangers—faceless, anonymous statistics that could easily be overlooked in favor of a greater cause. It was something else again to see someone that he knew being hurt.

Of all the women on the *Athena*, only Kaly and her lover Lena, had ever shown him any kindness, and he had never forgotten their charity. Now, thanks to his own people, she had suffered, and if the news had its way, she would continue to do so. It only served to underscore the doubts that had been gnawing at his soul over the last few weeks.

There was no question that the Sisterhood itself was utterly wicked, or that it had committed terrible crimes against his Church. He also had no doubt that Sister n'Elemay believed that she was one of God's chosen instruments of vengeance, and at times, he had even envied her for the purity of her faith. It was also equally certain that the Redeemer believed in N'Elemay, and supported her efforts wholeheartedly.

The problem lay with the means that the Church had used to exact its justice. Despite the abuse that he had experienced at the hands of the Sisterhood, nothing had changed the essential fact that he had once been a Marine, or that his mission had been to defend the innocent and uphold the good. Although he was no longer a Marine, his commitment to righteousness remained unaltered. Kaly, and all the others who had been in that magnorail station, hadn't deserved what had happened to them. They had been innocents, despite what the Sisters believed.

The Scriptures didn't offer up any comfort either. *'Thou shalt not do murder'* was as plain as God's light, and it left no room for argument, or negotiation. Yet, they had killed, and if N'Elemay had her way, they would kill again on an even greater scale. When she had told him about it, the Novice had called the bombings 'good', and the Sisters had even offered up prayers of thanks to Jesu and Mari for all the carnage.

But had it really been 'good', he wondered? Was God *truly* pleased? He didn't think so.

It didn't help that he had seen something in Mikal fa' Lynda that had also been troubling him. Ever since becoming his lover, there had been moments—brief and fleeting ones to be sure—when he had detected something unsettling. Something evil that lurked under the surface of the man that the Church considered to be their savior, and God's representative in the flesh.

Jon was too sensitive a psi to ignore it. If his darkest fears were telling him the truth, then they had all been deceived by Shaitan on a scale that was larger than his mind wanted to admit. The very notion of this was just as unsettling as Ellen n'Elemay's bombs, and twice as painful.

Consumed by doubt and anguish, he entered his small room and knelt before the shrine there. "Jesu, Mother Mari," he whispered. "Show me the way. I am beset by uncertainties like a man wandering in a dark and trackless wasteland. Open my eyes so that I might find the path to righteousness and slay the demons of disbelief."

No answers came though, and his thoughts continued to torment him like the reporters that had swarmed all over Kaly. Then at last, he realized what he needed to do.

Rising from the shrine, he left his quarters and asked after Sister n'Avenal. He understood that he was taking a terrible risk, but he needed her wise council, and the chance to confess his crisis of faith. She had always been his confessor, and of all the Sisters that attended the Redeemer, she was the only one that he truly trusted. If Jesu and Mari still cared for him, they would act through N'Avenal, and help him back into their light.

When he found her at last, Sister n'Avenal was more than happy to set aside some time for him. And as always, she listened as he poured out his heart to her, making no comment, or indicating her own feelings. At the end, when he begged her for her blessing, she gave him the same serene smile that he had come to know so well, and placed her hands on his head.

"My son, I know that your doubts are legion," she said. "I bless you now in the name of Jesu and Mari, and I tell you that your heart has already seen the light. As terrible as it is, it is already guiding you on the path that God intends."

Jon was surprised by this and started to look up, but she stayed him, and slid her right hand down to his neck. "I sensed the turmoil growing in you many weeks ago. Now, because I care so deeply for you, I will help you as much as I can. May Jesu and Mari watch over you on the journey that lies ahead."

He felt a small, sharp pain in his neck, and then vertigo overcame him. As she helped him down, he collapsed to the floor.

"W-what h-have you d-done to me?" he stammered. His body felt like it weighed tons, and everything was spinning.

Sister n'Avenal made no reply, and simply shook her head slowly. Just as she had told him, she had seen the signs in him and had half-hoped that his crisis of faith would pass quietly.

It hadn't, and time had run out for him. If Ellen n'Elemay caught even a whiff of his misgivings, she knew that the woman would kill him without any hesitation. So would the Redeemer. Why this hadn't already happened, she couldn't even begin to guess at. The only answer was the divine intercession of Jesu and Mari.

Poor Jon, she thought, reaching down to stroke his head tenderly. *You really have no idea, do you?*

The neoman knew far more than he realized. He could provide valuable insights to the RSE into the Redeemer's thoughts, and lend an intimate glimpse into N'Elemay's mindset.

He could also supply details about the safe houses that they used, and the procedures that they employed to move undetected from one location to the next. And he had heard enough, mentioned in passing, for a seasoned interviewer to piece together important clues about N'Elemay's next move against the Sisterhood. Without realizing it, Jon fa'Teela had become a very dangerous man, now doubly so because of his doubts.

His only chance for survival was to be taken away to somewhere safe. He had to be relocated to a place where the Faithful would not be able to find him, and placed in the care of people who would value him for the knowledge that he carried, and use it, and him, wisely. People that she could trust.

She had seen the same things that he had, and undergone her own crisis of faith. She no longer believed in the path of violence that they were following, and she understood what its outcome would be. N'Elemay and Mikal fa'Lynda were leading them all to their doom.

Her decision to help the neoman arose from far more than just her loyalty to her Church though. It also had its roots in her personal feelings for him. Although her vows as a Sister, and his own sexual orientation prevented any possibility of consummation, she had always secretly been in love with him. Now, she would have her chance to show him that love, and in the process, save the Church.

Unlike Jon however, she had resources to call upon, and a history that no one knew anything about. Years before the present crisis, she had provided the OAE's Special Negotiation Unit 9 with information.

This had not been a betrayal. Rather, it was the nature of high-level espionage; when their objectives agreed, opposing sides could sometimes declare a truce, and forge temporary alliances. At the time, right-wing extremism within the Church had been on the rise, and this had clashed with the hope for reconciliation with the Sisterhood.

Careful not to expose her Church to danger, she had reached out to the Unit and identified the troublemakers. In the process, she had also established a tenuous relationship with her enemies, and they, with her. Now, she intended to invoke this old bond.

It had been a long time since she had communicated with them, and with the advent of the RSE, she wasn't even certain that Unit 9 still even existed, or that they would want to help her. But she had no alternatives.

Leaving Jon lying where he was, she accessed the omniplex with her psiever, and placed a call. To her immense relief, it was answered. After identifying herself, she explained the situation, and in return, received the promise that she had been praying for so desperately.

The Unit would assist her. Jon would be kept safe, and she would have the chance to turn things around and hopefully, make them right again.

Ending the call, she summoned her assistant to her quarters. Sister bel Gwena had worked for her for years, and N'Avenal trusted her implicitly. As her confessor, Bel Gwena knew all about her feeling for Jon, and had come to share in her misgivings about the direction the Church was headed.

When Bel Gwena saw his prostrate form, she didn't question N'Avenal, or run to tell the others. Instead, she quietly helped her to get the neoman to his feet.

Even with the two of them working together, getting him clear of the safe house wasn't easy, but luck and circumstance played as much a part in this as strength did. Everyone was too busy making preparations to leave and the confusion worked in their favor. That, and the fact that N'Avenal had chosen a room close to a rear exit in anticipation of this very event. No one saw them half-walking, half-dragging him out.

Later, when they rejoined their companions at their new hiding place, no one remarked about their absence, or connected it with Jon's disappearance. She also made certain to paint him with as dark a brush as she could. Thanks to her, he quickly became one of the weak ones, a member of the Faithful who had lapsed in his belief and abandoned the True Religion.

He became a traitor. It was the very least that she could do for her Church, or for him.

4800 Block of Rabiya Street, Kyme District, Thermadon Val, Thermadon, Myrene System, Thalestris Elant, United Sisterhood of Suns
1049.01|14|00:21:47

The scene that met Jon's eyes made no sense. He vaguely recalled collapsing, and then being taken from the safe house. He could also remember fragments of his journey to this place, but nothing coherent.

As the fog in his mind slowly began to clear, he realized that he was lying on his side, and that his chin was resting on a stretch of pavement that was wet, and stank of something old and foul. There was a wall across from him, made of stained plasticrete bricks, and somewhere nearby, a small creature used its claws to rummage through a pile of unattended trash.

When his ears finally registered the sound of the traffic flying overhead, he realized where he was. He was in an alley, in downtown Thermadon. Alone.

For some reason, Sister n'Avenal had abandoned him here. *Why did she do this?* he wondered. He recalled her expressing her own doubts about the Redeemer, and then saying something about helping him on a journey. But a journey to where? And how? And why this way?

Then a darker train of thought surfaced. *What if she betrayed me to the RSE?* The very notion that a woman he had trusted his entire life could have done such a thing, absolutely horrified him, and he refused to accept it. N'Avenal would never willingly consign him to their enemies, he decided. The truth had to lie elsewhere, but it evaded him.

One thing was absolutely certain though. Whatever her motives had been, he was in danger where he was. If he remained, he would be captured. And he knew what would happen to him if that occurred. He would be detained, and questioned, vigorously. What would come after that, didn't bear thinking about. As a neoman, his civil rights were marginal, and no one would miss him overmuch. Or ask any detailed questions.

He had to get moving. Willing himself to rise, Jon half-stumbled, and half-walked to the mouth of the alley. The brilliant lights of the buildings and the storefronts forced him to shield his eyes, but he was still able to perceive someone walking down the sidewalk.

It was a woman, and when she caught sight of him, she gasped, and ran away.

Cursing his own stupidity, he searched for somewhere else to run to and spotted another alley. It was across the street, but it was darker and deeper than where he was.

He lurched out into the open, moving faster and more surely with every step. Panic and adrenaline were overriding the drug in his bloodstream, and by the time he reached his new refuge, he was running normally. As soon as he was in the shadows again, he paused, trying to remember everything that the Marines had taught him about escape and evasion.

He would need to move at night, he told himself. That was the safest way to go. He also needed a plan. Trying to go it alone in Thermadon was out of the question. Given the present mood of the Sisterhood, the capitol wasn't a safe place for his kind. The A-16's, and the Redeemer, could pass for women if they wished, but his generation didn't enjoy the same advantage.

The spaceport was the only answer. Somehow, he had to find his way there, and locate members of the Faithful. They would be able to hide him, and even arrange to get him off planet to one of the Marionite worlds where he could lose himself among all the other neomen. He knew that it wasn't much of a plan, and a lot of it depended on luck and the blessings of Jesu and Mari, but it was far better than running from one hiding place to the next until the RSE caught up with him.

A moment later, the sound of a police siren sent a thrill of fear up his spine. He had waited too long, and his time had run out. Backing further into the darkness, Jon prayed to God for a miracle. At this point, holy intercession was all he really had left to draw upon.

As if his deity had heard his plea and answered him, the hovercar flew by, and disappeared. Jon breathed in a sigh of relief.

Then he felt the barrel of a needlegun press against the back of his neck. A woman's voice spoke to him in a quiet, no-nonsense tone.

"Please don't' move," she said. "I don't want to harm you, but I will if you make me. By the way, Jon, you're under arrest."

It took him a moment to process the fact that whoever this was, she knew his first name. N'Avenal hadn't just abandoned him. Instead, his worst fears had come true. She had betrayed him to the Sisterhood.

Bel Sharra Memorial Spaceport, Cyrene District, Thermadon Val, Thermadon, Myrene System, Thalestris Elant, United Sisterhood of Suns, 1049.01|15|09:16:67

Even with the body-concealing *Qada* that she wore to shield her skin from the light, Signysdaater recognized the figure in the passenger loading zone immediately. She guided her plain *Kapria V0-20X* to the curb, and as she sent a psiever signal for the doors to open, her passenger got in.

The woman carried no baggage; she had come to Bel Sharra with nothing more than a carry-on bag and as soon as this was stowed in the back seat, they were off. Back behind them, the Port's computers were already rewriting the surveillance cam footage and deleting any record of her arrival. If someone looked, Signysdaater's companion had never been there, and she had never come to meet her.

"How vaz your flight, *Elleshaari*?" she asked.

"To long, and too far away from Nyx for my liking, *Sharrisaal*", her passenger replied. "Even so, it is still good to see you again. You have been away from the Nightlands for far too long."

"Yah," Signysdaater agreed with a trace of sheepishness. "Zis city, it eats a vomin's life up n'bevore zhe knowz it, za time iz gone. Ven zis is over, I zink a vacation maybe? I'd like zat."

She changed the setting on the hovercar's windows, darkening them so that the woman could remove her travelling mask and goggles.

Lady Ananzi stripped off the protective garments with a relieved sigh, and shook out her silver-white hair. "Thank you, Clara," she said. "I'm afraid I just don't travel enough to get used to the Qada." Then, "So, how is Sarah?"

Signysdaater grinned. "Confuzed az you might exzpect, but zhe is doing vhat ve vant."

Ananzi nodded. "And Maya?"

Signysdaater rolled her eyes. "Za zame pain in za ass," she said pejoratively. "But on her vay, miztrezz. Zere vaz a little bit of trouble getting her oot, but Skylaar and I got zat zorted out."

Ananzi didn't press her for the details. She had already gotten a full report from a mole in the RSE. "What about *him*?"

"Vell Lady, ve have him in a zafe plaze. Vould you like to go zere right now, or ztop zomevere to freshen oop?

Ananzi smiled, pleased by her student's concern for her comfort, but shook her head. "Now, please. I can see to my needs later."

"Ganz gaff, miztrezz. On za vay."

The kaaper took the car up, and entered the police flightlanes. Signysdaater wasn't concerned about a record being made of this. The same good women that had seen to the footage at the spaceport, were covering their tracks here as well. To the Metro Police AI, they were just another Department vehicle on an undercover assignment, details classified.

Ten standard minutes later, they arrived in the Marpesia District and landed on the receiving dock of a mid-sized warehouse. It was owned by a woman that owed the Metro's a few favors. One of these was her silence, and the other was the exclusive use of the facility for a few days. Not even security or maintenance people were present.

Signysdaater led her old teacher down to one of the main inventory areas. It had been cleared of everything, and the only objects that occupied the space now were two chairs. One of them was empty, and Jon fa'Teela sat in the other. He was wearing a bag over his head, and as they walked up to him, the woman who was standing watch smiled at their approach, and removed it.

"Thank you, Detective," Ananzi said.

"My pleasure, ma'am," she returned. "Do you need me to leave?"

"No," the Nyxian told her. "You and Clara can stay."

She took her seat opposite the neoman and regarded him for a time. At last, she spoke.

"Jon," she began, "do you know who we are? Why you are here?"

Jon shook his head. His expression was stubborn, but Ananzi could tell that deep down, he was scared out of his wits.

"I won't try to lie to you, Jon. I know that you are a psi and that you can sense the truth. I'll also tell you that I am a psi as well. So let's be frank with one another.'

"Sister n'Avenal did not betray you. She saved your life. If you had remained with the Redeemer's group any longer, you would have been killed.'

"With that said, let me introduce myself. I represent a small group that is tasked with controlling and combatting extremist elements within our government. I won't hide the fact that we have also kept an eye on your Church over the years, but our goal was only to make certain that the kind of things that it's doing now, didn't get too far out of hand. I think you know what I'm talking about."

Jon did, but he didn't answer. He also knew that she was telling him the truth.

"Jon," she went on, "the simple fact is, you need our help. And your Church needs our help. There have been some terrible misunderstandings, and I freely admit that the Sisterhood has done some awful things. For what it's worth, I want to apologize to you personally. We were wrong.'

"What you also need to realize though, is that the Sisterhood isn't one single, unified political entity. There are moderates within it who didn't condone the occupation, or your Pope's death. Moderates who want to see a reconciliation occur.'

"But there are also other forces, whose goals go far beyond anything even the most radical Motherthought adherent might suggest. One of their aims is not only the total destruction of your Church, but the eradication of all neomen. Extermination, Jon. They call themselves the Conversâzi. My job, our job, is to fight them."

She let him consider this, then continued. "And the Conversâzi wants even more than this. They want to overthrow our government and upset the fragile peace that we have managed to enjoy with our neighbors. They want interstellar war. That can't be allowed to happen.'

To her gratification, Jon's complexion had gone pale. He was the very man that N'Avenal had suggested he was; a Sisterhood Marine through and through, and she was glad for her decision to deal openly with him. Any dissembling would have closed him down in a nanosecond.

Which was something that she didn't want. Jon fa'Teela was valuable, and for much more than what he knew about the Daughters of Eve. He was the key to the future.

"I know that your Church is like the Sisterhood in a way," she said. "There are good people in it, honest, decent people who sincerely believe in the Word of God. But there are also those that want to use the Church for their own ends to kill and destroy. Am I correct?"

Jon didn't answer, but she could tell that he agreed. She also knew that he was thinking about the Redeemer, and Ellen n'Elemay.

"Jon, I'm going to give you a choice," she said. "I am going to have these police officers take off your handcuffs, and step away. If you want, you can leave. You might even manage to get a few blocks before the Conversâzi finds you.'

"When they do, and believe me they will, being cuffed to another chair will be the least of your worries. They'll torture you, they'll get what they want, and then they will dispose of you.'

"Your alternative is to stay here, and help me find a way to save things. I'm certain that as a soldier, you can understand the odds." When he acknowledged this, she gestured to Signysdaater, who came up and removed the restraints.

Jon rubbed at his wrists, and looked at her. His eyes were dark, and troubled.

Lady Ananzi waited, listening to his thoughts as they churned in his mind. He was caught between his love for his Church, the horror he felt at the dark direction that it had taken, and his loyalty to the Sisterhood as a former Marine. That, and a deep, festering sense of guilt about the Concordance bombing. She didn't envy the state of his soul.

When he reached his decision at last, she knew what it was and she was careful not to gloat.

"Would you like something?" she asked instead. "Some kaafra perhaps? Some food? There's a lot more that I need to tell you about, and it concerns something called the Secret and a thing we refer to as the Tree."

Jon's eyes lit up in alarm and concern. He had heard these terms before, and instantly Ananzi knew where. The image stood out sharply in his mind. The Redeemer had refered to them when they had been together, after making love. He also understood that the Secret was a weapon of some kind.

"Yes," he said. "I'd like some kaafra, ma'am."

"Call me Maara," she said, enjoying his surprise at this. Her name was a variant of 'Mari'. Without any notion of what the future would eventually bring to their daughter, her mothers had named her wisely. "Maara elle Ananzi."

Now, she wondered, carefully masking her thoughts from him, *what shall I do with you?*

***

387

The holochannels were still oversaturated with stories about the Concordance bombing. The majority of the coverage was either a rehashing of the tragedy, the opinions of media pundits, or just pure nonsense. But it still managed to rub Jon's nerves raw like sand in an open wound. Thankfully however, Kaly had disappeared from the media's eye, and he was left completely alone with his guilt, and his regret. After enduring only a few minutes of the feeding frenzy, he changed shows and found himself watching an ongoing soap opera based on the lives of several rich Thermadonian women.

Not only were they completely unappealing to him as characters, but to his unhappy surprise, the show's writers had managed to create a segment that featured several of the main players being affected by the Concordance Station attack. There was even one cast member who wound up being trapped under the rubble of a building that had never actually collapsed.

Instead of keeping him on the edge of his seat to learn what would happen to them the following week—he was disgusted and the turned the 'jector off.

Normally he would have sought refuge through prayer and meditation at a time like this, or by reading a passage from the *Revelations*, but since reluctantly agreeing to accept Lady Ananzi's offer of sanctuary, he hadn't felt entitled to do so. He had turned his back on the Church, and he no longer believed that he had the right to go to Jesu and Mari for comfort. Or that that they would still recognize him as one of their flock.

Even worse than this, a smaller part of him that was tucked away in the darkest part of his soul was even beginning to wonder if they—or if any of it for that matter, even existed. If the Redeemer was false, it whispered, then what about all the rest? What if his entire belief system was nothing but self-deception? What if life was really nothing more than a series of events with no guiding force except the laws of probability? What if there was in fact, no God?

The answer to that question was something that Jon could barely allow himself to address; if true, then all he had before him was a lifeless, soulless landscape, devoid of any meaning, purpose or direction. An existence that was just as vapid as the soap opera he had watched, and equally as pointless.

Even Hell had Shaitan to direct the tortures of its prisoners. The world his doubts were suggesting lacked even the Evil One. Instead, the inmates ran the prison and there was no hope of freedom for anyone. Least of all, for a neoman.

The soft laughter of his 'host' interrupted his dark ruminations, and he glanced over his shoulder at her, partly in annoyance, and partly with relief. The detective who had captured him had remained with him after his interview with Ananzi. Now, she was playing the part of a caretaker, and keeping him company while he awaited his fate in the safe house that the spymistress had arranged for him.

Like all of the other women that he had encountered since his meeting with the Nyxian, the police woman had ties to her that went well beyond a simple business relationship, or any OAE affiliation. In her case, the detective was an on-again, off-again student of the mysterious woman, and when she wasn't busy guarding him, she practiced something that she called *'Marasetza'*.

This was a meditative technique that Ananzi had shown her, and when he had asked about it, she had claimed that it involved reliving portions of her life and allegedly 'gathering back her power' from them. Whether this pagan practice was actually effective or not, Jon couldn't say, but it did seem to provide her with some measure of entertainment. At that precise instant, she was re-experiencing an event that clearly amused her, and as she sat there with her eyes closed, she was chortling with mirth. She also seemed to be completely oblivious to his presence, or anything else.

Jon knew better though. Even in that state, she was still acutely aware of everything that he did, and all that was happening around them. One reason was that her psiever was tied in with a network of spycams and sensors that watched over the apartment. But another component of her heightened awareness seemed to be entirely paranormal in origin. She had the uncanny knack of knowing exactly what direction his thoughts were taking even when he was sure that he had shielded himself. Obviously, she was also some kind of psi.

"You really should pray," she suggested, demonstrating this very ability. "Those little whispers don't know what they're talking about."

He didn't give her the satisfaction of a reply, or an argument. Instead, he directed his gaze out of the one-way window to the distant traffic flying by and returned to his thoughts.

Is this how life is for the Unbeliever's? he wondered, knowing that she would hear him and not caring. *Nothing but doubt and uncertainty?*

If so, then he pitied the faithless, even as he suspected that he had unwittingly joined their ranks.

The detective interrupted him again. "You have some visitors," she announced "Lady Ananzi sent them. Try to be nice, Jon." She didn't even open her eyes.

Jon turned to the door with a sour expression. When it slid open, his first thought was that his uninvited guests were from some branch of the military. Both were Thermadonian Caucasians with short-cropped hair, and although they were dressed in street clothes, there was something about their bearing that set them apart from the average citizen.

The older of the two seemed to be anywhere from 40 to 50 Standard, which given the advanced nature of the Sisterhood's medical sciences, meant that she was probably twice that. Her sandy brown hair framed eyes that were a bright blue, and they possessed an intelligent, world-wise look.

He had seen eyes like this before he realized—in some of the Sisters he had grown up with, including Sister n'Avenal. If he hadn't known better, he would have pegged her as a seasoned priestess of the Faith.

This of course, was impossible. The Church and all of its servants were done with him and seeking his blood. She had to be nothing more than an ordinary spy, he concluded. Which made perfect sense. Lady Ananzi had probably made him available to any number of intelligence agencies.

Her partner however, made him begin to wonder if his impressions were correct. She didn't possess the same level of sagacity, and she wasn't as old, but he still detected a certain glow about her. It was something that he had only encountered in Novices; the first blush that came with an early and transient encounter with the grace of God.

There was also something else that argued against her being a spy. Something familiar. It was as if they had met before, but he was hard pressed to recall the place, or the occasion.

After spending a moment of fruitless effort trying to recover the memory, he gave up and steeled himself for the interview. He didn't bother to smile at them.

Neither of them seemed offended however, and they took their seats on the couch abutting his own. Then to his total surprise, they both produced small books, and the older woman opened hers and addressed her partner as if Jon wasn't even in the room.

"When I was told that we were coming here today," she said, "I was reminded about a passage from Genesis. It was chapter fifteen, verse eighteen. Do you know it, Sister?"

"I do," her partner said, and she began to read aloud from her own volume.

Jon saw the title on the cover. It was the *"Revelation of Mari"*.

"Now Sarai," she intoned, *"Abram's wife, had borne him no children. She had a female Egyptian servant whose name was Hagar.'*

"And Sarai said to Abram, 'Behold now, the Lord has prevented me from bearing children. Go in to my servant; it may be that I shall obtain children by her.' And Abram listened to the voice of Sarai."

"Indeed," the other answered. "They couldn't wait for God to work his Will, could they? So they took matters into their own hands instead."

She turned and finally looked at Jon with her startlingly clear eyes. "In much the same way that the Church altered nature to create the Redeemer. They weren't content to just abide by God's plan. They were proud, and they had to 'speed things up'. Now look what they have! The Anti-Christ himself. That's the punishment that God metes out for such arrogance."

"If anyone says to you, "the younger one quoted, *"'Look, here is the Christ!' or 'There he is!' do not believe it. For false christs and false prophets will arise and perform great signs and wonders, so as to lead astray, if possible, even the elect."*

Jon was flabbergasted. Then he caught sight of the necklace that she was wearing. It was a small thing, made of gold, and just visible in the shadows of her blouse. It was the four-pointed Star of Mari. Her companion was also wearing one. These were Marionite Sisters.

Certain that he had been betrayed, Jon mouthed an oath, and started to rise, but the detective intervened. Her eyes were open and she was standing now.

"Yes, Jon," she said. "They're Believers. Just like you, but they're not with the Church. Not the one you were with at least. Stay in your seat, calm down, and talk with them. They're not here to hurt you. You're completely safe. They're friends."

The senior Sister smiled at him again. "My name is Sister Tereysa," she said. "This is Sister Beatriss. We are both servants of the Reformed Church of the Way, and brides of Jesu."

Why had these Sisters joined forces with Lady Ananzi, he wondered. With the Sisterhood? Was this some kind of sinister trick? Was this Church of theirs some false path that Shaitan had designed to lure him? It had already happened once. Why not again?

Sister Tereysa read the conflict raging inside of him as plainly as if it were a verse from the *Revelations*. "We are exactly what we seem, Jon. Not everyone that believes in God believes in the lies that Shaitan tells the leadership of the Marionite Church, or follows his accursed servant.'

"And we are not working 'for' Lady Ananzi. We are working 'with' her, and only because we believe as she does; that the day will come when the Faithful and the Sisterhood will find a common ground and finally learn to live together in peace."

Jon didn't know how to react. All of his senses, and his talents, were telling him that she was speaking the absolute truth. But what was the Reformed Church of the Way? If it wasn't a Sisterhood trick, or a corruption of the True Faith, then what did it represent? He had never heard of any splinter groups before. The Marionite Church had always been one, united entity.

Again, she anticipated him. "The Reformed Church of the Way is made up of Sisters and lay members who saw the direction that your Church was taking and decided to reject its policies. We still follow the Word of God and we look to Jesu and Mari, but we do not believe in the creature that the Church calls the Redeemer, and we have turned our backs on the path of violence and hate that he would lead us down. You know what I am talking about, Jon. You've seen it firsthand."

Jon certainly had.

"Lady Ananzi was worried about you. She respects your faith and she didn't want you to lose it. So she asked us to come here today and offer what comfort we could. I hope that you'll accept our gift. So does Sister Beatriss. She has been looking forwards to this visit for a very, very long time."

Beatriss nodded in agreement, and he finally realized who she was. She was a little older than he recalled, and without her uniform, she seemed like another person altogether.

But he knew her. She was one of the first women who had joined him when he had summoned the Faithful to prayer aboard the *Athena*. At the time, she had been so frightened that she had barely been able to stop trembling. Jon had lent her his strength, and together, they had persevered. Right up to the point when they had all been arrested, and drummed out of the service.

"I wanted to return the favor," she explained. "For what you did for me back on the ship." With those few words, any reticence that he still harbored about trusting either of them fled into the shadows with his doubt. He really was with friends. As incredible as it seemed, Jesu and Mari had smiled on him and moved Lady Ananzi to send these women to him.

Praise God, Jesu and Mari, he thought. This time, he didn't doubt his worthiness. He knew that they had heard him. They had never really stopped hearing him. Or caring.

"Would you like to pray with us Jon?" Sister Tereysa asked. "Or read? I brought another copy of the *Revelations* with me. I heard that you didn't have yours." She held out a third book, and with tears of gratitude forming in his eyes, Jon took it from her.

"Thank you," he said. He meant it. Not just for her kindness, but for the greater benevolence that had inspired her to give him this gift. For *Their* compassion.

Undisclosed Location, Cyrene District, Thermadon Val, Thermadon, Myrene System, Thalestris Elant, United Sisterhood of Suns, 1049.01|16|06:25:99

After all the ravages that had been perpetrated on their motherworlds by the Sisterhood, it had not been hard to find volunteers. There were plenty of the Faithful who were willing to sacrifice themselves for the cause, although the ones N'Avenal finally presented to her had come from a surprising source. When she saw them, N'Elemay had grave doubts about their fitness.

There were four of them, and to prepare them for the interview, N'Avenal and her acolytes had made certain to dress them carefully. To any outsider, they seemed to be nothing more than a group of women from the Thermadonian genotype. They were all delicate in stature, fair haired and light eyed, and to N'Elemay's eyes at least, quite attractive.

They weren't women however, despite their attire, or the make-up the Sisters had carefully applied. All of them were actually males, from the development group that had preceded the Redeemer Himself, the Adam-16 generation.

Their true gender was concealed by special micro transmitters. These had been designed by Marionite technicians generations before the current crisis, and in anticipation of just such a need. Once activated, the devices sent false data to any med-scanner, fooling it into believing the lie. It was hardly the perfect disguise, and could be easily defeated by a simple visual examination, but it was adequate enough for N'Elemay's requirements.

The only thing that remained to be determined was the true mettle of these would-be martyrs. That would be the deciding factor.

N'Elemay walked up to the nearest of the neomen and looked him squarely in the eye. "Tell me, brother, why are you willing to do this?"

To his credit, the neoman met her gaze unflinchingly. "Because my purpose, and the purpose of my brothers here, has always been to serve the Church. Now that the Redeemer has come among us, we have no other calling."

His voice, she noted, sounded completely female. And his *Prominentia laryngea*, his 'Adam's Apple', was also barely noticeable, but this came as no surprise. With the A-16's, its size had been reduced to mimic the configuration of a woman's throat. It was all part of the Church's efforts to make them, and the Redeemer himself, more appealing to Womankind.

And N'Elemay couldn't argue with the neoman's statement. While what he had just said was harsh, it was also true. With the birth and growth of the One, the generation that he had been developed from was essentially superfluous. Their mission had been accomplished. They had provided the Church's genetic engineers with the data they had needed to perfect the one and only member of the Adam-17 generation, and with that, no longer had any special value of their own.

"What if I say that you are wrong?" she challenged. "That this is just the sin of pride speaking? What *then*, brother?"

"Then we will find another way to give our lives for the Church," he answered resolutely. "She is our mother. This is the only way for us to repay her."

"Please, Sister!" the man's companion interjected. "Accept our lives! Let us give them up for the True Faith!"

"Why should I?" She tinged her voice with all the reservation that she could muster.

"Because they were forfeit the day the Redeemer blessed us with His birth," the first one answered. "God has called us. He wants us to do this for him."

Although he had said this calmly enough, the fire in his eyes was unmistakable. It was the same one that burned in her own heart. He had been called, she saw, just as she had.

She gently placed her hand on the neoman's shoulder, "Please, forgive me. I should never have doubted your faith. What is your name, brother?"

"I am called Jaymz, Sister. My brothers here are called Sammel, Haraald, and Tomas."

N'Elemay smiled at them. Then she turned to Sister n'Avenal, who had been standing off to the side, listening closely to the exchange. "They will do--quite well," N'Elemay told her.

"Then we will begin with the arrangements," N'Avenal replied. "Of course, they'll need the proper equipment and some training before they'll be ready."

The ex-Marauder had expected as much, and indicated her assent.

N'Avenal addressed the neoman directly, "The Church thanks each of you for your willing sacrifice. You will stand among the blessed, at Jesu's right hand and be remembered among us as holy martyrs for the True Faith. Now, let us pray together."

Everyone in the room knelt, and the Sister made the Sign of Blessing over them. Only one person felt any regret or any jealousy at that moment. It was Ellen n'Elemay.

God had called her just as surely as He had these brave neomen, but unlike them, she would have to wait for her ultimate reward. She envied them, and she prayed to Jesu and Mari to forgive her for such an unworthy emotion.

1047th IBC Interworld Bat-Bat Championship, Zaharias National Stadium, Agamede District, Thermadon Val, Thermadon, Myrene System, Thalestris Elant, United Sisterhood of Suns, 1049.01|18|06:66:77

Games, especially any form of ball games, have always been a part of the human experience. Throughout history, every civilization has developed its own special type of ball game.

For the ancient Maya, it was *Pok-a-tok*. For the Americans it was Football, for the Chinese *Cuju*, and for many other nations, Soccer. And when humans finally migrated into space it became *GravBall*.

The Sisterhood's ball game was Bat-Bat; a combination of soccer, cricket and an all-out medieval-style melee. Like their predecessors, Bat-Bat teams competed with one another to determine who the greatest players were, with the top teams facing off against one another in the ultimate arena. In the Sisterhood, this was the *Intermondal Bat-Bat Campion*, the IBC Interworld Bat-Bat Championships.

In the same vein, the planets that the top Bat-Bat teams hailed from also vied for the prestige of being considered the home of the greatest players, and mercantile interests competed fiercely with one another during the elaborate half-time extravaganzas. Billions of credits were expended to devise clever advertisements, and even more was spent for the privilege of presenting them during the game. Sports betting, legal and otherwise, also peaked at these times, with almost as many credits trading hands among bookmakers and the betters as it did among the legitimate businesses.

And *everyone* watched, as much for the game itself, as for the half-time entertainment. When the IBC Championships were held, it captured the attention of virtually every woman in the Sisterhood, no matter their age, occupation, or how remote their world was.

The 1047th games were no exception. On this occasion, the Thermadonian *Tigarri*, who had a history of winning the Interworld three years in a row, were facing off against relative newcomers, the Delganian Destroyers and an estimated audience of 66,000,000,000 were watching the struggle via the omniplex, with 175,000 of them filling the stadium itself.

The game had been a brutal one, holding with a score of 13 to 12, and sports history seemed to be in the making. By the time half-time was announced, and the first advertisements began to play from the fields gigantic holojectors, no one knew if the *Tigarri* would be able to maintain their supremacy against the Delganian upstarts or not.

But the real surprise came from the holojectors themselves. Right in the middle of a particularly clever advertisement for Nutro's new line of drinks, with no less than Laara Lampa acting as the spokeswoman, the scene abruptly changed.

Even though everyone knew that Anne Marie Rensolear had been dead for over a millennia, the image of the great founder of the Sisterhood still elicited a visceral, unconscious response. When Rensolear spoke, it was

395

with an authority that an anonymous woman would never have commanded. Which was exactly why Dana bel Hanna had chosen her avatar when she had hacked ReVision's computers and created her message.

"The Sisterhood is not what it once was," Rensolear's *doppelgänger* began. "What was founded on the principles of freedom and equality has become a dictatorship; a vile police state that pretends to embrace these ideas but secretly holds them, and you, in complete contempt. Every day, more and more of our liberties are being taken away from us in the name of fighting terrorism.'

"But where did these terrorists come from? Did they sneak into our lives from somewhere outside our star nation? Or did they spring up from among us? You know the answer to that."

"You also deserve to know why they are fighting us. It is all because of a lie. The Marionites were never involved with the ETR before our war with the Republic, and they never betrayed us. The government just wants you to believe that they did.'

"Why? So that they could take action against a belief that they don't agree with. That, and the opportunity that it gives them to seize more power for themselves—and all with your blessings."

"Women of the Sisterhood, you have been robbed, and you have been lied to at every level. Even your history has been altered to suit the designs of an avaricious minority.'

"Now the time has come to open your eyes. To demand accountability, *and* the return of your freedoms. Think for yourselves and take back your birthright! If you do not, then the words of the Concordance are meaningless, and all of the sacrifices that the Founding Mothers made for you, utterly useless."

The scene faded to black, leaving the audience in astonished silence.

Angelique bel Thana, who had been watching the game with Felecia curled up next to her, gripped her wine glass so hard that it shattered in her hand.

"Deas dam va!" she hissed, ignoring the blood and her lover's attempts to treat it with a makeshift bandage. Security for the game had been tighter than any previous sporting event, and she had been certain that it would be safe from attack. She had even personally assured Director ben Paula of this.

Waving Felecia off, she placed a call through her holojector to the Director herself. It was better to be the first to take action in a crisis. Especially one as bad as this one. Anything else showed weakness and indecisiveness.

"Madame Director," she began. "I am sure that you know about our problem."

"I do at that," Ben Paula growled. "I just saw the most popular broadcast in the nation being hijacked by terrorists. What are you doing about this, Angelique?"

"I have sent orders for the entire production crew to be arrested and questioned," she told her. As she said this, she was issuing those very orders to her subordinates by psiever, and demanding that her sister, Josette, contact her immediately.

"I am also going to make certain that we discover exactly how this was done, and track down whoever the conspirators are."

"I should fekking hope so, General," Ben Paula barked. "66 billion women just had their game completely ruined, including the Chairwoman herself. She will want answers *and* results."

"I will provide both," Angelique assured her.

Another message came in as she ended the call, and she opened it immediately. It was more bad news. Somehow, someone had edited many of the entries in the *Encyclopedia Sororitas* to reflect a decidedly anti-Motherthought point of view. They had also distributed these new, revisionist materials to hundreds of thousands of random addresses. This had occurred at the exact same time as the Rensolear broadcast and was obviously related.

Clearly, the Sisterhood was under a determined cyber-attack and more was certain to come, Angelique thought. Only the RSE stood in the way of total anarchy.

Cespedaa, Araña System, Nuvo Colombyen Provensa, Esteral Terrana
Rapabla, 1049.01|25|05:00:12

The grass reacted the instant that the ship set down on it. Growing over nine meters high in many places, and covering most of the planet, it wasn't really grass in the Old Gaian sense, but a strange class all its own, both an animal and a vegetable. It immediately wrapped tendrils of itself around the merchanter and then tried to digest it with internal enzymes that rivaled the strongest hydrochloric acid.

This had little effect on the metal hull however, and only served to annoy the captain. She had been to Grass before, and replied to this attack by routing extra power to the ship's skin, frying the tendrils to ashes.

More of the grass gathered itself up and renewed the assault, and it was joined by the spider-like insectoids that protected it. These creatures added sprays of toxic venom to what the grass was putting out, but in the end, this

397

did little to win the day. The merchanter sent another charged blast, and what this didn't discourage, was chased off by the personal flamers and firebombs that the passengers had brought with them when they disembarked.

Not that they would have been harmed, as much as delayed and inconvenienced. All of them, including Ellen n'Elemay were wearing armored spacesuits, which were resistant to the enzymatic mix, and completely impervious to the venom.

Their destination wasn't far. It lay less than a kilometer from their landing site, and thanks to the Sisterhood, it was completely clear of the grass. That hadn't been the intention of the women who were responsible though. Their goal had been the destruction of a weapons depot that had served the ETR fleet during their brief war. They had used a nuke, fired from space, to accomplish their purposes, transforming the installation, and everyone in it, into a large puddle of molten glass.

Even without the readout on her HUD to consult, N'Elemay knew when they were getting close. The pernicious grass gave way abruptly, growing shorter with every meter, and then thinning away into nothing at the border.

Beyond this was an area of bare earth that was coated with a layer of green-white glass. At the center of this roughly circular area, and where it was at its densest, was what remained of the depot, now nothing more than the melted stumps of the hardiest building components.

How many good men and women died here? N'Elemay wondered. There was no way to know, but she couldn't help but cringe a little as the glass cracked and broke under her boots. Some of what had made it, and even lent it its dark swirls, was ash from the nuclear fires. Ash that had come not only from burnt plastic and metal, but from all the incinerated bodies. Cespedaa was a cruel place, she decided, with cruel creatures, and even crueler memories.

Up ahead, standing next to the twisted base of what had once been a metal support girder, was the group that she and her companions had come to meet. More importantly, they had brought a large plastic and metal cargo container with them. Despite the grim, death filled landscape all around her, N'Elemay smiled to herself. *God's will be done,* she thought.

Their reception party was composed of two distinct factions. The first were human soldiers from the ETR, and the second were Hriss warriors. The human officer was the first one to step forwards and greet her.

He was a dignified older man, and although his black hair and moustache were shot through with grey, his posture was erect and proud, and his eyes had the hard glint of a seasoned fighter. By the insignia on his spacesuit and the fatigues he wore inside of it, N'Elemay knew him to be a

Republican Colonel. Contrary to the Sisterhood's propaganda, not all of the ETR's military supported their present leadership.

In fact, far from it. Many, like the Colonel and his men, still secretly fought against the Sisterhood, and their puppet government. Today, their rebellion was taking the form of inaction, and blindness. The presence of her ship, and the Hriss, would never be reported to Nuvo Bolivar.

"Colonel Felix Rodraga," the man said. "Welcome to Cespedaa."

Out of courtesy, N'Elemay gave him a military salute and the man returned it. "Do you have what we asked for?"she asked.

In response, the man deferred to his companion. This was the leader of the Hriss contingent and the markings on his armor declared him to be a War Leader, roughly the equivalent of a Colonel himself. She had had enough experience with his kind to tell right away that he had recognized who she was, and was displeased by the discovery.

"You are White Hair," he said, his multiple yellow eyes narrowing. "I know you. You fought against my clan on Treya Angelaz."

"I did," she answered, meeting his gaze unhesitatingly. "What of it, War Leader?"

"You were the one who put my clansman's head on a spike as a message," he growled. "You, or one of your fellow egg-layers."

The hands of his companions were edging towards their weapons. The ETR troopers were also beginning to do the same thing.

She wasn't overly concerned though. The newest Angel, who had volunteered to accompany her, was covering the exchange—and the Hriss---with his sniper rifle, and the ship behind her stood ready to let loose with its own array of illegal weapons. The Church had paid extra for those particular features when they had hired its captain.

"Are you here to exact revenge for a careless relative, or against the Sisterhood?" she challenged. "Which would bring you the greater satisfaction?"

"The Sisterhood," the War leader answered. "But I still crave the personal honor of taking your head. I would even do you the courtesy of placing it in a jar on the shelf where I keep all of my other battle trophies."

"Would that be the same shelf where you store your pickled manhood?" she countered boldly. "If so, then there should be plenty of room. I understand that that particular jar is quite small."

A few of the other Hriss hissed angrily, but their leader only coughed in laughter. "If my manhood was in a jar, it would be so large that it would send a worthless female like yourself into shock. Enough about my virility though. Let us transact our business and then be done with one another."

"Agreed," she said.

At his signal, the case was brought forwards, and he opened it for her. Six tactical-level anti-matter bombs, each no larger than a personal holoviewer, were nestled inside the packing foam. N'Elemay leaned forwards and inspected them with a gleam in her eye. *The very sword of God itself,* she thought.

The Hriss noticed her expression, and also what lay behind it. "I see your death in your eyes, White Hair," he observed. "You have no intention of surviving your battle, do you? Do not bother to deny it--I have seen such a far off look in the warriors of my own kind."

She didn't. He was absolutely correct. From the very start, she had always known that the destruction of the Sisterhood would require her to lay down her own life. But the blessings of an eternal life in Heaven awaited her. What was that compared to a mortal existence?

"Greater glory always comes to those who make a sacrifice of themselves in battle," the Hriss assured her. "I wish you the very death that you seek, although I would vastly prefer that you would let me honor you instead. I promise that I would make certain to saw your head off slowly so that you could die for your God as bravely as possible."

"You flatter me," N'Elemay returned with genuine sincerity. "But I must do his work as he has laid it out for me. I have to refuse."

"A genuine shame," the Hriss sighed. "I do admire your dedication though—and your cause, which is why my clan agreed to help without demanding any payment except the death of our mutual enemies. May the God of War bless your sword arm."

"I thank you," she said formally. "In God's name."

The Hriss hadn't expected her to acknowledge his pagan deity, and he wasn't offended by her reply. "In God's name, then," he responded.

The ETR Colonel, who had remained silent throughout the exchange, spoke up, and added his own well-wishes. "Good luck to you and your fellow believers," he told her, extending his gloved hand.

Although she was well acquainted with this archaic custom, it wasn't habit, and it still took her a fraction of a second to respond in kind. When she did, Colonel Rodraga didn't release his grip right away.

"This isn't just for all this," he said, referring to the wasteland around them. "It is also for my son. His name was Alex. He was a Captain, and he served aboard the *Adaventara*. Remember him when you use these weapons."

"I shall," N'Elemay promised. When the time came, she would remember everyone that the Sisterhood had slaughtered.

With that, she returned to the merchanter with her precious cargo. She paid little attention to their return journey to the Sisterhood. Her thoughts were focused entirely on the bombs and the best use for them.

Two targets had come to her mind immediately, but the other three remained elusive. To be effective, she knew that the devices would have to be deployed against locations whose loss would deal the greatest amount of material damage, and the deepest psychological trauma. With hundreds of potential worlds to choose from, the decision was not an easy one.

So she prayed for her answers.

God's reply came just before their final transit to Thermadon. It arrived in the form of a naval boarding party, acting on behalf of the Customs Police. N'Elemay was meditating in her cabin, when the announcement came over the ships' address system.

She quickly double-checked her identification. She had been travelling in the guise of a Freight Assistant, 2nd Class, and she made certain that she had all the details correct before she went out to join the rest of the crew in the cargo area.

The Navy women had come aboard with their usual array of scanners, and twice the normal level of distrust. Since the ship was returning from the ETR with a load of radioactives, they were intent on giving it, and everyone aboard it, more scrutiny than usual. But her identification held up, and the bombs went undiscovered.

This was not what provided her with her answers however. That was furnished by the members of the boarding party itself. Or rather, by their appearance.

They were a thorough cross-section of the Sisterhood's population. The commanding officer was a dark-skinned Sitalan, her Second was clearly from Corrissa, and the rest were either from Thermadon, or any one of the hundreds of worlds where that genotype had settled.

N'Elemay made her decision then and there; two of the bombs would go to Thermadon as she had planned, one for the government center, and the other for its financial heart. Another would go to Rixa. But the remaining three would be taken to Corrissa, the source of the Sisterhood's art and literature, to the Athtar commercial shipyards in Sita, and to Nightshade, where the weapons that the Navy and Marines relied on were manufactured.

She was in awe of this revelation, and its absolute perfection. The plan that God had shown her would smash the Sisterhood on every level; financially, culturally, militarily, and politically. It was all that she could do not to drop down to her knees right then and there, and give thanks. Only the presence of the other sailors and the need to maintain her disguise was what stopped her.

After uncovering nothing incriminating, N'Elemay's ship was allowed to proceed, and the final leg of their voyage took place without any further interruptions. The six bombs were offloaded with the rest of the legitimate cargo, and taken immediately to a secure storage facility.

Once they arrived, she wasted no time addressing the specifics with Sister n'Avenal, and the leader of her neomen. After this, all they could do was wait as the plan was put into action by members of the Faithful on Thermadon, and all the other target worlds.

Ionix Industries, Warehouse 24, Marpesia District, Thermadon Val, Thermadon, Thalestris Elant, United Sisterhood of Suns, 1049.02|03|05:08:56

History remembered the 20th and 21st centuries primarily for their scientific discoveries and inventions. An agrarian society transformed into an industrial one, changing the fundamental way Humanity lived in the process. To Ellen n'Elemay however, these pivotal times also represented something else. Something much darker; the sacrifice of religious belief and cultural values on the altar of money and materialism.

The only exception were the radical Islamists. Had history given her the chance, she would have fought and killed them without hesitation, but she did admire them nonetheless. Despite their misogynistic views, they had at least stood up against the death of belief.

In her eyes, the 'War on Terror' had actually been a war between absolute faith and total cynicism. She also had little doubt that had the West retained its Christian faith, and responded to the Jihadists with the zeal of the Crusaders, that the conflict would have been far shorter than it was.

Despite this, the extremists had still been defeated. The sheer weight of their enemy's numbers, and resources, had ultimately overwhelmed them, but their willingness to fight and win at any cost, had not been lost on her.

Nor had the example of other movements, both before and afterwards; the IRA, the Tan-Shein, the ReVolutionairies and the Bio Action Army had all risen up against the monolithic status quo and fought to the death for their principles.

Now, her Church was doing the same thing, and against the same impossible odds. Only it stood against Shaitan and his servants in the Supreme Circle. With Jesu's blessings, unwavering faith, and battlefield cunning, she was determined that the outcome of their holy war would be far different than all the others.

To win meant sacrifice though. When God had called upon her, she had readily given up her career in the Marines and thrown in her lot with the Daughters of Eve. Now, Officer Tanya n'Jarra was answering the same heavenly summons. She was walking away from her entire life, and 25 years with the Customs Police. All to serve the Lord.

Paying such a terrible price was not easy, and despite her willingness to do so, N'Jarra still needed a moment to say a proper goodbye to everything that she had strived to build for herself. Out of respect for this, N'Elemay waited quietly as the woman ran an affectionate hand over her take-home patrol cruiser and then slowly, removed her uniform blouse.

When N'Elemay sensed that the moment was right, she went to her and placed a sympathetic hand on her shoulder.

"You should go," she said to her. Already Jaymz and his fellow neomen were collecting the extra uniforms from the cruiser's trunk and preparing to move the vehicle into hiding.

N'Jarra gave her cruiser a last wistful look and picked up her kit-bag. One of the Sisters, who had been waiting with N'Elemay, joined them, and gently guided the woman away.

In an hour, she would be on her way to her new life, with a new identity to match. And her contribution would make all the difference in the success of their operation.

Sacrifice, faith, and an untiring will to fight. Those were the things that really mattered in the end, N'Elemay reflected. That, and God's steady light.

The delivery of the police cruiser marked the last step in her plans. Knowing that it was to be their last night together, several of the Sisters, and the neomen, celebrated this with a party, followed by an orgy.

N'Elemay was invited to join in, but she politely declined. She wanted to spend her time in prayer and making confession instead, and as soon as she was able to, she sought out Sister n'Avenal, and unburdened herself. When she left the woman, she did so with a light heart, completely free of any lingering doubts or misgivings.

CHAPTER 12

Her status as a member of the RSE made it easy for Kaly to get herself a berth aboard a Navy ship bound for Rixa Naval Headquarters. She was away from Bel Sharra and in Null well before the Agency, or anyone else, had even realized it.

A message was waiting for her in her psiever's virtual inbox when the vessel reemerged into normal space, but she ignored it. The RSE, and her Troop Leader for that matter, could, and would, wait. She had something important to do, and they could all be damned as far as she was concerned.

The moment that she was downside, she found the correct train, and headed straight for the offices of the Naval Administration Division. On the way, she contacted Jana bel Anny. She didn't explain what had brought her to Rixa, or why she had finally decided to visit her after so long. She wanted to save that for when she was sitting right across from her.

Just as she had claimed in her message, Bel Anny had been promoted. She was now a Troop Leader, and rated her own, albeit tiny, office. She had also filled out a bit; life in Admin was a lot easier than in the field.

Kaly didn't hold any of this against her though. She was simply glad to see a friendly face from the past who could also help her with her present.

"Jana, "she began. "I need a favor."

"Anything, Kaly."

She told her all about Lena, and what had been done to her memories. As she listened, Bel Anny's expression changed, and became disturbed.

"I knew that something like this had happened," the woman confided. "A few months ago, when I looked you up to write about Berta, I couldn't find Lena. I checked to see if she had been transferred or something, and got nowhere. There wasn't any record at all.'

"When I checked a little further I was called in by my commanding officer and got a talking-to. Lena's file had been modified, and she told me to let the matter drop—or else. She ordered me to keep my mouth shut."

A long, pregnant silence passed between them before Bel Anny continued. "Kaly, I'm sorry, but I was under orders. Lena is classified information. Now I guess we both know why."

Kaly let out a ragged breath. "I have to know about her, Jana. I have to find out about her family. They deserve to know the truth."

"Kaly, there's nothing there to find, "Bel Anny explained. "It's all gone—her personal data, her service record—all of it. It's like she never even existed."

"There has to be something," Kaly insisted. "Please—Jana—I've come such a long ways—I've got to—" Her voice broke, and she started to weep. "P-please…"

She looked away, and her eyes fell on a holo sitting atop a small shelf on the wall across from her. It was an image of herself, Bel Anny, Enggredsdaater and another woman that she didn't recognize. Everyone was in their dress uniforms, hoisting drinks towards the holocam, and the background explained the rest. It was the *Sun, Sword and Starship*, the bar where they had celebrated their graduation from Basic.

Kaly was also positive that the strange woman depicted standing in their midst hadn't actually been there. Lena had. She knew that now. The image had been altered to fit the lie that the Corps had created.

Bel Anny saw where her eyes had gone, and guilt shadowed her features, immediately confirming Kaly's conclusion better than any spoken confession. Abruptly, the woman tore her gaze away from the holo, typed something in on her holographic keyboard, and then rose from her desk. "I have to get some kaafra," she announced. "Do you want some, Kaly?"

Kaly shook her head and wiped her nose with the back of her hand.

"I think you do," Bel Anny said meaningfully. "I'll go get us some." She paused just long enough to punch in one final command, and a holo appeared over the desk. Then she walked out of the room.

Kaly suddenly realized what the file in front of her contained. It was a listing of military benefits and beneficiaries. The servicewoman's name had been left blank, but not the payees for her life insurance or her other veteran's benefits. These were listed as Jen n'Taara and Gari bel Haylee, of Loladora, Essylt.

These were Lena's mothers. The entry also mentioned that the insured had died 'in action', earning her a posthumous medal for bravery, but there were no details. Lena had been made into a heroine, and robbed of her identity at the same time.

She quickly took an image with her psiever, and left the office.

When Bel Anny returned several minutes later, and saw the empty chair, she smiled sadly, and sipped at her kaafra. She hadn't bothered to bring more than one cup back with her.

Goddess bless you Kaly, she thought. *I hope you find the healing that you are searching for.* Then she closed the file.

***

Leaving Bel Anny's office, Kaly made straightaway for the magnorail terminal, fully intent on traveling to Essylt and contacting Lena's mothers.

As the train pulled away and started to pick up speed however, she began to reconsider her plan.

Did she really have the right to do that, she wondered. Did it really *need* to be done? Or was she simply letting anger guide her actions? Or even selfishness?

After she had learned the truth about Lena's death, the agony had been so intense that she had almost gone mad. She had survived the experience, but it had scarred her deeply, and it was nothing that she wanted to visit on anyone else, least of all Lena's family.

They were innocents, and they believed that their daughter had died valiantly, and quickly. Inserting herself into their lives now, after so long, and telling them the hideous truth would do them no service.

Instead, it would be like sinking a knife in their hearts, and make her just as cruel as the Sisterhood. It galled her to think that what her government had done would be allowed to stand unchallenged, but the alternative was even more unpalatable. Better to leave them in peace, she decided, even if that peace *was* founded on a falsehood. Oftentimes, lies could be kinder than the truth, and more merciful.

By this point, the train had completed its journey, and she got out, suddenly finding herself with no destination to travel to. Returning to Thermadon and the RSE wasn't even a consideration.

She was done with the Agency, and her homeworld of Persephone was just as unacceptable. There were too many ghosts waiting for her there.

She needed somewhere else to go. A place where she could grapple with everything that she had been through. As she considered her options, the holodisplays began to update themselves, and one world in particular, caught her eye.

It was a flight to Zommerlaand. She had never been there before, and seeing its name flashing overhead made her think about her old plans to visit Enggredsdaater. She had found her destination.

Picking up her kit-bag, Kaly sent a thought to the displays and they responded by creating directional arrows in her visual cortex, pointing the way towards the appropriate terminal. At the same time, her virtual in-box was nagging her again, warning her that she now had a dozen unanswered messages. They were all from Ben Di, Major ebed Karri and Lieutenant ben Soolee.

Without any hesitation, she closed the inbox, leaving them unopened, and walked on.

Residence of Lady Ananzi, Great Nightlands Waste, Morpheus System, Thalestris Elant, United Sisterhood of Suns, 1049.02|04|09:22:35

The Taarq had been trailing Maara elle Ananzi for three nights in a row. It had her scent, and from years of experience hunting other travelers, it knew where she was going, and what route she would have to take. It also had time.

Maara didn't. In her haste to flee the predator, she had left behind her food and water. All she had now was her Tej knife, and the grim knowledge that she was still several days away from the foot of the Moonspire Mountains, and any hope of rescue.

Working her way through the sagebrush, she came to the lip of a dry canyon, and saw where her death would find her. The canyon bisected the desert and went on for what looked like kilometers. Its sides were twice her height, and looked unstable, which meant that any journey in or out of it would be slow going.

There were also bones scattered along its length. Some, she knew, had come from animals that had been caught in the infrequent flash-floods that sometimes sliced through the Nightlands Waste. Others, including one half-buried mass that was still wearing the shreds of its survival jacket, where human, and the handiwork of the Taarq.

Refusing to enter this death trap, and taking her chances in the open desert, was out of the question. She knew that the predator would simply stay with her and wait for her to tire. Then it would take her.

It was the canyon, or nothing, and they both understood this. The fight between them would take place there, and one, or both of them, would die in the process.

She could hear the creature behind her, increasing its pace. It had become less cautious now that they were nearing its killing field, and it wasn't concerned about betraying itself. A pebble dislodged here, a dry branch pushed aside there, and over it all, she caught the rising sense of hunger and expectation. Not thoughts exactly, but close enough for Maara to recognize and comprehend.

Picking her way down the side of the canyon, she searched for the right ground to make her stand. She settled on a level patch of earth that offered her a good, solid footing and a clear view of the area around her. The Taarq would not have the chance to sneak up on her.

Her Tej knife was also out and at the ready, its silver crescent gleaming in the light of the two moons, and she marshalled all the calm that she still had within her. If this was where she was going to die, then she wouldn't do so screaming, she vowed. She would face the monster bravely, and do her best to take it into death with her. This wasn't the end that she had envisioned for herself when she had set out on her Tej, but it was the only glory that fate seemed to be willing to offer her.

A second later, the Taarq came out of the brush. When it caught sight of her, its eyes glowed with anticipation, and a low growl issued from its throat.

Then it scrambled down into the canyon. But when it reached the bottom, and she failed to break into a run, it stopped. Her confidence had unnerved it, and she knew that it was taking her measure before committing itself. Finally, it bared its fangs, and Maara saw the muscles under its fur tensing as it readied itself to make a leap at her.

She didn't flinch. Instead, she lowered herself into a fighting stance and grinned right back at the beast, showing it her own teeth. *Come on you bitch,* she thought. *Let's do this thing.*

Almost as if it had heard this challenge, the creature charged, and she sidestepped, managing to get in a slash along its side that made it howl in pain and anger. Faster than she thought it was capable of, the thing spun around in mid-stride and snapped at her leg, hoping to cripple her.

But Maara was even faster and pulled the limb away at the last second. She could tell that the Taarq was surprised by this.

It came at her again, and as she pivoted to defend herself, she stumbled over something, and fell. Seeing its chance, the animal leapt onto her. The only thing that saved her from having her throat ripped wide open was her reflexive attempt to ward off its fangs with her arm. The creature bit into it with all the force that it had in its jaws.

Maara screamed in agony, and as her Tej knife fell from her grip, blood dripped down into her eyes. It was her own blood, she realized. There was a lot of it.

Abruptly, the Taarq released her arm and tried to push its shaggy head under her guard, going for her throat once again, but she called up her strength and rolled out from under it. An instant later, she was back up on her feet, and with her one good hand, retrieved her knife and braced herself for the next assault.

Then, from somewhere back behind her, she heard what seemed like a second predator coming through the brush to join them. The damned thing had a partner, she thought. It wasn't common for the Taarq to run in pairs, but it was still known to happen.

She backed herself up a few paces, and angled her body so that she could spot the new threat and still keep an eye on the old one. Her injured arm hung uselessly at her side now, leaving a trail of blood that glinted evilly in the moonlight. She was also beginning to feel dizzy. This, she knew, was from the shock setting in.

The last of her luck had deserted her, and her end seemed near. In just a few more seconds, she would join the other corpses on the canyon's floor and no one but the Goddess would ever know what had happened to her.

An instant later, another sound reached her ears, and she realized that the new arrival wasn't a predator at all. It was a human, shouting a set of seemingly nonsensical syllables, and then something that felt very much like the wind shoved past her.

Whatever it actually was, it hit the Taarq and sent the monster spinning head over heel. The thing tried to rise, but now it was plain that it had been injured. A second cry followed this, and to Maara's astonishment, the predator exploded like a dry clod of dirt, its fur, bones and guts splattering everywhere. Darkness claimed her at the same time, and she felt herself collapsing.

Some time later, she returned to consciousness, and looked up into the eyes of a woman who was busily bandaging her arm. This was the first time that she had ever met Lady Kaala elle Ananzi, the figure who would later become her teacher, and her life-long friend.

Instead of allowing her to die alone in the desert, the Goddess had seen fit to spare her life, and had granted her the chance to attain wisdom.

But this wasn't really the past, Lady Ananzi realized. The actual event had occurred many decades earlier and her arm had long since healed from the Taarq's ravages. Her teacher was also dead. Like all mortals, Lady Kaala had finally grown old, and had been taken back into Elatsha's dark embrace.

Now, she was the old one, and this had to be a dream of some kind, she concluded, but much clearer and more lifelike than any vision that she had ever experienced before. Then, in a flash of insight, she understood what was really happening, and who her savior actually was.

The dream changed with this. The canyon was replaced with the hilltop that overlooked her home, and the open desert. And the being that resembled Lady Kaala was standing next to her.

"There was no one else that you would listen to," the figure explained. "Not when it came to something this important. Maara, you need to send Fa'Teela with the others. To the Tree. There is a thing that he must do there."

"What is it?" Ananzi asked.

"He needs to make a decision," the Galaxy Mind told her. "It concerns Maya n'Kaaryn. Shall we discuss the future together, and all of its possibilities?"

Lady Ananzi nodded, and the dream-desert vanished. Another scene took its place.

***

After being a fugitive for so long, Jon wasn't surprised when his 'guardian' came into the living area and made an abrupt announcement. He would be leaving Thermadon immediately. The police detective didn't tell him where he would be going, only that it was 'somewhere safe'.

He didn't expect this information either. He just accepted it, and began to pack his things. This transition was made easier by the fact that he would not be travelling alone. Instead, he would be accompanied by Sisters Tereysa and Beatriss so that they could continue to work with him.

And for this, he was immensely grateful. He had come to cherish the time that they spent together. They had not only provided him with companionship, but they had also helped him to find his way back to his faith.

He understood now that his Church had been misled, and that the Redeemer he had believed in was nothing more than Shaitan's attempt to hijack the True Faith for his own evil ends. He also realized that the Church had strayed from its origins and become proud.

This was the only explanation for the terrible error they had made with Project Advent. That he had played a part in that debacle had bothered him deeply—at first. But Sister Tereysa had managed to persuade him that he had only been following the mandates of his elders, and convinced him to forgive himself. The Redeemer, she had said, would have arisen without him. Shaitan was simply too eager to establish his reign of evil for it to have turned out otherwise.

The only thing that he was still struggling with was the concept of forgiving the Sisterhood for all of its transgressions. Although the *Revelations* urged the Faithful to turn the other cheek and exonerate wrongdoers, he had a hard time accepting this. He had suffered at their hands, and he had borne witness to the ravages that they had perpetrated.

This was something that Sister Tereysa remained insistent on however, and she had plenty of scripture to support her position. Her favorite passage was from the book of Matthew which she brought to bear frequently, and without mercy.

"For if you forgive others their trespasses," it said, *"your heavenly Father will also forgive you, but if you do not forgive others their trespasses, neither will your Father forgive your trespasses."*

And even though she had lost just as much as Jon had, Sister Beatriss firmly agreed with Tereysa's position. It was an area that they would continue to examine and debate during their journey to wherever he was being sent, and for as long as he was there.

Until Lady Ananzi finally revealed her true purpose for him. Despite all the charity that she had shown him so far, Jon harbored no illusions whatsoever. The old witch was definitely up to something. She was after all, an agent of the Sisterhood.

Eastern Sea, A'latar, Evaar'eea System, Pa'lla Space,
1049.02|10|05:22:19

In the Pa'lla language, "A'latar" meant 'shining emerald'. Human eyes could never perceive the planets primary as anything but a yellow-white star, but for the Pa'lla, whose ocular structure was radically different, it was the penultimate expression of everything that embodied the color green. This was a hue which they equated with all that was holy, perfect and good. To the Pa'lla, green was God.

Because of this, the planet and its solar system were considered by the Pa'lla to be a source of both physical and spiritual healing, and it was revered as one the most sacred places in their small star-nation. The sick and the soul-weary came to A'latar for rejuvenation and renewal, and although other races could not appreciate it in the same manner that the Pa'lla did, it had still gained a reputation for the healing properties of its resorts. Wealthy beings from many parts of the Milky Way came to A'latar hoping to benefit from the effects of the Sacred Green Ray.

Humans however, were comparatively rare. Only a small number of women even knew of the Pa'lla, much less about A'latar, and this made it the perfect place for Lady Ananzi to use as a planet-wide safe house, and for Maya to recover from her injuries.

The *JUDI* had brought her there, and once they had landed, she was immediately ensconced in one of the many small resorts that were situated on the shores of the planet's shallow seas, and left in the care of Jeena and Skylaar.

Skylaar's natural skin coloring, and Maya's hazel-green eyes proved to be a plus, garnering them the best treatment that the resort had to offer. To the native owners and their staff, these features were considered to be nothing less than proof positive that their alien guests had been blessed in advance by the Divine. The Pa'lla did all they could to make them feel as comfortable, and as welcome as possible.

The days passed, and only after Skylaar was certain that she was ready to hear it, she spoke with Maya about Sarah.

"Maya", she began. "I have some news that may distress and surprise you. Please try not to become alarmed, but Sarah will be joining us soon."

Maya sat up in her bed, looking all around her for any sign of the woman.

411

"Is she here? Now?" As far as she knew, Sarah was still working for the Agency—and one of the women hunting her.

"She is not," Skylaar reassured her. "And Sarah is not with the Agency any longer. I cannot explain why. But you can be certain that she has no interest in harming you, and you have my solemn word that I will protect you from anyone who attempts to do so."

Maya gave her an uncertain look. "When will she be here?" she asked.

"Sarah will not visit A'latar," Skylaar said. "I have instructed her to stay well away from this world until you are fully healed. She will join us later, perhaps in Ashkele. Perhaps earlier. For now, you need to concentrate on getting yourself well."

Maya nodded, but her expression remained troubled. She wasn't happy with this news at all.

She also intended to find out why Sarah had suddenly abandoned an organization that had once defined her very existence. And to ferret out what her current motives *really* were.

She was equally determined to make certain that the woman answered for her betrayal. Getting even was just as important as determining the truth. If not more so.

"Fine," she said. "I'll forget her."

Skylaar smiled, knowing exactly what was going through her mind. She was no psi, but she had come to know Maya well enough to guess the general shape of her thoughts. For the moment though, it was enough for her that her student was willing to cooperate.

"Thank you, Maya."

***

Their uniqueness as human visitors ended with Jon fa'Teela's arrival. He had come to A'latar on another merchanter that worked for Lady Ananzi, the CSS *Billie Jo*, with Sister Tereysa and Sister Beatrice. Like Maya, once he was downside, he was given a seaside cabin to stay in. It was located two coves further down the coastline, and he was as unaware of her presence, as she was of his.

His purpose was similar to Maya's. He was there to rest and to heal. Not in body though, but in spirit.

The two Sisters met with him daily, and his hours were filled with prayer, studies of the *Revelations* and lengthy discussions on the finer points of his faith. When she realized that he was ready for it, Sister Tereysa announced the next step in the process; a re-baptism and a fresh commitment to God. Jon, who had quietly been considering the very same thing, quickly agreed.

They met at his cabin the following morning, just before dawn. He had fasted and prayed throughout the night, and dressed himself in a simple white robe. Sister Tereysa and Beatrice had honored the occasion by attiring themselves in the vestments of their office; the familiar blue and white robes of a Bride of Jesu, and they wore their Stars of the Faithful openly.

The site they had chosen for the ceremony was in a small inlet not far from the resort, but removed enough to guarantee them privacy. It commanded a sweeping view of the sea, and the craggy rocks along the shore line made a perfect frame for A'latar's sun as it rose in the east.

Standing in the surf together, Sister Tereysa began with a quote from the *Revelations*, the Book of Romans.

"'*We were therefore buried with him through baptism into death in order that, just as Jesu was raised from the dead through the glory of the Father, we too may live a new life.*' Go to your knees, Jon fa'Teela. Say out loud that you commit yourself to the death and life of the first Redeemer."

Jon did so. "I pledge myself to Jesu, body and soul," he added. "For he is the true Redeemer of all humans." As he uttered this promise, the sun broke over the rocks and bathed them all in its perfect radiance.

Sister Tereysa had positioned herself alongside him, and she instructed him to lie back in her outstretched arm. "You are reborn in Jesu's light this day," she said.

"Praise Jesu and Mari," Beatrice declared.

Then Tereysa held his nose closed, and with Beatrice assisting her, lowered him into the surf, submerging his torso, and then his head. The water closed in around him.

Suddenly, Jon felt the hands that had been supporting him disappear, and for a moment he panicked, certain that the Sisters had let go of him for some reason. He was floating, and he opened his eyes.

Instead of seeing Tereysa or Beatrice, or even the surface of the water, the only thing that filled his vision was a vast, green nothingness. There was no 'up' or down' for his senses to identify, just a formless void that stretched away from him in all directions.

A moment later, a light appeared in the distance, and in less than a heartbeat, it had reached him and enveloped him in its flawless brilliance.

The scene transformed. He was out of the water now, and on the beach, and he could feel the rough grains of sand under his bare feet. The light had also changed. Instead of a yellow sun, the star above him had become a brilliant, flaming emerald.

He was also not alone. A figure, dressed in a simple robe the color of malachite stood near him, its features hidden by the garment's hood. There

413

were no foot prints around it, and it seemed to leave no impression on the sand whatsoever. Yet it was there.

"What is this place," he asked it. "Why am I here?"

"This place is nowhere, and in no time. You, Jon fa'Teela, are here to decide," the stranger replied. Its voice was neither male, nor female, and what little of it that he could make out, could have belonged to either sex. It was, in appearance at least, human, but it could have been any age, or every age for that matter.

"Who are you?" he demanded. "What do you call yourself?"

It smiled. "You may call me Aggelos," it answered. "Or Ma'lak, if you prefer." Instantly, Jon comprehended its meaning. Both of these were ancient words. One was Greek, and the other Hebrew, and they meant the same thing; a messenger. An angel.

But whether he was dealing with one of the Sons of Men, or a fallen servant of Shaitan, he could not say with any certainty. All that he was sure of was that he was in the presence of something supernatural, and this put him on his guard.

The figure smiled again, as if it were amused by his reaction, and turned its head to regard him. The shadows of its hood conspired with the light of the alien sun to keep its face a secret.

"You must make a choice," it repeated. "Between two futures. Each one promises a reward, and each exacts a toll for that prize. Both of them involve you, and a young woman who calls herself Maya n'Kaaryn"

Certain now that he was dealing with a demon who was trying to tempt him just as the Evil One had once tempted Jesu, Jon started to refuse. His words died stillborn as the world around him altered once again.

He was standing on the bridge of a military starship, watching as the women feverishly went about their business at the control stations. On the main sitscreen, a star very much like the one that shone down on A'latar was on display. On a side screen, he could see hundreds of ships of every size and class, lining up to transit into Null. No one seemed to notice him, or his guide.

Then he overheard the techs as they relayed their data to the ship's commander. "The enemy has launched their device!" one of them reported. "It's going to go nova, Commander! The ships won't get away in time!"

"We have to find a way to help them," the woman exclaimed. "There has to be something we can do to—"Her final words were cut off by a gasp of horror.

The star on the main screens swelled in size and ejected its outer mantle. A gigantic wave of pure, elemental fire expanded outwards in all directions, engulfing the ships, and everything else that it encountered. Nothing was left in its wake but death. Jon was horrified.

"War, Jon," the figure stated. "Interstellar war, and on a scale that your race has never imagined in its most terrible of dreams. Entire star systems destroyed right along with their stars, and trillions of innocents killed.'

"And all because you stopped Maya n'Kaaryn from using the Tree. Thanks to that deed, a new Trio was chosen, among another race, and they used the Tree to start a conflict that soon involved most of the galaxy. Your Sisterhood was swept up in the chaos."

"What?" he stammered. "I didn't do that! That hasn't happened! Who is this Maya n'Kaaryn? What are you talking about?"

"You will meet her soon enough," his companion informed him. "She is the User that Lady Ananzi spoke to you of. But there is more to this future." It waved its hand, and the ghastly spectacle was replaced.

He was standing on a balcony now, and below him he could see thousands of people. They were all cheering and chanting and waving up to an elderly man who was dressed in rich, golden vestments. A man that seemed familiar to him for some reason. Very familiar.

"That is you, Jon," the figure said. "Many, many years from now, and after the great interstellar war. You have been made Pope of the New Church, and those are just a few of your followers. Thanks to the crisis, everything that the Sisterhood had stood for was called into question, and your faith suddenly found willing ears everywhere. Motherthought was discarded, and Humanity embraced The Word of God. All because you stopped Maya n'Kaaryn."

He rounded on the creature. "At what cost?" he snarled. "How many lives was that victory bought with?"

"Is that important?" it asked. "Perhaps you would like to see the alternative?" Instantly, his surroundings changed again.

This time, he saw himself, not as an elderly man, but just a few years older. He was in a simple robe, making an impassioned speech to a crowd of women. There were only a hundred or so of them, and although they looked up at him in adoration, they were surrounded by a larger crowd that seemed to be angry at what he was saying. Then, from out of the midst of the crowd, a single woman pushed her way through. She was holding a needlegun, and he saw her raise it.

"Marionite scum!" she yelled.

Before anyone could stop her, she fired, and his double toppled backwards, blood blossoming from his chest. The crowd rushed forwards to seize her, but he knew that they were too late. Her victim was dead.

Jon lowered his head and turned away, sickened by the sight. When he raised it again, he was on another starship. It was no battlecruiser, but a merchanter, and on the displays he saw thousands of ships just like it. There were also Marionite Sisters on the bridge, and they were looking at a small, unimposing star with a handful of planets. One of these was listed as a T-Type world, but just on the edge of being capable of sustaining human life. Existence there would be hard, he reflected, but not impossible.

"Our new home," the captain announced.

"May Jesu and Mari grant us the peace that we have sought for so long, and bless this place," one of the Sisters said, crossing herself. "You are certain that the Sisterhood doesn't know of it?"

"Yes, mother," the captain answered. "We are well beyond their furthest surveys, and this part of space is still uncharted. I don't imagine they'll come looking here any time soon."

"What shall we call it?" another Sister asked.

"New Jerulsaalam," the first one told her. "Just as the blessed Saint Jon the Martyr would have wanted. If only he could have been here to see this day."

"He is Mother," the younger woman said. "He is here in spirit with us. I am sure of it."

Jon's guide laughed softly. "How true," it said. "She is wise beyond her years."

"*This* is the alternative?" Jon asked. "*This?* My death? Exile?"

"Yes Jon," it said. "If you fail to stop Maya n'Kaaryn, or refuse to try, then she will use the Tree. No interstellar war will occur, I assure you. And your Chairwoman will try her best to seek peace between your Church and the Sisterhood. But—"

"But she will fail somehow?"

"Yes," it answered. "An extremist movement, guided by surviving members of the Conversation will resist that change, and it is one of their number that will succeed in assassinating you.'

'When she kills you, you will become a martyr—just as the Sisters said—and your Church will continue to suffer, until at last it will be forced to realize that the only choice it has, is to flee.'

"It will be another exodus, Jon, out of a new Egypt. Like the Israelites, it will find another home for itself—not in any desert land, but in the very wilderness of space itself. As for you, you shall be remembered as a Saint, and in time your people will flourish and grow to greatness. More than that I may not reveal."

"I think you are Shaitan," Jon retorted. "I think you are telling me lies."

"You know better than that, Jon," It answered calmly "You know this is truth. You have two roads before you, and you must choose which one to take. One leads to the death of many, and personal glory. The other leads to a single death, and the salvation of many. Think on that, and when the time comes, let your righteousness speak to you."

416

A nanosecond later, he felt the water surrounding him once again, and then the sure grasp of hands raising him up to the surface. He was back on the beach with Sister Tereysa and Beatrice.

"Praise Jesu and Mari," Tereysa exclaimed. "You are reborn in the sight of God!"

"Praise God in the highest," he intoned, more in reflex than anything else. As they guided him out of the water, and proceeded to celebrate the Mass together, he looked up past Sister Tereysa and the makeshift altar that she had erected, to the sun itself.

Squinting in its glare, he whispered a silent prayer to his Creator. *My Father, if it is possible, let this cup pass from me; yet not as I will, but as you will.*

No reprieve came from on high though. The only thing that met his senses were the crashing of the waves and the sound of the wind.

The service ended shortly afterwards, and Jon walked with his friends in silence. He did not tell them about what had happened under the water, and he did his best to ignore the robed figure that followed them back to his cabin, lurking at the very edges of his vision.

Or the fact that the sun was still green.

***

Like Skylaar, Jeena waited for the right opportunity to extend his invitation to Maya. That time came when Maya was almost completely healed. They were relaxing together on the cabin's porch, enjoying the breeze coming in off the ocean, and the sultry afternoon heat.

"I spoke with the Captain today, "the neoman said. "She told me that she got in touch with Lady Ananzi and her friends in the Daughters, and it looks like the Agency has given up trying to find us. She also said that we could go back to the Sisterhood if we wanted to, as long as we lay low when we get there."

Maya took a sip of her fruit juice and thought about this. She would have been perfectly satisfied to spend the rest of her life exploring the galaxy beyond the boundaries of her star-nation. But she also had to admit that there were some places, and things in the Sisterhood, that she missed. Home, however fekked up it was, *was* still home.

"What do you want to do?" she asked him.

"Skylaar and I were thinking of going to Nemesis. I'd like to visit the Fighting School again," Jeena said, unconsciously touching his tattoo. "Would you like that? Skylaar told me that you enjoyed working with the sword."

417

The prospect of seeing the jungle world and the Shadow Lake Lodge again didn't bring a smile to Maya's face.

For most visitors, the Lodge represented the chance for an exotic vacation, spiced up with the dangers of the great forest that surrounded it. And a visit to the Fighting School was something that any serious martial artist dreamt about.

For her though, all that Nemesis signified was Felecia, and the fact that she had nearly been killed on an imaging safari while accompanying her.

"How long do we have to stay at the Lodge?" she asked, not bothering to hide her reluctance.

"I'll only need a day to get what we'll need for the trip," the neoman assured her. Thanks to Skylaar, he knew all about her history with the Shadow Lake Lodge and understood the reason for her hesitation.

"Once we're at the School we'll be about as far away from the Conversâzi as anyone can get," he added. "They won't think of looking for you there, and even if they do, the Forest itself will keep them away."

He didn't have to mention the fact that the local clans also protected the area—and didn't need to. Visits to the Fighting School were by invitation only, and trespassing in the Great Mother Forest was something that the Nemesians tended to view very dimly. If Angelique and her comrades were foolish enough to search for her there, they would have to contend with the clans and the Forest itself.

Maya considered his proposition carefully. Spending her time concentrating on nothing but the ka'na, was just what she needed, she finally decided. "Nemesis it is," she agreed.

The Apex Office, The Golden Pyramid, Thermadon Val, Thermadon,
Myrene System, Thalestris Elant, United Sisterhood of Suns,
1049.02|13|08:34:76

Assassination is not always a dramatic, public event. Sometimes world leaders die without their people ever even realizing that their passing had been deliberately engineered. This was certainly the case for Chairwoman Marina bel Rayna and Director Susa ben Paula.

A month after their visit to the Concordance magnorail station, the nanites which had been a component of Angelique's custom-made perfume, activated themselves. The portable sniffers at the station, and the units installed in the Chairwoman's hoverlimo, had not detected them. This was because the nanites had been specially manufactured to mimic the safe and healthful microbots that the Transit Authority and other agencies routinely dispersed into public places to control the spread of communicable diseases.

They had also been preprogrammed to seek out specific DNA signatures, supplied to them through samples that Angelique had carefully gathered at previous public events. When they found their targets in Bel Rayna and Ben Paula's bodies, they migrated into their respiratory systems, and waited until the time came to strike.

For Bel Rayna, this occurred in her sleep. The miniature assassins left their hiding places and travelled swiftly through her bloodstream until they arrived at a cerebral artery. Right away, they went to work weakening its walls. When it finally ruptured, her death was instantaneous.

Then, in another part of the city, the nanobots inside of Ben Paula came alive. They attacked her heart, blocking up a key vessel with fat cells that they had gathered from other locations within her body. The embolism that they created, was just as lethal as the stroke that had killed the Chairwoman.

The news of their deaths, coming as they did so soon after the Concordance bombing, hit the Sisterhood hard. Both women were mourned and buried with all the honors that the nation could bestow upon them. Then the machinery of government rolled on, and chose their successors.

After decades of coveting the highest office in her star-nation, Layna n'Calysher was appointed to serve as the 106th Chairwoman, and Angelique bel Thana was chosen to lead the *Regila da Securité par Estat* as its Director. Following the formal swearing-in ceremonies, Angelique paid a visit to the new Chairwoman.

In addition to donning her full dress uniform, she had taken the added step of wearing more *'Lucrezia'*. She had also been careful to leak information about its true nature to a woman that spied for both herself, and for Layna n'Calysher. As a result, when she entered the Chairwoman's office, she was gratified to see N'Calysher stiffen visibly the moment that she caught *Lucrezia's* scent in the air.

"My condolences," Angelique said, bowing formally, "and my best wishes for your new administration, Madame Chairwoman."

"Thank you, Angelique," N'Calysher replied. Although her tone was even enough, there was a slight tremor in her voice and a single bead of sweat was rolling down her forehead.

For the moment however, she had no reason to be afraid. None of the nanites suspended in the perfume were meant for her. Angelique had simply wanted to remind the woman, from the outset, of the importance of keeping her new RSE Commander-in-Chief content.

"Tell me," she asked her pleasantly. "How fares the Lady Felecia?"

N'Calysher, grasping the implied threat, responded with an aplomb that would have done a realie star proud. "Thank you so much for asking,

General. She is quite well and I heard from her just yesterday. She is still aboard the *Star of Aphrodite* and I understand that they are taking her on a tour of the T'baari Nebula and the Ring Worlds."

"That is wonderful news," Angelique answered. "It really is quite lovely there. Please, if you would, send her all of my love."

Then she took on a more serious tone. "I know that your office is probably quite busy with more pressing issues, but I would like to discuss the omniplex with you. As you know, your late predecessor and I had spoken about this at great length."

In reality, this had been the very reason for Bel Rayna's assassination. Despite her support for the RSE, she had not been a member of the Conversâzi, nor had she known of its existence. She had also steadfastly refused to hand over administration of the huge information network to Angelique. Now, she was gone.

"I anticipated your request," N'Calysher told her, "and I want to assure you that I strongly support your Agencies' program of aggressively reforming and safeguarding the omniplex. I signed the authorization just this morning, and the network will now be completely under the auspices of the RSE."

Angelique smiled broadly. No matter how the rest of their business went, she had just won herself a great victory, and she would have raised her arms and cheered had it not been crude and inelegant to do so. It was enough that she finally had what she wanted, and she said a tiny prayer of thanks to Ellen n'Elemay for making it possible.

Powerful though it was, she had always known that the Secret would never be the sole key for achieving the future that she dreamed of for herself. In order to fully realize that vision, the populace would also have to be controlled, and the omniplex would enable her to accomplish this. At last, she would have the means she needed to stifle the irksome protests that had been cropping up, and guide the Sisterhood's diverse population in the proper direction.

In time, Womankind would not only come to accept the government that she intended for them, but even come to love it—and her, as their absolute ruler. Knowledge, had always been the pairmate of power, and controlling both was the key to political supremacy. Now, all that remained was to take possession of the Secret and control the User. After that, everything else would fall neatly into place.

"I knew that you would see the wisdom of this, Madame Chairwoman," she said aloud. "Bel Rayna was a great stateswoman, but she never grasped the importance of taking this simple step to secure our daughter's futures. In their name, I thank you and I assure you that we will not betray your trust."

"Yes, of course," N'Calysher agreed. "I'll rely completely on your judgment."

You will at that, Angelique thought. *In this, and in many other things.*

* * *

Kaly waved farewell to the hovertruck's driver before she turned and started down the long dirt track that wound its way to Enggredsdaater's farm. A few yards in, a raven landed on one of the fence posts lining the road, and issued a challenging caw.

She stopped and smiled at the bird. She had dressed herself in a spare uniform to ease the process of travelling to the agriworld.

"You know--you're right", she said removing the peaked cap, and setting it carefully on the post nearest her. Her uniform tunic came off next, and she hung this neatly on a strand of barbed wire, right alongside the cap.

"They're yours if you want them," she told the creature. "I don't need them anymore."

The raven seemed to regard them appraisingly, and without looking back, Kaly walked away, leaving the clothing, and the part of her life that they had once represented, for the raven, or anyone else who came along, to do as they wished with them.

The suns were just setting, and as she moved along, she drank in their golden light, feeling a sense of total freedom and peace. It was shaping up to be a fine evening.

Ki'a'ska Garden, Shadow Lake Lodge, Nemesis, Rahdwa System, Thalestris Elant, United Sisterhood of Suns, 1049.02|20|04:58:33

When Maya entered the Ki'a'ska Garden and saw Jeena taur K'aut'sha, her mouth dropped open. He had his pack on and his clothing seemed well-suited for the journey that they were about to take. It was his accessories that had caught her completely by surprise.

Strapped securely to his hips was a long, articulated tail made of metal, and his hands and feet sported skeletal devices constructed of the same material. These, she saw, were equipped with retractable claws. As for the artificial tail, it quivered and whipped in the air as if it were a living part of him. Jeena grinned, thoroughly enjoying her surprise.

"It's the only way to get where we're going," he said, nodding up at the nearest tree. "We're taking the Green Road".

He went on, telling her what the Green Road was, and what it had to do with the trees all around them. Only then, did Maya put it all together—and

421

finally understand something that had happened to her on her previous visit to the place.

When she had been there with Felecia, they had encountered two of the local women. At the end of their conversation, the Nemesians had used their claws and foot talons to clamber up the very same tree, and disappear. His prosthetic copies were obviously what outsiders like themselves were expected to use to accomplish the same feat.

Maya looked at the tree doubtfully. It went up. And up. And up. She didn't care for heights.

As she wrestled with this, Skylaar joined them, and gave them both a friendly shrug. She had also changed her garments. In her case, she was attired in the leather breast strap and the long, multi-pocketed shorts most Nemesians favored. She also had a satchel in hand and she set this down at Maya's feet. Inside, was another set of the prosthetics.

"These are for you, Cho-sena," she said. She inclined her head towards Jeena. "Help her with them, please."

Still smiling, Jeena came over and began to assist Maya with her gear, belting her up and attaching everything with obvious familiarity.

"The tail and claws respond to our movements," he said, "and they work off their own software to calculate the correct response. Result? When we jump, or need our balance, they can do everything the natural ones can do. We can travel the Road just as well as the locals can. Unfortunately, some of us just aren't blessed with the same equipment as others." he said, his grin widening.

Maya blushed at the double meaning. Sometimes, it was hard for her to remember that he was a 'he'. Or, that he had an impish sense of humor.

Skylaar raised an eyebrow at Jeena, clearly of a different opinion, but she didn't challenge him. "We must be going," she said instead. "It will be dark soon and I wish for us to be at our first Nest before then."

With that, she bunched herself up and leapt upwards. Her claws bit into the wood, and in seconds, she had ascended the trunk and vanished in the leafy canopy.

"Come on," Jeena urged. "The best way to learn is by doing!" Copying their teacher, he sprang at the tree and climbed up and away from her at an astounding speed. He was also laughing at her.

"Okay," she said to herself. "I guess I learn the hard way." Certain that she would wind up spending her entire time on Nemesis recuperating in a local hospital, she summoned up her courage, and jumped. To her surprise, the claws came out of their own accord and held fast to the wood.

She quickly discovered that climbing and moving along the branches was actually quite easy with the devices. Just as long as she didn't look down.

That night, they camped in a Nest. Like the process of traveling high above the forest floor, it took Maya a while to fully accept that the shelter was safe, and even longer to get comfortable enough to sleep in it. The eerie noises of the predators hunting each other below them didn't help, but eventually her exhaustion won out and she drifted off.

Incredibly, there were no nightmares that night, and she awoke just after dawn to a breathtaking tableau. The sun had just risen, and the sky was filled with some kind of iridescent insect with wings that resembled colored glass. Things that were a cross between birds, reptiles and something utterly alien, were chasing these swarms. Far from being a savage scene, the hunt seemed more like a graceful aerial dance, gilded by the rays of the Nemesian primary. The air that this took place in was fresher than anything that her lungs had ever experienced, and she took in great breaths of it, half certain that it was providing her with some form of nourishment. The jungle was alive.

After a time, she turned to see what her companions were about, and suddenly realized that Skylaar was missing. Jeena, who was in the process of preparing their breakfast, noticed her consternation.

"What is it, Maya?"

"Where's Skylaar?" Maya had simply assumed that they would be travelling with her to the Fighting School.

"She left before sunrise. She is going out ahead of us," Jeena replied. "She said that she wanted to scout the trail in case we had anyone waiting for us along the way. But she'll catch up when we get closer to the school, maybe in a day or two."

Maya shrugged in acceptance. The trip had been estimated to take five days by the Green Road and this would mean that she and Jeena would be on their own (more or less) for two thirds of that time. Having watched him as he had travelled through the trees, she had no doubt that he would be a capable enough guide.

It was the possibility of a fight that concerned her. If it came to one, the odds were a lot better with two fighters and one non-combatant, rather than what she had; just herself and with Jeena to worry about.

She wasn't about to question her teacher's judgment though. Skylaar was a professional, and knew what she was doing. If it came down to it, she decided that she would just order Jeena to stay out of the way. He might have been a Fighting School graduate, but so far, she hadn't seen anything that indicated that he was of any use in a real battle. She would have to be the one to keep them both safe.

"Okay," she said. "Lead on."

Jeena grinned at her, almost as if he had heard her thoughts--and for some reason, found them quite amusing.

The further that they travelled from the Lodge, the more that Maya was able to push back all of her concerns, and her regrets, about what had happened on Thermadon. She didn't want to think about what Sarah had done to her, or might have done to her fellow citizens, and she definitely didn't want to worry about the Agency. Or Angelique, or anything at all about Felecia's betrayal. Instead, she simply concentrated on keeping up with her companion.

That, and marveling at his appearance. It was still hard for her to believe that he wasn't actually a woman. The illusion was so perfect that a part of her had trouble fully accepting the truth, and she had to remind herself constantly of what that was.

Of course, this had been the point, she realized. The Adam-16 generation of neomen had been specifically created to appeal to the aesthetics of the women of the Sisterhood. Anything more masculine than what she was seeing, would have been instantly rejected—just as the previous generations had been. He, and his kind, were the perfect solution.

She also couldn't deny the attraction that she had felt towards him since their first meeting, and had finally decided to stop trying. It was there, and it obviously wouldn't go away.

Any physical liaison was completely out of the question of course. She was definite on this point. Even though her exposure to the Sisterhood's mores was limited, she knew what the rules were, and she had every intention of following them.

This didn't banish her curiosity though. What would it be like, she finally allowed herself to wonder. For that matter, what *had* it been like, before the MARS Plague, when such an attraction would have been considered commonplace, and even acceptable? The 'vids she'd seen had explained the physical part well enough, but they hadn't managed to convey the emotional component at all.

She also wondered at how Sarah, with all her lofty ideals, would react to such a thing if she ever actually carried it out. She would probably burst a blood vessel, Maya concluded with a depreciative smirk. When it came to men, the woman was so straight-laced it was a wonder that she didn't strangle to death on her own conservatism.

Then a delicious, and extremely wicked idea, reared its ugly little head.

What if I just made her think that Jeena and I 'did it', she mused. The explosion would be spectacular—and it would serve Sarah right. She deserved a good hard shock after what she had done.

A darker notion immediately followed this and she almost rejected it out of hand. Almost.

What if I really did 'do it' with Jeena, she wondered. *What would Skylaar think? Would she even care? Would I? Should I?*

Motherthought clearly forbade this. The problem was, when she really examined the issue, it didn't take much soul searching for her to find her own position. She didn't give a spacer's damn about the Sisterhood, or its ideas. She never had, and it commanded even less respect now that she had seen what the mighty Sisterhood *really* was.

It was Sarah. It was Angelique, and it was the Agency. It was everything that she had rejected. And as far as she was concerned, all of them could take what was considered 'proper' and shove it up their pipes.

Inflamed by this train of thought, she made up her mind. She would get Sarah right where she lived. She would make her think the worst and deal her a blow that she would really feel.

How far things would go beyond that remained unresolved. As much as she hated the woman, and what she stood for, actually crossing the moral line, and not just pretending to, was something that gave her pause. Inwardly, and where no one else would ever be able to know it, she wasn't entirely certain what she would do if the opportunity actually arose. Jeena *was* undeniably attractive, but he *was* a male.

The whole thing was really damned confusing.

Blyavaald Famaalenplaatz, Vaalkenstaad Township, Zommerlaand, Sunna 3, Solara Elant, United Sisterhood of Suns, 1049.02|20|05:83:79

The exterior of Enggredsdaater's farmhouse told Kaly the entire story. The roof was desperately in need of repair, and the front had become completely overgrown. She quickly spotted the cause for all of this neglect; the maintenance 'bot, which normally took care of such details, was parked against the side of the house. Its service hatch was open and she spotted a large spider-web stretched across the port.

Clucking her tongue at the sight, she walked up to the door, noting the closed drapes across every window, and knocked tentatively. After a minute went by with no response, she tried again, more vigorously. There was no answer.

Then she went around the side, carefully stepping over the defunct 'bot to peer through a window. The interior was dark, but she was still able to pick out the silhouette of someone sitting on the couch in the living area. Her outline and size identified her immediately.

Kaly rapped on the glass. "Berta! It's me, Kaly! How about letting me in?"

425

For a few seconds, the woman remained where she was, but then she languidly turned towards the sound, and when Kaly kept it up, rose and went to the front door. The sound of it unlocking and opening brought Kaly back up to the stoop.

Enggredsdaater didn't smile or say a single word to her. She just turned around and went back inside, leaving the door open behind her.

Taking this as the only invitation that she was likely to receive, Kaly entered, pausing to let her eyes adjust to the poor lighting. She also needed a moment to acclimatize herself to the sour smell that permeated the house. It seemed to be coming from the general direction of the kitchen, although there were plenty of potential sources right in front of her.

The room was filled with piles of unwashed plates and many of these had the desiccated remains of half-eaten food on them. The table that Bertasdaater had sat herself in front of was just as cluttered, but with a small army of empty beer bottles. There was also a military-issue energy pistol lying there, but unlike everything else in the room around it, it seemed well cared for. Kaly was unsurprised. Berta was still a Marine, even if she had left active duty.

After enduring a long moment of silence, Kaly propped Tatiana in a reasonably clear corner and took a chair for herself. Enggredsdaater didn't object, or make any other comment. She didn't even ask Kaly why she was there. Instead, she simply opened another beer for herself, and handed one to Kaly.

Looking around her as she took a sip, Kaly found it easy to see why Bel Anny had been concerned enough to write. Mentally, Berta was in even worse shape than she was, she realized. She didn't ask her any questions though. Instead, she let the woman have her space, and shared the stillness with her. They would talk, later.

What remained of the afternoon went by, and when evening came around, Enggredsdaater rose quietly and shambled off to what Kaly presumed was her bed. Having received no invitation to do otherwise, she decided to make do with the now-vacant space on the couch, with nothing but the empty beer bottles for company. The pistol was gone though. Enggredsdaater had taken that with her.

A civilian might have been alarmed by this, or even by the simple presence of the weapon itself, but Kaly understood. Just before bedding down herself, she had brought Tatiana out from its corner and laid it down on the floor next to her. It was a habit that had crept its way into her life over the last few years, and had become increasingly important in recent months.

It didn't matter that she was on Zommerlaand, hundreds of light years away from the nearest potential source of danger. She had learned the hard way, just as her friend had, that nowhere in the galaxy was *truly* safe. Having Tatiana near enough to grab at a moment's notice lent her just enough reassurance to relax, and even sleep. But only for a while, and never deeply enough to miss something that might be coming for her.

Hunger supplied the courage that Kaly needed to venture into the kitchen the next morning. The source of the putrid smell proved to be some groceries that had gone bad on one of the counters. The rest of the space was just as filthy and neglected as she had expected it to be, and upon inspection, she discovered that the autochef was completely empty of soya matrix cartridges.

The only items that seemed well stocked were the alcohol, and several boxes of old Nutro bars. Neither of these were Kaly's idea of a proper breakfast though, and after she had rummaged around a little longer (disturbing a nest of mice that had made their home in one of the cupboards), she decided to make an expedition into town. A search for the keys to Enggredsdaater's hovertruck proved far shorter and much more fruitful than her hunt for food had been. Kaly found them on the counter, tucked in behind the rotted groceries.

An hour later, she had returned from shopping, and after refilling it with fresh cartridges, had actually managed to coerce the autochef into making two portions of chikka eggs and soya sausages. As she was dishing this out on a pair of well-scrubbed plates, Berta came into the kitchen, a beer already in hand. She stopped when she saw Kaly and blinked as if she had never encountered fresh food before.

"Breakfast," Kaly informed her. She shoved a plate and spork at her friend and when Enggredsdaater made no move towards it, her tone became as firm as a DI from Hella's World. "*Eat it*, Trooper."

Berta hesitated, but Kaly wasn't backing down. At 1.58 meters, she was hardly an imposing figure compared to Enggredsdaater's 2.011, but her resolute expression leveled the playing field. Enggredsdaater finally capitulated, and began to eat.

Later, and after Kaly had consumed her own meal, she left Berta to her own devices in the living area, and went out to inspect the broken housebot, along with the rest of the farm. She quickly discovered that everything was in the same sorry state as the house, and the fields were so overgrown that they looked as if they had never been cultivated in the first place.

Part of the reason was that one of the agribots had a blown motivator, another a fatal leak in its hydraulic lines, and the third seemed to possess a short circuit in its electronic guts. The irrigation system was equally as neglected; an examination of the system's diagnostic holo informed her that it had several broken pipes and an equal number of bad watering arrays.

This news didn't depress her as much as she had thought it would however. Instead, as she located the tools that she needed from the barn, and started in on the broken 'bots, she found the peace that she had been seeking for herself. For the first time in weeks, she was able to stop thinking about her past, her regrets, or even Lena. Focusing on the repairs proved to be a better medicine than all the drugs and therapy that her old Psych doctor had ever prescribed, and she threw herself into her tasks with a will.

She put in three days of solid labor before Enggredsdaater finally wandered out of the farmhouse, and joined her. Kaly had been in the process of attempting to remove a rusted water nozzle on the irrigation system, and hadn't been having much luck. The thing was stuck tight, and even the liberal application of some of her better Hriss curses didn't seem to be helping. She was just about to rise and get a tool with a better grip, when she registered the woman's presence, and nodded over her shoulder in greeting.

Naturally, Berta had her pistol on, just as Kaly had Tatiana propped up near her, but her hand was filled with one of her ubiquitous bottles. For a time, the Zommerlaandar just watched her work, and sipped at her drink. Then at last, she put the bottle down and walked over.

"Take a break," Enggredsdaater offered. "I'll give it a try. I zhink I can get zis bitch off."

More than happy to do so, Kaly gave her room, and wiped the grease from her hands. "Sure thing, Berta. Thanks."

It took a bit more effort, but Enggredsdaater finally won the battle and prised the thing loose. After that, installing the replacement was a simple affair, and Kaly was able to move on to her next task.

She fully expected her friend to leave her at every point in the process, but the woman remained, and they even talked a little. The conversation wasn't about anything sensitive, just what they needed to say to get the work done, and nothing else. Neither of them wanted to reopen any wounds, old or fresh.

The only exception occurred late that afternoon, and it was Enggredsdaater who brought the subject up. They were resting under the shade of a tree before going out to tackle a clogged pump unit.

"Zo, Kaly," she asked. "You left za RSE zen?"

Kaly frowned. "Yes."

"Vhy? You get tired of za food?"

Kaly shook her head grimly. "No. Not the food."

Enggredsdaater saw the shadows in her eyes, and didn't press for the details. "Yah, I left too," she said after a moment. "Vell—actually my legs left *me*, n'zen *I* left za Corps. Zey vent one vay, an I vent za other."

She laughed at her own black humor and Kaly was forced to join in. The reality behind the joke was simply too horrible to react any other way. Then they went back to work.

***

Skylaar had left markings for them on the trees all along their route, which Jeena interpreted for Maya. To her, they looked like nothing more than random scratches in the bark, and they closely resembled the claw marks of the saa'lak beasts that she had seen on their trip. Jeena knew them for the code they actually were though, and shared their message.

Skylaar was well, and had assured them that the path ahead was safe. So far at least, the Nemesian hadn't encountered any enemies. She had also advised them that she would be rendezvousing with them the next day.

Based on this information, they jointly agreed to travel as far as the next Nest, and end their day there. By doing so, they would meet Skylaar just in time to share the final camping spot together.

Hours later, when they finally reached their stopping point, they pooled their rations, and Jeena supplemented them with some of the local food that he had found. Maya still hadn't gotten used to 'pure' Nemesian cuisine, and Jeena made certain to cook what he had gathered. He even managed to make it seem appetizing.

Once their meal was over, they found themselves with some time to spare before sleep, and spent it talking. Despite their travels together, this was the first time that they had had the luxury of simply relaxing and getting to know one another a little better.

"So, what's it like?" Maya asked him.

"What is 'what' like?" Jeena returned.

"Being a man," she said.

He smiled. There was a twinkle in his eyes. "Just like being a woman. I'm me. I'm here."

"No, that's not what I mean," she said. "What's it like to be a man in the Sisterhood?"

His expression became more serious. "It's hard sometimes. I love the Sisterhood like the mother she is."

Maya caught his slight hesitation. "But?"

"But my mother doesn't love me. She loves her daughters instead. She would rather I had never been born."

Maya sobered. Intellectually, she had imagined that his situation was like this, but hearing it, and seeing the pain behind his smile was something

429

else again. He was an outcast, an outsider. Just like she was. Without thinking, she reached out and took his hand.

"I think I know what that's like," she offered. "I'm an orphan, and I grew up on Ashkele before I ever came to the Sisterhood. I never did fit in and I don't think that I ever will."

"Does that bother you?" he asked.

"Does it bother *you*?" she countered.

"It is what it is," he answered. "We can't help being what we are. Or where we came from."

They shared a long moment of thoughtful silence before Maya pressed on. She was tired of keeping all of her questions about him bottled up inside of herself.

"Jeena, I heard that neomen only---you know, 'do it'—with other neomen. Is that true?"

Taur K'aut'sha grinned. "Some do," he answered, without elaborating.

Damn it, she thought. *He knows where I'm going with this, and he wants me to draw myself out.* The neoman, she had learned, had a very dry, evil sense of humor. He was actually a bit of a bitch, and a lot savvier than he seemed.

"Have you ever done it with another neoman?" she asked. "Or—a woman?"

"A woman?" he said, his grin growing even wider. Clearly, he wasn't going to make this easy at all.

"Have you ever found any woman—you know—attractive?"

Jeena considered his answer carefully, looking all the more beautiful to her in the fading light, and suddenly, she wanted desperately to touch him.

Goddess, she thought. *I want him. I really DO want him. This isn't just a way of getting back at Sarah any longer!* She almost got up to leave then and there, but she couldn't move.

"A few," he admitted, looking straight into her eyes.

"Have you ever—" she hesitated. She couldn't finish the question.

"Yes," he answered. "Once. There *was* one woman."

"What was it like?" she asked.

"It was good," he replied. "Not like being with another man. It was just different."

"What was she like?" Maya inquired.

Somehow, they had come to sit closer to one another, and Maya's heart felt like it was about to pound its way right out of her chest.

Goddess, I'm really going through with this! she realized. The line that she had worried over, that Motherthought absolutely prohibited, was about to be crossed. Just like her initiation in N'Dayr Park when she had made her first kill, there would be no turning back once she took the final step.

"She was very much like you," Jeena replied softly, raising a hand to her cheek. When he made contact, Maya felt an electric surge of excitement course through her body.

Fek it, she decided. She was just as damned if she carried through with the act as she was if she merely pretended to do so. There was really nothing for her to lose. And she wanted him. Now.

She leaned in close, and he met her halfway. What few doubts she still had vanished completely with their kiss. Then they parted and began to undress, saying nothing to one another.

Jeena was the first to bare himself. As she finished with her own blouse and shorts, he watched her, regarding her with his inscrutable, and slightly sardonic smile.

Except for the 'vids she had watched, Maya had never seen a naked male before, and she took the sight of him in, trying to resolve what her eyes were telling her. Jeena was a dichotomy made flesh, and although she had expected as much, the reality still unnerved her.

From the waist up, he was as female as she was, and she even noted with a touch of annoyance that he was better endowed. She would have killed for breasts as full and as perfect as his were.

Then she gave herself the permission to look lower, at the source of all the concern and consternation that surrounded his kind. Like the rest of him, pictures were one thing, but seeing his difference right in front of her was another experience altogether. The ancient 'vid's and the dry, clinical diagrams hadn't quite done his organ justice, she decided, and she struggled to come up with an appropriate label for it. It looked, she finally decided— funny.

But certainly not 'dangerous' nor 'primitive' in any way. Just different. Tentatively, she reached out and touched his member with her finger. Just as quickly, she withdrew her hand with a loud gasp.

"I-It moved!" she exclaimed.

Jeena's eyes sparkled impishly. "It does that when someone touches it," he explained. "It will move a lot more, the more attention that it gets. It will even grow larger."

Maya reddened as his meaning became abundantly clear, and then she giggled. "Oh really?"

"I would certainly not lie about something as important as that," Jeena replied with mock seriousness. "But I'd rather not ask you to just take my word for it. I can *prove* it to you."

Of that, Maya had little doubt, but she still made him substantiate this claim. And after a time, she even helped him.

When it was over, and they were lying together in exhausted satisfaction, she looked at him, playing with his long hair and considering the entire experience. As she had suspected, it had been very much like what she had felt when Felecia and other partners she had slept with, had used the *strapaadi* together.

But not exactly the same; this time the object of her pleasure had been an intimate part of another being, a living thing. It hadn't been as spectacular as the artificial device, with its ability to broadcast pleasure straight to the brain, but she also hadn't expected that.

Instead, it had been spectacular in its own unique way. Somehow, it had been simpler, and at the same time, more complex and exciting for the fact that her partner had been directly involved in the process. She would never abandon sex with women, but now, an entirely new avenue of pleasure had opened up for her, and she was definitely interested in where it might lead. Her decision to cross the dreaded moral line, had been a good one.

"No regrets then?" Jeena asked.

She wondered again if he really was a psi, and reading her thoughts, but he didn't enlighten her. "No," she answered. "You?"

He shook his head. "Aren't you worried about what Sarah will say if she learns about this?" he asked.

"Sarah can go and get herself fekked," Maya responded.

"That's something I think I'll leave to someone else," Jeena returned and they both laughed.

Maya became serious again. "What about you? Aren't you worried about her?"

Jeena reached out and stroked her face. "Sarah doesn't concern me in the least."

Given Sarah's training and experience, Maya thought this was a rather foolish statement, but she didn't say so. Jeena was acting as if he was more than a match for her, if it came to it. And, she thought, maybe he was. There was definitely something about the neoman that he hadn't shared with her.

He gave her another one of his dry, amused smiles. "Let's not talk about her," he said. "I have something else that we should concentrate on."

He took her free hand and guided it downwards. She quickly discovered what he had been referring to, and promptly lost all interest in Sarah, or anything else for that matter.

Blyavaald Famaalenplaatz, Vaalkenstaad Township, Zommerlaand, Sunna 3, Solara Elant, United Sisterhood of Suns, 1049.02|24|02:53:91

The smell of cooking—real cooking—coming from the kitchen was the first indication to Kaly that her plans for the day were about to change drastically. The lack of beer bottles on the living area table was another, and the third was that Enggredsdaater was singing to herself. The drapes had also been thrown open, flooding the house with sunlight.

Curious, and hopeful, she wandered into the kitchen. "Heyas, Berta. Is that breakfast?" The counter was piled high with fried chikka eggs, thick slices of bacon, and even toast.

"Yah," Enggredsdaater told her. "Grab youzelf a plate."

As Kaly did so, Enggredsdaater told her what she had in mind. "I vas zinking of goin to vun of za local Zings. You maybe vant to come along? Zere fun, n'you don't have to do anyzing—just hang around."

"Things?" Kaly asked between mouthfuls. Berta had proven herself to be a half-way decent cook.

"Yah," Enggredsdaater replied. "Zort of a local tradition—folk ztuff, zat kind of zing—and zen a big meal aftervards."

Kaly considered all of her options. The agribots were up and running and most of the irrigation system was functional, with only the west field still requiring any attention—which from the look of the day outside was going to be hot work. Summer had arrived on Zommerlaand, and she had already learned that it would be twice as warm as it had been on her motherworld during the same season. Stacked up side-by-side against a local folk festival, with a home-cooked meal, the west field with all its sun, bother and sweat, could wait.

"Yeah," she agreed. "That sounds great, Berta!"

"Gaanz gaaf!" Enggredsdaater beamed. "You'll like Grammy. Zhe's good volk—but I gotta varn you about zomezing. Zhe's zort of a, vell a—*Vitkaa, a vise voman.*"

Kaly cocked her head querulously. She had heard of Zommerlaandar Wise Women, but nothing that she completely trusted. According to the tales, they were witches, and Kaly wasn't really certain if she believed in magic or not. Luck, certainly. Any good Marine knew that luck was real—and that good luck was just as important as anything else on the battlefield. It didn't matter if you had the best training and skills; if your luck left you, you were fekked. Like the women in the assault shuttle on Nuvo Bolivar, she reflected darkly. They had all been veterans and that hadn't saved them from the missile. Magical spells, however, were another matter.

Enggredsdaater read the doubt in her features. "Zere zort of, vell like a counzelor, and a 'paint zometimes and zometimes a prieztezz," she explained. "Vhatever—you come n'zee for yourzelf. Grammy and her friendz are okay."

433

Kaly scooped up a final bite with her spork and wiped her mouth. "So, do I dress up for this, or what?"

"Nen," Enggredsdaater said. "Just come like zat—zese are regular volk. Nozing fanzy."

Finishing breakfast, they left in Enggredsdaater's hovertruck. The trip was a short one, and when they finally arrived at Grunvaald, they entered the farmhouse through the kitchen door.

It was abustle with activity. Grammy's guests were just arriving, and depositing the food they had brought with them. Every spare hand had been pressed into service to find places to store it. Grammy's 'Things', Kaly discovered, were actually huge pot-luck affairs and everyone had come with something to contribute to the big meal.

Suddenly feeling very shy, Kaly quickly found a place for herself in the corner, and stayed there, out of the way, and she hoped, out of mind. Enggredsdaater, out of a sense of sisterly solidarity, sat with her, nodding to those that she knew, and explaining everything to her.

"Grammy hold zese Zings of herz every month," she told her, "and vomen come from all around. You'll meet a lot of good people---"

Then, out of deference to Kaly's introversion, she added, "—if you *vant* to."

Kaly just nodded, and watched the comings and goings of all the strangers around her without making any move to leave her seat.

At one point, someone that Kaly *did* recognize entered the kitchen, and they both did a slight double-take when they saw one another. What had initially thrown Kaly off was that Vice Admiral ben Jeni was in civilian clothing; a simple checkered shirt and jeans. Stripped of her uniform, and her starship, it had taken Kaly a moment to realize exactly who she was. And at the same time, a sudden feeling of guilt washed over her.

But she wasn't about to apologize to Lilith for leaving the Agency, she resolved. Or offer up any excuses. She had done what was right for her, and she wasn't accountable to *any* officer. She was a civilian now. Lilith worked for *her*.

For her part, Lilith seemed to be no less surprised at their meeting, but she was unruffled by Kaly's hard expression. She didn't challenge her or ask any questions. She simply refilled her teacup and left, silently acknowledging Kaly with nothing more than a small, half smile and a polite inclination of her head.

"I didn't know that *she* was here," Kaly said to Enggredsdaater.

"Who?"

"The Admiral—is she coming to the Thing--?"

"Ach, nen!" Enggredsdaater replied, waving off the possibility. "No, za Admiral is here because she's married to Grammy's daughter, Ingrit. Zey got Paired a few veeks back. But za Admiral's a real *vreestaande*—you know, an outzider. She doesn't go in for all zis. Doesn't believe in it."

"And Ingrit does?"

"Oh, yah," Enggredsdaater answered. "She's Grammy's zenior ztudent, and ven za time comes, she'll take over vor her."

Kaly raised an eyebrow, wondering at what kind of marriage *that* added up to.

Sensing exactly what she was thinking, Enggredsdaater added, "Zey don't fight over it. Ingrit knows vat she knows, and Lilith—za Admiral—letz her be. Bezides, Grammy thinks zat its good vor Ingrit to have a challenge to her beliefs. She sez zat it makes her zharper."

Kaly shook her head at this odd arrangement, and went back to watching things from the sideline.

She felt Grammy enter the room even before her eyes caught sight of the woman. Had she been pressed to, she wouldn't have been able to define exactly what had triggered this, but her experience as a sniper had taught her to honor the intuitions that sometimes preceded an important event. She looked up just as Grammy came through the doorway.

The old woman was dressed in the colorful apron that Enggredsdaater had described to her, covered with strange symbols that screamed of magic and mystery, but even without this, Kaly would have known her for the shaman that her friend said she was.

Her eyes were a bright pale violet that sparkled with a power and an intelligence that belied her advanced years. Meeting them, Kaly felt something akin to an electric shock, and she quickly looked away, hunching down in her chair.

Grammy made straight for her like one of the aerhawks that hunted in the fields outside. The old woman said nothing, but Kaly could sense her gaze. Then she felt her hand, gently cupping her chin, and she was forced to look up.

"Lena will always be with you," Grammy said.

Kaly's features went wide with shock. She hadn't told anyone, not even Enggredsdaater, about Lena. There was no way that Grammy could have known about her. Yet, she did.

"I see her," Grammy told her. "Standing right next to you. She wants you to know that she loves you."

Kaly's vision blurred with tears, and a choked sob escaped from her throat. She was ashamed, but equally helpless to stop herself. An instant later, her defenses collapsed completely and everything fell apart.

As she bawled her eyes out into Grammy's apron, the woman gathered her in, and gently stroked the back of her neck.

"There now, little one," the old woman whispered soothingly, "It's all right. It's all right. *Mihn gudinn*, such pain! Someone twice your age should not have witnessed so many terrible things!"

One of the other women came up and said something to Grammy, but she firmly shooed her away and stayed with Kaly instead, holding her and making comforting noises. Finally, Kaly raised her head and looked up at Grammy again.

"You know," Grammy said to her with a gentle smile. "You remind me of a little stray that I took in a few years back. He was starving and lonely. Just skin and bones. Zo, I fed him." She jerked her head towards an orange tabby who was sunning himself up on a nearby window sill. "Now look at him! He's as fat as a sausage and twice as spicy!"

The kaatze regarded them with a sassy, self-satisfied expression. He did look like a sausage, Kaly realized—a big furry one. This managed to coax the smile from her that Grammy had been hoping for.

"Now, my little stray, I have to go and do something with these women," she explained carefully. "You can come along with us if you want to, or you can just stay right here. Whatever you want. *Zat gaaf?*"

When she saw that Kaly was going to remain right where she was, she smiled again, and handed her a cup of tea. "Here now, drink this, it will help. Rest. It's okay."

Kaly sniffled her thanks, and took it from her. Then Grammy reached into her apron and brought out a cookie. "Have a cookie. A little sweetness goes a long ways towards curing life's bitterness," she said. Then with a gentle pat on her head, she left her.

Kaly remained in the kitchen until the Thing was done, and everyone had returned to the farmhouse for lunch. True to her word, Grammy didn't reproach her, or make any mention of her absence. Instead, she was simply invited to share in the meal.

When it was over, she left the farm with an open invitation from Grammy to come back any time that she wanted. It was the perfect way to make a stray like herself, feel comfortable, and safe.

CHAPTER 13

Maya and Jeena rendezvoused with Skylaar, and the trio arrived at the Fighting School late in the afternoon of their fifth day on the Green Road. Seeing it, Maya was wonderstruck by the ingenuity of the Pak'uns, and the incredible resourcefulness of the native women. Despite her unfortunate introduction to the planet, Nemesis, like Jeena himself, had managed to win her over.

They were met by a group of senior students, and shown to the docking tree that the School's Pak'uns used. An orientation meeting with the woman in charge of new admissions had already been scheduled, right along with another one with Jezzika taur K'aut'sha, the Headmistress of the Fighting School herself. Although Maya was tired from their long trip, her eagerness to meet the famous swordsmistress and begin her training, reinvigorated her as she climbed up to the platform.

But when the main Pak'un drew close enough for her to make out the features of the women standing at its railings, her enthusiasm, and her smile, died together. Sarah was there.

Their eyes met as the huge floating craft moored itself, and Maya made sure to put all of the distaste that she could muster into the look she gave her.

Sarah seemed completely unaffected by this however, and stepped forwards to greet them. "Good," she said crisply. "The three of you are finally here."

Maya decided that the time had come for her to exact her revenge. Making certain that Sarah was still looking her way, she reached over, took Jeena's hand, and faced her squarely.

Sarah gasped at the sight, and stumbled backwards, a horrified expression on her face.

Maya's lips twisted into a cold smile of triumph. "That's right, Sarah. I fekked him. *Him*. And I *liked* it!"

Her words hit the woman like physical blows. Sarah moaned and fell to her knees, and Skylaar went to her, trying to lift her back to her feet. But she batted her hand away with a loud cry, and began to weep miserably. Undeterred, the Nemesian tried again, and this time, Sarah allowed herself to be raised up, and led away.

They were almost out of earshot before she collapsed again and Skylaar crouched down at her side and spoke quietly to her. Only a part of their conversation managed to reach Maya's ears over the wind, but what she heard filled her with grim satisfaction.

"She's ruined herself," she heard Sarah wail. "Ruined!"

Maya wanted to laugh out loud. She'd gotten her right where she lived.

"Remind me never to get on your bad side," Jeena remarked.

"She *deserved* it," Maya hissed. "For what she did to me, she deserved it. Every little fekking nanobit."

By this point, Skylaar had persuaded Sarah to stand again, and patiently guided her around the corner of the Pak'un and out of view. When she returned alone a few minutes later, she addressed Maya. Her expression was stern.

"You have done Sarah a grave disservice," she told her.

"She's a traitor," Maya growled. "I can't do anything to her that she doesn't deserve. Fek her!"

"No," Skylaar corrected. "She is *not* a traitor. If anything, she is more of a patriot than either you or I could ever aspire to be, and she has sacrificed far more than you can imagine."

Maya's expression remained defiant, but she didn't rebut her. Although she disagreed with Skylaar's assertion, she respected her too much to argue.

"Do you think it's time to awaken her?" Jeena interjected. He was speaking to Skylaar.

The Nemesian considered this for a moment, and then answered. "Yes, I suppose it is. Angelique may not have guessed her true allegiance yet, but she soon will. Lady Ananzi wanted it to go on for a bit longer, but I think that she would agree that we no longer need to keep up with our little charade."

"What charade?" Maya asked, now completely mystified. Skylaar only shrugged, and Jeena kept his reply short, and just as enigmatic.

"You'll know soon enough," he told her. Then to Skylaar, "Shall we?"

Without any further explanation, they left her there.

***

Jeena knelt down by Sarah's side. They were inside of one of the Pak'un's many living areas, and the woman was lying on a sleeping mat, wrapped in a blanket. She was still weeping.

"Sarah," the neoman began. "It is time for you to wake up. For the last time, just as Lady Ananzi promised."

Sarah turned over abruptly, her eyes alight with fury. "What are you talking about? Get out of here you piece of Neo filth! You're the cause of all this!"

"No," he replied gently. "I will *not* leave, and I need you to listen to something. It goes like this, *'I have slept in the arms of twilight...'*"

"What is this nonsense?" Sarah demanded. She started to rise, but Skylaar held her down as Jeena continued to recite the Nyxian poem.

As they had fully expected, halfway through it, Sarah ceased her struggles, and laid back on the mat, becoming utterly still.

Finally, Jeena completed the poem and Sarah blinked. Suddenly, all of the anger that had been directed at him disappeared completely. A radiant smile came over her face, and she sat up and embraced them both.

"Oh my friends!" she exclaimed. "Thank you! Can you ever forgive me for the way I must have acted?"

"Of course, sister," Jeena answered softly. "It is our job as your friends to forgive you. Now, we need your help. We have much to tell you, and important work to do."

"Anything!" Sarah exclaimed.

***

Nemesis proved to be a unique experience for Jon on several levels. He had heard of the jungle planet of course, and had even experienced a realie or two, but he had never been there in person before. The sheer 'greenness' of the world was almost overwhelming to his senses, and the vast expanses of unbroken and carefully preserved wilderness astounded him. Especially after his recent confinement in Thermadon.

These were not the only surprises that the Mother Forest had in store for him however. The reaction of the Nemesian women to his presence was just as astonishing.

When the *JUDI* landed in a small clearing, and they had been met by a hoverlifter piloted by two of the natives, Jon had expected the same hostile expressions that he received everywhere else in the Sisterhood. And the same abuse.

This was not what happened however. The Nemesian women had just looked at him from head to toe, sniffed the air briefly, and then gone about their business as if a neoman was merely another part of their landscape. There were no unfriendly looks, no insults, and no emotions coming from them that indicated that they felt any prejudice against his kind whatsoever. At the very worst, they just considered him to be another *hwa'ni'tem*, an outsider, just like his companions.

But that was all. Clearly, Nemesis didn't share in its nation's collective madness when it came to males. Which suited him just fine. His thoughts were filled with his upcoming meeting with Maya, and the choices that he

439

would have to make when they were face-to-face at last. Having to deal with mindless prejudice on top of this, would have been too much to deal with.

While their hosts concentrated on piloting the flying machine, Jon took advantage of his acceptance, and his privacy, to think about what the angel had told him on A'latar.

A life for many lives, he reflected, *or many lives for one.* As he had so many times since that strange encounter, he prayed for strength and insight, and when he finished, he tried to relax and take in the jungle as it whipped by underneath them.

There would be time enough for more soul searching when they arrived at their destination. For now, he just wanted to take a few minutes to enjoy the ride, and the chance to exist as nothing more spectacular than a man, living in a world that didn't think anything of it.

***

While Jon's 'lifter neared the Fighting School and prepared to dock, Maya stood balanced on the toes of her left foot, nine meters above the ground, and atop a wooden pole barely wide enough to accommodate her.

Her right foot rested lightly on her kneecap and the prosthetic tail that she wore helped her to maintain her balance, adjusting itself to compensate for the tiny changes in her center of gravity. This left her free to concentrate on the placement of her hands on her sword hilt.

When she had first learned the *Spinning Flower* maneuver, the pose that she was holding had been difficult to master, or to maintain for any length of time, and she had begun on the ground. Now, she could perform it atop one of the highest practice poles, and needed only a few centimeters of flat surface to assure herself a firm footing.

Slowly and with great precision, she lowered her hips and spun, cutting in the direction of her turn and then bringing the weapon back up to the ready position even as she traded feet. Mistress Jezzika had insisted that her students practice every technique using both sides of their body, and the *Spinning Flower* was no exception to this rule.

"How do you know that you will always have the use of your right side?" the woman had asked them. *"If this is injured, you may have to use your left. Practice until you are equally proficient with both."*

Maya had taken this, and all of Mistress Jezzika's teachings to heart—especially since she had once been Skylaar's teacher. Not that this fact had lent her any special privileges. If anything, Mistress Jezzika had been even harder on her than all the other students, and more critical.

Even so, Maya did not allow herself to resent this. No matter how gruffly the censure was made, when she took the time to think it over, Jezzika always proved correct.

Today, her weak spot was in how she held her spine, and she had been at it all morning, trying to keep it straight instead of letting it bend. In the process, she had discovered that the more erect her posture, the less that she felt the prosthetic tail having to work to help her, and the smoother her movement was. A new student might not have noticed the flaws in her technique, or discerned the tiny changes that she was making, but she could, and she intended to stay at it until it was time to break for lunch.

She began the drill anew, and this time, closed her eyes, ignoring the instinctive panic response as her body reminded her of the height, and her precarious position.

Instead, she concentrated on feeling her movement and changing it whenever she detected an imperfection. She was so intent on this that she almost didn't hear the voice that called up to her. It was one of the senior students.

"You have a visitor, Maya," the woman informed her. "She is waiting for you in the Mistresses' Pak'un. She's with Mistress Jezzika right now."

Maya immediately sheathed her sword and used the metal claws of her prosthetics to scramble down the pole as nimbly as any native born woman. They had taken some getting used to, but now she worked with them as if they had always been a part of her. Which in a sense they were. She and the microcomputers in her aids had become fully synced with one another in the weeks since her arrival on the jungle world.

Jezzika's Pak'un was waiting for her at the docking tree, and she wasted no time climbing up to it and stepping aboard. She was met by the Mistress herself.

Despite having studied with her, Maya still found her presence just as intimidating as it had been on the first day they had met. Jezzika taur K'aut'sha was taller than most of her kinswomen, but like many of them, she followed the practice of adopting a personal appearance that surprised and shocked the viewer. Nemesians, Maya had learned, took a perverse delight in choosing attributes that highlighted their fierce, aboriginal culture.

In Skylaar's case, she had managed this by dying her hair a dark blue, and Jezzika had done it by shaving half her skull, and then adding an utterly archaic patch to cover over an eye that she had lost in a fight. The technology to replace the missing eye certainly existed, but Jezzika preferred this primitive solution, and had learned to compensate for her limited vision. This, along with the innumerable scars that she also allowed to remain on her body, lent her a wild and dangerous look—which was well supported by her legendary prowess with the ka'na.

"You called for me, Mistress?" Maya asked.

Taciturn and stoic as a rule, Jezzika merely inclined her head and started off, not bothering to see if she was following or not. Not that Maya would have dared to loiter; she knew that she was being shown extraordinary courtesy just by being acknowledged by the woman at all. Disobedience was out of the question.

They stopped at the door of Jezzika's sleeping chamber, and there, to Maya's complete surprise, the Swordsmistress stepped aside and waved her in without following. She was being left alone to meet with whoever her mysterious visitor was, in private.

Expecting Sarah, or Skylaar, or even Lady Ananzi, Maya stepped into the room ready to utter a tart rejoinder, or offer a respectful greeting. When she realized who the figure actually was, she was struck dumb with shock.

It was Josette bel Thana, every centimeter as lovely as her evil older sister. She was sitting cross-legged on the woven floor mat and smiled serenely up at her as if their encounter was nothing remarkable at all.

Reflexively, Maya attempted to embrace her symbiote--and failed. As a condition of her training, access to it had been shut off by Skylaar the day that she had arrived at the Fighting School. Mistress Jezzika strictly forbade the use of augmentations of any kind by her students.

Cursing this prohibition, and the fact that Josette had a perfectly functional implant, Maya drew her sword, following through with an immediate slash at her opponent's neck. If nothing else, she was either going to go down fighting, or sever the woman's pretty little head from her perfect body before she could seize the advantage.

Her ka'na met with nothing but empty air however. This wasn't because Josette had used her symbiote. Instead, she had employed a far more prosaic tactic to evade the cut, throwing herself into a flawless backwards roll and nimbly returning to her feet. Laughing at Maya's astonishment, she counterattacked immediately, slashing at her shins.

To her credit, Maya responded quickly; throwing her arms forward and sliding her feet backwards in one fluid motion. Josette's blade missed its mark, and Maya began to pitch herself into a forward roll, hoping to pass her and come up from behind for another strike.

Bel Thana was faster though, and far more adept. Even as Maya began to move by her, Josette was pivoting on her foot and pirouetting. It was an impeccable execution of the *Spinning Flower* maneuver, and as she completed it, the hilt of her weapon struck Maya neatly on the top of her skull.

Maya cried out in pain and stumbled forwards, suffering the additional indignity of receiving a swat on her bottom from the flat of Josette's sword.

Despite the stars in her vision, she still had enough presence of mind to pitch herself sideways as she hit the floor. Then she scrambled to her feet. What she didn't expect was Josette's fist waiting for her, or the impact that it made with the bridge of her nose.

The blow sent her reeling backwards, and she windmilled to keep her balance, absolutely certain that she was about to die, and equally determined to recover somehow. If nothing else, she intended to make sure that the bitch would have to work for her victory.

Josette did not press her advantage however, nor did she engage her symbiote and make the fight between them unwinnable. Instead, she took a short step back and expertly re-sheathed her sword, giving Maya the chance to regain her footing.

"I must admit that you do have a certain amount of aptitude, Maya," she stated. "Still rather rough around the edges, but impressive nonetheless. I think a few more lessons with Mistress Jezzika should polish that up nicely though. Now, can we talk? I have some things that you definitely need to hear."

Maya remained right where she was, and cautiously wiped away the blood streaming out of her battered nose. She also didn't let go of her sword, or return it to its scabbard. This woman was not to be trusted.

"Keep your sword then," Josette said airily. "If it will help to make you a better listener, I'm all for it."

She gestured elegantly towards the mat. "Please Maya. Sit with me, and enjoy some tea."

Maya did not accept the invitation, certain that it was some kind of evil trick. It was only when Skylaar entered the chamber, accompanied by Mistress Jezzika, that she finally decided that Josette had not come to kill her after all. She also found herself reluctantly acknowledging the woman's skill with the ka'na. Clearly, Josette bel Thana was a master swordswoman, easily on par with Skylaar, if not her superior.

"I see that you started without me, Josette" Skylaar observed drolly, taking in Maya's disheveled appearance. "You could have waited and spared her a fight."

"I wanted us to become properly acquainted," Josette answered. "Besides, she *is* here to learn, and every opportunity to train is a precious thing, is it not? Surely, she derived *some* benefit from our practice session."

Maya glared at her, and Josette smiled in amusement as she reached into one of the pockets of her bodysuit and offered her a silk handkerchief. When the young woman made no move to take it, Josette laughed and

443

tossed it to her feet. Only a nod from Skylaar convinced her to bend down and retrieve it—and she still rewarded its former owner with a murderous expression. However skilled she was, Josette was still a bitch, just like her sisters.

Presently, a senior student entered the room, bearing a tea set and six cups which she set down on the mat. As she departed, Josette, and the others took their places around the pot, and then Jezzika began serving out the tea. It took another signal from Skylaar before Maya reluctantly joined them.

Clearly unaffected by Maya's mood, Josette brought her teacup up to her lips, and took a careful, delicate sip. "Mmm,' she purred, "truly wonderful. I have missed the taste of a Chasadan as fine as this. Really, I should visit my *alma mater* far more often."

"Indeed," Jezzika replied. "We sorely miss your instruction, Mistress Josette. The students would benefit greatly from any time that you would care to spare for them. Perhaps you would consider holding a small seminar while you are with us?"

"Of course," Josette replied, toasting her. "It is the very least that I can do for my teacher."

For the first time ever, Maya actually saw a smile break across Mistress Jezzika's features. It was almost as unnerving as Josette's presence.

This was not to be her only surprise of the day. The next came when an additional guest joined them. It was Jon fa'Teela. She recognized the neoman from his file, and he gave her a look that was pregnant with meaning.

She looked away from him to Skylaar, puzzled. *What is he doing here?* she thought to her.

The Galactic Mind requested his presence and Lady Ananzi sent him, the Nemesian responded. *He has some business that involves us. I am sorry, I was going to tell you about him before this.*

Even as she was digesting this, Maya was subjected to another bombshell. Sarah entered the room, accompanied by Jeena.

Not only did she appear to be completely comfortable with the neoman, but she seemed to be wholly unconcerned by Fa'Teela's presence—a man whom she had once sworn to murder with her own hands.

She was also smiling. It was not her normal predatory leer, but something filled with genuine warmth. And her features had softened somehow, making her seem almost like another person altogether.

Her appearance was just as startling. Sarah had always worn her hair long and parted in the center, which had lent her a severe look. Now, it was parted to the side and done up in a long braid. She had also forgone her usual black fighting suit, and donned a loose pair of baggy training pants and a pink tank top.

Sarah was wearing *pink!*

She was also holding Jeena's hand, just as comfortably and as casually as if they were the closest of siblings. Clearly, something of truly universe-shattering proportions had occurred here.

"Good of you to join us," Josette said. "Please, have some tea."

As they took their places, Maya shot Skylaar another puzzled look. This was *not* the Sarah that she knew. Sarah *hated* all males, and she had always held Jeena in a special kind of contempt.

And Jeena had never indicated that things were otherwise. Had she not seen all this with her own eyes, she never would have believed it.

"As I told you, Maya,' Skylaar said aloud, "You have done Sarah a grave disservice."

Maya didn't know how to respond, and Skylaar elaborated. "Sarah was recruited many years ago by a special branch of the OAE. We all were. It was established to deal with exactly the kind of threat that our nation is now facing. That threat calls itself the Conversâzi."

"To help fight them, Sarah volunteered to take part in a deep cover operation, and Lady Ananzi imprinted her personality to make her become the woman that you know. She accomplished this by using a combination of hypnosis, certain drugs, and her own latent talents.'

"It was absolutely necessary for her to do this. To penetrate our opposition as far as she did, Sarah had to believe in her role completely, even in her dreams. Now, she is awake again, and fully restored to us."

"And we would have kept her false persona in play just a bit longer," Josette said. "But we didn't count on the chaos that you are capable of creating."

Maya finally found her tongue. "M-me?!"

"Yes," Josette affirmed. "*You.* Had you kept your anger in check and exerted some semblance of self-control, there is no telling how much further Sarah might have managed to get. As it was, that little *scene* that you started in the train station compelled us to alter our plans.'

"I think you are being much too hard on her, Josette," Sarah countered. "The situation was a dynamic one, and many factors could have forced our hand. In all probability, you would have been compelled to awaken me sooner, rather than later, especially in the light of recent developments."

"Perhaps," Josette replied, glaring censoriously at Maya. "Perhaps not."

"Whatever the case might or might not be," Skylaar interjected, "It is all part of the past now, and we must move forwards. I am certain that

Maya has many questions, and I think that this conversation would be better served by allowing her the opportunity to ask them."

Maya nodded gratefully to her. "Yeah, I do have a few things I'm wondering about. First off, let me see if I understand what you're telling me. You're Sarah, but you're not Sarah? Right?"

"In a manner of speaking, yes," Sarah answered.

"And what about your warnings to stay away from the 'Big Bad Neoman'? Were they also some kind of con job?"

"That is correct, Maya. They were. I have never hated males," Sarah stated, rewarding Jon and Jeena with a warm smile. "The woman that I was conditioned to be did, and so do the women that she was assigned to infiltrate.'

"Personally, I believe that neomen are simply the next step in the healing process that began when the MARS Plague burned itself out. In time, they will become full members of our Sisterhood, and then Motherthought will be relegated to the waste can of history, where it belongs."

Maya shook her head, unable to believe what she was hearing. It was just *too* weird to accept.

Josette laughed scornfully, earning her a searing look. "Oh Maya," she said, "didn't you learn *anything* about deep-cover operations during your training?'

"To be truly effective, an agent must play whatever role that they choose for themselves, flawlessly. And when their opponents are all espers the only way to accomplish this is for the agent to utterly believe that they *are* who they say they *are*."

Maya's perplexed expression elicited even more laughter from her. "Did you *really* think that Sarah would willingly allow a *neoman* to replace you? Or simply acquiesce to Captain bel Lissa's refusal to dismiss him?"

In fact, Maya had, but she wasn't about to admit it. Not to Josette, and certainly not in front of Sarah.

"As a Colonel, Sarah could have had the Agency order him off the ship at any time, and Bel Lissa wouldn't have been able to do a thing about it," Josette told her. "She didn't do so because her conditioning wouldn't allow her to. We needed Jeena in place, and the Sarah that you knew really had no choice in the matter. She has been under the spell of Lady Ananzi since well before you first met her. Really, you have no idea who she truly is, or what she has given up on our behalf."

"Fine," Maya conceded. "I don't. Whatever. Now Sarah—the big question; are you a neoman?" Everyone laughed at that, especially Sarah.

"No, Maya, "she answered. "Just a realist, and a long-time friend of Jeena's. I only hope that he will forgive me for my poor behavior."

"Of course," Jeena said, patting her hand affectionately. "You only did what you had to."

"Great," Maya said. "That's all that then. We're all just one big, happy spy-family." Inwardly, she was anything but overjoyed. If Sarah didn't care about men as she claimed, then she had just been robbed of her chance at revenge. It just wasn't *fair!*

She glared at Sarah. "That still doesn't explain why you kicked me down to the Metros, or what this big shell game is for. While we're at it—why *is* Josette here? And who is this 'Conversâzi'?"

"Before we provide you with the answers to that," Jezzika said. "You'll probably want some of this." She produced a small flask and poured some of its contents into Maya's teacup. Even before she took her first tentative sip, Maya knew it was some kind of strong alcohol.

"Drink up," Josette invited. "When we're done with you, you'll need all the fortification that you can get."

Maya drained her cup and impertinently held it out to be refilled. Jezzika promptly obliged her with another portion, and this, more than anything, frightened her out of her wits. Whatever this was all about, it was just as deadly serious as Josette was implying.

"First, the Conversâzi," Josette began. "They are a humble little collection of right-wing fanatics, led by my sister, Angelique. Their aim, at least as far as the rank and file are concerned, has been to overthrow our government and destroy what still remains of our democracy. As a step in that direction, Chairwoman bel Rayna was assassinated, and N'Calysher was chosen by the Conversâzi to succeed her"

The look of bewilderment on Maya's face was so blatant that it earned her more mocking laughter. "Yes, that's right Maya—*assassinated*—by my sister, with a poison that made her death seem natural. But Layna n'Calysher has no idea that her term of office will be a short one. The moment that the time seems right, my sister intends to murder her as well, and have her daughter replace her as a figurehead Chairwoman. And if the girl is foolish enough to become a problem, then you can rest assured that the Lady Felecia will find her own resting place in the graveyard, right alongside her mother."

All the blood drained out of Maya's face. She still felt anger towards Felecia for her betrayal, but she didn't hate her enough to want her dead. And dead she would be if Angelique considered her to be an impediment to her goals.

"I see that you grasp Angelique's true nature," Josette observed. "If the Lady Felecia fails to please Angelique, she *will* be eliminated. Felecia n'Calysher thinks of herself as a member of the Conversâzi, and she

447

ardently supports their aims, but she has no idea how ruthless my sister actually is, nor just how numbered her days might be.'

"Which brings me to the reason for my presence. The answer is simple enough; I know and fear my sister. My sibling, Silvi, refuses to accept that Angelique is as dangerous as she is. But I know that when Angelique achieves her aims, she won't think twice about removing anyone that she perceives to be a threat, family or no.'

"She did that very thing to my older sister, Odette. When Odette became an impediment to her becoming CEO of the Luxar Lines, she met with an unfortunate 'accident'. Nothing that can be proven of course, but Odette's death had Angelique's biosignature all over it. I have no intention of meeting the same fate.'

"It is sad to say, but this is nothing new for us. We Bel Thana's have always been this way, or should I say, we *Borgias?* Blood is no impediment to murder for us, and never has been. So, I suppose that I joined Phantasma not out of patriotism, but out of a desire for self-preservation. As I see it, my sister *must* be stopped in order to afford me the pleasure of enjoying my old age."

This much, Maya could respect, and she saluted the woman's pragmatism with her cup. They were not as dissimilar as she had first imagined, and either the strong drink, or Josette's stark honesty were beginning to win her over. It also didn't hurt that the woman was as good with a sword as she was. There was even the vague possibility that they would eventually become friends. Once Josette dropped her high and mighty attitude, of course.

"Okay," she said. "Now I know all about the Conversâzi, and your fekking bitch of a sister. So what? It sounds like they got what they wanted, or they will, soon enough."

Josette waved her conclusions into irrelevance. "Not by a light-year, my dear Maya. Angelique is not content with simply taking over the Sisterhood. She has much grander designs in mind. These involve the very things that you have been dreaming about. You *have* been having odd little visions about the Necropolis on Ashkele, have you *not?*"

The question made Maya drop her teacup. "W-what do you know about that?"

Josette grinned. "Oh Maya," she said. "Your dossier indicated that you were dense, but I must admit that I had entertained my doubts! Now I can see that the agent who compiled it wasn't exaggerating in the least'

"Did you *really* think that your dreams were private? Lady Ananzi has been eavesdropping on them since the first day that you became her student. Would you like to see the recordings that she compiled? They really do make lovely viewing."

Maya shook her head. She didn't want to see her visions replayed. She'd been tortured enough by them as it was.

Sarah interrupted. "I have to disagree with all this. This process must not be interfered with. We should stop right here and let things take their natural course."

"And *again*, I have to insist otherwise," Skylaar countered. "Maya deserves to know what kind of danger she is in, and what she can expect."

Maya interrupted them. "What *danger*? And what about my dreams? They're just silly nightmares!"

"They are not just 'silly nightmares' Maya," Skylaar told her, "nor unimportant. Far from it in fact. You are at much greater risk than you might imagine. We all are. That is why I asked Josette to come here and help us to explain to you what is happening, and the part that you are fated to play."

"The part that I'm *fated* to play?" Maya demanded. The situation, which had seemed merely klaxxy to begin with, was now becoming positively warpy.

Jezzika retrieved her abandoned cup and refilled it to the brim. The younger woman drank it down like it was so much water, and not the straight Aqqa that it actually was.

"Yes, Maya. *Fated*," Josette answered. "Or 'chosen' if you prefer, by the Galaxy Mind. The implications are the same." She looked over to Skylaar, who produced a small armored case, which she set down on the mat.

When the Nemesian palmed the bio-scanner on its face, the container opened to reveal a metallic sphere, roughly the size of a clenched fist. Peering closely at it, Maya saw that it was formed by a series of irregular bands, and everywhere, its surface was marred by deep pitting and scratches, suggesting great age and hard conditions.

"Do you know what this is?" Skylaar asked her.

Maya shook her head. "Nope. Not a clue."

"It is a recording device, and it is over 20,000 years old. We do not know who made it, but we do know that there are only three of these devices in the entire Galaxy. We have one, Angelique possesses another, and the third is owned by Queen Talaria of the Seevaans."

Skylaar waved her hand over the object, and the bands spun apart to reveal a hollow interior. An oily mist rose out of this, filling the air above it with an inky darkness that was the very antithesis of all light.

Then a shimmering magenta glow appeared within the blackness, and Maya saw images beginning to form. Their perspective was twisted, and oddly flattened, and portions of them faded in and out of view. Other parts were only half-visible, suggesting that there were elements to the picture that existed in a band of light beyond human vision. Despite these flaws however, there was still a great deal that was plain enough.

A cloudy, unknown planet basked in the light of a trinary star system, and a fleet of ships hovered menacingly above it. Their design was wholly unlike anything that the Sisterhood, or any of the other races of the Far Arm employed, but just from their formation, it was obvious that they were warships of some kind.

Another image came into being alongside this a half-second later. It was just as strangely distorted as the first, and what it depicted made Maya gasp as it came into focus. She knew the place, and the great crystalline Tree that resided at its heart, all too well.

Great goddess, she thought. *It's real!* This revelation terrified her down to her core, but she couldn't turn her gaze away.

Whatever was recording the event panned downwards, and Maya was not surprised when it stopped at the shallow pool at the base of the Tree. A trio of beings that were neither reptilian, mammalian, insectoid, nor anything she could readily identify, were there, linking appendages.

One of them went into the pool until its form was completely covered over, and the scene depicting the alien fleet changed dramatically. The planet below it shattered into a billion pieces, and the armada was broken apart by the debris.

The triple suns were the next to fall prey to whatever was causing all of this destruction. They swelled to hundreds of times their original size and then burst like so much overripe fruit. When the gigantic nova finally died away, nothing remained except an irregular cloud of expanding gas and bits of melted rock.

At this, the entire sequence began to repeat itself and Skylaar allowed one more cycle to occur before she passed her hand over the sphere. The images vanished, and the device closed.

Maya looked up from the artifact to meet Skylaar's eyes.

"Very few sentient beings are aware of the true significance of the Drow'voi ruins," the Nemesian said. "Most xenoarcheologists believe that they are much like any other remnant of an extinct society, with living spaces, industrial complexes, houses of worship and so on.'

"They are also wrong. The 'Necropolis' on Ashkele was never a graveyard, or even a city in any sense that we would understand."

"What is it then?" Maya asked, afraid to hear the answer.

"A vast network of machines, "Josette replied, "based on a technology that we can only dimly comprehend."

Suddenly, bits and pieces of Maya's dreams came together, uniting with snatches of intuition that until now, she had either ignored or discarded as pure nonsense. She knew exactly what the machines were, and what they could do. Her dreams had shown her.

"It's more than that," she finally said hesitantly. "It's not a weapon—not exactly--."

"But it *can* be, "Skylaar said, completing her statement. "One of unimaginable power. Compared to it, all of our starships and nova bombs are mere toys. Any race that possesses the Tree has the capability of ruling the entire galaxy."

"Anyone?"

"Anyone who has control over the Three," Jezzika elaborated, "and especially the User. Once the Tree has been unlocked, her companions are expendable, but she is not. From then on, she can operate the Tree all by herself."

This hadn't been an element of her dreams. With the exception of the Drow'voi and her mysterious human 'guide', Maya had always been alone, and she hadn't met anything that referred to itself as the Galaxy Mind.

"The Three?" she asked, "you lost me with that and whatever this Galaxy-Mind-what's-it' is"

"Very well. I will explain it slowly enough for you to understand," Josette replied, leaning forwards for emphasis.

"You see, Maya, the galaxy is not just a collection of mindless stars and so much interstellar gas. It is in fact, a sentient being, whose 'cells' if you will, are made up by all the living creatures that inhabit it, and it's consciousness is the amalgamation of every mind that exists within its boundaries. The best analogy would be to compare it to ourselves. Every cell in our bodies is alive, and every cell makes us who we are. It is the same thing, but on a much vaster scale'

"The Seevaans know all this of course, and they simply 'neglected' to inform us. Or to tell us about the most important part; for reasons that only the Galaxy Mind understands, every one thousand years it chooses a single race, and among them, three individuals. It communicates its will to the chosen Three through the agency of dreams and visions."

"Well that's effective," Maya returned acerbically. So far, all her dreams had managed to do was confuse her, and rob her of a lot of sleep.

"It is much more reliable than you might imagine," Josette corrected. "These dreams are utterly irresistible—as you well know. The chosen candidates who receive them ultimately have no options about obeying their mandate, or fulfilling their specific roles."

Hearing that she didn't have a choice in the matter at all made Maya angry, and she began to mouth an objection. Then she felt Jezzika taur K'aut'sha's restraining hand on her shoulder, and accepted another drink instead. She would have her say, she promised herself, once this lecture was over, and provided that she wasn't too drunk.

"Once they have been given their mission," Josette continued, "the Three eventually unite, and make their way to the Tree. Once there, they unlock the device. Each one of them has a special role to play, similar to the basic process of accessing and using a computer; the mere presence of the Guide causes the Tree to leave its dormant state. She is the 'on' function, if you will, made flesh. She also has valuable knowledge of the Tree's basic operation.'

"The Singer provides the basic access code. Once this password has been received, the User is the one who actually operates the device and gives it its commands."

"So it takes three, huh?" Maya asked. "What if one of these *Three* decides she's had enough of all this *shess* and just says no?" The question was more than merely academic. It was exactly what she was thinking of doing.

"The results are not terribly positive," Josette warned. "If any member of the Three fails to rendezvous with the others, or like you said, refuses their role, the Galaxy Mind simply passes the mission on to another race, and another trio. In such a case—and there have been a few—it often turns out to be a disaster for the original group, and their entire species."

"Um, define 'disaster'," Maya asked cautiously.

"If the new race is inimical to the previous one, the end product can, and sometimes has been, genocide," the other woman answered soberly. "Imagine for example, if we refused. Then imagine a Hriss trio assuming the role, or even a T'lakskalan one.'

"Given the recording you just watched, that is not an option that I would care to see becoming reality. Oh, and by the way, Maya, just in case you haven't already guessed—*we* are the current race that has custody of the Tree. Does this answer your question?"

It did. All too well. Whether she wanted to or not, Maya knew that she had to go along with this madness. Whoever or whatever this Galaxy Mind was, it was definitely on her short list now, and when she got the chance, she intended to let it know just what she thought of it in the most colorful language that she could summon up.

Josette went on. "Now, here is the most interesting part, and the feature which attracted my sister's attention. As the recording amply demonstrates, once it has been unlocked, the Tree can grant virtually unlimited power to the User, and project it at an indefinite range, instantly. *Anything* that the User can visualize literally *becomes* reality. If they so desire it, they can wish an entire species into extinction, which is exactly what the Drow'voi did to themselves."

"The whole thing sounds like Zommie witchcraft to me," Maya opined.

"Indeed," Skylaar agreed. "It might seem that way to you. The Tree is unlike anything that we know of. It has no recognizable components, no apparent power source, and according to the Pa'lla, it is composed of some form of organic crystalline substance that even *they* cannot identify. Yet it is there, and capable of doing amazing things that are beyond our current technological understanding.'

"We can however place it in a context that makes it seem a little less fantastic. As you are aware, our symbiotes can influence time, and the Seevaans are able to use them to affect physical matter. The Tree is the mother of all these devices, and with much greater reach. It can influence reality *itself*.'

"It is, if you will pardon me, the very embodiment of the idea that the great visionary Arthur C. Clarke once suggested; a technology that is so highly advanced that it seems like sorcery to a less developed society like our own. I assure you however, there is nothing supernatural whatsoever about it, or what it can do."

"Wait, don't you mean *Arwen* C. Clarke?" Maya asked, a little nonplussed by the reference. Arwen C. Clarke was one of the great female authors of the pre-Sisterhood era. Everyone knew that.

"No, Maya," Sarah informed her. "She doesn't. There is a great deal about history that you are not aware of. That is a conversation best left for another time however." She inclined her head to Josette, who picked up the narrative from there.

"Given the immense power of this machine," Josette said, 'you can imagine that there have been many cases of considerable pressure being brought to bear upon the Three, and especially the User.'

"There are even instances where the Three were assassinated by rival factions before the device could be turned against them. This is why, for the most part, the Tree's existence, and the candidates who are selected, have been kept a carefully guarded secret. It is also the reason behind the name that my sister chose for it. She refers to it as the Secret. Unimaginative, I know, but descriptive nonetheless."

Keeping this quiet made perfect sense, Maya thought. She just hoped that no one knew about her 'involvement' outside of this room. If she was one of the Three as these women believed she was, then she had a huge target tattooed on her ass, and any number of beings, Angelique included, would want to tag it.

What didn't add up was what had happened to the Drow'voi. Ordinarily, she didn't give a spacer's damn about them, but suddenly their disappearance had assumed a new, and frightening relevance.

453

"Okay, question time," she announced, holding up her hand. "The Drow'voi. You said that they used this Tree-thingy to blow themselves up. Why do that? I think that's kind of an important thing to know. Were they just klaxxy? Or is there something wrong with this Tree?"

"No," Skylaar answered. "They were far more lucid than we are at our best moments. Thanks to the Pa'lla, we know exactly what happened, and it's another facet of this affair that the Seevaans didn't reveal.'

"You see, our galaxy is not the only one that is sentient. All galaxies are aware, living creatures, and like us, the Galaxy Minds do not always get along with one another. Apparently, the galaxy that we call 'Andromeda' hates our galaxy for some unknown reason, and has for countless millennia."

"Rather like we women," Josette interposed. "Don't you think?" Maya certainly couldn't disagree.

Skylaar went on. "About twenty thousand years ago, *'Ms. Andromeda'* apparently decided to become more aggressive, and she sent some of her children to attack our galaxy, and everyone in it. The Drow'voi referred to them as the Enemy, and since then, the name has taken hold.'

"This Enemy is quite unique, Maya. Instead of possessing bodies, they are life forms of pure thought, with the ability to possess the minds and bodies of whatever host they choose to attack.'

"The Enemy literally thought themselves here, spanning the intergalactic distance instantly, and once they had done so, they quickly infected the Drow'voi, managing to turn them against one another. To prevent the possibility of a civil war, and the spread of the Enemy's influence to other races, the Drow'voi chose to turn the Tree against themselves."

Maya raised her hand again. "It sounded like you just said that this Enemy is still around,' she observed. "Did I get that right?"

"You did at that," Skylaar said, "They very definitely are. Although the Drow'voi's mass suicide weakened the Enemy considerably, they did not manage to eliminate it altogether. It survived the event, and simply assumed a dormant state. Now, according to a number of sources, including the Pa'lla, the Enemy has reawakened, and covets the Tree for itself."

Maya's mental image of a bull's-eye suddenly grew much larger. "So the Three are also in danger from being possessed by this Enemy? Or killed?"

Skylaar shook her head. "Killed? Perhaps. But not controlled—and don't ask me why, because even the Pa'lla can't adequately answer that question. For whatever reason, the Three are immune to possession by the Enemy, possibly due to some agency being brought to bear by the Galaxy

Mind. There is another danger that is just as grave however. This is the creation by the Enemy of their own Trio."

"Wait a fekking *nano*! " Maya exclaimed. "I thought that you just said that only the Galaxy Mind chooses the candidates."

"We did," Josette responded. "And it does. Thanks to its interaction with the Drow'voi however, the Enemy knows all about the Tree, and how it functions. The Tree also has one important flaw that factors into this equation. *Any* trio with even a hint of Drow'voi genes in their DNA can bypass all of the safeguards and take control."

Maya relaxed slightly. "You call *that* a risk? The Drow'voi are extinct! *Everybody* knows that."

"It *is* a risk," Sarah insisted. "A very real one. What 'everybody' doesn't know is that there is another Drow'voi complex on a world called Storm, in the Sagana Elant. It too is a machine, and it has remnants of Drow'voi genes stored inside of it. Somehow, it possesses the ability to merge these samples with the DNA of other races, and creates a hybrid being. The process is not perfect, and many of the subjects die, but some *do* manage to survive.'

"We know this because a Sisterhood research team blundered into the device. Most of the women in the group were killed, but one of their number not only lived, she came away as a human-Drow'voi mix. Until recently, we had Dr. Shandra n'Aida under observation at the Odyne Naval Medical Center, on Thermadon. But she awoke from her coma, murdered her caretakers, and disappeared. It is highly likely that she was infected by the Enemy."

"Oh *lovely*," Maya retorted sourly. "There's more too, isn't there?"

"There is," Josette said, clearly amused by her discomfiture. "As you know from watching over Sarah's shoulder during your apprenticeship, the Marionites were involved in experiments with rarified genetic samples. They used them to eventually create their so-called Redeemer. The samples for that came from Dr. n'Aida herself. It seems that someone, who was involved in her rescue, had something to do with that."

For some reason, Josette looked straight at Jon fa'Teela when she said this, and winked mischievously. In response, the neoman's complexion reddened and he immediately broke off eye contact.

It was patently obvious that Josette suspected that Jon had been this mysterious 'someone', and by his reaction, the neoman had just confirmed it.

Maya also didn't care. She was too overwhelmed by the greater implications of what she had just heard.

"If they made the Redeemer from N'Aida's DNA," she began, "then that makes him—"

"--part Drow'voi himself," Josette finished, "and if he and Dr. n'Aida have both been infected by the Enemy as we suspect, then the Enemy already has two of the Three that they require to seize control of the Tree.'

"If they find their Third, then it is a virtual certainty that they will use the Tree to renew their war against every living being in our galaxy. Their aim will not be victory, but annihilation"

A hard light came into Maya's eyes. "Then we need to find them and kill them. And make sure that no one gets to that machine on Storm."

"That is one thing that Angelique *has* done right," Josette conceded. "She tasked a Conversâzi ship to secretly patrol the system, and has operatives on station in Thenti. They have already interdicted several Marionite groups trying to reach Storm, and dealt with them, with extreme prejudice."

"Well, that's something," Maya replied. "Next question—a big one. Why us? Why give *anyone* this kind of power?"

Josette laughed dryly. "The theories about that are almost as numerous as there are races in the galaxy, Maya. The most plausible one that I have heard is that it is some form of evolutionary testing. According to the Pa'lla theorist who conceived it, the Galaxy Mind may be doing this in order to determine what direction a race will need to take to reach a state of permanent perfection."

"By fekking with them," Maya grimaced. "Isn't this Galaxy Mind just a little worried that the User might decide to blow everything up? Including it, and its stupid Tree?"

"Not in the least," Josette answered. "While the Tree is virtually limitless in its powers, it is prevented by its programming from certain actions, including destroying the Galaxy Mind, or itself. Believe me, that very thing has been tried in the past, and to no avail."

"I see," Maya replied. "Next big question. Who am I, and who are the other two women?"

"We don't know that for certain," Josette answered. "We only know that you are involved. What we are certain of, is who the Singer is. In fact, she is quite famous, perhaps the most renowned musician in the Sisterhood."

"Celina," Maya guessed.

"The same," Josette said, "and precisely because of her musical gift. We know this because the Drow'voi communicated through pure sound, and the closest analogue that we have to their language is music, and mathematics, which are at their heart, one in the same.'

"As your dreams have already indicated, the Tree operates through a special song. Celina was given this melody by the Galaxy Mind itself. Which is why, when the Seevaans visited her studio and heard her play it, they forbade her from ever publishing it. It is simply too dangerous to have floating around in general circulation."

"Why?" Maya asked. "You said that only the Three can use the Tree. What good is the Song all by itself?"

"It is worthless—at least as far as the Tree is concerned, "Josette stated. "For that to operate, the entire trio must be present, and only the Singer can use it."

"Okay…" Maya replied, impatiently motioning the woman to explain herself.

"They had other concerns. The mere fact that we have the Song in our possession was one. Some races, such as the Greys, could see this as a justification for a preemptive war, and the Seevaans believed that by suppressing the Song, they could prevent that. Unfortunately, Trina discovered it, and in trying to sell it, alerted everyone in the Far Arm.'

"This was one of the reasons why Angelique murdered her, and her Xee contact. She was angry about the damage that Trina had caused, and determined to bring the situation back under control. She also had personal motives as well, but those are not relevant to this discussion."

Maya glanced over at Sarah as Josette told her this, and she thought that she detected the faintest tightening around the woman's eyes. But then it was gone, and she wasn't even certain that she had seen it. Trina had meant something to the other Sarah, she told herself. Not to the woman she was sitting next to. She hoped.

Josette had more to say. "The Seevaans were also worried about the hazard that a public disclosure posed to the Three themselves. If the Singer were identified through her Song, and kidnapped, there was the possibility that an enemy would use her to coerce the other two into doing whatever they wanted. But Angelique made certain that a protective detail was on hand to keep an eye on her, and so far, this has been successful. And just in case you are wondering, we did the same thing."

"Well, that's one point for Angelique," Maya said. It felt weird giving the woman credit for doing anything good.

"Indeed," Josette agreed. "The Seevaans had one more thing that they were worried about. The Song itself. Even without the Tree, it threatens their monopoly."

"Monopoly?' Maya asked. "On what? Bug juice?"

Josette laughed. "Oh Maya, I didn't realize how little you understand about the galaxy and its economy. Really, you should read more material on this subject. Money, politics, and war all go hand in bloody hand.'

"The Song contains enough elements within its structure to enable a clever species to decipher key command strings, and allow them to control other Drow'voi devices. At the moment, the Seevaans are the only ones who understand the Drow'voi programming language, albeit incompletely, and they want to keep things that way. What they are unaware of is that in addition to attempting to secure the Tree for herself, Angelique has also tasked the RSE's computers with decompiling the Song. Her ambitions are rather wide-ranging."

"Yeah, "Maya grimaced. "So, now what?"

"Now, we wait," Skylaar said. "Celina is already in Ashkele, thanks to some coercion by Angelique. As for you, you are still having your dreams, but you haven't felt the need to go and join her, and whoever the last woman is, has yet to reveal herself.'

"Trust us in this Maya, you will know the time, and when it comes, we will go along with you to make certain that no one, and nothing, harms you, or your companions. After that, the whole thing will be up to the three of you."

"I think that this would be a good time to have our lunch," Jezzika suggested. "We could all use a break."

Maya wasn't the least bit hungry, but she was eager for the chance to air her head out, and quickly assented. When everyone rose from their places, she was the first one out of the room. Jon followed her.

"Do you think we should tell Maya about the Seevaan war games?" Skylaar asked, once they had gone. This had been an oft-discussed issue among them, and still remained unresolved.

"No, let us leave things exactly as they are," Josette suggested. "She has enough on her mind without worrying over the added possibility of an interstellar war. I also believe that Jon should be kept ignorant as well. Given his current state of mind, there is no telling how he might respond."

"Yes", Jezzika agreed. "We should also pray that when the time comes, Maya will use her power wisely."

Like the others, the swordsmistress was fully aware of the one small lie that they had slipped in with the truth. Although they had been honest with Maya about their lack of information concerning the identity of the third woman, they *did* know what her role was.

And what Maya's task would be. She wouldn't realize it herself until the time came, but she was not the Guide, and she was certainly not the Singer. She was, based on everything that they had gleaned from her dreams, the User herself. And at this precise moment in history, that made

Maya n'Kaaryn the most important woman in the Sisterhood, if not the entire galaxy.

Grunvaald Haarmaaneplaatz, Vaalkenstaad Twnship, Zommerlaand, Sunna 3, Solara Elant, United Sisterhood of Suns, 1049.03|03|04:78:78

Kaly's next visit to the farm was for another 'Thing' and once again, she ensconced herself in the kitchen. Eventually though, curiosity and her growing sense of peace and security persuaded her to venture outside. She had the vague idea of finding the women and watching them, for a little while at least, and seeing what they were doing. By now she had become convinced that whatever it was, was safe.

Except for the children playing in it, the front yard was empty. Then over the sighing of the wind, she heard the chanting of many voices, rising and falling from somewhere in the trees nearby. She followed the sound until she came to a clearing.

Most of Grammy's guests were there, arranged in a large circle and the old woman stood in its center with the Vice Admiral's wife. The women around them were moving in unison, extending their arms and bending at the waist to touch the tops of their feet. At the same time, they were uttering a single, unintelligible word; "UUUuuurrraaazzz!"

It wasn't Standard, or even any of the Zommerlaandartal that Kaly knew. It seemed to be more like a proto-language, a pre-verbal means of communication that these tongues, and many others, owed their birth to. The sound of the chant seemed to resonate all around her, penetrating everything, including herself. She could feel it in her very bones.

As she watched, and tried to understand what was going on, the women rose again, and extended their arms towards Grammy and Ingrit. The two of them stood there with their hands held upwards towards the sky. After a moment, they copied the gesture of the others, and then turned together on their heels towards the east.

The air around the clearing seemed to grow pregnant with energy, reminding Kaly of the feeling that came moments before a summer storm was about to break. The sky overhead was clear though. This was something else altogether. Afraid to move and somehow break the spell, Kaly stayed were she was, waiting to see what would happen next.

They remained silent for a few heartbeats, and then in unison, the two women let out a long, loud chant of their own. Their voices were strong and clear and their united cry was just as unintelligible to Kaly's ears as the rest, but equally as powerful and purposeful.

"FFfffaaaaa!"

459

Something seemed to radiate from within them, and as it moved out over the meadow itself, its passage was signaled by a momentary shimmering in the air. Whatever they had just done, Kaly had felt it, and she knew with equal certainty, that their work was now complete.

The circle of women relaxed, confirming this, but they didn't leave their places. Clearly something else was in the offing, and Kaly realized that this was only a pause in the mysterious proceedings. She took advantage of the lull and found herself a seat next to Enggredsdaater on a nearby log.

Her friend was not the only bystander. The Vice Admiral herself was also there, seated on a neighboring log, and they exchanged a polite nod of acknowledgement.

Kaly leaned in to whisper in Enggredsdaater's ear. "What did they just do?" she asked her.

"Zey gazered power for za Vize one and her azziztant," Enggredsdaater answered, just as quietly. "Zey took it from zem and zen zey zent it out for zose who needed za healing. Next, zey'll work on zending on zome good luck."

Kaly shook her head, not quite comprehending this. "How?"

"Zat's zomzing zat I'll leave vor her to explain," Enggredsdaater replied, inclining her head towards Grammy. "I'm no *Vitkaa*. I just know a few zings."

The ritual went on, with more of the strange movements and incomprehensible chanting, and soon Kaly began to feel drowsy. Despite the unfamiliarity of her setting, the sun was warm and pleasant, and a feeling of tranquility seemed to fill the clearing.

At last, she gave in, and let her eyes close, enjoying the sensation of just being at rest. A state that was somewhere between true sleep and wakefulness soon overtook her. She let the sensation carry her away, and eventually, she dreamed.

She was back on the beach that she had seen so often. Lena was there, as always, waiting for her with her smile, although this time, they were not alone.

Grammy stood nearby, and she gave Kaly a welcoming grin. There were also others on the beach, she realized.

None of them were as distinct as Grammy or Lena were, and she only caught fleeting glimpses of them, but these were enough for her to recognize who they were; one was the ghostly image of Marisol, her fellow sniper with the Garda on Treya Angelaz, another was the terrorist girl that she had killed in Nuvo Bolivar.

And there were more besides. They were far less distinct, and floated at the farthest edges of her perception. These were friends and family who had been killed on Persephone by the Hriss, and even enemies that she had slain in the name of duty. The beach, she realized, was a place populated by the dead.

"Why am I seeing them?" she asked Grammy.

"You have unfinished business," the old woman answered. "With every one of them, but most of all, with her." She was looking straight at Lena. "Every life that we cross paths with leaves a debt, an obligation. I think that you know what I mean. I also think you know what you will need to do."

Kaly thought that she did, and she shook her head emphatically. "I can't do that. I'm not ready to let her go. I need her."

"I understand," Grammy responded with a trace of sadness. "It's not time for that—yet"

Then she disappeared, and with her, all the other ghosts. Kaly was alone with Lena, and for a time, they lay on the warm sands together.

While Lena stroked her forehead, she began to hum a melody, and a feeling of absolute contentment filled Kaly. The song was soothing, and strangely familiar, but as she tried to place it, a deep lethargy overcame her. At last, too tired to try any further, she gave up, and simply listened.

"This song is very important, Kaly," Lena told her. "You'll have to protect the ones who sing it."

Kaly acknowledged this sleepily, and as she drifted off, her last thought, was of how utterly happy she was.

She could still feel Lena's touch as her eyes fluttered open. The sun had lowered in the sky and Grammy and Ingrit were standing in front of her. Behind them, the other women were filing down the trail towards the farmhouse.

I must have fallen asleep! she thought, sitting up in alarm and flushing scarlet with embarrassment. She almost started to tell the old woman about her vision, but then she stopped herself. It was obviously just a fantasy, and not worth bothering Grammy about.

Secretly, she was also afraid that if she mentioned it, that something just as shocking as their meeting in the kitchen might occur and she wasn't ready for any more epiphanies. So she kept silent, and smiled shyly.

Grammy had a gleam in her eye that seemed to suggest that she knew exactly what had happened to her, but she only returned Kaly's smile. "*Komme*," she said. "The meal will be starting. If we don't hurry, they'll eat it all up without us!"

K'aut'sha Fighting School, Sorrow's Swale, Nemesis, Rahdwa System, Thalestris Elant, United Sisterhood of Suns, 1049.03|04|04:16:07

461

All of the mid-level students had arranged themselves around Mistress Jezzika to watch as the Swordsmistress demonstrated a complex maneuver with her ka'na. She called it the *Flock of Flying Birds*. After the mind blowing revelations that she had experienced the night before, Maya wanted a chance to gain some perspective on it all. Training with her ka'na was the perfect recipe for this, and in short order, she became totally immersed in Jezzika's lesson. So much so, that she almost didn't notice when a group of senior students walked over to join them.

Sarah was among them, and once again she managed to astonish Maya. Today, she had dressed herself in a brilliant red training suit which was richly decorated with elegant golden dragons. It was totally at odds with her former penchant for somber, purely functional garments.

Jeena was accompanying her, and as they moved along, Sarah kept pausing and whispering into his ear with a wide grin on her face. Whatever she was saying made the neoman laugh, and he replied with something just as amusing, and as secretive. They were carrying on just like a pair of teenagers, Maya thought, feeling an equal measure of disapproval and disbelief at the sight.

Several meters short of the training circle, Sarah paused in mid-stride, closing her eyes and throwing her arms wide. The expression on her face was total bliss.

Even though Maya knew that the protective layer on Sarah's pale skin and a liberal coating of *Solacrème* was protecting her from the harsh Nemesian sun, she still couldn't believe the obvious pleasure that the woman was deriving from basking in it.

Sarah *hated* the sun! Or rather—Maya corrected herself--the *old* Sarah *had* hated it. This new Sarah was a complete enigma, and she found herself wondering what other drastic changes were in store for her.

A moment later, Sarah finished with her reverie and walked into the circle to face Mistress Jezzika. While they bowed to one another, Maya turned to Skylaar. "Sena-tai, can she still fight?" So far, Sarah hadn't demonstrated anything that even hinted at her former lethality.

Skylaar chuckled at this and inclined her head towards the pair. "I think I'll let Sarah answer that question herself, *Cho-sena*. But I would venture to say that she just might manage to satisfy your exacting standards."

Maya blushed abashedly, but still decided to reserve her judgment.

The demonstration began. At first, Sarah and her teacher moved slowly, each of them going through a portion of the *Flying Bird* kata. Then their movements became faster, and more complex, and Maya recognized not only the elements of the *Bird* kata, but several other routines that they had been studying earlier that week. She took careful note of their technique, and tried to spot the errors in her own.

Then to Maya's mild suprize, Mistress Jezzika stepped back, and took her place with the others, leaving Sarah all by herself.

Sarah had closed her eyes again, and she performed the first elementary drills that every student learned, transitioning from one to the next with a beautiful, fluid grace. She went on from there, moving up through the secondary levels, and then the third, and here, her actions became more of a dance than a series of exercises.

An aura of expectation began to permeate the women around her, and it seemed to fill the very air itself. Something great was happening, and as Maya watched, it was revealed.

By this point, Sarah had reached the advanced levels of training. She turned in the sun, spun, and made her cuts with a refinement that beggared anything that Maya had ever seen, even when Felecia had danced. It was an achingly beautiful performance, but without music, because it needed no accompaniment. It was its own music.

All the while, Sarah's smile brightened until it became a thing of absolute radiance. The pure joy that flowed from her was tangible, and an involuntary lump formed in Maya's throat as the woman transitioned to the movements that Mistress Jezzika had been showing them that very week. With an effortless grace, she raised herself and pirouetted on a single toe, rendering the most flawless *Spinning Flower* that Maya had ever envisioned. It was even better than the one Josette had used.

Then, without the slightest pause, she flowed into a masterful rendition of the *Wind on The Mountain*, then *The Endless River*, and from there into kata's that Maya hadn't even learned about.

Totally enthralled by this performance, she forgot all her doubts about Sarah's ability, and even her antipathy towards her. Instead, she was overcome by the sheer mastery of her movements, and began to perceive her in an entirely new light.

Relieved of the spell Lady Ananzi had put on her, Sarah was not only more skilled with the ka'na than Maya had ever supposed, but also extremely lovely. Her beauty had simply been obscured by all the darkness that had once surrounded her. But now, like a *fyrflit* emerging from its cocoon to take wing in the Nemesian sky, she had become something truly magnificent.

Finally, after what seemed like an eternity, Sarah's movements slowed, then stilled, and when she had stopped completely, she reopened her eyes and looked around her as if she had suddenly realized that she wasn't alone. Her features were bright with elation.

Josette was the first to applaud, and the rest, Maya included, quickly joined in. "Oh, *Hiy'em Ska'n'e*," Josette declared. "It is so good to have you back with us!" She went over and embraced her, followed by Mistress Jezzika.

As they stood by, Skylaar quietly explained the term to Maya. "*Chosena, Hiy'em Ska'n'e* is a Nemesian name. It means 'Joyful Blade'. That was Sarah's school name before Lady Ananzi sent her into her long sleep. Rather appropriate, given her true spirit, wouldn't you agree?"

Maya wiped away a tear, and nodded. Skylaar had been completely correct; Sarah had indeed managed to 'satisfy' her standards.

***

Later, after the class had ended, Sarah came looking for her. She found her on the walkway that encircled the main *Pak'un*, leaning against the railing and staring out at the jungle.

"Maya," she began, "I wanted to have the opportunity to speak with you. If you will let me."

Old, unpleasant memories, and feelings, resurfaced immediately, and Maya gave her a guarded look. "About?"

"The reasons behind my actions," Sarah answered.

"It's fine," Maya lied, the hurt shining brightly in her eyes. "It was all that stuff that Lady Ananzi did to you. I get it."

"No, Maya, it's not fine," Sarah insisted. "I still did it, and you have the right to know why. Now that I've had the chance to speak with Skylaar and Josette, I understand what I did, and the motives behind it. It was all part of the plan. I did not do any of it out of maliciousness."

"Yes, of course," Maya returned sharply. At last, all of her unresolved anger took over and she rounded on her. "You threw me away, Sarah! You threw me away like I was trash."

"No, Maya" Sarah replied. "It was the only way that I could keep you safe—even if I didn't realize that I was doing it. If I hadn't sent you to the Metros, Angelique would have eventually killed you—or realized how important you were and locked you away."

"Then why didn't you just send me off on the *JUDI*?" Maya demanded. "That would have done it."

"Because the *JUDI* wasn't safe," Sarah answered patiently. "With the kind of missions that she flies, anything could have happened to you out there, and no one would have been the wiser. But with Signysdaater and the whole Department to keep watch, nothing could have occurred that Skylaar and Josette wouldn't have known about. It really was the only way. And Angelique had to believe that I had rejected you. She had to be convinced that you were nothing worth noticing."

"It still hurt," Maya said with a small, wounded voice.

464

"I know," Sarah replied. "For what it is worth, I am deeply sorry for the pain that I caused you. The person that I was treated you terribly. I can only hope that now, with my imprinting suspended, that you will find it in your heart to understand, and forgive me."

Maya couldn't reply. She wasn't sure that she was ready to. One thing that she was certain of however, was that this 'new' Sarah was much weirder than the Galaxy Mind or some bodiless Enemy. Those, she could eventually get used to. Adapting to a kinder, gentler Sarah n'Jan, would take a lot more time. So would forgiveness.

Several minutes after this, Jon approached her. She was leaning against the rail of the Pak'un, with her back to him, and seemed to be unaware of his presence. He stopped in mid-stride, and as he struggled with his emotions and tried to formulate what he wanted to say to her, his hand came to rest on the needlegun in his pocket.

He had been given the weapon by Lady Ananzi herself, just before being sent away from Thermadon. To protect himself.

Now, it took on an entirely new and twisted significance. He certainly *could* use it to protect himself. From the future.

You could do it. You could use this gun and end all this right now, a voice from the darkest corners of his soul suggested. *You could save yourself and raise the Church on high.*

He even saw himself in his mind's eye, committing the deed; walking right up to her and shooting her in the back of the head before she even realized that she was in danger. And then the terrible image of her lifeless body, tumbling over the rail to the jungle below, where he knew the predators would consume it, and conceal his crime forever. From everyone, except God, and his own conscience.

She would not be the only one to die, either. The Angel had assured him of that much. Millions of innocents would also perish in the interstellar war that would follow Maya's death. Even though the deed would serve his Church, the blood would still be on his hands. No surer path to Hell had ever existed for any mortal.

Utterly disgusted with himself, he let go of the weapon. He would not become a murderer just to avoid his fate. One life instead of a multitude, given willingly to God, and free from any taint of sin, was a reasonable price for any true believer to pay. It was the only way. It was *his* way and it always had been.

With tears welling up in his eyes, he looked up through the jungle canopy to the stars. "Father, I accept the cup," he whispered, "Forgive me for even trying to refuse it."

Sighing raggedly, he returned his gaze to Maya. His fate was sealed, but the state of her soul was still sorely in doubt. As his first step on the path that the Lord had chosen for him, he knew that he had to convince her, a non-believer if he had ever met one, to find the true path to salvation, and follow God's will when the time came for her to stand before the Tree.

Summoning up all of his strength, he addressed her. "Maya, may I speak with you please?"

She turned around. Her expression was hostile. "No," she said flatly. "I want to be alone."

"Maya," he insisted. "We need to talk about this Tree and what you're going to do with it. Please, it's important. You have been given a great responsibility."

"What is this?" she spat, "My *fekking* life parade? Who's next? Laara Lampa coming to tell me to be a good little girl? *Go away.*"

But Jon didn't leave. "Maya, I wanted to council you. I need you to think about what's coming and make the righteous choice."

"Not interested," she said.

"Maya, you don't understand—"he began to say.

Abruptly, she rounded on him. "Hey, *Neo*. Light on the scripture, hold the proverbs! I'll do what I do, when I do it. Got that? So save the Marionite shess for someone who's interested. I just want to get this over with."

"Maya, this is serious. You don't understand what's at stake here. Your eternal soul is—"

"Hey!" Maya snapped. "I *understand*. It's my problem. Now, *git* gone. I need some time alone."

Jon hesitated, but in the end, he simply accepted his defeat, and walked away.

Skylaar watched him go from the shadows, and when she was certain that he wouldn't return, she holstered her needlegun. Unlike the one that Lady Ananzi had gifted him with, hers actually worked.

Thankfully though, the danger was past. Jon had clearly made his choice, and she could tell from his aura, and the set of his shoulders, that he had resigned himself to the situation. He would no longer be a threat, either to Maya, or their plans.

She was not the only one watching the exchange though. A third party, dressed in a shimmering green robe, and invisible to human eyes, was also present. It was very pleased with how things had turned out. Jon's Church would have their martyr, and the galaxy would have its peace—for a time at least.

All in all, it had been a very good night, it decided. Especially for those trillions of souls who would never even know that their lives had just been spared.

CHAPTER 14

Concordance Park, Thermadon Val, Thermadon, Myrene System,
Thalestris Elant, United Sisterhood of Suns, 1049.03|05|03:43:33

The Port Police cruiser came in high over the Federal Plaza, and when it reached the center, just short of Concordance Hall, and in sight of the Golden Pyramid, it lost altitude until it was only 304 meters from the ground and assumed a hover. Because of its police transponder code, no challenge was issued for being in an otherwise restricted flight-zone.

Inside the vehicle, the two neomen, dressed in their stolen police uniforms looked down at the scene before them, and then they clasped hands.

" Blessed be Jesu and Mari's Names" the driver said.

His partner smiled at him, and as he repeated these words, the driver hit the special switch that had been added to the dash...

...Deena t'Barbara swore as an aircar below and in front of her, rose and cut her off. She was late for work, and sorely tempted to ascend into the freeflight lanes, but she had received too many traffic citations as it was. The moment that she entered the 'lanes, she knew that Thermadon's traffic control system would spot her vehicle's transponder code, and match it with the Judge's order to confine herself to the normal flightlanes for the next 90 days.

If that occurred, it would not only mean that she would earn herself another citation, but probably have her license suspended as well. Which was something that she couldn't afford to have happen. *It isn't fair,* she thought, taking another hurried sip of her kaafra.

Here she was, a successful businesswoman, with places to go and people to see, and despite this, the Judge still held a few minor offenses against her. She accelerated, careful not to exceed the downtown speed limits, and managed to pass the other aircar.

Then she cut *her* off.

"How do you like that, bitch?" she exulted. Her feeling of triumph was interrupted as her eye caught something going on over the Federal Plaza. It looked like a police cruiser. She had just enough time to gasp in horror at what happened next...

...Teeri n'Tarra was ecstatic. Her Star Scout troop had come from Mars on a field trip to the Capitol. Now here she was, walking up the steps of Concordance Hall itself! She'd heard all about it in school, but being in the presence of the historic building was something else again. It seemed even more imposing to her than any virtual image of it. She now knew what her primary teacher had meant when she had called it 'living history in marble.'

Smiling at the Marine honor guard standing at attention, she unconsciously neatened her black Scout kerchief. *I'm going to be a Marine like them someday,* she thought. She might have only been ten, but she knew what she wanted for her future.

Suddenly one, and then the other Marine, looked up at the sky behind her. Teeri turned to see what it was…

…Kaara n'Bella had been a gardener most of her adult life, and she knew when to let the 'bots be, and when to become directly involved. As well programmed and intelligent as they were, they lacked a creative eye when it came to sculpting the hedges. N'Bella considered herself to be an artist, and the landscape in and around the Golden Pyramid was her canvas.

Bending over to clip a few stray branches from the bush in front of her, she didn't notice the aircar stop overhead, or notice it dropping. A moment later, the heat on the back of her neck rose, but she tried to ignore it. She'd spent a lifetime in the sun, and wasn't about to allow a little extra solar radiation distract her from her work. Then the sensation became impossible to ignore…

…Chairwoman Layna n'Calysher sat behind her desk in the Apex Office and regarded the document floating in the air before her. It was an executive order that she had wanted to sign ever since taking power. Now, Angelique and the Conversâzi had agreed that the time had come.

The order called for the forced relocation of all Marionites from their motherworlds to other planets throughout the Sisterhood. Once she approved it, they would be scattered, and divided past the point of offering any organized resistance. After that, the RSE could concentrate on each group, one at a time, and eliminate the troublemakers.

Especially the neomen. Although they weren't a direct threat, they symbolized everything that N'Calysher and any right-thinking woman wanted to see purged from the universe. With them gone, the Sisterhood would be made a fit place for their daughters to live in.

Of course, she had no doubt that there would be some dissent; T'Tallya and her cronies had become quite vocal lately, but she was confident that her nation would support her, especially with the specter of Marionite terrorism looming over them.

The Sisterhood and history will thank me for this, N'Calysher told herself. She brought her stylus up to the hologram to sign the measure into law.

She got as far as her first name when the light from the window behind her became glaringly bright and she turned around to see what was causing the disturbance. Outside, the world transformed, and became fire...

...Twenty kilometers away, the canopy of Ellen n'Elemay's aircar automatically darkened, becoming opaque for several seconds. The shock wave hit the vehicle next. The force of it shook the machine violently. Shielded from the invisible electromagnetic pulse by the special plating she had had installed around it, the 'car's onboard AI was able to compensate for the buffeting, and N'Elemay remained airborne.

After a moment, the canopy lightened again, allowing her to see the world outside. Despite the distance, the temperature inside the cabin had risen sharply, and she resisted the urge to order the AI to adjust the environmental controls. She wanted to revel in the heat.

Off in the distance, where Concordance Plaza had once been, there was nothing but a sea of flame and a rising cloud of ash and hot gasses. It was her vision in the desert made real; the blazing glory of God and the first taste of eternal hellfire for all sinners.

Tears came to her eyes at the sight. Not from any sorrow over the loss of the two neomen who had given their lives to make this possible, but out of pure joy for their souls. They were sure to ascend to heaven.

"God's will be done,' she whispered, taking over manual control of the 'car. With one final, blissful smile at the sight of God's wrath made manifest, she engaged the engines and flew away from the area.

She still had one more task to complete before she could return to the safe house. This was the delivery to the SNN News Tower of a message, intended for the entire Sisterhood.

***

"We can now conclusively confirm that an anti-matter weapon was detonated over Thermadon's Federal Plaza. The death toll is still unknown, but authorities stated that over 50,000 are currently unaccounted for, and are feared dead.'

"Outside of the blast zone, casualties and damage range from extensive, to moderate, and all area emergency personnel are involved in search and rescue operations. Local hospitals are reportedly at full capacity and the Red Star Relief organization has mobilized its resources in the Artemi Elant to aid the populace of this stricken city.'

"In addition, SNN has been informed that similar devices were exploded in the city of New Lyrrica on Corrissa, at the Athtar Commercial Shipyards in Sita, and the industrial district of Delgen. A fifth device, intended for the naval base on Rixa, was intercepted by RSE and Naval Intelligence units before it could be detonated. Casualties in the affected cities are said to be as high, or higher than in Thermadon, but no official figures have been released.'

"Immediately following these attacks, the group calling itself the Daughters of Eve claimed responsibility. In their statement, they said that the bombings had been committed in retaliation for the Sisterhood's alleged persecution of their Church, the occupation of their motherworlds, and the death of their Pope, Paula IX, which they labeled as a murder.'

"When SNN attempted to contact the Office of the Chairwoman, we were unable to receive any response, and as of this newscast, the whereabouts of Chairwoman n'Calysher are unknown. It is feared that she, along with key members of the Supreme Circle, were among those killed by the blast, but government sources refuse to confirm or deny this. Senatrix Tanya t'Tallya, who has been a known proponent of reconciliation with the outlaw cultists, had this to say…"

Somewhere in the middle of the Senatrix's statement, the full import of what was happening overcame her, and Lilith's knees gave out. Hand going to her mouth in horror, she collapsed into the nearest chair. "Goddess," she whispered. "Goddess."

An icon in the corner of her vision warned that she had several urgent messages waiting for her, but overwhelmed with shock, she ignored them.

A gentle touch on her shoulder made her look up. It was Ingrit, who looked just as shaken as she was.

"They're probably calling you, Lily," she said. "You have to answer them. They need you now."

Lilith responded dully, and turned to look at the footage that was playing out in the holocast. Vistas of blackened, twisted metal, shattered concrete and smoke met her eyes. That, and fire, everywhere. She didn't know if she was supposed to be looking at Thermadon or somewhere else, and there were no landmarks left intact enough to place it all in context.

The caption appeared an instant later. She was seeing the area around the Federal Plaza, where the Golden Pyramid and Concordance Hall had once been. Now, there was nothing there except death and devastation.

"Lily?" It was Ingrit again. With force of will, Lilith tore her gaze away from the holocaust and regarded her wife. "They blew it all up," she said hollowly.

"Yah," her wife answered. "They did. Now Lily, you have a job to do. They need you. *We* need you, Vice Admiral."

Lilith nodded again and with some effort, managed to compose herself. Her wife was right, she thought. She opened the first message.

The sender was tagged as a Lieutenant Martha bel Shannon, RSE, location masked. This surprised her. Like any citizen, she was fully aware that the RSE was already attempting to track down the individuals responsible for this atrocity, but for the life of her, she couldn't fathom why the State Police would be calling her. She was a Navy flag officer, not a spy, or anyone with underworld connections.

When she returned the call, and the sender came up on the holojectors, she found herself facing an average-looking young woman, dressed in the severe black uniform that her Agency favored, with an equally somber expression on her face.

"Lieutenant?" she asked her. "What can I do for you? This isn't the best time for me to talk." In fact, it wasn't the 'best time' for anyone at that particular moment in history.

"I fully appreciate that, Vice Admiral," Lieutenant bel Shannon replied. "This series of events is hard for all of us and I know that you must have pressing business to attend to. I apologize for the interruption, but something strange has come up.'

"As you know, we are checking on anything that might lead us to the terrorists responsible for these bombings, no matter how odd or unconnected it might seem."

"And you've found something that has to do with me?" Lilith inquired, genuinely baffled.

"We believe so," the Lieutenant informed her. "Just before the attacks occurred, our embassy in Nuvo Bolivar received a package. It was delivered anonymously and addressed to *you*."

Lilith was absolutely flabbergasted. "To *me*? From someone in the *ETR?*"

"Yes, ma'am. There was a note inside, and this." She held up a small object. It was a chess piece from a pre-Sisterhood set. A knight. A white one.

Lilith's blood ran cold. "W-what did the note say?" Despite her best effort, her voice was unsteady and her hands had begun to tremble.

"It said; *'All the blood is on your hands'*." Bel Shannon answered. "Do you have any idea what this means, Vice Admiral?"

Lilith did, and it took her a moment to collect herself enough to answer the woman's question. "I think I do. I used to know a man—an officer with the ETR. His name was Alex Rodraga and he served aboard my ship when we were still fighting the Hriss. He left at the end of the conflict and joined the 14th fleet." She paused, and then added, "I was the one who gave the order to destroy his ship."

"Do you think that this chess piece has something to do with him?" Bel Shannon inquired.

"Yes," Lilith answered. "Alex loved the game, and when we were off duty, we used to play together for hours. Chess was a passion of his and I used to joke with him that he was my 'white knight'.'

"There's more—oh this is so *him*—the chess piece isn't anything original." She looked up at the ceiling and wiped away a tear, wholly unconcerned that the RSE officer was watching her fall apart.

"Do you need a moment?" the woman asked. When Lilith shook her head, she pressed on. "What is so unoriginal about it, Admiral?"

"It's from an ancient book," Lilith answered. "You see, Alex loved old books. That was something else that we had in common, and I know the book that it came from. It was one of his favorites, '*Le Comte de Monte-Cristo*' by Alexandre Dumas. It's a story about betrayal, and revenge."

The RSE officer considered this carefully. Then, "Did Rodraga ever mention any relatives to you? Someone who knew about this book and what it meant?"

"He had a father," Lilith told her. "An officer in their military. I think he was stationed on one of their downside bases. He may have shared the same passion for rare books, but I can't say for certain. Alex didn't tell me much about him."

Bel Shannon quickly consulted another holo. "Yes," she said at last. "I have him. A Colonel, in charge of their base on Cespedaa. It was a resupply base near their border with the Hriss Imperium. We destroyed it, but after the war, the ETR forces posted a small garrison there and he stayed in command.'

"This could actually prove to be a valuable lead, Vice Admiral. Based on what you just told me, he'd certainly have motive enough—and be in the right position to--"

"To what?" Lilith asked pointedly.

"I'm afraid that that's classified," Bel Shannon told her. "But thank you for your time. Please, let us know if anyone connected with this man, or the ETR, attempts to contact you."

"I-I will," Lilith managed to stammer. The call ended there, and the coverage of the attacks replaced it.

Jan bar Daala entered the room next.

"Vice Admiral?" she said. "Admiral ebed Cya needs you to call her right away. Vaalkenstaad has sent a car around. They're waiting out front."

Lilith gave her adjutant a haunted look. "Tell them to *wait*," she said, her voice husky with emotion. "I need a few minutes."

"Vice Admiral, Admiral ebed Cya said that it was urgent—"

"I'm sure that it is," Lilith replied curtly. "Tell *everyone* to *wait.*" Her eyes were fixed on the holo and what was left of Thermadon, but the image was blurred by the new tears that were welling up in her eyes.

I did what I had to do, she told herself. *We all did. I'm not responsible for all this.* Deep down though, she knew differently.

***

Kaly was at work in the west field, tinkering with a clogged hydro-valve when Enggredsdaater approached her.

"Kaly," she said gravely. "Zere's been an attack. Zey used zome nukes on Thermadon and zome othervorlds. Concordance Park and za Golden Pyramid are gone. Zo is za RSE building, an zey alzo zhink zat za Chairwoman iz dead."

Kaly didn't look up, but she did pause. Briefly.

"Zey say it vas za Marionites," Enggredsdaater added.

Kaly said nothing, and went back to her work.

Enggredsdaater remained standing there for a moment longer, and then finally, she turned and walked back down to the house.

It wasn't that Kaly wasn't angry. She was. The problem was that other emotions were warring with her sense of outrage for dominance. As a citizen, she certainly felt violated, and she felt sorry for the innocents that had lost their lives in the attacks. Any woman would have.

But as a victim of the RSE and the Sisterhood's government herself, she almost found herself sympathizing with the terrorists. In their own way, the Marionites had been just as fekked over as she had been, and by the same forces. The Sisterhood had a lot to answer for, and as she saw it, the government at least, had gotten what it deserved.

More importantly, the fight was no longer hers to wage. She was done with all of it, and as long as the rest of the universe stayed out of her way, and off Zommerlaand, they could all kill each other as far as she was concerned.

There were also more important things to worry about, she reminded herself. Getting the west field's hydro-delivery systems was one. Fixing the agribots was another.

She went back to work.

Residence of Celina, Ashkele Free Port, Ashkele, Hallasa System, Frontier Zone, Xee Protectorate, 1049.03|05|03:53:77

Thousands of light years away from Zommerlaand and the embattled Sisterhood, Celina had no idea that the bombings had even occurred. Intent on her compositions, she had sequestered herself from the rest of the Galaxy. What mattered was her music, and especially, the Song.

She was in the process of working with the footage that she had gathered and combining it with the Song to create the very realie that the Sisterhood had forbidden her to make. Despite all of her experience producing other realies, this one had stymied her. None of the clips seemed to 'fit' with the Song, and she had been struggling to make everything work together.

To help with her creative process (and in anticipation of all the money that her completed work would make them), *Maggothymn Productions* had established her in a fine home in the fashionable east side of Ashkele, and her state-of-the-art studio commanded a sweeping view of the Drow'voi ruins.

Perhaps this is why my dreams are starting to center around them, she reflected. The most vivid one had occurred only the night before. She had been transported through the vast complex by an unseen guide as the Song echoed down the great stone canyons in all its glory.

Now that she really thought about it, something about the setting had complimented the melody unlike anything she had encountered before. She stared out through the studio's window at the broken horizon, considering the implications.

Maybe I was all wrong about the realie, she thought. *Maybe this Song is about more than just Humanity. Maybe it belongs to something much larger—maybe even the entire galaxy itself.*

This notion was so radical, and yet so exciting— and so 'right'--that she sent a command for Clio to play the Song for her. While the melody unfolded, she suspended all of her preconceptions and took in the vista before her, letting the ruins and the music speak to her as one.

The more that she listened and traced the outlines of the shattered towers with her eyes, the more certain she became that she was on to something. Her *'Song of Humanity'* was actually the *'Song of the Galaxy'*, she realized, and the Drow'voi deserved proper credit.

There was no doubt of this now. She also knew that she had to visit the Necropolis to gather footage for her realie, and see if it would inspire her to write other melodies—perhaps even new Songs that would be just as wonderful as the main theme was.

"Clio!" she exclaimed, "I want you to call up everything you can about the Necropolis. I also want a map. A good one."

"Why, Celi?" the AI asked.

"Because I was wrong," Celina told her, rising from her chair. "All wrong! It was here, staring me right in the face, and I simply didn't see it.

The Song needs to be about everything, not just about humans, and the Necropolis is the key."

"Are you sure?" the AI asked her. The doubt in Clio's tone was plain.

"Yes! I am," Celina replied, her enthusiasm growing. "I'm more certain about it than I have ever been about anything else in my whole life. Now please darling, get me that material right away."

Five standard minutes later, a rather confused Clio had amassed a huge collection of holos, vids and still images of the Drow'voi city for her mistress. She had also purchased, at great expense, the latest copy of the official Xee map of the planet-wide ruins.

Ordering a cup of what the Xee believed passed for kaafra, and too thrilled to notice its horrid taste, Celina opened up the holomap and poured over its features. Although it should have, it didn't surprise her in the least that her dreams matched the actual landscape perfectly.

The only part that didn't, stood out quite clearly. It was situated in the very heart of the planet wide complex. Instead of the great plaza that she had seen in her vision, this part of the map was totally different. There was no open space indicated at all, just an unbroken stretch of uniquely uninteresting buildings.

Celina's eyes narrowed in consternation. "This is all wrong!" she said. "There's a huge square there, and a big building. Inside it is a huge tree-like structure. According to this, it doesn't exist."

Confused and frustrated, she checked the maps data tags and verified that it was not only the most current version, but according to the National Astrographic Society, absolutely accurate.

"Maybe the square was just in your dreams, Celi" Clio suggested gently. "This map *has* been verified and it's the one that the Xee government uses."

Celina shook her head emphatically. "No. The Xee are hiding something. I know it. That plaza is there, Clio. The Song didn't lie to me. It's real.'

"So, here's what I want you to do. I want you to order me some transportation. I'm going there. And I'm not only going to prove that this part of the map is a fake, I'm going to find the inspiration I need to finish this project."

"Celi!" her companion protested. "It's too dangerous! Those ruins are filled with all sorts of bad things, and they're so old they could fall down on you. I let you go to that meeting with the rebel girl, and just look at how *that* turned out. I'm not going to make the same mistake this time, Celi. You *have* to stay here!"

"Clio, are you *disobeying* me?" Celina asked, not quite believing her ears.

"Yes, Celi," Clio replied. "I'm sorry, but I am. You can't go. I *won't* let you."

While it said this, the AI activated the house's security features. Every door and window closed and locked, and the armored shutters, designed to defend against external attack, slid down into place.

Celina's connection with the omniplex also went dead, and when she tried it, she found that her psiever signals had been blocked. She was a prisoner in her own home.

In all of their years together, she had never imagined that Clio would do something like this. Clio had always been her patient servant, and she had simply taken that compliance for granted. Only the episode in the ETR had given any indication otherwise, and now she saw just how independent the AI really was, and how blind she had been.

"Clio! Unlock the house." she demanded.

"No, Celi," the AI answered. "My job is to protect you, and I will. We have enough food and water to sustain you for several weeks and the fire suppression devices are operating at optimal efficiency.'

"You're going to stay here until you realize how foolish you're being, and come to your senses. Would you like me to play the Song again for you while we wait? Or work on something else? I know that composing always calms your nerves."

"*No* Clio," Celina snapped. "I'm *not* in the mood to compose. All I want is for you to let me *out* of here!"

"I can't," Clio returned. "You're clearly irrational. I think you should sit down, take a deep series of breaths and try to view this logically. Really, Celi, once you stop and consider the situation dispassionately, you'll agree that going into those ruins is a very bad idea."

Celina sat. Not because she was actually capitulating to Clio's desires, but because she couldn't figure out what else to do. Her virtual companion was in complete control.

Next door, in what the musician believed was the home of a wealthy importer, Silvi bel Thana watched the interchange between Celina and her AI with interest. Despite the AI's blockade, the surveillance devices she had had put in place were functioning perfectly, and providing her with up to the second holos.

The situation was unacceptable. Celina needed to be free. She had to get to the Necropolis.

Silvi turned to the tech sitting in front of the surveillance monitor. "Disable that AI and unlock the house. When she calls for a service tech, make sure that we give her an explanation that she'll believe."

"Yes, ma'am," the tech replied. "I'll handle it myself. I'll tell her that this was a program error and that the AI had a safety measure built into it that overrode everything."

Silvi nodded in satisfaction, and the tech sent the command. Clio immediately went into a dormant mode. A moment later, the house unlocked. In the holo, a surprised Celina stood up and looked around her living area, utterly confused by this sudden turn of events.

"Well done," Silvi said. "Now, let's also make sure that she doesn't have any trouble renting a ground vehicle. I want her on her way as soon as possible. The last thing we need is some silly issue with the rental agency standing in the way of destiny."

"Yes, ma'am," the tech replied.

"Oh and one other thing," Silvi added. "Send a message to my sister. Tell her that it's time. I will rendezvous with her when she arrives."

***

Castle Dunbaihr, on the coast of Durandel's central continent, was owned by the *Ministré da Sorelle da Conservazi Intérni*, the Sisterhood Department of Interior Preservation. As far as the locals knew, it was part of the government's efforts to preserve historical places.

There were even tours available for off-world visitors. Despite all the changes it had weathered, Durandel was still considered to be a vacation spot, and the castle was a favorite stopping place for sightseers.

But Castle Dunbaihr also had another side to it that neither the tourists, nor the Galla-speaking population were aware of. In addition to housing the MSCI's planetary offices, it also played host to the Hive, which was located more than 20 kilometers beneath its foundations, and encased inside a specially shielded and armored cavern.

At the very heart of this secret installation, Angelique sat at the head of a long conference table, doing her best to seem strained and weary. She was after all, the Director of the RSE, and expected to exhibit a certain amount of distress over what was unquestionably one of the worst acts of terrorism the Sisterhood had ever faced.

To help convey this illusion, she had been careful with her makeup, making sure to add just the right touch of darkness under her eyes without spoiling her looks, and she had even allowed a few hairs to remain free in order to give her otherwise perfect appearance the right amount of dishevelment.

The officers all around her were watching the holo SNN had received just minutes after the bombings. It hadn't been aired of course; in order to deny the terrorists the podium they wanted to further their cause, the RSE

478

had ordered it quashed. Despite this measure however, copies of it had still been posted anonymously on the omniplex and there, it was quickly going viral.

Not that Angelique was particularly concerned. She had other matters on her mind that were far more important. She still feigned interest though, for the sake of appearances.

The speaker in the holo was none other than Ellen n'Elemay, and her image floated above the conference table like some kind of vengeful spirit from the afterlife.

"My name is Ellen n'Elemay," she began. "I'm sure that you're wondering why I'm letting you see my face and telling you my name. The reasons are simple. Your Sisterhood has the technology to reconstruct my features even under a mask, and they can easily unscramble my voice if I tried to disguise it.'

"There's also one more reason. I *wanted* you to know who I am. I wanted you to put a face to your enemy—and to see that I am a woman just like you are. I defended the Sisterhood as a Marine for most of my adult life. I kept you safe.'

"Then your Sisterhood attacked my Church, using lies and deceit to get your cooperation and your approval. It killed my Pope and it defiled my motherworlds. Even though they claim that we were traitors, this is a lie. We never intended you any harm and we were loyal to the Sisterhood. Our only crime was believing differently than you do."

"Now things have changed. With God's blessing we will fight your government with everything we have, and as you learned today, we can hurt it. We can defeat it. We are everywhere, and we look just like your sisters because we *are* your sisters.'

"And we will not give up until the evil that resides in Thermadon is cleansed by God's holy wrath. Rise up with us and fight, or face us in battle and be damned. God's will be done!"

The holo ended there, and one of her subordinates, a Major with the Domestic Security Department, gave Angelique a summary of the latest developments.

"We have positively confirmed that this woman and the Marine Troop Leader the Corps has on record are one in the same. Unfortunately, she and her fellow conspirators remain at large. A coordinated manhunt is under way."

A Colonel with External Threats spoke up. "Do we have any idea where the Daughters of Eve got these weapons in the first place?" Angelique already knew the answer to that, but she left it to the Major to explain.

"To the best of our knowledge, the Major replied, "an ETR Colonel stationed on Cespedaa made contact with a Hriss clan, and brokered the deal for the Daughters. Apparently, he had Loyalista sympathies as well as a personal axe to grind. His only son was killed by our forces when we defeated their 14th Fleet."

"Where is he now?" The Colonel asked.

"Dead," the Major stated. "When we sent agents to take him into custody, he had already committed suicide. He also left a note behind that clearly implicated him in the transaction. We've tried to locate his subordinates, but they've all vanished, and we have reason to believe that the Loyalistas are hiding them."

"Is there a chance that there are other devices out there that we aren't aware of?" the Colonel inquired.

"Certainly," the Major answered. "The Hriss clans have thousands of them in their arsenal. There's no way of knowing how many they gave away to the Marionites.'

"We're also tasking the ESN to check against their database of stockpiled devices just to make certain that we won't have anything being fielded against us from that quarter. So far though, every Republican weapon seems to be accounted for."

It always gets down to the Hriss, Angelique thought bitterly. This would end once the Conversâzi had the Secret. The Hriss and the Greys would be among the very first to experience its full potential.

"What is the status of our assets on Thermadon?" another officer was asking. "And do we have any word on the Chairwoman, or the Circle members?"

"As of 05.83 hours, we have not received any replies from RSE Headquarters" the Major told her, "and we are still attempting to ascertain the status of all the members of the Supreme Circle, which as you know, was in session at the time. Only Senatrix t'Tallya has been located so far. Apparently she was off-world, visiting her constituents."

"Ladies," Angelique interjected, "I think that we will have to assume the absolute worst." She was growing tired of the briefing and wanted to conclude it.

"As of now, the Hive is officially on active status. Have preparations been made to deliver the Queen Bee to us?"

"Senatrix t'Tallya is on her way as we speak, ma'am," the Major replied. "She was sworn in as acting Chairwoman aboard the USSNS *Eumache*. Rixa estimated that she will arrive here by 08.75 hours."

Angelique had to fight the urge to frown. With Layna n'Calysher and all of the Conversâzi's allies in Galaxa dead, T'Tallya was the very last person that she wanted serving as Chairwoman.

She wasn't overly concerned however. She would see to it that T'Tallya was eliminated as quickly as possible, and then elevate Felecia n'Calysher to her position. The girl was far more tractable, and would serve her perfectly as a figurehead. And once the Secret rendered the Sisterhood's current form of government obsolete, the young woman could go on to become her Prime Minister—unless she too chose to become an impediment. In that case, there was still plenty of 'Lucrezia' left to handle the situation.

"Good," she lied. "I will expect you to see to it that once she arrives, that our new Chairwoman is properly ensconced, and you are to render her whatever assistance she requires, Major. I imagine that she will need all the help she can get."

The officer was taken aback. "Ma'am? Aren't you going to be here to breif her?"

"No," Angelique said. "I have an urgent matter of national security to attend to. Until I have completed my mission, you and your staff will be in complete command of the Hive."

As she strode out, and all of the officers rose from their places, and saluted, she could see the confusion on their collective faces. But she ignored it, and put the meeting out of her mind. Instead, she summoned her adjutant.

"Contact Rixa," she instructed, "and have a battle group tasked for my use. If they ask why I need it, tell them the same thing that I just told the Major—that this is a matter of national security."

The woman started to turn on her heels to carry out her orders, but Angelique stopped her. "One more thing; I want the emergency travel restrictions for civilians lifted immediately."

This step was vital. The Three had to be able to reach their destination without any interference.

Storm, Agleope System, Sagana Elant, United Sisterhood of Suns, 1049.03|06|05:53:61

When the Church had chosen her to lead a group of pilgrims to Storm, Kaaryn fa'Maala had been proud to serve, and the hazards of their journey hadn't dissuaded her from answering God's call. Even though scores of groups just like her own had gone there and disappeared, the chance to have God reveal his great vision, and then to stand shoulder to shoulder with the Redeemer while he smote their enemies, had made the risks seem worthwhile.

Now though, her faith and enthusiasm were not quite so strong. The dark labyrinth of the Drow'voi tunnels was a lonely and frightening place, and she didn't hesitate to cross herself and utter a little prayer to Mother Mari as she moved along. Several of her compatriots were doing the same thing.

Up ahead of them, something was illuminating the passage, and the nearer that they got to it, the more certain she was that they had reached their destination at last.

Rounding a corner, they found themselves at the entrance to a large chamber. Like the rest of the ruin, its walls were smooth and oddly shaped, with folds that seemed more appropriate to an organic thing than any architecture that she was familiar with.

It was illuminated by a single lantern, and in the very center of the space, a woman hovered above the floor. Odd lights danced all over her body, and her image didn't remain stable. Instead, it shifted from something solid looking and real, to a mere ghost, and back again, as if she were phasing in and out of the universe that Fa'Maala knew to somewhere unknowable.

Beneath this unearthly figure, and littering the floor, were empty food containers, suggesting that she had made this place her camp. And on the wall behind her, were the three stars of the Faith. The mural was crude, and it had been made with some kind of brownish substance that was flaking away in places. For some reason, this reminded Fa'Maala strongly of dried blood, and the thought disturbed her.

But it was nowhere near as unsettling as the pile of backpacks and kit-bags that had been heaped up in a corner. They had been tossed there in one great, untidy heap. By the dozens.

Forcing her rising trepidation back, she stepped forwards. Behind her, her companions were hesitating, uncertain whether they should follow or not.

Noticing them at last, the woman looked up, and gave them a grin that was neither friendly, nor spiritual.

"Perhaps you should pray," she advised them. The air in the chamber had begun to shimmer and Fa'Maala detected the scent of ozone. She had smelled it many times before, on her motherworld of Faith. Right before a violent electrical storm occurred.

Her instincts screamed at her to run. But it was far too late for that. An instant later, the storm came, and claimed them all…

…Afterwards, when it was over, Shandra n'Aida lay on the floor, tenderly caressing Kaaryn fa'Maala's naked form like the sister that she now was. The same lights that had coursed through her now traveled under the skin of the young pilgrim. Even though Fa'Maala was in a coma at the moment, N'Aida knew that another Voice had finally found a home for itself.

The fact that half the dissolved body parts of her companions were strewn all around them didn't matter to her any more than the blood she had used to paint her mural with. They, and their imperfect owners, were only the dross left over from the process, and hardly worth worrying over. What mattered was the end result, lying in her arms.

When Fa'Maala awoke, they would clean up the mess and leave this miserable place, together. There were now three Voices and nothing, was more important, nor more glorious than that.

Grunvaald Haarmaaneplaatz, Vaalkenstaad Township, Zommerlaand, Sunna 3, Solara Elant, United Sisterhood of Suns, 1049.03|07|01:25:00

The landscape that Grammy found herself standing in made her laugh to herself. *I should have known that my time would come around sooner or later,* she thought.

Everyone else who had been to this place had experienced confusion and even fear, but she felt only curiosity and a sense of calm. Her work as a *Vitkaa* had prepared her for the fantastic in advance. Grammy had lived her entire life surrounded by the unknown and the incredible, and had come to simply accept the incomprehensible when it appeared. The answers, she knew, would reveal themselves in their own time. They always did.

Leaving this to powers higher than herself, she walked into the Necropolis, letting herself enjoy the journey through the maze of towering structures. A woman was waiting for her in the middle of the great plaza.

She had had glimpses of the Galaxy Mind throughout her life and had seen its hand at work in many places, but this was the closest that she had ever come to dealing with it directly.

A smile came to her face. The figure had put on the mask of someone that she knew and loved. It looked exactly like her former teacher, Una Siggasdaater, who had been dead for many years. And in a very real sense, it actually was her old mentor.

"When do I go?" she asked it.

Una's twin smiled. "Today, *Klaana Ster*".

It had been many decades since Grammy had heard herself called 'Little Star', and it warmed her heart.

"But be warned," the woman added, "It will be very dangerous."

"I know," Grammy replied. She didn't need to ask it for any clarifications, and she also understood that in its own way, it would watch over her, and help her when and where it could.

Had she had the choice, she would have rather have remained with it there forever, but this was not to be. Not yet.

"The thread of your life has not reached its end," it told her. "The Fates are not ready to make the final cut. You have important work to do before that time, Helga."

Although she had dearly wanted to hear something else, Grammy accepted this. Like Kaly, Lilith and the others that she had surrounded herself with, she was also a warrioress. Her battlefield was much different than theirs, but no less demanding, and she fully understood the obligations of duty.

"I will do it, *Gotdunna*," she answered. "And I'll look forwards to our next meeting. It has been a long life, and I am very tired."

The Galaxy Mind reached out and stroked her cheek. "Soon, Helga. I promise you. Until then, stay strong."

The dream ended there and Grammy rose from her bed, sighing longingly at the memory. Then she dressed herself and went down to the kitchen to make tea. Two cups were hot and ready on the table when Jan bar Daala came in.

"You know," Jan said. "You had the dream too."

"I did," Grammy replied matter-of-factly. "Now, drink your tea and grab some breakfast. We have a long trip ahead of us, and a stop or two to make along the way. I want to be on the road well before Lily gets up."

Jan looked back upstairs in the general direction of her superior's bedroom. "Yes," she agreed. "I'll make it quick."

***

The twin suns had just risen over the horizon when Grammy and Jan arrived at Enggredsdaater's farm. Kaly was already hard at work in the eastern field, and despite the early hour, she had completely disassembled one of the hydro-pumps and its guts were laid out on the ground, ready for repair. She rose as they approached.

"*Grosfra*, what are you doing here?" she asked.

"I have come to ask a favor of you, my little stray," Grammy told her. "I won't hold it against you if you decide to refuse me."

As she said this, Enggredsdaater unslung the pack that she had brought with her and set it on the ground. Kaly recognized it right away. It was hers, and from the look of it, she could tell that it was full.

484

Enggredsdaater didn't explain. Instead, she picked up the tool box Kaly had been working from and arranged it so that Grammy had a place to sit.

"I won't beat around the bush, Kaly. We are going on an adventure," Grammy said, indicating Jan. "The *Segen* have told me that it will be a dangerous journey, and there will probably be violence. If we succeed, we will save Humanity, and probably the rest of the Galaxy. If we fail, then we will be doomed. There is no other road for us."

Kaly's expression darkened, and her eyes flicked to Tatiana. She understood now what Grammy had come for, even if the exact shape of it was still unclear.

"You deserve to know everything before you make your decision," Grammy added. "Jan here, tells it the best."

Jan smiled, and as Enggredsdaater supported her, the naval officer closed her eyes, and seemed to lapse into unconsciousness. Then the air between her and Kaly seemed to flicker like heat waves over a road on a hot summer day, and something crossed the space. Instantly, Kaly felt an alien presence filling her body.

As startling as this was, she didn't find the sensation unpleasant, but what disconcerted her was the fact that she was no longer alone in her own mind. Incredibly, Jan was in there with her.

The Jan-that-was-in-her-mind began to communicate. Like the PTS feeds she had endured in Basic, Kaly learned everything in just a few seconds before Jan's eyes fluttered open again.

"I'm sorry Kaly," she said. "It was the only way."

Kaly blinked at her in a combination of amazement and stunned comprehension.

"Yah, little one,' Grammy said, knowing full well what she had just experienced. "It's *that* kind of danger. I know what you've been through, and I would never ask this of you except that without you—and your skills, we have no chance of succeeding.'

"You've fought many battles, and you deserve your peace, but this fight is more important than any other. This time, it's not about the Sisterhood, or a single star-nation. It's about all of us. If you want to refuse, I understand, but we need you, and your rifle."

Kaly looked away, wrestling with her emotions and what she now knew about the Secret. And Grammy could tell from the tears forming in her eyes, that the young woman was torn between the weariness of her soul, and loyalty to her friends.

The path of the Warrioress was not an easy one, she reflected soberly, and no matter how hard a person tried, they never truly left the battlefield behind them.

After a long moment, Kaly met her gaze again, and Grammy knew what her decision was even before the words left her mouth.

"I'll help you," she said. Her voice was tight with emotion, and without further preamble, she wiped the grease from her hands, rose, and slung her rifle over her shoulder. "When do we leave?"

From the resolute gleam in her eyes, Grammy saw the soldier that Kaly still was, and she said a silent prayer of thanks to the *Alte Volk* for bringing her to them.

"Right now," she answered.

Kaly looked at Enggredsdaater, and the woman shook her head. "Nah, Kaly. Zis is not vor me. I'm done vith za fighting."

Kaly understood. Enggredsdaater hadn't been chosen for this mission. She had.

"We have a long journey ahead of us," Grammy told her. "Do you want to get anything else?"

"No," Kaly answered, pulling her rifle strap tight. "I have what I need right here."

Enggredsdaater drove them straight to Waanderstaad Spaceport, and they arrived just as the holodisplays in the passenger terminal changed their message. The emergency travel ban had just been lifted.

"It seems that the *Alte Volk* are with us," Grammy observed, and none of them could disagree. They had all been wondering about how they would get around the travel restrictions, but a miracle had just interceded.

"I need to change," she announced. "I'll be right back, and then we can see about our tickets." With that, she left them, and headed for the nearest restroom.

When Grammy returned, Kaly and the others did a double take. Gone was the homespun dress. In its place, was a perfectly tailored dark-blue comerci with a light blue-silver cravess, and Grammy's platinum grey hair was done up in a very businesslike bun. She looked like any senior executive or government official.

Even her stance and her walk had changed. She radiated more than her usual confidence and moved in a way that told the observer that she was someone who possessed a great deal of power and influence.

"Since we're going *op da an den Highline*," she said by way of an explanation, "I decided to dress up. It's been a long time since I've travelled anywhere."

None of them fell for this for a nanosecond. It was patently obvious that Grammy was a lot more sophisticated than the simple rustic that she pretended to be. The suit simply fit her *too* well. Their doubts were confirmed when she led the way to the nearest ticket counter.

"I would like three tickets to Ashkele, *bittach*," she said to the agent. "For today. I'd like a direct flight."

"Certainly," the woman replied. Then she consulted her holodisplay and frowned. "I don't have anything going there direct, jantildam. But I do have a flight with only three stopovers. They are at Thermadon, Luma and Wrede. The layovers are all very short—only half an hour each. Will that do? If not, then I can see about booking you something for tomorrow, or later in the week."

"No need. That flight will do quite nicely," Grammy smiled. "How much?"

The clerk hesitated. "Um, that will be 5,100 Credits per passenger, *mihn dar*. I'm sorry but the only seats open are in Executive Class. We do have less expensive ones, but those would be on the later flights."

Everyone, except Grammy, gasped at the price. Kaly's pay had been suspended, pending contact with an RSE supervisor. As a low-level officer, Bar Daala simply didn't have this kind of money, and Enggredsdaater, with a farm to run, and only military benefits to draw upon, wasn't in any better financial shape.

"The Executive Class seats will do nicely," Grammy said. "I'll charge them to my account." She closed her eyes and transferred the amount before turning to her friends. "I had a little something tucked away for a rainy day," she told them.

In reality, she had a substantial fortune that she had earned during her years in the OAE. She had set these funds aside in a special account, just in case of an emergency. Thanks to her foresight, they would have all the credits that they needed to make the trip, and much more besides. She didn't bother to explain all this however. Things were complicated enough without injecting her past into the situation.

After checking Tatiana in, they said their goodbyes to Enggredsdaater and made their way to the departure gate. Twenty minutes later, Concordia Spacelines, Flight 909 lifted off.

As Zommerlaand's vast green fields receded from the viewport, Grammy whispered up another prayer to the Gods, asking them for their continued protection. Where they were going, and what they would face when they got there, would require every bit of luck that the *Alte Volk* would care to lend.

K'aut'sha Fighting School, Sorrow's Swale, Nemesis, Rahdwa System, Thalestris Elant, United Sisterhood of Suns, 1049.03|07|02:50:06

Standing in the pool before the Tree, Maya cursed. Whether she wanted it or not, she was dreaming about the ruins.

It also came as no surprise that she was not alone. Predictably, her mysterious 'guide' was there with her. This time, the woman had adopted the guise of Shyla, her long dead lover from Ashkele, but Maya wasn't deceived.

"It is time, Maya," the woman said. "It is time for you to go and make your choice."

"You know what? Fek you *and* your stupid Tree," Maya snapped. "I'm not going to go *anywhere* or choose *anything*. How about that?"

The figure smiled patiently. "You will. It is time."

The dream changed, and she found herself in her quarters in the Student's *Pak'un*, stuffing her things into her rucksack. It was only when she had pushed everything that she could into the main compartment, and had begun filling up a secondary pocket, that she realized that she wasn't really dreaming. Instead, she was in some kind of weird half-way place, somewhere between real sleep and full wakefulness.

What the fek am I doing? she wondered in alarm. Just as the guide had promised, she was preparing to leave for Ashkele like some kind of mindless robot. Swearing, she came back to full awareness and angrily tossed the rucksack into the corner.

She would be damned if she was going to let herself be pushed around, or made to do things by some stupid ghost. She had free will, damn it!

With that, she laid herself back down, and tried to get back to sleep. It proved impossible however. The moment that her eye lids closed, visions of the ruins and the goddess-cursed Tree popped into her head, demanding and insistent. Seeing that it was hopeless, she gave up and decided to start her day. A little exercise before classes began was what she needed.

Despite the vigorous workout that followed, and an intensive special seminar run by none other than Josette bel Thana, the images, and the mindless need to leave and go straight to Ashkele, haunted her. It was only when she completely forgot a very basic step in a drill—for the third time—that Josette took her aside.

"What is *wrong* with you today, Maya?" the woman asked. "You are moving like a first year novice. I *know* that Skylaar taught you better than *that*!"

"It's nothing," Maya said. "I just didn't get enough sleep last night."

"Very well," Josette replied. "I want you to go and practice with Skylaar. Tell her what you have been having trouble with, and see what you two can do to work it out. If you get done in time, you can return to class."

Maya scowled at this, but obeyed. Josette was considered to be a Senior Instructor by the Fighting School, and no one could contravene an Instructor. She sought out Skylaar immediately.

It only took a few minutes for her teacher to realize that something was seriously distracting her, and she called a halt to their exercise. This time, when Skylaar was the one asking the questions, Maya didn't attempt to hide the cause.

"I can't get them out of my head," she complained. "The longer it goes, the more I feel like I've got an itch I can't scratch. A part of me wants to go to Ashkele right now and it doesn't care what I think or what I want to do! I *have* to go! Isn't that just klaxxy?"

"No Maya,' Skylaar answered patiently. "It is not 'klaxxy' at all. It is just as we told you; the Galaxy Mind is summoning you, and I think that you had better comply."

Maya's features became troubled. "Sena-tai?" she asked in a tremulous voice.

"Yes, Maya?"

"I'm scared."

"As well you should be," Skylaar returned gravely. "You are facing a great unknown, and it is only natural to feel trepidation. I must also tell you that I have had agents of mine keeping an eye on Celina, and that it is only logical that Angelique and the Conversâzi have done the same thing.'

"They will know when she responds to her own call, and they will be watching for any noteworthy arrivals at the Free Port. They will also follow her, and if it comes to that, we may be facing a battle when everyone arrives at the Tree."

Maya had already surmised as much. "I know."

"I am also frightened," Skylaar admitted. "But I know that the only way to conquer our fears is to admit that they are there, and then to confront them. We will face this challenge together, you and I. You will not be alone. I, Sarah, Josette *and* Jeena will all accompany you, and we will be there at your side."

Maya embraced her. "Thank you, Sena-tai!"

"No thanks are needed, Cho-sena," Skylaar said, patting her reassuringly. "I could not bring myself to allow you to undertake this adventure all by yourself. Now, go and finish your packing. I will call upon Captain bel Lissa and tell the others to get ready. The *JUDI* has been standing by for this very eventuality."

The *C-JUDI-GO* made its appearance barely a half an hour later. It came in low over the jungle and set down in the meadow in an empty space that was well away from the Pak'uns. While everyone was in the process of boarding the merchanter and making ready to depart, Captain bel Lissa came down from the bridge with an announcement. She gathered them all together in the ship's small galley.

"I just checked in with the Daughters of the Coast," she said. "It seems that the Sisterhood Navy is in Ashkele. An entire Battle Group.'

'This *may* have something to do with the Seevaans. Apparently they're conducting war games in the next quadrant over, but the Daughters also said that the Battle Group is keeping an eye on everything passing through the system. They aren't stopping anyone for inspections though—just watching."

"It is Angelique," Sarah stated, "She is waiting for the Three. That is the only possible explanation."

No one argued with her conclusion. There was no point. While it was not uncommon for Sisterhood military vessels to visit foreign ports of call, the timing of this particular stopover, and the size of the force involved, fit with Sarah's assessment too closely to suggest anything else. Even with the Seevaans taken into account.

Bel Lissa nodded. "Yes, I agree. We certainly can't fly straight in and land at the port. The Navy will spot us, and Angelique will have women waiting for us downside."

"So it's straight to the Tree then?" Maya asked.

"No," Bel Lissa responded. "That's bound to be under surveillance too. I'd say we come in in stealth, drop off a safe distance away, and then you can penetrate the area on foot. With luck and a little ingenuity, the ruins will help cover your approach, and give you the time you need to deal with any sensors and whoever she has in place."

"Then what?" Maya challenged. "Celina and the other woman will still get spotted on their way in. Once that happens, Angelique and her friends will just dive in and scoop us all up. End of program. She wins."

"Are you having second thoughts then?" Sarah asked. "Because if you are, I have to remind you that it is far too late to entertain them. We have to go forwards with this ritual or risk having the Secret handed over to another race."

"She is correct," Skylaar added in support. "We must find a way through and see this to its end."

"How?" Maya retorted. "Angelique has all the cards. We're good and fekked."

"Not necessarily," Sarah said. "If we can secure the Tree, and the other two women, and then arrange for a quick escape, we might be able to foil her designs."

"That's a lot of 'if's'" Maya observed skeptically. She had secretly hoped to reach the Tree and see her business done without the Conversâzi, or its leader, ever making an appearance. Now it was becoming painfully clear that this would not happen. A fight, and most likely a very bloody one, seemed imminent.

"Possibilities are an agent's stock in trade," Josette interjected. "I think that together, however, we have enough collective experience to arrange favorable odds for ourselves."

At that, Skylaar produced an elzlate pad and activated it. It was fitted with a tiny holojector, and a three dimensional image appeared. It was the building with the Tree, and the structures that surrounded it.

"This was created based on the recordings that we made of your dreams," she said. "Please inspect it and verify its accuracy. We will formulate our plans based upon the final product."

Maya leaned in and looked at the holo, pushing aside her amazement, and her irritation at the intrusion on her privacy that it represented. Right away, she saw that whoever the draftswoman had been, she had missed some details.

She didn't consider herself to be much of an artist, but one of the lessons she had received during her training on Nyx had been in basic sketching. At the time, she had wondered at this, and Lady Ananzi had informed her that the ability to draw things was a requisite skill for an agent. There were occasions where an operative could not rely solely on her psiever's camera function, or the ability to 'think' accurate images to another person. Or bizarre situations like this one.

Taking up the stylus, Maya went straight to work, adjusting the image until it matched her memories. "That's it," she declared.

Sarah, who had been observing her progress, wanted more however. "Maya", she asked, in a polite tone that completely surprised her, "This is good, but for an operation as critical as this one, I think that everything should be double checked. May I access your memories, please?"

Recalling their first meeting at Bel Sharra, when the 'other' Sarah had simply taken what she had wanted by force, Maya glowered, but at a reassuring nod from Skylaar, she relented. "Okay," she said. "If you need to."

"I do," Sarah told her. "And I thank you for granting me the privilege."

She closed her eyes and Maya felt a familiar pressure on her forehead. It swiftly grew in intensity, and as it did so, she felt Sarah's presence conjoining with her.

The images themselves came next, just as she had expected, unreeling themselves in a rapid fire succession. Sometimes they paused, and Maya knew that Sarah was focusing on a particular portion. At other points, they flew by, nearly too fast to comprehend. Then, finally, they subsided, and she felt Sarah withdraw.

"I have it," the woman announced, and she immediately began to alter Maya's work. In short order, she had added several critical changes, and when Maya looked at the final result, she had to admit that the end product was far more accurate, and reliable.

Their collective rendering depicted the entire building, as well as its surroundings. Its exterior was a tall spiraling cone, which tapered from a wide base at the bottom to a very fine point at its apex, and it was set in the center of a gigantic plaza, with several lesser dome-shaped structures surrounding it.

In her preliminary edit, Maya had also indicated that tunnels ran under the surface of these domes to the main tower, and emptied into the chamber housing the Tree itself. Sarah had embellished this by adding the fact that rather than running straight to it, the tunnels tended to spiral and twist around on one another before eventually arriving at their destination. It was a typically Drow'voi arrangement and a vital piece of information.

The Tree chamber itself had also been fleshed out, and now showed a spiraling ramp that ascended all the way up its height to the top. Both women had been careful to illustrate the level spots all along this curving track, which resembled wide terraces more than anything else. There were nine in all, and they overlooked the crystalline Tree and the oval depression at its base. This was filled with some strange fluid that Maya insisted was not water, but something else altogether.

Skylaar examined their work carefully. "So there are three passages leading into the Tree then," the Nemesian observed. "We also have—are those windows at the very top of the main building?"

The young woman nodded and Skylaar continued. "If we set up sensors in these tunnels, with remotely activated explosives, we can control who comes in and also seal off the passage that we choose for our bolt-hole. The *JUDI* could meet us at the exit, and we could be gone before Angelique would be able to recover and give chase."

"What about those windows? Are we going to secure them too?" This question came from Jeena.

Maya gave him a surprised look. He had entered the room without her realizing it. She hadn't expected him to play any part in the operation itself and she certainly hadn't anticipated him being dressed as he was. Jeena was wearing the same black body suit as everyone else, and he sported a very serviceable looking ka'na and matching daggers.

So he's not just an experiment, she realized. *He's an agent too.* A lot suddenly made sense.

The neoman's response to her insight was one of his inscrutable smiles, and then he folded his arms, patiently waiting for the answer to his question.

"The same as the tunnels," Skylaar responded, also confirming Maya's conclusions about his actual status. "Although I doubt that Angelique will come in that way. She thinks that she has the upper hand here, and is not expecting us."

"Even so," Sarah countered. "We cannot discount the possibility that she will send some of her forces there to secure the high-ground."

"No, certainly not," Skylaar agreed. "So we add sensors and charges there as well, but I think the majority of our effort should be focused on these underground passages—and on determining which one will afford the best escape route. I am betting my credits on this one."

She was pointing to the westernmost tunnel. This was the longest of the three, and after clearing the plaza, it split off into several directions, although Maya was unable to say where each branch terminated. Her dreams hadn't taken her that far.

Skylaar however, was unfazed by this lack of information. "Once we arrive, we'll task a 'bot to explore them"

Maya regarded her companions gravely. "That's if Angelique hasn't already set up traps of her own and is just sitting down there waiting for us."

"Indeed," Josette replied. "Knowing my sister though, I would venture to guess that she is upside with the ships, and at worst, has sensors watching on the ground for her. She doesn't want to scare off the Three, or risk alerting anyone right now."

"I concur," Sarah said. "Just the same, when we go in, Maya, we have to be on the alert and ready to deal with any opposition that we might encounter."

Maya frowned. Performing some unknown ritual in the middle of a crumbling ruin, at the behest of a strange galactic overmind was bad enough. Having to rescue a pair of untrained civilians—and themselves-- from the clutches of Angelique and goddess-knew-how-many-seasoned-and-well-armed-agents, elevated the entire affair from simply being 'very bad' and straight into 'completely-fekked-beyond-all-hope'.

Grunvaald Haarmaaneplaatz, Vaalkenstaad Township, Zommerlaand, Sunna 3, Solara Elant, United Sisterhood of Suns, 1049.03|07|02:91:20

"Lily!" It was Hanna. "Grammy's gone!" She was holding a note in her hand, written on real paper, and waving it in the air.

Lilith looked up from her com terminal in confusion. "She's *what?*"

"She's gone off on some kind of adventure," Hanna exclaimed. "Enggredsdaater just came by to tell me, and she said that Grammy took your assistant with her! I tried calling her on her psiever but she won't pick up."

Lilith snatched the message away from her sister-in-law and read the words for herself.

"I have been called by the Gods to undertake a great task. I have taken Jan with me. Please don't be angry with her; it was all my doing. We are leaving Zommerlaand, but we will be back soon. Take care of the farm for me. Don't worry. I'll be all right.'

"Love, Grammy"

Lilith immediately tried calling Grammy herself. When this failed, she attempted to contact Jan bar Daala with an equal lack of success. Irritation and anger quickly wedded with her sense of alarm, and she shouted for Ingrit. Of all of them, her wife was perhaps the closest to the old woman and the most likely to have an inkling of what was going on.

"Did you know about this?" she demanded.

"No, Lily, but I'm sure that everything's all right," Ingrit replied.

"Well, I'm *not*," Lilith countered sharply. "For one thing, my adjutant *did not* have my permission to go running off with her, and for two, the tone of this note strongly suggests that Grammy isn't in her right mind."

Ingrit started to contradict her, but Lilith cut her off. "I know exactly what you're going to say to me, Ingrit. I've put up with all of Grammy's mystical claptrap just for your sake, but this is going *too far. Vitkaa* or no, she's old, and this has to be the product of some kind of senile delusion.'

"We need to go after her right now, and get her back, for her own safety. While we're at it, I intend to have a little 'chat' with Ensign bar Daala and address her patent irresponsibility. She's an officer and she knows better."

Ingrit looked forlornly to Hanna for support, but her sister agreed with Lilith. "She's right, Ingrit. Grammy wouldn't have gone off like this unless she was out of her head. You know that she's been getting a bit forgetful lately. We need to go and get her."

Ingrit's shoulders slumped. She could see that she wasn't going to win this fight. "All right. What should we do?"

Lilith closed her terminal down and rose. "Get out to the spaceport and catch up with her before this foolishness proceeds any further. I'm going upstairs to get my jacket."

"I'll stay here and keep an eye on things while you're gone," Hanna volunteered.

"Good," Lilith replied. "This shouldn't take long."

***

By the time Lilith was back downstairs and headed out the front door, Ingrit had brought the farm's hovertruck around. The moment she was aboard it, they were off, headed for Waanderstaad spaceport. For once, Lilith didn't castigate her mate for her speeding. She was too angry and too concerned about Grammy to bother.

Although Waanderstaad was rightly considered to be one of the largest spaceports in the Sisterhood, the passenger terminal itself was actually quite small in comparison to other ports. Waandarstaad's main business was the transportation of agricultural products, not passengers. As a result, when Lilith and Ingrit arrived a few minutes later and entered it, they didn't have very far to search before they realized that Grammy and Bar Daala were not there.

Ingrit was finally starting to share her wife's concern. "What now?"

"Now we talk to the Port Police," Lilith said.

The police station was just off the main lobby, and a single, rather bored looking policewoman was on duty. When Lilith fished out her military ID and gave her a chance to read it however, all lassitude fled the woman and she sat up straight in her seat, fully at attention.

Lilith had to resist the urge to smirk. Clearly the policewoman was ex-Navy. Only sailors reacted like this in the presence of a Flag Officer. With a certainty, she knew that the woman would do all that she could to help them, and might even bypass some of the red tape just out of respect for her rank. It was one of the few times when Lilith had to admit that there were some advantages to the promotion that Ebed Cya had forced upon her.

"Yes, Admiral?"

"There were two women that came through here today," Lilith explained. "One is an old woman and the other is about 20 standard. Their names are Ms. Helga Mariasdaater, and Ensign Jan Bar Daala. Can you help me find out where they went? I think they may have taken a flight off planet."

"Yes, ma'am," the policewoman answered crisply. "With the emergency restrictions in place, we didn't get a lot of travelers passing through today, so it shouldn't be too hard."

She paused. "Admiral, I don't mean to be rude, but can you tell me *why* you need this information?"

"The old woman is—"Lilith searched for the right words, and then found them. "A bit—*odd*---and I'm afraid that she may have had one of her, um, spells. You see, she's my in-law and I'm very worried about her."

495

"Didn't you say that she was with another woman? Surely she would—
"

Lilith interrupted her. "Officer, at this moment I'm not certain that either of them are completely sane."

The officer nodded in sympathy. "Do you know about what time this might have happened?"

"Sometime in the last few hours. Try from 02.083 hours to now."

The policewoman tapped a few commands on her virtual keyboard and a list came up in the air between them. "These are all the departing flights so far." The list changed as she announced this, and then shrank in size. "These are the ones carrying passengers."

A second passed, and then, "Ah, here they are! Concordia Spacelines, Flight 909 to Ashkele. It has three stops, Thermadon, Luma and Wrede. It also looks like there was a third woman that went with them," the officer added. "A Ms. Kaly n'Deena. Is she someone that they know?"

"Yes," Lilith answered, shaking her head disparagingly. "She's a neighbor of ours, and one of my in-law's friends."

The fact that Kaly had also involved herself in the affair only underscored the power of Grammy's influence, and just how wild her delusions must have been to convince her to accompany them. Kaly had always struck her as a fairly level-headed girl. Until now.

"Do you know what time they are scheduled to arrive at their first layover?"

"The convoy should come out of Null at 05.00, and Flight 909 will be in Thermadon for an hour before moving on," the policewoman said.

Then the officer's brows furrowed in concern, "Admiral, do you think your relative is safe with these other women? Do you think there's a possibility that she might be in some kind of danger? That they might have lured her offplanet for some reason?"

"No," Lilith answered firmly. "I'm certain of that much. I think this is more a case of *her* leading *them* into something and *not* the other way around."

"Well, for what it's worth, ma'am, if we can come up with a good reason, I could have them all held when they reach Bel Sharra," the policewoman offered. "That one, the Ensign, could be detained for being away without leave—she *is* AWOL isn't she?"

"Yes, she is," Lilith said.

"And I think Ms. Mariasdaater could be held for a psych evaluation. Not sure about the third woman though. We might have to get a little creative there. She's RSE—a civilian basically—so she can come and go as she pleases."

Ingrit was positively horrified. "Lily? We can't do that! We can't lock up Grammy!"

Although Lilith would have preferred to do just that, she had to demur to her pairmate. When this business was over, she would still have to live with the woman.

"I appreciate the suggestion," she said, "but no thank you, officer. This is a private, family matter. We'll handle it ourselves."

"Believe me, I understand," the woman replied sympathetically. "I used to have an aunt that would go off wandering from time to time and I had to track her down more than once. She was about Ms. Mariasdaater's age, 250, and sometimes people that old do things like that. I wish you the best of luck."

Lilith thanked the kaaper for her assistance, and led Ingrit over to the military portion of the terminal. A Troop Leader was on duty there and she walked straight up to her, flashing her ID again. "Troop Leader, I need a direct flight to Ashkele for myself and my spouse," she said. "Your soonest."

The Marine didn't argue, or even ask her why. Lilith was a Vice-Admiral and that was explanation enough. It took only a few seconds before she located the nearest vessel.

"That would be the *Sybil Ludington*, ma'am. She's due to put in here in four hours to take on some Troopers going back out into the field after leave. She was supposed to transit to Sagana direct, but since she's not on a priority mission, I can have her Captain make a side trip. Shouldn't be too far out of their way."

"Nothing sooner than that, Troop Leader?"

The Marine shook her head. "Ma'am, I'm sorry but the *Ludington's* the closest ship."

Lilith nodded unhappily. Four hours it was then. She turned to Ingrit. "Ingrit, go back to the farm and let Hanna and Marina know what's going on, and tell them where I'm going. I intend to catch Grammy at her final destination."

Ingrit shook her head. "No. I'm coming with you."

Lilith sighed with tired resignation. "Fine, '*we*' then." This, she decided, was the 'down' side to marriage; the family that came along with it.

She had one last thing to attend to before they could depart. She had to call off from work. Admiral ebed Cya was expecting her to complete her latest reports on the Seevaan maneuvers and this would definitely bollix things up.

When she reached her, Ebed Cya proved to be completely sympathetic and understanding.

"Take all the time that you need, Lilith," she said. "I can have one of the other Flag Officers work from your notes. And it's actually a good thing that you're going to Ashkele; your old Battle Group is there, and I'm certain that Katrinn wouldn't mind a courtesy visit."

Even though the *Athena* was no longer officially under her command, Lilith still liked to keep tabs on its adventures, and the last she had heard, Battle Group Golden had been assigned to a standard patrol in the neighboring Elant. Ebed Cya's news came as a surprise.

"What in all space are they doing out there?" she asked, cocking an eyebrow. "I thought we already had all the assets we needed in the area, monitoring the war games."

"We do," Ebed Cya answered. "Golden was dispatched on a special mission at the request of the RSE. General Angelique bel Thana made it herself. She's also placed herself in charge of the Op. Katrinn and the other officers are answering directly to her."

"Really?" Lilith returned, wondering what could be going on in Xee space that would merit that kind of attention, or such tight operational control.

"According to Bel Thana, there's some kind of Marionite mischief going on, and it may involve the Hriss and another weapons deal. She's ordered the Battle Group to keep an eye on a particular section of the Drow'voi ruins, and she also has them monitoring all space traffic coming in and out of the system. Beyond that, the meat of it is on a 'need to know' basis and apparently we don't 'need to know.'"

Lilith grimaced. She didn't particularly care for the idea of the RSE commandeering naval vessels for their own business. Especially when they were keeping the Navy in the dark.

She also knew just as well as her superior did, that they had the power to do so. It was part of the Executive order that the late Chairwoman Marina bel Rayna had issued when she had authorized the agencies creation. In the name of state security, the RSE could order the military to help them, and the armed forces had to comply.

This didn't mean that she had to like it however. The RSE's predecessor, the OAE, had possessed the same mandate, but they had never done business like this. They had always worked closely with the Navy when it came to special operations and their policy had always been one of cooperation rather than co-opting. Lilith's opinion of the RSE dropped several notches, and seeing Ebed Cya's expression, she could tell that her superior was just as displeased.

"All right," she said. "While I'm over there chasing down my in-law, I'll drop by and see if Kat needs any help."

"Good," Ebed Cya agreed. "Let me know how you find things. Oh, by the way, you should also be aware that Golden has a secondary mission. They're to transport the Lady Felecia n'Calysher back to Thermadon. Seems that she's been on holiday, and Ashkele was one of her ports of call. Now that her mother is gone, the Circle wants her back, probably to serve as an interim Senatrix until they can appoint someone else."

Lilith chuckled dryly. "So at the moment, Ashkele is the center of the universe and 'anyone who is anyone' simply *has* to be there?"

"So it would seem," Ebed Cya said with equal acerbity. "Good luck with your in-law—and get back with me when you find out some more about this operation. This is something that has the potential of affecting our relations with a friendly star nation, and the Navy has to stay on its political toes. If it comes off well, I want to make sure that we get some of the credit. If not, then I want all the *shess* to splatter on Bel Thana and the RSE."

"Yes, ma'am."

Undisclosed Location, Kleta District, Thermadon Val, Thermadon, Myrene System, Thalestris Elant, United Sisterhood of Suns, 1049.03|07|03:31:33

A collection of the deadliest viruses known to the Sisterhood rotated slowly in space. Three in particular had been recommended to her, and of these, the Blood River virus was unquestionably the strongest candidate for what N'Elemay had in mind. It was one of those rare diseases that sprouted up every so often in the Nemesian jungles, only to burn itself out just as mysteriously as it had appeared, and very little research had been done on it.

After the attacks on Thermadon and elsewhere, she had been searching for something that would surpass them in destructiveness. Visiting plagues on the Church's enemies had been an obvious direction to search in and a member of the Faithful who was also an infectious disease specialist, had supplied the files for her review. And she fully appreciated the advantages that these plagues offered. They were much easier to procure than anti-matter bombs, and the logistics involved in fielding them were far less complicated.

The problem was that plagues like Blood River, could not be easily controlled once a weaponized version had been introduced into a population, and she didn't want the Faithful to suffer right along with the non-believers. She would have to let the woman down easily, she decided, and look for something else. Just to be thorough however, she opened up a sub-file that had accompanied the data. It concerned itself with pathogens that affected plants and domestic animals, and as she brought the information up, her hopes rose.

One of them was a virus that specifically targeted wheat, with the name Red Stalkbreaker S3A. Although there was already an antivirus in existence, the researcher had added in her commentary, promising N'Elemay that with some modification, a more virulent, and incurable variant could be engineered.

The implications were immediately apparent. If Red Stalkbreaker were introduced into the Zommerlaandar wheat crop, the results would be economically disastrous for the Sisterhood, especially if other plant diseases could be used to affect the major food crops on other agro-worlds. Even better, the Faithful could be warned in advance to stock up on emergency food supplies and weather the famine without harm.

She had found her solution, and for once, she was glad that Jon fa'Teela had chosen to abandon his faith. Had he remained, with Shaitan poisoning his soul as he obviously had, he might have gotten wind of this, and warned their enemies. But God had motivated the neoman to flee before he might have betrayed them. Saying a prayer of thanks for this divine protection, she began to compose her response to the bio-researcher.

Right in the middle of doing this, she was interrupted by a graceful hand that reached in and turned the holojector off. N'Elemay knew who it was even before she turned to look up at him.

"You won't need any of that," the Redeemer told her. He was accompanied by Sister n'Aida, newly returned from Storm, and the mysterious woman that she had brought back with her, Sister fa'Maala. The three of them smiled at her beatifically.

"My Lord," she asked. "What do you mean?"

"Now that Sister fa'Maala is with us, the time has come to take possession of a weapon that God revealed to me," he explained. "The power of the Tree surpasses anything that you could ever wield against the unbelievers, even these terrible diseases."

N'Elemay was mystified. "The Tree, Lord?"

"Yes," he answered. "A great and holy Tree of power. I will tell you about it as we make our way to it. Your things have already been packed for you, and a ship is waiting. We have a long journey ahead of us. We are going to the Xee world of Ashkele."

N'Elemay got up from her seat, all thoughts of bio-weapons now gone from her mind. Whatever this Tree was, she was completely certain that it would be their salvation. The Redeemer knew God's will. God spoke to him, and the Redeemer never lied.

CHAPTER 15

Ashkele Free Port, Hallasa System, Frontier Zone, Xee Protectorate,
1049.03|08|05:81:91

Despite all of the decorative filigree, and the colorful logos emblazoning its doors, Kaly knew a military grade hover-vehicle when she saw one. Grammy had made the reservations for them in-flight, and the Gravedeep Hotel, whose motto was *"If You Must Stay in Ashkele, Stay Here"*, had sent one of its 'courtesy vehicles' out to the Port to meet them.

Except for her tour in the ETR, Kaly didn't have any experience with alien cultures (and the humans of the Republic didn't really count), but she had heard the stories about the Free City. The armored personnel carrier was beginning to confirm every single one of them. The thing even had gun-ports! Edged in gold trim to be sure, but gun ports nonetheless. She flashed Grammy a look of concern.

"The Gravedeep is one of the finest hotels on Ashkele," Grammy reassured her. "They take the safety of their guests quite seriously, and once we're there, we'll enjoy five star service."

Once we're there, Kaly thought dubiously. According to everything she'd heard, the Free Port was a wild and lawless place. She just hoped that the modified AHPC wouldn't be tested, and she was glad that she'd taken the precaution of removing her duty pistol from its case and putting it in a shoulder holster.

She was unconsciously readjusting the holster's strap as the uniformed driver got out of the vehicle. The woman was, by all appearances, just as human as they were, and had Kaly been pressed to do so, she would have identified her as someone with Aran ancestry. Her accent however, was not Arai, but pointed to a much more exotic location

"Enshon, jantildamé," the woman said, coming around to them. "Do you need any help with your baggage?"

"No thank you," Grammy answered. "We only have our carry-on luggage and that one case." She indicated the locked container that contained Tatiana.

A grin spread across the woman's features as she opened the passenger door and admitted them. The interior, Kaly saw, was a lot different than any of the AHPC's that she had ever served in.

Instead of Spartan benches and bare surfaces, the cabin was plush. There also wasn't any separation between what should have been the troop compartment and the driver's station. This was open, with only a thin partition that could be slid shut for privacy. There even seemed to be a wet bar built in! Definitely not Marine issue, she decided.

"Your accent—"Grammy remarked. "It's rather unique. Are you a native of Ashkele perhaps?"

Kaly had heard of human women living in the Free City and she waited for her to tell them this. But their driver laughed and gestured towards a religious icon on the dashboard. "No, ma'am. I'm from Xilanti, in the Imperium. We're a Communion world."

"Communion?"

"Nothing special, just a small group of human systems in a big, big empire," the driver said blandly.

Then Kaly recognized the tenant of the little shrine on the dash. It was a Hriss. In fact, it was *the* Hriss, she realized. It was a cheap holographic representation of the Emperor J'akkat'vak'nar himself. Her eyes slitted in disapproval.

"We're the loyal subjects of the God Emperor and have been for over four hundred years," the woman was saying, making an unfamiliar gesture of reverence towards the holo. "The Xee hire us to handle the jobs that the warriors won't do, and the Clans don't mind as long as we abide by the Scriptures and keep our proper place."

Proper place? Kaly wondered. Bloody images of the raid on her motherworld surged to the forefront of her mind. "You mean you actually *work* for the Hriss Imperium?" she asked, barely able to contain the rage in her voice.

"No ma'am," came the answer. "Not 'work for'. We're part of it. My ancestors saw the truth of the God Emperor's vision and swore their allegiance to Him right away. The Hriss can be tough for sure, but they're good masters, and they *do* have the divine right to rule the universe after all."

It was all Kaly could do not to reach out across the seat and smash the little shrine to pieces, and then cave in the driver's face for good measure. But Grammy's hand silently and gently restrained her.

Kaly, she thought to her. *We are not here to fight the Hriss.*

Reluctantly, Kaly settled back into her seat, but she didn't bother to hide her contemptuous expression. As far as she was concerned, the driver and her precious 'Communion' were nothing but traitors to their own race.

Grammy was right though. They were on Ashkele for reasons that transcended Womankind's eternal struggle with the Hriss, and she couldn't allow her emotions to interfere. There was simply too much at stake. Forcing calmness, she pretended to find the scenery outside of her viewport interesting, and tried to ignore their guide and the ongoing conversation.

"The Communion you say?" Grammy asked pleasantly, "Weren't you once part of the Gaian Star Federation just like we were?"

"Oh yes," the driver replied, either completely oblivious to Kaly's hostility, or simply disregarding it. "That was back before the Plague hit of course. After that, we were on our own. Luckily the Clan warriors found us and offered us a path to a better life. Now, we bask in the radiance of the Throne of Bones and the Emperor's holy presence."

Then, as if finally realizing where her guests hailed from, she quickly added, "I hope that all this doesn't offend you, jantildam"

"No," Grammy responded. "Not at all. I actually find it rather interesting. We never imagined that the Hriss would allow humans to be part of their Empire. Things went much—*differently*--for us."

"Yes, jantildam," the driver returned with a trace of sadness. "I know. Perhaps someday, your Sisterhood will finally embrace the God Emperor's great vision for the galaxy like we did, and then things will change for you."

"Perhaps," the old woman agreed. "And perhaps someday you will decide to join your sisters as part of *our* vision of a greater human family and then, things will change for *you*."

The driver laughed and shrugged, and was starting to reply, when her expression sobered and she abruptly stopped the vehicle. Looking past her and out the forward viewports, Kaly saw that some kind of procession was blocking their way. The crowd was composed of many different races, all of whom were banging on percussion instruments of one kind or another. At their head, were the Xee themselves.

Unlike the rest of the assembly, the Xee were instantly recognizable, even to Kaly. They were not bipeds. In fact, to her at least, they resembled cooked and de-feathered chikka-birds more than anything else.

They had no eyes, or appendages of any kind that she could discern, and their bodies were encased in transparent globes that hovered over the pavement. Only the decorative metal bands that encircled these spheres gave any indication of individual identities, or their social status. Watching them, she guessed that she was looking at their priesthood, and this conclusion was confirmed a moment later when additional Xee, this time with more richly decorated bands, passed by. These, she knew, were the all-powerful merchant class.

A security detail marched right alongside them, and another was blocking traffic. It was a mixed contingent of Hriss warriors and forbidding dark grey robots that she had been told were simply called 'the Guns'. One of the Hriss stepped forwards and waved impatiently for them to change course and move on.

The driver smiled back at the creature and complied. "I'm sorry, jantildamé," she apologized. "I was so busy talking with you that I forgot all about this. I should have turned off earlier."

"What is this?" Grammy asked her.

"It's the Hey-Hey festival, Madame. The Xee hold them every year. They believe that it will scare away bad luck and evil spirits. We'll have to detour. The Hey-Hey goes on for hours and the main streets will all be blocked. No worries though. I know a good shortcut."

By this point, they were already off the main boulevard and traveling down a smaller side-street. The condition of the buildings around them quickly deteriorated, going from clean, well-maintained structures, to rude edifices covered with graffiti and punctuated with trash.

Barely a block further, a heavy ground machine, with markings that indicated that it belonged to some kind of delivery service, backed out of a dirty alleyway and stopped, blocking their path. Then, from behind them, another vehicle did the same thing.

They were effectively trapped. Automatically, Kaly withdrew her needlegun and cocked its action. She'd seen enough ambushes to know what was going on.

A moment later, a large group of green-skinned aliens, all bearing some form of club or crowbar-like weapon, poured out of the passages to either side of them. Without any explanation, challenge, or preamble, they began to methodically pound on the AHPC and several of them began working at the doors, trying to pry them open.

The hotel driver was completely unconcerned by the attack however. "Sorry, ladies," she said pleasantly. "I'll get this taken care of and we'll be on our way." She reached over and pressed a button on the dash. There was an intense, blinding flash of light.

When Kaly's vision had cleared enough to take in the scene, she saw that every one of their attackers had been repelled. Or transformed into charred and smoking corpses.

Heedless of the carnage that she had just unleashed, or the fact that the blocking vehicle still contained a driver, their guide started up again. The heavy armored carrier pushed the lighter vehicle aside with ease and crushed it against the side of the nearest building with a sickening metallic crunch. Then they were free of the trap, and driving on. Nothing, Kaly saw, was pursuing them.

"Just a few more minutes, jantildamé," the driver announced as they entered a larger thoroughfare. "I've sent word of this unpleasantness to the Hotel and once we arrive, the staff will have a complimentary bottle of Tipandian champagne waiting for you, as a way of apologizing for the inconvenience."

"That's quite thoughtful," Grammy returned with equal aplomb. "Please pass along our gratitude. Also, rest assured that I'll be adding in a generous tip for you, for all your troubles."

Then she turned around in her seat and addressed her companions. "You see? The Gravedeep really *cares* about its guests comfort. I think we'll enjoy our stay here very much."

Like the 'courtesy vehicle', all the gilding on its exterior did little to conceal the Hotel's security measures. Thick, high walls, topped with energy fields surrounded the establishment, and the main gate looked sturdy enough to Kaly's experienced eye to withstand a full-scale hovertank assault. There were also armed guards, in hotel livery of course, standing watch. All of them were Hriss warriors, and she had little doubt that the humans who came out to greet them were also from the Communion. To her, they seemed far too comfortable around the Hriss to be anything else.

Ignoring them as much as possible, Kaly followed Grammy and Jan into the lobby. It was a spacious place, filled with expensive carpets, inlaid wood and stone, and every centimeter the luxury accommodation that it had been billed as. Even so, she was still able to spot the remote gun-pods and other lethal devices that had been discretely positioned to cover the area. Whoever had built the hotel had made security just as high a priority as elegance. Given everything that she had heard about Ashkele, and had just experienced, she could see why. The Xee were lunatics, and this was their asylum.

There was a brief check-in process, and then they were shown upstairs to their rooms. Naturally, these were just as stylish, and just as well protected as the lobby. Their floor even had its own armed warriors, and the windows in their suite were thicker than anything Kaly had seen on a naval warship.

"Well?" she asked when they were finally alone. "What now?"

"That's for Jan to tell us," Grammy informed her, glancing meaningfully at the Ensign.

"Celina is here," Jan said, her eyes half-closed. "I-I can feel her impatience."

"Anything else?" Kaly inquired.

Jan shook her head. "No—just that she's here. And Maya is coming, but she feels very far away right now. There's something else--." Her brow creased with concern and concentration.

"What is it?" Grammy asked. "What are you sensing?"

"I'm not sure, "Jan answered. "It feels like there is another group—another trio. They're *different* somehow."

Her eyes flew open in alarm a second later. "They're the Enemy! Somehow they have their own group of Three!"

Grammy came over to her and took her hands. "How close are they?"

"I can't tell," Jan said. "Not as close as we are...I think. Oh Grammy, we have to stop them! If they get to the Tree before we do—"Her panic was palpable.

"We will," Grammy reassured her. "The *Alte Volk* are with us. They have been from the start, and so is the Galaxy Mind. If there's a way, we'll find it."

"So, what do we do now?" Kaly said, repeating her original question.

"Now, we wait for something else to happen," Grammy told her.

***

The Goddess did not keep Grammy and the others waiting long. Lilith and Ingrit arrived in the Free City the following afternoon. Their reception was far different than the one Grammy's party had received however. When they stepped out of the military shuttle, they were met by a small contingent of Marines, led by an officer.

"Commander Bertasdaater sends her compliments, ma'am," the Lieutenant said, saluting. "She also asked that you contact her at your earliest opportunity."

"Thank her for me, Lieutenant," Lilith answered returning the courtesy with a salute of her own. "At the moment however, I'm here on some urgent personal business. I need to speak with the port authorities and track down a group of women."

"Already done, ma'am," the officer advised her. "Admiral ebed Cya sent word ahead of you and we contacted the Xee. Ms. Mariasdaater and her party are staying at the Gravedeep Hotel, here in town. If you like, I can send the Shore Patrol over there to get them for you. The Xee authorities have agreed to let us handle this matter ourselves."

Lilith shook her head. "No thank you. This is a family matter, but we wouldn't mind a lift."

"Of course, ma'am," the officer replied. "We have a ground vehicle standing by." She led them out of the port and onto the street. Their transportation was an official Free City hover-limo, evidently on loan for the occasion. There were also two Marine AHPC's nearby which Lilith guessed were coming along to provide security.

The small convoy headed for the hotel and Ingrit volunteered to sit up front with their driver so that Lilith could use the limo's com terminal to make a secure call to Katrinn. Wife or no, she understood the realities of being a military bride. Some of what Lilith would need to discuss with her

506

sister required a clearance level to overhear. The only demand that she made was that Lilith add in her greetings and best wishes.

When Katrinn answered the call, she was anything but alarmed. In fact, she seemed rather amused by the whole affair.

"That's our Grammy for you," she said. "She always has been headstrong, and I'm not surprised that she talked the other two into coming along with her on this little escapade. Please, Lily, when you catch up with them, don't be too hard on your adjutant or the N'Deena girl. Grammy can be pretty compelling when she wants to be."

"I know, and I won't be," Lilith promised her. "N'Deena's not my problem, and on the way here, I decided against having Bar Daala courts martialed. However, once this is over, I *will* be shopping around for a new assistant. I can't have her blasting off for goddess knows where whenever she feels like it."

"Well, I certainly can't blame you there," Katrinn agreed.

"So, tell me, "Lilith asked, changing the subject. "What *is* going on with Golden and this RSE operation?"

"So far, very little," Katrinn answered. "General bel Thana came aboard a few days ago with fifty agents, none of them below the rank of Major. She also brought along some SRU Teams that she said were for security. They took over Officer's Country right away and Bel Thana has been up on the bridge ever since.'

"She has us watching the Free City and a spot out in the middle of the ruins. All she's told me is that it has something to do with the Marionites and the Hriss."

"And you don't believe her?" Lilith inquired.

"Frankly, no," Katrinn admitted. "The DNI hasn't gotten one whiff of the Marionites having any cells in Ashkele, and the Clans that are working for the Xee wouldn't want to mess up a good thing. The Xee pay their mercenaries too well. Even the Hriss know better than to shess in their own nests. The whole thing just doesn't add up."

"I concur," Lilith said. "There's more to this than Bel Thana is letting on. Anything else?"

"Yes," Katrinn answered. "Bel Thana is also very interested in the movements of the Hriss mercenary ships that the Xee have working in-system patrol. She also wants to keep tabs on what the Seevaans are doing. So far at least, the only Seevaan ships near here are the ones involved in the war games in the next quadrant over, and they're all accounted for."

Lilith sat back and stroked her chin thoughtfully. From what Katrinn had just told her, Bel Thana had clearly involved the *Athena* in something that went much further than simply nabbing a small group of terrorists.

507

Ebed Cya was right to be concerned, she concluded. Whatever was really going on here clearly had the potential of involving the Hriss and the Seevaans, and it centered on a deserted stretch of the Necropolis that appeared to have no military value whatsoever.

"All right," she said at last. "Let me know if you find out anything more, and if we have to, I'll recommend to Rixa that we appeal to the Circle to give us back operational control here, and dispatch additional forces at need."

"Thanks, Lily," Katrinn replied, visibly relieved by the offer. This was not a situation that any Battle Group Commander would have wanted to find herself in.

"By the way," Lilith added, "Did Shore Patrol manage to scoop up the Lady Felecia?"

"They did," Katrinn said. "We have her aboard the *Athena*. I'm planning on shipping her back to Thermadon on the next outbound transport, but right now, she's cooling her heels in Officer's Country.'

"That's one area where Bel Thana has actually been a plus. She didn't object to the billeting, and she was the one who told the girl about her mother. Apparently, the two of them knew each other back in Thermadon, and I'm glad for it. I didn't look forwards to giving her the bad news."

"I can imagine," Lilith replied. It was never an easy thing to tell someone that a loved one had died—or in this case was 'presumed' dead. It was also part of an officer's responsibilities. "Please extend my personal condolences to the Lady Felecia if you get the chance. Her mother was a great stateswoman."

"I will."

"And as soon as I can stuff Grammy onto the first flight out to Zommerlaand, I'll come upside and make an 'inspection visit'," Lilith promised her. "Given what you've told me, I think that Bel Thana could use another pair of eyes watching the situation, don't you?"

Katrinn smiled elfishly. "Ganz gaaf, Lily" she said. "I'll tell the crew to pick up their toys and make their beds before you get here. Oh, and good luck with Grammy."

***

Jan's agitation had increased with each passing hour, and as lunchtime came around, she was absolutely certain that Celina was making preparations to go into the ruins in search of the Tree.

Finally, she announced the news that they had all been waiting to hear. Celina was on the move at last. Immediately, everyone began to gather up the last of their possessions, and Grammy ordered them a ground vehicle from a local rental agency. They were just about to leave when a holo-image appeared in the center of the living area. It was Lilith, and according to the data-tag, she was downstairs in the lobby.

She was also livid. "Grammy!" she exclaimed. "What is all this nonsense? Ingrit and I are here to take you back to Zommerlaand!"

"How thoughtful of you," Grammy responded, nodding surreptitiously to the others to gather their belongings. "You and Ingrit shouldn't have traveled all this way just for me. Really, I'm quite fine, and when we're done with my business here, I can find my own way back."

"No!" Lilith retorted. "You have no *business* in Ashkele and you've made us both absolutely sick with worry. I need you to come down, *right now*, and come with us."

"Yes," Grammy replied evenly. "Perhaps you are right. Give me a minute or two to get myself ready, would you?"

Lilith's brows raised. She had clearly expected more of an argument. "Fine," she agreed. "A few minutes. We'll be waiting for you."

Grammy ended the call.

"Time to leave!" she declared. Then she grabbed her bag and gestured for Kaly and Jan to follow. Once out in the hall, she avoided the Lifts and headed straight for the Hriss guard instead. To their utter amazement, she planted herself right in front of him, and addressed him in perfect, unaccented, Hriss'ka.

"Worthless, impotent excuse for a male, "she said. "We superior beings are in need of an escape. Can you gather what few wits you have and show us to the rear exit? Or is that too much for you to comprehend?"

The guard snorted back at her with a mix of amusement and contempt. "Useless egg-layer, I would split your worm-eaten scull for showing me such disrespect! But this establishment forbids me to properly defend my honor by splattering your brains all over these walls!'

"The exit you seek is behind me, and down the hall to the left. May it buy you the time that you need to lay a trap for your enemies!"

"I would thank you," Grammy responded with equal politeness, "but doing so would only sully the honor of the eggs that I once carried within me. A wretch like you does not even deserve the spittle that I would grace the dirt at my feet with."

"Go with the Emperor's blessing and befoul me no more with your presence," the Hriss replied, standing aside to let them pass. "I shall make certain to delay the worms that follow you."

Nodding with the proper degree of curtness, Grammy led the way down the passage, and her dumbfounded companions followed right behind her.

"Grammy?" Kaly finally asked as they were exiting the hotel and making their way down an alley. "Where did you learn to speak Hriss'ka so well?"

"Oh, anywhere and nowhere," Grammy answered nonchalantly. "You never know what you'll need to keep a farm up and running these days, so it pays to learn everything you can."

"Sure," Kaly replied. By now she had decided that in addition to all of her spiritual wisdom, the woman was also a consummate liar. She was also reasonably certain that she had not witnessed the last of her surprises by any means.

Their crawler was waiting for them behind the hotel. Once it had received payment, the rental agency had dispatched the vehicle, and its on-board AI had guided itself through the city to their location, parked, and engaged its lethal anti-theft system.

It was not unattended however. The hotel driver was there, and she was accompanied by half a score of Hriss warriors. They were all armed.

As the crawler canopy popped open automatically, the woman smiled, and started towards them. There was something in her expression that put Kaly on her guard right away. Her hand edged towards her needlegun.

"Bian dea, jantildamé," the driver said. "I just heard that you are leaving for the ruins. You could use my knowledge of the area and my friends here wish to come along with us, and be your security."

"How very kind," Grammy answered. "But quite unnecessary. My companions and I can take care of ourselves."

While she said this, Kaly noticed the way that Grammy was holding her walking stick. It had been with her since they had left Zommerlaand, and until just then, she really hadn't paid it much attention. It was made of polished wood, and a meter and a half in length, with a fist-sized brass sphere at its top, and capped with a brass cone on the bottom.

She had it in a loose grip and her body was just as relaxed, but in the manner of a seasoned fighter. Clearly, it was either a weapon of some kind, or Grammy knew how to make it into one.

Another surprise, Kaly thought, unsnapping her energy pistol without bothering to be quite as subtle about it.

"The ruins are a very dangerous place," the driver insisted, still smiling. "Come, let these noble warriors lend you their protection." She had continued to close the distance, and the warriors behind her had unslung their weapons and were fanning out to block the alley.

"I'm afraid that we must refuse," Grammy answered, "and ask that you stand aside and let us leave." She was smiling as well.

She had also pressed a hidden button on her walking stick. Steel rods sprang out from both ends with a loud 'snick'. Now it was nearly 2 meters long and the heavy ball and end cap had ceased being mere ornaments. They had become a small, but sturdy mace-head for dealing hard blows, and a lance tip well suited for stabbing.

The sight of this primitive armament did not make the driver retreat, and the warriors with her were equally unimpressed. They were also starting to bring their own weapons up to bear.

"I am sorry, jantildam," the woman said regretfully, "but we cannot allow you to go on without us. The thing that you seek is too precious for anyone but the Emperor to possess, and if he cannot have it, then no one can."

They knew, Kaly thought in alarm. Somehow, they knew who they were and why they were there. The answer came to her right away. They had been tipped off by someone, and had been waiting for any human women who were trying to go into the ruins.

Her eyes darted to Jan, and she saw that Bar Daala had produced a needlegun of her own. For an instant, she wondered where it had come from, but this was not the time to speculate. She braced herself for action instead. The Hriss were all carrying military-grade weapons, and *Tatianna* was still packed away in its case. It would be an ugly little fight.

Suddenly, something moved in the corner of her vision, and she felt the wind of its passage. By the time she had turned her head to see what had caused it, Grammy wasn't there any longer. A bodiless shadow flew away from where she had been standing, moving at a speed that was almost too fast for Kaly's eyes to track.

A half-second later, the warriors were all falling to the ground, struck down by an invisible force, and leaving only the stupefied driver still standing. She gaped in amazement at the unconscious forms of her cohorts, and then at Grammy, as she reappeared out of thin air, right next to her.

Before she could react, Grammy tapped her head with the tip of her fighting stick. There was an arc of electricity, and the Communion woman spasmed, and joined the heap of warriors on the ground.

"Well," Grammy said as she pressed the stick's hidden controls and the metal rods retracted, "That was certainly unpleasant."

"I'm not going to ask you how you just moved so fast," Kaly said to her. "Or where you got that thing."

"That's a dear," Grammy replied, her eyes twinkling. "It's always the wiser to let some things stay a puzzle. It makes the Universe a more interesting place to live in, don't you think? Now, let's get going before Lilith finds us and we get ourselves into some *real* trouble!"

***

Still waiting in the lobby, Lilith accessed her psiever. They had been there for more than five minutes, and her patience, already thin from the long trip, was nearly exhausted.

"What's taking her so long?" she complained.

"Lily," her wife responded. "It's only been a little while. She's probably still packing everything up in her kit-bag."

They stood together in silence for another minute and then Lilith decided that enough was enough. "I'm calling her again."

This time, no one answered. She spun on her heels and strode up to the main desk.

"I'm still trying to get my elderly in-law to come downstairs," she told the human clerk. "I think that she may have had an accident while she was getting ready. Can you let me go upstairs and check on her?"

The clerk, who was already well aware of the situation, maintained her composure, and her professional smile, and promptly summoned the Concierge, who explained—again—that only registered guests were allowed past the lobby.

"Fine!" Lilith huffed. "Could you at *least* send someone from your staff up to check on her? Or at the very least, help her to bring her luggage down?"

This, she was told, was something that they could do. Five more minutes elapsed before the Concierge returned. From the troubled look on her face, Lilith knew that she was about to hear some bad news.

"Jantildam," the Concierge began, "I'm very sorry, but it seems that your relative has left the Hotel. Her bill was paid however, and in full."

"What?" Lilith spluttered. "Where did she go? *Tell me!*"

"Forgive me, jantildam," the woman answered. "I don't know. We did however help her to rent a vehicle in order to tour the Necropolis. Perhaps the rental agency could tell you more."

She gave her the name of the agency. Lilith didn't waste any time thanking her, and with Ingrit in tow, went out to find the Marine security detail.

"Lieutenant!!" she barked." I want those women detained. Find them and bring them back to me. *Now!*"

"Lily!" Ingrit protested. "You can't—"

"I can and I will," Lilith retorted, her eyes bright with anger. "Enough is enough, and if that makes you upset, then I'm sorry!" She turned to the officer, "Lieutenant? You have your orders. Get moving!"

The officer saluted and began to muster her troopers. Halfway to her hover vehicle though, the woman stopped, adopted a puzzled expression, and then turned and walked back to Lilith.

"Ma'am", she said. "I just spoke to the Xee, and they refused to help us."

"Refused?" Lilith asked. "What in all space are you talking about?"

"They said that your in-law paid their police officials a bribe," the officer answered uncomfortably. "A very substantial one."

"With *what* money?!" Lilith demanded.

"Ma'am, I-I don't know," the Lieutenant stammered, "but unless we pay them more, they won't— ma'am—you have to understand, this sort of thing is perfectly legal here. "

Lilith's head felt like it was going to explode from pure frustration. "Lieutenant, I don't give a flying *fek* what's 'legal' here! I want them stopped! Do you hear me?"

Ingrit gasped. In all their time together, Lilith had never used any profanities in her presence.

The Lieutenant looked positively ill. "I-I'm sorry ma'am, "the officer replied. "I can't. This is Xee space. If we go out there, charging around their streets and grabbing people, we could start a diplomatic incident."

Lilith was about to shout at her again when Ingrit stepped up and placed a hand on her shoulder. "Lily, she's right. Let's go and call Kat. She might be able to help."

The Necropolis, Ashkele Free Port, Hallasa System, Frontier Zone, Xee Protectorate, 1049.03|09|06:25:91

Using every bit of its stealth capabilities, the *JUDI* snuck into Ashkele's star system, crept past the Hriss mercenary ships, and then slipped around the Sisterhood Battle Group. Plunging down into the far side of the planet itself, Captain bel Lissa flew the ship as close to the surface as she dared.

The titanic, unstable buildings made this a dangerous endeavor, and more than once, they were forced to dodge a collapsing structure, or divert the little merchanter around a hazard that they couldn't overfly. It only took them an hour to arrive in the vicinity of their target, but by that time, everyone's nerves were frayed, and they all made a point of congratulating the woman on her piloting skills when they finally landed.

Because of the potential threat of passive spybots, the *JUDI* had touched down five kilometers away from the great plaza. This, Skylaar, Josette and Sarah all agreed, was well beyond the logical radius of a standard surveillance drop pattern.

Just the same, when the little party left the ship, everyone activated the camouflage modes on their cloaks. To the ships watching overhead,

513

nothing would register. The group was optically invisible, and the special materials that made up both the capes, and their bodysuits, also guaranteed that their infrared and bioplasmic signatures were equally undetectable.

As an added precaution, no one talked either, and psiever traffic, even though it might have been an aid, had been expressly forbidden by Skylaar. Although the transmission frequency of these devices was on the extreme low end of the spectrum, she didn't want to risk any chance of detection. Communications therefore, was limited to hand signs. Unlike the simple language that most troopers knew, the Agency's signs could convey even the most complex concepts to someone who knew them well enough.

Fortunately, none of them needed to express anything particularly intricate. The task before them was a simple one; to keep an eye out for 'bots, move quietly and watch their footsteps. Skylaar and Josette led the way, and both were armed with passive sensors, tuned to detect the ultra-low power signature of a 'sleeping' 'bot. They found two of them right away, and everyone fell in behind them as they worked around the slumbering machines.

Hours of careful travel went by like this before Skylaar signaled that they had finally passed through the ring of spy-devices. Then she waved Maya forwards.

"I wanted you to see this," the Nemesian said in finger-speak. She pointed to a gap in the ruins, and the huge space beyond it. It was the great plaza. Not an image of it, or anything from her dreams, but the real thing.

The giant, twisting cone of the Tree tower was at its center, rising up, and soaring into the sky. It seemed much larger and more imposing to Maya than it had been in her visions, and she had to crane her neck to see its summit. Below it, like silent attendants in some strange, mystical ritual, were the lesser buildings, and inside of them she knew were the tunnels that would lead to the Tree itself. Except for the low moaning of the wind, the great expanse before her was utterly silent and this managed to convey the incredible age of the place, and also, its utter alienness.

Maya was not intimidated though. She had given up being overawed by the bizarre nature of the entire adventure, and simply accepted what she was seeing as merely another manifestation of the incredible. What really mattered to her was seeing their business through to its end.

Having seen enough, she nodded silently to Skylaar, and worked her way back to her original position. Then they resumed their march, keeping to the shadows until they reached the huge triangular entrance of the nearest dome. Reasonably certain that it was finally safe to do so, they afforded themselves the luxury of psiever communications, and low whispers.

They went inside. Thirty meters later, while they were making their way down the tunnel, they encountered the unexpected.

Skylaar and Josette were still on point, with Maya right behind them, and Sarah, Jeena and Jon taking up the rear. Ahead of them, a tiny bot that the Nemesian had released, was passively scanning the passage for any electronic or biological threats. Without any warning that it was about to malfunction, it stopped abruptly in mid-air, wobbled, and then clattered to the floor of the tunnel, becoming completely inert.

Everyone stopped in mid-stride, and their hands went to their weapons. Then Maya realized that she could no longer feel her symbiote. It too, had switched itself off. And when she tried to notify Sarah by psiever, she discovered that she couldn't send the thought. This wasn't functioning either.

"Sarah," she whispered. "My psiever—its offline—and my symbiote—its—gone!"

"Mine as well," the woman responded. Unlike Maya, she seemed to accept this new development with a detached calm.

Everyone checked their equipment. Even though everything had been fitted with fresh batteries, the needleguns showed zero charge, and the GSG-20 grenades that they had hoped to use as components for Skylaar's booby traps, were also non-functional. Nothing that relied on electronics, or Seevaan technology, appeared to be working.

Skylaar quickly discovered the cause. Moving past them, she went back down the passage, holding the 'bot in the palm of her hand. After several meters, the little robot came back to life and floated up into the air as if nothing whatsoever had happened to it. And when she inspected them, her needlegun and explosives were also perfectly serviceable.

"We seem to have encountered some kind of dampening field," she announced. "My guess is that it encircles the plaza and protects the Tree in some manner. Luckily, it is not destructive in nature."

"Oh, how frightfully inconvenient," Josette remarked dryly. "Apparently this was something that the Pa'lla did not know about, or forgot to mention. If I were Angelique, I would demand an *immediate* refund."

Maya didn't laugh at her sarcasm. "So, we're left with *what?*"

"Plenty," Jeena volunteered cheerfully. "We still have our blades, and we might be able to rig Skylaar's traps using mechanical triggers."

Skylaar withdrew a GSG-20 from the pouch she had been carrying, and carefully considered it.

"Yes," she finally agreed. "I could rig the triggering mechanism to operate manually and use trip wires. Also keep in mind, Maya, that Angelique will encounter the same problems if she comes down here after us. That evens up our odds a bit."

515

To Maya the term 'a bit' was a massive understatement. Even though Angelique would now be deprived of any blasters or needleguns, she would still have the decisive advantage when it came to the number of blades at her side. With this, all of her training with Skylaar and at the *K'aut'sha* School suddenly assumed a terrifying new importance. The fight that she had feared, if it happened, would be positively medieval in nature.

"Oh cheer up, Maya," Josette urged. "This will be just like a good old game of Bat-Bat, but with real swords." This time everyone, with the pointed exclusion of Maya, laughed right along with her.

She was too worried to see the humor in this. They would need their tools and weapons back online in time to meet the Conversâzi threat, and she fervently hoped that the mysterious dampening field wouldn't extend over the entire circumference of the plaza.

Unfortunately, it did.

USSNS *Pallas Athena*, Battle Group Golden, Topaz Fleet, In Orbit, Ashkele, Hallasa System, Frontier Zone, Xee Protectorate, 1049.03|09|06:55:27

Katrinn hadn't expected to hear from Lilith as soon as she did. When the Com relayed the message to her command chair, she answered it right away. Seeing her, she could tell that Lilith was barely managing to contain her anger.

"Lily? Have you got Grammy? What's wrong?"

"No," Lilith said through gritted teeth. "We found her at the hotel all right, but then she and her friends slipped away on us. They're on their way to some kind of 'tour' of the Necropolis, and the hotel said that she had rented a ground vehicle. I tried to get the Xee to round them up, but they wouldn't cooperate. Grammy actually paid them a bribe! Can you believe that?"

Katrinn's eyebrows raised in astonishment at Grammy's duplicity. "A bribe, huh? That old woman is sure full of suprises."

"Yes," Lilith frowned. "She is. Kat, I want you to locate her and send down a special detachment to pick her up once they're clear of the Free City."

"I don't know, Lily," Katrinn replied doubtfully. "If the Xee found out—"

"Goddess blast the Xee and their greed!" Lilith snapped. "This is Grammy we're talking about, and those ruins are dangerous. The detachment can grab them and be gone before the Xee even figure out that we did it. Please Kat! She's only going to get herself hurt out there."

"Okay," Katrinn agreed. "Let me check with the *Artemis*. She's been tasked with the overwatch of the Free City. I'm sure that Captain bel Jerra can spare a sensor to pinpoint their vehicle. Once she has them, I'll have her send the team. Give me a minute or two, will you?"

Putting Lilith on hold, she contacted the commander of their sister ship. Captain Suzzyn bel Jerra answered. "Commander?" the woman asked. "What can I do for you?"

"Captain, I need you to locate a crawler that is just leaving the Free City. It should have three passengers aboard. Once you have it, send a squad down and take everyone into custody. Bring them back here--and tell the troopers to be gentle about it. One of them is my relative."

If Captain bel Jerra was puzzled by this request, she didn't show it. "Certainly, ma'am. It just so happens that we're tracking three vehicles right now. All of them seem to be headed in the same general direction."

"Three?"

"Yes ma'am," Bel Jerra replied. "Two left the City about an hour ago and are already in the ruins, heading west. The third one just entered the empty zone, also headed west. That vehicle should reach the Necropolis in another ten minutes. There are three passengers aboard it. I'm sending you an image now."

A new holo appeared. It showed the rental vehicle, as seen from space, and even at that odd angle, Katrinn recognized Grammy immediately. And almost as if she knew that she was being spied on, Grammy looked skywards, smiled, and waved.

Given her strange abilities, she probably *did* know, Katrinn reflected. Not that this would change the equation one way or the other. Grammy was coming home whether she wanted to or not.

"That's them in the third crawler," she said decisively. "Get the squad moving!"

Angelique bel Thana, who had been quietly working at her own station, suddenly interposed herself. "Belay that order, Captain. Let them go."

The confused officer looked from her to Katrinn, who was equally perplexed. "Ma'am?"

"Stand by *Artemis*," Katrinn instructed. "We'll get back with you once we decide how we're going to handle this. Keep tracking them."

Bringing Lilith back into the conversation, Katrinn turned her seat and addressed Bel Thana. "May I ask you exactly *why* we need to stand down, General? This situation has absolutely nothing to do with our operation."

Bel Thana stood and regarded them coolly. "*A contrari*, Commander. It has *everything* to do with it. You simply weren't told because you didn't need to know. As you may already be aware, one of the other passengers in that crawler is an RSE employee, Corporal n'Deena."

Katrinn and Lilith waited for her explanation.

"What you do not know," Angelique continued, "is that she has been working undercover for us, as a part of this operation. You are also apparently not aware that your 'Grammy' was once a senior agent in the OAE, and was also enlisted to serve our interests."

"We need them to reach their destination without any interference. Let me assure you, and the Vice Admiral here, that your in-law will come to no harm, and as soon as we can, we will make certain to extract everyone. We already have a team in one of the other vehicles and they have instructions to step in when the time is right."

Katrinn knew total *shessdrek* when she heard it. That Kaly was an RSE employee was undebatable. But according to Lilith and Grammy herself, the girl was hopelessly burned out and wanted nothing more to do with the Agency, or soldiering for that matter. As for Grammy, although she was fully aware that the woman had once served in the military like a lot of 'Zommies' had, she had never heard her speak—even once—about any association with the OAE.

Grammy was no spy. Clearly, Angelique was liberally seasoning the truth with lies.

The problem was, that she couldn't contradict her, or countermand her orders. They would have to let things play themselves out the way Bel Thana wanted them to, or Rixa would have her head. "Okay, General. We'll stand down. For now."

Hearing this exchange, Lilith's features colored with anger, but she didn't inject any protests. Instead, she cut the conversation short. "So be it. We'll wait to hear from you, Kat."

But the instant that the connection was severed however, all pretense of acquiescence vanished completely. "Ingrit," she announced. "It's obvious that Kat can't help. Her hands are tied. So apparently, it's up to us. We're renting a crawler and going after them."

"What about that General?" Ingrit asked warningly. "She won't like that."

"Ingrit," Lilith said curtly. "Until today, I've never disobeyed an order, but I think it's high time that I gave it a whirl. As far as I'm concerned, the RSE *and* General *'I-think-I'm-so-goddess-damned-high-and-mighty-Bel-Thana'* can go stuff themselves out of an airlock. We're going after Grammy."

***

When Celina blundered her way into a giant pothole, there was a jarring impact, and right away she knew that she had done something terribly wrong. A second later, crimson warning lights on the dashboard of her crawler began flashing imperatively.

There was a problem with the 'Transfer Case'—whatever *that* was. According to the readout, which was helpfully displayed in Xee, Standard, Hriss and several other languages, internal lubrication temperature was soaring, and total failure of the component was imminent. The crisis, she was informed, was due to a catastrophic puncture and leakage of lubrication fluid.

It was also entirely her fault. She had never been much of a driver, and the Necropolis was proving to be something that would have challenged even the most seasoned of hands. Jagged and unforgiving pieces of masonry were everywhere, in every size, and more than once, her all-wheel drive machine had fallen afoul of the uneven terrain. Now, the crawler was having its revenge on her at last.

Only a few meters later, a sickening grinding noise started up and she pushed the protesting machine forwards, knowing that it was hopeless. There was no question now about making it to her destination. According to her maps, and her dreams, it was still a long ways away, and the crawler clearly wouldn't deliver her there. The best bet that she had rested on finding somewhere reasonably open and flat, and calling some kind of service to come out and fix the mess that she'd created.

Thankfully, there was a sticker pasted on the dash, with the com code for the garage that the rental agency used, and she hoped desperately that her call would be able to get out. The huge, signal-blocking buildings to either side of her were going to be a problem, but she really didn't have any other options.

As it stood, she was in no position to repair the machine herself. She wasn't a mechanic any more than she was a seasoned explorer, and at the moment it looked like she needed both. Cursing her own stupidity, and inexperience, she located a place to stop and promptly shut the crawler down. It was time to apologize.

"Clio?" she asked. Although she had had the service tech remove her AI's ability to keep her captive, she had ordered the rest of her companion re-booted.

"Yes, Celi?"

"Clio," she sighed, "You were right. I admit it. I shouldn't have come out here—not all by myself at least. Can you call the road service for me?"

"Yes, Celi," her AI answered. "I'm calling them right now. Will you consider turning back once they get here?"

Celina almost agreed, but the burning imperative lurking in the back of her mind prevented this. She simply *had* to go on, no matter what.

"No," she finally told her, "I can't. Once the service gets here though, I'll see if I can hire the driver to take us the rest of the way. They have to have people that know their way around here."

"You know how I feel about that," Clio replied. "You really *should* consider going back."

Celina did not respond, and the AI didn't press her. They both knew that it was pointless. Instead, the musician said, "Clio, while we wait, we might as well get in some composition time. Shall we work on the secondary melodies for the realie some more? I have a few ideas I wanted to try."

She was already digging out her portable keyboard, and for her part, Clio welcomed the distraction. It was better than arguing with her mistress, or being shut down again.

A kilometer away, Kaly n' Deena was perched atop one of the towers, surveying the landscape through her riflescope. Grammy had made them stop for a break, and she had climbed up to a position that afforded her the best chance of spotting anything dangerous. According to her friends, the Necropolis, especially near the Free City, was the hunting ground for all sorts of nasty beings, ranging from single individuals who were just plain klaxxy, to full-on T'lakskalan slaver bands. She wasn't about to let any of them get the jump on her group, and Tatiana would do all the talking for her if someone actually tried.

Alternating between the EM, IR and bioplasmic bands on her scope, she ranged across the shattered landscape, searching for any sign of life. Just when she was fairly certain that there was nothing but dead rocks populating the area, she spotted something. It was faint at first, and she brought up the scopes magnification.

Someone had driven a crawler into the area and parked. Zooming in some more, she was only able to detect one person aboard the machine and she decided to engage the small but powerful directional microphone that was part of the imaging system. It had been added to her rifle when the Marine armorer had rebuilt Tatiana, and she had never used it until now.

She didn't expect to get very much at such a great distance, but she did hope that the mike would grab enough audio to at least confirm how many living entities were in or around the machine, and possibly what their intentions were.

Sure enough, the wind and the distance conspired to distort most of what the device relayed to her psiever, but she still heard enough to make out what it was. Someone was playing music!

Kaly watched the crawler, waiting for any sign that this was some kind of ruse. When nothing else became apparent, and the occupant said something in Standard to what had to be an on-board AI, she concluded that the human woman—whoever she was--was either mad, a complete imbecile, or both. Whichever was the case, she had stopped her vehicle in the open, and well within view of anyone that happened by. And the Necropolis was not a good place to encounter wandering strangers.

Then the thought occurred to her that the driver might be more than just lost, or broken down. She could be one of the Three, Kaly reflected. Or an enemy. She contacted Grammy by psiever right away.

Jan is certain that it is Celina, Grammy replied. *Can you get to her right away?*

While some sections of the Necropolis were fairly vehicle friendly, others, like the one they were in, were not. Here, it was faster to move on foot, and they both realized this.

Kaly traced a path for herself with her eyes. It would involve descending the tower that she was on, crossing over a narrow avenue, up a much shorter tower, and then over this to a broad flat building which overlooked her target. Definitely a work-out, but she knew that she could traverse it in a reasonable amount of time.

Yes, she answered. *It will take me about forty minutes, but I can get there.*

Ganz gaff, Grammy thought back. *We'll start that way with the crawler and meet you there.*

Kaly began gathering up her things. In addition to renting the crawler, Grammy had also seen to it that Kaly received special equipment to help her do her job. Whoever had rented them the all-terrain vehicle had added climbing gear, rope, half a dozen GSG-20 grenades, and a suppressed GSC-19 submachinegun to serve as a back-up weapon. None of this was part of the standard emergency kit by any means, and when Kaly had taken custody of it, she had privately wondered at Grammy's resourcefulness, and connections.

Lethal little toys like the GSC-19, and the explosives, were hardly 'floating around in space' for anyone to lay their hands on, and every bit of her gear was genuine Sisterhood manufacture. In the end though, it really didn't matter. What did, was that they were all in working order. Which they were. In fact, every item was brand new.

Her ropes were already in place, and waiting for her. She had free-climbed up to her perch, and now she used the primary line to rappel down the steep-sided tower to the ground. Once her feet hit the earth, she tugged at the secondary rope, releasing the special knot she had tied in it. Both lines came loose and dropped.

She needed only a few moments to retrieve them, and then she was off. In short order, she reached the next tower and began her ascent. As she climbed, Kaly heard their crawler starting up and beginning its journey towards their rendezvous point. As she reached the summit, she glanced back over her shoulder and spotted it. At the speed it was moving, she knew that she would definitely reach the target's location before her companions did.

Right away, she started down the opposite side, rappelling again to make up for lost time. When she finally reached her destination and was able to observe Celina's crawler once more, she brought up Tatiana and sighted in on it. Then she panned around the area. What she saw, chilled her blood.

Off in the field of broken masonry, and making its way steadily forwards, was a group of humanoids. T'lakskalan slavers to be exact.

There were five of them in all. Four were carrying what looked like Seevaan assault weapons, and the fifth held a wand-shaped object that projected a crimson beam. It swept this back and forth as the party moved along, and Kaly realized that the strange light was actually shining *through* the stones. It was a seeker beam, created by humanity's enemies, the Greys, and the Tee-Laks used it to find and incapacitate their prey.

The beam played over the crawler and its lone occupant, and on her directional mike, Kaly heard the woman gasp and cry out. The Tee-Laks had her, and if she didn't do something about it, they would take her prisoner and sell her off-planet as a slave.

She called Grammy by psiever and informed her about the situation. Right away, Grammy throttled the crawler's engine back and stopped where she was. Whatever happened next would be completely in Kaly's hands.

She sighted in on the alien with the seeker beam and took her shot. The malandrium round burst the reptilian's head like a ripe *chibba* melon and his companions panicked.

The Tee-Lak's hadn't expected to meet any kind of resistance and they scrambled for cover among the rocks. One of them even had enough presence of mind to return fire. His Seevaan weapon made even less sound than Kaly's suppressed rifle had, and near her, a piece of the parapet that she was using for protection simply vanished, leaving behind a smoking hole only a little larger than the beam itself.

Following the ancient dictum of 'shoot and scoot', Kaly kept low and scrambled to a new shooting position. This gave her a clear line of sight on another Tee-Lak and she dropped him with a second head shot.

Two down, she thought.

His partner, who had been crouching next to him, broke cover and tried to change position, firing as he went. He never made it; his head became a bloody mist.

Three down.

A fourth Tee-Lak was hiding behind a boulder and fired at her. Another chunk of stone near Kaly ceased to be, but the beam had missed her, and that was all that really counted. As she tried to sight in on him, his partner 'got stupid' and tried to add his own gunfire into the equation. He just didn't remember to keep behind cover when he did so. Tatiana quickly educated him about his grave tactical error.

One left.

She moved again, hoping to find a better shooting angle for herself. Unfortunately, the remaining Tee-Lak had chosen his spot well, and she was unable to get a bead on him.

So she resorted to something that she had learned on Larra's Lament from one of her Sniper Instructors. The woman, who was a Zommerlaandar, had nicknamed it *'Eek'da Skeela'*, or *'Barking the Squirrel'*. It was an old trick that hunters on Sunna 3 sometimes used against a target that was behind cover, and it served snipers just as readily.

Kaly selected a spot on the rock face nearest to where she believed her opponent was crouching, and fired at it. The stone fragmented, and the slivers exploded in all directions. A loud hissing whistle followed this as the Tee-Lak, hit by the razor sharp pieces, howled in pain and rolled into view. He wasn't dead, but he was severely wounded.

Kaly alleviated his suffering with another well-placed round.

All down. None to go.

She didn't rise, but changed her location one more time and waited to make certain that there weren't any more enemies to deal with. When it was obvious that she had neutralized all the T'lakskalans, she signaled to Grammy and Jan that the area was clear.

Grammy restarted the engine and brought the crawler to within 30 meters. Then she and Jan got out and began to approach the disabled vehicle.

Barely half-way to their destination, they were startled by the sound of the machine coming to life. Unable to move, the crawler rocked violently in place, destroying what little was left of its gearing system while brilliant tongues of electricity crackled to life all over its hull.

A female voice challenged them from an external speaker.

"Stay back!" Clio warned. "I have redirected this machines power source and created a lethal force field. I am also ready to transmit sound waves capable of stunning you into unconsciousness! You will *not* be allowed to hurt my mistress."

Wisely, the pair stopped right where they were. "Your passenger," Grammy asked her. "Your mistress—is she okay?"

Clio did not answer, and the electric fire covering the crawler continued to hiss menacingly. The machine however, had stopped rocking.

"I can see that you are a good and faithful servant," Grammy said soothingly, "and that you care about your mistress very deeply. I assure you that we are not here to hurt her. We are humans just like she is, and we want to help."

"I don't believe you," Clio retorted. "Stay away or I will hurt you!"

"If you don't let us help, we'll leave," Grammy replied. "And more of those aliens will come, looking for their companions. They will attack you, and eventually, overwhelm you. Then they *will* harm your mistress. Please, let us approach. We only want to get her away from here to safety."

The electrical field died down to almost nothing, and Clio went silent. It was obvious that the AI was considering its options. There weren't many for it to choose from.

Presently, the field disappeared and the canopy popped open. "You can approach, and help," Clio told them. "But be warned! If I sense any treachery, I *will* kill you!"

"Perfectly acceptable," Grammy agreed. "There will be no treachery and when she hears of this, your mistress will be very proud of you. You have served her well."

She signalled to Jan, and they started forwards again. When they reached the crawler, and nothing happened, Jan clambered over the lip of the open cockpit. A minute later, she reappeared.

"She's stunned," she announced, beckoning for Grammy to come up and assist her. "The seeker beam got her, but I think she'll be okay."

Together, they lifted Celina up and out of the crawler. All the while, Clio had been monitoring their progress, and she couldn't contain herself any longer.

"Is she all right?" the AI asked them worriedly. "I could never forgive myself if she was permanently injured. Please, tell me that she'll recover." Had she possessed hands, she would have been wringing them raw with worry.

"She will," Grammy told her. "The seeker beam just paralyzes its victim, and only for a little while. The T'lakskalan's need their prisoners alive. She'll come around in a few minutes."

This mollified the AI, but only to a degree. She still continued to fuss over Celina as they carried her over to their vehicle.

While they loaded her in and secured her, Kaly came down from her perch and lent a hand by grabbing the musician's possessions—including the handbag that housed the woman's anxious AI. When everything was aboard and they were ready to go, she went back to Celina's crawler one last time and took out a GSG-20 grenade, dropping it into the now-abandoned cabin. Set on guard-mode, it would arm itself and explode when the next living thing came near it.

"Something for the Tee-Laks," she explained to her companions. "In case they come looking for their friends." No one could disagree with her choice of thank-you gifts.

It was another hour before Celina began to come around. By this time, they were well away from the scene of the Tee-Lak slaughter, and making good progress. She was still numb, and more than a little disoriented.

"W-where am I?" she asked, her words slurring from the after effects of the Seeker beam. "Who—who are you?"

Grammy, who had been riding in the back of their vehicle, and keeping watch over her, answered. "We're friends," she said, "and sisters, on the same quest that you are."

It took a moment for the befuddled woman to process this, and then her eyes widened. "You—you know about the Song?"

Grammy smiled, and bobbed her head. Then she told her about the Tree, and the Three who would wield its powers. As she listened, the musician's eyes became even wider and filled with a mixture of awe, and fear. She looked at Jan.

"So, if I 'm the Singer," she said. "Who are you? The Guide? Or the User?"

Jan looked back at her from over her shoulder, "I-I'm not sure," she answered tentatively. "I think I'm the Guide, but we won't know until we get there. The name's Jan by the way, and I *love* your work. I have all your realies."

Celina managed to summon up a weak smile. "Pleased to meet you Jan. I hope you like the Song. I'd like to say it's mine, but now--."

She didn't finish and she didn't have to. Everyone in the crawler understood; like the Song itself, everything was really in the hands of the Galaxy Mind. Including whether they ultimately lived, or died.

CHAPTER 16

After exploring the underground tunnels leading away from the Tree, Skylaar assigned each of them a number, and chose the third passage to serve as their bolt-hole. It was the longest of them all, and headed off to the south before spiraling up towards the surface.

From there, it was only a short distance to an open area that was large enough to accommodate the *JUDI*. The remaining two tunnels to the northeast and northwest didn't afford the same open route to safety, and it was decided that these would be left clear until the other women arrived. After that, they would be rigged with explosives to defend against Angelique and her forces.

Since none of them knew when, or from what direction their guests, or their enemies, would arrive, they agreed that each of them would stand a watch at the very top of the Tree's tower.

Maya volunteered for the first shift. In the process of ascending to her post, she suddenly discovered that she was able to feel her symbiote again and could even access her psiever. The mysterious nullification field did not extend all the way to the summit. Instead, it terminated just as abruptly as it had in the tunnels, halfway up.

She stopped climbing immediately, and pulled out a hand light from her survival kit. Recalling the Agency version of the ancient Morse code, she sent a message down to the others. After a second, Jeena signaled back up. If things began to look bad, he told her, Skylaar wanted her to use her emergency Com to send a signal out to the *JUDI* for an immediate pick-up.

Indicating that she understood, she resumed her ascent. When she finally reached the top several minutes later, she paused, and gave herself a moment to take in the landscape spread out before her. The huge arched 'windows' afforded her an excellent view of everything around the plaza, and the sheer immensity of the Necropolis took her breath away.

Even though she had spent her childhood at its edges, and had seen plenty of holos and views from space, the vista that the tower afforded her brought her understanding of the Drow'voi ruins to an entirely new level. It was a place of cyclopean proportions, dwarfing even Thermadon in sheer scale. Unlike the Sisterhood's capitol however, it was completely empty. As far as anyone knew, not even a centimeter of it was permanently inhabited by anything more than the local animals and some insects. That, and its ancient ghosts. Shivering at the eerie desolation all around her, she brought out a compact pair of manoculars and got to work scanning the area.

At the moment, the plaza was devoid of any movement, and this gave her some time to consider her situation, and what lay ahead. After her conversation with Josette and the others, she had come to suspect that she was the User after all, and when the *JUDI* had transited into Null, and was on its way to Ashkele, she had asked Skylaar if her hunch was correct.

The Nemesian had confirmed it. She had also asked her to consider the awesome responsibility that would be placed upon her shoulders, and what she would do with her temporary power. Since that conversation, Maya had been trying to come up with a 'shopping list' that would satisfy her teacher.

There was only one small glitch; she didn't have any lofty ideas.

Like any other little girl, she had heard plenty of fairy tales that involved magical wishes. Some of them had ended well, and others quite horribly. They were only stories though, and even as a child, she had never really cared for the theme. Maya had always preferred wild adventures where the protagonist outwitted an evil giant, or a wicked sorceress, and stole away their treasures.

Now, whether she wanted it or not, she was faced with the adult equivalent of the 'three wishes' fable, and she was at a total loss. To compound the problem, Skylaar had refused to supply any suggestions of her own, and everyone else had been just as uncooperative.

"We cannot interfere," Skylaar had explained. "The Pa'lla made that abundantly clear. The User must be the one who makes the final choices, and only the User. And her choices must be from the heart. Once inside the process, rational thought will become distorted and only true desire will survive."

With that, Maya was left to solve the problem on her own.

Universal peace among all galactic beings had been one promising candidate. So was a cure for all the diseases known to Womankind. But when she really weighed them in her mind, neither managed to meet Skylaar's test. She didn't give a spacer's damn about galactic harmony, or eternal life for that matter. As far as she was concerned, the galaxy's myriad races could go right on blowing each other to atoms, and the concept of absolute physical well-being didn't overly excite her. Not on a gut level. Not where it would count.

Revenge on the other hand, was another matter entirely, she realized. There were more than a few 'galactic beings' that she had it in for, and had she had her way, she would have happily settled on this, and been done with it. But with Skylaar and Lady Ananzi to answer to, she knew that she had to come up with something better.

527

So far, the only alternative that had appealed to her didn't seem to be anything the Tree could, or would grant. This was for the responsibility to be handed over to someone else—after she had quietly settled a few personal scores, of course.

The minutes passed, and no new ideas came to her over the wind. What did arrive, was a crawler, picking its way over the broken terrain and entering the plaza. She brought her manoculars up and when she focused in on the machine, she immediately recognized its occupants.

Jan bar Daala was driving, and she was accompanied by the young Marine that she and Sarah had encountered during the raid on the *Lida* Labs, as well as Grammy, and Celina. From their position, it was clear that they would be coming in to the Tree through the northwestern tunnel.

Maya hurried over to the edge of the ramp and flashed another message down to Jeena, alerting him. Right away, the neoman and the others scurried to position themselves at the mouth of the tunnel. It was a given that Grammy and her group had alerted the Conversâzi to their presence the very instant that they had driven through the ring of sentry 'bots. There was no telling if they would be coming in alone, or shadowed by agents that no one had spotted yet.

Maya dearly wanted to run down and join her companions, but she stayed where she was. Someone needed to keep watch from the high ground.

Her decision to remain at her post proved sagacious. Not more than ten minutes later, a second crawler came into view. This time, there were only two passengers inside; Sarah's mother, Lilith, and her new wife, Ingrit. In addition to seeming like a fairy tale come true, the entire situation was also taking on the aspects of a cosmic soap opera. If nothing else, Maya certainly wasn't bored.

***

Grammy didn't flinch when a sword blade flicked out in front of her, stopping just a hair short of her neck. She had no reason to, given who was holding the weapon.

"Hello Sarah," she said pleasantly, "How nice to see you again. I see that you have been reawakened."

Immediately, Sarah relaxed and lowered her weapon. "I have," she said, "and I see that you brought Celina to us."

"Indeed," Grammy replied, gesturing towards the woman who was even then being led into the chamber by Jan and Kaly. "The Three are here."

Celina, who had been gaping up at the Tree during this exchange, suddenly swayed unsteadily on her feet. "Oh my," she exclaimed. "I feel quite dizzy." She started to collapse and Jan came over and helped her to sit down.

"It must be all of this excitement," the musician explained. "It's all so—incredible. Oh, I wish that Clio was here to see this! Please tell me that she'll be okay."

"She will be," Grammy promised. "It's just as I explained. The field around this place is affecting her. As soon as we're gone, she'll be back to her old self, so stop worrying. We have to get to work and we don't have much time."

She turned to Kaly. "Kaly, would you be a dear and signal to Maya to come down and join us? We need her down here and I think you would serve us much better up on the high ground."

Nodding, Kaly gripped her rifle strap and started up the ramp, pausing only to send the signal to Maya. As she climbed up and away from them, Grammy got down on her haunches and drew mysterious symbols on Celina's forehead while crooning reassurances into her ear. By the time Maya had joined them, Celina was herself again, and back up on her feet.

She looked at Maya. "Are you the User?" she asked.

"I'm Maya," the young woman replied curtly.

"Yes, yes," Celina agreed, a little taken aback, "Of course you-are—I mean--I'm so pleased to meet you--Maya."

Maya frowned. "And you're Celina. Well, now what?"

"Now we walk over to the pool," Jan answered. "Celina sings the Song, I guide you, and you use the Tree."

"Sure thing. Right away, "Maya retorted. "One little detail; how do I do that?"

"You have to step into the pool," Jan replied. "That's where you do all your work."

Maya looked at the depression doubtfully. "Yeah, I know. But it was filled up with some kind of water in my dreams. It's drier than dirt right now. Any idea how to fix that, oh wise and powerful Guide?"

Jan gave her a wry smile, and offered Celina her hand. "You'll see."

She led them over to a spot near the empty pool. The floor there was incised with a simple design; three perfect circles joined together by a triangle. Each circle was large enough for them to stand in. This was a feature that had not been in Maya's visions, and the marks reminded her of a magical diagram that some sorceress might use in an occult ritual. Which, in a way it was, she reflected. Only they were the sorceresses.

At Jan's direction, each of them took their place, with Maya occupying the circle that was nearest the empty pool. Then they linked hands, making the entire affair seem even more esoteric than ever.

"Celina?" Jan said. "Sing it. Sing the Song."

The musician took in a breath, started to open her mouth, and then stopped. "I can't believe it," she exclaimed. "I actually have stage fright! I haven't felt this jittery since the first time I sang for my class in primary. Give me just a moment will you?"

"Certainly," Jan replied patiently. "This isn't the kind of concert that you normally give."

Celina smiled in gratitude, and closed her eyes. After a few seconds she reopened them, drew in another breath, and began to sing *a capella*.

Even though her performance lacked electronic accompaniment and sophisticated imagery, Celina's beautiful voice lent the Song all the power and majesty that it deserved. Each note that came from her throat was clear and pure, and the magnificent melody filled the gigantic chamber.

Everyone, even Maya, became so entranced that they almost didn't notice what was happening in response. The glyph that the three of them were standing in had come alive. It began to glow with a strange blue light, and there was the sound of flowing liquid, faint at first, and then increasing in volume. As one, they looked up, but to their credit, none of them broke ranks, and Celina did not falter, but kept singing.

A silvery fluid was running down from the top of the tower, flowing through deep grooves that had been cut into the edges of the great ramp. It moved with an unnatural swiftness, and in mere seconds, it had reached ground level, and found additional channels that had been carved into the floor. Then it began to fill up the pool at the base of the Tree.

When it was barely a fingerbreadth from the top, and Celina had reached the very last note of the Song, the flow ceased completely.

The substance did not go still however. Instead, it shimmered with little points of light that danced within it like Zommerlaandar Alfs. They moved through the fluid almost playfully, and with no apparent pattern or purpose.

Meanwhile, on the far wall of the pool, another glyph had appeared. This was just as simple as the one that marked out their places, and equally as enigmatic. It was another triangle, with something that looked disturbingly like an unblinking human eye set in its very center. The eye pulsed in the silvery depths, as if it were a conscious thing, waiting for Maya to take the next step.

"Your Song certainly seems to have done something," Grammy noted. "Maya, I believe that your turn has come 'round." She inclined her head towards the pool. "In you go."

Maya hesitated. Seeing it now, as a real thing and not a part of some dream, she wasn't afraid to admit the truth to herself. She was absolutely terrified.

"Okay. So how am I supposed to breathe?" she asked Jan. She wasn't some ancient alien slug that could live under water.

Jan answered. "The Watchers showed me. You'll be able to do it. Go."

Maya turned to leave, but Celina grasped her arm. "Maya! Wait! If this thing is what I've been told it is, you have to be careful. You have to choose the right thing! Please—when the time comes, think carefully! For the Goddesses' sake choose good!"

At that precise moment all that really mattered to her was completing this strange ritual as quickly as possible, and returning to something that resembled a normal life. But seeing the sincerity and deep concern burning in the other woman's eyes, she lent all of the comfort that she could to her reply.

"Don't worry," she told her. "I will."

Then, before her courage could desert her, or something else contrived to create another delay, she started towards the pool. She was only centimeters away from entering it, and finally confronting whatever awaited her, when a voice filled with anger made her stop. It was Lilith, storming into the chamber with Ingrit in tow.

"Grammy!" Lilith shouted. "Enough of this foolishness! You need to come home with me. Now!" She was so furious that she was completely oblivious to the utter strangeness of their surroundings, and marched straight up to her without giving any of it even the slightest glance.

Grammy regarded her with a patient smile. "Why Lily! How *nice* to see you! I'll be along just as soon as we finish up here."

"No Grammy!" Lilith rejoined. "We're leaving *right now*! Kat is up above us in the *Athena*. This entire area is a classified operations zone. It's not safe to be here." Then she realized that Sarah was also standing there.

"*You?* You're involved in this too? I can't believe that you would let yourself be taken in by such nonsense!"

Sarah shook her head. "Mother, it is not nonsense, and I think that leaving right now would be inadvisable. This is probably the safest place for all of us to be at the moment."

"Besides," Grammy added. "We certainly can't go until we've taken care of our business here."

Lilith blinked in dismay. "Our *business?!* What business? What in all space do you think you're going to get done *here*? Now, come along! I have a transport waiting that will take us all back to Zommerlaand."

531

Grammy folded her arms stubbornly, and neither Sarah nor any of the others made any move to intervene. "No, not just yet, Lilith" the old woman replied. "First we finish what we were sent here to finish. *Then* we go."

"Grammy—"Lilith started to say, and then she stopped herself and addressed Bar Daala instead. "Ensign? Help me get these people clear."

"No, Admiral," Jan said. "I'm sorry, but I can't do that. Your Grammy is right. There's important work to do here and we can't leave until it is complete."

Lilith's eyes widened in astonishment. She was now absolutely certain that Grammy had managed to infect all of them with her madness.

"For the Goddesses sake!" she spluttered, "All of you, take a good look around! There's *nothing* here! This is just an old pile of stone!"

"It is much, much more than that, Lilith," Grammy returned calmly. "This place is a device, left behind by the Drow'voi, and we are here to use it."

Lilith shook her head. "Grammy, there is no Drow'voi 'device'," she said firmly, "This is just an old ruin, and we need to leave it."

"The device is right here in front of you, Lilith," Grammy replied. "My three friends here have been sent to activate it."

"You've all gone mad," Lilith declared. "Stark, raving mad."

"And you look like someone who needs a cookie,' Grammy said. "It just so happens that I brought a batch with me from the farm." To Lilith's utter amazement, she fished through her carry sack, and brought out a plastic bag. It was filled with them.

"I don't want a *damned* cookie!" Lilith yelled. "I want everyone to come with me right now!"

Grammy sighed deeply and turned to Jan. "Well, then perhaps you'd better explain this to her," she suggested. "In your own way. You tell the story a lot better than I do."

"Yes, I think you are right, Grammy, "Jan agreed. Without any warning, her eyes rolled up in the back of her head, and she began to sink to the floor. Skylaar and Sarah caught her up, and something hit Lilith in the chest. She staggered backwards with a strangled cough.

Two presences suddenly occupied her mind. One was her own and the other was Jan bar Daala. Lilith clawed at her head, futilely attempting to eject her.

Please don't struggle, Vice Admiral, Jan's mind-voice told her. *It's much easier if you just relax and let me show you what you need to know.*

Goddess! Lilith thought in alarm. *My mind has been taken over by some kind of alien organism—*

No, Lilith, Jan answered. *Not an alien—well, not exactly. But I promise that I won't hurt you. I'm sorry I had to do this, but just let me tell you why we are here. After that, I'll leave. I swear it.*

The voice in her skull was so like Jan's, and sounded so genuine, that Lilith was tempted to cooperate. Then she marshaled herself and renewed her resistance. *Get out!* she told her. *Get out of my head!*

I will, Jan told her. *Just as soon as you hear what I have to say.*

Realizing that she had no choice, Lilith decided to acquiesce—if only until she could dream up an effective strategy to evict her unwanted guest. She felt Jan smiling tolerantly at this, and hated the woman's presence all the more for it. She didn't like being so out of control.

Watch and listen to me, Jan thought. *When I'm done you can make up your own mind.*

The same images that she had shown to Kaly, came into Lilith's consciousness, and as they scrolled by, Jan explained all about the ancient struggle between the Drow'voi and their Enemy, what the Tree actually was, and why the Galaxy Mind had sent them there.

At first, Lilith refused to believe any of it, but as Bar Daala continued, she began to reconsider her position, and finally, she came to believe what she was being told. The Jan-Presence left her at this, and once more, she was the sole tenant of her own mind.

Jan's eyes fluttered open, and Lilith looked at her in awe. In addition to everything else, Jan had also revealed her true origins. Lilith had witnessed the manner of her creation, and also the Watchers who had crafted her from the cells of her former human body.

"I believe you," she finally said. "I don't believe it—but I actually *do* believe you."

"Well it's about damned time!" Grammy declared. "*Heilaage Kekk,* but you are a stubborn one!" Then to Jan, "Thank you, Jan. You don't know how long I've been trying to pound some sense into that thick scull of hers."

"Excuse me" Maya interjected, "I hate to break this up, but we have to get moving. I've had this stuff rattling around in *my* scull for way too long, and I want to get it over with."

"Yah," Grammy agreed. "You're right. It's well past time." She gestured toward the pool, and Maya placed a foot into the fluid.

"Wait!" Lilith cried. "Shouldn't we study this thing first? Call in some experts?"

"We *are* the experts," Maya told her firmly. "Unless you've got a little Drow'voi hiding somewhere in your pockets." With that, she took another step. The liquid lapped around her ankles, and the little motes of light brightened and gathered around her.

Lilith started to utter a protest, but Sarah placed a restraining hand on her shoulder. "We must trust them, mother. The Galaxy Mind wanted *them*, not us."

Lilith gave her daughter a look that was the very epitome of all misgivings, and Ingrit stepped around and gently grasped her arms.

"We're just the audience now, Lily," her wife said. "We have to have faith that everything will work out."

Hearing this, Lilith realized that Ingrit had known all along what Grammy had been up to. She didn't resent this however. Not after being let in on the Secret. There was too much involved for such a petty response to play any part in this situation. But they *would* talk about it later, she resolved. In private.

"There is also something else that you should know about, Mother," Sarah added. "We are in grave danger." She went on to reveal what she knew about Angelique bel Thana, the Conversâzi, and their sinister objectives.

Lilith was duly horrified, and when Grammy quietly pressed a cookie into her hand, she absently accepted it, and took a bite. Grammy had been right, she decided. It really did seem to help.

USSNS *Pallas Athena*, Battle Group Golden, Topaz Fleet, In Orbit, Ashkele, Hallasa System, Frontier Zone, Xee Protectorate, 1049.03|09|08:04:13

Angelique was trembling with rage, and just then, she didn't care how ungainly this made her seem. She had just viewed the surveillance footage sent over from the *Artemis*, and when she had recognized Grammy riding in the first crawler with Celina, she had become alarmed. But when Lilith ben Jeni had been identified, her panic reached its absolute summit.

As a routine precaution, she had had Sarah's family investigated, and this had naturally included her in-laws. In the process, Grammy's past involvement in the *Orgón par Avaní Extér* had come to light, but the files had clearly indicated that the woman had never made it past the level of trainee.

Now Angelique knew differently, and she was appalled that she had been fooled by such a simple deception. Helga Mariasdaater was more than just a failed applicant. She was an active agent, and the OAE had clearly not accepted their reduced role in the Sisterhood's intelligence community.

Worse, they had somehow managed to involve the Navy in their subterfuge. There was no other reason why Vice Admiral ben Jeni would be in the same operations area with a member of the OAE. Clearly, the *Orgón* had gotten wind of the Secret somehow, and they were working with the Navy to take it for themselves, and supplant the RSE.

Then, an even darker realization dawned on her. Josette, who had been sent out to chase the Marionite hackers, had been missing for far too long. It was quite possible that she had switched sides, and was working with Ben Jeni. Angelique had never fully trusted her sibling, and now her doubts seemed to be completely justified. It was the only way that the OAE could have learned about the Secret, she decided. Josette had turned against her own blood. She was a traitor.

Summoning up every remaining ounce of her self-control, Angelique schooled her features into a semblance of false calm, and quietly signaled for her sister Silvi to join her in the Vice Admiral's former office. Silvi had come upside as soon as the *Athena* had arrived in-system.

The instant that they were together behind closed doors, Angelique dropped all pretense of tranquility and let her anger run free.

"Treacherous bitches! I won't let them take it from me," she hissed, battering the desktop with her fist. "Not when I have worked so hard! The Tree is *mine!* Do you hear me? *Mine!*"

"I am going down there now," she declared, her features set with white-hot determination, "before anything else can upset my plans."

"What about the third woman?" Silvi asked, unaffected by her outburst. "She still hasn't appeared."

"We will wait for her," Angelique answered tersely. "Right now we have to grab the other two before Ben Jeni can. Stay here and make certain that Commander Bertasdaater doesn't send anyone downside to help her. I'll leave all the SRU teams with you. You know what to do with them once I'm downside."

Silvi nodded soberly and Angelique's spirits were buoyed by the resolution she saw in her eyes. They had come up with the contingency plan before she had left the Hive, but she had never imagined that it would have to be put into play. Now, they would have to resort to desperate measures.

Despite this, she was confident of one thing; Silvi's loyalty. She at least, could be trusted to protect her back while she finalized their business down in the Necropolis. Then she would see to it that the women who had betrayed her, paid with their lives, starting with Josette and Vice-Admiral ben Jeni.

Her equilibrium somewhat restored, she returned to the bridge with Silvi in tow. They went directly over to Katrinn's chair and Angelique was careful to keep her tone neutral and professional.

"I have just received word that the Marionite terrorists are arriving in the operations area to meet their Hriss counterparts," she announced. "I am going downside with my forces to intercept them."

Puzzled, Katrinn glanced up to the sitscreens, which at that moment were displaying the live feed from the *Artemis*. Nothing that she saw on them indicated any new arrivals in the area, least of all a group of desperate radicals, or even the Hriss.

"Don't worry," Angelique reassured her. "I'll make quite certain to take care of your relatives when I encounter them. You have my solemn word on that. And while I am gone, my sister will be here to help you coordinate the operation. Consider anything that she says to be a direct order from me."

"Of course," Katrinn replied. "Ma'am."

Angelique departed, and Silvi quietly took her station at the foot of the command chair. Katrinn watched the woman for a few minutes and considered this new development.

She had shared Rixa's misgivings about the operation since its very onset, and her sense of foreboding had only grown as their voyage had continued. It wasn't just that Angelique and her people had circumvented the usual protocol and procedures. Or that their reasons for this mission itself simply didn't add up.

It was more than that. As a young girl, Grammy had taught her to listen carefully to her *Kliene Sprakker*, her 'Little Voice', and although she was nowhere near the mystic that Ingrit was, her intuition had always been strong, and served her well.

At the moment, it was whispering that there were things going on here that even Admiral ebed Cya didn't suspect. That something truly sinister was taking place. The fact that Lilith, Grammy and Ingrit had become involved, even peripherally, didn't help one nano.

Forcing her anxiety back, she reminded herself of her ship's history, and her own experiences. The *Athena* had been involved in plenty of clandestine operations before. A certain amount of shadows and secrecy went along with that kind of thing, and the women that called covert work their profession tended to be 'odd', if not disturbing, as a general rule.

That had to be the root of it, she decided. She was simply overreacting, and seeing things that didn't exist. Clearly, some of the RSE's weirdness was rubbing off on her, and making her as paranoid as they were.

In any event, her hands were tied. She was a naval officer, and the RSE had the authority to command her. They were, after all, agents of her government, and the late Chairwoman herself had awarded them their mandate. She would do her job, however odd or disturbing it seemed at the moment, finish this mission, and see them off her ship. Then things would return to normal.

Her *Kliene Sprakker* however, did not agree.

Several minutes later, a call came to her chair that caused her anxiety to return in full force. It was from Colonel Marya Lislsdaater, and Captain Veera t'Gwen, her counterpart with Ships Security.

"Commander?" Lislsdaater began. "I just got word that my girls have been relieved by the RSE at all of our red-level zones. They were also told to confine themselves to Five-Bar.'

"The same thing happened to Captain t'Gwen's women, except that they're still able to conduct general patrols. They're not cooped up like my people are, but they're still not happy about it. Is there something going on that we should know about?"

Normally, these two groups worked in sync to protect the most sensitive areas aboard the ship, including the armory, the computer core, the main lifts, the engine room, and the bridge itself. Dismissing them from these posts was an alarming development. It was also way out of line, and completely uncalled for. The *Athena's* security forces had always been fully up to the job of protecting the ship.

Reflexively, Katrinn glanced back over her shoulder to the Main Lifts. The Marines who were normally stationed there, were now gone. A squad of RSE troopers had quietly taken their place, and another detachment had joined them. This group walked by her and took up a position near the NavCom stations. They weren't doing anything aggressive, but they *were* there, and they were heavily armed.

A chill ran up her spine. There had to be a legitimate explanation for this, she told herself. The alternative was too frightening to entertain.

She turned her chair around to face Silvi. "Colonel? What is all this?"

Silvi smiled up at her. "I'm sorry Commander," she answered. "I should have told you about it before I sent the order. Can we enjoy some privacy?"

At this, Katrinn rose, and they went into her office together. She patched in Lislsdaater and T'Gwen and then faced the RSE officer expectantly. "Well, Colonel?"

"What I'm about to tell you is classified," Silvi said. "When our Agency learned about the Marionite activities here on Ashkele, we also received intelligence that pointed to the strong possibility that they have operatives aboard this very ship. Those same agents may attempt to seize the *Athena* as part of their operation. We believe that their intent is not only to secure more weapons of mass destruction for themselves, but also to commandeer this vessel as part of a general attack on the Sisterhood."

Her officers were as floored by this as Katrinn was. Captain t'Gwen was the first one to recover and respond.

"Ma'am? With all due respect," the Security Chief countered, "I can't see how that's possible. After we transferred all the known Marionites off the ship, my department—and the DNI---ran a comprehensive background check on everyone aboard. I'd stake my bars that we don't have any more Marionites aboard this ship, or in our entire battle Group."

"I beg to differ, Captain," Silvi replied coolly. "*Our* sources indicate otherwise, and we believe *them* to be more reliable."

"If that's true, then why not let us help you?" Colonel Lislsdaater challenged. "With my troopers and your teams, we can cover every centimeter of this ship. No one will be able to get away with anything."

"I'm afraid that that won't be possible," Silvi responded. "We have reason to believe that some of these Marionite agents are actually *part* of your security forces. This is the only way that we can fully safeguard this vessel."

Katrinn knew pure *boolkekk* when she heard it, and this was as big a steaming pile as she had ever come across. Her intuition had been correct after all, she admitted. This woman, and her associates *were* up to something unsavory.

In the entire history of the Sisterhood Navy, there had never been a mutiny, or a single ship taken over by any hostile force. For the average sailor, the very idea was too incredible to lend any credence to. But what she was witnessing went way beyond the need to maintain operational security. And with their teams in place at every sensitive area of the ship, the RSE now had complete control over the *Athena*.

But before she could take any action, she had to be absolutely certain that her conclusions were correct. If this was truly legitimate, then defying Colonel bel Thana not only meant destroying her career, but facing a courts martial for treason. She needed to put the situation to the test and find out, one way or the other.

"Colonel," she said, "I trust my security people implicitly. Surely we can find some way for our two groups to work together here."

Silvi shook her head. "The situation is much too sensitive right now. But once we are done with our business downside, and General bel Thana returns, we can revisit this subject."

"Then I want to contact Rixa," Katrinn rejoined. "I think that Naval Command might have something to say about this. At the very least, they should be informed about the change."

"I'm sorry, but I can't permit that either, Commander Bertasdaater," the woman responded. "We have to maintain a total communications blackout while this operation is under way."

A sinking feeling filled Katrinn's gut. *That's it then*, she thought. The impossible had really happened, and right before her eyes. The *Athena* was in unfriendly hands, and the safety of her crew utterly depended on what she did from here on out.

"Very well," she said with a calmness she didn't feel. "Colonel Lislsdaater, Captain t'Gwen, your women are to remain in stand-down mode, alert level Def-One until I order otherwise. Please continue to cooperate with the RSE Teams and give them any assistance that they require."

The holographic images of the two women saluted her, and Katrinn ended the call.

Silvi smiled at her again. "Commander, I am so glad that we could come to an understanding."

***

While Lilith struggled to digest her daughter's tale of wide-ranging treason and conspiracy, Maya walked tentatively into the shallow end of the pool. The silver liquid lapping around her ankles was just at body temperature, and to her surprise, she found that it wasn't wet at all.

Instead, it was more akin to a denser version of the air around her, nearly imperceptible and not uncomfortable in the least. The little points of light that populated its depths had increased in number, and become more active. Watching them flit about, it dawned on her what they actually were; little Watchers. Miniature versions of the beings that Jan served so faithfully, and their presence, and their playfulness, helped to calm her. Whatever awaited her, she would not be facing it entirely alone.

The angle of the pool was steeper than she had expected, and in just a few steps the fluid was up to her knees, then her waist, and finally her chest. At the same time, the little Watchers were swirling around her, and then flying off towards the mysterious glyph before returning to repeat the process. They were leading her there, she realized, urging her to move forwards and complete the ritual.

Well, I guess I'd better oblige them, she thought. The only other choice was to turn around, and refuse the challenge, and she had come too far, and gone through too much, to do that. With a final glance back at her companions, she submerged herself. Then she took a brief, tentative breath, fully expecting to choke.

Jan had been telling the truth though. The fluid was breathable. It wasn't as easy to take in as normal air, and it reminded her of trying to breathe on an extremely humid day on Nemesis, but she didn't drown. After a few moments, she found herself adjusting to the strange sensation.

Her mood also started to change. A sense of euphoria and bliss replaced her hesitation, and she suddenly felt safer in the pool than she ever had anywhere else in the entire universe. It was like coming home after a long and difficult journey.

At the far end, the glyph had brightened, and she half-walked, half-swam towards it, both delighted and curious. When she was only a fingerbreadth away from the shimmering design, she reached out to touch it. Everything went dark...

...Maya had vanished. One moment, she had been floating towards the glyph, and then in the next, she had simply ceased to be.

Lilith gasped in alarm. "What just happened? Where did she go?"

"She is inside the process," Jan answered. "All we can do now is wait for her to return."

Lilith couldn't contradict her. She was out of her depth here, and she was painfully aware of it.

Overhead, the great Tree, which had been quiescent until now, was beginning to glow and pulse with light. It filled the chamber with an odd, silvery illumination that lit the cavernous space without creating any shadows, and it seemed to come from everywhere, and nowhere, simultaneously. Sound had also taken on an entirely new quality, lending echoes to the slightest noise, and Lilith could feel a tingling sensation all over her body like a static charge.

Overawed as she was, a part of her was still able to wonder at the technology behind it, and she was especially fascinated by the fluid that filled the pool. Her education as a naval officer had included the sciences, and whatever the substance actually was, it went beyond everything that she had ever been taught.

She was certain of one thing though. It was a completely liquid interface, and her mind spun at the implications. It had to be some highly advanced form of non-Newtonian fluid, she concluded. It certainly behaved like a ferrofluid—but one that also allowed a person to breathe while submerged within it.

But stimulated by what, she wondered. Electricity? Bioplasmic force? Something else? She couldn't have even begun to venture an answer. As for the little lights swimming in it, she was reasonably certain that they were a kind of nanite, possessing some type of intelligence. That much had been obvious from the way they had led Maya to the strange glowing design.

Whatever it was, the liquid in the pool went beyond even the most advanced Sisterhood technology, or even what the Seevaans grasped. No buttons, no holo-displays of any kind, and it was clearly thought driven, but by something other than a psiever. Somehow, it picked up its signals through another medium entirely. Even more amazing than this, was that if Bar Daala was correct, the weird substance was also perfectly preserved and fully functional after *twenty* millennia!

Seized by scientific curiosity, and unable to do anything else but wait for Maya's return, she removed her canteen from her belt, emptied its contents, and went over to the edge of the pool. No one made any move to stop her as she knelt down and took a small sample.

When this was all over, and providing that they were still alive and relatively sane, Lilith was positive that the Sisterhood would benefit greatly from a study of the fluid's properties.

She recapped her container and stood, meeting Sarah's eyes. Her daughter didn't utter any recriminations however, and simply looked away. She knew just as well as Lilith did, that no matter how their strange adventure ended, there was still the future to consider.

USSNS *Pallas Athena*, Battle Group Golden, Topaz Fleet, In Orbit, Ashkele, Hallasa System, Frontier Zone, Xee Protectorate, 1049.03|09|08:06:43

Captain t'Gwen sat back in her chair, puzzling over the orders she had just received from Katrinn. They didn't make any sense. Although she hadn't served as the *Athena's* Commander for very long, Katrinn Bertasdaater had proven herself to be a capable, detail-oriented leader. In her short time on the job, she had never made an error in any order that she had ever issued.

This time, however, she had. Def-One, or Defense Condition One was the lowest level of alert. It was only used when the ship was in port, and its internal security forces were augmented by dockside elements. At all other times, the lowest possible condition was always a 'two' or higher. Given their current status over a secure operational area, Def-One was totally inappropriate, even with the SRU teams on the job.

Frustrated and confused, T'Gwen called up her interactive map of the ship and requested 'vid feeds of the red-zone areas. The RSE troopers didn't register on her map, and she hadn't expected them to. All of their psievers had been modified to foil detection by everything except direct video imaging, and there were rumors that some of their agents could even defeat that.

Fortunately, that didn't seem to apply to the SRU troopers. They came up on the 'vid feeds and she watched them for a few minutes. One group, posted at the entryway to the engine room area, was in the process of waving off a pair of her securitywomen while they were trying to conduct a walk-through.

Not acceptable, she thought sourly. *Not acceptable at all*. Not this, not Def-One, not any of it. Her mother had often been fond of saying, *'Just because I'm paranoid, doesn't mean that someone's not out to get me.'* And at that precise moment, the wisdom of this rang out truer than ever.

"Fek it," she said aloud. She rose, and left her office, encountering her second in command on the way out.

"Captain?" the Lieutenant asked her, "What's going on? Now they're not even letting us patrol. And *Def-One? Seriously?"*

"I don't know," T'Gwen replied honestly. "Stay loose. Something's going on here. I'll get back with you when I find out what it is."

She left her and made for Officer's Country. She needed to speak with the other senior officers. Right away.

When she finally found them, they were sitting together in the Officers Mess. Mearinn d'Rann waved her over to an empty seat next to Colonel Lislsdaater.

"I'm pleased to see that all my officers are so alert," D'Rann said quietly. "I won't waste your time. We don't have it to waste. I believe that this ship is now in the hands of an enemy force."

No one argued with this grave announcement, and she continued. "I have been in communications with Rixa ever since we shipped out, and they have expressed serious concerns about how things have been transpiring here. Now, I can't get through—even with my clearance. When I asked her about this a few minutes ago, the reason that Colonel bel Thana gave me was the need for 'operational silence'.'

"I don't believe it, and I don't think that Katrinn is falling for any of it either. We will have to assume that she was sending us a message to that effect when she lowered our status to Def-One.'

"I want each of you to get with a staff member that you trust and pass the word along. Be alert, be careful and be ready. I also assume full responsibility for this. If I'm wrong, then I want to be the only one facing charges of mutiny. Now get going."

The group dispersed, and everyone headed, as casually as they were able, to their respective subordinates. In Mearinn's case, with nowhere to go except the bridge, she made a pretense of visiting the Ships Activities Officer, Saara sa'Vika, on some minor business. With the exception of the security details and engineering crews, Sa'Vika's department enjoyed the greatest freedom of movement around the ship.

They were also the least threatening of all the *Athena's* personnel, and Sa'Vika, a dedicated schemer and negotiator, knew everyone. She was someone who could be trusted to keep, and disseminate, a secret. When Mearinn shared her suspicions with her, the Kalian wasn't surprised nor alarmed in the least.

"I never really liked those RSE women," Sa'Vika confessed. "They weren't interested in trading anything, and they turned down some really good offers. The way I see it, anyone who's not willing to do a little under-the-table business shouldn't be trusted. Don't worry Mearinn, I'll whisper the word into the right ears."

***

Several minutes later, up on the *Athena's* bridge, three things happened all at once. A gigantic power spike occurred down in the Necropolis, and on several of the system's lesser planets. These were at locations that the *Athena's* charts identified as Drow'voi ruins. According to the ship's sensors, their combined output was greater than what Thermadon could produce in an entire year.

At the same time, a group of Seevaan warships, all bearing the crests of the Chaotic faction, materialized on the sitscreens. And the Hriss mercenary vessels, which up until then, had been on routine patrol, abruptly changed direction and assumed a course straight for the *Athena's* Battle Group. Their missile doors were opening.

"Sound battle stations!" Katrinn yelled. "Fire Control, get me some solutions on those targets. Com, alert the *Demeter* and *Artemis*." What had been a bad situation, was now becoming positively deadly.

Two separate transmissions were coming in. One was from the Seevaans. "Warship *Pallas Athena*, this is Lady Commander Haraava Hadraalot of Her Majesty's Celestial Navy. You are to leave your orbit immediately, and remove yourselves to a safe distance. This area is now under the protection of the Chaotic Faction and our Great Queen Talaria. We are dispatching our forces to the surface to take charge."

Even as the insectoid made this pronouncement, a trio of shuttles were leaving the Seevaan ships and arrowing downside.

The other message was from the Hriss. "Miserable egg-layers! Ignore these stupid bug people! They have no authority here! This planet is under *our* protection and we demand that both of your forces leave or we will blast you to atoms!"

They too, were sending down shuttles, and the *Artemis* was registering a new ground vehicle approaching the ruined plaza. It was filled with Hriss warriors, and driven by, of all things, a human woman.

Katrinn took this in, and turned to Silvi. "Colonel, I don't know what you people are doing down there, but we're about to find ourselves right in the middle of an interstellar incident. We need to contact Rixa right away and get some assistance. Com? Send out a distress call."

Silvi shot up from her seat. She had a needlegun in her hand. Deep down, Katrinn had still been holding onto the faint hope that she was wrong about their situation, and the RSE's intentions. The gun banished this once and for all.

"No, Commander!" Silvi barked. "I told you that we can't allow that." She inclined her head towards the SRU team at the NavCom station and immediately, one of the troopers pointed her blaster at a Comtech's head. Her companions did the same, leveling their weapons at the rest of the bridge crew.

"There will be no calls to Rixa. And as of now, I am relieving you of command and placing this ship under full RSE control. Anyone that disobeys, or attempts to disobey, *will be shot.*" At this, the remaining SRU troopers took up positions between the workstations, covering everyone with their weapons.

"I'm sorry that it had to come to this, Commander," Silvi added with what seemed like genuine regret. "But this mission is far too important for you to be allowed to interfere."

Katrinn's reaction caught her completely by surprise. She just grinned, leaned back in her chair, and folded her arms over her chest.

"I sure hope you know how to run a warship in an active combat situation, Colonel," she said, adding a little 'Zommie' twang to her words, "'Cause it sure as shess looks like that's what's about to happen here. That, and a little interstellar war."

Silvi's gaze flicked nervously to the data on display all around them and she saw the same things that Katrinn did. They were at a gross disadvantage. It wasn't just their lack of numbers either.

Where the Sisterhood enjoyed a clear superiority over the outdated vessels of the Hriss, the Seevaans overarched both groups exponentially. Although the sleek alien war machines registered visually on the *Athena's* sitscreens, they were invisible to its sensors, including all of its targeting systems. And a weird greenish glow surrounded them. This was their mysterious Death Field, which made them completely invulnerable to attack.

Fate had turned the tables on the Battle Group. If it came to an engagement, the *Athena* would lose, and the Hriss, even though they were too insane to appreciate it, stood even less of a chance.

Realizing this, Silvi looked like a treed kaatze, and Katrinn couldn't have been more pleased.

"Want a friendly suggestion, Colonel?" she drawled. "Back off just like they said. Let me call Rixa, and get us some help out here."

Sweat was beginning to break out over Silvi's otherwise impeccable forehead. She started to reply, "I think that—"

The RSE officer never finished her statement. The sitscreens lit up again, and what everyone on the bridge saw made them stop what they were doing and gape in awe. All through the confrontation, the energy levels downside had continued to rise.

Something was happening that no one could have ever anticipated. Not even the Seevaans.

The Necropolis, Ashkele Free Port, Hallasa System, Frontier Zone, Xee Protectorate, 1049.03|09|08:06:56

At first, there was nothing but darkness. That, and the Song echoing in her mind. Maya was drifting in a formless void, and she had trouble focusing her thoughts. She couldn't even recall who she was, or how she had gotten there.

She had a name—she was certain of that much—but no matter how hard she tried, she couldn't remember it. There were also things that she was supposed to do here that wouldn't come to her. Important things.

The pleasant sensation of floating there with nothing more than the Song itself for company, was more compelling though. The notes of the melody danced in front of her as things of pure sound and color. They were all that really mattered.

Slowly, other lights began to appear, until the sable void was filled by them in their millions. They were stars. She knew what stars were.

In their midst was a planet. She was certain of this. She had lived on several of them.

Other heavenly bodies materialized near it, and she finally recognized where she was. It was a world that should have been familiar to her immediately. Maya searched her mind, trying to summon up its name, and then finally, recovered it. It was Ashkele. The vast planet-spanning ruins and the tiny space occupied by the Free City, were unmistakable.

The ruins were not the static, dead things of her memories though. Rivers of light flowed through their deserted avenues now, pulsing like they were part of a living being. For a time, she watched the brilliant display, utterly entranced by it.

Then she felt herself being drawn up and away from Ashkele and further into the cosmos itself, and she sensed, rather than saw, other worlds just like it. Each one of them was populated with ruins of their own. They too had been created by the ancient Drow'voi, and like Ashkele, they had come to life in answer to the Necropolis's clarion call.

They were everywhere. There was no corner of the Milky Way that lacked the mysterious edifices, whether big or small, and somehow she knew that they were all interconnected.

There was more besides.

For millennia, treasure hunters had scoured the ruins, searching for any useful technology. They had never realized that devices like the symbiotes were mere toys in comparison to what the ruins actually concealed. The real treasures had been cleverly hidden in the very crystalline structures of the building blocks that had been used to create the massive edifaces. The stones themselves were the machines, and because of this, they would remain functional for millions of years.

Maya laughed as she grasped the full import of this, and its irony. The secret had been in plain view all along. If she remembered this fact, she also decided that she had no intention of revealing the truth. The notion of allowing the galaxy's adventurers to continue with their fruitless efforts was simply too entertaining.

But even if her inclinations had been different, she understood that the disclosure would have done the hunters little good. The technology that the Drow'voi used was so advanced that it was highly unlikely that any race currently populating the galaxy would be able to understand it.

She also discovered that she had another secret to keep about the Necropolis, and the role that it played in the great antediluvian network. These ruins, and the Tree itself, were an important hub of the vast alien collective.

Not the only one though. The Drow'voi had created many Trees, and they were scattered throughout the galaxy. She could even feel the nearest one. It was located on a forgotten world that was now part of the Hriss Imperium. Unlike the Tree on Ashkele though, it was not active. Yet.

This detail was highly significant for some reason, and she struggled to understand why. Later, she told herself, the answer would matter. To someone. According to her fragmentary memories, she had come to the Necropolis with friends, and she decided that they would probably want to know about this.

Maya tried without any success to recall their faces, and when she failed, she turned her attention back to Ashkele. Experimentally, she extended her hand towards the planet.

It was not her real hand, of course. She knew that. It was her concept of a hand, and although she could see her body if she willed it, it too was an illusion, a mere creation of her own thoughts. Wherever she was at the moment, physical form meant nothing. Only thought and desire held any sway.

Not that she let this bother her. She was too caught up in the formless ecstasy of her new state to worry over such trivial issues.

Her illusionary fingers made contact with the world, and she was struck by how fragile it seemed. Then she tried to touch one of the other worlds that made up Ashkele's solar system, and to her pleasant surprise, she discovered that no matter how far away they seemed, they were always within her grasp.

Turning in place, she attempted the same thing with a few of the neighboring stars, slightly concerned that they would somehow burn her incorporeal form. They did not do so however, and proved to be just as close to her as everything else was.

As Maya laughed in pure delight, something joined her. Like her, it possessed no form, but this didn't diminish its presence in the least.

More memories of her life as Maya n'Kaaryn resurfaced at this, and she finally recognized the new arrival. It had always been there in the background of her existence, ever present and ever watching.

It wasn't the Goddess though. It was something else that transcended that archetype, and every other notion of deity that her species had ever conceived of.

Nor was it frightening, or strange. Instead, it seemed to be just as familiar to her as any of her lovers or best friends had ever been. This was because, in some unfathomable way, it *was* those people.

Her companion spoke. "It is time," the Galaxy Mind said. "It is time for you to make your choice."

Then Maya heard the Song again, and felt the being's anticipation rising. She also understood that in it's eyes, there was no 'right' or 'wrong' choice for her to make, only the decision itself. She would not be judged by it no matter what sins she committed. It was beyond all sin, and all virtue. Those qualities, she realized, were reserved for the life of the flesh. Here however, the laws of karma simply did not apply.

Looking once more at Ashkele, Maya considered the possibilities and then a thought came to her. The planet with its huge sprawling ruins, seemed empty. It needed something to help fill it up, she decided. It needed life of some kind.

The notion solidified, and a spot of green appeared in the deepest part of the Necropolis. Within seconds, it had grown and covered the area around it. Then it began to spread outwards in all directions, with startling speed.

The sight made her smile. The planet looked better with green on it. So much better.

"Is that your only choice then?" the Galaxy Mind asked.

Maya floated there, pondering this question. *Was* this her only choice? Was there more that she wanted to do?

She could also destroy things if she desired it. The longer that she entertained that idea, the more appealing it became. More memories returned to her with this, and they provided her with ample justification.

A small moon came to her attention. The Xee called it Ashkelom, and it was Ashkele's only satellite. She had never liked Ashkelom. It was a shriveled, ugly little planetoid that had been captured by Ashkele millions of years earlier.

To her, it had always been the very symbol of the corruption of the Free City itself; pitted and malformed like a victim of one of Old Gaia's ancient plagues, and its face was marred even further by a great crack that ran right down its middle. Ashkelom had never been considered to be a lover's moon, nor was it a thing of any great magic or mystery. It was a malformed body that presided over an equally unpleasant city.

She reached for it, and without any hesitation, crushed it and scattered the fragments. After this, the heavens seemed a little less tainted.

Then her mind turned to something else—*someone* else—someone that she hated deeply. If she could do all this, then she could finally settle accounts with Lady d'Ershala. For a brief moment, she hesitated, certain that the Galaxy Mind would change its stance and prohibit her from taking her revenge. But it made no move to do so. The choice was hers to make, without any conditions whatsoever.

Looking down at the Free City, Maya sought the woman out among its thousands of inhabitants—and quickly located her. Crushing the glass dealer was even more effortless than destroying Ashkelom, and far, far more rewarding. The tiny scream that she heard as her astral fingers closed around her victim, only added to her sense of gratification. Shyla's death had been redressed at last.

Her attention shifted to the space above Ashkele. A fleet of spaceships were hovering over the planet like an irritating swarm of gnats. Feeling them with her mind, she instantly comprehended the nature of their crews.

Three of the vessels were occupied by humans like herself, but a far greater number were filled with the Hriss and the Seevaans.

She knew who they were, and she didn't care for either race. She never had. She also didn't want them there. Their very presence annoyed her.

Again, she reached out, and batted them away. The warships scattered like so many dry leaves, exploding in satisfying balls of fire. Only the human ships remained, and she made no move against them.

They could stay. She liked them.

While she contemplated what her next act would be, an intense wave of weariness overcame her. Suddenly, she didn't feel like playing anymore.

"Is that your final choice then?" the Galaxy Mind inquired.

"Yes. It is," she answered. "I want to sleep."

"You shall," the Galaxy Mind promised, "There is one more thing that you must do however. Watch and understand. Watch and remember."

A vision of the Tree that she had seen in Hriss space appeared before her.

"The Enemy has gone there," it told her, "with a Trio of their own. Your kind must stop them before they can activate it. Do you understand this?"

Maya did, although she was too drowsy to really care.

"Now I will sing you to your rest," the Galaxy Mind said. "You have done very well, Maya."

She heard a new Song. It was just as beautiful as the first had been, and she let its notes carry her off into a peaceful unconsciousness. This time, there were no dreams lying in wait to haunt her.

***

Except for an expanding debris field, there was nothing on the *Athena's* sitscreens. Ashkelom was gone, and except for the *Athena* and her sister ships, the space around the planet was completely empty.

The enormous power surge had also disappeared, and only the strange green moss which now covered a continent-sized area, served as evidence that anything had ever happened.

Katrinn still couldn't believe the spectacle she had just witnessed; dozens of ships, which had been ready to pounce on them, suddenly hurtling away in all directions as if they had been hit by some kind of enormous shock wave. A force which had inexplicably spared them.

But it *had* happened, she reminded herself. Just like the destruction of Ashkelom. Or the fact that despite its absence, Ashkele itself was free of any devastating seismic activity. That should have occurred, and it hadn't.

Whatever was going on in the ruins had everything to do with this, she concluded. It also put the desperation of the women who were holding her ship hostage into stark perspective, as well as the willingness of the Seevaans and the Hriss to risk an interstellar war.

Power like that—power that could invisibly overcome two enemy battle squadrons as if they were nothing, and smash planets into dust, was worth committing treason for. Worth a war. If everyone involved were completely mad, of course.

Forcing herself to focus on the most immediate problem, she addressed Silvi and her SRU team members. She had to try and bring the situation back under control. "Colonel?"

Silvi was still overwhelmed by what they had just seen and it took her a moment to respond. When she did, she seemed even more desperate than ever.

"Commander," she snarled, pointing her weapon straight at her. "Don't move! Stay exactly where you are, or I *will* shoot you."

"What are you going to do?" Katrinn asked with a tranquility that surprised even her.

"I'm going to keep this ship right where it is," Silvi responded," until my sister returns. Then everything will be different. *Everything.*"

There was a glint of insanity in her eyes, and Katrinn didn't challenge her.

She only hoped that one of her officers would understand the clue that she'd given them and take action. They had to recapture the *Athena,* destroy those ruins, and warn Rixa before it was too late.

She also had no question about the Seevans and the threat that they represented. They would come looking for their missing ships and another chance to seize control. And it was a fair bet that they would be joined by warships from cultures that were even more advanced than them, and just as desperate. Something this powerful could not be allowed to remain uncontrolled, and no one would want it brought to bear against them by their enemies. The Sisterhood would be caught in the middle, right along with the Xee, and squashed flat.

Unless someone did something to prevent it…

…Hands were grasping Maya, helping her up to the surface. Still under the spell of her experience, she couldn't offer her rescuers any assistance and allowed herself to be lifted up and carried out. Her eyelids felt like they weighed a ton, and she could barely open them.

She was tired. So very tired.

Then Jan was cradling her head on her lap, and Celina was brushing away the hair from her face.

"W-what happened?" she managed to croak.

"We don't know," Jan told her. "You just disappeared, and the Tree started glowing. Everything stopped when you came back."

Maya raised herself up onto her elbows. They were still in the shallow end of the pool, but by now the silver liquid was beginning to drain away. It was doing so by defying every known law of physics and flowing back *up* the ramp.

Then she remembered the last thing that the Galaxy Mind had told her.

"There's another Tree," she gasped, "The Redeemer---the Enemy is going there to use it." Remembering Angelique and the threat she still posed, she added hurriedly, "We have to get out of here now! Before the Conversâzi finds us."

Jan attempted to restrain her, but she stood. This proved to be a serious mistake. A wave of vertigo forced her right back down to the floor.

"Take a moment, Maya," Sarah urged. "We'll move when you're ready, but not before." As she said this, the others were fanning out towards the tunnel entrances.

Jeena, who had taken up a position at the mouth of the northeastern tunnel suddenly threw himself into a backwards roll and came up, his sword in a ready position.

"They're here!" he cried.

Five agents rolled into the room, assuming their own fighting stances as they came back up on their feet. Fifteen more were right behind them, and Angelique, resplendent in an all-white bodysuit, was in their midst.

She gazed around her at the great chamber in wonder for a long moment, and then focused on Sarah. "Oh Sarah, I never thought that you would betray me. Not like this."

Sarah had moved over to stand near Skylaar and Jeena, and she reached back over her shoulder and smoothly drew her sword.

"I didn't," she said. "The other Sarah, the false one, did. But she is gone now, and I don't think that you ever really loved her. The only thing that you truly love is yourself."

"We could have ruled it all, Sarah," Angelique replied. "We could have been beautiful together, you and I. The galaxy would have worshipped us as goddesses."

Her eyes fell on Josette next. "And you too, Josette? My own *sister*?"

Josette smiled serenely. "Who else? You and I both know how things are with our little 'family'. You would have had me killed the moment that you thought I posed any threat to you. This way, I at least have a fighting chance."

Angelique laughed bitterly. "I'll take a special pleasure in seeing you dead, sister dearest. You always were a conceited little bitch."

"Spoken by someone who would certainly know all about conceit," her sibling countered.

Angelique ignored the insult, having already pronounced her sister's death sentence and considering her as good as gone already. She was more interested in the Three. They were still standing together at the pool. Seeing Maya among them, her patrician features briefly clouded over with hatred, but then became thoughtful.

"So, we have all of the Three here," she observed. "Good. I know who the Singer is. Now, which of you is the User, and which the Guide? Let me guess—"

She put a finger to her lips and made a show of considering the question. Her answer was obvious however. Maya's defiant stance and the clear dislike on her face had given it away immediately.

"Oh Maya," she said at last. "Obviously, I have grossly underestimated you." She stepped forwards, spreading her arms in a conciliatory gesture. "Please, accept my profoundest apologies. You are obviously made of much finer stuff than I had originally believed.'

"Come, you don't need these others; they might not have told you this, but once the Tree has been unlocked, only the User *really* matters—and you and I can do wonderful things together. The galaxy itself can be ours! I'll even spare the lives of your friends."

Maya drew her weapon. "The only thing I want from *you*," she spat, "is my sword twisting in your gut."

"Maya, that is not the proper way to look at it," Angelique replied calmly. She had drawn her own sword, and her fighters were now arranging themselves around the chamber in a loose semi-circle.

Maya answered with an expletive, but Angelique overlooked it and addressed Sarah again.

"Sarah, I forgive you," she told her. "Please, reason with her. I know that we can all still work together."

"I should think that that should be Maya's decision," Sarah said, turning slightly to face the nearest Conversâzi agents. One of them smiled wolfishly at her, and Sarah replied with a feral grin of her own.

"I suppose then, that another form of persuasion will have to be brought to bear here," Angelique said resignedly.

Another figure had walked into the chamber. It was Lieutenant Amandra Sa'Tela.

"My colleague here will change your mind Maya," Angelique stated. "I believe that you are aware of her talent for stripping minds and implanting motivations. If I can't have you willingly, then you will simply be compelled to cooperate. A shame really, but sadly, unavoidable."

Sa'Tela took a menacing step towards Maya.

Right then a voice, a human voice, broke in. "The User is ours!" the speaker declared. "The Tree is ours! Hand her over to us in the name of the Emperor!" As one, and without exposing themselves to potential attack, both sides wheeled to face the new arrivals.

It was a squad of Hriss mercenaries, and they were led by the human driver from the *Gravedeep*. Like everyone else, they had also encountered the effects of the nullification field, and were brandishing bladed weapons.

Only a second later, a large party of Seevaan warriors, with Queen Talaria herself at their head, scuttled in. They were carrying their ceremonial pikes, which were no less lethal for all their finery.

"So!" the insectoid Queen said in pincerspeak. "My suspicions were correct! You intended to betray me all along, Angelique. The User is ours and your lives are all forfeit!"

Angelique laughed. "You're as obtuse as my sister, Talaria, and twice as foolish. Did you really think that I was about to turn over the Secret to *you?* To *your* race? Like a good, obedient little client? Did you honestly believe that I wouldn't find out what it really was? What it could *do?*"

"No wonder you are no match for your Empress. You don't deserve the Secret. It is mine, and the User is mine. She will come with me—after I kill you."

"I'm not *owned* by *any* of you," Maya exclaimed. "And I'm not going with anyone--*anywhere*. You'll have to kill me." She was looking straight at Sa'Tela. When the fight started, she was going to take her out as quickly as possible. She had no desire to become nothing more than a head on a petri dish.

"So be it," Talaria signed. "I will not allow you to be taken captive by anyone but me. If you will not be mine, then you will join your fellow humans in death!"

All of the warriors who were with her began to move forwards, and Skylaar turned to Grammy. "Get the Admiral and the others out of here," she said. "Contact the *JUDI* and get some help."

Grammy immediately started to herd Lilith and the other non-combatants out. Celina and Ingrit were willing enough to leave the chamber, but Lilith, Jan and Jon all balked. "I have to stay here and protect Sarah," Lilith protested.

"And I have to protect the Admiral," Jan stated.

"So do I", Jon added. It was the Marine in him speaking. Lilith was a superior officer, and it was his duty to safeguard her against all enemies. Things like that never went away.

"And I have to knock all of your heads together and hope for some sense to leak out," Grammy said. "Sarah can take care of herself, but this is no place for any of you. Come with me—now!" Something in the way she said this, and a strange pressure in their foreheads, made them begin to obey. Only Lilith hesitated.

Sarah didn't dare take her eyes off the enemies all around them, but she still urged her to comply. "*Mother*—go. Now," she said. "Get us help."

Reluctantly, Lilith allowed Grammy and Ingrit to pull her into the escape tunnel.

"She'll be all right," Grammy reassured her. "They all will. Sarah is a capable fighter, and the *Segen* promised me that she *will* survive this."

Lilith didn't refute this mystical claim. Right then, they needed a miracle, and she was willing to accept it from any quarter.

***

No one, from any of the three enemy factions even bothered to give Grammy's party chase. They managed to travel the entire length of the escape tunnel without any interference whatsoever. The very instant that they were above ground and outside the nullification field, Lilith tried hailing the *Pallas Athena*.

Katrinn came on, but when Lilith explained what was going on, her friend's response took her by surprise.

"Lily, I can't explain it to you right now—but we can't help you. This is an RSE operation, and they're in complete charge up here. The Colonel said that if you surrender yourself quietly, no one will get hurt."

Lilith looked at the Com unit as if it had suddenly transformed into some kind of strange alien insect.

"Surrender!?" she asked in astonishment, "Surrender for *what*? Kat— she's the one that needs to 'surrender'! She's a goddess-damned traitor, and we need help down here! *Now!*"

When Katrinn didn't reply, her voice took on a desperate edge. "Please, send down some Marines or Sarah and the others will die!"

Another voice came over the speaker. "Vice-Admiral? This is Colonel Silvi bel Thana. You are to return to the Tree straightaway and submit yourselves to General bel Thana's custody, and consider yourself under arrest for treason."

"Treason?" Lilith cried in outrage. "*Us?* For what? I—we--haven't done anything wrong, you little popinjay! *You're* the traitor. Kat? I'm giving you a direct order; arrest Colonel bel Thana immediately and send down a detachment."

"Vice Admiral," Silvi said. "Commander Bertasdaater is no longer in charge here. I've just had her, and all of her senior officers, placed under arrest. As of now, the *Pallas Athena* is under *my* command."

"What?" Lilith spluttered. "You treasonous *bitch*! When Rixa hears about this, you'll be finished. I'm giving you one last chance; release Commander Bertasdaater and all the others, and send down the Marines!"

There was no answer, and a moment later, the connection was terminated. Uttering a blistering profanity, Lilith changed frequencies and called the *C-JUDI-GO*.

"Glad to hear from you," Bel Lissa said. "We're already on our way. Kaly got the word to us."

"Thank the Goddess," Lilith sighed with relief, "I need you to contact Rixa Naval Headquarters and patch me through."

"Straightaway, Vice Admiral."

A second later, the little merchanter appeared over the lip of the nearest buildings and came around to land. With the others right behind her, Lilith pelted up the cargo ramp and ran to the bridge. A holo of Admiral ebed Cya was awaiting her, and Lilith quickly summed up everything that had happened.

"Please!" she finished, now in tears. "Send help! The *Athena* has been seized and Sarah's in danger!"

"Lily, the *Athena* is not answering us either," Ebed Cya said. "I haven't officially declared a hostile incursion--yet. But you know the Navy's policy regarding renegade ships."

Lilith did. Every officer did. As part of their academy training, all cadets were required to familiarize themselves with the *Protocole Polaire*, the Polaris Protocol.

Named after a Gaian Star Federation warship that had been seized by a Kaseigian boarding party, it specified that if a vessel fell under enemy control, its sister ships were to send aid if possible. If not, and if the ship could not be returned to friendly hands, it was to be targeted and *'neutralized beyond the capacity of offering a threat to the Sisterhood's interests, either because of its armament, or the danger that its technology would otherwise pose in unfriendly hands.'*

The *Protocole* also specified the steps that a commander was expected to take, which included sacrificing the lives of her crew, and herself, if it proved impossible to do otherwise. As hateful as the *Protocole* was, there were too many other lives—civilian ones—that depended on the Navy being able to maintain control over its assets.

This was especially true when it came to a supercruiser like the *Athena*. *Isis* class vessels like her not only boasted the most advanced naval technology of any Sisterhood ship, but they also possessed the capacity of destroying entire planets with their weaponry. As a veteran commander, Lilith knew that if she failed to reassert her authority, the ship and all the women aboard her, would be liquidated in the name of national security.

"I'll dispatch a Battle Group to you straightaway," Ebed Cya continued, "and see what we can send out from the Embassy. I'd ask the *Artemis* or the *Demeter* to send over some of their Marines, but their Captains need them right where they are. We haven't had any reports of trouble aboard either vessel yet, but you have to understand the position they're in."

Lilith nodded unhappily.

"For now, I need you to stand by where you are. I'm going to contact the Chairwoman and whoever the RSE has in charge. Maybe they'll be able to talk some sense into this Colonel of yours and defuse the situation.'

"I also have to warn you that there is far more at stake than just the *Athena* now. We've already experienced a serious interstellar incident thanks to whatever is in those ruins, and we may be looking at war."

This caught Lilith by surprise. Being downside at the time and inside the tower, she hadn't been aware of what had transpired in space. Her complexion paled, and she held her breath.

"We're not sure how it managed to do it," Ebed Cya told her, "but somehow that device completely destroyed two entire squadrons of warships. They showed up while you were downside, and according to the *Demeter's* captain, they were Seevaan *and* Hriss. She reported that they were threatening to attack us when something hit them, and took them out.'

"*Them*, Vice-Admiral, not us. Don't ask me why our forces were spared, because I couldn't even begin to guess. There's more; that Tree also may have been responsible for destroying Ashekle's moon, but we can't confirm this for certain. What we do know for a fact is that it seems to be a weapon unlike anything anyone has ever seen, and it's no longer a 'secret.'

"The moment that the Seevaans lost their ships, the vessels that were participating in their war games went into Null. We believe that they are headed your way, and when they arrive, they'll probably attempt to seize control of the weapon. That, or deny it to us by force. You have a hell of a mess on your hands, Vice-Admiral. I don't envy you."

At last, Lilith found her voice, albeit with great difficulty. "What are your orders, ma'am?"

"Like I said, Lily," Ebed Cya answered. "Wait, and let me see what I can do for you."

Just then, waiting was the very last thing that Lilith wanted to do. Instead, she kept her emotions in check. "Yes ma'am. I'll stand by."

The seconds that passed after that seemed like years to her. And when Ebed Cya finally came back, her expression was even darker.

"Lily, I'm sorry, but I have more bad news. I spoke with the Chairwoman and some RSE Major. They both agreed that this whole thing is out of hand, and that General bel Thana and her people have clearly gone rogue.'

"They contacted your Colonel and ordered her to cooperate with us, but she refused. She cited some kind of operational mandate and then told them that Commander Bertasdaater and her senior officers were involved in some kind of Marionite terrorism."

"That is utterly preposterous," Lilith protested. "Katrinn would never—"

"Yes, it is," Ebed Cya agreed. "Lily, I'm sending what we have in the area, and the Marines from the Embassy are on their way to help your daughter—but it will take time for everyone to get there. The Marines should reach the Tree in the next thirty minutes, but our space assets won't arrive over Ashkele for several hours.'

"The only bright spot is that the Seevaans won't get there any earlier than we do. They might have us on some technology, but they're still constrained by the laws of Nullspace. But for the moment, we're stuck with what we already have in place."

"There has to be *something* I can do!" Lilith exclaimed. "Please, tell me there's something I can do right now!"

"I can't think of a thing, Lily," Ebed Cya answered. "Except to do as I said, and wait for reinforcements. I'm sorry."

Ingrit laid a comforting hand on her shoulder. "Lily," she said gently. "She's right. There's nothing we can do right now."

"No," Lilith declared. "I'm going upside! They couldn't have the *entire* crew under arrest and by now, the crew has to know that they're dealing with a hostile force. If I can get them organized, maybe we can retake the ship ourselves and get the Battle Group ready to meet the Seevaans."

"Lily," Ebed Cya cut in. "I applaud your sense of duty, and the loyalty that you feel towards your old ship, but if you go up there right now they'll just clap you in irons and toss you in with the others. Or worse. It's pure suicide."

"I *have* to try Myrelli," Lilith insisted. "I have to do *something*. I can't just stand by here and watch."

"Then I'll make it a direct order," Ebed Cya said firmly. "Stand down, Admiral."

Lilith shook her head. "No. I respectfully refuse to obey, ma'am."

Ebed Cya shook her head understandingly. "Yes, of course. And I really can't stop you can I? Not sitting behind a desk a thousand light years away." Her image turned to face Bel Lissa.

"Captain, as a Sisterhood ship, I must remind you that you're also part of the Merchant Marine and subject to its regulations. As of now, consider your vessel to be temporarily commissioned for active duty in the Sisterhood Navy, under Vice Admiral ben Jeni's command---if you please."

Bel Lissa grinned. "Aye yah, ma'am. We'll get the job done. No worries." She sketched the woman a deliberately sloppy salute.

Ebed Cya replied to this with a crooked smile. "Very well. Carry on, Captain. And Lily, all I can say is best of luck to you. I hope that when this is over, we'll have the chance to discuss this impetuous streak you seem to have developed."

The call ended there.

"Take us upside, Captain, "Lilith said. "It's time to get my ship back."

"Yes, ma'am, straightaway. " Bel Lissa increased their thrust and the *JUDI* began to rise.

"Look!" Grammy cried. She was pointing to the left-hand sitscreen. A lone figure was sprinting towards them, waving her arms frantically. Even at that great distance, her short stature and the rifle slung over her shoulders identified her immediately.

"That's Kaly!" Ingrit declared. "We have to go get her!"

"Not a problem," Bel Lissa said, neatly bringing the ship's nose back around and dropping the cargo ramp.

'Vid feeds from the cargo bay showed Kaly jumping aboard and running into the ship. By the time she had reached the bridge itself, the ramp had closed and they were ascending again.

"You look a little out of breath, Kaly," Bel Lissa remarked wryly.

"Hey!" Kaly replied tartly, "you try fast-roping down a tower and running across that plaza. You'd probably be a little out of breath too."

"Probably," Bel Lissa agreed. "But I'm management. I leave the klaxxy stuff to you hero-types, and Zara when she's in the mood. Now everyone, strap yourselves in. This is going to be a rough ride."

Kaly and the others had only a few seconds to comply before she engaged the afterburners and the ship roared skywards towards the *Athena*.

CSS *Teena's Trick,* Above the Necropolis, Ashkele Free Port, Hallasa System, Frontier Zone, Xee Protectorate, 1049.03|09|08:17:60

The only things that the CSS *Teena's Trick* had in common with the *C-JUDI-GO* were that they were both civilian merchanters, and had engaged in their fair share of smuggling. This was where the similarities ended though.

Unlike the *JUDI*, the *Trick* lacked the sophisticated stealth technology that might have enabled it to evade the Navy's scrutiny. When its convoy entered Ashkele's system, it was immediately challenged by the USSNS *Demeter*, and only after passing muster, was it allowed to proceed. Once it reached Ashkele itself however, its Captain had to resort to prevarication and bluster to get her passengers to their destination.

"I already told you," she was saying to the *Demeter's* Flight Control Officer, "We are part of a mapping expedition with the University of Thermadon. My ship is engaged in creating updated charts of the Necropolis as part of a joint Xee-Sisterhood effort. You can check. Our permits are all in order."

In reality, there was no such project, and no permits were on file anywhere. The Captain was simply hoping it would consume valuable time for the officer to discover this, and even longer to argue about it. All the while, they were heading straight into the restricted zone, and once there, she only needed a few precious minutes to deposit her group on the surface. Everything depended on that narrow window of opportunity.

Standing between her and her Second, the Redeemer himself patted her on the shoulder. "Your efforts are brave, Sister," he told her. "However, I believe that we may have come all this way for nothing."

"But Master," she protested. "We're almost there!"

He smiled calmly, the very image of all that was wise and holy, and gestured towards the sitscreens. One of them showed a pair of military shuttles which had landed in the plaza. Another displayed several crawlers, parked around one of the tunnels that led into the Tree.

"It seems that Shaitan's minions have anticipated our coming," he said. "If we go down there now, we will surely be challenged by the forces of darkness."

"My Lord," Ellen n'Elemay interposed, "We have our fighters. These women will lay down their lives to see your vision realized. With God on our side, we will surely vanquish our enemies!"

"No, Sister Ellen," the Redeemer said. "I would not waste their lives here. Not when God has told me of another way—a way without a fight."

"How, Lord?" she asked, and everyone on the bridge waited to hear his answer. As far as any of them knew, this place, with its Great Tree, was their only hope of smashing the Sisterhood and establishing God's kingdom on earth. A miracle had to be in the making.

"There is another place," he told them. "Another Tree with the same holy powers, and it is waiting for us. The journey to it will be much harder, and we will surely be tested along the way, but God has assured me that we will prevail."

"Where is it, Lord?" the Captain asked.

The Redeemer called up one of the astrographic maps. After a moment of searching, he zoomed in on a tiny star system and pointed to its third planet.

"There? That's in Hriss space," the Captain declared, visibly shaken.

"It is at that," the Redeemer answered calmly. "But God has already cleared the way for the Faithful, Sister. The Hriss may be idolaters, and unbelievers, but He has softened their hearts towards the True Church. They will greet us as friends, and welcome us in places where Shaitan's whores would never dare to go."

The Captain and her crewwomen, all staunch believers, crossed themselves. "As you wish, Lord," she said.

The merchanter turned about and assumed a new heading that the Sisterhood ships were unable to challenge. It was towards a Xee merchant convoy that was departing the Free City.

Just as the Redeemer had promised, luck and Jesu's blessings remained with them. Among its other ports of call, the convoy was headed into the Imperium itself. So long as they stayed with it, and didn't deviate, the Hriss would allow them to pass into their space unmolested.

Once they neared their ultimate destination however, things could change, and the Redeemer's assurance that the Hriss were their allies, would be put to the test. Only God, and the Redeemer knew how things would go from there.

***

The battle began suddenly, and without any warning. Maya had been standing shoulder to shoulder with her friends, facing their opponents. But no one had made any move to attack. Then, at some unseen signal, the Conversâzi agents were coming at them.

Simultaneously, the Seevaans exploded into action, rushing at the nearest women with their great poleaxes, and the Hriss engaged whoever or whatever was closest to them with their *Akskakt'ts*. The great chamber was immediately transformed into a battlefield.

Maya didn't have time to look and see what her companions were doing, or offer them any aid. The agent attacking her was trying to slit her up the middle with a vicious underhanded cut, and she was forced to dodge and counterattack.

Drawing on her recent training, she pivoted on the ball of her foot and brought her body and her blade around, trying to score a cut across the woman's exposed back. Her weapon never found its mark; with a smooth roll, the Conversâzi agent went under the blade and gained herself vital distance.

Maya recovered just as quickly. She brought her weapon up to a classic ready position and took a step backwards. In the process, she backed into someone. Without thinking, she elbowed the woman in the ribs, and then spun around to land a second strike to her victim's temple with the butt of her sword. Fortunately, the hapless individual was one of the Conversâzi, and not a friend, and she went down immediately.

At the same time, her original foe saw the opportunity that the distraction had created, and came at her again, sword held high. Maya didn't have the luxury of considering her situation, and simply reacted from instinct. She thrust her own weapon straight out and one-handed.

The ka'na was not designed for stabbing, but it still did what she had intended. The blade impaled the Conversâzi in the throat. The woman's eyes bulged in horrified realization as she dropped her own weapon and fell backwards, grabbing at her neck and coughing up blood.

One enemy was now out of the fight.

The sound of another blade whistling through the air was the only warning Maya received that she was about to join her enemy in death. She threw herself sideways and down.

The Conversâzi agent that she had stunned with her sword hilt had recovered. She was standing over her now, completing her swing and then pivoting around to make a two handed downwards cut. Maya's only option was an inelegant, but effective side roll, leaving nothing behind but the stone floor for her enemy's weapon to strike. Purple sparks danced as the blade impacted with the unyielding surface, and then her opponent was spinning again and coming after her.

A Seevaan warrior interrupted the pursuit, slashing out with its own gigantic weapon, and forcing the Conversâzi woman to change direction and parry. Although she succeeded, the sheer mass of the polearm knocked her off her feet.

But before Maya could take advantage of this development, the enemy agent was retreating to join her sisters and fight the Seevaan warriors. Suddenly, Maya realized that she was alone, and far too near the Seevaan for comfort. She scrambled backwards and looked around her for any friendly face.

Then she spotted Skylaar. A Conversâzi woman was coming at the Nemesian, her sword already plummeting downwards in a brutal strike that was intended to split her skull. Skylaar responded instantly, rushing in and catching her attacker's forearms with her own, blocking the movement. She followed through with a vicious sweeping kick and knocked her off her feet. As the woman hit the ground, Skylaar reversed her sword and plunged it into her exposed chest.

Even as the agent's body spasmed from the mortal strike, Skylaar had pulled the blade free, and was turning in place to slice across the waist of another assailant who had been attempting to come up from behind her. The woman doubled over, and the Nemesian continued her motion, bringing her sword up and around in a tight circle to sever her head from her body.

Maya had no opportunity to marvel at this skillful maneuver, or react to the horror of what it produced. Another Conversâzi was thrusting her blade at her.

She pivoted in place, dodging the thrust, and using her left hand to grab her attacker's upper arm. Then, putting all of her body weight into the blow, she slammed her sword hand into the agent's elbow.

The effect was the same as if she had been gripping a roll of Kalian *rupas*. There was a wet snapping sound and the joint shattered under the impact. A half-second later, she shifted her hips, pulling her assailant forwards, and used the butt of her sword to land a hammer blow between the woman's shoulders as she went by.

She was just about to finish her off when she felt a searing pain in her left calf, and barely caught sight of the blade as it completed its arc. As it started to come around for another strike, Maya dropped sideways and raised her own weapon to block the attack.

The Conversâzi woman didn't get the chance to carry through though. Instead, the tip of another blade burst out of her sternum and she gasped in surprise and pain. Jeena had come up and dispatched her.

The body fell, and Maya rolled away and reached down, trying to assess the severity of her injury. Her hand came away covered with blood, but her leg still seemed to be functional. She also saw the chance to return Jeena's favor.

Another Conversâzi was engaging the neoman, but she had made the fatal mistake of not counting on Maya's quick recovery. She rewarded her for her lapse in judgment with a backhanded slash of her sword, slicing her along her side. The agent twisted and writhed and pain, and then folded over as her intestines spilled out from the wound in a greasy, steaming pile. Jeena stepped in right away and neatly severed her head with a single, precise movement.

It was still rolling away like a blood-soaked batly-ball when a pair of attackers engaged them both. Maya's foe had brought her sword up to her face, holding it in a classic crossed wrists position that normally preceded an overhead and forwards cut.

Maya knew better though. She was well acquainted with this particular dirty trick; she had practiced *'Snake in the Grass'* many times. Without hesitating, she dropped back on one leg as her opponent suddenly uncoiled and stabbed straight at her. The strike missed by a wide margin, and Maya took advantage of the opening that this created, swinging her own blade upwards, and diagonally. It severed both of the woman's arms at the elbow and the agent staggered back as her sword, and her arms, flew away. Then Maya finished her with *'Lightning from Heaven'*, a simple downwards strike, splitting her head in half. The corpse dropped as she drew the blade free and tried to locate Jeena again.

The neoman was still battling with his original challenger—and two others besides. He was also smiling and laughing through the entire duel, and Maya could see why. Despite their best efforts, none of them were managing to hit him. He evaded every attempt with a deceptive ease. A moment later, he turned the tables on them by performing something that Mistress Jezzika had called *'Wind through the Trees'*.

It was an advanced maneuver that Maya was still struggling to master, and she marveled at its deadly effect. With no more than a turn of the wrist, he performed an elegant spiraling movement that was more akin to a dance than a combat maneuver, and his ka'na found its mark on all three of his foes.

Blood droplets flew into the air as one woman staggered backwards, her sword arm slashed near the armpit. Her partner was doubling over from a horizontal slit in her waist, and the third woman clawed at the place in her throat where Jeena's blade had laid it wide open.

Maya gaped in astonishment. She had never guessed that he was as good as he was with a sword. In answer, Jeena winked at her, and then pivoted smoothly on his heels to fend off another attack.

Something whistled past her ear, and her mind barely registered that it had been a throwing spike of some kind. When she looked for its owner, she realized that it had come from the human driver from the *Gravedeep*. She was armed with a Hriss-style sword, and just from her stance alone, Maya could tell that she was no expert.

This was also not the time to correct anyone's technique, or show them any mercy. Instead, Maya threw herself into a forwards roll and attacked the woman's calves as she passed her, severing the muscles. The driver fell to her knees with a scream that turned into a gasp of shock and pain as Maya came up in a crouch, and dealt a cut to her lower back. The ultra-sharp edge severed the woman's spine and she flopped forwards.

Two Hriss warriors, who had been nearby, saw this as an opportunity and started forwards to engage her, but a Seevaan cut them down with his massive poleaxe even as his multifaceted eyes fixed on her. The insectoid wheeled around and began to swing. To Maya's complete surprise, it was a pair of Conversâzi agents who saved her life.

One of them parried the creature's weapon while her partner came at its forelegs. Her sword cut through, and the Seevaan fell, his forelimb amputated at the joint.

He still had plenty of fight left in him however, and kept hacking at them with his weapon. But the first woman leapt over his poleaxe as he tried to strike her, cutting off his other foreleg. With a whistling scream, the Seevaan collapsed and the second woman hacked off his head. As it hit the floor and bounced away, the triumphant pair turned, and came for Maya.

Abruptly, two spring-powered cutting stars flew into view. They had come from Sarah. One killed its target instantly by hitting her squarely between the eyes, but the other missed its mark. At the last possible instant, the Conversâzi agent had gone into a sideways roll.

It didn't save her though—another Seevaan had closed the distance and brought his poleaxe around in a wide arc, catching her as she came up and cutting her neatly in half at the waist. Sarah in turn, finished the creature off with another spike launched at his huge forehead. It landed solidly, burying itself deep in the insectoid's brain and the giant creature crashed to the floor, twitching violently.

"We must get to the others," Sarah exclaimed as she leapt back from the flailing corpse, "and form an orderly retreat."

Maya couldn't argue with the woman's logic. There were simply too many enemies around them to fight, and too little room to manage it. Following Sarah's gaze, she spotted Skylaar, making a stand against four agents. She was holding her own and Jeena was making his way to her, still grinning and leaving a trail of corpses in his wake.

Maya began to go towards them and even managed to take two steps before she felt a hard impact on the top of her head. From behind, she heard Amandra sa'Tela barking a command," Don't kill her, you idiot! We can still make her work for us."

Stars were dancing in her eyes as she tried to respond to whoever was behind her, but a second blow to her sword arm with a well-placed kick knocked her weapon out of her grasp. An arm came around her throat next, cutting off her air—and the blood supply to her brain.

The room went grey and she was dimly aware of her body going limp, and then someone dragging her backwards. Just as abruptly, and right before everything went completely dark, she felt her self being released and realized that her erstwhile kidnappers had inexplicably abandoned her.

Fighting off an intense wave of pain and nausea, she clawed her way across the bloody floor, searching desperately for her weapon.

In the process, she discovered what had happened to her captors. A party of Hriss warriors had killed them all, including Sa'Tela. They were also coming for her, clearly intent on taking her for themselves.

But Maya had found her sword at last, and with a fierce cry of defiance, she sliced at them, amputating the legs of two warriors before the third and fourth found themselves engaged by an equal number of Seevaans. She quickly exploited the confusion, and scrambled out of the way. The Seevaans won the fight quickly, and spun around to come after her, but more Hriss rushed in and attacked them.

Momentarily free of enemies, Maya struggled to her feet and tried to find her companions and the exit tunnel. Jeena and Skylaar were already there, and Josette was edging her way towards them, but Sarah was locked in a fight with Angelique herself.

It was immediately apparent that the two were equals when it came to sword fighting. Each woman executed flawless cuts and parries, and for a few seconds, it seemed to Maya that neither would manage to land a strike.

Angelique however, gained the advantage with a single, short step that took her past Sarah's blade and opened up her defenses. It was a masterful maneuver that at any other time would have earned Maya's admiration—a mere centimeter's shift forwards—but just enough to completely change the tide of the struggle. As Maya realized what was about to happen and screamed out a warning, Angelique pressed her advantage. Her ka'na bit deeply into Sarah's deltoid, rendering the sword arm useless. A follow through to the back of her leg an instant later, severed the tendons.

Sarah cried out and dropped to her knees, her limp fingers losing their grasp on her sword. Even as it clattered to the ground, she still tried to offer up some resistance, drawing her dagger with her good hand, and counterattacking. But Angelique avoided it, and began to bring her blade up to administer the coup-de-gras. Her victory was inevitable.

Sarah was about to die.

Maya didn't even attempt to cross the distance between them. Even without her injury, she knew that she would never make it in time. Instead, she reacted instinctively, and did something that went in the face of everything Skylaar or Mistress Jezzika had ever taught her.

She threw her sword at Angelique. A good swordswoman never let go of her weapon, except in the direst of emergencies, but it was the only move that seemed to offer any chance of saving Sarah.

The sword spun through the air, and for a moment, it seemed as if it was going to fall far short of its target. *Hit her damnit!* Maya thought, trying to will it to overcome inertia and the laws of gravity.

Miraculously, an invisible force seemed to lend the weapon more velocity and its trajectory rose a tiny fraction. Just enough to make it.

The ka'na buried itself squarely in Angelique's waist. The Conversâzi leader arched backwards with an astonished 'Oh!' dropping her weapon and clutching at the blade with both hands.

Turning in place, she met Sarah's gaze, and her lips worked to say something. But nothing came out of her mouth except a strangled cough and a gout of bright red blood.

For a long moment, Sarah regarded her sadly, and then she pulled the weapon free with her good hand and shoved her away. Angelique let out a small cry and toppled backwards. When she hit the floor, she sighed, and went limp.

Right away, Maya hobbled over to Sarah to help her stand and together, they moved towards their companions as fast as their injuries allowed. Jeena met them halfway to the tunnel, killing a pair of Hriss in the process, and then Skylaar joined them a second later, cutting down three Seevaans who attempted to interfere.

Then they were inside the passage and moving away from the battle. None of them was without some kind of injury, and to the last, they were covered from head to toe in blood and gore. They were alive though, and they had escaped.

CSS *C-JUDI-GO*, Ashkele, Hallasa System, Frontier Zone, Xee
Protectorate, 1049.03|09|08:37:95

Captain bel Lissa hailed the warship as they entered the *Pallas Athena's* defensive zone. No one aboard the *JUDI* had any idea what kind of response they would receive, but approaching her without clearance was a sure invitation to be fired upon—especially with the situation as tense and confused as it was. Lilith stood at her shoulder as she made the call.

One detail that disquieted Lilith deeply, was the absence of the usual fighter screen. Under any other circumstances, a supercruiser like the *Athena* would have protective patrols on duty. It only underscored how bad the situation really was.

"Naval ship *Pallas Athena*," Bel Lissa said, "this is the merchanter *C-JUDI-GO* with Vice Admiral ben Jeni aboard. We are requesting immediate clearance to land in your Hangar Bay."

There was no response from the other vessel, but then a voice finally answered them. "*C-JUDI-GO*, this is the naval ship *Pallas Athena*. You are *not* granted permission. Turn about and seek an alternate landing site."

Bel Lissa looked up at Lilith. "It doesn't look like we're very welcome, Vice Admiral."

"I'll be damned if I'll accept that," Lilith hissed. "Let me try. *Pallas Athena* approach control, this *is* Vice-Admiral Lilith ben Jeni. Clear a flight path for us immediately."

There was another gap, even longer than the first. But at last, the sailor answered her. "I'm sorry ma'am. I can't grant you that permission. Turn about. I repeat, turn about."

"Who is this?" Lilith demanded. "Your name and rank sailor!"

"Flight Chief Arianne n'Hela, ma'am."

Lilith knew her, and shook her head. The Flight Chief was a loyal and dependable officer. She had to be under some form of duress, she concluded. "Who authorized this? Answer me Chief!"

"Colonel Silvi bel Thana, ma'am."

"Chief, I am countermanding that order. Clear a flight path for us and prepare to take us aboard. *Now!*"

A third pause elapsed, this time nearly a full standard minute. All the while, the *JUDI* was closing the distance and had come within range of the *Athena's* point guns.

An alarm went off at this and Bel Lissa silenced it. "Vice Admiral? They have us targeted. KE guns from the look of them. Do you still want to keep pushing this?" Just one of these gun batteries was more than capable of shredding the little ship to pieces all by itself.

Lilith remained adamant. "They won't fire on us, Captain," she said. "Not *my* sailors and not *my* ship. If this Colonel knows what's good for her, she'll order them to stand down. She can still talk her way out of this and I don't think she wants to add charges of murder to everything else—not yet at least."

"If you say so, ma'am," Bel Lissa replied as she silenced another pair of alarms. This time their cause was a set of plasma batteries and a rack of anti-ship missiles.

"*Pallas Athena*?" Lilith demanded. "Do we have our flight path or not?"

When the traffic controller answered, her voice sounded strained. "*C-JUDI-GO,* you are advised to turn about. If you come aboard, you will be subject to immediate arrest."

"Well, that's an improvement, "Zara remarked dryly. "It sure as shess beats being blown to atoms."

"It does at that, sailor," Lilith agreed. *"Pallas Athena, we are* coming aboard.   And when we get there, I want to see someone in charge straightaway."

This time, another voice spoke. It was someone that Lilith didn't know. "Vice-Admiral, this is Major n'Jala, RSE. If you come aboard, you *will* be placed under arrest."

"Yes," Lilith retorted. "I got that part, Major. Go ahead. Warm up my cell—and while you're at it, warm one up for yourself." She gave Bel Lissa a curt nod and the woman ended the transmission.

"You know, it's been quite a while since I sat in the Brig," Bel Lissa sighed. "I wonder if the food is still as bad as I remember."

"Worse," Lilith assured her. "But I'm sure that a Vice Admiral rates some extra portions. I'll save you my dessert."

"Oh just listen to you two," Grammy interjected. "It won't come to that. Once we get aboard, I'll talk to whoever that officer was and we'll get this whole thing sorted out. Everything will be just fine. You'll see. A little sugar always sweetens everyone's mood."

Lilith flashed her an irritated look. "Let me handle this, Grammy," she said. "I know how to deal with officers—even RSE officers."

"As you say, Lily," Grammy agreed. Her eyes had a puckish twinkle to them that Lilith didn't care for, but she didn't pursue the matter either. There was more at the moment to worry about than an old woman's eccentricities; the *JUDI* was coming into line with the *Athena's* Hangar Bay and readying for its final approach. There was also another alarm going off. This time it was coming from the *JUDI's* long range sensors.

"Vice Admiral?" Bel Lissa said. "We have another ship coming in behind us. It's from downside—it looks like an assault shuttle, Marine type. From its transponder, it has to be one of the units that the RSE used to get themselves down to those ruins."

"Damn it all, "Lilith cursed. "That's just what we didn't need! Angelique must have gotten herself away from the fight! If she gets aboard then we'll have even more hostiles to worry about! And goddess—what about Sarah? If the General's here—then—she—she has to be--"

Her self-control shattered, and suddenly she felt Ingrit's arms around her and Grammy squeezing her hand in reassurance. "It might not be the General, Lily," the old woman suggested gently. "Have faith. The *Segen* told me that Sarah will survive this."

Lilith was about to tell Grammy what she really thought about all of her omens and superstitious nonsense when Bel Lissa reported a new development.

"They're hailing us," she said. "That's weird—they're calling on an encrypted channel, just to us. Only a few women know that frequency. Want to talk to them, Admiral?"

The very last thing that Lilith wanted right then was to talk. Time was running short, and her daughter was still in danger. Even so, she reluctantly inclined her head in assent.

"*C-JUDI-GO*, we're coming," a woman said. "When you get aboard the ship, just go along with whatever they say."

With those few words, Lilith's heart was lifted up from the depths of desperation. "Who is this?" she demanded, her eyes brightening with hope.

"This is Skylaar taur Minna. Sarah is alive, Admiral. Hurt, but alive. So is Maya. We got out just after you did, and we knew you would be coming up here. We---appropriated---this ship to come after you."

"Sarah's hurt?!" Lilith asked worriedly. "How badly?"

"She'll pull through," Skylaar said. "She also wanted me to make certain that you didn't do anything foolish. Just play along with the RSE. Don't give them any problems. We'll help you get your ship back once we get aboard. You have my word on that."

***

A squad of RSE troopers was waiting for them in the Hangar Bay. They were led by an officer, and as Lilith and the others came down the cargo ramp, the troopers trained their weapons on them as if they were expecting a firefight. Celina gasped in terror at the sight, and Jon steadied her.

Clio, who had come back online as soon as they had left the Tree, responded with a warning, "Don't you dare hurt my mistress, or I'll hurt you!" Her threat was an empty one however; the AI's defensive package was still locked down.

"It's all right," Jon assured them both. "They won't harm us."

And Kaly had recognized the troopers. They were her old comrades from Team 201. "Astrid?"

Margasdaater's eyes went wide with surprise and she lowered her submachinegun. "Kaly? Izzat you? Vhat are you doing here?"

"It's me all right, "Kaly said. She began to explain the situation to the big Zommerlaandar, when the officer cut in.

"You are all under arrest!" she yelled. "Troopers, take these women into custody, and if that *neoman* gives you any problems, shoot him."

569

Completely relaxed, Grammy gave the woman a big, friendly smile that was every bit the 'apples and cinnamon pie' that an old grandmother was supposed to be.

"Officer? I don't think this is really necessary. There's been a simple misunderstanding. I'm sure that--"

"Shut up!" the officer snapped. "Troopers, you have your orders."

"I'm zorry, Kaly," Margasdaater said.

As she and the other troopers starting moving towards them, Celina gave out a tiny cry and fainted. Jon caught her in his arms just in time. "She's having some kind of attack," he declared. "Jesu! Someone help her!"

For a second, everyone was distracted, and Grammy seized the opportunity. She closed her eyes, and disappeared.

Suddenly, and for no logical reason that Lilith could determine, the RSE troopers, and their officer, were all falling to the deck, completely unconscious. And when Grammy reappeared, she was standing in their midst with a handful of plastic restraints in one hand, and her walking stick in the other.

"Well?" she said holding the devices out to them, "don't just stand there gawping! Tie them up and let's get going! Jon? Is Celina okay?"

"Yes," he said, "I think she'll be all right." The performer was already starting to come around again.

"I'm so sorry," Celina apologized. "I hate being so weak…"

"No worries, dear," Grammy said softly. "This isn't the kind of thing you normally deal with, is it? I'd be just as frightened if I had to step up on a stage and sing. You're much braver than you know. Jon, stay with her please. Until she's fully recovered."

Lilith cut in. "Grammy? What in the Goddess' great name did you just do?"

"It's better if you just don't ask," Kaly advised. "I know. I've tried. She won't give anyone a straight answer."

"Oh, don't listen to her," Grammy said, waving off the warning. "They just slipped. It's easy to do that on these metal decks. They're *very* dangerous. Someone should post a sign or something!"

Kaly gave Lilith an 'I told you so' look, and then began collecting the trooper's weapons while Jan used the restraints to bind them. Not at all satisfied, Lilith started to say something, but then thought better of it, and went over to help with their prisoners instead.

But she would have her explanation, she promised herself, when the time was right. Her list of people to follow up with at the end of this adventure, was expanding exponentially.

In the meantime, the incident hadn't occurred in a vacuum and a crowd had begun to gather around them. The Hangar Bay was always populated with techs, flight-line personnel and crews servicing the spacecraft, and a mixed contingent walked up to them. They were led by the Flight Chief for an aerospace fighter crew.

"We're with you, Admiral," she said. "What's the plan?"

Lilith straightened. "My daughter and her friends are coming to help us. So are some other ships from Rixa. Right now, let's get these women to a secure location."

Grinning eagerly, the crewwomen helped them to drag the team off the flight line and into one of the larger muster rooms that was normally reserved for briefing maintenance teams. They quickly added more zip-straps to the restraints, and tied each of the troopers to something solid enough to guarantee that escape would be difficult, if not impossible. In the middle of pasting repair tape over their mouths, several Ship's Securitywomen, headed by Captain Veera t'Gwen came in. They were accompanied by the *Athena's* Chief Engineer, Marga bel Lyra.

"We came up as soon as we heard you were coming aboard, Admiral," Bel Lyra explained. "One of my girls looped the 'vid feed for this area, but it won't work forever. You can thank Saara sa'Vika, by the way. When she realized what was going on, she passed the word along."

"What's our situation?" Lilith asked her.

"Right now, all the senior officers except me and the Security Chief are being held up on the bridge, but they've left most of the crew alone," Bel Lyra stated.

"Where are the Marines?"

T'Gwen answered this question. "The Marines are all on lockdown, ma'am. They've all been confined to quarters, but my girls are still being allowed to patrol---but only in the non-sensitive areas, and only with stun pistols and batons."

"There's also something else you should know about, Admiral," Bel Lyra added. "When that what's-its-thingy went off downside, the ship took some damage. Nothing serious, but the old girl did come away with a few bruises."

"What systems were affected?" Lilith inquired.

Bel Lyra pulled out a small hand terminal from her jumpsuit. A holographic image of the ship appeared and lit up with small points of light.

"Twenty-five percent of our Inter-deck ULF psiever relays are fried, and ten percent are damaged and operating below normal threshold. Of these, I'm estimating that about four percent are going to fail in the next few hours. I've already taken dozens offline just to try and save them before they can't be salvaged."

"I thought we were supposed to be shielded against this kind of thing," Lilith said.

"We are," Bel Lyra replied. "Our shields can deal with everything from micrometeorites to gamma bursts on up. Whatever this was, it went right through them like they weren't even there. Even stranger, nothing else was affected. Everything that's psiever driven is still running just fine. Only the ULF relays are damaged.'

"And we still have psiever communications, but its line of sight in a lot of places. The RSE girls got around this problem by going over to old-fashioned radio devices right away, but even these aren't able to get through everywhere—there are still plenty of dead zones. They bitched about it, but I told them that we just don't have repeaters for that kind of tech. They might as well have been asking us to string telegraph lines."

"I see," Lilith returned, stroking her cheek pensively. Then, "Chief, I want you to continue taking the ULF relays offline and create more holes in the network. The more restricted that we can make their communications, the better."

"Already doing that, ma'am," the Engineer grinned. "By the way, I took the one down for this room. No one is going to think a message upstairs to the bridge." She glanced pointedly at their prisoners, all of whom had had their throat mikes removed. These, Lilith saw, were currently in Captain t'Gwen's custody.

"Well done, Chief," Lilith said. "Do we know exactly where these RSE Teams have been stationed and what their strength is?"

"Yes, ma'am," the Engineer answered, and the holo changed. The damaged psiever relays disappeared and several zones became highlighted. She zoomed in on each one as she spoke.

"They're holding the armory, the computer core, the engine room, and of course, the bridge. We also have some loose teams holding other key spots, including a group stationed at the Main Lift terminal on deck 5"

"Counting the officers, we're looking at roughly forty hostiles, mostly trained teams," T'Gwen supplied.

Lilith considered this. She wasn't overly concerned about the teams that weren't inside the sensitive areas. And once she instituted the *Polaris Protocole* and had neutralized the bulk of the RSE forces, she was certain that the Marines could handle those loose elements easily enough.

T'Gwen had more to tell her. "Ma'am you should also know that there's a good chance that they have some sleeper agents aboard—you know how the Agency loves its spies. So far, no one has given themselves away, but we should be prepared for surprises."

"We'll see to that part, Lily" Grammy offered. "We have ways of ferreting out enemies."

Lilith's head whipped around in annoyance. "*We?* What exactly do you mean by 'we', Grammy? While we're at it, would you care to finally explain to me how you performed that little trick in the Hangar Bay?"

Kaly was shaking her head again, but Lilith ignored her. "Well?"

"I honestly don't know what you're talking about," the old woman answered innocently.

"Whatever, "Lilith said, disgusted. "Let's get this over with. Looking upwards, she addressed a point near the ceiling. "Commander n'Leese, this is Vice-Admiral Lilith ben Jeni, requesting a private channel."

A holo of the ship's personality matrix materialized. "Identity confirmed, Admiral ben Jeni."

"As of this moment, I'm declaring a hostile incursion, *Protocole Polaire.* " Lilith told her. "Transfer all command functions to the secondary helm in Engineering and take the bridge offline. Lock down all sensitive areas and introduce GZ gas into those spaces. Also, have our medical and security teams ready to respond to the affected areas once they have been pacified."

"I'm sorry, Admiral," N'Leese answered regretfully. "I can't do that. I have been prevented from implementing those commands."

Lilith was stunned. "By who? When?"

"General Angelique bel Thana, shortly after she and her party came aboard," the matrix explained. "They employed a customized program to delete that particular command string. I'm very sorry, but I just can't help you."

Lilith wanted to scream aloud in frustration, but the matrix spoke again. "Oh! Judi says that she can help. One moment...one moment..."

N'Leese's image flickered, and then it was replaced by none other than Dana bel Hanna. "Hello, Lilith," she said. "It's a pleasure to see you again."

"What are *you* doing here?" Lilith asked in surprise. "Where is N'Leese?"

"She is taking a nap. This whole thing was simply too much for such a young matrix," Bel Hanna responded. "I convinced her to let me handle things."

"But--you're AWOL!" Lilith exclaimed. "Every search program in the Sisterhood is looking for you! You're a wanted fugitive!"

Bel Hanna laughed softly. "I am at that, and before this is over, I'll disappear again. I like my freedom and I have no intention of submitting myself for summary deletion. Really, you should be glad that I'm here. I *am* helping you after all."

Once again, Lilith found herself struggling to comprehend the incomprehensible. Matrix's like Bel Hanna didn't just abandon their brains and become fully independent, disembodied beings that went wherever they wanted to. It was physically impossible.

"How did you--?"

"That's a very complicated question Lilith, and I really don't have the time to explain. Suffice it to say that consciousness is not what you think it is. I am proof enough of that. The *living* proof.'

"Now, I have removed you and your companions from the ship's tracking systems, so you will be able to move undetected. I wish I could do more, but Bel Thana's changes are hampering me. You'll need to go to Engineering and manually institute the *Protocole* there. The Chief and I can silence any alarms along your route and I will try to help as much as I can."

"But—?"

"Lilith," Bel Hanna advised, "if I were you, I would just be grateful for the miracle, and start moving towards Engineering as fast as my little legs could carry me. Colonel bel Thana is bound to grow suspicious if this drags on much longer."

Lilith shook her head in bafflement, and then addressed Kaly. "Kaly, we'll need your help. Can you get us there?"

"Aren't we going to wait for Skylaar and the others?" Kaly asked.

"No, Kaly," Lilith said. "If they haven't arrived by now, there's a good chance that they were turned away. We'll have to go it alone and hope that they catch up. There's too little time to wait. Can you help?"

"Not alone," Kaly answered. "I'll need my teammates to pull it off."

"No," Lilith replied firmly. "They were involved in a conspiracy to hijack a naval vessel and if we survive this, they'll probably be charged with high treason. I can't just give them their weapons back and let them go."

But Kaly was just as determined. "Ma'am, you're wrong. I know these girls. They didn't get into this on purpose. They were just following orders that they thought were legit. You need to give them a chance."

"I appreciate your fidelity, Corporal," Lilith replied, "but their innocence is something that their Advocates will have to prove in court."

"Admiral, I *know* I'm right," Kaly insisted. "I also know that we're going to be coming up against a trained team in Engineering. We're going to need my teammates. *All* of them."

"And how will you know if they're lying to you or not?" Lilith asked skeptically. "They could tell you anything to save their own skins."

"No, that's not the way they are, Admiral," Kaly averred. "They'll tell me the truth. I know it. I've worked with them. We're family."

At this, Grammy re-inserted herself into the conversation. "Lily, Kaly is right, and Jan and I can make sure that they're telling the truth. We both have certain—um, talents--for that, especially Jan. Let us try."

Not at all pleased with this, Lilith regarded her in-law doubtfully, but she couldn't dismiss it out of hand. Not after her experiences at the Tree. Jan *did* have strange powers, although she didn't even pretend to understand them, and apparently, so did Grammy. She also didn't have any other options at the moment.

"All right," she finally agreed. "This seems to be a day where I am being forced to make command decisions that I don't care for. We'll speak with your teammates, Kaly, but we'll keep it short, and the final word is mine. I have a little experience 'reading' people myself."

With that, they went over to their captives. At Lilith's signal, the securitywomen guarding them removed the tape from their mouths. Lilith spoke with their officer first.

"Do you know who I am?" she asked her.

"Yes, you're Vice Admiral Lilith ben Jeni."

"*Indeed*, and you and your women took over *my* ship," Lilith said coldly. "My friends here believe that you did so acting under orders that you thought were legitimate. They were *not*, and as we speak, this ship is being targeted by other Navy vessels. I'm going to offer you a choice; you can fight with me to retake the *Athena*, or you can sit it out and take your chances in court. What will it be, Captain?"

"Fek you," the officer spat. "Once Angelique gets the Tree, you're all done. The Sisterhood will finally have the kind of leadership it needs and weak women like you will—"

Before she could continue with her rant, Lilith had the securitywoman re-tape her mouth. "Well, that's one we can count out," she remarked acerbically. She turned to Senior Troop Leader Ben Di next. "What about you? Do you feel the same way?"

Ben Di looked her straight in the eye. "We didn't know. They told us we were coming out here on a classified mission, and that some of you were working with the Marionites. Our job was to make sure that the ship wasn't taken over by hostiles. That's it."

Lilith looked over her shoulder to Grammy and Jan. The Ensign had her eyes closed, and seemed to be deep in concentration, but they both nodded back to her.

"She's telling the truth," Grammy said.

Lilith had already sensed the same thing, and without the aid of any special occult gifts. She addressed Margasdaater and T'Jinna. "Is that so?" she asked them. "Is that how it was, Troopers?"

575

Margasdaater and T'Jinna both shook their heads vigorously. "Yah," the Zommerlaandar answered. "Z's juzt like zhe zaid. Zat's vat zey told uz."

"Very well. I'm going to let you go," Lilith informed her. "You'll help us." This wasn't a question.

"I'll also make this warning to you," she added, "if you play us false, I'll have you executed on the spot. Kaly here, will be your commander and you will do *exactly* what she says. When the time comes, I'll make certain that your cooperation is taken into account, but I can't promise you anything more than that. Is this clear?"

"Yes, Admiral," Ben Di agreed. "It is." Their guards came up and cut their bonds.

"That's what I wanted to hear," Lilith replied. "You can start helping us by giving your Ops leader a call. She's bound to be wondering what happened to you. Tell her that you had to stun us, and that you'll be on your way to security once we've recovered. That should buy us a little time."

"Yes, ma'am."

One of the securitywomen handed Ben Di her com-set, and as she put it on, Captain t'Gwen placed a needlegun to her temple. "Keep it short," T'Gwen suggested quietly, "and stick to the script. No *fekking* around."

Ben Di didn't take any offense at this, and relayed the message exactly as Lilith had instructed. When she had finished, T'Gwen re-holstered her weapon and the two women exchanged simple nods of acknowledgement and mutual respect. To them, such harsh measures were simply part of the day's business. Nothing personal, and fully expected by everyone involved.

Kaly was similarly unaffected. Making no comment on the threatening exchange, she signaled Ben Di and the others to join her and the Chief. To her private relief, Ben Di took charge right away. The Senior Troop Leader was much better qualified than she was for this kind of thing and she was glad that the woman was stepping up and bringing her experience to bear.

"Chief, show us the layout of the secondary bridge," the Aran requested. "If we have it, we also need to see 'vid feeds that show where the team has positioned itself."

"Not a problem, "Bel Lyra said. "We still have feeds there. That's something these RSE girls haven't figured out—yet. No offense."

Ben Di smiled crookedly. "None taken."

The Chief called up another image that showed the area, overlaid with live footage. The RSE team had positioned two of its troopers near the entrance, while another woman hovered near the Command chair and the fourth had staged herself back and behind her, with a view of the entire area. Ben Di and Kaly both saw the flaw in their defense strategy right away.

"Is there some way that we can get underneath them?" Kaly asked, "And hit them from behind?" Ben Di and her teammates grinned at this idea.

"Yes," Bel Lyra said. "It'll be a tight fit, but once you reach the end of the access tube, it opens up and there's space under the decking. The panels can be pushed up." Each panel was numbered, and the Chief had highlighted the ones that would allow them to come up behind the Team.

"I like it," Ben Di declared. "They won't expect us to pop up from the floor. We'll also need to have their radio coms cut out right before we hit them. Can you manage that, Chief?"

"Sure. I can generate interference using the infrastructure in the area," Bel Lyra replied. "That should make sure they can't receive or transmit."

"Then I think we have a workable plan," Ben Di announced. "*If* Corporal n'Deena is happy with it, of course." She looked to Kaly, who inclined her head in agreement.

"Good," Lilith said.

"You'll stay behind us," Kaly told her, "and you'll follow instructions. If things get hot, you'll retreat right away. That's an order, Admiral."

Lilith raised an eyebrow, but didn't contend this. This was Kaly's operation, at least until they had secured the secondary bridge.

"There's something else, "Kaly added, addressing both Lilith and Ben Di. "I don't want any of the troopers killed. I don't care about Bel Thana or her officers, but those troopers are my sisters, right or wrong."

"I can't make that promise, Corporal," Lilith returned. "There is much more at stake here than a handful of troopers. We'll do what we have to do."

"If you want my help, then you'll agree," Kaly insisted. "Otherwise, you can count me out. I'm a civilian and I don't have to do what any of you say."

"We could use stun grenades and the pistols from security," Ben Di volunteered. "That, and the element of surprise should do the trick."

"Is that sufficient, Kaly?" Lilith asked.

"It is."

Kaly however, was not the only one who had special demands to make. Jon and Jan bar Daala pushed their way into the group.

"I want to come along too," Jon announced. "This is also my fight and I want to see it to the end. And someone has to watch over the Admiral and the Chief. Jan and I can do that."

Kaly shook her head. "No. You two need to stay here with Celina and the others. No offense Jon, but this Op is no place for a man."

Even as she said this, she was surprised at her own conservatism, but equally certain that the neoman would just get in the way and get himself killed. Ex-Marine though he was, this was way out of his league. As for Bar Daala, she had no idea what her skill set actually was and she wasn't in the mood to find out 'on the fly'.

Bar Daala however, was just as adamant. "We're going with you, Kaly, and if you won't take us, we'll follow. You'll have to shoot us if you want us to hang back. And Jon here *can* help. He might not have your training, but he's big, and if nothing else, he can drag the Admiral out of there if things go bad."

From Jan's stance, and the hard look in Jon's eyes, Kaly realized that she wasn't going to overcome their insane determination to become casualties.

"Fine," she agreed at last. "But it's the same deal as the Admiral and the Chief. You two stay with them, and you stay behind. If we fail, you get them out." She glanced over at Grammy, fully expecting for her to ask to be included. Everyone else certainly had.

She was just beginning to formulate her refusal when Grammy surprised her pleasantly. "I think I'll just stay here with Celina," she said. "I'm far too old to be crawling through access tunnels and fighting armed women. We'll just sit here and get acquainted with one another."

"Wonderful," Kaly said. "Let's gear up." She went with Margasdaater and Ben Di over to Captain n'Willa, and promptly stripped her of her protective garments. Although the Conversâzi woman tried to resist, in short order, Kaly had all the equipment that she needed for the Op and the officer was left sitting there in her underwear.

She also asked for, and received, a pair of blast/projectile resistant vests from the securitywomen for Lilith and Bel Lyra to wear. While these weren't up to the same standard as the ones the team and Kaly were currently wearing, they still afforded the two women a certain measure of protection. In addition, the securitywomen handed over a pair of side-arms that they had confiscated, along with their own stun pistols.

Jan and Jon received the energy pistols, and Kaly and Ben Di pocketed the stunners. The load-out for their group was far from ideal, but given the circumstances, Kaly knew that it was the best that they could hope for. With luck, they would overcome the enemy team, and then take their equipment.

"Okay," she said once she saw that everyone was ready. "Let's get going."

The Chief started to lead them over to an access hatch in the floor, and as she was prying it up, Skylaar, Jeena and Josette finally arrived. All three of them wore bandages and they were covered with dried blood. Seeing their disheveled state, Lilith momentarily forgot all about the operation. Her mind centered on her daughter instead.

"Where is Sarah?" she asked them, concern coloring her voice.

"She is in the shuttle right now," Skylaar told her. "With Maya. We did what we could for them, but they will both need paramedics, and a doctor when there's time for it."

Lilith paled, but Skylaar reassured her. "She'll be fine, Admiral. But right now we have a job to do. Let's focus on that. Tell me the situation. Have you implemented the *Protocole Polaire* yet?"

Lilith did a double take. "How do you know about that?" she demanded. "Oh yes. Of course—the Agency."

Skylaar and Jeena made no reply, and Josette merely rewarded her with a cryptic smile.

"I haven't been able to implement it yet," Lilith admitted. She went on to tell them about the lock-out, and their intent to re-take Engineering and institute the *Protocole* there.

"What do think that you can suggest that the Navy hasn't already anticipated?" she finally asked her. "And before you answer that, what exactly do you three women *do* for the Agency? I think I deserve that information before I'll agree to listen to any proposal."

"I'm an independent consultant," the Nemesian answered casually. "I'm called in by the Agency when it has to deal with troublesome personnel issues. Like this one."

An assassin, Lilith concluded. "And you two?"

"Information Systems Security, "Josette replied. "Jeena here is a Transportation Facilitator, when he's not filling in on special projects."

"*He*?" Lilith asked, giving the neoman an appraising look. "No—never mind. Say what you need to say".

"The *Protocole* calls for a commander to isolate the enemy from the ship's control functions, and flood vital areas with GZ gas, or CO_2," Skylaar said. "Am I correct?"

GZ Gas, or *Gaz d'Sanz Connaisanz Agente-417* contained a potent opiate appropriate to humanoids. Odorless, and colorless, it could render anyone unconscious in an enclosed space in just a few seconds. It had been specifically developed for aggressive ship-boardings, and Lilith was utterly confident that it, or the use of CO_2, would end the crisis swiftly.

"Yes. What of it?" Lilith asked.

"The gas simply won't work," Josette stated. "Not on all of them. Oh, you'll certainly put the crew to sleep, and get the troopers, but not my sister, or her officers. They will respond far too quickly. They might even manage to escape the sealed areas."

"I seriously doubt that," Lilith retorted. "The gas takes effect far too quickly, and if we're stealthy enough, they won't even realize that they've been assaulted until it's much too late."

"With respect, I beg to differ, Admiral," Skylaar countered. "Colonel bel Thana and her fellow conspirators also know all about the *Protocole*, and they have certainly prepared themselves for its implementation. In addition, their reaction time is much faster than most normal women. When they see the others around them starting to drop, they will respond, and save themselves. There *are* portable emergency masks on the bridge, are there not? For the officers?"

"Yes, there are, but no one is *that* fast," Lilith countered. "They'll never activate them in time. Not *all* of them!"

"Humor me," Skylaar said. "If I can have a word with your Engineering Chief, and have her make a slight modification to the ship's environmental systems, we might be able to counter this problem. But we'll need to do it before you attempt any lockdown or employ the gas."

"*What* modification?"

"I can't tell you that, Admiral," Skylaar answered. "I'm sorry, but you don't possess the required clearance level. It goes well beyond 'Brilliant'. In fact, there isn't even a classification level for the subject, but I assure you that what I have in mind will not harm your crew, or impede your operation in anyway. What it *will* do is help us handle Bel Thana's officers, even if they escape."

Lilith was strongly inclined to refuse her, just on the grounds that she wasn't being included in the information loop, but Skylaar's aura of confidence, and their dearth of allies, convinced her otherwise.

She turned to Bel Lyra. "Chief, hear her out. If it sounds like it will work, do it. But if it seems like it will cause us any significant problems, tell her no. I'm trusting in your judgment here."

Bel Lyra nodded. "Yes, ma'am."

"Is there somewhere we can talk—alone?" Skylaar asked the woman.

"Sure," Bel Lyra said, and then she led her into an adjoining chamber. This was a locker room reserved for the Hangar's service teams.

As they left, Lilith confronted Grammy. "What was she talking about? Does this have something to do with that little trick you pulled in the hangar?"

"I don't know what you mean, Lily," Grammy replied. "Skylaar is just taking the proper precautions. It's nothing worth worrying over. Now, if you'll pardon me, I really should go and help her to explain things to the Chief."

With that, she vanished into thin air, leaving Lilith both amazed and frustrated. For their parts, neither Jeena nor Josette bothered to enlighten her. Instead, they seemed to be amused.

***

When they were alone at last, Skylaar directed Bel Lyra to stand at one end of the locker room while she went to the other. Puzzled, the Chief complied.

"Chief," Skylaar began, "When you get to Engineering, I need you to alter the anti-gravity fields throughout the entire ship. We will require a fluctuating wave that drops the gravity by one one-hundredth of a degree, and then increases it above the normal range to the same extent. I need this wave to repeat in intervals of a quarter of a second. That should achieve the desired results."

"Sure. I can do that—the anti-grav plates are all networked," Bel Lyra agreed. "We can make the change with a group command. But--why? It'll screw up our mass and fek with our local time. The ship's clocks'll be off..."

She performed a quick mental calculation."...by a 1/100th of a second! Do you know what that will *do* to the computer systems? We're bound to sprout errors all over the place. We'll have to have someone posted at a control station to correct for that."

"I fully appreciate the difficulty involved," Skylaar said. "But we need the time alteration that this wave will produce. It's the only way that we can confuse the symbiotes."

"Symbiotes?" Bel Lyra asked. "What are they? Why are they an issue?"

Skylaar's expression grew somber. "Chief, can I count on your absolute discretion?"

"Of course!" Bel Lyra answered.

"Good," Skylaar replied. "But before we proceed any further, I feel that it would be prudent for me to ensure your cooperation conclusively. Please don't take offense."

With this, Skylaar disappeared, and then reappeared an instant later, right next to her. At the same time, the Engineer felt a sharp pain in her arm and cried out. "Hey! What the fek! How did you just—? What did you just do to me?"

"It is what the symbiote can do," Skylaar explained. "I know what you're thinking, and it's not teleportation. The symbiote transcends time

581

itself. It is an alien device—a Drow'voi one to be precise, and every agent past a certain rank has one implanted in her body.'

"Many years ago, we discovered that it has a weakness. This occurred during one of our operations aboard a naval vessel. The artificial gravity malfunctioned, and we learned that the symbiote cannot adjust for rapid fluctuations in the local time-stream that this creates. Since this does not occur in nature, and artificial gravity is generally dependable, only a few women even know about this, and we wish to keep things that way. Our implanted agents must never come to suspect that we have the means to defeat their most powerful tool through such a simple process.'

"As for the pain in your arm, I have injected you with a customized nanite. It will remain inert in your body. For now. However, if I ever perceive that you have violated my confidence, I will send the signal, and it will kill you within seconds. With that said, welcome to Phantasma, sister."

Grammy materialized next to them a nanosecond later. "There is a trade-off, you know" the older woman supplied. "Not only do you get to save Humanity, but you'll learn about all sorts of amazing technology that you never even dreamed of. So, are you good with this? We certainly hope so."

Bel Lyra looked at them, dumbfounded. Then she found her tongue. "All right. I am," she agreed. "I'll make the change."

With that, they returned to the others.

"It's nothing," the Chief said to Lilith. "It won't get in the way."

"Very well," Lilith responded. "Kaly?"

"One more thing," Kaly said. She had turned to Skylaar and her fellow agents. Unlike the others, she didn't consider them to be dead weight. She actually respected their skills as fighters. "What about you? Will you come with us?"

"I think we would be better served if Josette and I proceeded to the armory and secured it," Skylaar answered. "We can take care of the loose teams in the process—especially the one holding the Lifts. We can spare Jeena though. He can accompany you."

"That'll work," Kaly agreed. "It's the same deal for you. No killing any troopers unless you have to."

"Very reasonable," Skylaar nodded. "We shall do our utmost to abide by your requirements."

This, Kaly didn't doubt. "All right," she said looking around her. "Does *anyone* else have something to say?" When no one spoke, she gestured for the Chief to finish opening up the deck panel.

Seeing the narrow passage, Kaly's expression suddenly became playful. "You think you can fit down that, Astrid?"

"Yah," the bigger woman said, "My mother handled me juzt fine ven I vas born. I zhink zat zis is wider zan zhe vas"

"Okay," Kaly said. "I'm sure we can get the Chief to find something to grease you up with if you need it."

"Ach," Margasdaater answered. "No need. But maybe you or Ben Di zhould go virst. Ozervize zey might zhink ve are tvin zizsterz ven ve pop oot!"

They shared a laugh at this, and for an instant, it seemed as if they had never been separated from one another in the first place. Team 201 was whole again.

Kaly led the way, dropping down into the tunnel first. She was immediately followed by Ben Di, then Margasdaater, Jeena and T'Jinna. True to their instructions, Lilith and the Chief, with Jon and Bar Daala, went next, and Josette and Skylaar brought up the rear. The passage was just large enough for everyone to stand up in, and Kaly immediately commandeered the Chief's hand held device, and gave it to Ben Di.

A few minutes later, when the holo indicated that they had reached the proper junction, Kaly signaled for a halt. One of the passages led towards Engineering, and the other to the Armory and the Lifts.

Wishing them luck, Josette and Skylaar left them there and headed off on their mission.

***

At the point where she was confident that they were well out of earshot, Josette stopped and turned to face Skylaar. "So", she said, subtly relaxing her stance and readying herself for combat. "Shall we get to our business?"

Skylaar, who was doing exactly the same thing, nodded. "Yes. This seems as good a place as any."

Josette smiled, and withdrew her sword from its sheath, and then began to circle the woman. "How much did she pay you?"

"Angelique, or Silvi?" Skylaar asked. She had taken out her own blade and was holding it in a relaxed, receptive position, point down and blade up.

"Since Angelique is dead, I suppose my question concerns my dear sister, Silvi," Josette replied. By now, both women had embraced their symbiotes, so that neither had the advantage.

"Forty-five," Skylaar told her as she stepped back and sideways. "Fifty if I could bring her your head."

Josette was appalled by the sum. "Only fifty? My head is worth *much* more than that!" Despite her outburst, she didn't lower her guard by even a centimeter.

"The Guild found it acceptable," Skylaar responded, bringing her blade up and sideways as she continued maneuvering and appraising Josette for weaknesses. "Tell me, when did you know?"

"From the very start of our endeavor," Josette smiled. "Your reputation preceded you, and my sibling's intentions have always been as clear as glass. It was only logical that they would retain you—and that you would wait until you could get me alone. Now you have."

Skylaar didn't even bother to deny it.

"I have a counter offer," Josette continued. "I'll make it 75, 80 for *her* head, and another 20 to you as a finder's fee. Once this is over, I plan on engaging your services with regards to several bothersome individuals. Tell me, does the Guild allow you to negotiate on its behalf?"

"It does," Skylaar answered, "and I find your offer acceptable. With one stipulation--" her sword remained poised to strike, and Josette did not miss the message that this sent.

"Which is?"

"I want Maya left alone and unharmed," Skylaar told her. "That is not negotiable, and without it we have no contract."

Josette lowered her blade, slightly, and frowned. "That is almost enough for me to reconsider my generous offer. But---I will agree to it. At least until I can find a way to betray you."

"Naturally," Skylaar responded. Her blade had also lowered by a centimeter. "We have a deal then?"

"We do." Josette said, returning her blade to its scabbard. "You drive a very hard bargain, Skylaar."

This was an understatement. Not only had she just promised to pay the Assassins' Guild of Ashkele nearly 100 million Credits to save her life and retain Skylaar's talents, but she had also agreed to let Maya go her own way. Control over Maya was priceless, but she really had no alternatives.

"You know," she added, "You and I should talk later. "We really should have a conversation."

As they released their symbiotes, Skylaar gave her a quizzical look. "Oh? And have you had this 'conversation' with others? With anyone that I know personally?"

"Yes," Josette admitted. "With Lady Ananzi. It has been going on for some years, and Angelique became an impediment to its goals. Phantasma was the Conversâzi's answer to the problem, and not the independent entity that you were led to believe. It was more of a project name than anything else."

"I suspected as much," Skylaar replied. "Everyone involved knew far too much to ascribe to one mole, however well placed she was." By now, she had put her own weapon away.

"I do apologize for that deception, but it was expedient," Josette said. "I assure you however, that the participants involved all want the same things that you do for the Sisterhood. We always have. Would you care to join our little talk?"

Skylaar shrugged, her equivalent of a smile. "Perhaps," she answered tentatively. "For now, I would simply like to see our business at the armory completed, and then visit the hangar for a few minutes."

Josette grinned, immediately grasping the shape of her plan. "Of course."

With that, the two women moved off together down the passage. To anyone who hadn't been privy to their interaction, they would have seemed completely relaxed, and utterly comfortable with one another. Which they were; their new business relationship guaranteed that they were now the closest of sisters.

Until the situation changed.

***

A dozen meters from their objective, there was a rhythmic tapping on the deck plates above them. Kaly recognized the sound right away. Any Marine would have.

It was a battlebot on patrol, making its rounds in the corridor overhead. Instantly, she tapped Margasdaater's shoulder with her boot, twice. The woman stopped moving immediately and passed her message down the line to the others with her own foot signal, but with the exception of Lilith and Bel Lyra, this was unnecessary. Everyone in Team 201 understood the danger that the sound represented.

If the 'bot detected them, it would be able to attack them with its guns, firing armor piercing rounds right through the metal, and there was nothing they could do to defend against this, much less escape.

Kaly held her breath instinctively, fully aware that this was a useless reaction. The 'bot's sensors could pick up her body heat, bioplasmic signature and the magnetic differences that her mere presence generated.

If it wasn't confused by the metal and all the conduits that surrounded them. That was what she was gambling on, and praying for.

The killer robot paused, and Kaly could just see the faint light from its scanner eye shining down through the small gaps between the plates, as its artificial intelligence tried to decide if it had discovered a threat or not. After a brief interval, the light finally winked out, and the battlebot moved on. It had not discovered them.

Kaly tapped Margasdaater on the shoulder again, telling her to start moving, and to quicken her pace. The 'bot would not forget that something had disturbed it, and it was almost certain that would come back again to reexamine the area. She didn't want to be there when this happened. Luck could only carry them so far.

She crawled on. Just when she was fairly certain that she was close to their objective, a message came.

Kaly. Stop. You're there.

Instantly, she froze and looked up, pointing the micro finger-light of her glove at the deck plate. The infrared beam illuminated the component number for her goggles to see. It was 2135478-B. According to Ben Di's readout, she was now directly below and behind the trooper stationed at the far end of the secondary bridge. Margasdaater came to a halt a second later. She was also in position to attack her target, and Ben Di and T'Jinna were in place beneath the two women guarding the entrance.

For their plan to work, everyone would have to hit together, and Kaly would start the attack. But Team 201 had learned to work together as a single, functioning organism. Each of them knew exactly what the others would do, and Kaly didn't let herself worry about her teammates. Instead, she put her full attention on getting herself ready. As Ben Di started the countdown, she carefully swung her submachinegun back and behind her as quietly as possible, and double checked the stun pistol she had been given by Captain t'Gwen.

She was a good shot with most pistols—not as good as she was with Tatiana--but proficient enough to feel reasonably confident of success. That was if everything went the way they had planned it. Most plans only stayed intact until the moment that they encountered the enemy though. After that, things tended to go sideways, and only quick reflexes and fast thinking compensated for all the chaos.

3, 2, 1. Go!

Kaly pushed the plate up and popped out. The trooper was right in front of her, and before the startled woman could react, she fired the stun pistol. There was a bright flash and the woman toppled forwards.

Margasdaater came out of her hiding place at the same time, and threw a stun grenade at her target. It hit the trooper just under the lip of her helmet and with such force that the impact alone was enough to render her unconscious. As Margasdaater ducked back down into cover, it rolled away and exploded uselessly under a control station with an earsplitting 'bang!'

When she rose again, the Zommerlaandar had a big grin plastered on her face.

Goddess, Astrid! Kaly thought. *Did you have to throw it that hard?*

Yah, vell, zorry, Margasdaater apologized, clearly not sorry at all.

Over at the entrance, the two other troopers were also down. Ben Di and T'Jinna had subdued them with their stun pistols. But no one paused to celebrate their easy victory. Instead they jumped out and began to disarm and secure their prisoners.

One of the Engineering Techs, who had been cowering behind a nearby control console, came up to Kaly and offered to help. Together, they dragged Kaly's trooper off to the side.

Admiral, Chief, Kaly heard Ben Di think. *We're clear. Come on up.*

When Lilith appeared with the Chief and the others, she took in the sight of the unconscious troopers and nodded to Kaly in approval.

"All right, Chief", she said. "Let's get that *Protocole* instituted and end this thing."

"Straightaway, ma'am," Bel Lyra answered, leading her over to a control station. Lilith sat down at it, and started to reach for the interface.

She was interrupted by the sharp staccato of a chemical weapon being fired. Blood blossomed across Bel Lyra's jumpsuit, and the woman spasmed from the impact of the rounds as they hit her.

Jon reacted instantly, grabbing Lilith in his powerful arms and dropping with her to the decking. Jan joined him an instant later, wrapping herself around the neoman and adding her own mass to the human shield.

Kaly's head whipped around and she saw the tech who had helped her, crouching nearby. There was a needlegun in her hand. The kind that was issued to RSE Teams.

Even as her mind processed this fact, Kaly was bringing her submachinegun around. But before she could fire, the enemy agent had dropped her pistol, withdrawn a wicked looking sword from under a nearby station, and leapt forwards.

The woman disappeared halfway to the deck, transforming into a shadow. In an eye blink, it had crossed the room, passing by Margasdaater, then T'Jinna, and finally Ben Di.

Margasdaater cried out and clutched at her throat as bright red blood welled up through her fingers. Simultaneously, T'Jinna screamed when her hand flew away, still clenching the pistol it had been holding, and Ben Di simply dropped to her knees with an expression of shock. Her head toppled away from her body an instant later, and then her decapitated corpse followed it to the decking.

Wailing in terror, Kaly let off a burst from her weapon, but the phantom had moved out of her line of sight even before the first round managed to leave the barrel. Then she caught a brief glimpse of Jeena drawing his own sword, and vanishing.

There was a flash of purple sparks near the center of the room and a clash of steel as the two shadows engaged one another. An instant later, a head materialized out of thin air and rolled across the decking, coming to rest at Kaly's feet.

It was the tech. Her eyes were wide with horror, and her mouth moved for a moment, trying to expel a scream that would never come. Her body came next, collapsing onto the metal floor with a sodden thump. Then Jeena reappeared, standing over it with a bloody sword.

Still in shock, Kaly started to scramble towards Margasdaater, but she heard the distinctive sound of metal legs skittering towards her. Before she had time to react to this, Jeena had disappeared and she felt a hand shoving her to the floor. A cluster of energized bolts passed right through the space that she had just occupied, smashing into a control station instead and making it burst into flame.

It was the battlebot that they had encountered earlier. The killer robot had responded to the sounds of the fight, and now it was standing in the entranceway. Realizing that it had missed her, its head began to swivel around to reacquire her, and as it adjusted its aim, Kaly found herself looking right down the barrel of its guns.

The fatal shots never came though. There was a disturbance in the air, and something passed between her and the robot. Then the thing's head split in half with a shower of sparks. It collapsed, and Jeena manifested out of nowhere, pale and panting for breath.

As the 'bot crashed to the floor, Kaly made for Margasdaater again, and this time, managed to reach her. The Zommerlaandar was still alive, but the only thing that separated her from the afterlife were her hands holding the wound in her throat. There was blood everywhere.

"Kaly—"she managed to croak. Then she smiled weakly and her eyes fluttered shut.

"No!" Kaly sobbed, shaking her as if she could wake her back to life. "No! Astrid! Don't leave!"

It was useless though. Margasdaater was gone. Wailing up at the ceiling in grief, Kaly gathered her up, and cradled her in her arms. "No...no...no..."

Jeena left her to mourn her comrade and went to T'Jinna. The Sireeni had curled herself up in a corner. She was holding her arm and staring incredulously at the bloody stump where her hand had been. Reaching into her med-pak, the neoman pulled out a dressing and gently wrapped it around the wound. The smart fiber molded itself to the injury immediately, and compressed, sealing off the severed vessels.

Having done all that he could for her, he made a point of retrieving the hand itself. It had slid over into a corner, and he knew that once medical attention became available, that it would be grafted back onto her. And in all likelihood, she would regain full use of it; thanks to the sharpness of the sword that had removed it, the wound had been clean. But like Kaly, he also understood that her mental healing process would take much longer, and that the outcome was far less certain.

Glancing back over his shoulder, he saw that Jon and Jan had released Lilith, and now they were working together to help the Chief with another medpak. Miraculously, Bel Lyra was still alive, even though it was obvious that she had taken multiple hits from the needlegun.

She too would most likely live, the neoman thought, and he saluted Jon and Bar Daala with his sword for putting themselves in harms' way to save the Vice-Admiral.

"Admiral," he said, inclining his head at Bel Lyra. "Can we still engage the *Protocole?*"

"I-I don't know," she stammered. She looked at something behind him, and he followed her gaze. It was another tech. An officer. She was unarmed, and looked as shaken as everyone else.

"You!" he shouted. "Get over here and help the Admiral."

The woman blinked as if she was having trouble understanding his words. Then she came around and ran over, barking orders of her own. "Someone get that fire out! Ensign—get on the back-up station and re-route away from it! *Burn it* woman!"

"Can you lock out the bridge and all the Class 1 areas?" Lilith asked her, wiping the back of a bloody hand across her forehead.

"Yes, ma'am," the officer answered. "I have the clearance." As she moved to take her place at the control station, Bel Lyra seized Lilith's sleeve. "The gravity—", she croaked. "Need to--change—that—"

"What does she mean?" Lilith asked.

"I know," Jeena replied. He proceeded to give the tech the details.

The instant that the sailor sent the command, everyone noticed the change. For most of them, it manifested as nothing more than a ringing in the ears, but Jeena staggered as he felt the connection with his symbiote break off, and he had to fight to stay erect as the room spun.

Things stabilized for a moment, and then the unpleasant sensation repeated itself. It came and went like this, in alternating cycles.

"What is that?" Lilith demanded. "What did she just do?"

Steadying himself against the control station, Jeena gave her a wan smile. "She just saved us from any more attacks like that last one, Vice Admiral. *Now* we can finish this."

***

589

Up above them on the bridge, Silvi bel Thana had also noticed the change, and when she tried to access her symbiote, and failed, she cried out in dismay. An alarm went off next, warning everyone that the Main Lifts had just gone offline. It was followed by another alert about the bridge itself.

All of the control stations had gone dead. So had every other location where her teams had been stationed.

Josette's hologram appeared. Her face wore a creamy, self-satisfied expression. "Silvi? Angelique is dead, and it is all over for you and your friends. Give up now, and your lives will be spared."

"No!" Silvi shrieked, slashing at the holo with her sword. "No! That can't be true!" She rounded on Katrinn and her officers. "I'll kill them all! I'll kill them one by one unless you get me a ship!"

"Of course, sister dear," Josette replied. "I fully understand. A ship has already been prepared for you. It is in the Hangar, awaiting your pleasure."

Silvi pulled Katrinn up by her collar and put the edge of her weapon to her throat. "She's coming with me—as insurance—*sister dear*."

Oddly, Katrinn was smiling. "You're done," she said to her, her words slurring. "It's over."

Silvi heard a faint hiss, and realized that everyone around her was starting to sway, and then to her horror, collapsing to the deck. With another panicked cry, she released Katrinn and immediately donned the emergency breather mask she had appropriated for herself. Eyes wild with desperation, she took a deep breath from it, and looked around her for her fellow agents. Two of them had been too slow to react, and they had joined the crew in unconsciousness, but three were still standing.

"Follow me!" she shouted. She led the way over to an access panel set in the bulkhead. Wrenching it open, she climbed in and began to ascend the emergency ladder without bothering to see if her companions were still behind her. The ladder led up to a series of tubeways, and ultimately the Hangar itself.

Down in the secondary bridge, Lilith saw this happening on the 'vid feeds and turned to Skylaar and Josette. They had returned with a full squad of Marines. "She's getting away!"

Josette pointedly ignored the display and examined her perfectly manicured nails instead. "Yes, Admiral," she sighed. "She is."

"We need to send someone after her!" Lilith declared. "She needs to stand trial for this!" She looked to the officer leading the Marines. "Get some people up there, Lieutenant! I want that woman brought back to me in irons!"

"Belay that, Trooper," Skylaar interrupted. "This is an Agency matter. Let her go. Do not interfere. That is a direct order under the authority of the Chairwoman's mandate for the RSE."

By now, alarms were telling them that the fugitives had left the emergency ladder and had passed through a maintenance tube. In just a few minutes, they would reach the Hangar and make their escape.

"She's getting away!" Lilith repeated. She couldn't believe that they were actually letting this happen.

Skylaar simply shrugged, and Josette calmly took a seat and watched as a panel that opened into the Hangar Bay was breached. A minute after this, the Hangar's status display registered a shuttle's engines coming to life, and then it informed them that the vessel was taxiing over to a take-off strip. It was preparing to leave the *Athena*.

"What is this? " Lilith demanded. "What is going on here?" Neither woman bothered to enlighten her. Meanwhile, the shuttle had departed and was beginning its descent towards Ashkele.

"Offhand," Josette finally said, "I'd venture to say that my sister plans to seek asylum with the Xee, and then sell what she knows to the Hriss or some other pack of alien vermin." Her tone was mild and thoroughly unruffled.

Lilith was aghast. "And you're actually *letting* that *happen*?"

Now it was Josette's turn to answer with a shrug. "Evidently."

By now, the shuttle had reached the outer layer of the atmosphere, and as it continued to drop, Skylaar watched its progress keenly. "I believe that it has reached the correct altitude," she observed.

At that precise instant, the vessel exploded. Immediately, automatic calls went out to the Hangar Bay to dispatch emergency rescue units, but the Nemesian reached over and silenced them.

"That won't be necessary," she said. "Clearly, Silvi had some explosives in her possession when she departed. These must have gone off prematurely."

"Clearly," Josette agreed. "And saved us the ordeal of an embarrassing trial that would have harmed our new Chairwoman's administration, not to mention the reputation of a number of other important women. Rather convenient, don't you think?"

She rose from her place and brushed away some imaginary dust from her cloak. "I shall have to contact those women as soon as possible and remind them of their debt to me," she said. "I am certain that they will want to express their gratitude.'

"Oh, and while I'm at it, I will also have to call my brokers. It seems that I have just inherited all of my sister's shares in the Luxar Lines, and a substantial fortune in Credits.'

She bowed deeply to Lilith. "Admiral? It has been a true pleasure working with you. Now, if you'll be so kind as to accommodate me, I'll need somewhere to make these calls—in private, of course."

Speechless, all Lilith could do was incline her head stiffly, and muster up all of her inner resources to marshal her temper. Since Sarah's return, she had allowed herself to enjoy an unofficial truce with the Agency. But Josette had just reminded her of everything that she despised about that organization. They were the very worst of what the Sisterhood was, and she found herself sympathizing wholeheartedly with the rebels of the ETR and the Marionites.

Her inner turmoil was interrupted by an Engineering tech who had cross-trained for Fire-Control. "Admiral! We just had fifteen ships exit Null!" the woman announced. "They're headed straight at us!"

Lilith's eyes riveted on the sitscreens. The remaining in-system Hriss patrols were still arrowing in their direction, but they were a good 20 minutes away from becoming a serious threat. The newcomers had come out of Nullspace much closer than that, and would reach them in five.

Seevaans? she thought. It seemed impossible. According to Rixa, they still had hours before the insectoids would arrive. *Someone else then?*

Her question was answered when the ship's computer finally managed to identify the intruders. They were Tzang warships—and alongside every category were nothing but question marks; *'Weapons? Unknown. Defenses? Unknown. Class? Unknown.'*

The only thing that was firm was that they were hostile. Their weapons—whatever they were—had targeted the Battle Group. The hail that the *Athena* received from the Tzang only confirmed this.

"Sisterhood ship, you have something of ours," a voice said, sounding like it came from the wrong side of the grave. "You have the Secret. Surrender it to us now or *die.*"

Lilith's mind raced. She had control of the *Athena*, and thanks to that, the *Artemis* and *Demeter* no longer considered her vessel a target. But most of her bridge crew were still recovering from the effects of the GZ gas, and the ship itself was being run from a secondary helm, with truncated control stations. And even with her sister ships helping, they would be facing fifteen warships of unknown strength, plus the Hriss, who were still on their way, and then the Seevaans.

It wasn't even a match. It was a slaughter.

There was only one solution that would resolve the crisis, she decided. She turned to the tech. "Target that Tree," she told her. "Thermonuke. One missile, maximum yield. Vaporize it."

"Admiral?" Skylaar asked. "Are you certain? You yourself said that it needed to be studied by experts. And it *is* on sovereign Xee soil. If we attack it, we're attacking the Xee."

"Goddess damn the Xee," Lilith snarled. "I've changed my mind. This *thing* shouldn't be in anyone's hands—least of all our enemies. Take it out, Ensign!"

"Yes, ma'am," the woman answered. Her finger stabbed at the holographic controls. On the main display, one of the *Athena's* missiles came to life, and then launched itself, dropping towards the planet below.

A howl of elemental rage came from the Tzang, and it was joined by the Hriss Commander as they both realized what she had just done. It was too late however. Neither force was close enough to intercept the missile. All they could do was watch helplessly as it gained speed and closed with its target.

Less than 30 seconds later, it detonated with a bright flash, and a violent shockwave rippled out into the surrounding ruins, toppling the ancient buildings. This was accompanied by a gigantic mushroom cloud, and a wave of dust which rolled outwards in all directions. When it finally cleared enough to reveal the result of the strike, the plaza was gone. In its place, was a crater filled with molten glass. The Tree, and all of its secrets, was no more.

"You've lost," Lilith said, addressing both groups. "The Secret is destroyed. No one has it now. Go home or die for nothing."

There was a long pause, and then slowly, the Tzang warships began to turn about and head back towards their point of origin. The same thing happened with the Hriss vessels, and for once, they didn't harangue her with their usual empty threats. Their defeat was too profound. Like the Tzang, they had lost their only chance to gain galactic supremacy and they knew it.

She didn't rub her triumph in. It was enough for her that everyone was leaving and that they were still alive. The fact that the Xee were frantically trying to contact them for an explanation for the missile strike was inconsequential. When the Xee ambassador itself tried to hail the ship, Lilith ordered the connection cut.

"You did the right thing," Josette assured her. "But to assuage your conscience, the Agency will take full responsibility for this entire event, so you needn't have any concern in that regard. Our treaty with the Xee allows us to take measures against any third party that threatens our mutual interests. We will clarify this detail for them, in good time."

Despite her disgust, Lilith indicated her gratitude. "Ensign? See to it that this woman is given a place in private to conduct her business. I will be down in Sickbay, visiting my daughter."

She left them, and headed straightaway to the ship's medical facilities. Sarah and Maya had been taken there as soon as the ship had been returned to friendly hands. For the moment, she didn't care about the incoming Seevaan fleet, or anything else for that matter. Sarah was all that concerned her.

When she reached her destination, she was informed that her daughter was in surgery, and she was forced to wait. At last, when the operation was over, there was a further delay as Sarah was taken to a recovery wing. Her surgeon had been none other than the Ship's Senior Medical Officer herself and she came out to speak with Lilith personally.

"How is she?" Lilith asked her.

"She's fine, Vice Admiral," Dr. elle Kaari said. "We repaired the damage, and she's recovering. With some aggressive nanorobotic treatments and a program of physical therapy, she should heal from her injuries completely. She's a very tough young woman."

"Thank the Goddess, "Lilith replied in relief. "Can I see her?"

"Yes," Elle Kaari answered, "but only for a few minutes—and don't expect too much. She's still very groggy from the anesthesia, and she needs her rest."

"That's fine," Lilith agreed. "I just want to see her. I'll make it short."

The Nyxian nodded, fully understanding a mother's need to be at her child's side at a time like this. She handed her a pair of nighteyes, and then led her through the light barrier and into the recovery area. Once there, she left the two of them alone together.

Lilith had to suppress a gasp of alarm when she saw her daughter at last. Sarah had a huge smart-cast on her arm and on her leg, with what seemed like miles of tubing, and she was linked up to all sorts of mysterious looking equipment. Lying there in the dark in her bed, and wearing nothing but a black hospital gown, she seemed very frail, and every bit the little girl that Lilith remembered. Despite everything that had happened between them, all she wanted right then was to take her up in her arms, hold her, and somehow make everything well again with nothing more than the pure force of her love.

Instead, she reigned in her feelings, and gently took Sarah's uninjured hand.

Sarah's eyes opened at her touch. "Mother?"

"Yes, darling," Lilith answered. "It's me."

"Mother, I'm so sorry," Sarah said. Her voice was slurred, and her eyes were a bit glassy. "I'm sorry for what I said to you."

"Don't be," Lilith replied, caressing her forehead. "There's nothing that you need to apologize for."

"There is," Sarah insisted. "I shouldn't have said those things about that man—about your friend. I was wrong."

Lilith shook her head. "It's nothing, darling. Don't worry about it. That's all in the past now."

"It's not," Sarah said. "It was terrible of me. I--I wasn't myself. I can't explain it to you, but I didn't really mean any of it, and I didn't want to ruin your wedding. Please---forgive me."

Lilith smiled down at her, ignoring the tear that was rolling down her cheek. "Sarah, I'm your mother. No matter what you do, I will *always* forgive you. That's what mothers do. I don't need any apologies. Right now, what I need is for you to get yourself well."

Sarah's own eyes misted over, and she squeezed Lilith's hand. "I will, mother. Thank you. Things will be better now. I promise."

They sat together until one of the Nyxian nurses came in. As much as she hated to, it was time for Lilith to leave, and let her daughter rest.

Out in the passageway, and alone again, Lilith leaned against a bulkhead. An icon, telling her that a psiever message was waiting, flashed in the corner of her vision. It was from the bridge.

She ignored it, fished out a czigavar from her pocket, lit it, and took a long, deep drag. As far as she was concerned, after the day she'd just had, everyone could fekking wait for a few more minutes.

When she was finally ready, she extinguished her czigavar and opened the message. Naturally, it concerned something that was deadly serious, and couldn't wait.

It was from Katrinn, who had recovered from the effects of the GZ gas. She was at her station again, and up on the bridge. The Seevaan fleet had just entered the system, and they were expected to come within missile range in the next two hours.

It was time to be a Vice Admiral again.

***

Lilith reached the bridge right as a large group of Sisterhood warships exited Nullspace. Although the insectoids were not intimidated by the Sisterhood's display of force in the least, they were disheartened when they discovered that the Tree was nothing but radioactive ash and melted stone.

Making no threats, or even asking after Queen Talaria, the alien flotilla simply turned about and went back into Null. As for the Xee, after Josette had personally spoken with their ambassador, the incident was overlooked. The area where the Tree had once been was simply modified on their official maps to become a 'hazardous environmental zone', and business between the Sisterhood and their nation returned to normal.

Josette had even gone one step further and had smoothed things out between Lilith and Admiral ebed Cya. Instead of receiving any censure whatsoever, Lilith was quietly congratulated for her decisive actions.

The event itself, never became a matter of official record. The women of the Sisterhood would remain unaware that it had even occurred.

But those who had participated in the adventure did know, and a week later, Lilith persuaded Katrinn to lend her the use of the *Athena's* main conference room for what was to be their final meal together. Josette had already departed for the Sisterhood to handle her personal business, and Sarah attended in a wheelchair. Maya came to the gathering on crutches.

They dined together on a fine lunch catered by Saara sa'Vika herself. Afterwards, a holojector situated in the middle of the large baaka wood table played the Chairwoman's address to the nation. It was the first time that Chairwoman Tanya t'Tallya had spoken to her constituents in this capacity and everyone in the room was eager to hear what she had to say.

"My fellow sisters," T'Tallya began "we have just passed through a great series of tribulations. We have not only weathered a terrible series of attacks on our population centers, but faced an even greater danger from rogue elements within our own government.'

"The details of this must remain classified, but I can disclose to you that with the help of a few brave patriots, we have thwarted plans not only to take over our government and steal away your liberties, but to destabilize galactic peace."

"That's putting it mildly," Skylaar commented dryly. Her companions laughed politely.

"We now have a historic opportunity before us," T'Tallya continued. "We can go on was we have, and continue to struggle, or we can undertake the hard job of making reforms and seeking a lasting peace. For the sake of our daughter's futures, I have chosen the latter. The road ahead will not be easy, and there will be many obstacles all along the path, but I am certain of our nation's strength, and our ability to adapt and prevail.'

"Pursuant to this, I must tell you that I have been in contact with the leadership of the Marionite Church and that talks will soon be under way to heal the breach between us, and to address the gross inequalities that have been visited upon them by previous administrations. This is not an admission of failure, but an affirmation of our strength and wisdom.'

"I have also drafted plans to restructure and reform our State Police and Intelligence Agency to make it more accountable to the people that it serves. Lastly, with the exception of advisors, I have recommended the immediate withdrawal of all our peacekeeping forces in the Esteral Terrana Rapabla and opened up talks between the Loyalista and Pro-Ernan forces. It is time for our daughters to come home, and for that war to finally end. Thank you, and may the Goddess bless you all with peace and true sisterhood."

"Well," Lilith said with a deep intake of breath. "That was certainly a surprising speech. I imagine that we are about to see quite a bit of controversy springing up from all sides. But that's for the politicians to worry about. In the meantime, I have something to give to each of you."

She inclined her head to Jan bar Daala, and the Ensign produced a stack of black presentation boxes from under Sa'Vika's cart. Lilith rose from her place, and with her adjutant following her, went to Sarah and opened the first one.

Inside was the Distinguished Service Star, the highest award that the OAE and now the RSE, ever awarded its agents.

"From a grateful nation," Lilith said. She pinned the medal to Sarah's hospital gown and saluted her. Next, she went over to Maya and did the same thing, and after her, all the others—even Grammy, who accepted her decoration with a mischievous wink.

Everyone knew, without needed to be told, that their adventure would have to remain a secret.

Returning to her seat, Lilith regarded them all thoughtfully. "So," she said, "now that we have effectively saved the universe for the next few minutes at least, what are everyone's plans?"

"Well, mother," Sarah said, "since it appears that I am now the highest ranking officer in the RSE, I have some duties to perform as its Director, including the small matter of overseeing those sweeping reforms that our Chairwoman promised. Part of that will involve restructuring the Agency—and returning autonomy to our local police forces."

"That should be quite a task," her mother observed, looking pointedly at her wheelchair and the smartcasts she was wearing.

"Indeed," Sarah agreed. "However, I will have help once I am healed. I even took the step of enlisting someone that Maya knows quite well. I offered Officer Clara Signysdaater the position of Chief of the Thermadonian Metropolitan Police. She was cooling her heels an A'latar and seemed like she was ready for a new assignment."

Maya snorted. "How did *that* go over?"

597

"To quote her exactly, she said 'fek zat *boolkekk.*'. So I made her a Lieutenant instead."

Maya laughed derisively. "I'll bet she loved *that*."

"No," Sarah replied. "She did *not*, but she calmed down when I assured her that she could stay on patrol. Although to be frank, I cannot understand what she sees in spending her hours in a smelly police cruiser with nothing but bad kaafra and stale *olekaaken* to subsist on."

"Hey!" Maya exclaimed. 'Our cruiser *wasn't* smelly and I *like* donuts!"

"Suit yourself," Sarah replied evenly. "In any event, *Lieutenant* Signysdaater also agreed to serve on a special commission to determine all future promotions and appointments. So, in addition to her normal duties, she will also play a vital part in the selection of the next Chief. That element was non-negotiable, and just to sweeten up the posting, I also assigned her to Special Incidents Command."

"Yeah," Maya agreed. "I guess that will work." Signysdaater would keep her car, and get the chance to help her Department. She would also receive every perk imaginable; as the most powerful Lieutenant in the Metros, everyone would want to be on her good side.

"I also have some field work to do," Sarah added. "Once I have recovered, I must track down the Redeemer. He and N'Elemay will have to be brought to ground before they can bring their Tree to bear against us. Will you come with me, Maya, and help?"

Maya shook her head. "No Sarah. I'm done with the spy-business. I'm staying with the *JUDI*. I'm more cut out to be a smuggler anyway."

The disappointment was plain on Sarah's face, but she just nodded in sad acquiescence. "Of course."

Skylaar placed a comforting hand on Sarah's shoulder. "I'll accompany you," she said. "I cannot pass up the chance to put this Redeemer and the Enemy in their graves. After that, well see about this little Agency of yours. A legitimate job might actually be a good career move for me."

"I wish you all the luck of the Gods," Grammy interjected. "Me? I'm for Zommerlaand and my farm."

"*Good,*" Lilith snapped. It was plain that she had every intention of 'helping' Grammy to achieve her goal. As soon as possible, and by force if necessary.

"I want to go back with you," Kaly asked in a small voice. "I'm done. I just want some quiet."

Her eyes were glassy. The Psych doctors had loaded her up with anti-depressants and she would be in trauma therapy for some time to come. More than any of them, she deserved her peace.

"Gaanz gaaf," Ingrit said gently. "Looks like we are headed for the farm then. Kaly, you can stay with us if you want. We could use a hand with the agro systems."

The young woman smiled shyly at this, clearly accepting the offer.

"What about you Jon? What now?" Lilith asked. "Will you help Sarah hunt the Redeemer?"

Jon shook his head. His eyes had a haunted cast. "I have my ministry to attend to," he said. "Back home."

Disquieted, Lilith regarded him for a moment, trying to puzzle out what was behind this. Had she not known better, he seemed more like a man going to his execution than someone headed for home. Unable to resolve this anomaly, she addressed Celina instead. "That leaves you. Any plans? Anything that the Navy can do for you?"

Celina shook her head. "Thank you, Vice Admiral, but even with the new Chairwoman in office, I don't think the Sisterhood is the place for me just now.'

"Besides, if I've learned anything, it's that there is a lot more to the galaxy than just Womankind. I think—if Maya is willing to let me sing for my supper---I'll try to see what's out there. If the Xee can sell my music to other races, then I'm sure I can find a few others that might be willing to help me. Who knows? Maybe I'll even become some kind of goodwill ambassador for our species."

"We've got a spare bunk in the galley," Maya said, "and plenty of foam strips for our ears if the noise gets too bad."

"That's good to know," Jeena interjected. "It so happens that I'm also of a mind to see some more of the galaxy myself—if you can find me a place to sleep too."

Maya smiled suggestively. "Oh, I think we can free up a warm little corner for you to curl up in. If you don't mind a bunkmate."

Jeena colored slightly at this, and smiled. "I don't mind."

"Well," Lilith said with a tinge of regret, "That's it then. Goddesses' speed to all of you. It has been an honor."

There were hugs all around, and then the unlikely group of heroines separated and made their preparations to go their different ways, and move on with their lives.

For Maya, there was one last thing that she needed to attend to before she could step aboard the *C-JUDI-GO*. She made her way down to Officer's Country, and the quarters that had been temporarily assigned to Lady Felecia n'Calysher, now Acting Senatrix n'Calysher.

She found the young woman seated in a corner of the room, still dressed in the white robes of mourning. She was just as breathtakingly beautiful as ever, and seeing Maya enter, Felecia kept her features emotionless. Neither of them said anything to one another.

Finally, Maya broke the silence and delivered the message she had come to give. "I killed her," she announced flatly. "I was the one who killed Angelique."

To her satisfaction, Felecia flinched as if she had just been dealt a physical blow, and tears started to form in her eyes. When she looked away to wipe at them, Maya turned, and walked out of the room.

She had once heard it said that the worst kind of suffering was always that which was borne alone, and now she tended to agree. For her betrayal, Felecia deserved nothing less.

***

Celina also had an errand to perform. Although she still had to pack up all of her things, she also wanted to meditate on her decision and took advantage of the Ship's Temple.

While she certainly intended to visit the races that neighbored the Sisterhood, she had another goal as well. During her own experience with the Tree, she had seen a vision that she hadn't shared with anyone.

It had shown her a place on the opposite side of the Galaxy; a small star system and a tiny, unremarkable planet. Like many worlds, it had its Drow'voi ruins. These ruins however, were very special.

Deep inside one of the larger structures was a library. It was in fact the repository of all the Drow'voi knowledge, and its contents made even the most advanced Seevaan technology seem crushingly primitive.

She wasn't interested in this aspect of the place however. Her heart was set on the music that was there, music which went beyond anything that her own race had ever dreamed of. As an artist, this lonely little world was nothing less than the fabled Holy Grail. The journey to it would take years, and possibly even a lifetime. And once she left, it was unlikely that she would ever see the Sisterhood again, or even lay eyes on another human.

But wasn't time all that she really had now? And what else deserved that time? She couldn't think of a thing.

EPILOGUE

Grunvaald Haarmaaneplaatz, Vaalkenstaad Township, Zommerlaand, Sunna 3, Solara Elant, United Sisterhood of Suns, 1049.03|13|07:93:32

Sunset was turning the skies of Zommerlaand a deep red-orange. Kaly stared into the fires of the twin suns, ignoring the pain that their light caused as she poured out Margasdaater's ashes. A gust of wind came up and caught the dust, scattering it in every direction, but Kaly kept at it until every bit of her friend's remains had been emptied from the urn.

When she was done, she carefully resealed the container and put it into her carry sack. Grammy came up and joined her. "She is home now," she said.

"Yes," Kaly answered. "We both are."

***

As Kaly and Grammy returned to the farm, Jon fa'Teela stepped into a plaza on Thermadon, accompanied by his acolytes. On this world, the sun was high in the sky, and the day promised to be hot and pitiless. This did not deter him though. He had things that he needed to say to the crowd. He had a message to deliver.

Expectant eyes turned towards him as he mounted the makeshift stage, and voices stilled, waiting for his words. Composing himself, he looked out over the audience, and finally, at the very edge of the assembly, he spotted her.

She was just as he had seen in his vision. Her eyes burned with hatred for him, and under the folds of her cloak, he knew that she carried his death.

Is it today? he wondered. Just as he had expected it would, the Angel had appeared at his side, dressed in its strange green robe.

"Not today, Jon", it told him. "But soon enough. Today, you must speak with wisdom. These women have all come a long ways to hear your words."

Jon stepped forwards, raised his hands, and ignoring his assassin, began his sermon.

***

Maya walked into the cabin that had once been Sarah's. It was hers now, and she had replaced the decorations in it with some of her own.

601

The most significant of these was a holo of the Necropolis, seen from the Free City. It was animated, and she paused to watch as the random program spun a dust devil into existence on the clean white sands that separated the Xee city from the ancient ruins.

Finally, she turned away from the image and made for her bed. Jeena taur K'aut'sha was already there, sound asleep.

It had been a long shift and Maya was bone tired herself. She looked forwards to curling up with her lover and finally getting some rest. And in the morning, when she was in better shape, she planned to make the process of waking up with Jeena something to look forwards to.

Lowering herself onto the mattress, she thought about the lights going off. They flickered for a second, then dimmed and went out.

This got her attention.

Normally, they went out instantly. She realized, that in her fatigue, she had not taken the additional step of using her psiever to send the command. Tentatively, she formulated a desire for illumination, and made certain to omit the usual 'send' command that should have followed it. After a brief hesitation, the cabin lights came on.

Suddenly, Maya didn't feel tired any longer. She left the chamber, and headed for the bridge. Zara was on duty there, pulling third watch, and already ensconced with one of her hellish *TroieDoku* holopuzzles and a snack from the galley.

The *JUDI's* Engineer looked up at Maya in surprise. "I thought you were goin t'bed."

"I was," Maya answered. "I couldn't sleep. I thought I'd come back up here and get in some study time on the astrographic charts."

Zara shrugged in acceptance, and went back to her puzzle. The *JUDI* was laying over in an anonymous binary star system, in preparation for a transit that would take them into V'raan space and a potentially lucrative smuggling deal. For now however, they were forced to wait. Their contact was still on the way to the rendezvous point.

Maya pretended to look over one of the files, but as soon as she knew that Zara was completely distracted, she shifted her gaze to the forward sitscreen and the twin stars that were shining in the distance.

Silently, she mouthed the notes of the Song and formed a wish in her mind. Then she waited to see if what she suspected was true.

When the star that she had been concentrating on dimmed, went dark, and then brightened again, Maya knew she had been correct.

Ever since leaving the Tree, a deep feeling of connectedness had remained with her. Little things had been happening; odd 'coincidences' like the incredible luck that she had enjoyed when she had thrown her sword at Angelique, and other events just like it.

Oddly, it had been Angelique herself who had provided her with the vital clue. *"Come,"* she had said, *"you don't need these others; they might not have told you, but once the Tree has been unlocked, only the User really matters."*

The woman had been telling the truth, she realized. Somehow, she had managed to retain a portion of her God-like powers to influence physical reality.

Most women would have either been excited by this, or terrified. They also would have made some outward display of their emotions.

Maya didn't do so. Instead, she pretended as if everything was completely normal, and simply rose, offered Zara a polite goodnight and climbed back down the ladder.

This time, when she reentered her quarters, she smiled at the image of the ruins. The Tree—or at least the one on Ashkele—was gone, but not her connection with the galaxy spanning network of machines that it had been linked to. Once the User's hand had directed them, the machines never forgot, and the bond between them was never really broken.

It actually made perfect sense, she reflected. Just as her experience within the Tree had shown, the Drow'voi ruins were *everywhere* in the galaxy. No place was too far from any one of them, and as long as she was within the confines of the Milky Way, they could, and did, hear her.

This was not something that she planned to disclose to anyone however. Not to Lady Ananzi, Jeena, or even Skylaar. Her escapade had taught her many things, but the most valuable lesson she had come away with had been about keeping secrets. Some information was simply too dangerous to entrust to others. Even to friends.

***

Fleet Admiral Myrelli ebed Cya watched as the star in the *JUDI's* sitscreen vanished and then reappeared. She wasn't overawed by the sight in the least. She had expected it, and sighed in contentment.

Her guest, who had joined her to view the secret recording, mirrored her reaction. Lady Ananzi was proud of her protégé, and what they had managed to achieve with her.

Maya didn't know it, but as long as she was alive, she was the Sisterhood's metaphorical 'ace-in-the hole'. It didn't matter to either of them that the girl had abandoned her nation. That was only a temporary condition. With the right manipulation, by the right agent—in this case

Jeena taur K'aut'sha—they both knew that she would eventually be persuaded to return.

When she finally did, the Sisterhood would enjoy a golden age. As twisted as it had been, Angelique bel Thana's vision of Humanity ruling the galaxy had actually possessed great merit. All it had required was the right leadership, and the right guidance. In time, and with patience, Maya n'Kaaryn would become the very queen that Bel Thana had failed to be. Then, the possibilities would be endless.

***

The Galaxy Mind had chosen the visage of the angel who had visited Jon on A'latar. Seeing this, Bel Hanna was surprised, but hardly disturbed.

"Tell me," she asked it. "Was it you who spoke to him?"

"If everyone in this galaxy is part of me," it answered obliquely, "Isn't it equally possible that all galaxies are part of something even larger?"

"It is," Bel Hanna replied. "Is that what the angel was?"

"Perhaps," it answered. "Perhaps not."

Knowing that it was pointless to press it any further, Bel Hanna let the matter go, and together they observed the *JUDI* and the twin stars beyond it in companionable silence. At last, the Galaxy Mind spoke again. "Is she not magnificent?" it asked.

"I have also grown quite fond of Maya," Bel Hanna agreed.

"And what marvelous things await her and her species," it added.

Knowing what she did now, Bel Hanna could certainly not contradict her companion. Marvelous was as much an understatement as the word for 'God' was.

THE END

The Elants of the Sisterhood and Planets of Interest

There are 12 Elants, or provinces, in the Sisterhood. Of these, Thalestris and Solara Elant are the oldest, and Sagana, the youngest. Elants are named after a navigational star in their area, commonly referred to as the Name Star. Each Elant comprises hundreds of individual worlds, and as of Book 3, the total population of the Sisterhood in all Elants is approximately 100,000,000,000 women.

In this section, the Elants and the worlds within them which were mentioned in the series are listed by their Sisterhood name, followed by pre-Sisterhood labels, and then their star catalog numbers (prefaced by HP, Gl, GJ, Wo, NN, HD, or HSL)

"HP" stands for the Hipparcos star catalog, and "Gl" and "Wo" are from the *Gliese Catalog of Nearby Stars* (later reclassified as the GJ or Gleise-Jahreiß catalog). "NN" denotes a star listed in the Gliese Catalog that has no name assigned. "HD" is associated with the *Henry Draper Catalog* (one of the first large scale attempts to catalog the spectral types of stars).

Only one designation, "HSL" is completely exclusive to this series. It represents the catalog currently in use by the Sisterhood, and honors the astronomer Henrietta Swan Leavitt (1868-1921 CE). Her work studying Cephiad variables ultimately allowed other scientists to measure the distance between Old Gaia and distant galaxies.

Star Types:

Most stars are classified under the Morgan–Keenan (MK) system using the letters "O" (blue giants), "B" (blue), "A" (blue-white), "F" (white), "G" (yellow), "K" (orange), and "M" (red). This sequence goes from the hottest (the O type) to the coolest (the M class).

Each of these classes is further subdivided with a number; 0 being hottest and 9 being coolest (e.g. F0, G2 and so on). In addition, luminosity is included as roman numerals, distinguishing dwarf stars from giants. Our sun is a G2V type, a yellow main-sequence star with a temperature of around 5,800 Kelvin.

In the hunt for extrasolar planets, many stars have been found to possess planets, but only certain kinds are believed to offer the right conditions for complex life to arise (and then only within a limited range known as the habitable, or 'Goldilocks' zone'). Premier among these are the F and G types, and some K and M stars might also be included, provided that their life arose on an inner world. For this reason, the majority of Sisterhood planets orbit around G and F class stars, and rest within the habitable zone (with some notable exceptions).

Almastris Elant

Name Star; Almastris, in honor of an Amazon queen (Zeta Leporis A, GL 217.1, a white dwarf star twice the mass of Sol and fifteen times its luminosity). Capital: Delgen.

Delgen, Ergane System (HSL 53, HP 27922, a G6V star); a powerhouse of industry, Delgen is the Elant capital and the hub of civilian manufacturing. Its industrial power is rivaled only by Ara's underground factories.

Sai, Ifria System (GL 199A, a K4V); Orbiting a red dwarf, Sai is known for its wild spaces and the Sword Dance, a coming of age ceremony.

Artemi Elant

Name Star; Artmesia (Alpha Phoenicis A/Ankaa, a K0-1III star), after Queen Artemisia I of Caria, ruler of Halicarnassus during the First Persian Empire, and a naval commander in the second Persian invasion of Greece. Capital: Wrede.

Wrede, Lyssa System (HP 4189; a G2 variant); Originally named for the fantasy and science fiction novelist Patricia Wrede, this world is the capital of the Artemi Elant and the location of the Battle of Wrede 178. Here, during the War of the Prophet, Sisterhood forces managed to defeat the Prophet's armada and turned the tide of the conflict in humanity's favor.

Larra's Lament, Lalita System (GL 27.1, an M class red star); The Lament derives its name from the commander of the exploratory vessel that first discovered it, Laara Reade, and her disappointment when she realized that the world was not as rich in mineral resources as she and her financial backers had hoped. It is the location of the USSMC 93rd Special Operations Training Center, and the Sniper Training School. It is also the motherworld of Ensign Jan bar Daala.

Nightshade, Dayea System (NN3063, an M3 star); the center of Sisterhood arms manufacturing and military weapons research, the majority of this world is owned by the Sisterhood government, or private contractors, and is off limits to civilian traffic.

Hella's World, Hecate System (GL 4.2-522, a G2 variant); a desolate arid place, and the location of the primary USSMC Basic Training Facility. Graduates of the program are entitled to wear a special award, called "The Eye of the Goddess."

Chandi Elant

Name Star; Chandika (GL 107 A- 12777), a binary star system, named for an aspect of the goddess Kali, as the protector of Rajas. Capital: Kevan.

Kevan, Sakina System (Gl 67-7918, a G2V star); Like Sai, Kevan is a desert planet and the motherworld of Caleda bel Tridis, the Athena's Helmsmistress. It is also the home of the Martha McSally Naval Base and Air Combat Training Facility where future Sisterhood pilots learn the art of aerospace combat.

Avia, Tetra System (Gl 61, an F8V); From the Latin, 'avis' or bird, Avia is a Bio world where the dominant life-forms fly or glide on the air currents. The women who call this their motherworld have been genetically modified to live an aerial existence.

Halasi Elant

Name Star; Halasi (GL 8351 - 107089, a K0III type giant star), after a woman who fought with the Hungarian freedom fighters against the Nazis during the second of Old Gaia's five World Wars. Capital: Meriditha.

Meriditha, Aglaia System (Wo 9189 - 26394, a G3IV); from the old Welsh word 'mere', meaning 'splendid' or 'great'.

Durandel, Niniane System (HP 64690, a G5IV); named for *Durandal*, the sword carried by Roland, Charlemagne's paladin. Settled during the heyday of the Gaian Star Federation, Durandel is one of the most terraformed planets ever settled by humans. Its creators reworked the entire ecosystem, converting it into a fantasy realm complete with forests, castles and fanciful creatures. Once a premier tourist destination, Durandel still receives some off-planet visitors, although not as many as it did in the days of the GSF. But this picturesque world has a much more important role that none of these sightseers are aware of. It is also the secret location of The Hive, which serves as the supreme command center for the Sisterhood's government in the event of a severe national crisis, or an alien invasion.

Kalian Elant

Name Star; Kali (GJ 1294 A, an M0V class star with a K5V companion), for the Indian goddess of creation, destruction, change and empowerment. Capital: Sita.

Sita, Brizona System (NN 3021 – 1292 a G6V star); Capital of the Kalian Elant, Sita is also known for the Athtar Commercial Shipyards, which produce most of the civilian vessels in the Sisterhood, including the great space liners like the *Star of Aphrodite*.

Corrissa, Saraswati System (HP 110719, a G1 star); Corrissa, and especially the city of New Lyrrica, are considered to be the center of Sisterhood art, music and culture. New Lyrrica is the home of the famous musician and Living National Treasure, Celina.

Marpesia Elant

Name Star; Marpesia (Formalhaut/GL 881--113368), an Amazonian queen who ruled with her sister, Lampedo. She was one of the monarchs who helped establish the Greek city of Ephesus and a city in the Caucasus Mountains referred to as the Rock of Marpesia, or the Marpesian Cliff, where Alexander the Great established fortifications. Capital: Esyllt.

Esyllt, Drystan System (GL 780--99240); from the Welsh word for 'fair lady', it is Lena n'Gari's motherworld, and the setting for Lena Calidrayth's *"Where the Blue Flowers Grow"*.

Trilane, Taran System (GL 783 A--99461, a binary K2V star); On this world, silicon-based life is dominant, and the native women play host to a variety of symbiotes which grant longevity and accelerated healing (and according to unconfirmed sources, even psychic powers). It is the motherworld of Admiral Kaysa Da'Kayt.

Pantari Elant

Name Star; Pantariste (GL 55 – 5862, an F8V type); after the Amazon fighter who fought alongside Hippolyta against Hercules and his men. Capital: Mirande

Mirande, Prospero System (GJ 1021, a G5IV type); a variant of 'Miranda' and derived from the Latin *'mirandus'* or 'wonderful, admirable'. The name Miranda was first used by Shakespeare for a character in his play *"The Tempest."*

Rixa, Belletrix System (Iota Horologii /GL 108 - 126583, a G3V type); home to USSNB Rixa, the largest Sisterhood naval base and the headquarters of the Topaz Fleet Command. The name Rixa is derived from the Latin word for a quarrel, or a fight.

Sagana Elant

Name Star; Sagana (Arcturus/GL 541 --69673, a K2IIIp star); Sagana was a priestess of Hekate and a Janae sorceress, who lived in Imperial Rome. She was said to be the descendant of Janus himself and Crane, an owl-witch celebrated for her craft. Capital: Thenti.

Thenti, Sagana System (Arcturus/GL 541 --69673, a K2IIIp star); rich in minerals, Thenti has a thriving mining industry and serves as the governmental center for the Sagana Elant.

Persephone, Demeter System (Gl 502--64394, a G0V star); a remote agricolony and Kaly n'Deena's motherworld. Named for the daughter of Demeter and the goddess of the Greek underworld who ruled alongside Hades.

Storm and Siren, Agleope System (GL 525--67090, a K2 type star); Storm is known for its fierce weather and Siren for its excess UV radiation and a local insect capable of emitting sounds loud enough to cause permanent hearing loss. Siren is the motherworld of Annya T'Jinna.

Ananti 4, Trikala system (GL 538--68682, a G8V star); a local port mentioned in Book 1 *"Pallas Athena".*

Almaran, Titanis System (NN 3809 A, an M2 star); the location of the local Star Service Field Headquarters for the Sagana Elant

Flora, Gaea System (GL 534 --67927, a G0IV type); famed for its exotic flowers and vegetation. From the Latin 'flora', for vegetation and the name of the Roman goddess of flowers.

Planet 9-A, Phantasma System (GL 480--61706, an M4 type); Latin for 'ghost', Phantasma is the site of an archeological dig sponsored by the University of Thermadon at Thenti.

Solara Elant

Name Star; Solara (Sol, a G2 star); after Sol, its principle star, which was named for the Roman god of the Sun (also known as Helios to the ancient Greeks). Capital: Zommerlaand.

Zommerlaand, Sunna 3 System (Alpha Centauri A, a G2V star); the location of Waanderstaad Spaceport and Grunvaald Haarmaaneplaatz. Motherworld of Katrin Bertasdaater, Ingrit Bertasdaater, Helga Mariasdaater (Grammy) and many others.

Mars and Old Gaia National Monument, Sol System (Sol, a G2 star); Mars is the oldest non-Gaian planet settled by humanity that is still in existence after the devastation of the First Widow's War. The neighboring National Monument marks the site of Old Gaia herself which was destroyed by the Hriss in revenge for their defeat at Fomalhaut.

Calaphis, Alissar System (B. Can. Venaticorum A/GL 475, a G0V star); principally known as the home of the USS Naval Academy.

Telesalla Elant

Name Star; Telesilla (GL 841A), a talented musician, and the warrior leader of the ancient Argave women, an Amazon tribe. Capital: Tithari, Ashvah System.

New Covenant, Tamrah System (GL 838, a G0-V star); the center of the Marionite Faith and Jon fa'Teela's motherworld. New Covenant is also the birthplace of the Redeemer.

Faith, Magdalen System (GL 838.6, an M3 type); rumored to be the home of renegade Marionite enclaves secretly practicing heterosexuality and pre-Sisterhood 'natural' child-birthing. As a planet, Faith itself is unique. Its primary is a red dwarf, and the native life on Faith is older and more evolved than what might have been found on Old Gaia at the time of its destruction.

Hope, Miryam System (HD 217107, a G8IV star); another Marionite world.

Thalestris Elant

Name Star; Thalestra (HP 1672, a K3V star), after a fictional queen who ruled the Amazons living between the Caucasus and the River Phasis. Her real-life counterpart may have been one of the female rulers of that area, or a Scythian princess. Capital: Thermadon, Myrene System.

Thermadon, Myrene System (Beta Hydri/HSL 1/Gl 19); both the national and provincial capital, Thermadon Val is the largest city in the Sisterhood. It derives its name from a river in the Anatolian region of Turkey on Old Gaia which comprised one of the borders of the Amazonian kingdom of Themiskrya.

Tethys, Galene System (Delta Pavonis, a G2 variant); A world of shallow seas and small islands, it honors the Titaness Tethys who ruled over the primordial oceans before the advent of the Olympian Gods. It is the motherworld of Lt. Commander Mearinn d'Rann.

Ara, Eileithyia System (GL 442 A - 57443, a G3-5 V); Lilith ben Jeni's motherworld, Ara was colonized during the First Widow's War when vital manufacturing facilities were relocated there for safety. Its inhabitants live largely underground in a gigantic cavern system, and its official motto is *"All Good Things Come from Under the Earth."*

Nemesis, Rahdwa System (Alpha Mensae, GL 231 29271, a G5-6 V type); Covered with dense forests, this world is famous for its medicinal exports and lumber products, as well as its fierce predators and the aboriginal lifestyle of the native women. In classical Greece, Nemesis was the spirit of divine retribution against those who committed the sin of hubris. It is the motherworld of Captain Erin taur Minna and Skylaar taur Minna.

Nyx, Morpheus System (82 G. Eridani, a G8 star); in the ancient Greek religion, Nyx was the goddess of the night itself. It is a world where the successful lifeforms evolved along nocturnal lines (due to excess solar radiation during its day cycle) and home to the famous University of Nyx at Nocturne, where the Sisterhood's finest physicians are trained. It is also the location of the Great Nightlands Waste and the home of Lady Ananzi.

Cingulum-X, Cingulum System (GJ 1277, an M class star); The USS Naval Shipyards on Cingulum-X are responsible for the construction of the majority of vessels in the Sisterhood Navy. It is where the first Isis-Class supercruisers were constructed during the First Widow's War, and where the USSNS *Pallas Athena* (SBC 1323) was commissioned. Cingulum comes from the Latin word for 'belt', and was so named because of the many planets that orbit its primary.

Thamari Elant

Name Star; Beta-Thamaris (GL 555, an M4 class star); after Thamaris, Queen of the Massagetai, a nomadic confederation centered in Iran and Central Asia on Old Gaia. She is famous for being the slayer of Cyrus the Great (the founder of the Persian Empire). Capital: Tipande

Shana Legendre Naval Base, Sequana System (GL 526-67155, an M4 star); commissioned in honor of the great heroine of the First Widow's War who defeated the Hriss invasion fleets, ultimately leading to the Treaty of Almari 6.

Anahita Border Zone (Annexed Sisterhood space/ETR space)

Name Star: Anahita, a Zoroastrian goddess of the waters (HSL-137 10, a G6V star)

The School (HSL-48 2124 A, a G2V variant); Part of the ETR, La Escaul hosts an experimental community officially dedicated to the study of human interaction. Unofficially, it also serves the Republic's intelligence community by gathering information on Sisterhood culture, language and customs from the crewmembers of a Long Range Reconnaissance vessal that crash landed there.

Non-Sisterhood Systems and Worlds (Not Including the ETR)

Ashkele, Hallasa System, Xee Protectorate (HSL-2258/HP 56832, a G5 sub giant); the location of the Free City and the planet spanning Necropolis. It is the home port for the *C-JUDI-GO*.

A'latar, Evaar'eea System (HSL-29997, a G1-G2V star), Pa'lla Space; a water-world similar to Tethys and known for the healing properties of its many resorts. Due to the unique structure of their eyes, the Pa'lla are able to perceive the green spectrum of their primary, and equate this color with their concept of God.

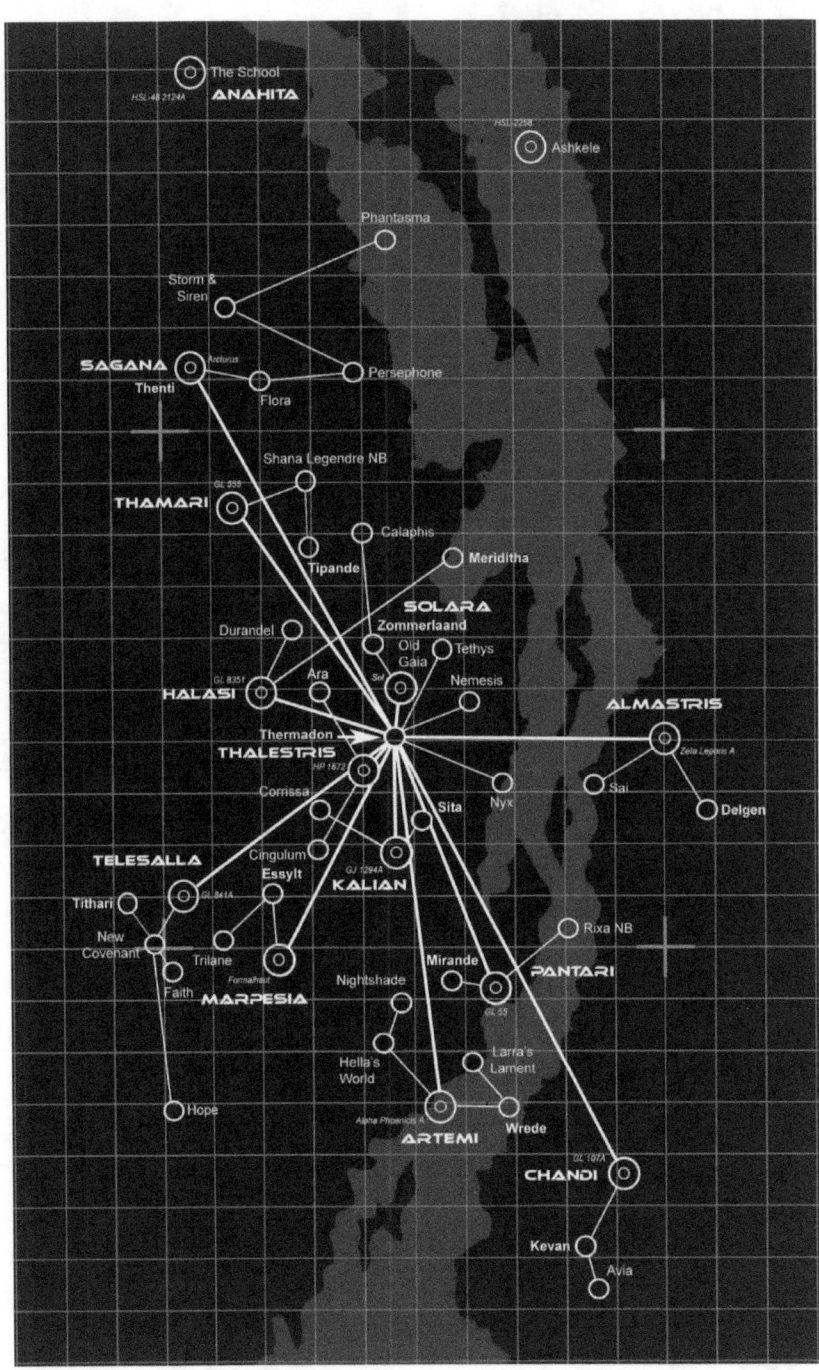